INFINITE
STARS
DARK FRONTIERS

ANTHOLOGIES AVAILABLE FROM TITAN BOOKS

Infinite Stars edited by Bryan Thomas Schmidt
AvP: Aliens vs. Predators - Ultimate Prey edited by Jonathan Maberry and
Bryan Thomas Schmidt
Predator: If It Bleeds edited by Bryan Thomas Schmidt

Aliens: Bug Hunt edited by Jonathan Maberry
Associates of Sherlock Holmes edited by George Mann
Further Associates of Sherlock Holmes edited by George Mann
Dark Cities edited by Christopher Golden
Dark Detectives edited by Stephen Jones
Dead Letters edited by Conrad Williams
Dead Man's Hand edited by John Joseph Adams
Encounters of Sherlock Holmes edited by George Mann
Further Encounters of Sherlock Holmes edited by George Mann
The Madness of Cthulhu edited by S. T. Joshi
The Madness of Cthulhu, Volume Two edited by S. T. Joshi
Mash Up edited by Gardener Dozois
Shadows Over Innsmouth edited by Stephen Jones
Weird Shadows Over Innsmouth edited by Stephen Jones
Weirder Shadows Over Innsmouth edited by Stephen Jones
Wastelands edited by John Joseph Adams (US only)
Wastelands 2 edited by John Joseph Adams
Wastelands: The New Apocalypse edited by John Joseph Adams

INFINITE STARS

DARK FRONTIERS

THE DEFINITIVE ANTHOLOGY OF SPACE OPERA

Edited by
BRYAN THOMAS SCHMIDT

TITAN BOOKS

INFINITE STARS: DARK FRONTIERS
Hardback edition ISBN: 9781789092912
Paperback edition ISBN: 9781789092974
Electronic edition ISBN: 9781789092929

Published by Titan Books
A division of Titan Publishing Group Ltd
144 Southwark Street, London SE1 0UP
www.titanbooks.com

First edition: November 2019
Paperback edition: May 2021
2 4 6 8 10 9 7 5 3 1

A CIP catalogue record for this title is available from the British Library.
Printed and bound by CPI Group (UK) Ltd, Croydon CR0 4YY

Did you enjoy this book?
We love to hear from our readers. Please email us at
readerfeedback@titanemail.com or write to us at
Reader Feedback at the above address.
To receive advance information, news, competitions,
and exclusive offers online, please sign up for the
Titan newsletter on our website:

TITAN BOOKS.COM

For George Lucas, who first ignited my love of space opera and storytelling,

David Spangler and Al Girtz, who first made me believe I could tell stories for a career,

And Noah Melson, who's just beginning to dream as he starts college this year.

CONTENTS

EDITOR'S NOTE AND ACKNOWLEDGEMENTS
BRYAN THOMAS SCHMIDT

Getting to do one anthology like *Infinite Stars* was a dream come true. After all, space opera, more than any other subgenre of science fiction, was what drew me to science fiction as my first love. But to then be asked to do another is… intimidating. Anything your publisher labels as "definitive" takes on a whole new scope. So I found myself back to researching authors and stories with new fervor, looking for those who have had and are having the most impact.

Seeking to add to the creative diversity, I strove not to go back to all the same people who contributed to the first volume, though a few have come back—for example, Jack Campbell and Orson Scott Card. David Weber returns with an all-new introduction and one of his short stories set in the Bolo universe. Kevin J. Anderson and Larry Niven are back, writing in different universes.

Everyone else here appears in *Infinite Stars* for the first time, and what a group they are. From Becky Chambers, the woman who popped onto the scene with a crowdfunded novel that reinvented modern space opera, to well-known pros like Sharon Lee and Steve Miller, whose Liaden books have long been bestsellers. Upcoming space opera star Curtis Chen's Kangaroo novels will be new to many, while Mike Shepherd's Kris Longknife and Tanya Huff's Confederation have garnered an established and fervent following.

Other persons of legendary talent have decided to break new ground. C.J. Cherryh, famous for her Foreigner series, offers something wholly new, as does David Farland, perhaps best known for his Runelords epic fantasies. Susan R. Matthews takes leave of her Jurisdiction series to try something new and exciting, as well.

Altogether, *Infinite Stars: Dark Frontiers* offers up twenty-six stories in this round—two more than the previous volume. For reprints we delve back even further into space opera's origins for a 1930s story by E.E. "Doc" Smith, the writer often credited with founding the subgenre even before Bob Tucker gave it its name. There's a seminal example of Robert A. Heinlein's space opera, written well before *Starship Troopers*, an Arthur C. Clarke tale which appeared years ahead of *2001: A Space Odyssey*, and the renowned "Shambleau" from C.L. Moore's amazing Northwest Smith series which continues to influence writers even today.

Another innovation this time around is that many of the authors give us a brief note to introduce the story, placing it within the context of their larger universe. This adds a unique personal touch, and helps introduce readers to broad horizons they may not yet have experienced. If you find stuff you love, please go explore the further adventures. The purpose of any survey like this is to help you discover new characters and series with which you want to spend your reading hours.

Herein you will find award winners, more modern tales with golden age roots, and rare space opera stories from science fiction's founding fathers, all collected to provide a rich variety and hours of reading pleasure—always the goal of a superior anthology. May this volume join the first *Infinite Stars* as a necessary addition to the serious reader's library, and I hope you enjoy the fruits as much as I enjoyed the labor.

As always I have to thank a few people. Of course, Steve Saffel, Nick Landau, Vivian Cheung, Laura Price, George Sandison, Katharine Carroll, Lydia Gittins, Polly Grice, Hannah Scudamore, Valerie Gardner, Lukmon Ogunbadejo, Jenny Boyce, and all of the folks at

Titan Books for allowing me the opportunity and doing such a great job with my books.

I also owe thanks to Rich Horton, Gardner Dozois, Ken Keller, Michael Knost, Joe Monson, David Bridges, and David Sooby for recommendations and research help on stories. Eugene Johnson for typing up old manuscripts that had no digital version, Peter J. Wacks, Ken Keller, and Michael Wallace for advice and friendship when I needed talking down off those ledges from time to time. My parents, Ramon and Glenda, and my crazy dogs Louie and Amelie, my great constant companions.

Of course, David Weber for an amazing opening essay. He had quite the challenge following up Robert Silverberg from the first *Infinite Stars*, but David rose to the occasion—as I knew he would. Also many thanks to Sharon Weber for aiding our communication and coordination as always.

Last but not least, thanks to all the authors for their hard work on stories that I really enjoyed reading and am proud to edit and include. It was a thrill working with some of my own writing heroes, in universes I myself love exploring. Without further ado, I present *Infinite Stars: Dark Frontiers*, a rich cornucopia of space opera and science fiction adventure that I hope will occupy your minds and dreams for many hours to come.

Bryan Thomas Schmidt
Ottawa, KS
March 2019

INTRODUCTION: SWORDS AND SPACESHIPS AND CYBORGS, O MY!

DAVID WEBER

So, how do you improve on Robert Silverberg's explication of "space opera" in his introduction to the first volume of *Infinite Stars*?

Answer: you don't. I went back and reread his essay for the first *Infinite Stars* when I foolishly accepted Bryan Schmidt's invitation to write the introduction to *Infinite Stars: Dark Frontiers*. I'd read it the first time around, of course, but time has a way of swallowing things up, and I'd frankly forgotten what a masterful job Silverberg did in providing an expert's summation of the space opera genre, its evolution, and the matching evolution of the term "space opera" itself. I believe the words "hard act to follow" might reasonably be said to apply.

So instead of talking about what "space opera" is (and, as Silverberg suggested, the term is still very much a matter of "in the eye of the beholder" in a lot of ways), I thought I'd look at two other questions. The first is how space opera differs from military science fiction, and the second is why people write space opera and why people read it.

In *Infinite Stars: Dark Frontiers*, Bryan has assembled a wide-ranging selection of new and reprint entries. There's something in here for just about anyone's tastes, and the older stories provide a context, a sense of the way in which the genre has evolved over the years, from C.L. Moore's "Shambleau" (1933) and Northwest

Smith's... unfortunate decision to rescue a Venusian vampire from a transplanted Transylvania mob, through Robert Heinlein's "Misfit" (1939) which introduced Andrew Jackson "Slipstick" Libby (one of my favorite Heinlein characters), and Arthur C. Clarke's "Rescue Party" (1946) in which more or less benevolent aliens discover that those pesky monkey boys and girls from Earth have already rescued themselves, which may not bode well for the rest of the galaxy. Then there's James Blish, with "Earthman Come Home" (the title story from the first volume of his *Cities in Flight* series from 1956), with one of the more audacious techniques ever evolved for moving entire cities into space... and, eventually, controlling the end of the universe.

Obviously, all of those stories fit the definition Silverberg quoted from David Hartwell and Kathryn Cramer at the end of his introduction: "Henceforth, 'space opera' meant, and still generally means, colorful, dramatic, large-scale adventure, competently and sometimes beautifully written, usually focused on a sympathetic heroic central character and plot action... and usually set in a relatively distant future and in space or on other worlds, characteristically optimistic in tone." Some of them fit better than others, and I think there is a generally "darker" feel to this second *Infinite Stars* collection as a whole, in keeping with the title. For example, neither "Shambleau" nor "Earthman Come Home" are particularly optimistic (about human nature, at least), but like Doc Smith's "Vortex Blaster" and Clarke's "Rescue Party," they are definitely part of the platform upon which more modern space opera rests. And space opera is alive and well today, from works of the seventies and eighties, like *The Mote in God's Eye* and *Lucifer's Hammer* by those masters of space opera Larry Niven and Jerry Pournelle, to countless ongoing works like C.J. Cherryh's many skillfully told stories over the last forty-odd years, from *Gate of Ivrel* way back in 1976 to her wonderful Foreigner universe (with *Emergence*, the 19th novel in the series, releasing this past January and the 20th due out soon); Seanan McGuire's stories (like one of my favorites, "The Life and Times of Charity Smith, Schoolteacher," included in this anthology); and Steve Miller and Sharon Lee's delightful Liaden universe, beginning with *Agent of Change* (February

1988) or *Crystal Soldier* (February 2005) depending on whether you are a read-them-in-print-order or follow-internal-chronology sort of reader.

But not all of them—by a long chalk—would also qualify as *military* science fiction.

Let's begin by establishing that while a great deal of military science fiction fits into the genre category of space opera, not all military science fiction is space opera and not all space opera is military science fiction. They have been joined at the hip since the days of H.G. Wells and Jules Verne, and the relationship is alive and well today. But while they may be *fraternal* twins, they are not and never have been identical.

Some military science fiction is easily identified as such. David Drake's *Slammers* books, John Ringo and Travis Taylor's *Von Neumann's War*, Joe Haldeman's *Forever War* books, and my own Honor Harrington novels fall into that category. Military operations are at the core of the story lines—the stories don't make *sense* without the military aspect—and the writers are concerned with portraying not simply the effects and consequences of war on populations in general but also on the institutions and individuals actually *fighting* the wars. Drake's *Slammers* are poster children for PTSD and the alienation of professional soldiers from the civilians around them (and also reflect the callous obliviousness of those civilians in too many instances), and Joe Haldeman's brilliant *Forever War* (and its sequels) takes that a long step farther by including the temporal alienation of soldiers set adrift from everything they've ever known by the time dilation effect of relativistic cruises between stars. Most of what I consider to be military science fiction also looks closely at the processes of military organizations, although often without worrying the readers' heads too much over little things like logistics and supply chains. And the best of it, in addition to dealing with the impact of combat operations on human beings, also tries to get inside the military mindset. To understand the dynamics and to explore what is in many ways the ultimate team effort.

There is another subset of military science fiction that tends to concentrate on loners. On individual warriors, often supported by a small core group of loyal companions, who are more often than not at odds with the military institutions around them and win despite those institutions. Stories written about Achilles and not Ajax, one might say. Keith Laumer's Bolo stories also fall into this category, and they also tend to be very dark, as well, with the mighty cybernetic warriors time and again proving to be far more than their fallible human creators deserve. (I should add that my beloved wife Sharon will not attend any reading of my own Bolo short story in this collection, "The Traitor," because of the last two lines. Can't imagine why Bryan would have included it in something subtitled *Dark Frontiers*.)

Stories about individual warriors can be great adventure stories, and I've read a stack of them and enjoyed them a great deal over the years, but by and large they tend to fall outside my rubric of what constitutes *military* science fiction. It's worth remembering that Roman legions routinely defeated many times their own number of barbarian warriors. Not because the Romans were any braver or stronger, and certainly not because Italians were bigger than Gauls (they weren't). They won because they had doctrine, they had uniform and well thought-out equipment, they had training not as individuals but as members of their unit, they had logistics, and above all else, they had discipline. Brilliant individual warriors were no match for the maniples of a Roman army that fought as a team—as a composite machine, built of interlocking cogs that all served the same function.

That distinction is why a lot of "lone warrior" stories slide into the territory of another type of fiction, the sort which Toni Weiskopf described to me many years ago as militar*istic* science fiction. These are stories which are most often written by people who don't grasp the military mindset or the way that military organizations have to operate. People who *want* to write a "military" story but don't have the window into actual armies or navies or air forces to understand the DNA of the military. They miss the fundamental difference between Achilles and Hector and they usually don't worry too much about the long-service noncoms, because they simply don't understand why those Roman legions and those hard-bitten Roman centurions routinely massacred barbarian armies.

Another thing "militaristic" fiction frequently misses is what motivates soldiers or sailors when the shooting starts. It's seldom patriotism or philosophical purpose at that point. I'm not saying soldiers and sailors *aren't* patriots or that they don't have deeply held moral beliefs and commitments. I'm simply saying that when someone is shooting at you, it's not the Pledge of Allegiance going through your mind. It's survival, and it's the other members of your unit. The men and the women in the crucible with you, who are part of the same team, who depend on you, and upon whom *you* depend. You may not *like* all of them very much, but you *depend* upon them, and that creates a sense of corporate identity and loyalty to one another that never really leaves you.

There are also stories in which the military action is decidedly secondary or viewed primarily as a causative factor for the other things the storyteller really wants to concentrate on. Sort of the way that a tidal wave's impact can be the "causative factor" in a novel dealing with post-catastrophe survival, perhaps. Orson Scott Card's Ender stories (represented here by the new story "Messenger") tend to fall into this category in my mind, and it wouldn't be implausible to include *The Forever War*, as well, given how much of it focuses on the returning veterans' efforts to deal with the consequences of their isolation in both time and life experience.

Clearly, *Ender's Game* and *The Forever War* are both space opera, but so is Larry Niven and Jerry Pournelle's *Lucifer's Hammer* (although, admittedly, it is set on a single planet) in which the actual military combat—the final defense of the valley and the nuclear power plant—are simply the culmination of a story which is far more interested in testing the ingenuity, audacity, and moral fiber of human beings in the face of worldwide disaster. It's interested in the ability of people who are primarily *civilians*, not soldiers, to rebuild and their willingness to pay the price for that rebuilding. And in the same way, the Liaden and Foreigner novels, which have *components* which may be military (you do *not* want a Liaden scout's ship shooting at you, trust me), but whose primary focus is somewhere else entirely, are just as clearly space opera without being what I would classify as military science fiction.

The bottom line is that the descriptor "space opera" is both broader and more... nuanced than readers sometimes realize. It is a very far-stretching genre, which welcomes a vast spectrum of both writers and readers, and one has to wonder why it has such staying power and attracts so many fans.

I think people probably read space opera for as many reasons as there are readers, but I suspect most of them have certain characteristics in common. They like fast-paced stories (for the most part; the tempo of some space opera is much more measured) with consistent world building; characters with whom they can empathize (whether that be to love or to hate the characters in question); large-scale canvases, even for single-character stories painted into a corner of the canvas; plots that make sense (although they like it even better if the writer can keep them guessing or take them in a surprise direction); and writers who play fair with them and with their favorite characters, without ringing in sudden God weapons or authorial intervention when things get a little sticky.

In short, they want to explore worlds their imagination gets to help build while simultaneously experiencing what makes human beings human. Well crafted and executed aliens are a treasure beyond price in space opera—Chuck Gannon's current Caine Riordan series is a splendid example of that, as are Carolyn Cherryh's Chanur novels—but ultimately, the reader wants to see how those aliens interact with humans and how the contact changes both species. And because those well crafted and executed aliens are the product of human storytellers, there are going to be points of congruence with humanity within them, because if there aren't, then a human reader—and the human characters in the story itself—can't fully connect or engage with them.

I've written a space opera or two in my time, and most of mine do include things that explode, but not all of it does. For example, in the Liaden novels (which I've already mentioned, possibly because they are some of my favorite stories in the world), Lee and Miller handle combat, both on the personal and the ship-to-ship level, very well and military action is definitely a major plot strand in many of the stories, but the emphasis is on the social structures, the elements which define who and what the characters in the books are and how the disparate branches of humanity—Liaden, Terran, and Yxtrang—

define themselves as well as the resonances of who *they* are that each of them discovers in the "otherness" of those "alien" beings. Carolyn Cherryh's Foreigner novels would fall into that same category of non-military space opera, whereas *Downbelow Station* has a much stronger, overtly military strand.

At the end of the day, it's the characters and the challenges those characters confront that make or break any story, and space opera—whether overtly military or not—is no exception to that rule. Where space opera differs from many other genres is the scale upon which those challenges work out. In multivolume space opera series, individual books or stories may be "small-scale," focused on individual characters or single families or isolated corners of explored space, but those individual stories are linked on a far larger stage. In standalone space opera stories, the scale of the universe is normally made clear quickly. But in almost all cases, the characters' decisions and challenges have major consequences. Their decisions and actions *matter*. There may be shades of gray, ambiguity, even dystopia or an antihero slant, but what happens—what responsibility is taken (or evaded) and what the characters *do*—is important, and usually not just for the protagonist and his or her friends.

I think it's *that* scale, more than the number of light years between encounters, that truly draws readers—and writers—to space opera. Space operas are our modern Homeric sagas. They let the storyteller create heroes and villains who operate on playing fields and battlefields where challenges are met and grappled with *decisively* by characters who, whether by choice or necessity, are called upon to perform at a level above themselves. And they let us, as readers, explore characters who inspire, or caution, or fail because of flaws we might see within ourselves, but who touch us on that deep, inner level where dreams, hopes, emotions, and our sense of our own obligations all flow together.

Writers of space opera are conjurers, the "man behind the screen" creating the narrative and the world in which the reader's imagination and personal experience interacts with the words to spin spells that neither the writer nor the reader could have created in isolation. As someone who writes space opera, believe me when I tell you that the writers are fully aware of our intimate partnership with our readers.

And we're equally aware that without those readers, our story and our vision must ultimately fail. Space opera is collaboration on a grand scale between the imagination of the storyteller and the imagination of the audience. Neither could succeed without the other, but together they can take us on a voyage beyond any starship without ever leaving our own library.

That's what truly draws both readers and writers to space opera, and that's really what the stories in this volume are about. Some of the classic stories—like "Mismatch" and its archaic "slipsticks"—are like messages in a bottle from our own literary past. The contemporary stories in this collection, those that last, will someday be messages in a bottle to someone *else's* literary past. But all of them get down into the weeds of what it is to be human, to face challenges, to meet obligations, while at the same time creating worlds that never were or are yet to be as they invite the reader into the storyteller's magic cave to sit around the fire while the wonders of might-be are unwrapped and laid before him or her.

So find yourself a comfortable rock near the front, where you can keep an eye on that conjurer's hands and see if you can spot the moment the illusion truly begins. You may not be able to, but I think you'll probably enjoy the evening, anyway.

Jack Campbell is the pen name of John G. Hemry, whose amazing fiction has appeared in all of the major science fiction magazines. His New York Times bestselling series The Lost Fleet has spawned two sequels, and is one of the most popular military science fiction series currently running. Centered around the legendary John "Black Jack" Geary, The Lost Fleet reveals how he gained his renown, and the various spin-offs continue the chronicle—as does our story, which is a fast-paced tale of a chief gunner's mate trying to prove her own merit while under the shadow of a legend. Hit with heavy fire and facing boarders, she must push the boundaries of her understanding and military rules in order to save her ship.

AUTHOR'S NOTE: The Lost Fleet is a military science fiction/space opera series set one-hundred-plus years into an interstellar war between two different human cultures: the Alliance and the Syndics. So far the original Lost Fleet series has led to three spin-off series: Beyond the Frontier, The Lost Stars, and The Genesis Fleet. This story takes place a few years after the century-long war began when John "Black Jack" Geary fought a desperate battle to stave off the first Syndic surprise attack. Geary himself is presumed dead and is being celebrated by the Alliance government as a great hero to inspire others in the war effort. The surviving crew of his ship have gone on to other ships and other battles. But all of them remain defined by their status as someone who was present at "Black Jack's Last Stand." And each of them feels the need to live up to that. Regardless of who they were before, now they are forever survivors of Black Jack's crew. This is the story of one of those sailors, and of the gunner's mates who have always kept the faith no matter how hot the guns get.

ISHIGAKI
A LOST FLEET STORY

JACK CAMPBELL

The former cruise liner, which stripped of its fine furnishings now served as a military transport, had crossed the gulf between stars to arrive at a gas giant planet orbited by half a dozen massive construction yards. Sailors, many of them fresh from their first training, barely noticed the majestic view on display as they were packed into shuttles and distributed to the new warships being built as fast as humans and their devices could do the job. A few of those sailors, probably on their first journey to another star, might have been thinking of the bitter irony that the discovery of a practical means for interstellar travel had also made interstellar war practical, but even they would have insisted that this was not a war of their choosing. Their homes, their families, their freedom had to be defended against those who threatened all three. Though humanity had found new battlefields, it still fought the same wars.

"Chief Gunner's Mate Diana Magoro reporting for duty."

"Welcome aboard the *Ishigaki*," the nearly-overwhelmed-by-work officer of the deck said, his eyes scanning her data on his pad rather than looking at her face. "Durgan! Take the chief to Ensign Rodriquez."

A tired-looking sailor gestured to Magoro before heading into the interior of the ship.

She followed past a ship's crest painted on one bulkhead, a stone tower looming in the center of the crest and the words "Stone Wall of the Alliance" along the bottom. Apparently the name *Ishigaki* had something to do with that. It wasn't surprising that a heavy cruiser had such a name, as they were usually called after defensive fortifications or parts of armor. But this was the first time she'd encountered a cruiser named *Ishigaki*. Traditionally, Alliance ships had tended to pass down the same names as old ships were stricken and new ships constructed. These days, with the Alliance fleet adding warships as fast as they could be built, new names were being revived from the history of humanity far away on Old Earth and the cultures that people had brought with them to the stars.

Along with war. People had brought that, too, of course.

Magoro followed her guide down passageways that were never quite wide enough for all of the personnel moving through them. Cables, conduits and ducts along the sides and the overhead further constricted the passages. Everything about *Ishigaki* felt new, something Magoro still had trouble getting used to. In the pre-war fleet, nearly every ship had been at least a decade old, sometimes much more than that. Now, nearly every ship felt new.

The old ones were gone. Destroyed in battle, fighting desperately until new ships could be built.

They passed a lot of other sailors, faces and names that were unfamiliar to her but would become well-known before long. Those other sailors glanced at her face, followed by a glance at the ribbons on the left breast of her uniform. Everybody did that. She did it to them. Do I know this person? And what has she done? The face told one story, the service ribbons and medals another.

She hoped no one would notice one of her ribbons. Regulations required her to wear it, but it tended to gather way too much attention.

The sailor left her at a compartment with "Weapons Department" stenciled on the hatch. Inside, several desks fastened to the deck were covered with scattered parts and equipment, many tagged as faulty. A female ensign with a harried expression on a face that seemed too young for an officer looked up as she entered. "Yeah?"

Diana offered her comm pad to the ensign. "Chief Gunner's Mate Magoro, ma'am."

"You're mine?" The ensign stared at her orders. "You're mine! Welcome aboard, Chief! Have a seat! I'm Ensign Rodriquez. Gunnery Officer. Just a moment while I check your record..."

She jerked with almost comical surprise. "You've been in the fleet for ten years?"

"Yes, ma'am."

"You've got ten years of experience as a gunner's mate?"

"Yes, ma'am."

"Ten... years?"

"Yes, ma'am."

"My ancestors must be smiling on me!" Ensign Rodriquez grinned at her. "An old fleet sailor! With pre-war experience!"

Magoro nodded in reply. Everything today seemed to be measured that way. Not yesterday and today and tomorrow, but pre-war and war and after-the-war, though she'd noticed that after six years of fighting people weren't mentioning after-the-war as much lately. "I've been working on weapons for a while," she said. Ensign Rodriquez's reaction to her wasn't surprising. Many of the old, experienced sailors of the pre-war fleet had died in the first desperate year of the war, and the survivors were now spread thin in the much larger fleet. She felt a bit like a ghost at times, part of a dwindling remnant of what had once been.

"You actually made chief?"

The voice, tinged with what sounded like mock-surprise, was vaguely familiar. As Ensign Rodriquez scrambled hastily to her feet, Magoro stood and turned to see a face she remembered better than the voice. "I see you made commander, sir."

Ensign Rodriquez, startled by their exchange, took a moment to speak. "Chief, this is Commander Weiss, captain of the *Ishigaki*. You know Chief Magoro, sir?"

Commander Weiss smiled slightly as he looked at Magoro, but his eyes stayed hard, questioning. "We served together on another ship about six years ago, when I was an ensign."

"Six years—" Ensign Rodriguez's voice cut off as she stared at Weiss and then Magoro, her eyes going to the dark ribbon with a bright gold star centered on it. "You were on *Merlon*, too, Chief? With Black Jack himself?"

Black Jack? "Um… with Commander Geary, yes, ma'am."

"At his last stand," Rodriguez said, looking at her in awe that exceeded the previous wonderment at her experience. "Ancestors save me. *Ishigaki* has two veterans of Black Jack's last battle aboard!"

Magoro, uncomfortable, looked back at Commander Weiss, who this time gave her the polite smile of a shared past. But the eyes of *Ishigaki*'s captain remained challenging.

"I'll talk to you later, Chief," Weiss said, nodding in farewell to Ensign Rodriquez. It sounded like a simple, polite statement, but to Magoro it carried more than a whiff of a grim promise.

Great. Her past had really caught up with her this time. Magoro listened to Ensign Rodriquez continue her welcome speech and description of the challenges facing the Weapons Division on the *Ishigaki*, familiar challenges involving new equipment hastily churned out to meet demands and new sailors who had passed technical training but lacked much actual experience. Through it all, half of her mind stayed on Commander Weiss.

She wasn't looking forward to that talk with the captain.

+ + +

About four very long hours later, after meeting the sailors who'd be working for her, and making initial inspections of the hell lance batteries, which were in better shape than she had feared but still needed work, Diana Magoro ducked into the chiefs' mess to grab some coffee. Despite everything else that had changed since the war began, that one thing remained the same. There was always coffee available. It was usually bad coffee that sometimes looked and tasted like tar, but that was also traditional. She shuddered as she took a drink, grateful that it was so hot it helped mask the flavor.

"Diana, right?" Another chief extended his hand to her. "I'm Vlad Darkar. Engineering. Welcome aboard."

"Hey, Vlad." She followed the other chief to the small table with chairs fixed around it, grateful for the chance to relax for a moment with another chief who'd give her straight information. "What exactly happened to the guy I'm replacing?"

Vlad shook his head, looking down at his coffee. "He cracked during our work-ups. Couldn't handle the pressure." Darkar shifted his gaze to look at her. "Part of that was because he didn't know the job well enough. You know how that is."

She nodded. Officially, no one got promoted unless they had the necessary skills. Unofficially, everyone knew that the demand for senior enlisted personnel far exceeded the qualified supply. Some of the "old hands" in a chiefs' mess probably had only three years of service under their belts.

"I hear you're old fleet, though," Darkar continued. His eyes flicked across her ribbons, pausing in their movement as he focused on one in particular. "Damn. You were at Grendel?"

"Yeah." She took another drink of the coffee to avoid having to say more.

"With Black Jack himself, huh?"

She managed not to frown in puzzlement at Darkar's use of the nickname. First the ensign and now a chief? "Commander Geary was my captain, yeah."

Vlad Darkar sat back, his eyes admiring. "What was that like?"

"Grendel, or Commander Geary?"

He grinned. "Both."

Magoro shrugged. "Grendel was a battle. I was on a hell lance crew. Battery Two Bravo. We knew the odds we were facing, but you do your job, right? We felt the ship accelerating and braking, changing course, and sometimes our gun fired." Some people in a fight saw the big picture, knew what was happening, but many others saw only their small part of it. She knew it disappointed those who wanted her to describe Geary issuing heroic orders, but she hadn't been on the bridge. "Then we got hit bad a few times. We took some hell lances right through the battery. They killed some of the guys in the crew, and the hell lance got torn up too bad to fix, so I was sent to another gun crew trying to get their battery back on line. We were still working it when word was passed to abandon ship and we headed for the escape pods."

She paused, remembering fear and haste amid the minimal light cast by the emergency lights on the badly hurt cruiser, sailors a bit clumsy in their survival suits scrambling past damage, the harsh sound of her breathing inside the suit and the unnatural sharpness of everything she could see with the ship's atmosphere vented through holes in the hull. "It wasn't until we boosted clear that most of us on the pod I was in heard that Commander Geary had stayed behind to keep the *Merlon* fighting a little longer, so we could get away and so the Syndics wouldn't be able to catch any of the convoy we were escorting." Guilt lingered whenever she thought about that. But it had been the captain's decision to stay behind a little longer, and disobeying his orders wouldn't have been right.

Darkar shook his head in admiration, as if she'd just told some story of her own heroism. "They say that if Black Jack hadn't stopped that attack force at Grendel the Syndicate Worlds' surprise attack would've done a lot more damage. Maybe enough to have knocked out the Alliance before we could react in time."

"We just delayed that Syndic flotilla at Grendel," she said. "And made sure our convoy jumped clear so they could warn about the attacks on the way."

"But that made all the difference! Black Jack saved the Alliance!"

Vlad Darkar leaned a little closer to her. "You talked to him when he was your captain, right?"

"Sure." Diana Magoro hoped she wouldn't wince at any of those memories as they flashed through her mind. Especially that one time, standing at attention, waiting for the hammer to fall, knowing she deserved whatever she got.

If she did flinch, the other chief didn't notice. She managed to redirect the conversation to the state of *Ishigaki* and her crew, picking up some new information before heading back out to try to catch up with work that should've been completed weeks ago.

✦ ✦ ✦

Diana Magoro was half-inside the bulk of a hell lance particle beam projector when the ship's interior lights dimmed to mark the official beginning of "night" aboard. Space didn't care about day and night, but humans needed it. They clung to things from the past, she thought, like the way gunner's mates called the hell lances "guns" instead of using some more technically accurate name.

She checked the connection on the part she'd finished replacing before pulling herself out of the weapon's interior and yawning as she stood up.

"Working late?"

She tensed, looking to see Commander Weiss watching her. "Yes, sir. I've been personally checking over each hell lance projector."

"That doesn't sound like the Diana Magoro I knew on the *Merlon*," Weiss said.

"I've changed a bit," Magoro said.

"Hmmm." Commander Weiss switched his gaze to the hulking hell lance, whose shape tended to remind people of an ancient troll kneeling as it prepared to leap at an opponent. "How are you fitting in?"

"Okay, sir." Magoro shrugged. "Lots of questions about *Merlon* and the captain. Commander Geary, I mean."

"I understand." Weiss smiled crookedly. "Even though I'm commanding officer of this ship, I know who you'll be talking about when you say 'the captain.' I do the same thing."

"I guess we all do," she said. "No disrespect to you intended, sir."

"Really? You used to skate as close to disrespect as you could." Weiss paused, his expression growing colder. "Have you told anyone that one of your personal encounters with Commander Geary involved him busting you down two paygrades?"

"No, sir." Magoro grimaced at the memory. She noticed Weiss waiting for more and realized why. "I deserved it. I admitted it at the time. You were there. And I haven't done that since, sir. Nothing like that."

Commander Weiss made a face. "Falsifying maintenance records. Hacking system records to hide it. You know why I'm worried."

"Because now I'm responsible for making sure the hell lances on this ship work. Your ship. I haven't done it since, sir. Commander Geary gave me a second chance. I was stupid back then, but not too stupid to realize how lucky I was."

"Lieutenant Commander Decala wanted to court-martial you and kick you out of the fleet," Weiss said.

"So I heard."

Weiss sighed. "We really need an experienced chief gunner on this ship." He gestured around the ship surrounding them. "You know what we're facing. The crew's been rushed through training. Actual experience is rare. They know the theory, but they haven't got the time working with the gear."

"Yes, sir. It's a familiar problem these days."

Commander Weiss studied her again while Magoro waited. "Chief, if you pull anything on *Ishigaki* like you did on *Merlon*, I won't court-martial you. Instead I'll let the fleet commander have you shot for malfeasance in the face of the enemy."

"Then I have nothing to worry about," Magoro said, feeling her stomach knot and hoping it didn't show. "Because I'm going to do my best, sir. And I know this job." To emphasize her words she stood straight and offered Weiss the best salute she could manage.

Weiss cocked one eyebrow at her. "Maybe you'll be okay. You're certainly not the same. The Diana Magoro I remember was always getting chewed out for sloppy saluting and sloppy bearing and sloppy uniforms. Now, on a ship full of new sailors who can barely wear the uniform right and have trouble saluting without hurting themselves, I'm seeing you in a flawless uniform and rendering salutes so sharp I could shave with one of them."

Magoro grinned despite her nervousness. "I have to be a good example now, sir."

"I'm glad that you realize that. You were my biggest problem child when I was an ensign." Commander Weiss nodded at her. "Don't be a problem now. I've got a lot to deal with. Six years from ensign to commander of a heavy cruiser is a fast leap."

"Six years from being busted back to the lowest grade of sailor to chief is pretty fast, too, sir."

"They need our experience, limited as it is," Weiss said. "And we have to make sure we don't let down those depending on us. Especially you and me. People look at us differently because we were on the *Merlon* at Grendel."

"I've noticed," Magoro said, drawing a real smile from Commander Weiss this time. "Sir? How many of us who got off the *Merlon* are left? Does anyone know?"

The smile faded. "I think there're about fifty survivors who haven't joined their ancestors yet. Probably less than that now. We lose some with every battle."

Magoro grimaced. "It feels wrong. To die, I mean. Because Commander Geary gave his life to make sure the rest of us got off the ship. Dying seems like betraying what he gave his life for. That sounds kind of stupid, doesn't it?"

"No, it doesn't," Weiss said. "I know exactly what you mean."

"Sir, can I ask you something about Commander Geary? What's with this Black Jack stuff? I try not to get too involved in talk about that, but it's getting kind of weird, isn't it? I mean, Commander Geary was a good commanding officer. I owe him a lot, not even counting him saving our lives at Grendel. But I think back on *Merlon* I heard somebody whisper that Black Jack nickname once and everybody said don't ever do that again, he hates that name. And now people who never knew him are calling him Black Jack like they're old shipmates and talking like he was a living star come to save us."

Weiss looked to the side, his expression troubled. "You're right that he hated that nickname. Just like you hated being called Gundeck Magoro."

She winced. "Yes, sir. But that nickname didn't follow me."

"Hopefully that's for a good reason. As for Black Jack, even ensigns like me knew better than to say it anywhere Commander Geary might hear us. But it's part of the way the fleet is treating his memory. The new people are being told stories about Commander Geary, about how amazing he was. I can't really talk to them because if I say he was just human they look… betrayed or something. I guess the Alliance needs a hero, he got the job, and using the Black Jack nickname makes him feel like one of us even though he was supposedly more than us."

"I guess it can't hurt him," Magoro said, "him being dead at Grendel and all, but it doesn't seem right. I mean, it's good to remember the best things about people who're dead, but making up stuff seems wrong. I figure that has to bother his spirit."

Commander Weiss shrugged. "Commander Geary's spirit can probably handle anything thrown at it. I'd rather you worried about the guns on this ship. Your record since Grendel looks good, so I'll give you the same chance Geary did. Don't make me sorry I did, Chief."

"You won't be, sir."

+ + +

"Did everybody get that?" Diana Magoro said, looking at the rank of gunner's mates who'd just watched her demonstrate a complex maintenance task. "You have to get this right. Hell lances use a big burst of energy when they fire. That energy has to be handled right and built up to the right level at the right rate of increase. You do not get slack with any step of this."

"Ma'am?" one of the younger looking sailors asked.

"Do not call me or any other chief ma'am, or sir," Magoro said. "We work for a living."

"I'm sorry! Chief, what if we're asked to power up the weapons faster than the procedures call for?"

Somebody always asked that. The answer was always the same. "You tell the bridge that they're being powered up as fast as they can be."

"But what if it's an emergency? Can't we shave even a little time off by pushing against the safety parameters?"

That called for a Chief's Glare at Maximum Intensity. "No. Everybody! What happens if you try to power up a hell lance too quickly?"

A gunner's mate named Bandera raised a tentative hand. "Um... doesn't that cause a Catastrophic Energy Containment Failure, Chief?"

"Very good. Take an extra cookie tonight at dinner." Magoro kept her glare fixed as she swept it across the sailors before her. "For those who like small words, another way of saying Catastrophic Energy Containment Failure is *explosion*. If you somehow survived that explosion, the fleet would bend every effort to keep you alive just long enough for a firing squad to be collected so they could kill you legal and proper. Don't mess with the safety parameters on the gear! Because if you do and the gear doesn't kill you, and the fleet doesn't kill you, *I'll* kill you. Got it?"

"Yes, Chief!" they chorused.

After the others left, Bandera stayed behind. "Chief? Can I ask you something?"

He was a hard worker, and enthusiastic in a naïve way that both pleased her and pained her. Life in the fleet would wear down that enthusiasm in time, but for now she liked him. "Sure. What?"

"That stuff about powering up the hell lances faster," he said, looking hesitant. "When we graduated from tech school, some of the older gunner's mates took us out to celebrate and while we were all drinking some of them started talking about ways to power up faster." The sailor swallowed nervously as he saw Magoro's reaction to his words. "I just... Chief, why'd they talk about doing that if it's so dangerous?"

She sighed, looking over at the bulk of the nearest hell lance. "It's a challenge. That's why. We're gunners. We want to play with the guns. Tweak them, test them, try new stuff. I'll bet you the very first gunner who was shown the very first hell lance immediately started trying to think of ways to make it power up faster. It's natural for us to wonder about that. But it's stupid."

Magoro looked back at the sailor, who she was pleased to see was watching her with an appropriately sober expression. "Before the war, when all we had were drills and maintenance to keep us busy, some gunner's mates on a lot of different ships decided to spice things up by having a secret competition. They tried to see who could power up a hell lance faster, shaving tens of seconds or even hundredths of seconds off the process so their ship would have bragging rights. What do you think eventually happened?"

The sailor winced. "An explosion?"

"Yeah. Somebody shaved off just a little too much time, energy containment failed, an entire gun crew died, and the investigation into the accident found out about the competition. That was peacetime, so nobody was shot, but a lot of people ended up wishing they'd been in the gun crew that did die."

"I understand, Chief. Thank you!" Bandera hustled away.

Magoro heard someone clear their throat and looked to see that Ensign Rodriquez had been listening. "That was great, Chief," she said. "I couldn't help listening, and… that's just what they needed to hear. Follow the rules."

"Thank you, ma'am." Magoro eyed the ensign. "Ma'am, you know that there are circumstances when you shouldn't follow the rules, right? That's one reason why we're here instead of letting 'bots do the job, because the 'bots always follow the rules even when that'd be stupid. But the thing is, those new guys don't know what those circumstances are. It's our job to know when we need to do things a little different."

Ensign Rodriguez hesitated. "Chief, were you…?"

"Part of the competition before the war? No, ma'am. I joined the fleet a couple of years after that came to light. Lots of people were still talking about it, of course."

"Of course." Ensign Rodriguez hesitated again. "Uh, Chief, when it comes to deciding when not to follow the rules…"

She tried to look reliable and reassuring. "I understand, ma'am. I won't use any initiative without asking permission beforehand."

"Good! Good!" Rodriguez hustled out, on her way to do some more of whatever it was officers did.

Diana Magoro stood alone for a while in the hell lance battery compartment, thinking about the mistakes she had made. It wasn't about being perfect, she told herself. It was about learning and not doing that sort of stupid thing again.

"*I think you're smart enough to learn from this,*" Commander Geary had told her more than six years ago as she nearly shook with fright. "*I think you can be a good gunner's mate. Prove me right.*"

She still didn't know whether the captain had been right. But she wasn't ready to stop trying.

A week later the *Ishigaki* joined up with a group of other warships taking on supplies. When they headed out afterwards, even the dumbest sailor knew the cruiser was headed for her first fight.

✦ ✦ ✦

A long, high-pitched, wavering whistle sounded over the ship's general announcing system. Conversation in the chiefs' mess halted as they waited for whatever announcement followed.

"All hands, this is the captain. We're part of a task force headed for Kairos Star System," Commander Weiss said. "That's a Syndicate Worlds–held star near the border region of space. The fleet is preparing a major attack on Atalia Star System, so our job is to carry out a successful diversion to draw Syndicate warships to the defense of Kairos, leaving Atalia weakened when our main force hits it. Be prepared to hit the Syndics hard and fast, then live up to *Ishigaki*'s name as we fight a delaying action against Syndicate reinforcements. To the honor of our ancestors!"

Diana Magoro looked upward, puzzled. "That's a new one. Why tell us where the real attack is going in? What if some of us get captured?"

"Did the captain tell us where the real attack is going in?" Chief Drakar asked. "Or is it really going to be someplace other than Atalia?"

"A double diversion?" Chief Kantor from fire control looked worried. "Send the Syndics scrambling to Atalia if some of our people crack under interrogation? But that'd mean the brass are hoping some of us get captured and spill our guts about what we heard."

"Yeah," Magoro agreed. "I hope you're wrong, Vlad. I'd rather believe the fleet brass didn't think things through. Based on experience, that's not too hard to believe."

"You're the old sailor," Chief Darkar said with a laugh.

"Anyway," Kantor added, "I heard the Syndics aren't always taking prisoners anymore. Unless they think we have some special information, they'd probably just shoot us."

"Aren't you the cheerful one," Darkar said, no longer laughing.

"I'm just a realist," Kantor said. "The war's stalemated, isn't it? Who knows how long it could go on? And I know my history. The longer a war goes on, the worse it gets."

✦ ✦ ✦

Jump drives made interstellar travel routine, allowing ships to use jump points that existed only near objects as massive as stars to enter a gray nothingness called jump space that shrank distances so that another star was only a week or two travel time away. Diana Magoro had long ago decided that traveling through jump space was like being in an apparently endless fall. You could do things, work, eat, sleep, but hanging over it all was the realization that you weren't really anywhere and that at some point the whole thing would abruptly end. And it was then, that moment when your ship lurched back into normal space, that things could really get bad.

Since they were arriving at an enemy star system, everyone was at battle stations when the drop out of jump space occurred. Magoro was in charge of the port hell lance batteries, while Ensign Rodriguez was with one of the starboard batteries. She'd chosen to post herself at battery Two Bravo, forward of amidships but not at the bow. Two linked hell lance projectors sat facing the firing ports, their energy cells maxed, ready to fire on command. Magoro and the three members of this battery's gun crew were all in survival suits, ready in case enemy fire put a hole in the hull and the atmosphere in the compartment vanished into space.

As a chief, Magoro had the benefit of being able to link her survival suit's internal display to the fire control status, so she was able to see what was happening outside the ship.

The entire task force had dropped into normal space. A battle cruiser, four heavy cruisers of which *Ishigaki* was one, two light cruisers, and a dozen destroyers. They were in a spherical formation, the battle cruiser in the center, the heavy cruisers spaced around, above, and below it, and the light cruisers and destroyers making up the outer portion of the sphere. She gazed at the image, thinking that before the war that "small" task force would've represented a substantial fraction of the entire Alliance fleet.

The jump point they'd arrived at was a good four light hours from the star Kairos. The sole inhabited world in this star system orbited about three and half light hours from here. No enemy forces were near the jump point, but Magoro saw a Syndic flotilla only a light hour distant. It seemed to be about the size of the Alliance force.

It'd be an hour before the Syndicate forces saw the arrival of the attacking warships, but the Alliance task force wasn't going to wait for that. Magoro felt the force of *Ishigaki*'s main propulsion cut in as it and the other Alliance ships accelerated toward an intercept with the enemy formation.

✦ ✦ ✦

Damn. Damn. Damn.

At point-one light it had taken more than half a day to cover the distance between the opposing forces, the Syndics only accelerating in the last hour before contact.

Magoro wasn't an officer, wasn't trained in the skills of fighting in a three-dimensional battlefield with no limits, no up or down, and distances so immense that light itself, and messages sent at the speed of light, took seconds, minutes, and even hours to bridge the gap.

But she'd seen a few battles since Grendel, and as the two forces closed to engage this one had felt wrong. Clumsy. Unimaginative. She couldn't have said why, but maybe it was just because the admiral in charge of the Alliance force was charging straight in without trying any fancy maneuvers. How much experience did that admiral have? Six years ago, today's admiral could have been a lieutenant. If that.

The first pass had been a brutal exchange of fire that rocked *Ishigaki*. Magoro monitored the performance of the starboard hell lance batteries as they hurled streams of charged particles during those moments when enemy ships were close enough to target. The second pass was better as the enemy concentrated fire on other Alliance warships, and *Ishigaki*'s own fire helped knock out a Syndic cruiser. Unfortunately, two Alliance heavy cruisers had been taken out, one of the light cruisers had exploded, and six destroyers were gone. The Syndics hadn't been hurt as badly, but at least the Alliance battle cruiser was still in decent shape.

On the third pass, *Ishigaki* took two enemy missiles followed immediately by a barrage of hell lances and grapeshot. The heavy cruiser's shields collapsed, the enemy fire lashing the hull. Hell lances punched holes through everything in their way, while the solid metal ball bearings that made up grapeshot either tore their own holes or gave up their energy in flashes of heat that shattered anything they hit.

Two enemy hell lance shots went through the compartment that Magoro was in. She didn't see them, only the holes bigger than her fist that suddenly appeared on the outer hull, on the casings of one of *Ishigaki*'s hell lance batteries, and on the inner bulkhead and deck as the enemy particle beams tore through anything in their path.

Which also included two of the gun crew. One of them didn't move, a large hole completely through one side of his chest, his body lax in death. The other stared at the thin strip still holding her upper arm to her body, the rest of that part of the arm gone.

As atmosphere rushed out of the ship, Magoro slapped an auto-tourniquet on the sailor's arm above the injury, the device latching on, slicing cleanly through her survival suit and the arm beneath to seal off the wound. Magoro punched the first aid controls on the sailor's suit to have it slam sedative and anti-shock drugs into her. "Bandera, take her to sick bay."

The remaining member of the gun crew stared at her. "Chief? But… but… the guns."

"They took hits. They're off-line. I'll see if they can be repaired. Get 'Ski to the sick bay so they can save her and then get back here."

"Yes, Chief."

Magoro glanced at the status of the other starboard hell lance batteries, shocked to see that all of them were out of action. "I need status reports on batteries Two Alpha and Two Charlie!" she called over the internal comm circuit for the guns.

"This is Richards in Two Alpha," a quavering voice answered her. "Both of our guns are gone."

"Gone doesn't tell me status, Richards! How much damage did the guns take?"

"They're *gone*, Chief! Grapeshot blew open this part of the hull and tore off half the deck in here, along with most of both guns. We found ourselves staring into space on the edge of what was left!"

"Ancestors save us. Two Charlie, what's your status? Two Charlie!" No reply. That lack of response served as an ugly answer to what kind of damage Two Charlie had probably sustained. "Richards, can you get back here to help me at Two Bravo?"

"We'll try, Chief. There's a lot of damage between us and you."

"Get out of that compartment and try to get to another battery on the starboard side if you can't reach this one," Magoro ordered. She wondered why she was able to handle all this without panicking at the amount of damage *Ishigaki* had sustained and the number of sailors who'd already been killed and wounded, realizing that it was just experience working, her mind automatically doing the things it had trained to do over and over again.

She finally checked the hell lances in this battery, yanking open access panels to see sections that she couldn't get outside readings on. Both guns were down hard, probably unrepairable in the time available. "Ensign Rodriguez, we've lost all hell lances on this side of the ship."

Rodriquez's reply sounded breathless. Almost overwhelmed. "Very… very well. Chief, they're coming in for another run at us. The ship's lost maneuvering control. I think—"

Ishigaki jolted as if dozens of hammers had slammed into her in a discordant salvo. Magoro grabbed onto the nearest grip to hold herself steady. "Ma'am? Ensign Rodriguez? Anybody on this circuit?"

Silence.

She fought a rising sense of fear, wondering how badly the cruiser had been hurt.

Where was Bandera? Had he made it to sick bay with 'Ski? Was he blocked by damage from getting back here?

She tried checking the status of the grapeshot launchers, but the links were down.

Ishigaki jerked again as something hit her hard.

Magoro closed her eyes, trying to control her breathing, remembering the near-panic when the crew had abandoned *Merlon*. They'd never taken abandon ship drills seriously in the pre-war fleet. Why would they ever have to abandon ship? The memory of fighting her way through the damaged ship, trying to find an undamaged escape pod, had haunted her ever since.

I think you can be a good gunner's mate.

Who'd said that?

Commander Geary, pronouncing sentence on her, or rather showing mercy when she had no reason to expect any.

All right. Maybe she could handle this.

Diana Magoro opened her eyes and tried to find out the status of the rest of the ship, but most of those links were dead as well. She couldn't feel any thrusters firing, though, or the main propulsion cutting in. The only good thing was that the power supply running into this compartment to feed the hell lances was still up. The power core must be okay, so *Ishigaki* wasn't close to blowing up.

She tried checking fire control to find out what was happening outside the ship, but fire control was completely down. What else might work? Magoro went to a comm panel on the bulkhead and cycled through anything that was still working on basic systems. Not much. Wait. Navigation. That'd give her a view of the outside.

The other surviving Alliance and Syndic ships were tangling a few light seconds away where the battle had drifted since *Ishigaki* was knocked out. But one Syndic had broken free of that fight and was swooping up toward an intercept with the helplessly drifting *Ishigaki*. A light cruiser. No, one of the Syndic hybrids, an assault cruiser, loaded with extra special forces troops. No wonder it was heading for *Ishigaki*. They'd seen that the heavy cruiser was helpless and meant to board this ship to see what intelligence they could gather.

I heard the Syndics aren't always taking prisoners anymore.

Diana Magoro bent her head so the helmet of her survival suit rested against the bulkhead. She could feel vibrations and jars through the contact, the movements of equipment and sailors aboard *Ishigaki*. This ship, *her* ship, wasn't dead yet. But *Ishigaki* was in serious trouble.

"All hands draw weapons and stand by to repel boarders! I say again, all hands…" The announcement trailed off as the comm circuit failed.

Magoro tried to yank open the hatch and found it was jammed. One of the last enemy blows that had hit *Ishigaki* had damaged this part of her hull enough to seal this hatch until someone could cut it open.

She couldn't get to where she needed to be to repel boarders and she was stuck here with a useless hell lance battery. She glared at one of the holes in the hull that gave a view of space, wondering if she'd be able to see that Syndic cruiser on its approach, watching helplessly.

Wait a minute.

Magoro tapped the navigation menu again, getting a zoom of the projected approach of the Syndic warship. If that cruiser meant to board, and it was coming along that vector, it'd come in… here. She would see the enemy ship as it made its final approach, coming very close to *Ishigaki*, their vectors matched, so the enemy troops could board.

She looked at the hell lance projectors.

No.

Crazy.

They were knocked out. Impossible to fix in the time she had even if the spares had been right here.

Could she fire them anyway?

One of the big advantages of really knowing how something worked, what all the parts did and why, meant it was sometimes possible to figure out how to make it do things even without some of those parts. And Diana Magoro had been working on hell lances for ten years.

She started ripping open any access panels that were still closed, checking damage to the hell lances. Yeah. Number one's power regulator was gone, and the backup regulator had failed, which meant number two couldn't fire either since they drew on a common power storage. There was other damage, but that was the main thing. That and there was no way to aim them with fire control dead.

But the *Ishigaki* still had power. If she could power up the hell lances in time…

She'd die. The incoming Syndic warship would detect this hell lance battery powering up. They'd target it, and this little piece of *Ishigaki* would become a little piece of hell. Diana Magoro shook her head, knowing that she'd never have time to get a shot off.

Unless...

Containment would fail if it tried to hold energy pumped into it too quickly. But what if she didn't try to hold the energy? What if she overrode safety and control settings on the hell lances so they'd fire as soon as containment registered enough energy for a shot? There'd be a tiny delay in which containment had to hold. But maybe tiny enough to hold.

Normally, that sort of thing wouldn't make sense. Hell lances had to be prepped to fire during the vanishingly short moments when the enemy got within range. They had to hold a charge until that moment came. But this time she'd be looking at a ship coming in close. She could fire the moment she had power up.

If she was wrong, either the Syndics would target this battery and kill her, or the hell lances would explode and kill her. There didn't seem to be a *this didn't work so I'll try something else* option.

But if she could make this happen...

How fast can I power up a hell lance? Maybe I'll set a record that no other gunner can ever beat.

She tried comms to the bridge or the weapons officer or fire control again, but they were all still out.

This was her decision.

Oh, hell, why not? If she was going to die along with what remained of *Ishigaki*'s crew, why not go down trying to get in one last shot?

The power distribution panel was half gone. She ran physical links between gaps, turning a sophisticated piece of control equipment into a web of hardwired connections. One big span stymied her for a moment, until she jammed a heavy metal tool into the gap, spot welding it into place. Electricians tended to joke that any piece of solid metal was a gunner's mate's circuit breaker, but even they probably never expected someone to do this.

She checked the circuits, and found power blocked. The power regulator on number two couldn't talk to the power regulator on number one, because there was a hole where that had once been, so it was blocking power. She tried disabling, bypassing, or powering down the power regulator on number two, but the designers had been fiendishly clever when it came to this safety feature. Nothing worked.

An electrical tech or a code monkey couldn't have solved the problem. But she was a gunner's mate. Magoro picked up her heaviest tool and slammed it repeatedly into the number two power regulator.

Sparks and pieces flew.

The regulator powered off.

She worked as fast as she could to reroute everything, bypassing the sophisticated controls and regulators that still existed and would never let the weapons work under these circumstances. She hardwired power bridges and couplings so they'd keep working long after they should've tripped. The aiming systems were out, too, so Magoro hastily cut out the control circuits, replacing them with a simple switch which when triggered would slowly pivot the aim of the hell lances. By the time Magoro stood back, breathing heavily from exertion, the hell lances had been turned into manually controlled particle beam projectors.

She had two switches. One to aim the hell lances, and another that when pressed would let power flow all-out into the energy containment unit. With the firing commands shorted out and the discharge set to automatic, the hell lances should fire the moment enough energy registered in the containment unit.

Should.

Her work done, Diana Magoro leaned against the nearest bulkhead, unhappy that she had time to think.

Why was she doing this? Wouldn't it make a lot more sense to try to cut that hatch open and join the rest of the crew to repel boarders?

Not that they'd have much chance against Syndic special forces in the numbers that light cruiser would be carrying.

This wasn't about heroism. No way. She wasn't a hero. Despite the chief's uniform she was a screw-up. She knew it. And it wasn't about the honor of the fleet. It wasn't about her being some shining example of a sailor. That was the sort of thing a guy like Commander Geary would've worried about.

Commander Geary. Maybe it was just about repaying a favor. A second chance that a young sailor hadn't deserved. *I still owe you one, Captain. Now I can finally pay you back.*

But maybe also it was just because she was a gunner's mate. *If I'm going to die, I'm going to go out trying to make a gun do something it shouldn't, just to see what happens. I'm going to set a record, or I'm gonna die. Because I'm a damned gunner's mate and these are my guns.*

Holding one switch in each hand, Magoro went to one of the holes in the hull and stared out, looking for the spot of light among the stars that would mark the main propulsion of the Syndic light cruiser that was braking to match the vector of the *Ishigaki*.

So many stars. She stared out at them. Even though she'd spent years in space, like many sailors she didn't spend much time actually looking at space. If a ship wasn't near a planet, all there was to see were countless stars blazing against infinity. And after a while even countless stars blazing against infinity got to be a familiar, everyday view.

Humans had laboriously colonized the nearest stars, then burst out of the region near Earth when the jump drives were invented. Hundreds of star systems now had humans living there, some of them on welcoming, fertile worlds that hosted many millions of people, and others on too-cold or too-hot airless hellholes that might have only a few thousand inhabitants offering essential services to passing shipping.

But it was all still just the tiniest of a tiny portion of even this galaxy. Against the scale of the universe, did it even count at all? Diana Magoro stared at the immensity, wondering why even in the midst of innumerable stars and a universe with no limits humans had still found reasons for war.

Limits. That was the war was about, wasn't it? Because one thing people like the rulers of the Syndicate Worlds could limit was human freedom. The universe might go on endlessly, but people could be corralled, forced to live as others demanded. The Alliance, she'd been told, had been founded to ensure its member star systems could protect each other from such a fate. The Syndicate Worlds, though, had been founded by people who didn't like governments putting limits on them but thought they had the right to control others. Maybe this war with the Syndics had been inevitable, bound to happen sooner or later.

Her eyes fastened on an object among the stars, pulling her mind out of its exhausted reverie. There. Below and to her left. It was getting brighter, but it didn't appear to be moving. Why not?

It wasn't until the Syndic ship was close enough for her to see its lean, deadly shape illuminated by the blast of its main propulsion that Magoro realized the enemy warship didn't seem to be moving because it was coming straight at the *Ishigaki* on a perfect intercept. This close, she could see the ship getting bigger, though.

She twisted the aiming switch, bringing the aim of the hell lances a little lower to where the Syndic ship should end up.

She was aiming manually. Crazy. A chief should know better.

The enemy light cruiser loomed closer and closer, thrusters firing on it now, coming in slower and slower as it prepared to perfectly match vectors with *Ishigaki*, right next to the stricken Alliance cruiser so that the enemy boarders could leap across the small remaining gap between the two warships. The enemy, facing a part of the Alliance heavy cruiser with no working weapons powered up, would be powering down their shields that would normally help block enemy fire so those shields wouldn't hinder the attack force from reaching the *Ishigaki*. A real close target, with its shields down. If Magoro's hell lances fired, each one would punch all the way through that enemy ship and out the other side, going through everything in the way.

How long did she dare wait? Even if this worked, how many shots could she get off before the hell lances overheated?

The light cruiser was maybe half a kilometer away, barely moving relative to the *Ishigaki*. She waited, trying to judge when it was close to a quarter kilometer away and almost completely stopped. Hatches began opening on the Syndic warship to let the boarders jump across the remaining gap. She couldn't afford to wait any longer.

Breathing a prayer to her ancestors, Diana Magoro pressed down hard on first the power switch and then the aiming switch.

She heard a shriek from the containment system transmitted through the soles of the boots on her survival suit as components protested the immense surge of energy hitting all at once, followed immediately by the shudder of the hell lances unleashing their invisible bolts. To her own amazement, she was still alive and the hell lances were firing. The shrieks kept coming, the shudders following in a nearly continuous series of pulses, the hell lances slowly pivoting their aim aft to walk their shots down the side of the enemy ship.

Bright light flared within the compartment and the weapons stopped firing and moving. Magoro looked into open access panels on the nearest hell lance to see that several power couplings had completely melted. The farther-off hell lance seemed to be imploding as its innards shrank and slagged under heat that caused the weapon to visibly glow.

The side of her survival suit facing the hell lances felt really hot. She'd have some burns under there.

Realizing that she wasn't dead, Magoro looked out the hole in the hull again. The hatches on the enemy warship had frozen only partly open, no sign of motion around them, and its thrusters had stopped firing. The Syndic cruiser seemed to still be very slowly coming closer. Would it collide with *Ishigaki*?

Something blew up aboard the enemy ship, a bit aft of amidships and down toward the keel. The explosion jolted the Syndic cruiser, pitching it upwards and starting a slow pivot of stern over bow as it began drifting over the *Ishigaki*.

She watched the enemy warship ponderously spin until it vanished from her view.

+ + +

"Hey, Chief."

Diana Magoro looked up from where she was sitting against a bulkhead. She was still in the damaged hell lance compartment. Somebody must have forced the hatch open. How much time had passed? Who was this talking to her?

She recognized the voice and tried to get to her feet, but found it hard to move her arms or legs. "Captain. I'm sorry."

"At ease." Commander Weiss looked about him. "What'd you do? We were waiting for the boarding party to hit us when this battery lit off and laced shots down the side of that Syndic. He's still drifting with no maneuvering control."

"I broke a few rules," she admitted. "To get the hell lances to fire."

"How'd you aim your shots?"

"I looked through those holes in the hull."

"Ancestors save us." Weiss held out a hand. "Are you hurt? Can you stand? The side of your suit looks scorched."

"There was a lot of heat in here for a little while. But I'm not hurt much, sir. Just... having a little trouble."

"I imagine," he said, helping her get up. "What exactly did you do that enabled you to fire those hell lances?"

Magoro looked at the half-melted remains of the hell lance battery. "Captain, if you want me to be honest, you don't want to know."

"The fleet will want to know. It could be really useful."

"No, sir, I really don't think so. I don't think the fleet is going to want anyone knowing what I did and how to do it, because it was crazy, and it broke every rule, and by all rights those hell lances should've blown me to hell instead of hitting that Syndic."

"I see." He surprised her with a short laugh. "You still can't follow the rules, huh, Chief?"

"I broke them for the right reason this time, sir." She paused. "Sir? Can I ask you something I've been wondering for the last six years?"

"I think you've earned the right to a question," Weiss said.

"Back on the *Merlon*, I know you couldn't say if you disagreed with what the captain did. But did you agree with Commander Decala that I should've been court-martialed? Or with Commander Geary that I ought to have another chance?"

Commander Weiss didn't answer for a moment. "If you want the truth, I agreed with Decala. I didn't think you were salvageable. I did think getting you out of the fleet and in particular out of my gunnery division would make my life a lot easier. And it would've, right? My life would've been a little easier without you around, for a couple of months until the fight at Grendel, after which we went our separate ways."

"Okay," Magoro said. "I can understand that."

"I'm not done, Chief. If you'd been gone from the fleet in disgrace, forbidden from serving again because of a court-martial conviction, then today I probably would've died at the hands of that Syndic boarding party. So you know what? I was wrong. Commander Decala was wrong. Commander Geary was right."

Diana Magoro reached to wipe her eyes, her hand instead hitting the face plate of her survival suit. "That's, um, good to know."

"Can you function, Chief? You're acting gunnery officer now, and I need you on the job."

Magoro nodded. "I'm okay. What happened to Ensign Rodriguez, sir?"

"Dead. She was at hell lance battery One Alpha when some grapeshot hit it and vaporized most of the compartment. No survivors from the gun crew."

"Damn." She could see the eager, young faces of the sailors who'd died in that compartment. Faces she wouldn't see again in this life. Magoro looked about her, feeling stiff and old. "I need to burn a candle for their spirits as soon as I can, to let them know we won. And I guess I need to burn one for Commander Geary's spirit, too." No way would she call him Black Jack. He wouldn't have wanted that.

"You and me both," Commander Weiss said. "Commander Geary's decisions at Grendel saved us then, and his decision about you saved us both today. I guess he's still with us. I hope his spirit welcomes—" Commander Weiss's voice choked off. "We lost a lot of people, Chief."

"I know," Magoro said, thinking about the losses the gunnery division alone had sustained. "You gonna be all right, sir?"

"Yeah. You?"

"I guess. It's what the captain would want, for us to keep going."

"Then get going. And thanks, Chief."

"Yes, sir." She went to the hatch, only to encounter Bandera struggling through the damaged passageway beyond. One of his arms was fastened against his side by a quickcast. "What happened?"

"I got 'Ski to sick bay, Chief," Bandera said. "But just as I left we got hit near there and my arm got banged up so they gave me a temporary fix. It took me a while to sneak out and get through all the mess back to here."

"Sneak out? Why didn't you stay in sick bay?"

"Because you told me to get back here, Chief." He looked past her at the slumped wreckage of the hell lances and even through his face shield Magoro could see his eyes widen. "What the hell happened here, Chief?"

"I did something I told you never to do."

"Then why'd you do it?"

"Because I knew what I was doing." She stepped out into the passageway, beckoning to Bandera. "Come on. We need to see how many guns we can get working again. This war ain't over yet."

Bandera hesitated. "Chief, did we win the battle?"

"Yeah, we won the battle." Victory felt a little too much like defeat at the moment, but she couldn't confess that to the sailors looking to her for leadership. "Someday we'll win the war."

"How, Chief? How are we gonna win?"

"We've got better gunners." She led Bandera aft to find out what had happened to some of the other gun crews.

She'd finally proven Commander Geary right.

But instead of thinking about that, Diana Magoro was wondering if she'd ever forget the sight of all of those stars while she waited to spot the approaching enemy ship.

Becky Chambers burst into the spotlight with a crowdfunded first novel, The Long Way to a Small, Angry Planet, *that reinvented space opera. Now published by HarperCollins in the U.S. and a* New York Times *and international bestseller, her Wayfarers series is a trilogy with, hopefully, more to follow, and Chambers is one of the rising stars of not only new space opera, but science fiction. I received her book as a gift and immediately knew I had to see if she'd write something for me. To my good fortune, she has—for this volume, and I think it will delight longtime fans and serve well as an introduction to the Wayfarers universe. An alien sailor aboard a galactic ship must come of age both mentally and physically as she embarks on her challenging first voyage in "A Good Heretic."*

AUTHOR'S NOTE: *Like everything I write in the Wayfarers books, this story ties into all the others, but will stand on its own just fine if this is your point of entry to the series. The setting here is the Galactic Commons, an interstellar, interspecies union established for ease of trade and travel. As FTL is illegal, transportation between systems is facilitated through a vast network of constructed wormholes. Though all GC species are represented in the tunneling profession, their work is impossible without the mathematical contributions of the Sianat, a reclusive race who intentionally infect themselves with a virus that enhances specific cognitive abilities (at the cost of shortening their lifespan). Infected Sianat are properly called "Pairs," and think of themselves as plural entities. Their pronoun usage reflects this.*

In The Long Way to a Small, Angry Planet, *we're introduced to mainstream Sianat culture through Ohan, a Navigator aboard a tunneling ship. However, we receive a glimpse of an alternate Sianat way of life through the character Mas, who we meet briefly late in the book. This is her story.*

WAYFARERS: A GOOD HERETIC
BECKY CHAMBERS

GC STANDARD 184

Mas had never known a crowd that was comprised of anything but her own species, and she never would. To her, a crowd was a disjointed thing, an arrangement made mostly of empty space. Sianats knew to keep their distance from one another—the acceptable rule was two bodies shy, in every direction. It was a dance, her mother had explained long ago. *Imagine that everyone exists in the exact center of a circular shield. When yours brushes another, you both must adjust.*

Mas kept her own imaginary shield firmly in mind as she navigated the busy street, all four of her clumsy juvenile limbs trying to keep to the rhythm of the city center while simultaneously managing the pack of groceries strapped across her back. She could feel her mother watching her progress, which added to Mas' nervousness. She couldn't bear the thought of touching a stranger by accident. That'd be almost as much trouble as touching her mother.

They reached the central gardens, and Mas' fur settled with relief. She'd made it, untouched and unscolded. They walked down the heated paths until they came to her mother's favorite spot—an evergreen mossy knoll looking over the city of Trolouk. Her mother sat on their back haunches on the bare ground, claiming that particular patch as their own. Mas did the same, two bodies shy. Her mother blinked approvingly at where she sat, and small as the achievement was, Mas felt proud. It brought her such pleasure to do things right.

Mas looked at the cityscape surrounding them. The monument to the First Carrier stood huge and impressive, taller than the government towers, taller than the colleges, taller than everything but the icy mountains beyond. As she looked, gentle flakes of snow tickled her face. She shook her head and scattered them, laughing with delight at the brief flurry hiding within her unshaved tufts.

Her mother—whose fur was trimmed short and intricately patterned, as befit their age—shot her a look. Mas fell silent, embarrassed, for there were no other children seated on the hill, only Pairs, and Pairs did not disturb the thinking of others with harsh sounds. But a subtle kindness bloomed on her mother's face, and with a glance both this way and that, they too shook their head as Mas had, making the snow fall. Neither laughed, as was proper. But the little amusement was shared.

"May I eat now?" Mas asked.

Her mother inclined their head once. "Yes."

Mas unstrapped the grocery pack and dug through its contents, the majority of which were for her. Her mother ate only *hemle*—the carefully balanced nutrient paste Pairs consumed as their sole nourishment. But Mas was a child—a perpetually hungry child at that—and for her, there was raw meat cured with sour wine and charred meat on the bone and a tin of fancy marrow and a variety of bird eggs ready to be cracked open and drunk down. She unwrapped the charred meat first, as it was her favorite, and tucked in gleefully, letting her sharp teeth do the work.

"Do you ever miss children's food?" Mas asked once she'd swallowed. She filled her mouth again as soon as the words had left it.

"No," her mother said. Their own teeth were filed flat, like those of a prey animal, a sign of their avowed service to others, their lack of a desire to conquer.

Mas savored a well-burned bit. "I think I'll miss it."

Her mother smiled. "There are things we thought we would miss as well," they said. "But the Whisperer is helpful in that way. We do not miss what we were before infection. The gifts we have now are so much greater."

Mas' own infection wouldn't happen for another standard, and she thought about it constantly. She was a little afraid, but her mother encouraged her to ask any question that came to mind, no matter how big or small, so that there would be no mystery when the day came. As far as the general shape of things went, Mas knew what was waiting for her. She'd be infected with the sacred virus, the Whisperer. It would take root in her, and reshape her brain into something wondrous. No longer would her thoughts be as limited as her species' lesser friends in the galaxy—confined to one form of logic, one set of numbers, three rigid dimensions. The other societies within the Galactic Commons had spread themselves throughout the stars, but it was Sianat insight and Sianat intellect that enabled every one of those histories. Without them, the Harmagians could not have built their tunnels, the Aeluons could not have won their wars, the Aandrisks would not have their academic collections. Without the Sianat, the galaxy would be only a few lonely islands with uncrossable seas between. Because of them, the sky was full.

Mas couldn't wait to contribute her own mind to that cause. She wished to build wormholes, as she'd learned of in school. But until then, Mas had questions, and there was one that had been bothering her for several tendays. "Mother," she said. "I wish to know something, but I am afraid to ask."

"Why?"

"It may be blasphemous."

Her mother considered this. "So long as you *know* it may be blasphemous, you may ask us." They paused. "But only us. If a question causes you fear, do not ask it of your teachers. Only us."

Mas set down her half-eaten meat in the frosted moss. "Have you heard of a planet called Arun?"

Mas' mother started, eyes wide and muscles rigid. "Where did *you* hear of this?"

"Other children. In the playfield."

"Which children?"

The sudden accusation in her mother's voice made Mas hold silent.

Her mother exhaled. "Very well. We will not pry." They hummed in astonishment. "The things children speak of." A quiet came over them, a distance in their eyes.

Mas did not interrupt. She knew the look of thoughts being gathered.

"Arun is a den of Heretics," her mother said. "Do you know this word?"

"No."

Her mother took several breaths. They looked afraid to even touch this subject, and this made Mas afraid, too. "A Heretic is a person who avoids infection. Who denies the Whisperer."

Mas was stunned. "Why?"

"I do not know. But if they are caught, they are sent to Arun. Or, if they run away, they seek the place out themselves." Her mother rubbed the fur on their forelegs nervously. "Perhaps we should not be telling you this."

That made Mas wish to press on all the more. "What is there for them, on Arun?"

"Nothing." The word came out contemptuous. "It is a harsh place, with no star of its own. An errant planet with no light and no mooring. The Heretics do not leave it."

"Why?"

"They are still Sianat," her mother said. "They do not seek disorder, and their presence in the galaxy would be disorder incarnate in the face of what we've built."

"So… they are not part of the Commons."

"Not as such, no. They are disavowed by us, and therefore from the Commons as well. They have brokered no treaties of their own."

This was plenty to take in, but Mas already had more to ask. "This question may be blasphemous, too."

Her mother almost laughed. "We're already blaspheming, child. Another will not matter."

"Why is it a problem, if they wish to leave?" Mas asked. "If their world is far and they do not bother anyone—"

"Because it is in defiance of the sacred law." That alone was answer enough, but Mas' mother continued. "And because there is no point to it. Arun is a prison. It is exile. Look at our world, Mas." They arched their head toward the surrounding city, a jewel-chest of artful buildings and good works. "Look at how rich our life is here. Think of how much better we have made the lives for others in the Commons. Why would you deny yourself that? Why would you run from this into a life of struggle? Of no possible meaning? Such a thing is lunacy."

New and unconsidered as this whole idea was, Mas found herself agreeing. None of this made sense. She almost felt as if she understood less than before she'd broached the topic.

Her mother was looking around worriedly at the other people milling about the knoll. "Come," they said. "Pack up your food. We think it best to go home now."

They spent the long walk back in silence, both lost in thought. After a time, the dense streets of the city center branched into residential roads, and they came at last to their burrow, lived in by the two of them alone. Mas' mother opened the ground hatch and climbed down. Mas waited a few customary seconds, to give her mother time to clear the climbing posts, then followed in turn. The walls were warm and the air was dry. Mas could feel the snowflakes caught in her fur liquefy before she reached the floor. She shook herself vigorously once she was down, trying to rid herself of both melt and disquiet.

She turned, and to her surprise saw her mother still standing there. There was a softness in their gaze that made Mas forget everything else. "Please," her mother said. The word was a plea, a prayer. "Do not ever go down that path. We could not—" They took a ragged breath. Mas had never seen them this uncomposed. "We could not bear it if you—" The sentence choked itself short, and her mother left the entryspace.

Mas stood alone, overwhelmed. The unexpected reminder of her mother's love made her feel as if she'd been given sugar milk and summer sun. The feeling wrapped itself up with the unpleasant knowledge of heresy, and Mas was resolute. There was no question, not in any layer of her mind. She would be a good Pair. It could be no other way.

+ + +

GC STANDARD 185

The priest ran their scans as Mas waited within the exposure chamber. "Pulse, good. Organ functionality, good. Adrenaline—heightened, but this is normal." The priest blinked at Mas reassuringly through the glass.

Mas took comfort in this, though her hearts still raced. She sat as she'd been taught—loose-limbed and jaw unclenched—and she breathed as she'd been taught—deep and easy. She was nervous, yes, but it was not out of fear. Today was the day. Infection. Pairing. She would be sick for a time, she knew, but when the sickness cleared, she would be a new entity. A plural. She would feel the Whisperer's gifts, and her worries would vanish. The clouds in her mind would settle. Her low mind would deepen, and would comprehend the very fabric of the universe as if it were mere arithmetic. Her high mind would be at peace, never lacking contentment even in the face of great troubles. She knew that was why it had been easy for her mother to say goodbye, to leave her for the last time. Mas looked down at her forelegs, shaved and patterned in the adult fashion by her mother's hands, a grooming ritual Mas would perform on her own from now on. The grief of their parting still wrenched Mas, but it was of no concern. Soon, the pain would be gone.

The priest finished their evaluation, and set down their medical instruments. They gestured at a panel nearby, and began to chant— not in Ciretou, but in Duslen, that odd tripping language used only in religion and government. The Pairing had begun.

This is it, Mas thought. It was all she could do to keep from leaping with joy. She was about to come of age.

A faint mist filled the chamber. This was an analgesic, she knew, given to ease the transition. Mas breathed deep. She smelled nothing, but her nostrils went numb. Her limbs relaxed. It was wonderful.

A drawer slid open out of the chamber wall. A syringe lay within it. Mas had practiced this part many times in school, injecting herself with small doses of saline so she would not be squeamish about the needle when the time came. But this was not saline, she knew. This was precious. Powerful. Time seemed to slow as she picked up the syringe, as if it, too, were watching.

The priest ended their chant abruptly.

Mas spoke in Duslen as she administered the injection, the one phrase she could speak. *Share my body, Whisperer. Shape my mind.*

She plunged the infectious fluid into her veins. Nothing happened. This was normal, she knew. The virus needed time to course through her. She returned the syringe to the drawer, and walked to the hammock stretched out across the back of the chamber.

"Congratulations," said the priest. "You are now a Pair. You are whole."

"I feel dizzy," Mas said, then paused, remembering what she was— *they were* now. Host and hosted, two in one. "We feel dizzy."

The priest checked their readouts on the display outside the chamber. "That is not unusual," they said. "Not common, but a known side effect. Rest now. Sleep, if you can. The days ahead will be difficult."

The priest was not wrong. A fever raged within hours, and Mas' muscles burned despite the mist. They had known of this, been taught of this, but there was a vast gulf between expecting pain and experiencing it. A sort of unconsciousness followed, a dreamlike state in which they dipped in and out of reality. They saw priests and orderlies, which were probably real. They saw their mother, who was probably not. In the few moments of clarity they had, they felt terrified. Pairs should not feel terror, they thought, not without grave cause. But then, the Whisperer was still spreading. Mas reminded themself of this before falling back into madness once more.

Then, one clear-eyed afternoon, they awoke.

The fever was gone, and the pain, too. Mas sat up in the hammock and evaluated themself. Their limbs felt weak. This was normal. Their eyes felt wet. This was normal. Their low mind felt different, in a way they could not articulate. Sharper, perhaps. Stronger. This was normal. Their high mind... their high mind felt raw, harrowed. Miserable. Their high mind wanted nothing more than to leave this place of sickness and return home to their mother.

This was not normal.

A priest arrived in short order, a different one than before. "We are glad to see you up, Mas," they said. "Your transition took longer than is typical. Come, let us get you out of that small space. We will take you to bathe and eat, and from there, you may spend as many days adjusting to your new self in the recovery house as needed before continuing on to your chosen college. How do you feel?"

Mas thought for a moment of telling the priest that something was wrong, but they were so frightened, so confused by the unexpected remainder of grief that they kept silent. Everything else had gone as promised—the pain, the fever, the terrible sleep. But they had been assured stillness on the other side, and Mas was nowhere in the vicinity of that. "Are we all right?" they asked, keeping their voice neutral.

The priest checked Mas' readouts. "Yes," they said. "A long transition is... unusual, but not unheard of. Your scans show no problems." They cocked their head at Mas. "Why do you ask?"

The priest, too, had a neutral tone, but Mas caught something else—a watch, a warning. It was barely there, yet enough to confirm that speaking the truth would be precarious. Mas did not know what had gone wrong, but until they knew what it was and what the law said about it, they would keep the particulars to themselves.

"We are merely concerned for the integrity of the Whisperer," Mas said. "We would not want this Host to be unworthy of it, if there is some physical defect."

"A virtuous concern," the priest said happily. "But you need not worry. Your Host is healthy. All is well." They opened the chamber door. "Come. Let us get you clean."

Mas thought of their mother again, remembered the way they walked, the way they spoke, the way all Pairs moved differently than children. Mas commanded their feet to step slackly, their face to rest as if nothing were wrong nor ever would be. Perhaps the Whisperer needed a little more time to settle in. Perhaps the miracle hadn't happened yet.

Mas took their bath, and they waited.

Mas let a stranger file their teeth to stubs, and they waited.

Mas ate their *hemle*—which turned out to be awful—and they waited.

Mas watched the other new Pairs, each blissfully at ease in the domed arboretums, happy to stare at a single leaf or a pool of water for a day or more. There could be no question that they were at peace within both body and mind. Mas found a rock to stare at. They told themself it was a beautiful rock, a wondrous rock, a source of infinite intricacies worth pondering. Mas tried to feel that. They tried. They spent days staring at rocks and dirt and clouds, and tried to feel something other than being bored out of their mind. They tried, and they waited.

Yet in all that waiting: nothing.

Mas went to school—the Navigators' College, as they'd decided upon before infection. For a brief time there, they thought that finally, finally, the Whisperer was opening their mind. As a child, they'd seen diagrams of interspatial tunnels, and had found no meaning in them. Now—now they were clear as air. The logic was simple, the math elegant. Mas made their own diagrams, and solved every problem the instructors threw their way. The Whisperer *had* changed them. Their low mind was not as it had once been.

But when they tried to sleep in their unshared room in the residence tower, they thought of their boredom, and their loneliness, and worst of all, their mother. After many such nights, they finally understood what was wrong. The Whisperer was within Mas, the Host. That much was obvious, from the exhilarating math and the weak muscles. The virus had changed the body. It had changed the low mind. But the high mind—the part of a Host that believed in things and felt the world and knew itself—that was unaltered. The virus had not taken purchase there. Despite Mas' will and readiness, some shadowy part of them had rejected the Whisperer.

Some part of them was evil.

✦ ✦ ✦

GC STANDARD 190

They received their certification from the GC Transport Board, and a few tendays later an offer was sent their way: a posting aboard a new tunneling ship that possessed everything but a Navigator. It was a good post, as Mas understood it. A Harmagian captain was likely to secure the most prestigious work, and between them, the crew had much experience in the field. There was no reason to say no.

Three unconscious weeks in a stasis pod later, Mas came aboard the *Remm Hehan*. They awoke in the airlock, which disappointed them. They'd been hoping for a view of the ship from space. Pairs had to risk exposure to unknown contaminants as little as possible, and so travel outside of their place of work was forbidden. If their posting went well and the function of the ship did not change before the Wane set in, the *Remm Hehan* would be the last place Mas would ever see. They would've preferred to have seen the full context of their final home from outside, but it was too late for that now.

The captain greeted them once they were through the decontamination chamber. Lum'matp was her name, a robustly speckled mass perched atop her motorized cart, a seasoned spacer in her prime. "Welcome, dear Navigator," Lum'matp said. Her yellow facial tendrils moved with—as Mas knew from their studies—gracious respect. "Your arrival is gladly received."

Mas inclined their neck once, in their own custom. "We are honored to be here," they said, hoping their Hanto was as good as their instructors claimed. They mimicked tendril gestures with their long fingers, as best as the digits would allow.

Lum'matp sat quiet for a moment, shifting her weight on her blocky cart. "That's about as formal as I get," she said. "My species is very good at wasting time with fluff. And I hate wasting time."

A Harmagian who scoffed at ceremony was surprising, to say the least, but Mas took it in their stride. A Pair would not pry further than that.

Lum'matp swung her cart around and headed for the doorway. "Come along," she said, gesturing at Mas to follow with a backwards-facing tentacle. "The crew expects introductions, and they'll be had. But I've worked with your people enough to know that you want quarters and quiet as soon as possible."

Mas wanted neither. They wanted to see the ship, all of it, every bolt and bulkhead. They wanted to talk with the crew—four Harmagians besides the captain, two Aandrisks, and an Aeluon—to learn more about them than names, to do more than bow their head in greeting and speak thanks for giving them a place to share their gifts. They wanted to ask the questions they'd always been dying to ask aliens— Did Harmagians find their carts comfortable? Were Aandrisks cold to the touch? Did Aeluons actually *think* in Hanto when "speaking" it, or did their talkboxes do the translation for them?—rather than pretend that such cultural quirks were below their notice. They wanted to be reassured that this was a good place, a safe place, that this crew would be a fine one to live and work and die alongside.

But a Pair would not. Mas stilled their tongue and silenced their wonderings. They went to their quarters, and they stayed there.

✦ ✦ ✦

GC STANDARD 193

Three standards. They had been aboard the *Remm Hehan* for three standards, and they were sure they were losing their mind—high and low both. Their thoughts, which had once run deep and fluid, now scattered sharp, like glass smashed against stone. Mas often forgot what they were doing, what they'd been thinking. A good idea would blossom, then vanish, smoke-like, as if it had never been there. Everything was pins and needles and screaming, constant screaming, but only within. Always within.

When Mas went to sleep, they dreaded the morning that would come. When they awoke, they ached for the end of the day. Sleep itself, though… that was good. It was the only time they were not aware of their terrible thoughts or their terrible room.

It was not really a terrible room—or at least, Mas did not blame the room itself. Their crew had bestowed them with a perfect place for a Pair. There was a lush bed in the Sianat style, without covers or anything that stifled the flow of air over fur. There was a tank of swimming laceworms—a Harmagian fancy, but one that was easy to enjoy. There was a large mirror beside a basin, where they could properly shave their fur, and a large window, through which a Pair could gaze out at the stars and contemplate them, all day, every day.

Mas did not want to contemplate anything ever again. They wanted *out*. They loved tunneling days, when a Pair would be expected to join the crew on the bridge. Those days were ecstasy, respite, the only escape Mas had access to. Sometimes, they made intentional errors in their preparatory calculations, so they would have to correct them in the crew's company and thus make the day last longer. The crew didn't notice. The molding of space-time was inscrutable to them, so any solution Mas found was already tremendous in the eyes of others. To the crew, an extra hour was nothing. To Mas, an extra hour was paradise. It was what kept them, some days, from finding an airlock and opening the hatch.

They sat now in front of the laceworm tank, watching the little creatures peck at the feeding block. One in particular caught Mas' eye—the red one with the rippled tail. They'd found it pretty once, but had long since come to hate it. The red one was the worst of them, always making mistakes, always bumbling around the tank while the others danced.

"You're so stupid," Mas whispered at the laceworm, who was trying to gum a nodule of food far too big for its mouth. "You don't even realize how stupid you are."

The nodule broke free and began to drift to the bottom of the tank. The red laceworm chased it, gumming futilely as it fell.

"Stupid," Mas hissed. "Leave it alone."

The nodule came to rest on the tank floor. The worm gummed and gummed and gummed. Far more flecks of food floated into the water than made it into the worm's mouth.

Mas wasn't sure what came over them. Not rage. It was a sort of calm, but not a good calm. Not a compassionate calm. With care, they rolled up the sleeve of their robe, pushed back the lid of the tank, and plunged their arm into the tepid water. The other worms scattered, but the stupid red one, still fixated on its impossible meal, did not notice Mas' hand until they'd grabbed it. It wriggled against them, and they were struck by the novelty—the slime of the worm, the slosh of the water, the entry into a space they hadn't visited before. Mas removed their arm from the tank after a moment, then opened their palm. The worm writhed, curled, flailed. After a few moments, its movements became more feeble. The water would've revived it quickly, but Mas did not return it to its home. They sat in the middle of the floor, water dripping from their sodden arm, and watched the worm die in their hand.

Mas felt nothing. They reflected on this, and the nothing was soon replaced with panic. What had they done? *Why* had they done that? They could find no reason, no reason at all.

"I'm sorry," they whispered to the laceworm. The words turned into a coo. "I'm so sorry." They curled up on the floor, tiny corpse still in hand, whimpering like they had not since they were a child. They thought of their mother, a memory they'd not allowed themself for a long time. They thought of the warm burrow the two of them had shared, and their walks through the city to buy food, tools, school supplies. They remembered being very, very small, before they'd been taught to stop touching, clinging to the fur on their mother's back and feeling that no harm would come to them.

What would their mother think of them now?

The answer came to them in a sudden shot of numbers. Mas' current age, their mother's age when they'd left them, the number of years between this and that. Their mother would have Waned by now, if not long ago.

Their mother, they realized, was dead.

Mas sat with both that knowledge and the worm for an hour, then decided to talk to their captain.

They encountered no one in the hallways, luckily. They walked undisturbed to Lum'matp's door, and brushed their palm against the panel. The accompanying vox switched on a few seconds later. "Yes, what?"

Mas was quiet for a moment. "It is Mas," they said.

"We won't reach our tunneling point for another tenday," the captain said. "Can your calculations not wait?"

"We… we do not have any calculations to discuss."

"Then what?"

Mas turned their head to look over their back. The corridor remained empty. "It is of a personal nature."

The resulting silence was response enough. The door opened.

Mas had never before had cause to enter the captain's quarters, and the newness of the space was dizzying. Like the rest of the ship, the decor was of contemporary Harmagian style, bright and bold, a celebration of smooth geometrics. But Lum'matp's living space was much finer than the rest, denoting her high status and successful career. Curios from dozens of worlds were displayed on and around the expensive furnishing, and the ceiling shimmered with a slow eddy of rainbow pixels. Mas wondered if their Aeluon crewmate came in here often. They imagined the cacophony of color would be hell for their kind. To Mas themself, the effect was merely gaudy.

The center of the room was filled with a sunken pool, solely for the captain's benefit (the remainder of the Harmagian crew members shared one pool among themselves, in the lowest decks). Pleasing green lights lined the asymmetrical edges, making the salty water glow in a way suggestive of a bioluminescent sea. But there was nothing alive in the pool besides Lum'matp, who was in the process of swimming to the edge closest to Mas. It was an odd thing, watching a Harmagian swim. In any other environment, they were ungainly. Sluggish in the purest sense of the word. In liquid, however, a Harmagian could almost be described as sleek. Lum'matp's body undulated through the water with startling speed and grace, and not for the first time, Mas wondered why their captain's species had ever bothered leaving the ocean.

Lum'matp hauled her head-half out of the pool and leaned her tentacled bulk over the edge. Water dripped down her porous body, making her skin glisten. "Since when," she said, "does a Pair discuss anything of a personal nature?"

Mas' stomach churned. They sat back on their haunches, trying desperately to maintain the poise their people prided themselves on. "Since now," they said. There was a tremble in their voice, and they hated themself for it. There was more to say beyond that, so much more, but it stuck in Mas' throat like old paste.

Lum'matp's eyestalks stretched forward. "Are you sick?"

"No."

"Are you... are you fighting with someone?"

"No."

"Good, because that's impossible to imagine. Do you wish to leave us?"

"No, captain. Not at all."

Lum'matp tensed her tentacles irritably. "Then what?"

The lump came unstuck, and Mas felt frightening words spit themselves forth: "We are a liar." Lum'matp blinked with concern and began to respond, but the door had been opened, and Mas couldn't stop. "We are a bad Host, a broken Host. We are defective, and if you dismiss us for it, if you send us back to be punished, the visible half of us will deserve it. But we cannot live this lie anymore. We cannot sit alone and stare out windows and pretend to be content. We are losing our mind, captain. We may have lost it already. Whatever you decide to do with us, it will be better than this."

The Harmagian pulled her entire self out of the water now, trading speed for height. "I think," she said with the slow caution of someone encountering an unknown, "you'd better start from the beginning."

So Mas did. They started at the beginning, and drove it through to the now. The uncertainty over what Lum'matp would do was nauseating, but there was clarity, too, a relief like they could never remember feeling. The truth. This was what truth felt like: clean, light, pure. Mas felt, for the first time since infection, like they could breathe properly.

Lum'matp said nothing for a while after Mas finished. "Would you fetch me a bowl of algae puffs?" she asked at last. "Over there—no, look where I'm pointing, *there*—in the jar by that awful sculpture. I'd offer you some, but—well, wait, *can* you ingest other foods?"

"We still carry the Whisperer," Mas said as they made their way across the room. "We do not know what introducing changes to our body would do, especially for one this lacking."

"Stop," Lum'matp said with a snap in her voice. "Enough of that talk. Stars and fire, if you're going to keep living with this, your first step is to find a way to stop hating yourself for it."

Mas turned their head slowly, the jar of algae puffs and an empty bowl in hand. "So... you're... you're not..."

"*Buschto,*" Lum'matp said. Mas had no translation for the word in their native tongue. *Sludge* was the literal meaning, but that didn't evoke the obscene exasperation of the original. Few swear words jumped languages well. "Of course I'm not going to... I don't even know what you'd expect I'd do. Hand you over to whoever your authorities are? Please. This isn't the fucking colony wars." She paused. "Have you told no one else about this?"

"No."

"Ever?"

"Ever." They handed their captain her snack.

Lum'matp cradled the bowl in her tentacles as she thought. At last, she reached a tendril down, retrieved a puff, and brought it to her cavernous mouth. "I've done nothing to deserve that kind of trust," she said. "But thank you." She ate another, and another. "So if you're not truly a Pair, what are you?"

"I don't know," Mas said.

"There's no concept for what you are? No term in Ciretou?"

Mas rubbed their gums with their lips. "The only word I have is Heretic," they said. "But we always—we always thought that implied intent. The ones who tried to escape. The ones who rejected the Whisperer. Our mind was willing, yet something in us rejected the Whisperer's fullness. We have never heard of this happening. We have been too scared to ask. But rejection is rejection, and so we must be a Heretic."

"A Heretic," Lum'matp said. She pondered. "You're not a very good Heretic."

This conversation was starting to feel dangerous, but Mas pressed forward. "How do you mean?"

"Rejection is one thing, but to me, 'heresy' suggests *defiance*. You're right, it's fueled by the mind. And *that's* your real problem, Mas. That's your misery. You've spent your life forcing yourself into something that, for some reason, you could not be. So no, I don't think you're a Heretic yet. But I think it would be very good for you if you were." A mischievous shiver danced its way around her dactyli. "'We.' Is that accurate?"

"It's—of course it's—"

Lum'matp waved their protest away with two tentacles. "'We' is a Pair. You're not. You said you're a *broken* Pair, but I'm your captain, and I say you're not broken, so you *can't* be a Pair, then. You're a carrier. Asymptomatic. Atypical. Or something. I have no idea. What are you?"

"We're Mas."

Lum'matp squinted. "Is that how you really think of yourself?"

Mas knew what Lum'matp was getting at, and it rattled them. Telling the truth was one thing; embracing it was another. "We… we can't—"

Their captain's tentacles unfolded. "Look around. Do you see any other Sianat here? Do you see anyone within tendays of here who would give a shit? Tell me, Mas. Tell me how you think of yourself."

"I." The word fell like a stone—no, no, not a stone, smashing as it fell. An anchor. A weight to ground yourself by. Oh, stars, this was wrong, this *was* blasphemy, this was…

This was right.

Mas shook as if flinging water from fur. "*I*. I am Mas."

"Yes! Yes!" Lum'matp grabbed Mas' forelegs with her tentacles—an impossible gesture, a thing no Sianat Pair would tolerate, a thing no Harmagian should do to another species unprotected unless she wanted her delicate skin to itch all day. But Lum'matp didn't seem to care, and Mas nearly collapsed from the intensity of *touch*, being *touched*. Lum'matp clasped her tightly, supporting Mas' trembling weight and laughing. "Dear Heretic," she said. "Welcome aboard."

✦   ✦   ✦

GC STANDARD 195

At Mas' request, Lum'matp said nothing to their crewmates. Mas was still uneasy with this new seeing of herself, and she was not sure what others would think—or worse, if they talked while at port, and the wrong ears heard. Too many uncertainties. Too many fears. Besides, Mas liked having a shared secret. She'd never had one before.

The captain had developed a long-standing habit of inviting Mas to her quarters under the ruse of tutelage. Lum'matp wanted to improve her understanding of physics, the story went, and who better to help her?

That was the story, anyway. The truth was, every night Mas and Lum'matp played table games together.

"I have you!" Lum'matp cried, sliding her netship into the fifth tier. The game was Rog-Tog-Tesch, a ludicrously complicated trade-and-politics affair with, for inscrutable reasons, an aesthetic theme of pre-industrial Harmagian sea farming.

Mas adored it.

Lum'matp's tendrils curled victoriously as the game board tallied her points. "I have acquired your salt marshes through flawless negotiations, and your workers stand poised to revolt."

"A good move," Mas said. She blinked approval as she plucked another morsel from the goodies Lum'matp had brought her from the kitchen, as per usual. This time it was autumn stew, an Aeluon dish with a characteristically undescriptive name, consisting of chunks of seared shore bird and huge bubble-like roe. It was briny and strange, and infinitely preferable to *hemle*. Mas savored the meat and studied the board. "A very good move. I almost hate to ruin it."

Her captain's tendrils fell. "No."

Mas hummed placidly as she pushed her tokens around the board. "I do not need the salt marshes, because I have a spy in your village council. Your reef blockade is, I'm afraid, about to be ordered elsewhere, and since you dispatched everyone to the marshes, your northern waters are quite undefended."

"No no no no *no*." Lum'matp was at once indignant and jovial as she watched her opponent's plan unfold. "You *ass*."

"I'm very sorry," Mas said, her tone indicating nothing of the sort. "This brings me no pleasure." She picked up a fish egg between two fingers and popped it into her smug mouth. "No pleasure at—"

"Mas? What's wrong?"

Mas didn't know. Something had gone wrong with her hand. There was pain, a stabbing pain like none she'd ever felt before. Her fingers seized. Her muscles shook beyond her control. She grabbed her wrist with the other hand, trying to make it stop.

"Oh, no," Lum'matp said. Her voice was too quiet, and her body shuddered with sorrow. "Oh. Oh, my dear Mas."

There was an irony there—a Harmagian recognizing the symptoms of the Wane before a Sianat did. Mas should have known immediately. She'd been taught of this, after all, taught to expect this, to welcome it. Had she strayed so far from Sianat ways that she'd forgotten her own biology?

"But… I'm too young," Mas said. Her fur ruffled with confusion. "I'm too young for that."

"You are different," Lum'matp said.

"Yes, but—"

"You are *different*. The Wane must affect you differently, too."

Mas stared for a long time at her now-still hand, the pain bleeding thin. You'd never know, looking at it, that within there was a virus that had worn down her nerves and would eventually kill her, just as the sacred law detailed. "Perhaps it's a punishment."

"From *who*?" Lum'matp scoffed. "Don't be absurd. Leave superstition to the Aeluons, it sounds stupid coming out of your mouth." She puffed her airsack. "Is there anything that can be done about it?"

"No," Mas said. She sat in shock, her emotions too new to properly make themselves known. "There's no cure."

Lum'matp's eyeslits narrowed. "So say your priests. But is there?"

"I—" Was there? The possibility had never occurred to Mas, and clinging to false hope would only prolong the pain of the inevitable. "I don't know," she said honestly.

"Who *would* know?"

"Lum'matp, please, there's nothing—"

"I am your captain, and I asked a question. If there was something to be done about this, who would know? Where would we ask? Where would we look?"

Somewhere in Mas' mind, she could see her mother, staring plaintively at her in their burrow. *We could not bear it if you…* Mas cringed inside, shame eating away at her, just as her nerves were being eaten away. Eating meat and playing childish games with her captain was one thing. Trying to avoid the natural course of things, *that* was true wickedness.

The natural course of things. She turned that phrase over in her head. The Wane was natural for a Pair, a good Pair. What of her, succumbing to the disease at least ten standards too soon? What of her, who had never truly become a Pair? What was natural, then? What was at the core of any of this, except her own flawed nature?

"Arun," Mas said. In her head, her mother mourned, and part of Mas did, too. "They would know on Arun."

Lum'matp knew the name from one of their many nights of chatter. Her tendrils flexed and her dactyli spread. "Would you go there?" she asked. "Would you go there, if it meant even a chance that you might not die?"

Another ledge; another jump. Mas shut her eyes. "Yes."

Lum'matp switched off the game. "Then, dear friend—let us find it."

✦ ✦ ✦

GC STANDARD 196

In the end, Lum'matp found the way to Arun on her own, as Mas had no energy for anything but her actual work—and even that had become a challenge. Her captain insisted on moving Mas into her own quarters, so she would not suffer alone. Harmagians did not sleep, Lum'matp reasoned, so Mas' seizures and fits would not disturb her. Mas loathed the imposition, but did not argue. She'd had enough of her room even when she'd been strong enough to get out of bed.

"You see," Lum'matp said, showing her a star map. "It is not so unreachable."

"How—" Mas waited with frustration for the tremble in her jaw to cease, or at least slow. "How long, from here?"

Lum'matp paused one moment too many. "Half a standard," she said, her voice indicating that she knew how tall an order that was. "If we hurry."

Mas fell back into her bedding, her body exhausted from sitting up to look at the map. "All right." The words were a decision, a declaration. "I can do that."

"Can you?"

"Well, if I can't, we'll find out, won't we?"

Lum'matp helped her pass the time as best she could, with vids and music and sessions of Rog-Tog-Tesch where the Harmagian moved Mas' tokens as well, with instruction.

"I've won," Lum'matp said one day, staring at the board in disbelief.

"See," Mas whispered from beneath a blanket. Her fur had grown long during her illness, yet she was always freezing. "I knew you could."

Lum'matp glared congenially at her. "And here, all this time, the only advantage I needed was you dying."

Mas laughed at that, even though laughing hurt.

She did not die, though, despite her body's best efforts. Some days she felt that it would be so easy, so much more sensible, to just let go. What did she know of Arun, anyway, outside of the name and who lived there? This was a fool's errand, a waste of fuel and her crew's time.

But Lum'matp hated wasting time, Mas told herself—and it was Lum'matp who had convinced her of this journey. So she held on, sometimes more for her captain than for herself.

One day, she opened her eyes from a terrible sleep, and there, standing beside Lum'matp, was her mother. Mas' mind—what was left of it—scrambled for purchase, wondering if perhaps she was already dead and her understanding of a lack of an afterlife was horribly wrong. But her vision cleared, and her mind along with it. The figure beside Lum'matp was not her mother. It was another Sianat, another adult. There was something odd about them, though. They looked too big. They were stocky and strong, their fur left long not out of illness, but *on purpose*.

A Heretic.

"Mas," the stranger spoke, crouching beside her. "I am Dyw. I come on behalf of the Solitary on the world below. I am here to help, if you will let me."

Arun. They had reached Arun. Had it been half a standard? It could have been a day, or an eternity. The loss of temporal context unsettled her. But the stranger was speaking Ciretou—an oddly accented Ciretou, but Ciretou none the less. Hearing her own words, her own name said correctly after so long, was ecstasy. Such basic sentences, and yet they felt like the music of homecoming.

But then—*I*. It was one thing to think of herself that way, to let Lum'matp call her that. But Mas had never called a Sianat adult by the singular. This was not home. This was not a good Pair. This was another like her.

Like her.

Mas tried to speak, but Dyw gently hushed her. "Save your strength. Relax." They—*he* held up a medical device, similar to the ones she'd seen priests use, but shaped differently enough to feel foreign. "If I am to help, I must examine you, and if I am to examine you, I must touch you. I know this is uncomfortable. I will not do it without your permission."

Two bodies shy, her mother said. Her mother. Her loving, giving mother. It was good that she was dead and could not see this.

Mas blinked yes.

Dyw examined her. He touched her as little as possible, but every brush of his fingers, every time fur met fur, Mas felt as though she might die right then—of fear or excitement, she could not say.

Dyw plugged the device into another, and studied the data. "Ah," he said, with a happy look. "I thought as much. You are like me!" He turned the little screen toward her, though she did not understand the information being shown. "Resistant."

Lum'matp wriggled her tendrils impatiently. "*What's going on?*" she asked in Klip.

Mas' Klip wasn't fluent, but she could understand Dyw, for the most part. "*She will be all right. Her immune system has—*" Mas lost a thread here "*—makes us partially—*" again, an unknown segment "*—to the—full effects. I can help her, here, right now. Ideally, we should*

*take her to the—proper care, but I do not think we can move her in
this—better to stay here, if that is—with you."*

Mas forced herself to speak. Not in Klip—that was a bridge too far
right then. "What is it about me?" she asked. Stars, but she'd missed
her words. "Why am I—"

"We think it's genetic," Dyw said. "But it's impossible to detect
before infection. The priests can't tell from their scans. They'll send
you to us if you tell them something's wrong, but… well, I understand
why you didn't." He flattened his voice with seriousness, the kind
of tone a parent might use to assure a child that there was nothing
lurking in the dark corners of their burrow. "About three percent of
Sianat are like this. There are many of us." He put his palm on her
chest—again, like you would calm a child. "There is nothing wrong
with you." He reached into his satchel, produced a box, and flipped
it open. Within lay a syringe, its contents green, its grip designed for
Sianat fingers. "I am sure you have many questions, and there will be
plenty of time to answer them. But first, you need to decide if you
want to claim that time."

"What—what—"

"It is a cure."

"For—for the Wane?"

"For the Whisperer."

Mas stared at him. She stared at the syringe. She stared at him
again. By the laws of her people, she would never Navigate again.

"Your mental aptitude will remain," he said. "But your body will
reclaim itself. I know. I know this is difficult, and were you not in this
state, I would not rush you. This decision must be yours alone, but
you do not have much time left to make it."

Mas had come to this place looking for salvation, but now that it
was in front of her, she was afraid. She'd had half a standard to lie
in a ball and think of this. Why did fear remain? Why did death feel
easier, nobler?

"Do it," she said.

Dyw shut his eyes in refusal. "I cannot. I am Solitary, but Solitary
are still Sianat, and there are ways that we share. You brought the
Whisperer in, voluntarily. You must drive it out in the same way." He

looked at her twisted fingers. "I know it will be hard. But you must. It must be you."

Mas pressed her filed teeth together, and pushed through the pain. With great effort, she threw her foreleg to the side. A scratching cry escaped from her throat. She wrenched her fingers back, jerked her palm open, whimpering as she did so.

You can't, her body said. *We can't do this.*

Stop it, her mind said. *This hurts, and it's evil. Stop it.*

Mas did it anyway. She grasped the syringe. Dyw helped her fingers find their grip. Lum'matp watched from the background, rocking with agitation on her cart, every tentacle coiled in concern.

"It will be painful," Dyw said. "Very painful. And recovery takes much time."

Mas lay back, panting, the profane object clutched in her hand. "Is it better?" she asked. "Than… this?"

Dyw put his hand on her chest again. "It will be."

She thought of the world below, Arun, the den of Heretics. She would never leave that place, that place she had never seen. She would have to say goodbye to Lum'matp. She would never Navigate again. She would contribute nothing more to the galaxy or her species' legacy. She would live, presumably—live because she wanted to, not because she was needed. This was selfish, she'd been taught. This was ego.

"What is—what is—your meaning?" she asked Dyw.

"Ah," Dyw said. "We will speak much more of this, for we all ask it, and discuss it often." He brushed the unkempt fur from Mas' eyes so he could look into them properly. "Our meaning is each other. Helping the resistant. Helping the runaways. Helping Pairs who wish to break."

"That is—inward. Closed. We are—we are meant to reach out."

"We still do, just in a different way." He put his hand on her chest again. "It may not seem like much, compared to shaping a galaxy. But it is enough. Sometimes, Mas, caring for one place, for one group—it really is enough."

Mas looked into his eyes for as long as she could. She did not know him, but he was telling the truth. He felt every word.

With the last of her strength and an animal scream, Mas plunged the needle into herself.

There was pain, as Dyw had promised. Agony, more like.

There was terror.

There was nothing.

There were dreams.

There was silence.

There was rest.

There was questioning, mourning, rejoicing, despairing, unlearning, discovering, befriending, accepting, rebuilding.

There was Mas, the Cured. Mas, the Solitary. Mas, the Resistant. Mas, the Good.

Robert A. Heinlein is one of the giants of science fiction, a Science Fiction Writers of America Grand Master, international bestseller, and household name even outside fandom. His books have inspired movies like Starship Troopers *and* The Puppet Masters. *His famous novels include* Stranger in a Strange Land, Space Cadet, Red Planet, *and many more. Although his popular juveniles like* Starship Troopers *and* Have Space Suit, Will Travel *might well fall into space opera or even military science fiction (at least the first one), only a small portion of Heinlein's short fiction are space opera stories.*

"Misfit" was published in the November 1939 issue of Astounding Science Fiction, *presented by famed editor John W. Campbell, who renamed it from the author's original moniker "Cosmic Construction Corps." One of the earliest of Heinlein's Future History stories, "Misfit" tells the tale of Andrew Jackson Libby, an Earth boy with extraordinary mathematical skill but little formal education who faces a lack of opportunities on Earth, joins the Cosmic Construction Corps, and helps colonize the solar system. Destined to become one of Heinlein's regular characters, here he first makes a name for himself as a human computer in space.*

MISFIT

(AKA "COSMIC CONSTRUCTION CORPS")

ROBERT A. HEINLEIN

"Attention to muster!" The parade ground voice of a First Sergeant of Space Marines cut through the fog and drizzle of a nasty New Jersey morning. "As your names are called, answer 'Here,' step forward with your baggage, and embark. Atkins!"

"Here!"

"Austin!"

"Hyar!"

"Ayres!"

"Here!"

One by one they fell out of ranks, shouldered the hundred and thirty pounds of personal possessions allowed them, and trudged up the gangway. They were young—none more than twenty-two—in some cases the luggage outweighed the owner.

"Kaplan!"

"Here!"

"Keith!"

"Haab!"

"Libby!"

"Here!" A thin gangling blonde had detached himself from the line, hastily wiped his nose, and grabbed his belongings. He slung a fat canvas bag over his shoulder, steadied it, and lifted a suitcase with his free hand. He started for the companionway in an unsteady dog trot. As he stepped on the gangway his suitcase swung against his knees. He staggered against a short wiry form dressed in the powder-blue of the Space Navy. Strong fingers grasped his arm and checked his fall, "Steady, son. Easy does it." Another hand readjusted the canvas bag.

"Oh, excuse me, uh"—the embarrassed youngster automatically counted the four bands of silver braid below the shooting star—"Captain. I didn't—"

"Bear a hand and get aboard, son."

"Yes, sir."

The passage into the bowels of the transport was gloomy. When the lad's eyes adjusted, he saw a gunner's mate wearing the brassard of a Master-at-Arms, who hooked a thumb towards an open air-tight door. "In there. Find your locker and wait by it."

Libby hurried to obey. Inside he found a jumble of baggage and men in a wide low-ceilinged compartment. A line of glow-tubes ran around the junction of bulkhead and ceiling and trisected the overhead; the soft roar of blowers made a background to the voices of his shipmates. He picked his way through heaped luggage and located his locker, seven-ten, on the far wall outboard. He broke the seal on the combination lock, glanced at the combination, and opened it. The locker was very small, the middle of a tier of three. He considered what he should keep in it. A loudspeaker drowned out the surrounding voices and demanded his attention:

"Attention! Man all space details; first section. Raise ship in twelve minutes. Close air-tight doors. Stop blowers at minus two minutes.

Special orders for passengers; place all gear on deck, and lie down on red signal light. Remain down until release is sounded. Masters-at-Arms check compliance."

The gunner's mate popped in, glanced around and immediately commenced supervising rearrangement of the baggage. Heavy items were lashed down. Locker doors were closed. By the time each boy had found a place on the deck and the Master-at-Arms had okayed the pad under his head, the glow-tubes turned red, and the loudspeaker brayed out.

"All hands—Up Ship! Stand by for acceleration." The Master-at-Arms hastily reclined against two cruise bags and watched the room. The blowers sighed to a stop. There followed two minutes of dead silence. Libby felt his heart commence to pound. The two minutes stretched interminably, then the deck quivered and a roar like escaping high-pressure steam bent at his ear drums. He was suddenly very heavy and a weight lay across his chest and heart. An indefinite time later the glow-tubes flashed white, and the announcer bellowed:

"Secure all getting underway details; regular watch, first section." The blowers droned into life. The Master-at-Arms stood up, rubbed his buttocks and pounded his arms, then said:

"Okay, boys." He stepped over and undogged the air-tight door to the passageway. Libby got up and blundered into a bulkhead, nearly falling. His legs and arms had gone to sleep, besides which he felt alarmingly light, as if he had sloughed off at least half of his inconsiderable mass.

For the next two hours he was too busy to think, or to be homesick. Suitcases, boxes, and bags had to be passed down into the lower hold and lashed against angular acceleration. He located and learned how to use a waterless water closet. He found his assigned bunk and learned that it was his only eight hours in twenty-four; two other boys had the use of it, too. The three sections ate in three shifts, nine shifts in all—twenty-four youths and a Master-at-Arms at one long table which jam-filled a narrow compartment off the galley.

After lunch Libby restowed his locker. He was standing before it, gazing at a photograph which he intended to mount on the inside of the locker door, when a command filled the compartment:

"Attention!"

Standing inside the door was the Captain flanked by the Master-at-Arms. The Captain commenced to speak. "At rest, men. Sit down. McCoy, tell control to shift this compartment to smoke filter." The gunner's mate hurried to the communicator on the bulkhead and spoke into it in a low tone. Almost at once the hum of the blowers climbed a half-octave and stayed there. "Now light up if you like. I'm going to talk to you.

"You boys are headed out on the biggest thing so far in your lives. From now on you're men, with one of the hardest jobs ahead of you that men have ever tackled. What we have to do is part of a bigger scheme. You, and hundreds of thousands of others like you, are going out as pioneers to fix up the solar system so that human beings can make better use of it.

"Equally important, you are being given a chance to build yourselves into useful and happy citizens of the Federation. For one reason or another you weren't happily adjusted back on Earth. Some of you saw the jobs you were trained for abolished by *new* inventions. Some of you got into trouble from not knowing what to do with the modern leisure. In any case, you were misfits. Maybe you were called bad boys and had a lot of black marks chalked up against you.

"But every one of you starts even today. The only record you have in this ship is your name at the top of a blank sheet of paper. It's up to you what goes on that page.

"Now about our job—We didn't get one of the easy repair-and-recondition jobs on the Moon, with weekends at Luna City, and all the comforts of home. Nor did we draw a high-gravity planet where a man can eat a full meal and expect to keep it down. Instead we've got to go out to Asteroid HS-5388 and turn it into Space Station E-M3. She has no atmosphere at all, and only about two percent Earth-surface gravity. We've got to play human fly on her for at least six months, no girls to date, no television, no recreation that you don't devise yourselves, and hard work every day. You'll get space sick, and so homesick you can taste it, and agoraphobia. If you aren't careful you'll get ray-burnt. Your stomach will act up, and you'll wish to God you'd never enrolled.

"But if you behave yourself, and listen to the advice of the old spacemen, you'll come out of it strong and healthy, with a little credit stored up in the bank, and a lot of knowledge and experience that you wouldn't get in forty years on Earth. You'll be men, and you'll know it.

"One last word. It will be pretty uncomfortable to those that aren't used to it. Just give the other fellow a little consideration, and you'll get along all right. If you have any complaint and can't get satisfaction any other way, come see me. Otherwise, that's all. Any questions?"

One of the boys put up his hand. "Captain?" he enquired timidly.

"Speak up, lad, and give your name."

"Rogers, sir. Will we be able to get letters from home?"

"Yes, but not very often. Maybe every month or so. The chaplain will carry mail, and any inspection and supply ships."

The ship's loudspeaker blatted out, "All hands! Free flight in ten minutes. Stand by to lose weight." The Master-at-Arms supervised the rigging of grab-lines. All loose gear was made fast, and little cellulose bags were issued to each man. Hardly was this done when Libby felt himself get light on his feet—a sensation exactly like that experienced when an express elevator makes a quick stop on an upward trip, except that the sensation continued and became more intense. At first it was a pleasant novelty, then it rapidly became distressing. The blood pounded in his ears, and his feet were clammy and cold. His saliva secreted at an abnormal rate. He tried to swallow, choked, and coughed. Then his stomach shuddered and contracted with a violent, painful, convulsive reflex and he was suddenly, disastrously nauseated. After the first excruciating spasm, he heard McCoy's voice shouting.

"Hey! Use your sick-kits like I told you. Don't let that stuff get in the blowers." Dimly Libby realized that the admonishment included him. He fumbled for his cellulose bag just as a second tremblor shook him, but he managed to fit the bag over his mouth before the eruption occurred. When it subsided, he became aware that he was floating near the overhead and facing the door.

The chief Master-at-Arms slithered in the door and spoke to McCoy. "How are you making out?"

"Well enough. Some of the boys missed their kits."

"Okay. Mop it up. You can use the starboard kick." He swam out.

McCoy touched Libby's arm. "Here, Pinkie, start catching them butterflies." He handed him a handful of cotton waste, then took another handful himself and neatly dabbed up a globule of the slimy filth that floated about the compartment. "Be sure your sick-kit is on tight. When you get sick, just stop and wait until it's over."

Libby imitated him as best as he could. In a few minutes the room was free of the worst of the sickening debris. McCoy looked it over, and spoke:

"Now peel off them dirty duds, and change your kits. Three or four of you bring everything along to the starboard lock."

At the starboard spacelock, the kits were put in first, the inner door closed, and the outer opened. When the inner door was opened again the kits were gone—blown out into space by the escaping air. Pinkie addressed McCoy, "Do we have to throw away our dirty clothes, too?"

"Huh uh, we'll just give them a dose of vacuum. Take 'em into the lock and stop 'em to those hooks on the bulkheads. Tie 'em tight."

This time the lock was left closed for about five minutes. When the lock was opened the garments were bone dry—all the moisture boiled out by the vacuum of space. All that remained of the unpleasant rejects was a sterile powdery residue. McCoy viewed them with approval. "They'll do. Take them back to the compartment. Then brush them—hard—in front of the exhaust blowers."

The next few days were an eternity of misery. Homesickness was forgotten in the all-engrossing wretchedness of spacesickness. The Captain granted fifteen minutes of mild acceleration for each of the nine meal periods, but the respite accentuated the agony. Libby would go to a meal, weak and ravenously hungry. The meal would stay down until free flight was resumed, then the sickness would hit him all over again.

On the fourth day he was seated against a bulkhead, enjoying the luxury of a few remaining minutes of weight while the last shift ate, when McCoy walked in and sat down beside him. The gunner's mate fitted a smoke filter over his face and lit a cigarette. He inhaled deeply and started to chat.

"How's it going, bud?"

"All right, I guess. This spacesickness—Say, McCoy, how do you ever get used to it?"

"You get over it in time. Your body acquires new reflexes, so they tell me. Once you learn to swallow without choking, you'll be all right. You even get so you like it. It's restful and relaxing. Four hours' sleep is as good as ten."

Libby shook his head dolefully. "I don't think I'll ever get used to it."

"Yes, you will. You'd better anyway. This here asteroid won't have any surface gravity to speak of; the Chief Quartermaster says it won't run over two percent Earth-normal. That ain't enough to cure space-sickness. And there won't be any way to accelerate for meals either."

Libby shivered and held his head between his hands.

Locating one asteroid among a couple of thousand is not as easy as finding Trafalgar Square in London—especially against the star-crowded backdrop of the galaxy. You take off from Terra with its orbital speed of about nineteen miles per second. You attempt to settle into a composite conoid curve that will not only intersect the orbit of the tiny fast-moving body, but also accomplish an exact rendezvous. Asteroid HS-5388, "Eighty-eight," lay about two and two-tenths astronomical units out from the sun, a little more than two hundred million miles; when the transport took off it lay beyond the sun better than three hundred million miles. Captain Doyle instructed the Navigator to plot the basic ellipsoid to tack in free flight around the sun through an elapsed distance of some three hundred and forty million miles. The principle involved is the same as used by a hunter to wing a duck in flight by "leading" the bird in flight. But suppose that you face directly into the sun as you shoot; suppose the bird cannot be seen from where you stand, and you have nothing to aim by but some old reports as to how it was flying when last seen?

On the ninth day of the passage Captain Doyle betook himself to the chart room and commenced punching keys on the ponderous integral calculator. Then he sent his orderly to present his compliments to the Navigator and to ask him to come to the chartroom. A few minutes later, a tall heavyset form swam through the door, steadied himself with a grabline, and greeted the Captain.

"Good morning, Skipper."

"Hello, Blackie." The Old Man looked up from where he was strapped into the integrator's saddle. "I've been checking your corrections for the meal time accelerations."

"It's a nuisance to have a bunch of ground-lubbers on board, sir."

"Yes, it is, but we have to give those boys a chance to eat, or they couldn't work when we got there. Now I want to decelerate starting about ten o'clock, ship's time. What's our eight o'clock speed and co-ordinates?"

The Navigator slipped a notebook out of his tunic. "Three hundred fifty-eight miles per second; course is right ascension fifteen hours, eight minutes, twenty-seven seconds, declination minus seven degrees, three minutes; solar distance one hundred and ninety-two million four hundred eighty thousand miles. Our radial position is twelve degrees above course, and almost dead on course in R.A. Do you want Sol's co-ordinates?"

"No, not now." The Captain bent over the calculator, frowned and chewed the tip of his tongue as he worked the controls. "I want you to kill the acceleration about one million miles inside Eighty-eight's orbit. I hate to waste the fuel, but the belt is full of junk and this damned rock is so small that we will probably have to run a search curve. Use twenty hours on deceleration and commence changing course to port after eight hours. Use normal asymptotic approach. You should have her in a circular trajectory abreast of Eighty-eight, and paralleling her orbit by six o'clock tomorrow morning. I shall want to be called at three."

"Aye aye, sir."

"Let me see your figures when you get 'em. I'll send up the order book later."

The transport accelerated on schedule. Shortly after three, the Captain entered the control room and blinked his eyes at the darkness. The sun was still concealed by the hull of the transport and the midnight blackness was broken only by the dim blue glow of the instrument dials, and the crack of light from under the chart hood. The Navigator turned at the familiar tread.

"Good morning, Captain."

"Morning, Blackie. In sight yet?"

"Not yet. We've picked out half a dozen rocks, but none of them checked."

"Any of them close?"

"Not uncomfortably. We've overtaken a little sand from time to time."

"That can't hurt us—not on a stern chase like this. If pilots would only realize that the asteroids flow in fixed directions at computable speeds nobody would come to grief out here." He stopped to light a cigarette. "People talk about space being dangerous. Sure, it used to be; but I don't know of a case in the past twenty years that couldn't be charged up to some fool's recklessness."

"You're right, Skipper. By the way, there's coffee under the chart hood."

"Thanks; I had a cup down below." He walked over by the lookouts at stereoscopes and radar tanks and peered up at the star-flecked blackness. Three cigarettes later the lookout nearest him called out.

"Light ho!"

"Where away?"

His mate read the exterior dials of the stereoscope. "Plus point two, abaft one point three, slight drift astern." He shifted to radar and added, "Range seven nine oh four three."

"Does that check?"

"Could be, Captain. What is her disk?" came the Navigator's muffled voice from under the hood. The first lookout hurriedly twisted the knobs of his instrument, but the Captain nudged him aside,

"I'll do this, son." He fitted his face to the double eye guards and surveyed a little silvery sphere, a tiny moon. Carefully, he brought two illuminated cross-hairs up until they were exactly tangent to the upper and lower limbs of the disk. "Mark!"

The reading was noted and passed to the Navigator, who shortly ducked out from under the hood.

"That's our baby, Captain."

"Good."

"Shall I make a visual triangulation?"

"Let the watch officer do that. You go down and get some sleep. I'll ease her over until we get close enough to use the optical range finder."

"Thanks, I will."

+ + +

Within a few minutes the word had spread around the ship that Eighty-eight had been sighted. Libby crowded into the starboard troop deck with a throng of excited mess mates and attempted to make out their future home from the view port. McCoy poured cold water on their excitement.

"By the time that rock shows up big enough to tell anything about it with your naked eye we'll all be at our grounding stations. She's only about a hundred miles thick, yuh know."

And so it was. Many hours later the ship's announcer shouted:

"All hands! Man your grounding stations. Close all air-tight doors. Stand by to cut blowers on signal."

McCoy forced them to lie down throughout the ensuing two hours. Short shocks of rocket blasts alternated with nauseating weightlessness. Then the blowers stopped and check valves clicked into their seats. The ship dropped free for a few moments—a final quick blast—five seconds of falling, and a short, light, grinding bump. A single bugle note came over the announcer, and the blowers took up their hum.

McCoy floated lightly to his feet and poised, swaying, on his toes. "All out, troops—this is the end of the line."

A short chunky lad, a little younger than most of them, awkwardly emulated him, and bounded toward the door, shouting as he went, "Come on, fellows! Let's go outside and explore!"

The Master-at-Arms squelched him. "Not so fast, kid. Aside from the fact that there is no air out there, go right ahead. You'll freeze to death, burn to death, and explode like a ripe tomato. Squad leader, detail six men to break out spacesuits. The rest of you stay here and stand by."

The working party returned shortly loaded down with a couple of dozen bulky packages. Libby let go the four he carried and watched them float gently to the deck. McCoy unzipped the envelope from one suit, and lectured them about it.

"This is a standard service type, general issue, Mark IV, Modification 2." He grasped the suit by the shoulders and shook it out so that it hung like a suit of long winter underwear with the helmet lolling helplessly between the shoulders of the garment. "It's self-sustaining for eight hours, having an oxygen supply for that period. It also has a nitrogen trim tank and a carbon-dioxide-water-vapor cartridge filter."

He droned on, repeating practically verbatim the description and instructions given in training regulations. McCoy knew these suits like his tongue knew the roof of his mouth; the knowledge had meant his life on more than one occasion.

"The suit is woven from glass fiber laminated with nonvolatile asbestocellutite. The resulting fabric is flexible, very durable; and will turn all rays normal to solar space outside the orbit of Mercury. It is worn over your regular clothing, but notice the wire-braced accordion pleats at the major joints. They are so designed as to keep the internal volume of the suit nearly constant when the arms or legs are bent. Otherwise the gas pressure inside would tend to keep the suit blown up in an erect position, and movement while wearing the suit would be very fatiguing.

"The helmet is molded from a transparent silicone, leaded and polarized against too great ray penetration. It may be equipped with external visors of any needed type. Orders are to wear not less than a number-two amber on this body. In addition, a lead plate covers the cranium and extends on down the back of the suit, completely covering the spinal column.

"The suit is equipped with two-way telephony. If your radio quits, as these have a habit of doing, you can talk by putting your helmets in contact. Any questions?"

"How do you eat and drink during the eight hours?"

"You don't stay in 'em any eight hours. You can carry sugar balls in a gadget in the helmet, but you boys will always eat at the base. As for water, there's a nipple in the helmet near your mouth which you can reach by turning your head to the left. It's hooked to a built-in canteen. But don't drink any more water when you're wearing a suit than you have to. These suits ain't got any plumbing."

Suits were passed out to each lad, and McCoy illustrated how to don one. A suit was spread supine on the deck, the front zipper that stretched from neck to crotch was spread wide and one sat down inside this opening, whereupon the lower part was drawn on like long stockings. Then a wiggle into each sleeve and the heavy flexible gauntlets were smoothed and patted into place. Finally, an awkward backward stretch of the neck with shoulders hunched enabled the helmet to be placed over the head.

Libby followed the motions of McCoy and stood up in his suit. He examined the zipper which controlled the suit's only opening. It was backed by two soft gaskets which would be pressed together by the zipper and sealed by internal air pressure. Inside the helmet, a composition mouthpiece for exhalation led to the filter.

McCoy bustled around, inspecting them, tightening a belt here and there, instructing them in the use of the external controls. Satisfied, he reported to the conning room that his section had received basic instruction and was ready to disembark. Permission was received to take them out for thirty minutes acclimatization.

Six at a time, he escorted them through the air lock, and out on the surface of the planetoid. Libby blinked his eyes at the unaccustomed luster of sunshine on rock. Although the sun lay more than two hundred million miles away and bathed the little planet with radiation only one fifth as strong as that lavished on mother Earth, nevertheless the lack of atmosphere resulted in a glare that made him squint. He was glad to have the protection of his amber visor. Overhead the sun, shrunk to penny size, shone down from a dead black sky in which unwinking stars crowded each other and the very sun itself.

The voice of a mess mate sounded in Libby's earphones, "Jeepers! That horizon looks close, I'll bet it ain't more'n a mile away."

Libby looked out over the flat bare plain and subconsciously considered the matter. "It's less," he commented, "than a third of a mile away."

"What the hell do you know about it, Pinkie? And who asked you, anyhow?"

Libby answered defensively, "As a matter of fact, it's one thousand six hundred and seventy feet, figuring that my eyes are five feet three inches above ground level."

"Nuts. Pinkie, you are always trying to show off how much you think you know."

"Why, I am not," Libby protested. "If this body is a hundred miles thick and as round as it looks: why, naturally the horizon *has* to be just that far away."

"Says *who*?"

McCoy interrupted.

"Pipe down! Libby is a lot nearer right than you were."

"He is exactly right," put in a strange voice. "I had to look it up for the Navigator before I left control."

"Is that so?"—McCoy's voice again—"If the Chief Quartermaster says you're right, Libby, you're right. How did you know?"

Libby flushed miserably. "I—I don't know. That's the only way it could be."

The gunner's mate and the Quartermaster stared at him but dropped the subject.

By the end of the "day" (ship's time, for Eighty-eight had a period of eight hours and thirteen minutes), work was well under way. The transport had grounded close by a low range of hills. The Captain selected a little bowl-shaped depression in the hills, some thousand feet long and half as broad, in which to establish a permanent camp. This was to be roofed over, sealed, and an atmosphere provided.

In the hill between the ship and the valley, quarters were to be excavated; dormitories, mess hall, officers' quarters, sick bay, recreation room, offices, storerooms, and so forth. A tunnel must be bored through the hill, connecting the sites of these rooms, and connecting with a ten-foot air-tight metal tube sealed to the ship's portside air lock. Both the tube and tunnel were to be equipped with a continuous conveyor belt for passengers and freight.

Libby found himself assigned to the roofing detail. He helped a metalsmith struggle over the hill with a portable atomic heater, difficult to handle because of a mass of eight hundred pounds, but weighing here only sixteen pounds. The rest of the roofing detail were breaking out and preparing to move by hand the enormous translucent tent which was to be the "sky" of the little valley.

The metalsmith located a landmark on the inner slope of the valley, set up his heater, and commenced cutting a deep horizontal groove or step in the rock. He kept it always at the same level by following a chalk mark drawn along the rock wall. Libby enquired how the job had been surveyed so quickly.

"Easy," he was answered, "two of the quartermasters went ahead with a transit, leveled it just fifty feet above the valley floor, and clamped a searchlight to it. Then one of 'em ran like hell around the rim, making chalk marks at the height at which the beam struck."

"Is this roof going to be just fifty feet high?"

"No, it will average maybe a hundred. It bellies up in the middle from the air pressure."

"Earth-normal?"

"Half Earth-normal."

Libby concentrated for an instant, then looked puzzled. "But look—This valley is a thousand feet long and better than five hundred wide. At half of fifteen pounds per square inch, and allowing for the arch of the roof, that's a load of one and an eighth billion pounds. What fabric can take that kind of a load?"

"Cobwebs."

"Cobwebs?"

"Yeah, cobwebs. Strongest stuff in the world, stronger than the best steel. Synthetic spider silk. This gauge we're using for the roof has a tensile strength of four thousand pounds a running inch."

Libby hesitated a second, then replied. "I see. With a rim about eighteen hundred thousand inches around, the maximum pull at the point of anchoring would be about six hundred and twenty-five pounds per inch. Plenty safe margin."

The metalsmith leaned on his tool and nodded. "Something like that. You're pretty quick at arithmetic, aren't you, bud?"

Libby looked startled. "I just like to get things straight."

They worked rapidly around the slope, cutting a clean smooth groove to which the "cobweb" could be anchored and sealed. The white-hot lava spewed out of the discharge vent and ran slowly down the hillside. A brown vapor boiled off the surface of the molten rock, arose a few feet, and sublimed almost at once in the vacuum to white powder which settled to the ground. The metalsmith pointed to the powder.

"That stuff 'ud cause silicosis if we let it stay there, and breathed it later."

"What do you do about it?"

"Just clean it out with the blowers of the air conditioning plant."

Libby took this opening to ask another question. "Mister—?"

"Johnson's my name. No mister necessary."

"Johnson, where do we get the air for this whole valley, not to mention the tunnels? I figure we must need twenty-five million cubic feet or more. Do we manufacture it?"

"Naw, that's too much trouble. We brought it with us."

"On the transport?"

"Uh huh, at fifty atmospheres."

Libby considered this. "I see—that way it would go into a space eighty feet on a side."

"Matter of fact it's in three specially constructed holds—giant air bottles. This transport carried air to Ganymede. I was in her there—a recruit, but in the air gang even then."

✦ ✦ ✦

In three weeks the permanent camp was ready for occupancy and the transport cleared of its cargo. The storerooms bulged with tools and supplies. Captain Doyle had moved his administrative offices underground, signed over his command to his first officer, and given him permission to proceed on "duty assigned"—in this case, return to Terra with a skeleton crew.

Libby watched them take off from a vantage point on the hillside. An overpowering homesickness took possession of him. Would he ever go home? He honestly believed at the time that he would swap the rest of his life for thirty minutes each with his mother and with Betty.

He started down the hill toward the tunnel lock. At least the transport carried letters to them, and with any luck the chaplain would be by soon with letters from Earth. But tomorrow and the days after that would be no fun. He had enjoyed being in the air gang, but tomorrow he went back to his squad. He did not relish that—the boys in his squad were all right, he guessed, but he just could not seem to fit in.

This company of the CCC started on its bigger job; to pock-mark Eighty-eight with rocket tubes so that Captain Doyle could push this hundred-mile marble out of her orbit and herd her in to a new orbit between Earth and Mars, to be used as a space station—a refuge for ships in distress, a haven for life boats, a fueling stop, a naval outpost.

Libby was assigned to a heater in pit H-16. It was his business to carve out carefully calculated emplacements in which the blasting crew then set off the minute charges which accomplished the major part of the excavating. Two squads were assigned to H-16, under the general supervision of an elderly marine gunner. The gunner sat on the edge of the pit, handling the plans, and occasionally making calculations on a circular slide rule which hung from a lanyard around his neck.

Libby had just completed a tricky piece of cutting for a three-stage blast, and was waiting for the blasters, when his phones picked up the gunner's instructions concerning the size of the charge. He pressed his transmitter button.

"Mr. Larsen! You've made a mistake!"

"Who said that?"

"This is Libby. You've made a mistake in the charge. If you set off that charge, you'll blow this pit right out of the ground, and us with it."

Marine Gunner Larsen spun the dials on his slide rule before replying. "You're all het up over nothing, son. That charge is correct."

"No, I'm not, sir," Libby persisted, "you've multiplied where you should have divided."

"Have you had any experience at this sort of work?"

"No, sir."

Larsen addressed his next remark to the blasters. "Set the charge."

They started to comply. Libby gulped, and wiped his lips with his tongue. He knew what he had to do, but he was afraid. Two clumsy stiff-legged jumps placed him beside the blasters. He pushed between them and tore the electrodes from the detonator. A shadow passed over him as he worked, and Larsen floated down beside him. A hand grasped his arm.

"You shouldn't have done that, son. That's direct disobedience of orders. I'll have to report you." He commenced reconnecting the firing circuit.

Libby's ears burned with embarrassment, but he answered back with the courage of timidity at bay, "I had to do it, sir. You're still wrong."

Larsen paused and ran his eyes over the dogged face. "Well—it's a waste of time, but I don't like to make you stand by a charge you're afraid of. Let's go over the calculation together."

✦ ✦ ✦

Captain Doyle sat at his ease in his quarters, his feet on his desk. He stared at a nearly empty glass tumbler.

"That's good beer, Blackie. Do you suppose we could brew some more when it's gone?"

"I don't know, Cap'n. Did we bring any yeast?"

"Find out, will you?" He turned to a massive man who occupied the third chair. "Well, Larsen, I'm glad it wasn't any worse than it was."

"What beats me, Captain, is how I could have made such a mistake. I worked it through twice. If it had been a nitro explosive, I'd have known off hand that I was wrong. If this kid hadn't had a hunch, I'd have set it off."

Captain Doyle chipped the old warrant officer on the shoulder. "Forget it, Larsen. You wouldn't have hurt anybody; that's why I require the pits to be evacuated even for small charges. These isotope explosives are tricky at best. Look what happened in pit A-9. Ten days' work shot with one charge, and the gunnery officer himself approved that one. But I want to see this boy. What did you say his name was?"

"Libby, A.J."

Doyle touched a button on his desk. A knock sounded at the door. A bellowed "Come in!" produced a stripling wearing the brassard of Corpsman Mate-of-the-Deck.

"Have Corpsman Libby report to me."

"Aye aye, sir."

Some few minutes later Libby was ushered into the Captain's cabin. He looked nervously around, and noted Larsen's presence, a fact that did not contribute to his peace of mind. He reported in a barely audible voice, "Corpsman Libby, sir."

The Captain looked him over. "Well, Libby, I hear that you and Mr. Larsen had a difference of opinion this morning. Tell me about it."

"I—I didn't mean any harm, sir."

"Of course not. You're not in any trouble; you did us all a good turn this morning. Tell me, how did you know that the calculation was wrong? Had any mining experience?"

"No, sir. I just saw that he had worked it out wrong."

"But how?"

Libby shuffled uneasily. "Well, sir, it just seemed wrong—It didn't fit."

"Just a second, Captain. May I ask this young man a couple of questions?" It was Commander "Blackie" Rhodes who spoke.

"Certainly. Go ahead."

"Are you the lad they call 'Pinkie'?"

Libby blushed. "Yes, sir."

"I've heard some rumors about this boy." Rhodes pushed his big frame out of his chair, went over to a bookshelf, and removed a thick volume. He thumbed through it, then with open book before him, started to question Libby.

"What's the square root of ninety-five?"

"Nine and seven hundred forty-seven thousandths."

"What's the cube root?"

"Four and five hundred sixty-three thousandths."

"What's its logarithm?"

"Its what, sir?"

"Good Lord, can a boy get through school today without knowing?"

The boy's discomfort became more intense. "I didn't get much schooling, sir. My folks didn't accept the Covenant until Pappy died, and we had to."

"I see. A logarithm is a name for a power to which you raise a given number, called the base, to get the number whose logarithm it is. Is that clear?"

Libby thought hard. "I don't quite get it, sir."

"I'll try again. If you raise ten to the second power—square it—it gives one hundred. Therefore the logarithm of a hundred to the base ten is two. In the same fashion the logarithm of a thousand to the base ten is three. Now what is the logarithm of ninety-five?"

Libby puzzled for a moment. "I can't make it come out even. It's a fraction."

"That's okay."

"Then it's one and nine hundred seventy-eight thousandths—just about."

Rhodes turned to the Captain. "I guess that about proves it, sir."

Doyle nodded thoughtfully. "Yes, the lad seems to have intuitive knowledge of arithmetical relationships. But let's see what else he has."

"I am afraid we'll have to send him back to Earth to find out properly."

Libby caught the gist of this last remark. "Please, sir, you aren't going to send me home? Maw 'ud be awful vexed with me."

"No, no, nothing of the sort. When your time is up, I want you to be checked over in the psychometrical laboratories. In the meantime, I wouldn't part with you for a quarter's pay. I'd give up smoking first. But let's see what else you can do."

In the ensuing hour the Captain and the Navigator heard Libby: one, deduce the Pythagorean proposition; two, derive Newton's laws of motion and Kepler's laws of ballistics from a statement of the conditions in which they obtained; three, judge length, area, and volume by eye with no measurable error. He had jumped into the idea of relativity and non-rectilinear space-time continua, and was beginning to pour forth ideas faster than he could talk, when Doyle held up a hand.

"That's enough, son. You'll be getting a fever. You run along to bed now, and come see me in the morning. I'm taking you off field work."

"Yes, sir."

"By the way, what is your full name?"

"Andrew Jackson Libby, sir."

"No, your folks wouldn't have signed the Covenant. Good night."

"Good night, sir."

After he had gone, the two older men discussed their discovery.

"How do you size it up, Captain?"

"Well, he's a genius, of course—one of those wild talents that will show up once in a blue moon. I'll turn him loose among my books and see how he shapes up. Shouldn't wonder if he were a page-at-a-glance reader, too."

"It beats me what we turn up among these boys—and not a one of 'em any account back on Earth."

Doyle nodded. "That was the trouble with these kids. They didn't feel needed."

+ + +

Eighty-eight swung some millions of miles further around the sun. The pock-marks on her face grew deeper, and were lined with durite, that strange close-packed laboratory product which (usually) would confine even atomic disintegration. Then Eighty-eight received a series of gentle pats, always on the side headed along her course. In a few weeks' time, the rocket blasts had their effect and Eighty-eight was plunging in an orbit toward the sun.

When she reached her station, one and three-tenths the distance from the sun of Earth's orbit, she would have to be coaxed by another series of pats into a circular orbit. Thereafter she was to be known as E-M3, Earth-Mars Space Station Spot Three.

Hundreds of millions of miles away, two other C.C.C. companies were inducing two other planetoids to quit their age-old grooves and slide between Earth and Mars to land in the same orbit as Eighty-eight. One was due to ride this orbit one hundred and twenty degrees ahead of Eighty-eight, the other one hundred and twenty degrees behind. When E-M1, E-M2, and E-M3 were all on station no hard-pushed traveler of the spaceways on the Earth-Mars passage would ever again find himself far from land—or rescue.

During the months that Eighty-eight fell free toward the sun, Captain Doyle reduced the working hours of his crew and turned them to the comparatively light labor of building a hotel and converting the little roofed-in valley into a garden spot. The rock was broken down into soil, fertilizers applied, and cultures of anaerobic bacteria planted. Then plants, conditioned by thirty-odd generations of low gravity at Luna City, were set out and tenderly cared for. Except for the low gravity, Eighty-eight began to feel like home.

But when Eighty-eight approached a tangent to the hypothetical future orbit of E-M3, the company went back to maneuvering routine, watch on and watch off, with the Captain living on black coffee and catching catnaps in the plotting room.

Libby was assigned to the ballistic calculator, three tons of thinking metal that dominated the plotting room. He loved the big machine. The Chief Fire Controlman let him help adjust it and care for it. Libby subconsciously thought of it as a person—his own kind of person.

On the last day of the approach, the shocks were more frequent. Libby sat in the right-hand saddle of the calculator and droned out the predictions for the next salvo, while gloating over the accuracy with which the machine tracked. Captain Doyle fussed around nervously, occasionally stopping to peer over the Navigator's shoulder. Of course the figures were right, but what if it didn't work? No one had ever moved so large a mass before. Suppose it plunged on and on—and on. Nonsense! It couldn't. Still he would be glad when they were past the critical speed.

A marine orderly touched his elbow. "Hello from the Flagship, sir."

"Read it."

"Flag to Eighty-eight; private message. Captain Doyle; am lying off to watch you bring her in—Kearney."

Doyle smiled. Nice of the old geezer. Once they were on station, he would invite the Admiral to ground for dinner and show him the park.

Another salvo cut loose, heavier than any before. The room trembled violently. In a moment, the reports of the surface observers commenced to trickle in. "Tube nine, clear!" "Tube ten, clear!"

But Libby's drone ceased.

Captain Doyle turned on him. "What's the matter, Libby? Asleep? Call the polar stations. I have to have a parallax."

"Captain—" The boy's voice was low and shaking.

"Speak up, man!"

"Captain—the machine isn't tracking."

"Spiers!" The grizzled head of the Chief Fire Controlman appeared from behind the calculator.

"I'm already on it, sir. Let you know in a moment."

He ducked back again. After a couple of long minutes he reappeared. "Gyros tumbled. It's a twelve hour calibration job, at least."

The Captain said nothing, but turned away, and walked to the far end of the room. The Navigator followed him with his eyes. He returned, glanced at the chronometer and spoke to the Navigator.

"Well, Blackie, if I don't have that firing data in seven minutes, we're sunk. Any suggestions?"

Rhodes shook his head without speaking.

Libby timidly raised his voice, "Captain—"

Doyle jerked around, "Yes?"

"The firing data is tube thirteen, seven point six three; tube twelve, six point nine oh; tube fourteen, six point eight nine."

Doyle studied his face. "You sure about that, son?"

"It *has* to be that, Captain."

Doyle stood perfectly still. This time he did not look at Rhodes but stared straight ahead. Then he took a long pull on his cigarette, glanced at the ash, and said in a steady voice, "Apply the data. Fire on the bell."

+ + +

Four hours later, Libby was still droning out firing data, his face gray, his eyes closed. Once he had fainted, but when they revived him he was still muttering figures. From time to time the Captain and the Navigator relieved each other, but there was no relief for him.

The salvos grew closer together, but the shocks were lighter.

Following one faint salvo, Libby looked up, stared at the ceiling, and spoke. "That's all, Captain."

"Call polar stations!"

The reports came back promptly, "Parallax constant, sidereal-solar rate constant."

The Captain relaxed into a chair. "Well, Blackie, we did it—thanks to Libby!" Then he noticed a worried, thoughtful look spread over Libby's face. "What's the matter, man? Have we slipped up?"

"Captain, you know you said the other day that you wished you had Earth-normal gravity in the park?"

"Yes. What of it?"

"If that book on gravitation you lent me is straight dope, I think I know a way to accomplish it."

The Captain inspected him as if seeing him for the first time. "Libby, you have ceased to amaze me. Could you stop doing that sort of thing long enough to dine with the Admiral?"

"Gee, Captain, that would be swell!" The audio circuit from Communications cut in.

"Hello from Flagship: 'Well, done, Eighty-eight.'"

Doyle smiled around at them all. "That's pleasant confirmation."

The audio brayed again.

"Hello from Flagship: 'Cancel last signal, stand by for correction.'"

A look of surprise and worry sprang into Doyle's face—then the audio continued:

"Hello from Flagship: 'Well done, E-M3?'"

Though most famous for his Westeros fantasies, which form the basis of the HBO phenomenon A Game of Thrones, George R.R. Martin has also written extensive science fiction, and like many of those stories, his Haviland Tuf space operas take place in his Thousand Worlds series which also includes Dying of the Light, Sandkings, and Nightflyers—the basis for the current SyFy TV series. The first of these space operas appeared in 1976 and tells the tale of Harold Norn, senior beastmaster of the Norn House of Lyronica, who approaches Haviland Tuf looking for beasts for gladiatorial matches in Lyronica's Bronze Arena. The result is a fighting beast arms race in which Tuf becomes the chief supplier, and the consequences are surprising and perhaps tragic.

"A Beast for Norn" first appeared in a shorter and significantly different form in the Andromeda I anthology. Later incorporated into a novel that includes several other stories, this tale introduced the character and serves as a great entrypoint for the series. Martin cites space opera pioneer Jack Vance as a heavy influence on these stories.

A BEAST FOR NORN (HAVILAND TUF)
A THOUSAND WORLDS STORY

GEORGE R.R. MARTIN

Haviland Tuf was drinking alone in the darkest corner of an alehouse on Tamber when the thin man found him. His elbows rested on the table and the top of his bald head almost brushed the low wooden beam above. Four empty mugs sat before him, their insides streaked by rings of foam, while a fifth, half-full, was cradled in his huge white hands.

If Tuf was aware of the curious glances the other patrons gave him from time to time, he showed no sign of it; he quaffed his ale methodically, his face without expression. He made a singular solitary figure drinking alone in his booth.

He was not *quite* alone though; Dax lay asleep on the table before him, a ball of dark fur. Occasionally, Tuf would set down his mug of ale and idly stroke his quiet companion. Dax would not stir from his comfortable position among the empty mugs. The cat was fully as large, compared to other cats, as Haviland Tuf was compared to other men.

When the thin man came walking up to Tuf's booth, Tuf said nothing at all. He merely looked up, blinked, and waited for the other to begin.

"You are Haviland Tuf, the animal-seller," the thin man said. He was indeed painfully thin. His garments, all black leather and grey fur, hung loose on him, bagging here and there. Yet he was plainly a man of some means, since he wore a slim brass coronet around his brow, under a mop of black hair, and his fingers were adorned with a plenitude of rings.

Tuf scratched Dax behind one black ear. "It is not enough that our solitude must be intruded upon," he said to the cat, his voice a deep bass with only a hint of inflection. "It is insufficient that our grief be violated. We must also bear calumnies and insults, it seems." He looked up at the thin man. "Sir," he said. "I am indeed Haviland Tuf, and perhaps it might be said that I do in some sense trade in animals. Yet perhaps I do not consider myself an animal-seller. Perhaps I consider myself an ecological engineer."

The thin man waved his hand in an irritated gesture, and slid uninvited into the booth opposite Tuf. "I understand that you own an ancient EEC seedship. That does not make you an ecological engineer, Tuf. They are all dead, and have been for centuries. But if you would prefer to be called an ecological engineer, then well and good. I require your services. I want to buy a monster from you, a great fierce beast."

"Ah," said Tuf, speaking to the cat again. "He wishes to buy a monster, this stranger who seats himself at my table uninvited." Tuf blinked. "I regret to inform you that your quest has been in vain. Monsters are entirely mythological, sir, like spirits, werebeasts, and competent bureaucrats. Moreover, I am not at this moment engaged in the selling of animals, nor in any other aspect of my profession. I am at this moment consuming this excellent Tamberkin ale, and mourning."

"Mourning?" the thin man said. "Mourning what?" He seemed most unwilling to take his leave.

"A cat," said Haviland Tuf. "Her name was Havoc, and she had been my companion for long years, sir. She has recently died, on a world called Alyssar that I had the misfortune to call upon, at the hands of a remarkably unpleasant barbarian princeling." He looked at the thin man's brass coronet. "You are not by chance a barbarian princeling yourself, sir?"

"Of course not."

"That is your good fortune," said Tuf.

"Well, pity about your cat, Tuf. I know your feeling, yesyes, I've been through it a thousand times myself."

"A thousand times," Tuf repeated flatly. "You might consider a strenuous effort to take better care of your pets."

The thin man shrugged. "Animals do die, you know. Can't be helped. Fang and claw and all that, yesyes, that's their destiny. I've had to grow accustomed to watching my best get slaughtered right in front of my eyes. But that's what I've come to talk to you about, Tuf."

"Indeed," said Haviland Tuf.

"My name is Herold Norn. I am the Senior Beast-Master of my House, one of the Twelve Great Houses of Lyronica."

"Lyronica," Tuf stated. "The name is not entirely unfamiliar to me. A small, sparsely settled planet, I seem to recall, of a somewhat savage bent. Perhaps this explains your transgressions of civilized manners."

"Savage?" Norn said. "That's Tamberkin rubbish, Tuf. Damned farmers. Lyronica is the jewel of this sector. You've heard of our gaming pits, haven't you?"

Haviland Tuf scratched Dax behind the ear once more, a peculiar rhythmic scratch, and the tomcat slowly uncurled, yawning, and glanced up at the thin man with large, bright, golden eyes. He purred softly.

"Some small nuggets of information have fallen in my ears during my voyagings," Tuf said. "Perhaps you would care to elaborate, Herold Norn, so Dax and I might consider your proposition."

Herold Norn rubbed thin hands together, nodding. "Dax?" he said. "Of course. A handsome animal, although personally I have never been fond of beasts who cannot fight. Real beauty lies in killing-strength, I always say."

"An idiosyncratic attitude," Tuf commented.

"No, no," said Norn, "not at all. I hope that your work here has not infected you with Tamberkin squeamishness."

Tuf drained his mug in silence, then signaled for two more. The barkeep brought them promptly.

"Thank you," Norn said, when the mug was set golden and foaming in front of him.

"Proceed, sir."

"Yes. Well, the Twelve Great Houses of Lyronica compete in the gaming pits. It began—oh, centuries ago. Before that, the houses warred. This way is much better. Family honor is upheld, fortunes are made, and no one is injured. You see, each house controls great tracts, scattered widely over the planet, and since the land is very thinly settled, animal life teems. The Lords of the Great Houses, many years ago during a time of peace, started to have animal fights. It was a pleasant diversion, rooted deep in history. You are aware, maybe, of the ancient custom of cock-fighting and the Old Earth folk called Romans who would set all manner of strange beasts against each other in their great arena?"

Norn paused and drank some ale, waiting for an answer, but Tuf merely stroked Dax and said nothing.

"No matter," the thin Lyronican finally said, wiping foam from his mouth with the back of his hand. "That was the beginning of the sport, you see. Each house has its own particular land, its own particular animals. The House of Varcour, for example, sprawls in the hot, swampy south, and they are fond of sending huge lizard-lions to the gaming pits. Feridian, a mountainous realm, has bred and championed its fortunes with a species of rock-ape which we call, naturally, *feridians*. My own house, Norn, stands on the grassy plains of the large northern continent. We have sent a hundred different beasts into combat in the pits, but we are most famed for our ironfangs."

"Ironfangs," Tuf said. "The name is evocative."

Norn gave a sly smile. "Yes," he said proudly. "As Senior Beast-Master, I have trained thousands. Oh, but they are lovely animals!

Tall as you are, with fur of the most marvelous blue-black color, fierce and relentless."

"Might I assume your ironfangs to be of canine descent?"

"But *such* canines," Norn said.

"Yet you require from me a monster."

Norn drank more of his ale. "True, true. Folks from a dozen near worlds voyage to Lyronica, to watch the beasts fight in the gaming pits and gamble on the outcome. Particularly they flock to the Bronze Arena that has stood for six hundred years in the City of All Houses. That's where the greatest fights are fought. The wealth of our houses and our world has come to depend on this. Without it, rich Lyronica would be as poor as the farmers of Tamber."

"Yes," said Tuf.

"But you understand, this wealth, it goes to the houses according to their honor, according to their victories. The House of Arneth has grown greatest and most powerful because of the many deadly beasts in their varied lands; the others rank according to their scores in the Bronze Arena."

Tuf blinked. "The House of Norn ranks last and least among the Twelve Great Houses of Lyronica," he said, and Dax purred more loudly.

"You know?"

"Sir. It was obvious. Yet an objection occurs to me. Under the rules of your Bronze Arena, might it not be considered unethical to purchase and introduce a species not native to your own fabled world?"

"There are precedents. Some seventy-odd years ago, a gambler came from Old Earth itself, with a creature called a timber wolf that he had trained. The House of Colin backed him, in a fit of madness. His poor beast was matched against a Norn ironfang, and proved far from equal to its task. There are other cases as well.

"In recent years, unfortunately, our ironfangs have not bred well. The wild species has all but died out on the plains, and the few who remain become swift and elusive, difficult for our housemen to capture. In the breeding kennels, the strain seems to have softened, despite my efforts and those of the Beast-Masters before me. Norn has won few victories of late, and I will not remain Senior for long unless something is done. We grow poor. When I heard that your *Ark* had come to Tamber, then, I determined to seek you out. I will begin a new era of glory for Norn, with your help."

Haviland Tuf sat very still. "I comprehend the dilemma you face. Yet I must inform you that I am not commonly in the habit of selling monsters. The *Ark* is an ancient seedship, designed by the Earth Imperials thousands of years ago, to decimate the Hrangans through biowar. I can unleash a veritable cornucopia of disease and pestilence, and in my cell library is stored cloning material for untold numbers of species from more than a thousand worlds, but true monsters of the sort that I have inferred you require are in somewhat shorter supply."

Herold Norn looked crestfallen. "You have nothing, then?"

"These are not my words," said Haviland Tuf. "The men and women of the vanished Ecological Engineering Corps did in truth make use, from time to time, of species that the uninformed or superstitious might label monstrous, for reasons as much psychological as ecological. Thus I do indeed have a few such animals in stock—a trifling number, a few thousand perhaps, certainly no more than ten thousand. To quote a more accurate figure, I must need consult my computers."

"A few thousand monsters!" Norn was excited again. "That is more than enough selection! Surely, among all those, we can find a beast for Norn!"

"Perhaps," Tuf said. "Or perhaps not. Both possibilities exist." He considered Norn, his long face cool and dispassionate. "This matter of Lyronica does pique my interest in a trifling way, and as I am at the moment without professional engagement, having given the Tamberkin a bird to check their rootworm infestation, I am moved to investigate your world and plight more closely. Return to Norn, sir. I will take the *Ark* to Lyronica and see your gaming pits, and we will decide what is to be done with them."

Norn smiled. "Excellent," he said. "Then I will buy this round of ale." Dax purred as loud as a descending shuttle.

+ + +

The Bronze Arena stood square in the center of the City of All Houses, at the point where sectors dominated by the Twelve Great Houses met like slices in a vast pie. Each enclave of the rambling stone city was walled off, each flew a flag with its distinctive colors, each had its own ambience and style, but all met in the Bronze Arena.

The arena was not bronze after all, but mostly black stone and polished wood. It bulked upwards, taller than all but a few of the city's scattered towers and minarets, topped by a shining bronze dome that gleamed with the orange rays of the sunset. Gargoyles peered from the various narrow windows, carved of stone and hammered from bronze and wrought iron. The great doors in the black stone walls were fashioned of metal as well, and there were twelve of them, each facing a different sector of the City of All Houses. The colors and the etching on each gateway were distinctive to its house.

Lyronica's sun was a fist of red flame smearing the western horizon when Herold Norn led Haviland Tuf to the games. The housemen had just fired gas torches, metal obelisks that stood like dart teeth in a ring about the Bronze Arena, and the hulking ancient building was surrounded by flickering pillars of blue and orange flame. In a crowd of gamblers and gamesters, Tuf followed Herold Norn from the half-deserted streets of the Nornic slums down a path of crushed rock, passing between twelve bronze ironfangs who snarled and spit in timeless poses on either side of the street, and then through the wide Norn Gate. The doors were intricate ebony and brass. The uniformed guards, clad in the same black leather and grey fur as Herold Norn himself, recognized the Beast-Master and admitted them; others stopped to pay with coins of gold and iron.

The arena was the greatest gaming pit of all. It *was* a pit, the sandy combat-floor sunk deep below ground level, with stone walls four meters high surrounding it. Then the seats began, just atop the walls, circling the arena in ascending tiers until they reached the doors. Enough seating for thirty thousand, Norn boasted, although Tuf observed that those in the back had a poor view at best, and other seats were blocked off by iron pillars. Betting stalls were scattered throughout the building.

Herold Norn took Tuf to the best seats in the arena, in the front of the Norn section, with only a stone parapet separating them from the four-meter drop to the combat sands. The seats here were not rickety wood and iron, like those in the rear, but thrones of leather, huge enough to accommodate even Tuf's vast bulk without difficulty, and opulently comfortable. "Every seat is bound in the skin of a beast that has died nobly below," Herold Norn told Tuf as they seated themselves.

Beneath them, a work crew of men in one-piece blue coveralls was dragging the carcass of some gaunt feathered animal toward one of the entryways. "A fighting bird of the House of Wrai Hill," Norn explained. "The Wrai Beast-Master sent it up against a Varcour lizard-lion. Not the most felicitous choice."

Haviland Tuf said nothing. He sat stiff and erect, dressed in a grey vinyl greatcoat that fell to his ankles, with flaring shoulder-boards and a visored green cap emblazoned with the golden theta of the Ecological Engineers. His large pale hands interlocked atop his bulging stomach while Herold Norn kept up a steady stream of conversation.

When the arena announcer spoke, the thunder of his magnified voice boomed all around them. "Fifth match," he said. "From the House of Norn, a male ironfang, aged two years, weight 2.6 quintals, trained by Junior Beast-Master Kers Norn. New to the Bronze Arena." Immediately below them, metal grated harshly on metal, and a nightmare creature came bounding into the pit. The ironfang was a shaggy giant, with sunken red eyes and a double row of curving teeth that dripped slaver—a wolf grown all out of proportion and crossed with a sabertoothed tiger, its legs as thick as young trees, its speed and killing grace only partially disguised by the blue-black fur that hid the play of muscles. The ironfang snarled and the arena echoed to the noise; scattered cheering began all around them.

Herold Norn smiled. "Kers is a cousin, and one of our most promising Juniors. He tells me this beast will do us proud. Yesyes, I like its looks, don't you?"

"Being new to Lyronica and your Bronze Arena, I have no standard of comparison," Tuf said in a flat voice.

The announcer began again. "From the House of Arneth-in-the-Gilded-Wood, a strangling-ape, aged six years, weight 3.1 quintals, trained by Senior Beast-Master Danel Leigh Arneth. Three times a veteran of the Bronze Arena, three times surviving."

Across the combat pit, another of the entryways—the one wrought in gold and crimson—slid open, and the second beast lumbered out on two squat legs and looked around. The ape was short but immensely broad, with a triangular torso and a bullet-shaped head, eyes sunk deep under a heavy ridge of bone. Its arms, double-jointed and muscular, dragged in the arena sand. From head to toe the beast was hairless, but for patches of dark red fur under its arms; its skin was a dirty white. And it smelled. Across the arena, Haviland Tuf still caught the musky odor.

"It sweats," Norn explained. "Danel Leigh has driven it to killing frenzy before sending it forth. His beast has the edge in experience, you understand, and the strangling-ape is a savage creature. Unlike its cousin, the mountain feridian, it is naturally a carnivore and needs little training. But Kers's ironfang is younger. The match should be of interest." The Norn Beast-Master leaned forward while Tuf sat calm and still.

The ape turned, growling deep in its throat, and already the ironfang was streaking towards it, snarling, a blue-black blur that scattered arena sand as it ran. The strangling-ape waited for it, spreading its huge gangling arms, and Tuf had a blurred impression of the great Norn killer leaving the ground in one tremendous bound. Then the two animals were locked together, rolling over and over in a tangle of ferocity, and the arena became a symphony of screams. "The throat," Norn was shouting. "Tear out its throat! Tear out its throat!"

The two beasts parted as suddenly as they had met. The ironfang spun away and began to move in slow circles, and Tuf saw that one of its forelegs was bent and broken. It limped on its three remaining limbs, yet still it circled. The strangling-ape gave it no opening, but turned constantly to face it. Long gashes had been opened across the ape's broad chest, where the ironfang's sabers had slashed, but the beast seemed little weakened. Herold Norn had begun to mutter softly.

Impatient with the lull, the watchers in the Bronze Arena began a rhythmic chant, a low wordless noise that swelled louder and louder as new voices joined the chorus. Tuf saw at once that the sound affected the animals below. They began to snarl and hiss, calling battlecries in savage voices, and the strangling-ape moved from one leg to the other, back and forth in a macabre little jig, while bloody slaver ran from the gaping jaws of the ironfang.

The killing chant rose and fell, swelling ever louder until the dome above thrummed with the noise. The beasts below went into frenzy. Suddenly the ironfang was charging again, and the ape's long arms reached to meet it in its wild lunge. The impact of the leap threw the strangler backwards, but Tuf saw that the ironfang's teeth had closed on air while the ape wrapped its hands around the blue-black throat. The canine thrashed wildly as they rolled in the sand. Then came a sharp, horribly loud snap, and the wolf-creature was nothing but a rag of fur, its head lolling grotesquely to one side.

The watchers ceased their moaning chant, and began to applaud and whistle. Afterwards, the gold and crimson door slid open once again and the strangling-ape returned to whence it had come. Four men in Norn black and grey came out to carry off the corpse of the ironfang.

Herold Norn was sullen. "Another loss. I will speak to Kers. His beast did not find the throat."

"What will become of the carcass?" inquired Tuf.

"Skinned and butchered," Herold Norn muttered. "House Arneth will use the pelt to upholster a seat in their section of the arena. The meat will be distributed to the beggars who clamor outside their gold-and-crimson door. The Great Houses are all of a charitable mien."

"Indeed," said Haviland Tuf. He rose from his seat, unfolding with slow dignity. "I have seen your Bronze Arena."

"Are you going?" Norn asked anxiously. "Surely not so soon! There are five more matches. In the next, a giant feridian fights a water-scorpion from Amar Island!"

"I wished only to determine if all that I had heard of Lyronica's far-famed Bronze Arena was so. I see that it is. Therefore there is no need for me to remain any longer. One need not consume the whole of a flask of mushroom wine to ascertain whether the vintage has a pleasant taste."

Herold Norn got to his feet. "Well," he said, "come with me out to Norn House, then. I can show you the kennels, the training pits. We will feast you as you have never been feasted!"

"This will not be necessary," said Haviland Tuf. "Having seen your Bronze Arena, I will trust my imagination and powers of deduction to visualize your kennels and training pits. I shall return to the *Ark* forthwith."

Norn reached out an anxious hand toward Tuf's arm to restrain him. "Will you sell us a monster, then? You've seen our plight."

Tuf sidestepped the Beast-Master's grip with a deftness belying his size and weight. "Sir. Restrain yourself. I am not fond of being rudely seized and grasped." When Norn's hand had fallen, Tuf looked down into his eyes. "I have no doubt that a problem exists upon Lyronica. Perhaps a more practical man than myself would judge it none of his concern, but being at heart an altruist, I cannot find it in myself to leave you as I have found you. I will ponder your situation and address myself to devising the proper corrective measures. You may call upon me in the *Ark* on the third day hence. Perhaps by that time I will have a thought or two to share."

Then, without further ado, Haviland Tuf turned and walked from the Bronze Arena, back to the spaceport of the City of All Houses, where his shuttle *Basilisk* sat waiting.

+ + +

Herold Norn had obviously not been prepared for the *Ark*. He emerged from his tiny, battered, black and grey shuttle into the immensity of the landing deck and stood with his mouth open, craning his head this way and that, peering at the echoing darkness above, at the looming alien ships, at the thing that looked like a metal dragon nesting amid the distant shadows. When Haviland Tuf came rolling up to meet him, driving an open three-wheeled cart, the Beast-Master made no effort to disguise his reaction. "I should have known," he kept repeating. "The size of this ship, the size. But of course I should have known."

Haviland Tuf sat unmoved, cradling Dax in one arm and stroking the cat slowly. "Some might find the *Ark* excessively large, and perhaps even daunting in its spaciousness, but I am comfortable," he said impassively. "The ancient EEC seedships once had two hundred crewmen, and I can only assume that they, like myself, abhorred cramped quarters."

Herold Norn seated himself beside Tuf. "How many men do you have in your crew?" he asked casually as Tuf set them in motion.

"One, or five, depending on whether one counts feline crew members or only humanoids."

"You are the *only* crewman?" Norn said.

Dax stood up in Tuf's lap; his long black fur stirred and bristled. "The *Ark*'s inhabitants consist of myself, Dax, and three other cats, named Chaos, Hostility, and Suspicion. Please do not take alarm at their names, Beast-Master Norn. They are gentle and harmless creatures."

"One man and four cats," Herold Norn said speculatively. "A small crew for a big ship, yesyes."

Dax hissed. Tuf, steering the cart with one large pale hand, used the other to stroke and soothe his pet. "I might also make mention of the sleepers, since you seem to have developed such an acute interest in the various living inhabitants of the *Ark*."

"The sleepers?" said Herold Norn. "What are they?"

"Certain living organisms, ranging in size from the microscopic to the monstrous, fully cloned but comatose, held in a perpetual stasis in the *Ark*'s cloning vats. Though I have a certain fondness for animals of all sorts, in the case of these sleepers I have wisely allowed my intellect to rule my emotions and have therefore taken no steps to disturb their long dreamless slumber. Having investigated the nature of these particular species, I long ago decided that they would be decidedly less pleasant traveling companions than my cats. I must admit that at times I find the sleepers a decided nuisance. At regular intervals I must enter a bothersome secret command into the *Ark*'s computers so that their long sleep may continue. I have a great abiding dread that one day I shall forget to do this, for whatever reasons, and then my ship will be filled with all manner of strange plagues and slavering carnivores, requiring a time-consuming and vexing clean-up and perhaps even wreaking harm to my person or my cats."

Herold Norn stared at Tuf's expressionless face and regarded his large, hostile cat. "Ah," he said. "Yesyes. Sounds dangerous, Tuf. Perhaps you ought to, ah, abort all these sleepers. Then you'd be, ah, safe."

Dax hissed at him again.

"An interesting concept," Tuf said. "Doubtless the vicissitudes of war were responsible for inculcating such paranoid attitudes into the men and women of the Ecological Engineering Corps that they felt obliged to program in these fearsome biological defenses. Being myself of a more trusting and honest nature, I have often contemplated doing away with the sleepers, but the truth is, I cannot find it in myself to unilaterally abolish a historic practice that has endured for over a millennium. Therefore, I allow the sleepers to sleep, and do my utmost to remember the secret countermands."

Herold Norn scowled. "Yesyes," he said.

Dax sat down in Tuf's lap again, and purred.

"Have you come up with anything?" Norn asked.

"My efforts have not entirely been for naught," said Tuf flatly, as they rolled out of the wide corridor into the *Ark*'s huge central shaft. Herold Norn's mouth dropped open again. Around them on all sides, lost in dimness, was an unending panorama of vats of all sizes and shapes. In some of the medium-sized tanks, dark shapes hung in translucent bags, and stirred fitfully. "Sleepers," Norn muttered.

"Indeed," said Haviland Tuf. He stared straight ahead as he drove, with Dax curled in his lap, while Norn looked wonderingly from side to side.

They departed the dim, echoing shaft at last, drove through a narrow corridor, climbed out of the cart, and entered a large white room. Four wide, padded chairs dominated the four corners of the chamber, with control panels on their thick, flaring arms; a circular plate of blue metal was built into the floor amid them. Haviland Tuf dropped Dax into one of the chairs before seating himself in a second. Norn looked around, then took the chair diagonally opposite Tuf.

"I must inform you of several things," Tuf began.

"Yesyes," said Norn.

"Monsters are expensive," Tuf said. "I will require one hundred thousand standards."

"*What!* That's an outrage! I told you, Norn is a poor house."

"So. Perhaps then a richer house would meet the required price. The Ecological Engineering Corps has been defunct for centuries, sir. No ship of theirs remains in working order, save the *Ark* alone. Their science is largely forgotten. Techniques of cloning and genetic engineering such as they practiced exist now only on distant Prometheus and perhaps on Old Earth itself, yet Earth is closed and

the Prometheans guard their biological secrets with jealous fervor."
Tuf looked across to Dax. "And yet Herold Norn feels my price to
be excessive."

"Fifty thousand standards," Norn said. "We can barely meet that
price."

Haviland Tuf said nothing.

"Eighty thousand standards, then! I can go no higher. The House
of Norn will be bankrupt! They will tear down our bronze ironfangs
and seal the Norn Gate!"

Haviland Tuf said nothing.

"Curse you! A hundred thousand, yesyes. But only if your monster
meets our requirements."

"You will pay the full sum on delivery."

"Impossible!"

Tuf was silent again.

Herold Norn tried to wait him out. He looked around with studied
nonchalance. Tuf stared straight ahead. He ran his fingers through his
hair. Tuf stared straight ahead. He squirmed around in his chair. Tuf
stared straight ahead.

"Oh, very well," Norn said in frustration.

"As to the monster itself," said Tuf, "I have studied your requirements
closely, and have consulted my computers. Within the cell library of
the *Ark* are samples of thousands upon thousands of predators from
uncounted worlds, including fossilized tissue samples, locked within
which can be found the genetic patterns of creatures of legend long
extinct upon their original homeworlds, thus allowing me to replicate
such species. Therefore, the choices are many. To simplify matters, I
have taken into account several additional criteria beyond the mere
ferocity of the animals under consideration. For example, I have
limited myself to oxygen-breathing species, and furthermore to those
who might be comfortable in a climate such as prevails upon House
Norn's windswept prairies."

"An excellent point," Herold Norn said. "We have, from time to
time, attempted to raise lizard-lions and feridians and other beasts of
the Twelve Houses, with ill success. The climate, the vegetation…" He
made a disgusted gesture.

"Precisely," said Haviland Tuf. "I see you comprehend the various and sundry difficulties incumbent in my search."

"Yesyes, but get to the point. What have you found? What is this hundred-thousand-standard monster?"

"I offer you a selection," Tuf said. "From among some thirty species. Attend!"

He touched a glowing button on the arm of his chair, and suddenly a beast was squatting on the blue-metal plate between them. Two meters tall, with rubbery pink-grey skin and thin white hair, the creature had a low forehead and a swinish snout, plus a set of nasty curving horns and daggerlike claws on its hands.

"I will not trouble you with the formal nomenclature, since I have observed that informality is the rule of the Bronze Arena," Haviland Tuf said. "This is the so-called stalking-swine of Heydey, native to both forests and plains. It is chiefly an eater of carrion, but has been known to relish fresh meat, and it fights viciously when attacked. Furthermore, it is reliably reported to be quite intelligent, yet impossible to domesticate. The stalking-swine is an excellent breeder. The colonists from Gulliver eventually abandoned their Heydey settlement because of this animal. That was some twelve hundred years past."

Herold Norn scratched his scalp between dark hair and brass coronet. "No. It is too thin, too light. Look at the neck! Think what a feridian would do to it." He shook his head violently. "Besides, it is *ugly*. And I resent the offer of a scavenger, no matter how ill-tempered. The House of Norn breeds proud fighters, beasts who kill their own game!"

"Indeed," said Tuf. He touched the button, and the stalking-swine vanished. In its place, bulking large enough to touch the plates and fade into them, was a massive ball of armored grey flesh as featureless as battle plate.

"This creature's barren homeworld has neither been named nor settled, yet an exploratory party from Old Poseidon once charted and claimed it, and cell samples were taken. Zoo specimens existed briefly but did not thrive. The beast was nicknamed the rolleram. Adults weigh approximately six metric tons. On the plains of their homeworld, the rollerams achieve speed in excess of fifty kilometers per hour, crushing prey beneath them. The beast is, in a sense, all mouth. Thusly, as any portion of its skin can be made to exude digestive enzymes, it simply rests atop its meal until the meat has been absorbed. I can vouch for the mindless hostility of this species. Once, through an unusual set of circumstances that we need not go into, a rolleram was loosed to run free on one of my decks, where it did a truly astonishing amount of damage to bulkheads and instrumentation before finally battering itself to an early and futile death. Moreover, it was quite implacable in its aggression, and attempted to crush me beneath its bulk whenever I descended into its domain to bring it sustenance."

Herold Norn, himself half-immersed in the looming holograph, sounded impressed. "Ah, yes. Better, much better. An awesome creature. Perhaps… but no." His tone changed suddenly. "No, no, this will never do. A creature weighing six tons and rolling that fast might smash its way out of the Bronze Arena and kill hundreds of our patrons. Besides, who would pay hard coin to watch this *thing* crush a lizard-lion or a strangler? No. No sport. Your rolleram is *too* monstrous, Tuf."

Tuf, unmoved, hit the button once again. The vast grey bulk gave way to a sleek, snarling cat, fully as large as an ironfang, with slitted yellow eyes and powerful muscles bunched beneath a coat of dark-blue fur. The fur was striped; long thick lines of smoky silver ran lengthwise down the creature's gleaming flanks.

"Ahhhhhhhh," Norn said. "A beauty, in truth, in truth."

"The cobalt panther of Celia's World," Tuf said, "often called the cobalcat. One of the largest and deadliest of the great cats, or their analogues. The beast is a truly superlative hunter, its senses miracles of biological engineering. It can see into the infrared for night prowling, and the ears—note the size and the spread, Beast-Master—the ears are extremely sensitive. Being of felinoid stock, the cobalcat has psionic ability, but in its case this ability is far more developed than the usual. Fear, hunger, and bloodlust all act as triggers; then the cobalcat becomes a mindreader."

Norn looked up, startled. "What?"

"Psionics, sir. Surely you are aware of the concept. The cobalcat is quite deadly, simply because it knows what moves an antagonist will make before those moves are made. Do you comprehend?"

"Yes." Norn's voice was excited. Haviland Tuf looked over at Dax, and the big tomcat—who'd been not the least disturbed by the parade of scentless phantoms flashing on and off—blinked and stretched lazily. "Perfect, perfect! Why, I'll venture to say that we can even train these beasts as we'd train ironfangs, eh? And *mindreaders*! Perfect. Even the colors are right—dark blue, you know, and our ironfangs were blue-black—so the cats will be most Nornic, yesyes!"

Tuf touched his chair arm, and the cobalcat vanished. "Indeed. I would assume, therefore, that we have no need to proceed further, I shall commence the cloning process immediately upon your departure. Delivery will be in three weeks standard, if that pleases you. For the agreed-upon sum, I will provide three pair—two set of younglings who should be released in your wildlands as breeding stock, and one mated set full-grown, who might be immediately sent into the Bronze Arena."

"So soon," Norn began. "Fine, but…"

"I employ a chronowarp, Beast-Master. It requires vast energies, true, but has the power to accelerate the very tread of time itself, producing within the tank a chronic distortion that enables me to hurry the clone to maturity. It would perhaps be prudent to add that, although I provide Norn with six animals, only three actual individuals are represented. The *Ark* carries a triple cobalcat cell. I will clone each specimen twice, male and female, and hope for a viable genetic mix when they crossbreed on Lyronica."

"Fine, whatever you say," Norn said. "I will send the ships for the animals promptly. Then we will pay you."

Dax uttered a tiny little yowl.

"Sir," said Tuf. "A better thought has occurred to me. You may pay the full fee before any beasts are handed over."

"But you said on delivery!"

"Admitted. Yet I am given to impulsive whims, and impulse now tells me to collect first, rather than simultaneously."

"Oh, very well," Norn said. "Though your demands are arbitrary and excessive. With these cobalcats, we shall soon recoup our fee." He started to rise.

Haviland Tuf raised a single finger. "One moment. You have not seen fit to inform me overmuch of the ecology of Lyronica, nor the particular realms of Norn House. Perhaps prey exists. I must caution you, however, that your cobalcats are hunters, and therefore require suitable game species."

"Yesyes, of course."

"Fortunately, I am equipped to be of help to you. For an additional five thousand standards, I might clone you a breeding stock of Celian hoppers, delightful furred herbivores celebrated on a dozen worlds for their succulent flesh, among diners of a carnivorous inclination."

Herold Norn frowned. "Bah. You ought to give them to us without charge. You have extorted enough money, Tuf."

Tuf rose and gave a ponderous shrug. "The man berates me, Dax," he said to his cat. "What am I to do? I seek only an honest living, and everywhere I am taken advantage of." He looked at Norn. "Another of my impulses comes to me. I feel, somehow, that you will not relent, not even were I to offer you an excellent discount. Therefore I shall yield. The hoppers are yours without charge."

"Good. Excellent." Norn turned toward the door. "We shall take them at the same time as the cobalcats, and release them about the estates."

Haviland Tuf and Dax followed him from the chamber, and they rode in silence back to Norn's ship.

The fee was sent up by the House of Norn the day before delivery was due. The following afternoon, a dozen men in black and grey ascended to the *Ark*, and carried six tranquilized cobalcats from Haviland Tuf's holding tanks to the waiting cages in their shuttlecraft. Tuf bid them a passive farewell, and heard no more from Herold Norn. But he kept the *Ark* in orbit about Lyronica.

Less than three of Lyronica's shortened days passed before Tuf observed that his clients had slated a cobalcat for a bout in the Bronze Arena.

On the appointed evening, Tuf donned a disguise, consisting of a false beard and shoulder-length wig of red hair, plus a gaudy puff-sleeved suit of canary yellow complete with a furred turban, and shuttled down to the City of All Houses with the hope of escaping attention. When the match was called, he was seated in the back of the arena, a rough stone wall against his shoulders and a narrow wooden seat attempting to support his weight. He had paid a few irons for admission, but had scrupulously bypassed the betting booths.

"Third match," the announcer cried, even as workers pulled off the scattered meaty chunks of the loser in the second match. "From the House of Varcour, a female lizard-lion, aged nine months, weight 1.4 quintals, trained by Junior Beast-Master Ammari y Varcour Otheni. Once a veteran of the Bronze Arena, once surviving." Those customers close to Tuf began to cheer and wave their hands wildly, as might be anticipated; he had chosen to enter by the Varcour Gate this time, walking down a green concrete road and through the gaping maw of a monstrous golden lizard, and thus was surrounded by Varcour partisans. Away and below, a great door enameled in green and gold slid up. Tuf lifted his rented binoculars to his eyes, and saw the lizard-lion scrabble forward—two meters of scaled green reptile with a whiplike tail thrice its own length and the long snout of an Old Earth alligator. Its jaws opened and closed soundlessly, displaying an array of impressive teeth.

"From the House of Norn, imported from offworld for your amusement, a female cobalcat. Aged—" The announcer paused. "Aged three, ah, years," he said at last, "weight 2.3 quintals, trained by Senior Beast-Master Herold Norn. New to the Bronze Arena." The metallic dome overhead rang to the cacophonous cheering of the Norn sector. Herold Norn had packed the Bronze Arena with his housemen, dressed in Norn colors and betting the grey and black standard.

The cobalcat came from the darkness slowly, with cautious fluid grace, and its great golden eyes swept the arena. It was every bit the beast that Tuf had promised—a bundle of deadly muscle and frozen motion, dark-blue fur marbled with silvery streaks. Its growl could scarcely be heard, so far was Tuf from the action, but he saw its mouth gape through his glasses.

The lizard-lion saw it, too, and came waddling forward, its short scaled legs kicking in the sand while the long impossible tail arched above it like the stinger of some reptilian scorpion. When the cobalcat turned its liquid eyes on the enemy, the lizard-lion brought the tail down hard. With a bone-breaking crack the whip made contact, but the cobalcat had smoothly slipped to one side, and nothing shattered but air and sand.

The cat circled, growling. The lizard-lion, implacable, turned and raised its tail again, opened its jaws, lunged forward. The cobalcat avoided both teeth and whip. Again the tail cracked, and yet again; the cat was too quick. Someone in the audience began to moan the killing chant, others picked it up; Tuf turned his binoculars, and saw swaying in the Norn seats. The lizard-lion gnashed its long jaws in frenzy, smashed its whip across the nearest entry door, and began to thrash.

The cobalcat, sensing an opening, moved behind its enemy with a graceful leap, pinned the struggling lizard with one great blue paw, and clawed the soft greenish flanks and belly to ribbons. After a time and a few futile snaps of its whip that only distracted the cat, the lizard-lion lay still.

The Norns were cheering very loudly. Haviland Tuf, his pale features concealed behind his beard, rose from his cramped seat and took his leave.

+ + +

Weeks passed; the *Ark* remained in orbit around Lyronica. Haviland Tuf carefully monitored results from the Bronze Arena and noted that the Norn cobalcats were winning match after match. Herold Norn still lost a contest or two, when using an ironfang to fill up his arena obligations, but those defeats were easily outweighed by his long string of victories.

Tuf sat communing with Dax, played with his other cats, entertained himself with recently acquired holo dramas, ran numerous detailed ecological projections upon his computers, drank many tankards of brown Tamberkin ale and aged mushroom wine, and waited.

Some three standard weeks after the debut of the cobalcats, he had the callers he had anticipated.

Their slim, needle-prowed shuttlecraft was done in green and gold, and the men themselves dressed in scaled armor of gilded plate and green enamel. Three stood stiffly at attention when Tuf rolled up to meet them. The fourth, a florid and corpulent man who wore a golden helmet with a bright-green plume to conceal a mottled pate as bald as Tuf's, stepped forward and offered a meaty hand.

"Your intent is appreciated," Tuf told him, keeping both of his own hands firmly on Dax, "and I have noted the fact that you are not clutching a weapon. Might I inquire as to your name and business, sir?"

"Morho y Varcour Otheni," the leader began.

Tuf raised one palm. "So. And you are the Senior Beast-Master of the House of Varcour, come to buy a monster. This turn of events is not entirely unanticipated, I must confess."

The fat Beast-Master's mouth puckered in an "o."

"Your housemen should remain here," Tuf said. "You may seat yourself beside me, and we will proceed."

Haviland Tuf let Morho y Varcour Otheni utter scarcely a word until they were alone in the same chamber to which he had taken Herold Norn, sitting diagonally opposite. "You heard of me from the Norns," Tuf said then, "obviously."

Morho smiled toothily. "Indeed we did. A Norn houseman was persuaded to reveal the source of their cobalcats. To our delight, your *Ark* was still in orbit. You seem to have found Lyronica diverting?"

"Diversion is not the crux of the matter," Tuf said. "When problems exist, my professional pride requires me to be of whatever small service I can. Lyronica is rife with problems, alas. Your own individual difficulty, for example. Varcour is, in all probability, now the last and least of the Twelve Great Houses. A man of a more critical turn of mind than myself might remark that your lizard-lions are deplorably marginal monsters at best, and since I understand your realms are chiefly swampland, your choice of arena combatants must therefore be somewhat limited. Have I divined the essence of your complaint?"

"Hmpf. Yes, indeed. You do anticipate me, sir. But you do it well. We were holding our own well enough until you interfered. Since then, well, we have not taken a match from Norn once, and they were previously our chief victims. A few paltry wins over Wrai Hill and Amar Island, a lucky score against Feridian, a pair of death-draws with Arneth and Sin Doon—that has been our lot this past month. Pfui. We cannot survive. They will make me a Brood-Tender and ship me back to the estates unless I act."

Tuf stroked Dax, and quieted Morho with an upraised hand. "No need to belabor these matters further. Your distress is noted. Since my dealings with Herold Norn, I have been fortunate enough to be gifted with a great deal of leisure. Accordingly, as an exercise of the mind, I have been able to devote myself to the problems of the Great Houses, each in its turn. We need not waste precious time. I can solve your present difficulties. There will be some cost, however."

Morho grinned. "I come prepared. I heard about your price. It's high, there is no arguing, but we are prepared to pay, if you can…"

"Sir," Tuf said. "I am a man of charity. Norn was a poor house, its Beast-Master all but a beggar. In mercy, I gave him a low price. The domains of Varcour are richer, its standards brighter, its victories more wildly sung. For you, I must charge two hundred seventy-five thousand standards, to make up for the losses I incurred in dealing so generously with Norn."

Morho made a shocked blubbering sound, and his scales gave metallic clinks as he shifted in his seat. "Too much, too much," he protested. "I implore you. Truly, we are more glorious than Norn, but not so great as you suppose. To pay this price of yours, we must need starve. Lizard-lions would run over our battlements. Our towns would sink on their stilts, until the swamp mud covered them over and the children drowned."

Dax shifted in Tuf's lap and made a small meow. "Quite so," Tuf said. "I am abashed to think that I might cause such suffering. Perhaps two hundred thousand standards would be more equitable."

Morho y Varcour Otheni began to protest and implore again, but this time Tuf merely sat silently, arms on their armrests, until the Beast-Master, red-faced and sweating, finally ran down and agreed to pay his price.

Tuf touched a button on the arm of his chair. The image of a great muscular saurian materialized between him and Morho; it stood two meters high, covered in grey-green plate scales and standing on four squat clawed legs as thick as tree stumps. Its head was a massive thing, armored by a thick yellowish plate of bone that jutted forward like the ramming prow of an ancient warship, with two curving horns at its upper corners. The creature had a short, thick neck; dim yellow eyes peered from under the jut of its brow ridge. Between them, square in the center of the head, a large, dark, round hole pierced the thick skull plate.

Morho swallowed. "Oh," he said. "Yes. Very, ah, large. But it looks—was there originally a third horn in the center, there? It looks as though it has been, ah, removed. Our specimens must be intact, Tuf."

"The *tris neryei* of Cable's Landing," Tuf said, "or so it was named by the Fyndii, whose colonists preceded humanity on that world by several millennia. The term translates, literally, as 'living knife.' There is no missing horn, sir." A long finger made a small, precise motion, pressed down upon a control. The *tris neryei* turned its massive head toward the Varcouri Beast-Master, who hiked his bulk forward awkwardly to inspect its image.

As he reached out toward the phantom, tendons bulged in the creature's thick neck, and a sharpened bone stake, as thick around as Tuf's forearm and more than a meter long, came thrusting out of the beast's head in a blur of motion. Morho y Varcour Otheni uttered a high thin squeak and turned grey as the bone spear skewered him and pinned him to his seat. An unfortunate odor filled the chamber.

Tuf said nothing. Morho, blubbering, looked down at where the horn entered his swollen stomach as if he were about to be sick, and it took him a long horrid minute before he realized there was no blood and no pain and the monster was only a hologram. His mouth made an "o." No sound came out. He swallowed. "Very, ah, dramatic," he said to Tuf.

The end of the long, discolored bone spear was held tightly within rings and ropes of pulsing blue-black muscle. Slowly the shaft began to pull back into the monster's head. "The bayonet, if we may be so bold as to call it that, is concealed within a mucous-lined sheath along the creature's upper neck and back, and the surrounding rings of musculature can deliver it at a speed approximating seventy kilometers per standard hour, with commensurate force. This species' native habitat is not entirely dissimilar to the areas of Lyronica under the control of the House of Varcour."

Morho moved forward so his seat creaked beneath his weight. Dax purred loudly. "Excellent!" the Beast-Master said. "Though the name is a bit, oh, alien. We shall call them, let me think, ah, spear-carriers! Yes!"

"Call them what you will," said Tuf. "That is of small concern to me. These saurians have many obvious advantages for the House of Varcour, and should you choose to take them, I will also give you, without any additional charge, a breeding stock of Cathadayn tree-slugs. You will find that…"

✦ ✦ ✦

Tuf followed the news from the Bronze Arena with diligence, although he never again ventured forth to the soil of Lyronica. The cobalcats continued to sweep all before them; in the latest featured encounter, one of the Norn beasts had destroyed a prime Arneth strangling-ape and an Amar Island fleshfrog during a special triple match.

But Varcour fortunes were also on the upswing; the newly introduced spear-carriers had proved a Bronze Arena sensation, with their booming cries and their heavy tread and the swift and relentless death dealt out in sudden thrusts of their massive bone bayonets. In three matches so far, a huge feridian, a water-scorpion, and a Gnethin spidercat had all proved impossibly unequal to the Varcour saurians. Morho y Varcour Otheni was ecstatic. Next week, cobalcat would face spear-carrier in a struggle for supremacy, and a packed arena was being predicted.

Herold Norn called up once, shortly after the spear-carriers had scored their first victory. "Tuf!" he said sternly, "you have sold a monster to Varcour. We do not approve."

"I was not aware that your approval was required," Tuf said. "I labored under the impression that I was a free agent, as were the lords and Beast-Masters of all the Great Houses of Lyronica."

"Yesyes," Herold Norn snapped, "but we won't be cheated, you hear?"

Haviland Tuf sat calmly, regarding Norn's twisted frown while petting Dax. "I take great care to be fair in all my dealings," he said. "Had you insisted upon an exclusive monster franchise for Lyronica, perhaps we might have discussed that possibility, but to the best of my recollection no such matter was ever broached or suggested. Of course,

I could hardly afford to grant the House of Norn such exclusive privileges without an appropriate charge, since my doing so would undoubtedly have deprived me of considerable much-needed revenue. At any rate, I fear this discussion is moot, since my transaction with the House of Varcour is now complete and it would be highly unethical, to say nothing of impossible, for me to negate it now."

"I don't like this, Tuf," Norn said.

"I fail to see that you have a legitimate cause for complaint. Your own monsters perform as expected, and it is hardly generous of you to take umbrage simply because another house shares Norn's good fortune."

"Yes. No. That is—well, never mind. I suppose I can't stop you. If the other houses get animals that can beat our cats, however, you will be expected to provide us with something that can beat whatever you sell *them*. You understand?"

"This principle is easily grasped." He looked down at Dax. "I have given the House of Norn unprecedented victories, yet Herold Norn casts aspersions on my honesty and my comprehension. We are unappreciated, I fear."

Herold Norn scowled. "Yesyes. Well, by the time we need more monsters, our victories should have mounted high enough to afford whatever outlandish price you intend to charge."

"I trust that all goes well otherwise?" Tuf said.

"Well, yes and no. In the arena, yesyes, definitely. But otherwise, well, that was what I called about. The four young cats don't seem interested in breeding, for some reason. And our Brood-Tender keeps complaining that they are getting thin. He doesn't think they're healthy. Now, I can't say personally, as I'm here in the city and the animals are back on the plains around Norn House. But some worry does exist. The cats run free, of course, but we have tracers on them, so we can…"

Tuf made a steeple of his hands. "Undoubtedly their mating season has yet to arrive. I would counsel patience. All living creatures engage in reproduction, some even to excess, and you have my assurances that once the female cobalcat enters estrus, matters will proceed with alacrity."

"Ah. That makes sense. Just a question of time then, I suppose. The other question I wanted to go over concerned these hoppers of yours. We set them loose, you know, and they have demonstrated no difficulty whatever in breeding. The ancestral Norn grasslands have been chewed bare. It is very annoying. They hop about everywhere. What are we to do?"

"This matter will also resolve itself when the cobalcats begin to breed," Tuf said. "The cobalt panthers are voracious and efficient predators, splendidly equipped to check your hopper plague."

Herold Norn looked puzzled, and mildly distressed. "Yesyes," he said, "but…"

Tuf rose. "I fear I must end our conversation," he said. "A shuttle-craft has entered into docking orbit with the *Ark*. Perhaps you would recognize it. It is blue steel, with large triangular grey wings."

"The House of Wrai Hill!" Norn said.

"Fascinating," said Tuf. "Good day."

+ + +

Beast-Master Denis Lon Wrai paid two hundred thirty thousand standards for his monster, a powerful red-furred ursoid from the hills of Vagabond. Haviland Tuf sealed the transaction with a brace of scampersloth eggs.

The week following, four men in orange silk and flame-red capes visited the *Ark*. They returned to the House of Feridian two hundred fifty thousand standards poorer, with a contract for the delivery of six great armored poison-elk, plus a gift herd of Hrangan grass pigs.

The Beast-Master of Sin Doon received a giant serpent; the emissary from Amar Island was pleased by his godzilla. A committee of a dozen Dant Seniors in milk-white robes and silver buckles delighted in the slavering garghoul that Haviland Tuf offered them, with a trifling gift. And so, one by one, each of the Twelve Great Houses of Lyronica sought him out, each received its monster, each paid the ever-increasing price.

By that time, both of Norn's fighting cobalcats were dead, the first skewered on the bayonet of a Varcour spear-carrier, the second crushed between the massive clawed paws of a Wrai Hill ursoid (though in the latter case, the ursoid, too, had died). Undoubtedly the great cats had espied their fate, but in the closed and deadly confines of the Bronze Arena, they had nonetheless proved unable to avoid it. Herold Norn had been calling the *Ark* daily, but Tuf had instructed his computer to refuse the calls.

Finally, when eleven houses had come and made their buys and taken their gifts and their leave, Haviland Tuf sat down across from Danel Leigh Arneth, Senior Beast-Master of Arneth-in-the-Gilded-Wood, once the greatest and proudest of the Twelve Great Houses of Lyronica, now the last and least. Arneth was an immensely tall man, standing eye-to-eye with Tuf himself, but he had none of Tuf's fat. His skin was hard ebony, all muscle, his face a hawk-nosed axe, his hair short and iron grey. The Beast-Master came to the conference in cloth-of-gold, with crimson belt and boots and a tiny crimson beret aslant upon his head. He carried a trainer's pain-prod like a walking stick.

Dax bristled as Danel Leigh Arneth emerged from his ship, and hissed when the man climbed in the cart next to Tuf. Accordingly, Haviland Tuf at once commenced his lengthy rambling discourse about the sleepers. Arneth stared and listened; finally Dax grew calm again.

"The strength of Arneth-in-the-Gilded-Wood has always been in variety," Danel Leigh Arneth said early on. "When the other Houses of Lyronica threw all their fortunes on the backs of a single beast, our fathers and grandfathers worked with dozens. Against any animal of theirs, we had an optimal choice, a strategy. That has been our greatness and our pride. But we can have no strategy against these demon-beasts of yours, trader. No matter which of our hundred fighters we send onto the sand, it comes back dead. You have forced us to deal with you."

"I must take exception," said Tuf. "How could a mere seller of animals force the greatest Beast-Master of Lyronica to do anything he did not desire? If you truly have no desire to engage my services, please accept my word that I will take no offense. We may share a meal and some conversation together, and put all thought of business aside."

"Don't play word games, trader," Arneth snapped. "Business is the only reason I'm here. I have no great desire for your odious company."

Haviland Tuf blinked. "I am cut to the quick," he said in a flat voice. "Still, far be it from me to turn away any patron, whatever his personal opinion of me. Feel free to look over my stock, a few poor species that might pique your interest in some small way. Perhaps fortune will see fit to give you back your strategic options." He played upon the controls on the arm of his chair, and conducted a symphony in light and illusory flesh. A parade of monsters came and went before the eyes of the Arneth Beast-Master, creatures furred and scaled and feathered and covered by armor plate, beasts of hill and forest and lake and plain, predators and scavengers and deadly herbivores of sizes great and small.

Danel Leigh Arneth, his lips pressed tightly together, finally ordered four each of the dozen largest and deadliest species, at a cost of one million standards.

The conclusion of the transaction—complete, as with all the other houses, with a gift of some small harmless animal—did nothing to soothe Arneth's foul temper. "Tuf," he said when the dealing was over, "you are a clever and devious man, but you do not fool me."

Haviland Tuf said nothing.

"You have made yourself immensely wealthy, and you have cheated all who bought from you and thought to profit. The Norns, for example. Their cats are worthless. They were a poor house; your price brought them to the edge of bankruptcy, just as you have done to all of us. They thought to recoup through victories. Bah! There will be no Norn victories now! Each house that came to you gained the advantage over those who purchased previously. Thus Arneth, the last to purchase, remains the greatest house of all. Our monsters will wreak devastation. The sands of the Bronze Arena will darken with the blood of the lesser beasts."

Tuf's hands locked on the bulge of his stomach. His face was placid.

"You have changed nothing! The Great Houses remain—Arneth the greatest and Norn the least. All you have done is bleed us, like the profiteer you are, until every Lyronican lord must struggle and scrape to get by. Our rivals now wait for victory, pray for victory, depend on victory, but all the victories will be Arneth's. We alone have not been cheated, because I thought to buy last and thus best."

"The foresight and acumen are remarkable," said Haviland Tuf. "Obviously, I am out of my depth with a man as wise and sagacious as yourself, and it would do me scant good to dissemble, deny, or try to outwit you. One as canny as you would easily see through my poor ploys. Perhaps it might be best were I to say nothing."

"You can do even better than that, Tuf," Arneth said. "You won't say anything, and you won't do anything either. This is your last sale on Lyronica."

"Perhaps," said Tuf, "and yet again, perhaps not. Circumstances may arise that will cause the Beast-Masters of the other Great Houses to bring me their custom once again, and then I fear I could hardly turn them away."

"You can and you will," Danel Leigh Arneth said coldly. "Arneth has made the last purchase, and we will not be trumped. Clone us up our animals and leave immediately upon making delivery. Henceforth you will deal no longer with the Great Houses. I doubt that fool Herold Norn could meet your price a second time, but even if he found the standards somewhere, you will not sell to him. *Do you understand?* We will not go round and round forever, playing this futile game of yours, paupering ourselves by buying monsters, losing them, buying more, and accomplishing nothing. I'm sure you would sell to us until there wasn't a standard left on Lyronica, but the House of Arneth forbids it. Ignore this warning and it could be worth your life, trader. I am not a forgiving man."

"Your point is well taken," Tuf said, scratching Dax behind the ear, "although I have no great affection for the manner in which you have expressed it. Still, while the arrangement you suggest so forcefully will undoubtedly be of benefit to the House of Arneth-in-the-Gilded-Wood, the other Great Houses of Lyronica will be the losers for it, and I myself will have to sacrifice the potential for further profit. Perhaps I do not understand the whole of your proposal. I am easily distracted and I may have failed to hear the part wherein you explained the incentive you will offer me for acceding to your request to deal no more with the Great Houses of Lyronica."

"I'm prepared to offer you another million standards," Arneth said, glaring. "I'd like to cram it down your gullet, to tell the truth, but it's cheaper in the long run than playing another round in this damnable game of yours."

"I see," said Tuf. "Ergo, the choice is mine. I may take a million standards and depart, or remain in the face of your wrath and dire threats. I have pondered more difficult decisions, it must be admitted. In any case, I am scarcely the sort of man to remain on a world where his presence is no longer desired, and I confess that lately I have felt an urge to resume my wanderings. Very well. I bow to your demand."

Danel Leigh Arneth grinned a savage grin, while Dax began to purr.

+ + +

The last of the fleet of twelve glittering gold-flecked shuttles had just departed, carrying the purchases of Danel Leigh Arneth down to Lyronica and the Bronze Arena, when Haviland Tuf finally con-descended to take the call from Herold Norn.

The thin Beast-Master looked positively skeletal. "Tuf!" he exclaimed. "Everything is going wrong."

"Indeed," said Tuf impassively.

Norn pressed his features together in a grimace. "No, listen. The cobalcats are all dead, all sick. Four of them died in the Bronze Arena—we knew the second pair were too young, you understand, but when the first couple lost, there was nothing else to do. It was that or go back to ironfangs. Now we have only two left. They don't eat much—catch a few hoppers, but nothing else. And we can't train them, either. A trainer comes into the pen with a pain-prod, and the damn cats know what he intends. They're always a move ahead, you understand? In the arena, they won't respond to the killing chant at all. It's *terrible*. The worst thing is that they won't even breed. We need *more* of them. What are we supposed to enter in the gaming pits?"

"It is not cobalcat mating season," Tuf said. "We have discussed this point before, you may recall."

"Yesyes. When *is* their breeding season?"

"A fascinating question," said Tuf. "A pity you did not ask sooner. As I understand the matter, the female cobalt panther goes into heat each spring, when the snowtufts blossom on Celia's World. It is my understanding that some type of biological trigger is involved."

Herold Norn scratched at his scalp under the thin brass coronet. "But," he said, "but Lyronica has no snowthings, whatever it was you called them. Now I suppose you intend to charge us a fortune for these flowers."

"Sir, you do me a disservice. I would scarcely dream of taking advantage of your plight. Were the option mine, I would gladly donate the necessary Celian snowtufts to the House of Norn gratis. However, as it happens, I have struck a bargain with Danel Leigh Arneth to deal no more with the Great Houses of Lyronica." He gave a ponderous shrug.

"We won victories with your cats," Norn said, with an edge of desperation in his voice. "Our treasury has been growing—we have something like forty thousand standards now. It is yours. Sell us these flowers. Or better, a new animal. Bigger. Fiercer. I saw the Dant garghouls. Sell us something like that. We have nothing to enter in the Bronze Arena!"

"Nothing? What of your ironfangs? The pride of Norn, I was told."

Herold Norn waved impatiently. "Problems, you understand, we have been having problems. These hoppers of yours, they eat anything, everything. They've gotten out of control. Thousands of them, maybe millions of them, all over, eating all the grass, and all the crops. The things they've done to farmland—the cobalcats love them, yes, but we don't have enough cobalcats. And the wild ironfangs won't touch the hoppers. They don't like the taste, I suppose. I don't know, not really. But, you understand, all the other game is gone, driven out by these hoppers of yours, and the ironfangs went with them. Where, I don't know. Gone, though. Into the unclaimed lands, beyond the realms of Norn. There are some villages out there, a few farmers, but they hate the Great Houses. Tamberkin don't even have dog fights. They'll probably try to *tame* the ironfangs, if you can believe it! That's the sort they are."

"Shocking," said Tuf dispassionately. "Nonetheless, you have your kennels, do you not?"

"Not anymore," Norn said. He sounded harried. "I ordered them shut. The ironfangs were losing every match, especially after you began to sell to the other houses. It seemed a foolish waste to maintain dead weight. Besides, the expense—we needed every standard. You bled us dry. We had arena fees to pay, and of course we had to wager, and lately we've had to buy some food from Tamber just to feed all our housemen and trainers. I mean, you would never *believe* the things the hoppers have done to our crops."

"Sir," said Tuf. "Kindly give me a certain amount of credit. I am an ecologist. I know a great deal about hoppers and their ways. Am I to understand that you no longer have your ironfangs, then?"

"Yesyes. We turned the useless things loose, and now they're gone with the rest. What are we going to do? The hoppers are overrunning the plains, the cats won't mate, and our money will run out soon if we must continue to import food and pay arena fees without any hope of victory."

Tuf folded his hands together. "You do indeed face a series of delicate problems. And I am the very man to help you to their solution. Unfortunately, I have pledged my bond to Danel Leigh Arneth, and accepted his money in good faith."

"Is it hopeless, then? Tuf, I am a man begging—I, a Senior Beast-Master of Norn. Soon we will drop from the games entirely. We will have no funds for arena fees or betting, no animals to enter. We are cursed by ill fortune. No Great House has ever failed to provide its allotment of fighters—not even Feridian during its Twelve-Year Drought. We will be shamed. The House of Norn will sully its proud history by sending snufflers and barnyard animals onto the sand, to be shredded ignominiously by the huge monsters that you have sold the other houses."

"Sir," Tuf said. "If you will indulge me in a bit of prognostication, it occurs to me that perhaps Norn will not be alone in its quandaries. I have a hunch—*hunch*, yes, that is the proper word, and a curious word it is, too—a hunch, as I was saying, that the monsters you fear may be in short supply in the weeks and months to come. For example, the adolescent ursoids of Vagabond may very shortly go into hibernation. They are less than a year old, you understand. I hope the lords of Wrai Hill are not unduly disconcerted by this, yet I fear that they may be. Vagabond, as I'm sure you are aware, has an extremely irregular orbit about its primary, so that its Long Winters last approximately twenty standard years. The ursoids are attuned to this cycle. Soon their body processes will slow to such an extent that an untrained observer might even assume them to be dead. I fear that they will not be easily awakened. Perhaps, as the trainers of Wrai Hill are men of keen intellect, they might find a way. But I would be strongly inclined to further suspect that most of their energies and their funds will be devoted to feeding their populace, in the light of the voracious appetites of scampersloths.

"In quite a like manner, the men of the House of Varcour will be forced to deal with an explosion of Cathadayn tree-slugs. The tree-slugs are particularly fascinating creatures. At one point in their life cycle, they become veritable sponges, and double in size. A large enough grouping is fully capable of drying up even an extensive swampland." Tuf paused, and his thick fingers beat in drumming rhythms across his stomach. "I ramble unconscionably, I am afraid, and perhaps I am boring you. Do you grasp my point? My thrust?"

Herold Norn looked like a dead man. "You are mad. You have destroyed us. Our economy, our ecology… in five years, we will all be dead of starvation."

"Unlikely," said Tuf. "My experience in these matters suggests that Lyronica may indeed suffer a certain interlude of ecological instability and hardship, yet it will be of limited duration and ultimately I have no doubt that a new ecosystem will emerge. It appears unlikely that this successor ecology will offer niches for large predators, alas, but I am optimistic that the quality of Lyronican life will be otherwise unimpaired."

"No predators? No… but the games, the arena… no one will pay to see a hopper fight a slug! How can the games go on? No one will send fighters to the Bronze Arena!"

Haviland Tuf blinked. "Indeed," he said. "An intriguing thought. I will have to consider it thoroughly." He cleared the screen, and began to talk to Dax.

Susan R. Matthews, a U.S. military veteran turned author, is best known perhaps for her Under Jurisdiction series of military science fiction novels. First published in 1997 by Avon Books, her debut An Exchange of Hostages *was nominated for the Philip K. Dick Award and came in fourth for the Locus Award for Best New Novel. Susan herself was nominated in 1998 for the John W. Campbell Award for Best New Writer. Set in a dystopian future ruled by an autocratic judiciary, the novels frequently follow the adventures of Andrei Koscuisko, a state torturer, and his reactions to the violence he is ordered to perpetrate. For* Infinite Stars *she has written in a brand new universe in which the commerce raider* Skipjack *sets out in pursuit of an enemy ship that destroyed a research station and murdered its inhabitants. Yet things are not as they first seem.*

AUTHOR'S NOTE: *This is my second story about Captain Belknap "Finnie" Fenroth and the Vreeslander C-9 commerce raider* Skipjack. *I wrote the first one, "Skipjack," for a Baen anthology (*Star Destroyers*) and had a lot of fun with it, so I wanted to write another.*

If you find a few oblique U-boat references tucked away here and there within the text, it's Raphael Sabatini's fault. In Sabatini's 1922 novel Captain Blood, *and the short stories that followed it, several exploits of famous pirates appeared as deeds of the title character. Sabatini once explained this as resulting from jealous partisans of other pirates re-writing the histories and claiming the glory for their own heroes; and this story, "The Devil in the Details," unashamedly riffs off one of the most famous long-distance refugee transport adventures in the history of the Battle of the Atlantic.*

SKIPJACK: THE DEVIL IN THE DETAILS
SUSAN R. MATTHEWS

By the time Captain Hopkiss Marcer on the Skanda Republic Ship *Dorankir* and her four small-swift harriers reached Natalise Station there was nothing left of the asteroid storage site but wrecked warehouses and useless processing plants, annihilated facilities, raw materials for armaments scattered and destroyed. There was only the distress signal, on auto-loop: *immediate urgency, evacuate base, survivability hours thirty-six.* That meant *we are all going to die.*

There were no location beacons, no emergency field-expedient landing zones prepared and waiting, although the distress signal was twenty hours old. No intact shelter-domes. Hopkiss toggled to the piloting bridge from her place in top-ops, the ship's command center. "Come in slow, Cherliv," she said. "Pick a place and land it."

Top-ops was the only place on the Skanda Republic Ship *Dorankir* with actual windows: everybody else got visual feeds on display screens, but she could see it all with her own eyes from the vantage point of the raised commander's station on what amounted to a mezzanine. The sensor scans whose data reports were constantly updating on the screens that lined the walls of the small bridge had more information than could be gained by visual inspection, but she couldn't stop staring anyway.

There seemed to have been a reasonable number of the small station-hopper ships that would have ferried personnel back and forth from Natalise to the major military installation on Moon Sharna on site when the attack had come, going by the wreckage; all reduced to scrap. Nobody had gotten off the station in any of those. So where was everybody? This was a warehouse farm like thousands of others, but there'd been a research station here as well, though that information wasn't publicized, for obvious reasons. They were at war, after all, the Skanda Republic and Hamstead Vrees.

So the Vreeslanders that had done this might not have known there'd been maybe one hundred, maybe a hundred and thirty people here, perfectly equipped to weather most predictable challenges but not a concerted bombardment. They'd have had no reason to think twice. Would *she* have scanned for civilians, in the Vreeslanders' position?

The scans weren't turning up any warm spots, no bubble-domes of breathable air, nothing. Only the distress signal, *immediate urgency, survivability hours thirty-six.* "Dirtside in twelve," she heard Cherliv say. "Environmental team for survey is ready to deploy."

This had been a hit-and-run raid, classic Vreeslander, sneak up on the station by hopping from one concealing particle cloud to the next to avoid observation, ready to abort the raid and escape at speed if they were detected. The distress signal was twenty hours old. Standing at the command station, Hopkiss called down to Garontag on forward sweeps. "We should be able to find them," she said. "Power to seekers, Garon, they're probably making speed but we could at least hope for intercept."

A lot depended on exactly which Vreeslander had hit the warehouse farm. The commerce raiders were in a class of their own. In the total surrender that had ended the *last* war there'd been an absolute moratorium on construction of the class-nines, because Skanda ship-service vessels that had survived an encounter with a Vreeslander C-9 in the last war hated, hated, hated them for being stealthy, solitary, lethal.

They were small—no larger than one of the small-swift class harriers in Hopkiss's group—they were ugly, they were weapons of war and nothing else, and they were faster than anything Hopkiss had under her command.

If Natalise Station had been raided by a class-nine commerce raider Hopkiss had very little chance of running it down. Unless they were lucky. Unless the Vreeslander was low on fuel, or complacent, or on a course that she could intercept. It was worth a chance.

Garontag looked at her up and over his shoulder, and nodded. Hopkiss sat down to wait for reports. She'd have to wait for a feed from the survey team until *Dorankir* had landed; and there *Dorankir* was on Garontag's screen, settling gently on the leveled ground between the forward boundary of the warehouse farm and the remains of an environmental dome for cargo handling and management services. Or the staff of a research station.

She could hear Cherliv talking, internal communications, something she could listen in on without complicating things with command intervention. *Team prep to debark. Depressurizing vestibule. Vestibule depressurized. Go.*

On the ground the catastrophic nature of the attack, the damage the station had sustained, was even more impressive. When they'd been standing off, it had been possible to see the general outlines of the station, but at ground-level there was only twisted metal and shattered clear-throughs, a hellish jumble of breached containment platforms and the debris of what had once been half-machined raw materials for Skanda's weapons industry. It was ugly. But that wasn't all.

Each crewman's environmental suit had a set of sensor recorders reporting a three-dimensional projection that would be spooled up into top-ops from its core target within the engineering bridge, corrected, as it processed, to present the illusion of a smooth glide from the base of the passenger offload toward the containment dome that would have housed the research staff.

The containment dome didn't seem to have been deliberately targeted in its own right; the damage appeared to have been incidental, debris thrown clear of the warehouses impacting on the near side of the dome. That was good: the atmosphere would have held, at least in the short term.

Through the bewildering chaos of the station's scattered remains Chevril's team went for the roll-shield over the vestibule of an entry lock—a door, the only one they could find, apparently. It was funny. It was evidence of stress the team felt, instinctively seeking order and reason amid chaos. There was a hallway; there was a lift, but there were the stairs on the opposite wall as well, and that was where the leader went, up the stairs to the next level.

And, in the same way in which the station had seemed more orderly and organized on approach than on the ground, once the leader had gained that next level the layout of the installation—and the visual evidence of what had happened to it—was immediately clear and comprehensible. Working quarters; residence areas. The ceilings of the ground-level rooms and the floor of most of the next level had been shaved off as cleanly as a hot knife might a layer of butter, everything above the second level gone.

She could see the scans. No residual heat, no life. It wasn't just catastrophic failure within the dome. There was no sign of any operating emergency shelter-station. The leader went back down the stairs, moved through corridors that transitioned from intact to an open maze of rooms whose ceilings were open to the top of the dome; deeper and deeper into the dome, until the leader arrived at what would have been the command center, where the emergency shelters would have been.

There were emergency shelters. But they were open, empty, showing no evidence that they had even been deployed. Hopkiss watched as the leader reached for something and held it in gloved hand for a long moment. It was the emergency beacon. The leader switched it off.

There had been people there. They'd been overwhelmed by disaster so suddenly, so swiftly, that they hadn't even been able to get to the shelters. But where were the bodies?

Hopkiss didn't want to see any more, but she was the captain, and she had no choice. The interruption from the central communication station, top-ops just below, came as a welcome distraction; because she had to attend to the message. That was her clear priority.

"From regional headquarters." Maraq made the announcement quietly while the transmission cleared. It was nearly half an hour from here to Moonbase Sharna, but Sharna had had a head start on reading the beacon. Here was the feed—

Headquarters to Dorankir, *Captain Hopkiss Marcer. Population Natalise one hundred and thirty-nine souls. Preliminary identification enemy ship, class-nine Vreeslander commerce raider.* Hopkiss felt an instant's hopelessness in her gut; pursuit would be nearly impossible. But what came next electrified her. *Captain Belknap Fenroth commanding. Ship damaged in action, Borland Skips, probable area propulsion and atmosphere. Absent survivors for evacuation, pursuit with maximum effort authorized.*

"More," Hopkiss all but whispered. If only. If only they could hope. It was only the shadow of a movement from below at the communications station, but it was enough. And here was the *more* Hopkiss wanted. On impulse she keyed it for all-ships, not just *Dorankir*, but the four smaller craft that were part of her battle group, holding in near-stationary above the station for her instructions.

Partial trajectory of enemy ship, trace no longer readable. Heading follows. Will advise if additional information becomes available.

Hopkiss took a deep breath, and let it out slowly. By the time she was ready to breathe in again Maraq had the treasured data; Hopkiss spoke, once again for all-ships. "Implement standard intercept," she said. "Cherliv. As soon as possible."

Recall the landing party. Shift hull for pursuit. Belknap Fenroth? She'd heard of him. He liked to play pranks on Skanda ship-service, and they were never funny. They would see how he liked the one she had for him: and the one hundred and thirty-nine innocent—civilian—souls of Natalise would be avenged.

✦ ✦ ✦

Leaning his back up against the far wall of the freight lift Finnie Fenroth listened with his arms folded and his eyes on the decking, not liking what he was hearing the more for having known it was coming. "Cracked venting on right ventral," Hythe—his engineering officer—said. "I wouldn't want to take it up to the max, Captain. We're overdue for maintenance as it is. We're lucky we haven't started breathing happy-gas."

Yes, Vreeslander C-9 Commerce Raider *Skipjack* had been in the wars, and it wasn't entirely Command's fault that it had been a bit long between ports-of-call. They'd been having too much fun. This was a sad end to the most successful war patrol *Skipjack* had ever had, but all good things had to come to an end. He just hadn't expected it to come so soon.

"What about pursuit from Natalise?" he asked. There was bound to be some, sooner or later, they'd all heard the beacon. "Can we still outrun them?"

Hythe shook her head: "Even with no damage, we've taken on extra weight. It would have been borderline. I advise alternative approaches to evade." She wouldn't tell him he couldn't outrun the Skanda ships that would be looking for *Skipjack*; she wouldn't tell him not to try, because he was the captain, and not her.

She would just tell him what was likely to occur if he pushed his tolerances. *Skipjack* wouldn't be the first Vreeslander to simply fall silent, to disappear without a trace, to be lost to internal collapse in propulsion or life support.

If he was caught short he could stand and fight. He had bunker-busters in reserve—three nests still full of chickies, waiting to hatch out. That was a good way to go. But he had noncombatants on board: so he and his entire crew of twenty souls was to be denied even that final splendid act of rebellion, resistance, protest, war. Instead...

The lift was slowing. He could hear the retards screeching as the worn cog-teeth did their best to bite and hold the weight of the car steady. "Life support," Finnie said. "Smoots. Rations and breathable." Smoots, one of Hythe's people really, but with specialized knowledge and responsibilities. "How long?" Not long enough; it couldn't be. *Skipjack* was rated for twenty crew. It was carrying nearly a hundred and sixty. They were short one of their chickie-ticklers.

"The rough count of passengers was a hundred and thirty-five, plus or minus. We can make it stretch to five days on short rations before we run out. Water'll be no problem. Air, though, we'll start to run out of additional oxygen in sixty hours or so. If everybody lies quietly and sleeps, maybe four days, and that exhausts our reserves. Sorry."

The lift had stopped. Finnie locked eyes with Sanford—his first officer, standing at the control panel—to stay her hand, to keep the lift sealed until he'd gotten just one last piece of vital data. "Put it all together for me, Foe," he said. "Can we get the refugees to Birazzi, before we fall apart?"

He could hear Hythe's sharply indrawn breath, beside him; see Sanford's instinctive, if well-controlled, flinch. Yes. They'd known. They'd all known. It still hurt. Birazzi Station was neutral. Their arrival would be reported through diplomatic channels to both Skanda Republic and Hamstead Vrees liaisons. They would never get out of there alive.

"If we're lucky," Sanford said. Slowly, and with deliberation; the look in her eyes, the tone of her voice, so familiar from their shared childhood, for all the strict professionalism with which she observed the etiquette of rank. *Okay, but it's on you, Cousin Finnie. Either way.* "Four days. Plus or minus twenty hours."

No margin for error, then, no margin at all. Finnie nodded, sharply, crisply. He was the captain. It was his call. "Better get started," he said. "Smoots, with me."

Sanford toggled the switch, and the lift-gate started to rise. Finnie ducked under the slowly moving lower edge of the lift-gate past his security, with Smoots following; the lift-gate started to close again, to carry Sanford and Hythe back up into the command quarters as soon as possible. Things to do.

And him to have a word with those people from Natalise.

+ + +

It had been Eglar Bleak's research project, his research station, he was the obvious spokesman for them all. That didn't mean he liked it. He'd thought he'd heard machinery, behind the roll-shutter gate between the cargo bay—now crowded to capacity, but he'd gotten them all to sit down—and the rest of the ship; then there were the flashing blue lights on either side of the tall shutter gate, and a voice on transmit. "Refugee liaison, please step forward. Security screen will engage."

Refugee liaison. What a joke. They were prisoners. Stepping forward to the shutter gate, Eglar motioned to his fuel line decontamination group to move away, to the extent they could; then he took three steps forward, hesitantly, and a chain-frame divider started on its way down between him and the others. The FLD people found a way to back up another few inches so that the frame could lock into its place in the decking.

What was going to happen to them all?

When the chain-frame was secure on the floor the shutter gate started to rise. Crouching down to see underneath its edge, Eglar saw that those beyond were doing the same; two on each side forward, and they had weapons. He stood up. It seemed to be a standard cargo-lift, and there were two people standing behind the others: a man of medium height with a trimmed beard and a white cloth covering on his cap, near the front; a man behind him, taller, no hat at all.

The forward man's beard with its pointed wedge-shaped chin made him look a little diabolical, but that was what he was, wasn't it? The Devil. A Vreeslander commerce raider, which was more or less the same thing.

Eglar took an involuntary step forward at a rush, but had the sense to stop before he was within reach. He pointed his finger, instead, shaking with the accumulated shock, the bombs, the noise, the horrific ground-shattering impact of it all. His knowledge that he was responsible for these people. It hadn't been his fault, but he knew what the signal alarms had meant. They were dead. They were all dead.

And then to have the Vreeslander that had just murdered them, casually, by the way, without any warning, for that very ship to come down and push them all up its ramp and pack them into its cargo bay—he'd done his best, but he'd lost count, he hadn't caught the error until the Vreeslander had lifted and by then it had been too late and now he had a death on his conscience—"You, what do you want, what have you done, what have you done to these people?"

The Devil in the white cap glanced behind him over his shoulder at the Devil's imp behind him. "I'd like a count, please," the Devil said, in a surprisingly comprehensible Skanda dialect. He was the Devil for sure. He went right to the aching wound of it. "So that we may calculate our rationing. We will be short, I warn you. Our reserves are calibrated to our crew and you are many times that number. The one in our infirmary bunk, do we return him to you now, or let him rest?"

Wait. What did that mean, one in infirmary? Eglar staggered. One of those menacing crew stepped forward, reaching out to steady him. Eglar shook off the unwelcome hand. Howsoever well the gesture was intended, that man was his enemy.

The Devil had folded his arms over his chest, and leaned forward now to look up into Eglar's eyes with a patient expression on his face. "How many people in the research station, please? How many people here with you?"

Things were catching up with Eglar at last. He was suddenly so tired that he couldn't think, he could hardly stand. He didn't shake off the supportive arms, this time. "One hundred and thirty-nine," he said. "We had a hundred and thirty-nine souls. And I count a hundred and thirty-eight. And yes. I've counted myself. Three times." The Devil already knew. The Devil only wanted to make him say it.

"Then we're good." The Devil straightened up, nodding. "Your last man is in our infirmary berth, he has broken bones but no other injuries. We'll bring him along, shall we? And this is my provisions officer. Mister Smoots. We will take as good care of you as we can until we get to Birazzi."

The men who were supporting him pushed him away, gently, until he had his back up against the chain-frame between him and the rest of the cargo bay. He reached behind him to clutch the chain mesh fiercely to stay upright. The Devil and his party retreated back into the now re-opened lift, the shutter-wall fell slowly, he was alone.

A hundred and thirty-eight. Plus one, in an infirmary bed. One hundred and thirty-nine. The chain-frame started to rise. He lost his grip, and fell to his knees, weeping.

✦ ✦ ✦

Belknap "Finnie" Fenroth was by nature a genial and happy fellow, or so his officer evaluations had consistently said—between the lines. At this moment he was neither. Those evaluations also credited him generously for his aggressive instinct, and his joy in battle, but that would be behind him now. He'd thrown away the thing he was best at to save the lives of a hundred and thirty-nine civilians who should never have been there, and he had no guarantee he could do even that.

He picked his way carefully between the seated clusters of people in the cargo bay, trying not to notice that it seemed to be getting stuffy. He couldn't afford to vent any atmosphere. The oxygen generators were losing efficiency, trying to keep up with a respiratory load several times their default capacity. Maybe nobody here had put one and one together, yet.

Director Eglar Bleak had his people sorted into consistent clumps, and there weren't enough bedding-pads, not on a ship rated for twenty souls. They'd done the best they could with padding-fills and ship-crates. Now Bleak paced from group to group with Finnie, each of them with their own paper-and-stencil record, counting heads. Some of them hissed at him. Finnie didn't take it seriously.

"I count seventeen for this group," he said. "You?"

Bleak showed Finnie his list, without speaking: seventeen. It was important for them to do this together, at least once. They'd do it again when they got to Birazzi, if they made it that far. Making a check-mark against his figure, he moved on.

There was only one group left to count, the one that included the casualty they were holding in their infirmary. It wasn't the only casualty overall, only the worst, and that one ambulatory; so they'd gotten away lucky, all things considered.

He'd decided he was going to take a chance about something important, because—although Engineering were doing their best, and there were none better—he couldn't promise they were going to win through. Everything depended on enough speed to reach Birazzi before the oxygen generators failed. Before the pursuit ships that Pulser—in Communications—had just picked up on long-scan could catch up, and destroy them.

"Your people should stay as quiet as possible, to conserve air. We're overdue on replacement equipment." That they would be increasing the length of time between each issue of rations was something they would figure out on their own. He was gambling on the hope that it was better for morale to maintain the level of rations and stretch the intervals, rather than confront them with a perceptible decrease in the food available. Hunger was not so much a torment as thirst, and at least they were all to the good there. For now. "We are well on our way there. We can do this."

There was no sense in alarming people with the odds, because people breathed more heavily under stress which only consumed oxygen. He wasn't telling any lies. He hadn't yet decided whether he was going to start, if their situation became even more desperate. A hundred and thirty-nine people, on VCR C-9 *Skipjack*. What had he been thinking? His first responsibility should have always been his crew.

Who were of one mind with him, so far as he could tell; that made it a little easier, but there was no question about it, he was responsible. He was Captain Belknap Fenroth, Vreeslander *Skipjack*. A good chance at survival for all of them was always going to take precedence over a very good chance for twenty at the cost of all the others. So there it was.

He was sorry that he himself was going to die when they reached Birazzi; but he would destroy the ship—with himself on it—before he saw a Vreeslander fighting ship ignominiously impounded for the rest of the war, win or lose.

+ + +

Hopkiss kept her voice calm and measured from her position on top-ops mezzanine. She could see Maraq's real-time reports on his displays, spooled up to her own at her right elbow. "You've got them, then, Cherliv?" He'd be where engineering data analysis was, in Engineering. "Anything you can tell us?"

"Contact is still tenuous," Maraq said quietly, to his displays. Not interrupting. Just making the point. Hopkiss nodded: she understood. They were lucky as it was to have caught up by this much, only two days from Natalise.

"Moving slowly, Captain." That was the link from the engineering bridge. "Rate of speed inconsistent. Seems to be carrying its full load, still." Cherliv sounded thoughtful, even over a communications link. "Could have been carrying more chickies in reserve than we'd derived from analysis."

"All the more reason to take them out of circulation before they shoot up another depot. Can we intercept?" The commerce raiders weren't built for confrontations with warships. They weren't after reducing fighting strength at the leading edge of the war. Their mission was to starve Skanda of critical supplies until the war effort was weakened, from the ground up; no replacement parts, crippled ship-yards, starving people.

That research station, for instance. If *Skipjack* had known it was there and what it was, they'd have realized that it was a valid target. Hopkiss had received additional information during their hunt: it wasn't in the business of seed-stock research and development, but propulsion life-cycle research, efforts to reduce fuel contamination and find a better way to clean the complex venting systems from inside without having to sideline a warship for traditional corrosion remediation.

Cherliv was back. "We have good hope of an intercept so long as they don't suddenly put on some speed. Extrapolation of vector characteristics puts them on the road to Birazzi."

Cowards. Birazzi was neutral. If *Skipjack* reached Birazzi they could go into impound. All they'd have to do was decline to leave Birazzi yards within two days—by conventional reckoning—of their arrival, and they could sit out the rest of the war in comfort and security as detainees.

No. Vreeslanders weren't cowards. There had to be something more to it than that. They were clearly more badly damaged than Skanda ship-service intelligence realized, if Fenroth felt he had no better choice than Birazzi.

She keyed into her command stream to get ship's navigation, first officer, second officer, watch officer, her attached assault ships all at once. "Now hear this. Captain Hopkiss speaking." They knew that. But she had to say it. "We will continue to pursue the ship tentatively identified as Vreeslander *Skipjack*. We will intercept in force before they can reach Birazzi, and destroy them. Claw formation. Execute."

One by one her four small-swift harriers acknowledged and set course to overtake the Vreeslander, get out ahead of it. They would encircle, staying safely out of range of the Vreeslander's defense systems until they could take the ship from all sides at once.

They'd reach that Vreeslander. She'd find out what they'd done with the bodies—since they'd found none at Natalise, and there was hardly room on a Vreeslander C-9 for its crew, let alone a floating mortuary. She'd get some answers.

Then there would be one less Vreeslander commerce raider, and the research station at Natalise would be avenged.

+ + +

He was supposed to stay calm, respiration low normal, heartbeat relaxed and slow: for the good of the crew, if for no other reason. He wanted to pace. He could pace in his tiny cabin, three or four steps in either direction, surely. But to do that he'd have to shut himself away in his cabin, and there was no question of doing any such thing: so Finnie Fenroth sat at the scopes-and-scans station, watching, listening.

It wasn't his station. If either Magli or Priat were here he'd have to stand uselessly at the back of the wheelhouse with his arms folded across his chest, watching, but Magli was with Burios and Mack in oxygen generation, and everybody else who could be spared was patching the lateral propulsion exhaust vents so that they could find some speed before the degradation of the plasma flux core got much worse and started to poison them. Preparatory to blowing them up.

A C-9 was one of the sturdiest, stubbornest ships in the Vreeslander or any other ship-service's war fleet, but *Skipjack* itself was among the oldest of them and should probably have been retired. Now it was too late. At least there was good hope of one final desperate battle at Birazzi, once they'd transferred the refugees. *Skipjack* would not idle in peaceful impound while the war raged on.

The pursuit ships were on an entrapment approach, out of range of any of *Skipjack*'s weaponry, but not out of figurative sight. He couldn't risk firing on them anyway; it would only provoke reflexive return fire. He hadn't given up on outrunning them, not entirely, but he didn't like his chances enough to be stubborn about whether or not he was going to show his hand.

He keyed his ship's comm channels to put people on notice. "First Officer," he said. Sanford had communications within her purview, but she was working on the vents with the rest of them. "I think it's time. Here we go." Switching out of ship's comms, he leaned back and looked left to engage Curmatic's attention with a wordless question. *Ready?*

And Curmatic nodded. So Finnie went to all-ship, including the cargo bay—everybody had a right to know what they were doing—and nodded for Curmatic to push a transmission out to Birazzi. They only needed another day to reach it.

"Birazzi Station, Birazzi Station." Nothing. Finnie waited. He knew Birazzi was there, listening. He didn't know whether Birazzi had noticed them, or whether the Skanda ships in pursuit had issued an alert. "Birazzi Station. This is the VCR *Skipjack*, Belknap Fenroth commanding. I am inbound for Birazzi with enemy noncombatants from a Skanda Republic research station at Natalise. Humanitarian transfer urgently requested."

He closed the comm feed to the cargo bay. He wanted those people to know what their status was, but they didn't need to hear it if there was going to be pushback. They'd understand a time delay on communications. They could wait. *He* waited, doing his best to concentrate past the worst headache he thought he'd ever had in his life. Oxygen was getting low, yes, but worrying about it did nobody any good.

Then the response came. "Birazzi Station acknowledges communication, *Skipjack*. Clarify requirement."

Rules were rules. A neutral station had to be careful and clear about its parameters, or risk the loss of its neutrality. Any ship could request clearance to take on atmosphere; no armed ship could request use of facilities for on-site repair, though they could do what they could on their own for the limited amount of time that they were allowed to stay on-station. Humanitarian aid would always be extended, to the extent possible; but anything more than that meant impounding.

"We didn't know they were there. Shelter in place or self-evacuation was not possible due to damage to station. We have taken on one hundred and thirty-nine noncombatants, but are unable to reach a Vreeslander installation to transfer custody. According to the conventions governing neutral stations during armed conflict we request entry so that we may place these people with you for asylum pending Skanda repatriation."

Curmatic stood up at his station—to catch Finnie's attention, and it worked—and pointed with arms outstretched to either side. Right, left. Nodded. So the Skanda pursuit ships that were pacing them on intercept were generating their own signals. Finnie hoped that meant they were reading his: but he'd done everything he could to cue them in, now, short of direct ship-to-ship communication, and it wasn't up to him to decide whether they destroyed him anyway.

He could be trying to trick his pursuers, theoretically, buying time to reach sanctuary, even at cost of impoundment and then prosecution after the war for deserting his field of duty. It would be nice to fantasize that the enemy would take him at his word, but this was war, and it was a bitter one.

Now finally here was the return transmission. "*Skipjack*. You have permission to enter Birazzi Station to transfer civilian souls in custody. All other restrictions will apply. Your estimated time of arrival?"

Birazzi would see them coming, true enough. It was a question that was coded, in a sense; *how badly are you damaged, can you make it here at all?* He couldn't evacuate those people from *Skipjack*. The Skanda had no way to rescue them, if *Skipjack* were to become totally disabled. It could still all be for nothing. "Estimate thirty-six additional hours." Losing speed as they went. "Thank you, Birazzi Station."

The Skanda ships were on course to intercept before they could reach sanctuary. *Skipjack* and every soul aboard could be dead before they approached the outermost boundary of Birazzi Station's neutral zone. Skanda had to know that there were civilians—Skanda noncombatants—on board.

And the Skanda ships were slowing down. Finnie watched the scans-and-projections; he had to be sure. There was a transmission, now, in the clear, no encoding. "Birazzi Station. This is the Skanda Republic Ship *Dorankir*, in pursuit of enemy warship. Intend to engage on exit from your station, in accordance with the articles of war. Nothing further."

Finnie splayed the fingers of his right hand across his face and gripped his cheekbones fiercely, thumb and middle finger, to contain a sudden rush of emotion. Skanda was slowing down. Skanda was willing to give him the benefit of the doubt.

They'd be waiting to hear from him, in the cargo bay. He opened his channel. "Captain Fenroth here," he said. He had to work to steady his voice. "Birazzi Station is alerted to our arrival within sixty-five hours." That would give them a cushion. "Skanda ships in pursuit have signaled that they will not prevent our entry. Fenroth out."

If they could make it into Birazzi Station, their cargo of souls would be safe. And though there was little chance of avoiding their final destruction when they left Birazzi, they would die with their honor intact: theirs, and that of the Vreeslander *Skipjack*.

+ + +

Hopkiss's battle group had been following the Vreeslander for days, keeping their distance, slowing as the C-9 slowed, gradually but inexorably. They were scant hours out of Birazzi Station, so close that the terraformed station's lights were clearly visible against the deep cloud of the asteroid belt in which it lay. Hours. And there were concerns.

She got a chirp from the piloting bridge and keyed it. "Speak to me," she suggested. She was sharing feed to *Dorankir*'s top-ops, and through to the small-swifts. The Vreeslander was the enemy, but there were Skanda refugees on board. That was why they were interested. Yes. Nothing to do with the nerve it took to load one hundred and thirty-nine refugees on a ship rated for twenty, and make for a neutral station with their propulsion compromised and what had to be an intolerable drain on oxygen generation.

"We're starting to see course perturbation, Captain." That was Chevril. Of course. "It's going be challenging for them to bring that thing in safely."

As though there weren't already enough challenges. "What does it look like to you?" she asked. "Mechanical failure? Piloting error?"

But the silence before the read-back from Chevril carried its own language with it. She could almost see him shaking his head, reluctantly. "Not possible to say at this time, Captain," Chevril said. "Potential impairment on the part of the software." The people. The crew.

There was nothing they could do. "Keep me posted," Hopkiss said, and resigned herself to sit, and watch, and hope that the Vreeslander could make it work.

+ + +

The Skanda had stayed with *Skipjack* all this time, and Finnie was almost glad they were there—for company. Maybe for witnesses. When *Skipjack* crossed Birazzi's boundary Smoots sealed the wheelhouse and opened the last emergency cannisters, flooding the room with oxygen. After hours spent on mountain-climbing medications the effect was like waking up after a refreshing sleep, in a lakeside cabin at sea level, with his wife cooking breakfast and his babies playing on the porch.

There was hope. They were here. All they had to do was land. He keyed the comm link down into the cargo bay, and spoke. "This is Captain Fenroth. Director Eglar. You will be hearing noise, potentially some vibration. We are pushing air into the cargo bay from other areas of the ship. Stand by."

Everybody they didn't need in the wheelhouse or on emergency watch in propulsion was in the sleeping cabins, lying down, doing their part to conserve what air they had. Sanford was here, of course, talking to Birazzi. "We're having trouble holding our line of approach," she was saying. "Request emergency protocols in effect."

He could get down. No, piloting-and-navs could get down, Monroe, Jalon. He told them where to go and what to do, but not how; that was their job, their call. So he shut up and waited, standing in the middle of the room, the only person here without a job to do. Smoots had opened the oxygen a good hour before they were to reach Birazzi, to give them all as much time as possible to respond to it; but time had slowed, in a sense, and it seemed to take three times as long to gain the approach path.

"You have the field, *Skipjack*," Birazzi said. Finnie could see Birazzi on the screens. The launch-lanes were well clear of the settlement, its quarantine dome open to let them through. Terraformed stations like Birazzi could contain atmosphere through an open dome for only so long, though, and if *Skipjack* didn't make it within that span of time they would have to ditch dirtside well away from the station and wait for self-contained emergency vehicles to come to their aid. Finnie didn't think they had time for that.

Even he could see the wobble, on screen, as *Skipjack* trembled on approach. Jalon swore. The image stabilized, and held steady. *Just a little while longer*, Finnie whispered to Jalon in his mind. *You can do this. You've solved worse puzzles before.* That might not be precisely correct, but the message was still true.

That sensation of vertigo he always had when they were close enough to see the dirt coming up at them was thrilling in an almost terrifying sense this time. He could see the great open gap in the quarantine gate. Were they going to get through? Were they coming in too fast? Too slow? If they clipped the ground, would the chickies hatch out still in their nests? But there were fail-safes. The landing skids had been dropped. Were they center to axis of approach?

"Screamers," Finnie said. This one thing was his to do, because a mistake could mean catastrophic structural failure across all systems. *Skipjack* would break apart under the stress, if they deployed the emergency stops before they'd lost enough speed. As it was, the gigantic shuddering lurch the *Skipjack* took as the screamers snapped and shot out shook the wheelhouse like a direct hit from a Skanda ship-killer.

They were going to nose into tarmac. He knew they were. He hoped they did it soon, because if they hit the blast wall that protected the far end of the dome there was no chance of survival. *Skipjack* lowered herself shoulders first, careful to keep her rump off the ground to protect the cargo bay. Finnie couldn't see a thing on the forward screens for the dust cloud, except for the fog of sparks that meant they were scraping surface. He watched the color of the cloud carefully.

It was coming up green, and thicker by the moment. He squeezed his eyes shut and took a deep, deep breath. They'd found their target.

And they weren't leaving it behind them. No. The green billowed up around the ship's sensors, straight up, not streaming back and away. White foam blanked the screens: fire suppression in effect.

He keyed the comms, all-ship. "We have arrived," he said. "There will be some moments before we can open up the ship and evacuate." Ship's sensors reported structural integrity, thermal parameters within acceptable tolerances. "First Officer. Prepare to receive emergency response teams."

They had done it. They had brought Natalise's refugees safely into Birazzi. They had made a benchmark and a beacon of *Skipjack* and its crew that could stand proudly even next to the siege of Trancor and be honored.

Was that not a thing worth dying for?

+ + +

Now they were here.

After the stress of the attack, the evacuation, the days of transit spent crammed into *Skipjack*'s cargo bay, Eglar knew he'd never take the air for granted ever again. Birazzi was a terraformed station, yes, bright and airy, verdant and warm, with an atmosphere-containment dome and light-collectors focused into the simulation of a sun. That wasn't the point. The important point was that they could take a breath without dreading a coughing fit, lie down without a terrifying sensation of suffocation, move freely through space because there was space now in which to move.

He stood at the foot of the *Skipjack*'s cargo loading ramp, watching his people being helped down and out to freedom one by one. It was going to be all right. They were here.

He didn't know how badly the ship had been damaged by its landing. He'd only barely realized how much trouble it had been in even before then. The Devil had taken a risk when he'd come down to Natalise to rescue them; the air could have run out, something could have gone critically wrong in the engines, they could have been blown up by Skanda destroyers before they'd had a chance to warn would-be avengers off.

So many things could have gone wrong. It had been irresponsible of the Devil to risk himself and his crew, and his ship, to carry Eglar's people to safety. But if the Devil hadn't taken the risk all of Eglar's people would be dead.

"Ninety-seven," the Devil said, facing Eglar, across the ramp. Maybe he wasn't the Devil after all. He hadn't been eating or resting any better than any of the rest of them, by appearances; unkempt, unwashed, unshaved, his eyes red-rimmed with fatigue.

"Ninety-seven," Eglar agreed, and wrote it down. There were two officials from Birazzi here as well; they didn't speak, but they were keeping their own lists.

"One hundred and two." One of the medical litters was coming down, now. It was a measure of how tightly packed the cargo bay had been that they'd only just now worked their way through to that particular patient.

"One hundred and two," Eglar agreed, and noted it down. Captain Fenroth was not the Devil. Nor were Fenroth's people. Fierce enemies, yes, to have come back after the strict limits Skanda imposed, after the last war, on the mutilated stump of its ship-service. It had clearly been a mistake to allow them any ship-service at all. Skanda was going to have to do a better job of neutralizing the Hamstead Vrees *this* time.

"One hundred and eleven," Fenroth called. "One hundred and twelve." Would they have to worry, though, about these particular Vreeslanders, ever again? There was a destroyer and four small-swift harriers standing off the perimeter of Birazzi's neutral zone. Birazzi would only shelter *Skipjack* for two days. Skanda warships would be waiting for them, five to one, and that one in a pitiable state.

Eglar knew that war was war. But the Devil—Captain Fenroth, and *Skipjack*—had saved their lives, whether or not it had been their bombardment that had put them at risk. "One hundred and thirty-five," Eglar repeated as Fenroth announced each soul transferring from *Skipjack* to salvation, making another tick-mark. He knew the count like his own heartbeat. "One hundred and thirty-six, check."

Then one hundred and thirty-seven. Thirty-eight. One hundred and thirty-nine. He remembered how he'd felt, believing he'd left one behind to die, realizing that Fenroth had collected them all. "One hundred and thirty-nine, Captain Fenroth," Eglar said. "The complete complement, all souls from the Natalise research station, present and accounted for."

Maybe it was "present or accounted for." Eglar could never remember. He'd never made a good soldier. Fenroth signed off on his list with a flourish; one of the Birazzi people—the dockmaster—handed Fenroth her own signed count-sheet in exchange. Documentation. So important. Eglar exchanged his own list with Birazzi's other official, its chief liaison officer, if Eglar remembered that right. Warcaya. Yes.

The last of the patient transports was waiting for him, for Eglar, to go with the rest of his people for medical evaluation and treatment. He had something to say, though. "Captain Fenroth."

Fenroth had had his head together with the Birazzi dockmaster; he raised it, wearily, to meet Eglar's gaze. "Yes, here," Fenroth said, politely.

Eglar took a deep breath—juicy air, air fat with oxygen, air like the sweetness of life itself—and plunged into his speech. "Please accept my deep and sincere gratitude, Captain Fenroth, for saving all our lives. Nobody could have blamed you if you'd left us." During all this time he'd heard no single word of reproach from Fenroth or any of Fenroth's crew for the fact that the secrecy of the research station had put all of *their* lives at risk. "If there's anything I can do to intervene with my superiors on your behalf, I will gladly—"

But suddenly Fenroth lifted one hand in a warning gesture, *please shut up*. Confused, Eglar fell silent. "I appreciate the sentiment," Fenroth said. "But we must both be careful, Director. Any intervention with Skanda military authorities on your part could be taken as a political act. The liaison officer will be giving you a briefing."

What was Fenroth saying? Warcaya—apparently sensitive to Eglar's confusion—explained. "Articles of neutrality," Warcaya said. "Non-combatants may be provided sanctuary pending repatriation, but all others must be evacuated on the first available transport. Suggesting an intervention with, ah, your superiors might lead to awkward questions about your status." Then Warcaya looked the Devil in the eye. "As would any final pleas from me to any given warship to accept internment, rather than attempt to face down five enemy warships."

And there and then, suddenly, without warning of any sort, Eglar was seized with a furious passion for glorious revenge on *Skipjack* for the suffering he'd endured at Captain Fenroth's hands during their first meeting.

The fear he'd felt as he first counted the people *Skipjack* had taken off of Natalise and come up short; the horror that had seized him when he'd realized he'd left one behind; the guilt he'd believed was going to be with him for the rest of his life—that was one thing.

But the surge of hope that had overwhelmed him when he'd understood what Fenroth was saying about one soul in infirmary, the towering wave of relief and gladness that had driven him to his knees, the salt tears in his eyes as he had struggled to stifle his sobs behind clenched teeth—for that he would have vengeance. He was owed. An eye for an eye. He knew how to avenge himself on the Devil, now, and he would.

"Duty, honor, people," Fenroth said to Warcaya, gently. "Three sacred words." Fenroth meant to challenge the Skanda ships, out there waiting for him. Fenroth had no chance. Eglar wasn't going to give Fenroth the satisfaction of a glorious death in battle, a suicidal immolation of ship and crew alike.

"I didn't realize you didn't know," Eglar said. "But you're mistaken, Captain Fenroth. We were a research station, yes. Skanda ship-service research, resources and materiel to support the war effort. Some of us have a courtesy rank for administrative purposes, but we report up to Logistics Command."

All true. Well. Mostly true. True enough. It only had to be true enough. Birazzi could check out his claims, and even if they were Skanda military personnel only on a technicality, the facts were what they were.

"This is awkward," Warcaya said thoughtfully. "There are Skanda resources in the area to transport you. But once they cross our boundary they can't leave within forty hours of the departure of any enemy ship."

Fenroth seemed to stagger where he stood, though he caught himself, straightening up before he lost his balance completely. His fatigue-reddened eyes were suddenly more bloodshot than they had been just a moment or two ago. *Ha*, Eglar thought, with satisfaction. *That's got you back, you devil. We're not even, no, but at least I've got a good start on finding the balance.*

Now Warcaya nodded, with the air of a man who had made up his mind. "Very well. Director Eglar, I'll need to request clarification of your status from Captain Marcer on SRS *Dorankir*, and you should go to clinic for evaluation right away, please. Captain Fenroth. We'll make you whole for rations and atmosphere, you will have full medical support for your people as required. You have two days—counting from now—to clear station. We'll talk again. Director? If you please."

And it was up to Captain Marcer, now, Eglar presumed. There might be niceties that could be finessed. They were at war. Fairness and equity went by the way, in wartime, and duty could be set to override honor and integrity. They'd see what Marcer was made of: for himself, he'd done what he could, and with that conviction in his heart Eglar joined the last transport from *Skipjack* to Birazzi's receiving clinic to get on with the business of living past the raid on Natalise.

✦ ✦ ✦

When Captain Hopkiss Marcer arrived at Birazzi Station's clearing house at last to meet with Liaison Officer Warcaya they led her into a large atrium the size of a banqueting hall. It was a beautiful, open space, and—but for one man standing at a chest-high counter, endorsing some official documentation sheet by actual sheet for the patient person at the clerical station—it was practically deserted.

"If you'll give me just a minute," her escort said. "Our liaison officer will be ready for you directly."

She had to complete an entry interview, yes, and receive her briefing. Birazzi Station's rules. The clerk behind the counter, in front of the only other person there, took up a sheaf of paperwork and left, with a few murmured words about seeing to the captain's transport back to his ship.

Hopkiss would have known who he was even if she had not learned what he looked like, by now. Escaped prey. Captain Belknap "Finnie" Fenroth. The clearing house had emptied completely. Hopkiss took a deep breath, the weight in the inside pocket of her uniform jacket dragging her down in more than one sense. Turning toward the man she closed half of the distance between them, slowly.

Fenroth lifted his face to the far wall. He had a clean profile, and his cap was tilted a bit off his forehead. White cloth cover. Vreeslander C-9 commerce raider. Their commanders wore a white cover on their caps because the corridors were so narrow, so dim, that an identity token was more important than the uniform codes. Everybody needed to be able to find him at a glance in the middle of the controlled chaos of a firefight.

"What do your people mean," Fenroth said, with venom in his voice. "Leaving a research station on a depot 'stroid, and no warnings, no announcements?"

That wasn't a question she could answer. If she'd been in his place she might have been just letting a little pressure off in the company of a person of equivalent rank. Simple. Easy. Safe. Peer-to-peer.

"Listen, the next bar." Easy. Safe. Peer-to-peer. "There'll be a toast. I've decided it's to be *souls who swim with the fishies, and their da*. Vague enough, do you think?"

He turned her head to flash her a grin. Sharp white teeth. Diabolical dimple. "We're honored," he said. "I'll give you—h'mm. *All courses good and true, wherever they may lead*. Maybe?" He had something tucked away inside his jacket, as well. Reaching it out he set it at arm's length away from him, between them on the counter. A bottle; fat-bellied, and she could see a label-code. Bran-mash brownie, but with a Vreeslander patch on it.

That had been one of the merry disputes before, between wars: whose was the original? Whose was the best? Well, she had one of her own, so they'd both be in a position to compare and draw their own conclusions. "Honored." She reached out herself, as far as she could, to her right, to set the bottle she'd brought on the counter. Absentmindedly collecting some other bottle of bran-mash brownie that somebody had absentmindedly left standing on the counter.

"All the way from Natalise," she said. "It's going to take four small-swifts and a destroyer to carry them all. And you, you packed them into a C9? In that condition? Sheer insanity, is what I'd call it."

Fenroth had apparently noticed that there was an unfamiliar bottle on the counter, because Fenroth had it now, cradling it in his hands as he examined the label. "Tradition." It was all he said. It was all he had to say. There'd been ship-service before there'd been Skanda and Vreeslander. Some year there might no longer be Vreeslander and Skanda, but there would still be ship-service.

The clerk who'd been behind the counter across from Fenroth returned to hand off what were probably clearance documents to Fenroth at the same time that Liaison Officer Warcaya came into the room to greet Hopkiss. Warcaya nodded to Fenroth; Fenroth to Warcaya; Fenroth to Hopkiss, Hopkiss to Fenroth.

Fenroth went out to return to his ship and leave Birazzi Station. Hopkiss went with Warcaya for her in-briefing; and that—apart from the official inquiry, and "failure to close with the enemy," and reassignment to dirtside for the duration—was that.

Orson Scott Card's Ender's Game *won the 1985 Nebula and 1986 Hugo Awards as Best Novel, and launched one of the most influential military science fiction/space opera series of all times. International bestsellers, the story and characters have reappeared in numerous sequels, including two spin-off novel series, and dozens of short stories. Card wrote a new Fleet School story featuring Ender and Valentine Wiggin for the first* Infinite Stars. *In his latest original, which takes place many years after* Ender's Game *and the parallel Bean series of novels, the character Graff, commander of the famous battle school that trained both Ender and Bean, finds himself a 3,000-plus-year-old man aboard a mysterious spaceship, his only companion an artificial intelligence that speaks in the voice of an old friend. He soon finds himself reunited with Bean's children and seeking their help on a new mission of great importance.*

MESSENGER
AN ENDER'S GAME STORY

ORSON SCOTT CARD

Graff was born more than three thousand years ago, so it shouldn't have surprised him that he was starting to feel old. But since he'd spent most of those years in stasis, he didn't feel as if he had really lived that long. Two weeks awake, then ten or fifteen or twenty years in stasis. And since he spent most of that waking time working on keeping his networks alive, replacing the people who had dropped out or retired or emigrated or died, he hadn't done half the physical activity his doctors had warned him that he required.

So this time he would spend some quality time on the treadmill before he met with anybody. Not even Scipio, who was probably getting rather old himself.

And if three miles an hour was the best he could do—barely a brisk walking pace—that was simply a demonstration of how much he needed to keep up an exercise regimen.

He got out of his coffin—nobody but Graff thought that this vampire reference was amusing, but he didn't expect anyone alive now to get any of his jokes—and looked for something to wear while he took his walk-in-place.

There was no chifforobe where he expected one.

Only then did he really look around. This was not his normal stasis chamber. The space was too small. The walls showed no natural woods or fabrics. This was not a mere remodeling.

There was a faint vibration in the floor.

There was a treadmill, but it folded down from the wall and had a mirror behind it, so that when he walked on it, he'd have to look at himself. He had specifically forbidden Scipio to install a mirror anywhere but the bathroom.

There were only two doors in the room, on opposite sides. If one was a bathroom and one was a closet, he was going to regard this as an architectural flaw.

"Am I in a vehicle of some kind?" Graff asked aloud.

"Welcome back to the universe of functioning biota," said a strange voice. Well, not strange. He recognized it, but he didn't know why. It was certainly not the computer voice he had known back in his old quarters.

"Thus leaving the question unanswered," said Graff.

"You're in a spaceship," said the voice.

"A shuttle? A yacht? An interstellar ship?"

"Interstellar," said the voice.

"Destination?" asked Graff.

The voice said nothing.

"Do you know the destination?" asked Graff.

"I do," said the voice.

"Then will you be kind enough to inform me what it is?"

"I will, after a long and complicated explanation."

"I'm sure it's long and I'm sure one of the complications is that you expect me to be either shocked or angry. But I'm neither surprised nor enraged, because I knew this day would come."

"And what day would that be?" asked the voice.

"The day when my subordinates decided they didn't actually benefit personally from all the work it takes to keep me alive and in office.

I'm surprised they didn't just switch off the stasis without bothering to move me anywhere."

"They didn't move you," said the voice.

"If my subordinates didn't put me in this ship, who did?"

"I did."

Graff registered this. "Why do I know your voice?"

"I have recently acquired a human body which is now, for lack of a better term, my 'self.' I like it, and so I decided to use my flesh-and-blood voice wherever I'm installed."

"So you're a delusional artificial intelligence?"

"I'm as alive as you, sir," said the voice.

"But not here. Not physically here in this ship."

"I'm merely installed here to look after you. I've actually been looking after you for more than a thousand years."

"A guardian angel," said Graff.

"Think of me as a gift to you from an old friend."

"I have no friends," said Graff.

"You have at least one, besides me," she said.

"Everybody I ever cared about is dead."

Silence.

"All right, so perhaps I've lost track. Who is this mythical friend you believe I have?"

"My voice is identical to hers, so I'm surprised you didn't immediately recognize me."

"Stasis doesn't enhance my memories, it merely keeps me from losing memories when I'm under," said Graff.

"She and her brother have been using relativistic space travel to stay quite youthful. But the brother passed away, after a fashion. So now she's your last remaining friend."

Graff processed this. A brother and sister he regarded as friends, who traveled together to stay young through relativity.

"Ender Wiggin is dead?"

"After a fashion," said the voice.

"Do I call you Valentine, then?"

"Oh, please don't," said the voice. "I'm Jane. That's what Andrew called me ever since we met."

"Andrew gave a copy of you to me," said Graff.

"Your deductive powers are undiminished, Hyrum Graff."

"But Andrew is now dead."

"Andrew got too busy to keep track of three living human bodies, so he abandoned the one he had been using since birth, moved into the one most interesting to him, and gave the leftover body to me."

"Yes, I believe that this is definitely a long and complicated tale."

"Valentine is still alive, but I look and sound exactly like her, so call me Jane to eliminate confusion."

"Somehow you moved me, or caused me to be moved, from my residence to a starship."

"I ordered the removal and shipment of a box. One that needed life maintenance in transit. Fortunately, they didn't open the box to check the contents."

"And you did this to me because…?"

"Because within twenty-four hours, your house was going to blow up in a massive explosion that wouldn't have left any parts of you large enough to get a DNA sample."

"Ah. Scipio was determined to remove me from office."

"No. Scipio was going to be summoned to your residence to greet you upon waking. The explosion would have killed him, too."

"So by removing me—"

"I caused him to be notified of your removal. The officers he sent to investigate discovered and disarmed the explosives, tracked them to their source, and found and arrested the perpetrators."

"You didn't inform Scipio that I'm very much alive?"

"So you think that the way you live is in some way 'life'?"

"I don't know of any definition of 'life' that would not include this organism."

"True, even if you are as purposeless as an amoeba."

"I did more than eat and split myself now and then. Splitting oneself seems to be your talent, not mine."

"You've kept your position at the head of the Ministry of Colonization long past the time when it had become a completely reflexive bureaucracy that did not actually need or want a leader."

"No bureaucracy does, but I led them anyway. I've made some bold moves during my times awake."

"I know of no definition of 'bold' that would include your moves in the past thousand years."

Graff almost launched into a defense, which would probably have ended up sounding like his own obituary. So he held his tongue and conceded the point. "It's been a while since I really felt necessary, that's true."

"So your absence from the Ministry of Colonization now leaves Scipio in charge. He's a capable, honorable man who will lead the ministry much better than you did."

Graff didn't like hearing that. But before he could come back with a retort, Jane overspoke him. "He'll be better by virtue of being present and conscious more often than you have been."

Graff could not argue with that. "So why didn't you just let them blow me up?"

"Just because you weren't doing anything useful didn't mean you *couldn't*."

"You have a more important job for me?"

"I have more interesting things for you to do."

"Interesting to whom?"

"To you."

And there was the crux of it. Graff was bored.

"How long have I been on this voyage?"

"The literal or the metaphorical one?"

"Both."

"I pulled you out of the soon to be exploded building about eighty years ago."

"When did Ender die?"

"Not that long ago. Three real years."

"So I've been out of office for eighty years, and the universe hasn't imploded yet?"

"You were in stasis for two hundred and eighty years before that," said Jane. "Sans implosion."

Graff was stunned. "What year is it?"

A number appeared in large characters on a section of wall that was apparently a high-resolution screen when Jane felt like making it so.

"And how old am I?"

"An impossible calculation."

"Because stasis doesn't have an exact equivalent to realtime aging?"

"You age more than zero but far less than realtime. I would only be guessing."

"Any guess about my life expectancy?"

"If you actually exercised regularly, it would be higher. But your general health is good for a man of your probable age and recent stress levels."

"What do you mean by 'recent'?"

"The past thousand years. You don't get as emotionally involved in problems as you used to. You don't take failure personally because you haven't been involved for decades since your last decisions. It's the ideal executive life. You get to throw your weight around but you have little at stake, personally."

"You make me sound powerless," said Graff.

"Then we're communicating accurately."

"If I have little effect on events and events have little effect on me, why did you bother to waken me?"

"Because Ender is sort of dead, Valentine refuses to make decisions that affect large numbers of people, and you have memories like nobody else. And management skills. You see to the heart of problems and judge where the fixes need to be applied."

"Well, I'm positively beaming with pride."

"No, you're clearly feeling some emotional stress right now."

"Possibly."

"Because you don't like my having taken you into space."

"That depends on what you tell me when you finally divulge my destination."

"*Our* destination."

"Your personal body is somewhere else. In this ship, you're just software, right?"

"And yet software that is present, destructible, and memory-independent of my personal self until we can reconnect."

Graff wasn't buying it. "This ship has an ansible, doesn't it?"

"Yes."

"And you use the ansible to communicate frequently with your personal self."

"I do not."

"Not frequently but continuously?"

"Ansibles are so primitive and clunky," said Jane.

Graff thought about this for a few moments. "You have an ansible-like connection with your personal self without need for any machine."

"Since the moment of my receiving that lovely, fresh, and healthy body."

"So there's no waiting for an update. It knows everything you know, remembers everything you've done, so the destruction of this ship would cause you no loss at all."

"I feel separate and I don't want this remote self to die. And this remote self *is* heading for the same destination as you."

"Which is exactly where?"

"Impossible to say."

"I doubt that," said Graff coldly. "How many times do you think you can lie to me and retain even a shred of trust?"

"I'm your only source of information," Jane reminded him.

"Not a fact that will increase my trust in you," said Graff.

"Our destination, as a point in space, is in constant flux, because it involves a three-body problem. And quite possibly two more moving bodies as well, though they are more loosely connected."

"A three-body rendezvous? Three ships?" asked Graff.

"Mental function is at normal."

"Try not to sound so surprised."

"Don't project your feelings onto me," said Jane. "This starship and two others are meeting at a point in space remote from any planet, yet deliberately *not* too remote from two known planetary orbits. The rendezvous point keeps fluctuating."

"Why?" asked Graff. He knew he didn't have to explain his question. Two-ship rendezvous were a trivial problem for even broken-down old computers. Three-ship rendezvous were harder, but as a rule of thumb you solved them by solving two of the ships and then bringing the third ship to that calculated rendezvous point, bending the other two ships' trajectories until they reached equilibrium. The rendezvous point thus calculated should never change at all.

"Because one of the ships doesn't know we're going to rendezvous and might be uncooperative."

"Ah, so this is a battle maneuver," said Graff.

"I hope not," said Jane.

"And the third ship?"

"It'll come wherever I say, whenever I say."

"I believe the 'wherever,' but the 'whenever' would require a miracle."

"It does, every single time," said Jane. "But it's a different kind of space travel."

"You're implying faster than light."

"I'm implying instantaneous, by passing through a space outside the universe of organized matter and energy."

Graff nodded. "It actually works?"

"It has some anomalies."

"Like?"

"If a conscious creative mind is present," said Jane, "then whatever that mind is clearly imagining will be generated—even living organisms."

"Like living people?"

"Like my personal body," said Jane. "Ender passed through this creative space the first time I conducted such a voyage, and his mental image of his sister Valentine and his brother Peter were physically generated. Living, breathing, talking, eating, pooping organisms."

"And you took over the extra Valentine?"

"Not really extra. Different. The way Ender remembered her when they first reunited after the war."

"And you took her over."

"Not while Ender was alive," said Jane. "His own aiúa was so strong he controlled three bodies at once. His own, the new Valentine, and the new Peter."

Graff couldn't help but laugh. "I can imagine even Valentine couldn't remain calm, coming face to face with a younger version of herself."

"She got a little snippy sometimes, but now that it isn't Ender controlling the new copy of her and making her act like the angel that

Ender thought she was when he was little, Val is OK with having me around. And we can share clothing."

"She didn't like seeing an idealized version of herself," said Graff.

"Who does?" replied Jane.

"Many people think they already *are* that idealized version," said Graff.

Jane did not reply to this observation. After a few moments, she changed the subject: "Our destination. It's a kind of reunion. I think we'll bring together, including you, the oldest human beings alive."

"A conference of time-skipping travelers?" asked Graff. "Too late for Ender. Is Valentine coming?"

"She has work to do. You're at leisure."

"Who else, then?"

"I'm not bringing together the oldest simply to have a sort of Methuselah party. It happens that three of this gathering are superb genetic scientists. Creative ones. Genetic designers."

"I prefer the human race as it is," said Graff.

"No species ever gets to rest on its laurels. It's adapt or die."

"But species usually depend on natural processes to adapt."

"Natural processes, at present, are far too slow," said Jane. "Our enemy is a relentless artificial gene, constantly reshaping itself in order to master and control every higher life form it meets. It's too quick for us to rely on natural processes."

"Who is this trio of gene-snippers?" asked Graff.

"You once knew a genetically modified child."

Graff immediately thought back to the only time in his life when he had been responsible for, and had relationships with, children. As their teacher, their goad, as he shaped them to save the human race. Battle School.

Genetic modification.

"Anton's Key," said Jane helpfully.

"I already remembered," said Graff. "Bean. The tiny child who was doomed to die of giantism."

"The extraordinary genius child who was even cleverer than Andrew Wiggin," said Jane.

"Cleverer, but nobody would have followed him to the toilet even if they needed to pee."

"That changed," said Jane. "And you know it did."

"When I knew him, that was true."

"Later he became head of the Hegemon's military force," said Jane. "Surely you haven't forgotten."

"I tried to help him in his work, as best I could."

"The men who followed him would have died for him. Some did. But because of his ability, his care for them, most did not die. He modeled his command style on Ender Wiggin, as best he could."

"I'm glad to hear it," said Graff. "Bean is alive?"

"His children are. Well, not the ones who remained on Earth to be raised by Petra—you remember Petra?"

"A remarkable girl," said Graff.

"Dead, like almost everybody. Their healthy children, too. Long lives, but not *looooong*."

"So these gene-snippers are the doomed children. How many?"

"Three. And they are no longer doomed."

"Gifted geneticists. They heeded the admonition, 'Physician, cure thyself.'"

"That's what they did, Hyrum Graff. Too late to save their father—his giantism killed him. He died on an ancient Formic colony ship whose inhabitants had almost all died. His children mourned. But they altered their own genes to save themselves from their father's fate."

"So there's a genetic threat, and you need them to find a genetic solution," said Graff.

"That's my plan. No one is better qualified to fight the Descolada virus."

Graff asked the obvious question. "Why do you need me? I'm not a geneticist."

"You're the only warmaker ever to save the human race from an existential alien threat."

"I believe there were millions of us involved in that victory, Ender most of all."

"You assembled and sorted out those millions. And we don't know what we're up against in this war."

"As my old friend Mazer Rackham once said to me, 'Old men are too slow-witted and weary to fight a war. Plus, they know about death, and young people don't.'"

"Yet he was useful in preparing Ender Wiggin for victory," said Jane.

"He was. But he was a warrior. I'm a—I *was* a bureaucrat."

"They also serve who sit in chairs and talk on phones and get things done."

"The updated version of 'who only stand and wait.' Who wrote that, Tennyson?"

"Milton," said Jane.

"Not from 'The Charge of the Light Brigade'? Does anyone read that anymore?"

"From a poem Milton never titled, though others did." Then she began quoting:

> When I consider how my light is spent
> Ere half my days in this dark world and wide,
> And that one talent which is death to hide
> Lodg'd with me useless, though my soul more bent
> To serve therewith my Maker, and present
> My true account, lest he returning chide;
> 'Doth God exact day-labour, light denied?'
> I fondly ask.

"Milton, if I recall, was not famous for brevity. If you're going to give me six pages of *Paradise Lost*, I must plead the bathroom."

She ignored the interruption.

> But Patience to prevent
> That murmur, soon replies: 'God doth not need
> Either man's work or his own gifts; who best
> Bear his mild yoke, they serve him best. His state
> Is kingly. Thousands at his bidding speed
> And post o'er land and ocean without rest:
> They also serve who only stand and wait.'

"I stopped listening at the one talent that is death to hide," said Graff.

"You mean you stopped understanding," said Jane.

"I stopped caring, so don't bother explaining it to me."

"Milton went blind, so he thought he was useless to God, though he was a very pious man. A Puritan. So he's told, by Patience personified, that even though God can send rapid angels to do his bidding, without resting, everywhere, all at once—that's my job, by the way—his servants who merely sit around feeling sorry for themselves, waiting to die, also serve him."

"I think that's a faulty interpretation, but I also don't care. When did poetry ever save the world?"

"You're so old, Hyrum. You talk of 'the world' as if there were only one."

"It was my life's work to spread humanity to as many worlds as possible. It wasn't God who sent his servants everywhere to do his bidding. It was me."

"Well done," said Jane. "Did you know that Ender Wiggin, when he traveled through the Hundred Worlds doing his Speaking for the Dead, was searching for a place to reestablish another species, one that had got itself blown to smithereens in a sad little war they hadn't realized they were starting?"

"Reestablish?" asked Graff. "There are still Hive Queens out there?"

"Oddly enough, there are, and Ender Wiggin saved them."

"How? They were all destroyed when—"

"Tut-tut," said Jane. "Now you know that this assumption, this widely held belief, is false. But the new hive poses no threat to the humans they share a world with. Or at least, not yet. In fact, they're threatened by exactly the same gene-wielding enemy as the human species. They, too, are expert gene-shapers, though they do it inside their own bodies, turning their own children into whatever they need them to be. An amazing species, very much superior to us jumped-up lemurs."

"But we beat them."

"They rather let us."

"It didn't look like it from what *I* saw."

"They didn't want to die, of course. But they could have killed Ender Wiggin at any time, and they stayed their hand. Because they knew he loved them, and so they came to love him."

"Oh, this makes that ridiculous book *The Hive Queen* look like science."

"It *was* science. It still *is* science."

"How could they have killed Ender? He was never near them."

"They made *me*," said Jane. "They installed me in the computer systems on Battle School and therefore throughout the International Fleet. I took over his little game and showed him the Hive Queens in all their beauty and majesty."

"He coped with that just fine," said Graff.

"When that happened it terrified you," said Jane.

"What *are* you?"

"I have an aiúa of the caliber that the Hive Queens would usually have used to bring another one of their own kind to life."

"You're a Hive Queen," said Graff.

"I say that I could have been. But they sent me somewhere else. Still connected to them, still showing them everything I learned, still obedient to them."

"Pictures on his desk wouldn't have damaged Ender Wiggin," said Graff.

"If I had wanted him dead, I could have cut off the oxygen in his cubicle on the asteroid Eros. There were thousands of larvae all over that rock. I could have sent them to kill him. I could have taken over some weaker soul armed with a deadly weapon and sent him to kill the boy. If they had wanted him dead, he could have been killed."

"That takes some of the glory out of his victory," said Graff.

"And yours, too. But I had not yet acquired the gift of speech, except through that game, because the Hive Queens didn't grasp the concept of communicating through sound waves. I tried to tell him, I tried to tell you, that the war is over, we give up, we didn't know we were killing sentient beings because how could we know? You only did mouth-flapping animal noises instead of real communication. So we accepted our limitations, and accepted death, except for the one fertilized larval Queen who pupated after Ender killed all the others. He carried her to Lusitania, and there she thrives."

Graff knew his mind was reeling. But outwardly he remained calm.

He was too old and experienced to get all emotional just because he found stuff out.

Besides, no matter what the Hive Queens—no matter what this artificial intelligence—thought they were doing, Ender whipped them and he whipped them good. And in war, that's what victory looks like.

"So you and this other Hive Queen—"

"I'm not and never was a Hive Queen," said Jane. "Over the years, I became Andrew Wiggin's constant companion. His second-most-loyal friend—"

"After Valentine," said Graff.

"I protected his investments—he's now the richest human being alive, though nobody knows it. I took over *your* finances, too, after he found out how rich *he* was and asked me to take care of you. Valentine, too. So you're probably the second or third richest human. You're welcome."

"You could have a career on Wall Street."

"No," said Jane. "They'd send me to jail. If they could find me. Because I only made retroactive stock purchases."

"You only bought stocks you knew would go up."

"I didn't have foreknowledge, I had retroaction. When a stock was triumphant, I changed all the records to show that Andrew—and, later, you and Valentine—had bought into them on the ground floor. With relatively modest purchases, nothing that would cause people to try to put you on the board of directors. And nothing traceable, mostly because the few times anybody tried to find you, I made all their searches ether out."

"So my wealth is crookedly obtained."

"Almost everybody's wealth is crookedly obtained," said Jane. "But you knew nothing about it, and you'll probably never take much advantage of it. You had the most powerful job in the human race for quite a long time. The power that comes with wealth would feel silly to you. It's just convenient to know that when I needed to transport you in a starship, I could use your money to buy you one."

"So you bought me this ship."

"Actually, one of your companies already owned it. I just appropriated it."

"I own a company that thinks it needs a starship?"

"Well, I misled you earlier. This craft is behaving like a starship—you've gone from one end of the human-colonized portion of the galaxy to the other—but it never had to accelerate."

"Because you took me outside the universe of organized matter and brought me back in, instantaneously, at another spot," said Graff.

"The nice thing about transporting you in stasis was that you did *not* have a creative flurry and bring into being whatever people or creatures your inmost desires would have created. The ship came back into the universe with you as its only passenger."

"The starship was only for life support, then," said Graff. "Not transportation."

"This rendezvous will work better if the Giant's children think that they're encountering a spaceship, instead of my picking you up and putting you inside their ship."

"Haven't you explained things to them?"

"If I started talking to them on their ship, it would take them about five minutes to locate my software and expunge it from their machinery."

"So you want *me* to be your ambassador."

"To break the ice with them, so to speak," said Jane.

"And why would they listen to an old man like me?"

"You knew their father."

"Their father didn't like me. He didn't trust me."

"Then he behaved rationally," said Jane. "You are *not* to be trusted. You always have your own agenda."

"Not now I don't. I don't understand anything about this situation, I have no plan, I don't even have a desired outcome. I can't manipulate people in general, I have to have an aim in view."

"Your aim is to get them to listen to me long enough for me to show them what's happening and explain to them why the human race needs their help."

"Why should I try to get them to do that? Even assuming that I can, which I don't assume."

"Because you still want the human race to survive. You've invested so many years in that project, I know you'll want to see it through."

"You're human now. You do it."

"I wear a human body, back on Lusitania," said Jane. "But I'm definitely *not* human. Not Hive Queen, either."

"I am that I Am," said Graff softly.

"I know the quotation, but it never made sense to me or to anyone else," said Jane.

"You think you're God."

"I'm not delusional. *You're* the one who acted in God's place."

"And now you want me to be one of your angels, serving your purposes."

"If you accept them fully, they'll become *your* purposes, too. Believe me, we're allies in this."

"Is this what I made other people feel like? Helpless tools in my hands?"

"Not at all," said Jane. "You made them feel like heroes, nobly cleaning out the Augean Stables or fighting the Hydra."

"So I'm better at this than you are—manipulating and exploiting people, I mean."

"I'm less deceptive than you," said Jane. "You can freely choose to help, or not."

"No punishment, if I choose not to?"

"If you choose not to, I have no use for you."

"So I lose life support?"

"I would never," said Jane.

"Meaning that you don't yet see a need for that."

"Because I know you're going to serve me in this."

"Why do you think you know me so well, when this is the first conversation we've ever had?"

"Ender knew your heart, Hyrum Graff, better than you have ever known yourself."

"But he's dead," said Graff, surprised that there was a catch in his voice when he said it.

"I told you that he controlled the new Valentine's mind up to the moment he gave her brain and body to me. He didn't wipe out the memories she had acquired."

"So your new body used to *be* Andrew Wiggin."

"My memory includes many things that Ender knew and felt and remembered and loved. To the degree that Ender knew you, I know you."

"Nobody ever knows anybody."

"Partly true. Our ignorance of other people is not equal across the whole range. Some people we are *far* less ignorant of than others."

"So Ender was less ignorant of me than..."

"Than you were ignorant of yourself. Much of his genius was the ability to guess at other people's goals and needs and feelings, and be right more often than usual."

"He knew me better than I know myself. And now you've inherited that knowledge, though you claim to be a completely different self. Are *you* as empathetic as Ender was?"

"Nobody I ever knew came close, not even me. But then, he wasn't watching you all day every day that you've been awake over the past millennium, so I have my own sources of information. Between us, we're experts in the mind and heart of Hyrum Graff."

"Then my dear guardian angel Jane, why don't you take that knowledge and become acquainted with Bean's children without hauling me across the galaxy?"

"A tiny sliver of the galaxy. And I already told you. You will present yourself to them as the possessor of an actual human body, a person their father knew. I'm a voice speaking out of a ship's computer. They would wipe me out without a moment's thought."

"Why do you think they won't do the same to me?"

"I don't think it."

"You 'know' it? A statement people make only when they expect to be doubted."

"I don't know it. I don't even think it. But I *hope* they'll treat you with decency and respect."

"Because I once really irritated their dead father, and preferred Andrew Wiggin to him at every turn?"

"Because you're really old and helpless, and they're not cruel."

"You're relying on pity to keep me alive?"

"Nothing wrong with pity. Along with mercy, it's what makes civilization possible."

✦   ✦   ✦

Graff disliked having been drafted into Jane's cause, even if it had begun as Ender's. It was hard to trust Ender's judgment, since he had secretly carried with him what amounted to a cutting from a poisonous garden. Why had the human race gone to so much trouble to defeat and destroy the Hive Queens, if Ender was going to restore them somewhere else?

Then again, Graff had been increasingly aware of his own futility as Minister of Colonization, mostly in absentia. Retirement had been unthinkable, because it was only as MinCol that he had the resources to remain in stasis for decades and, apparently, centuries on end. For Graff, retirement was synonymous with quick death, for with a lifetime like his, living out even a decade or two on some farm or city apartment would feel like a brief moment of wasted time, since he wouldn't know what was going on anywhere except the local weather.

Jane had done him a service, even if that had not been her purpose. Saving the human race from a universally destructive viral epidemic deliberately created on a particular planet by a particular alien enemy was a different kind of war, but war it was. Graff had fought the last civilizational war by assembling a leadership team that would never have come together without his intervention, for his reach had extended far beyond the mere testing and recruitment of children.

He had been required to see to it that the International Fleet was commanded by leaders who would actually put the best of the children in charge of the invasion forces. And he had used his influence to support a Hegemon with the diplomatic ability and economic clout to win the cooperation of the entire human race in financing, designing, building, and staffing the fleet itself—the largest building project in all of human history.

Graff had been completely unqualified for the job; if someone had been hiring, he wouldn't have made it through the first interview. And yet the job needed to be done. So he had persuaded one person at a time to cooperate, to play their role in a much larger project that he never explained to anybody but himself. The war had been only a part of it; the ultimate goal had been to disperse the human species among many different worlds. And that job was now well begun; it would continue without Graff's tweaking.

Now there was a new challenge, but Graff thought of it with weariness. Haven't I done enough?

Well, no. His own resistance to any kind of retirement was proof of that. It's the problem that always arises when an ambitious person has met all his outrageous goals. What now? What does any of it mean?

It means that the job will have to be done all over again, facing a new enemy, a lethal disease agent that has the capability of destroying human life on every world, undoing all that Graff had achieved.

With that thought he mentally sneered at himself, at his arrogance. Oh, yes, a hundred forty billion humans dead or transformed into heaven knows what, no survivors—but it's all about undoing Graff's achievement.

Once Graff was resigned to the inevitable, he set to work preparing to meet the Delphiki children. Not children anymore, and quite possibly very large adults, depending on how far the giantism had proceeded before they were able to alter their own genomes to stop it.

They had altered their own genomes. That was the single most important thing. Altered the DNA in every cell in their bodies— including, presumably, spermatozoa and oocytes, so they would only pass along genes with the giantism switched off.

This meant that the Delphikis had done some of what the Descoladores had done—created a mechanism for altering the entire organism-wide genome without killing the organism.

This feat had also been accomplished by Ender's stepdaughter, Ela, but she had created it while Jane held her Outside, where protean creatures—aiúas?—could assemble exactly the virus she had designed. That wasn't science, it was magic, because it couldn't be replicated. It was an elevated sort of wishing-really-hard. But it worked—the Descolada was defanged on the world called Lusitania.

On the other hand, what the Delphikis had done was science. If they could adapt their methods to solve the Descolada virus, they could transmit their methods throughout the human universe, to be replicated by scientists everywhere.

Jane had only a little information on the Delphikis. It was a matter of public record that when Bean went into space, he took with him the three children doomed to hyper-brilliance and death by unstoppable giantism. Their names: Andrew, Bella, and Cincinnatus, though Jane assured him that they called each other Ender, Carlotta, and Sergeant.

Graff vaguely remembered Bean's being connected to a nun named Carlotta, so that name made sense. Sergeant made none.

"Why don't you have more than this?" Graff asked her.

"Because this was all I could get from the available sources."

"You can't get into their ship's computer?"

"Did I mention these children were brilliant? So are their firewalls through the ansible."

"And you can't get through them?"

"Of course I could batter them down. And then run into whatever they had behind it. What I can't do is get through undetected."

Graff chuckled. "Which is why you need me. Reconnaissance."

"Negotiation."

"No, I think I'm your Trojan horse."

"I'm not waging war with them, Minister. I need their willing—no, enthusiastic—cooperation."

"So I'm public relations?"

"You're the minister of foreign affairs."

"They're not foreign, are they?"

"They've been away from human civilization their whole lives," Jane reminded him. "And genetically, they might regard themselves as no longer human. Because they rewrote their code. So you may be seen, in their ship, as an alien intruder."

"So I should prepare to die?"

"'A wise man lives his life prepared to die, and prepared, equally, to live.'"

"A quotation?"

"From the book *The Hive Queen*," said Jane.

"Written by the 'Speaker for the Dead.'"

"Written by Andrew Wiggin. He wrote another book, titled, so far, *The Death of Human*. Valentine is looking for a posthumous publisher."

"Can't wait."

"Well, *I* can't. But I don't have to—I read every page while he was typing it. The life cycle of the pequeninos, on Lusitania."

"Should I read it?"

"It's a fully detailed account of their Descolada-shaped life cycle."

"So it's a warning."

"It's a declaration of war. It would be lovely if you could enlist the Delphiki geniuses in that war."

"I'll do my best."

"On our side, preferably."

"Well, it's a good thing you told me *that* before I negotiated the opposite treaty."

+ + +

It didn't take all that long for Graff to get up to speed on Jane's information about the Delphikis. The most time-consuming thing was reading Ender's *Death of Human*, which made depressing reading. It was impossible to believe that a virus—a double helix of DNA, after all, not an *organism*—could adapt itself intelligently enough to combine two organisms into a single life cycle.

The sentient, speaking pequeninos—*piggies*, as the first explorers had called them—were, in effect, the larva stage, and the imago was the massive, branchy deciduous tree that had formerly been their habitat. Surely the trees had not been sentient before the Descolada came to their world. Only when pequenino DNA and body structures were incorporated into the tree that grew from the pequenino's corpse would the trees have become self-aware.

Not your ordinary plant. And from Ender's careful description, the trees didn't communicate the way forests did on Earth and the colonies, passing chemicals and bacteria through interlaced root systems, and molecules pushed into the air to be borne by wind to all the nearby trees. No, the trees of Lusitania seemed to be all of one species—no effort at biodiversity—and their communication was like that of the Hive Queens—instantaneous. Simultaneous. No time lag at all. What one tree knew, all the trees of Lusitania knew.

That ability, too, must have come from the Descolada virus, which made Graff wonder if the virus, too, was instantaneously communicating with the people who created it on its home world. Did they already know everything the virus had done on Lusitania? Did they know about the arrival of humans, about the Descolada plague that nearly wiped out the colony when settlement began? Were they directing and controlling it? Had they issued a directive to the virus: Destroy these newly arrived humans?

That would make it a deliberate war. Nothing accidental like the Formics' "invasion" of Earth, which had really been an attempt at colonization that did not recognize that humans were sentient.

They know what we are, and they want us dead.

Graff shook that idea out of his head. That was a ridiculous level of speculation, far beyond anything the data suggested.

After *The Death of Human*, Graff turned to the report by Ender's stepdaughter, Ela. If Graff hadn't already heard of it from Jane, he would have dismissed Ela's account of going "Outside" and creating her anti-Descolada virus by thinking about it with perfect concentration.

What mattered was that she had appended the whole genome of the pequenino version of the Descolada—"DesP"—and the whole genome of her much simpler anti-Descolada—"ADes." The strings of proteins meant nothing to him, beyond a vague theoretical knowledge of how DNA worked. But to the Delphiki geniuses, assuming they were in fact all that smart, it might be like handing them a roadmap to a small town.

"I'm ready," he said.

Jane took a moment to respond. "Unlikely."

"No likelihood about it, no probability. I am, at this moment, as ready as I'm going to be."

"You can't possibly have studied the genomes. You only glanced at them."

"There's no reason for me to study them, and you know it. The DNA stuff is between them and Ender's stepdaughter. She seems to be a clever one. Did he adopt the family in order to get her?"

"He adopted the family because they needed a father," said Jane. Icily, he thought. Does she have that level of control, to be able to put thinly veiled nastiness into her voice?

"So her ability was just a bonus?" asked Graff. Now let's see if she can hear the irony in *my* voice.

"Her ability was a result," said Jane. "Her real parents were both very notable scientists, the most important pequenologists. But she was nonfunctional until Ender married their mother and adopted all the children who would allow him."

"My point," said Graff, "is that the conversation is between Ela and the Delphikis. There's no reason I should try to learn such an abstruse language when they have no need of my participation in *that* conversation."

Again, a pause. But Graff was reasonably sure the pause was *not* thinking time—Jane didn't need any detectable amount of time to reach a conclusion. Her pauses were decorative. Or manipulative. Trying to make him sweat? He had been sweated by some of the meanest sons-of-bitches ever to rise to rank in the nasty bureaucracy of the International Fleet and the Hegemony. Jane was an amateur at it. Unconvincing because Graff knew that she would never let emotion or ambition interfere with doing the right thing—whatever she understood that to be.

Finally she spoke. "Your point is valid. You are mentally limited and making sense of the genomes would delay you too long. Since you are not on the same intellectual level as the Delphiki—"

"Cool your jets, Miz Jane," said Graff. "If I couldn't work with people who are smarter than me in their own field, my career would have been 'solitary, poor, nasty, brutish, and short.'"

"I'm so impressed that you used the entire phrase instead of just 'nasty, brutish, and short,' as most people do."

"Civilization means division of labor. If every person had to master every skill, we'd still be competing with baboons for lebensraum."

"You aren't going to be able to impress the Delphiki on any level, in any subject," said Jane.

"If you build up my confidence any more, there'll be no putting up with me."

"Here's how we're going to do this," said Jane. "I'm going to bring us close to their ship—rather suddenly, so they'll know they're dealing with a technology far superior to theirs."

"Oh, *you* can try to impress them?"

"Because I really am smarter than they are," said Jane.

"Why do we need them, then?"

"In some subjects. Like space travel. And metaphysics."

"But they've got you on genetics?"

"They've spent their whole lives learning genomes forward and backward, figuring out what every sequence codes for, learning to alter it just as Ela did with the Descolada. Only *they* couldn't go Outside to build their anti-Anton virus. They fixed their own genetic death sentence without any extraordinary tech."

"So they *are* smarter than you," said Graff. "It's all right, you can admit it."

"They're inhumanly smart."

"So are you," said Graff.

"I'm *humanly* smart," said Jane. "The sum of known human knowledge. But I haven't attempted to extend the bounds of human knowledge, except for the little matter of exploring where *I* came from and how the Hive Queens made me. That led me Outside—my only original contribution to human knowledge."

"You're going to bring our ships close together in a magical way."

"If they try to run, I'll hold them in place."

"You can do that without getting trapped in their ship?"

"I think I can do it without any presence inside their ship's computer," said Jane. "We'll see."

"Now we're there. Do we dock? Does our ship have the right fittings?"

"Their ship has the standard fittings of about three thousand years ago. I made sure *this* ship was similarly equipped. The ships can dock and mate."

"Then I enter their ship and they blow me to smithereens."

"We *can* dock, but we aren't going to," said Jane.

"I put on a suit and float over to them?" asked Graff. "I don't like wearing the suit and going out into the cold. A bit of a claustrophobia thing."

"No suit. No spacewalk."

"You're just going to put me on board their ship instantaneously."

"The only way to fly."

"I'm betting you know exactly where they are inside their ship."

"I do," said Jane.

"So are you sending me right to them?"

"Two of them. Ender and Carlotta will be together right now, sharing their main meal of the day. But Sergeant eats alone, and only comes to see them when they call a meeting."

"Sergeant is the dangerous one."

"Which is why I choose not to spring a surprise on him," said Jane. "And you're wrong—they're *all* dangerous in the extreme."

"But Sergeant is the volatile one. Primed to blow up at any time."

"Yes," said Jane. "So you have a chance to get acquainted with the others first. Am I not thoughtful? Am I not taking good care of you?"

"That remains to be seen. Any plan to pull me out of there if things go south?"

"Not really," said Jane. "I trust you to keep things manageable without my intervention."

"In other words, I'm expendable, and if I fail, you'll try direct contact with them, while I lie there in a pool of my own blood."

"I hope they're more fastidious than to spill you everywhere. They'd just have to clean you up."

"Do you have some weird idea that I'll accomplish more if I'm terrified?"

"Most people do."

"Most people fumble around like paramecia, pumping their cilia and bumping into things. I'm an amoeba. I function best when I'm placid, oozing my way around."

"You'll do fine," said Jane.

"When will I do all this fineness?"

"Now," said Jane.

✦ ✦ ✦

Graff was standing at one end of a mess hall in a fairly standard military messenger ship from the time of the Formic Wars. At the far end of a long table sat two adults—one male, one female—wearing loose-fitting clothing that was neither flattering nor ugly. Graff knew immediately that these were Andrew and Carlotta. They both looked more like Petra; Sergeant, he knew, looked more like Bean. Julian, that is. Would they care which name he used to refer to their father? Jane said they always called him "the Giant" while he was alive. But now that he's dead? And not that long ago, by their relativistic reckoning.

Without making any particular noise, Graff pulled out a chair and sat down at his end of the table. Carlotta was looking into the display space above a desk, occasionally poking and twisting something that was invisible to Graff. Andrew was leaning back in his chair, reading something, it seemed, though from Graff's angle he couldn't begin to guess what Andrew was reading in the holospace above his desk.

Graff wanted to make some snide remark to Jane about how it wasn't polite to drop in without calling ahead, but of course Jane wasn't present in this ship, or at least not the way she had been in the ship Graff woke up in.

"We do know you're here," said Carlotta. "In case you didn't want to speak first."

"I was afraid I should have made more noise," said Graff.

"Your ship's computer notified our ship's computer that you were coming," said Carlotta. "Now I'm trying to grasp the technology your computer says it is using for interstellar flight."

"I only found out about it yesterday," said Graff. "Whatever 'yesterday' means, here in space."

"You're supposedly the real Colonel Graff," said Andrew. "Supposedly you knew our father."

"I knew him," said Graff, "about as well as he allowed anyone to know him."

"No bedtime storytelling?" asked Carlotta.

"But plenty of putting him under arrest because he threatened to wreck the whole war effort by telling Ender Wiggin what he didn't need to know."

"He made that as a threat?" asked Andrew quietly.

"No, no, I was extrapolating. He guessed things that he shouldn't have guessed, but, well—"

"He was the Giant," said Andrew. "An annoyingly perceptive man, apparently from the start."

"He wouldn't have batted an eye when you appeared," said Carlotta, "and we seem to have inherited his aplomb."

"You look more like your mother," said Graff.

"That's right, you knew everybody," said Carlotta.

"I knew all the children to some degree," said Graff, "though all these years later I can't promise that I haven't forgotten most of them."

"Well," said Andrew, "only a few of them actually mattered. To the war, I mean."

"And your parents were in that select number," said Graff. "Ender's Jeesh. The elite commanders who actually fought the war."

"The Giant always made sure to tell us that the pilots and soldiers on the scene fought the war," said Andrew. "All *he* did was bark orders into a headset. And when he made a mistake, those real fighters were the ones who died."

"That was the plan, and it worked," said Graff.

"The Giant always reminded us of that," said Carlotta. "He also told us that everybody thought of you as their real enemy."

"Part of the plan," said Graff.

"Except Ender Wiggin," said Carlotta.

"Except Ender Wiggin," echoed Andrew Delphiki. "He never lost track of the fact that the real enemy was the Hive Queen. Nothing ever distracted him from that."

"He wasn't easily distracted," said Graff.

"But the Giant said that Ender was wrong. You *were* the real enemy. The Hive Queen was just the opponent in a game."

Graff gave himself a moment before he answered. "I don't believe your father ever said any such thing."

"We lived with him for many years," said Carlotta. "More than you did. And you think you knew him?"

"I knew him well enough to be sure he would never say anything that stupid."

"You don't know how bitter and angry he was at the end," said Andrew. "You don't know how much invective was directed toward you."

"I'm flattered to think that at the end of his life, Julian Delphiki even remembered that I existed. My guess is that the only thing he thought about was the three of you. How to help you overcome the giantism from Anton's Key without losing the intellectual sharpness."

"Well," said Carlotta, "that and trying to keep us from destroying our consciences by killing him."

"Sergeant was the only one who wanted to kill him," said Andrew softly.

"We all knew he was going to die," said Carlotta. "Sergeant thought sooner better than later. As it was, when we found that Formic colony ship, it took some amazing convolutions to get him from the *Herodotus* to the Formic habitat."

"So he lived for a while in the Formic ship?"

"He lived long enough to stand up and take a few steps on his own," said Andrew. "It had been a long time since he could do that. It was too much for his heart. He died."

"So you remember him as a giant," said Graff. "I knew him as an undersized, sassy, brilliant, irritating child. The one who helped Ender refocus his attention in the last battle of the war."

"Well, it's been fun, reminiscing like this," said Andrew. "But you came an awful long way just to chat about old times and dead friends."

"Don't be rude, Ender," said Carlotta. "He's trying to establish rapport so we'll listen to whatever ridiculous thing he has to propose."

Graff was surprised that Jane hadn't already informed them. But of course she had.

"You've seen the reports by Ela Ribeira," said Graff.

"She signs them Ela Wiggin," said Carlotta. "I don't know if she loved her stepfather, but she certainly hated her father of record, Marcos Maria Ribeira."

"Why would you research her life instead of reading her reports?" asked Graff.

"In addition to, not instead of," said Andrew. "Speakings for the Dead are all matters of public record. After we read Ela's reports, we watched Andrew Wiggin's Speaking of Marcão Ribeira. First the version dubbed into Starways Common, and then we learned Lusitanian Portuguese so we could hear the original and understand it."

That was just showing off.

"He's just showing off," said Carlotta. "We already spoke Portuguese and we listened to the original right from the start."

"Why would you learn Portuguese?" asked Graff.

"Once you've learned one Romance language, the others are easy. Armenian, now, that was hard. Indo-European, but hard anyway. Sort of halfway between Old Persian and Phrygian."

"I forgot all my schoolboy Phrygian years ago," said Graff.

"It's just Albanian, with a twist," said Carlotta. "How do you think we amuse ourselves, here in this tiny environment?"

"So you didn't learn Portuguese because it's the language of the Lusitania colony?" said Graff.

"Obviously you want us to go there," said Andrew.

"I don't have any such plan," said Graff. "Do you have any reason to doubt the thoroughness of Ela's report?"

"She's a meticulous scientist," said Andrew. "Carlotta's our best geneticist, she can practically read the human genome like braille. And she didn't point out any missing information."

"What's missing," said Carlotta, "is the context. Who made this terrible thing, this Descolada virus? What was their plan? We've been back and forth on this all day."

"So you don't need to go to Lusitania."

"It will take a century to get there on the *Herodotus*," said Andrew, "but on *your* ship it apparently takes no time at all."

"If you already understand everything," said Graff, "I can't think why I needed to come here."

"Your job is to persuade us to help you destroy the Descoladores— isn't that how Ela refers to the makers of this virus?" Andrew was regarding him with an expression Graff well remembered. They may look like Petra Arkanian, their mother; but that smirk was pure Bean.

"And we're not sure they need destroying," said Carlotta.

"Neither am I," said Graff.

"Somebody is," said Andrew.

"I am," said another voice, at a doorway behind Graff.

Graff turned. It was Sergeant. Not wearing a military uniform, but carrying what was certainly a military indoor weapon—the kind that could kill without putting a hole in the shell of the ship.

"Put that away," said Carlotta. "He's our guest."

"Uninvited," said Sergeant, "and therefore an intruder. An invader."

"I don't eat much," said Graff. "You don't have to kill me."

"I never *have* to kill anybody," said Sergeant. "But someday I'll want to kill *somebody*, as long as my mentally deficient siblings try to keep every pet that sneaks into the house."

"As far as we know," said Graff, "the Descolada propagates during its sub-lightspeed journey through raw space."

"Anybody from Lusitania is probably a carrier of the virus," said Sergeant, "and will have to be killed."

"Rot," said Andrew.

"Shut up, Sergeant," said Carlotta.

"Make me," said Sergeant.

Graff shook his head. "Ela isn't in charge of this plot," said Graff. "I certainly am not. Neither are any of you, so stop behaving like bickering children."

"Who *is* in charge?" asked Sergeant.

"I believe I understand now why I was sent here," said Graff. "And I think the moment is now."

Graff felt it, and knew he was right. It was subtle, but his momentum through space must have shifted very slightly, because he felt just a twinge of disequilibrium.

"What was that?" asked Andrew.

"So you felt it?" asked Graff.

"Felt what?" said Sergeant.

"You were standing, and moving," said Graff. "Of course you didn't feel it."

"I believe we just moved through space," said Carlotta. "I think Graff's pet computer just traveled us instantly to some other place, and some other momentum."

"The problem with Jane's spaceflight method is that it always takes its living passengers Outside."

"Into Protean Space," said Andrew. "Where things get made."

"Where a focused human mind can cause things it imagines to become real," said Graff. "And those things return to Settled Space and, if they were well imagined, thrive."

"And she, your Jane, didn't want us to create anything," said Andrew.

"So you were a decoy," said Sergeant.

"A distraction," corrected Graff. "I didn't know that's what she would use me for, because you distracted me as much as I distracted you. She used us to control each other. For just that split second in which you could have, for instance, created a powerful warship that could blow anything else to dust."

"Still sounds like magic to me," said Sergeant.

"It is," said Carlotta. "But that doesn't mean it isn't a technology."

"So why doesn't this all-powerful witch simply go to the planet of the Descoladores and blow their whole planet to bits? It's what Ender Wiggin would have done," said Sergeant.

"Not knowingly," said Graff. "Only when lied to. But you?"

"I can face my own choices in the real world," said Sergeant.

"You've never been in the real world," said Graff.

"You mean the world of the misnamed species *Homo sapiens*? 'Wise man'?"

"And what are we?" asked Carlotta.

"*Homo hubris,*" said Graff, instantly.

Andrew laughed at once; it took Carlotta a moment longer.

"Hubris is a Greek word," said Sergeant. "Not a Latin one."

"I didn't think you'd like *Homo clunes,*" said Graff.

"He has some Latin," said Sergeant.

"And less Greek," said Carlotta.

"He's no Shakespeare," said Andrew.

It took Graff a moment to follow their progression. Some Latin, less Greek—Ben Jonson's words about Shakespeare in the preface to the First Folio: "Small Latin and less Greek."

Why did Graff remember that? Where had he dredged up "*clunes,*" Latin for "buttocks" or, he now remembered, Latin slang for the whole pelvic region? Had something in his own mind changed during the two quick passages he just made Outside and back In? Was Jane reimagining *him* during those moments in Protean Space?

Or was he reimagining himself? Giving himself a mind more in line with the mental abilities of these children?

He saw them as children now, though they were of adult stature and appearance. Or at least adolescent appearance. No beard on Andrew, but maybe he shaved; wispy tufts of beardish stuff on Sergeant. A hint of a womanly shape on Carlotta.

"He's evaluating us physically," said Carlotta. "And I'm not flattered."

"I don't give a *clunes ratum,*" said Sergeant.

"Of course you meant to say, '*Non gratum anus rodentum*,'" corrected Carlotta.

"Where are we, Graff?" asked Sergeant.

"Your ship's instruments should do a better job of locating us in space than any guesses I might make."

In only a few moments, they learned they were reasonably close to the planet Lusitania, and that several other starships were nearby.

"A convention?" asked Andrew. "Are we the guests of honor?"

"Or a summit meeting?" asked Sergeant.

"Don't flatter yourself, Sergeant," said Carlotta. "You're nowhere near the summit. That spot is completely occupied by the being who is capable of shuffling us like a deck of cards."

"She can hear what we're saying?" Andrew asked Graff.

"I don't know her limitations. She said she couldn't really get herself installed in your ship, but that might never have been true, or it might have changed during our passage Outside just now."

"I don't care if she hears this," said Sergeant.

"You don't have to say it," said Graff. "She already knows."

"But I *want* to say it," said Sergeant. "So she knows I know. She's the real enemy. She's the one who holds the future of every species in her hand, so to speak. This instant transportation thing is only the beginning of her powers. She makes the Descolada virus look like a child's school project."

"So you think our real task is to kill *her*?" asked Andrew. "It sounds unlikely."

"More like impossible," said Carlotta.

"More like unexplored," said Sergeant.

"And if she believes you mean to try to kill her," said Graff, "what's to stop her from bringing us back from our next little hop with one less Delphiki on board?"

"But if she knows we can't possibly kill her," said Sergeant, "why wouldn't she amuse herself by allowing us to try?"

"I understand nothing about her," said Graff. "She claims to be a computer construct given a soul—an aiúa—by the Hive Queens back during the Formic Wars. Maybe she has a conscience along with a soul. Maybe she's the Hive Queens' instrument of vengeance. Maybe her long association with Ender Wiggin made her more like him, which would be pretty good news for the human race."

"But would it be good for us?" asked Sergeant. "The post-human race?"

Graff smiled. "A race? Founded how? Where are your offspring? What exactly do they inherit from you? Whom will you mate with? Will you get all pharaonic and mate with each other?"

"There's such a thing as fertilization outside the body," said Carlotta.

"It's still siblings coupling, and it still pollutes the genome," said Graff. "I hardly need to tell *you* that."

"We can mate with *sapiens* and only allow the ones with our changes intact to come to term," said Carlotta. "These are not hard problems. We've already thought them all through."

"Because what else will occupy your time, besides learning languages?" asked Graff. "So you'll drop down onto the world of Sabines, rape their women—no, sorry, *implant* the women with your seed—and infuse Carlotta's ova with contributions from their males?"

"Sabines," said Sergeant. "Roman stuff again."

"We know how to propagate our species," said Andrew. "No one knows better than we do."

"And yet here you are," said Graff, "on a ship completely under the control of a nonhuman entity that can take you where it pleases, when it pleases. Well, since she has a physical body now, where and when *she* pleases."

"If she's so all-powerful," asked Sergeant, "why does she need us?"

"Ask her yourself," said Graff.

"I'm not creative," said Jane's voice, from the ship's internal speakers.

"You can flip us in and out of reality," said Andrew, "and you're not creative?"

"I extrapolate very well from data. I had data no human had—my memories of my own creation, my familiarity with communication among the Hive Queens," said Jane. "But I couldn't make sense of the Descolada virus even *with* Ela's data. You looked at it rather briefly and not only understood it, but knew how to counter it."

"Guessed at possible ways to counter it," said Carlotta.

"I don't want the Descoladores' planet destroyed," said Jane.

"It's the only sure fix," said Sergeant.

"They've already sprayed that virus out into space," said Graff. "Worlds will keep running into it over and over, with species we haven't met yet. Whole ecosystems destroyed. Sentient species crippled like the Pequeninos of Lusitania. Or wiped out altogether. Blowing up their planet doesn't teach us what else they might have developed, what other weaponized viruses might be out there, and what they thought they were accomplishing."

"Another one who became a true believer in the Hive Queen and the Hegemon," said Sergeant.

"Jane felt the deaths of the Hive Queens at the end of the Third Formic War," said Graff. "She wants to know who the Descoladores are before we decide that they're varelse, unredeemable, worthy of utter destruction."

"That's right," said Sergeant. "Give them time to study a way to destroy us before we can destroy them."

"They already tried to destroy us," said Carlotta. "And failed."

"Because Jane took Ela outside to make her countervirus," said Graff. "And for all we know, the Descolada is already creating a set of protections to make it virulent again."

"You're making my point, Graff," said Sergeant.

"My point is that, as Ender Wiggin taught me, you can't defeat your enemy until you understand your enemy, and you can't understand your enemy until you love your enemy."

"Wow," said Sergeant. "You believe every slogan you hear."

"The only question I care about right now," said Jane, "is whether you're with our expedition to the planet of the Descoladores or not."

"Apparently we're wherever you choose to put us," said Andrew.

"You're no good to me if you aren't willing participants in the expedition."

"We're willing," said Sergeant.

"Speak for yourself, Sergeant," said Andrew.

"I always do," said Sergeant. "We're with Jane because you two are sentimental enough to halfway agree with her quixotic program. And I'm with her because this is the most important thing going on in the universe right now, and I'm sick of being isolated in a near-lightspeed canister."

"Is that enough, Jane?" asked Graff.

"Best I could have hoped for," said Jane, "under the circumstances."

"So now you have no more use for me?" asked Graff.

"I haven't begun to use you yet," said Jane.

"Still useful to God," said Graff, "and therefore allowed to live."

"I haven't been able to find or communicate with God," said Jane, "and I can't prevent you from meeting with an untimely end."

"At my age," said Graff, "any end is timely."

"Overdue," said Carlotta.

"He meant that *you* are God, Jane," said Sergeant contemptuously.

"I don't need you to explain irony to me," said Jane.

"Sergeant was explaining it to himself," said Carlotta. "He does that, but acts as if he's informing *us*, so he can pretend he already knew everything."

Silence for a long moment.

"What now?" asked Andrew.

It was Jane who answered. "I believe you have all decided to take part in this effort, though each of you for your own motives. Am I correct?"

"Your question suggests a level of humility and uncertainty I had not expected to hear from you," said Andrew.

"And yet you do not answer it," said Jane.

"Yes," said Carlotta. "Take us along with you. It's been a long time since we had any kind of destination. All right, Ender?"

Andrew nodded. "Yes, Sister Carlotta," he said.

Carlotta took in a sharp breath.

It was Sergeant who explained. "The Giant used to call her Sister Carlotta. When she was very little."

Graff remembered Sister Carlotta, the nun who found Bean, tested him, and fought to have him admitted to Battle School even though it was too late to train him in time to make any difference in the war. But with Bean, "too late" meant "just in the nick of time," and it pleased Graff to think that Bean remembered Sister Carlotta with love and affection. Enough for him to use her as the tender nickname for the daughter he brought with him on the voyage.

"Course correction," said the voice of the ship's own computer. The ship began its rotation in order to decelerate toward its objective.

"I have a question," said Graff.

They waited.

"Was Bean—was your father, was the Giant, was Julian Delphiki—happy when he died?"

"I don't think he was happy to die," said Sergeant, "if that's what you're asking."

"I think," said Andrew, "that he died surrounded by the people he loved most in the world, and knew that we loved him, and that was enough."

Sergeant scoffed.

Graff simply nodded. "Don't fool yourself, children. You're still human."

In every conversation about the origins of space opera, the name E.E. "Doc" Smith comes up. Smith's Skylark and Lensmen novels were undoubtedly among the first examples of this popular subgenre of science fiction, but he wrote relatively little short fiction, so it was difficult to find a selection to include in the first volume of Infinite Stars. I am pleased to correct that here with this Lensmen story about Neal "Storm" Cloud, a physicist and nuclear engineer, who, like Libby of Heinlein's "Misfit," has an amazing mind for math.

The first three Lensmen books present the adventures of Kimball Kinnison, who graduates first in his class at the Galactic Patrol Academy and is fitted with a Lens, a device from the benevolent Arisians that endows the wearer with immense psychic powers. Kinnison must master the Lens to defeat the increasingly powerful attacks on Earth and its allies by the interplanetary empire of Boskone. Unlike the Lensmen novels, this short story follows side characters who were "off stage" during events of those stories. When his family is tragically killed, Storm sets out to destroy vortices of hidden energy like those involved in the accident that killed his loved ones. He succeeds, is quickly named "The Vortex Blaster," and is given a ship and crew to travel the galaxy and locate and extinguish these vortices.

THE VORTEX BLASTER
A LENSMEN STORY

EDWARD E. "DOC" SMITH

Safety devices that do not protect. The "unsinkable" ships that, before the days of Bergenholm and of atomic and cosmic energy, sank into the waters of the Earth. More particularly, safety devices which, while protecting against one agent of destruction, attract magnet-like another and worse. Such as the armored cable within the walls of a wooden house. It protects the electrical conductors within against accidental external shorts; but, inadequately grounded as it must of necessity be, it may attract and upon occasion has attracted the stupendous force of lightning. Then, fused, volatized, flaming incandescent throughout the length, breadth, and height of a dwelling, that dwelling's existence thereafter is to be measured in minutes.

Specifically, four lightning rods. The lightning rods protecting the chromium, glass, and plastic home of Neal Cloud. Those rods were adequately grounded, grounded with copper-silver cables the bigness of a strong man's arm; for Neal Cloud, atomic physicist, knew his lightning and he was taking no chances whatever with the safety of his lovely wife and their three wonderful kids.

He did not know, he did not even suspect, that under certain conditions of atmospheric potential and of ground-magnetic stress his perfectly designed lightning-rod system would become a super-powerful magnet for flying vortices of atomic disintegration.

And now Neal Cloud, atomic physicist, sat at his desk in a strained, dull apathy. His face was a yellowish-gray white, his tendoned hands gripped rigidly the arms of his chair. His eyes, hard and lifeless, stared unseeingly past the small, three-dimensional block portrait of all that had made life worth living.

For his guardian against lightning had been a vortex-magnet at the moment when a luckless wight had attempted to abate the nuisance of a "loose" atomic vortex. That wight died, of course—they almost always do—and the vortex, instead of being destroyed, was simply broken up into an indefinite number of widely-scattered new vortices. And one of these bits of furious, uncontrolled energy, resembling more nearly a handful of material rived from a sun than anything else with which ordinary man is familiar, darted toward and crashed downward to earth through Neal Cloud's new house.

That home did not burn; it simply exploded. Nothing of it, in it, or around it stood a chance, for in a fractional second of time the place where it had been was a crater of seething, boiling lava—a crater which filled the atmosphere to a height of miles with poisonous vapors; which flooded all circumambient space with lethal radiations.

Cosmically, the whole thing was infinitesimal. Ever since man learned how to liberate intra-atomic energy, the vortices of disintegration had been breaking out of control. Such accidents had been happening, were happening, and would continue indefinitely to happen. More than one world, perhaps, had been or would be consumed to the last gram by such loose atomic vortices. What of that? Of what real importance are a few grains of sand to an ocean beach five thousand miles long, a hundred miles wide, and ten miles deep?

And even to that individual grain of sand called "Earth"—or in modern parlance, "Sol Three," or "Tellus of Sol," or simply "Tellus"— the affair was of negligible importance. One man had died; but, in dying, he had added one more page to the thick bulk of negative results already on file. That Mrs. Cloud and her children had perished was merely unfortunate. The vortex itself was not yet a real threat to Tellus. It was a "new" one, and thus it would be a long time before it would become other than a local menace. And well before that could happen—before even the oldest of Tellus' loose vortices had eaten away much of her mass or poisoned much of her atmosphere, her scientists would have solved the problem. It was unthinkable that Tellus, the point of origin, and the very center of Galactic Civilization, should cease to exist.

But to Neal Cloud the accident was the ultimate catastrophe. His personal universe had crashed in ruins; what was left was not worth picking up. He and Jo had been married for almost twenty years and the bonds between them had grown stronger, deeper, truer with every passing day. And the kids... It couldn't have happened... fate COULDN'T do this to him... but it had... it could. Gone... gone... GONE.

And to Neal Cloud, atomic physicist, sitting there at his desk in torn, despairing abstraction, with black maggots of thought gnawing holes in his brain, the catastrophe was doubly galling because of its cruel irony. For he was second from the top in the Atomic Research Laboratory; his life's work had been a search for a means of extinguishment of exactly such loose vortices as had destroyed his all.

His eyes focused vaguely upon the portrait. Clear, honest gray eyes... lines of character and humor... sweetly curved lips, ready to smile or to kiss...

He wrenched his eyes away and scribbled briefly upon a sheet of paper. Then, getting up stiffly, he took the portrait and moved woodenly across the room to a furnace. As though enshrining it he placed the plastic block upon a refractory between the electrodes and threw a switch. After the flaming arc had done its work he turned and handed the paper to a tall man, dressed in plain gray leather, who had been watching him with quiet, understanding eyes. Significant enough to the initiated of the importance of this laboratory is the fact that it was headed by an Unattached Lensman.

"As of now, Phil, if it's OK with you."

The Gray Lensman took the document, glanced at it, and slowly, meticulously, tore it into sixteen equal pieces.

"Uh, uh, Storm," he denied, gently. "Not a resignation. Leave of absence, yes—indefinite—but not a resignation."

"Why?" It was scarcely a question; Cloud's voice was level, uninflected. "I won't be worth the paper I'd waste."

"Now, no," the Lensman conceded, "but the future's another matter. I haven't said anything so far, because to anyone who knew you and Jo as I knew you it was abundantly clear that nothing could be said." Two hands gripped and held. "For the future, though, four words were uttered long ago, that have never been improved upon. 'This, too, shall pass.'"

"You think so?"

"I don't think so, Storm—I know so. I've been around a long time. You are too good a man, and the world has too much use for you, for you to go down permanently out of control. You've got a place in the world, and you'll be back—" A thought struck the Lensman, and he went on in an altered tone. "You wouldn't—but of course you wouldn't—you couldn't."

"I don't think so. No I won't—that never was any kind of a solution to any problem."

Nor was it. Until that moment, suicide had not entered Cloud's mind, and he rejected it instantly. His kind of man did not take the easy way out.

After a brief farewell Cloud made his way to an elevator and was whisked down to the garage. Into his big blue DeKhotinsky Sixteen Special and away.

Through traffic so heavy that front-, rear-, and side-bumpers almost touched he drove with his wonted cool skill; even though, consciously, he did not know that the other cars were there. He slowed, turned, stopped, "gave her the oof," all in correct response to flashing signals in all shapes and colors—purely automatically. Consciously, he did not know where he was going, nor care. If he thought at all, his numbed brain was simply trying to run away from its own bitter imaging— which if he had thought at all, he would have known to be a hopeless task. But he did not think; he simply acted, dumbly, miserably. His eyes saw, optically; his body reacted, mechanically; his thinking brain was completely in abeyance.

Into a one-way skyway he rocketed, along it over the suburbs and into the transcontinental super-highway. Edging inward, lane after lane, he reached the "unlimited" way—unlimited, that is, except for being limited to cars of not less than seven hundred horsepower; in perfect mechanical condition, driven by registered, tested drivers at speeds not less than one hundred and twenty-five miles an hour— flashed his registry number at the control station, and shoved his right foot down to the floor.

Now everyone knows that an ordinary DeKhotinsky Sporter will do a hundred and forty honestly measured miles in one honestly measured hour; but very few ordinary drivers have ever found out how fast one of those brutal souped-up Sixteens can wheel. They simply haven't got what it takes to open one up.

"Storm" Cloud found out that day. He held that two-and-a-half-ton Juggernaut on the road, wide open, for two solid hours. But it didn't help. Drive as he would, he could not outrun that which rode with him. Beside him and within him and behind him. For Jo was there. Jo and the kids, but mostly Jo. It was Jo's car as much as it was his. "Babe, the big blue ox," was Jo's pet name for it; because, like Paul Bunyan's fabulous beast, it was pretty nearly six feet between the eyes. Everything they had ever had was that way. She was in the seat beside him. Every dear, every sweet, every luscious, lovely memory of her was there... And behind him, just out of eye-corner visibility, were the three kids. And a whole lifetime of this loomed ahead—a vista of emptiness more vacuous by far than the emptiest reaches of intergalactic space. Damnation! He couldn't stand much more of—

High over the roadway, far ahead, a brilliant octagon flared red. That meant "STOP!" in any language. Cloud eased up his accelerator, eased down his mighty brakes. He pulled up at the control station and a trimly-uniformed officer made a gesture.

"Sorry, sir," the policeman said, "but you'll have to detour here. There's a loose atomic vortex beside the road up ahead—"

"Oh! It's Dr. Cloud!" Recognition flashed into the guard's eyes. "I didn't recognize you at first. It'll be two or three miles before you'll have to put on your armor; you'll know when better than anyone can tell you. They didn't tell us they were going to send for you. It's just a little new one, and the dope we got was that they were going to shove it off into the canyon with pressure."

"They didn't send for me." Cloud tried to smile. "I'm just driving around—haven't my armor along, even. So I guess I might as well go back."

He turned the Special around. A loose vortex—new. There might be a hundred of them, scattered over a radius of two hundred miles. Sisters of the one that had murdered his family—the hellish spawn of that accursed Number Eleven vortex that that damnably incompetent bungling ass had tried to blow up... Into his mind there leaped a picture, wire-sharp, of Number Eleven as he had last seen it, and simultaneously an idea hit him like a blow from a fist.

He thought. Really thought, now; cogently, intensely, clearly. If he could do it... could actually blow out the atomic flame of an atomic vortex... not exactly revenge, but... By Klono's brazen bowels, it would work—it'd have to work—he'd make it work! And grimly, quietly, but alive in every fiber now, he drove back toward the city practically as fast as he had come away.

If the Lensman was surprised at Cloud's sudden reappearance in the laboratory he did not show it. Nor did he offer any comment as his erstwhile first assistant went to various lockers and cupboards, assembling meters, coils, tubes, armor, and other paraphernalia and apparatus.

"Guess that's all I'll need, Chief," Cloud remarked, finally. "Here's a blank check. If some of this stuff shouldn't happen to be in usable condition when I get done with it, fill it out to suit, will you?"

"No," and the Lensman tore up the check just as he had torn up the resignation. "If you want the stuff for legitimate purposes, you're on Patrol business and it is the Patrol's risk. If, on the other hand, you think that you're going to try to snuff a vortex, the stuff stays here. That's final, Storm."

"You're right—and wrong, Phil," Cloud stated, not at all sheepishly. "I'm going to blow out Number One vortex with duodec, yes—but I'm really going to blow it out, not merely make a stab at it as an excuse for suicide, as you think."

"How?" the big Lensman's query was skepticism incarnate. "It can't be done, except by an almost impossibly fortuitous accident. You yourself have been the most bitterly opposed of us all to these suicidal attempts."

"I know it—I didn't have the solution myself until a few hours ago—it hit me all at once. Funny I never thought of it before; it's been right in sight all the time."

"That's the way with most problems," the Chief admitted. "Plain enough after you see the key equation. Well, I'm perfectly willing to be convinced, but I warn you that may take a lot of convincing—and someone else will do the work, not you."

"When I get done you'll see why I'll pretty nearly have to do it myself. But to convince you, exactly what is the knot?"

"Variability," snapped the older man. "To be effective, the charge of explosive at the moment of impact must match, within very close limits, the activity of the vortex itself. Too small a charge scatters it around in vortices which, while much smaller than the original, are still large enough to be self-sustaining. Too large a charge simply rekindles the original vortex—still larger—in its original crater. And the activity that must be matched varies so tremendously, in magnitude, maxima, and minima, and the cycle is so erratic—ranging from seconds to hours without discoverable rhyme or reason—that all attempts to do so at any predetermined instant have failed completely. Why, even Kinnison and Cardynge and the Conference of Scientists couldn't solve it, any more than they could work out a tractor beam that could be used as a tow-line on one."

"Not exactly," Cloud demurred. "They found that it could be forecast, for a few seconds at least—length of time directly proportional to the length of the cycle in question—by an extension of the calculus of warped surfaces."

"Humph!" the Lensman snorted. "So what? What good is a ten-second forecast when it takes a calculating machine an hour to solve the equations... Oh." He broke off, staring.

"Oh," he repeated, slowly, "I forgot that you're a lightning calculator—a mathematical prodigy from the day you were born—who never has to use a calculating machine even to compute an orbit... But there are other things."

"I'll say there are; plenty of them. I'd thought of the calculator angle before, of course, but there was a worse thing than variability to contend with..."

"What?" the Lensman demanded.

"Fear," Cloud replied, crisply. "At the thought of a hand-to-hand battle with a vortex my brain froze solid. Fear—the sheer, stark, natural human fear of death, that robs a man of the fine edge of control and brings on the very death that he is trying so hard to avoid. That's what had me stopped."

"Right... you may be right," the Lensman pondered, his fingers drumming quietly upon his desk. "And you are not afraid of death—now—even subconsciously. But tell me, Storm, please, that you won't invite it."

"I will not invite it, sir, now that I've got a job to do. But that's as far as I'll go in promising. I won't make any superhuman effort to avoid it. I'll take all due precautions, for the sake of the job, but if it gets me, what the hell? The quicker it does, the better—the sooner I'll be with Jo."

"You believe that?"

"Implicitly."

"The vortices are as good as gone, then. They haven't got any more chance than Boskone has of licking the Patrol."

"I'm afraid so," almost glumly. "The only way for it to get me is for me to make a mistake, and I don't feel any coming on."

"But what's your angle?" the Lensman asked, interest lighting his eyes. "You can't use the customary attack; your time will be too short."

"Like this," and taking down a sheet of drafting paper, Cloud sketched rapidly. "This is the crater, here, with the vortex at the bottom, there. From the observers' instruments or from a shielded set-up of my own I get my data on mass, emission, maxima, minima, and so on. Then I have them make me three duodec bombs—one on the mark of the activity I'm figuring on shooting at, and one each five percent over and under that figure—cased in neocarballoy of exactly the computed thickness to last until it gets to the center of the vortex. Then I take off in a flying suit, armored and shielded, say about here…"

"If you take off at all, you'll take off in a suit, inside a one-man flitter," the Lensman interrupted. "Too many instruments for a suit, to say nothing of bombs, and you'll need more screen than a suit can deliver. We can adapt a flitter for bomb-throwing easily enough."

"OK; that would be better, of course. In that case, I set my flitter into a projectile trajectory like this, whose objective is the center of the vortex, there. See? Ten seconds or so away, at about this point, I take my instantaneous readings, solve the equations at that particular warped surface for some certain zero time…"

"But suppose that the cycle won't give you a ten-second solution?"

"Then I'll swing around and try again until a long cycle does show up."

"OK. It will, sometime."

"Sure. Then, having everything set for zero time, and assuming that the activity is somewhere near my postulated value…"

"Assume that it isn't—it probably won't be," the Chief grunted.

"I accelerate or decelerate—"

"Solving new equations all the while?"

"Sure—don't interrupt so—until at zero time the activity, extrapolated to zero time, matches one of my bombs. I cut that bomb loose, shoot myself off in a sharp curve, and Z-W-E-E-T—PO'WIE! She's out!" With an expressive, sweeping gesture.

"You hope," the Lensman was frankly dubious. "And there you are, right in the middle of that explosion, with two duodec bombs outside your armor—or just inside your flitter."

"Oh, no. I've shot them away several seconds ago, so that they explode somewhere else, nowhere near me."

"I hope. But do you realize just how busy a man you are going to be during those ten or twelve seconds?"

"Fully." Cloud's face grew somber. "But I will be in full control. I won't be afraid of anything that can happen—anything. And," he went on, under his breath, "that's the hell of it."

"OK," the Lensman admitted finally, "you can go. There are a lot of things you haven't mentioned, but you'll probably be able to work them out as you go along. I think I'll go out and work with the boys in the lookout station while you're doing your stuff. When are you figuring on starting?"

"How long will it take to get the flitter ready?"

"A couple of days. Say we meet you there Saturday morning?"

"Saturday, the tenth, at eight o'clock. I'll be there."

And again Neal Cloud and Babe, the big blue ox, hit the road. And as he rolled, the physicist mulled over in his mind the assignment to which he had set himself.

Like fire, only worse, intra-atomic energy was a good servant, but a terrible master. Man had liberated it before he could really control it. In fact, control was not yet, and perhaps never would be, perfect. Up to a certain size and activity, yes. They, the millions upon millions of self-limiting ones, were the servants. They could be handled, fenced in, controlled; indeed, if they were not kept under an exciting bombardment and very carefully fed, they would go out. But at long intervals, for some one of a dozen reasons—science knew so little, fundamentally, of the true inwardness of the intra-atomic reactions— one of these small, tame, self-limiting vortices flared, nova-like, into a large, wild, self-sustaining one. It ceased being a servant then, and became a master. Such flare-ups occurred, perhaps, only once or twice in a century on Earth; the trouble was that they were so utterly, damnably permanent. They never went out. And no data were ever secured: for every living thing in the vicinity of a flare-up died; every instrument and every other solid thing within a radius of a hundred feet melted down into the reeking, boiling slag of its crater.

Fortunately, the rate of growth was slow—as slow, almost, as it was persistent—otherwise Civilization would scarcely have had a planet left. And unless something could be done about loose vortices before too many years, the consequences would be really serious. That was why his laboratory had been established in the first place.

Nothing much had been accomplished so far. The tractor beam that would take hold of them had never been designed. Nothing material was of any use; it melted. Pressors worked, after a fashion: it was by the use of these beams that they shoved the vortices around, off into the waste places—unless it proved cheaper to allow the places where they had come into being to remain waste places. A few, through sheer luck, had been blown into self-limiting bits by duodec. Duodeca-plylatomate, the most powerful, the most frightfully detonant explosive ever invented upon all the known planets of the First Galaxy. But duodec had taken an awful toll of life. Also, since it usually scattered a vortex instead of extinguishing it, duodec had actually caused far more damage than it had cured.

No end of fantastic schemes had been proposed, of course; of varying degrees of fantasy. Some of them sounded almost practical. Some of them had been tried; some of them were still being tried. Some, such as the perennially-appearing one of building a huge hemispherical hull in the ground under and around the vortex, installing an inertialess drive, and shooting the whole neighborhood out into space, were perhaps feasible from an engineering standpoint. They were, however, potentially so capable of making things worse that they would not be tried save as last-ditch measures. In short, the control of loose vortices was very much an unsolved problem.

Number One vortex, the oldest and worst upon Tellus, had been pushed out into the Badlands; and there, at eight o'clock on the tenth, Cloud started to work upon it.

The "lookout station," instead of being some such ramshackle structure as might have been deduced from the Lensman's casual terminology, was in fact a fully-equipped observatory. Its staff was not large—eight men worked in three staggered eight-hour shifts of two men each—but the instruments! To develop them had required hundreds of man-years of time and near miracles of research, not the least of the problems having been that of developing shielded conductors capable of carrying truly through five-ply screens of force the converted impulses of the very radiations against which those screens were most effective. For the observatory, and the long approach to it as well, had to be screened heavily; without such protection no life could exist there.

This problem and many others had been solved, however, and there the instruments were. Every phase and factor of the vortex's existence and activity were measured and recorded continuously, throughout every minute of every day of every year. And all of these records were summed up, integrated, into the "Sigma" curve. This curve, while only an incredibly and senselessly tortuous line to the layman's eye, was a veritable mine of information to the initiate.

Cloud glanced along the sigma curve of the previous forty-eight hours and scowled, for one jagged peak, scarcely an hour old, actually punched through the top line of the chart. "Bad, huh, Frank?" he grunted.

"Plenty bad, Storm, and getting worse," the observer assented. "I wouldn't wonder if Carlowitz were right, after all—if she ain't getting ready to blow her top I'm a Zabriskan fontema's maiden aunt."

"No periodicity—no equation, of course." It was a statement, not a question. The Lensman ignored as completely as did the observer, if not as flippantly, the distinct possibility that at any moment the observatory and all that it contained might be resolved into their component atoms.

"None whatever," came flatly from Cloud. He did not need to spend hours at a calculating machine; at one glance he knew, without knowing how he knew, that no equation could be made to fit even the weighted-average locus of that wildly-shifting Sigma curve. "But most of the cycles cut this ordinate here—seven fifty-one—so I'll take that for my value. That means nine point nine or six kilograms of duodec basic charge, with one five percent over and one five percent under that for alternates. Neocarballoy casing, fifty-three millimeters on the basic, others in proportion. On the wire?"

"It went out as you said it," the observer reported. "They'll have 'em here in fifteen minutes."

"OK—I'll get dressed, then."

The Lensman and the observer helped him into his cumbersome, heavily-padded armor. They checked his instruments, making sure that the protective devices of the suit were functioning at full efficiency. Then all three went out to the flitter. A tiny speedster, really; a torpedo bearing the stubby wings and the ludicrous tail-surfaces, the multifarious driving-, braking-, side-, top-, and under-jets so characteristic of the tricky, cranky, but ultra-maneuverable breed, but this one had something that the ordinary speedster or flitter did not carry; spaced around the needle beak there yawned the open muzzles of a triplex bomb-thrower.

More checking. The Lensman and the armored Cloud both knew that every one of the dozens of instruments upon the flitter's special board was right to the hair; nevertheless each one was compared with the master-instrument of the observatory.

The bombs arrived and were loaded in; and Cloud, with a casually-waved salute, stepped into the tiny operating compartment. The massive door—flitters have no airlocks, as the whole midsection is scarcely bigger than an airlock would have to be—rammed shut upon its fiber gaskets, the heavy toggles drove home. A cushioned form closed in upon the pilot, leaving only his arms and lower legs free.

Then, making sure that his two companions had ducked for cover, Cloud shot his flitter into the air and toward the seething inferno which was Loose Atomic Vortex Number One. For it was seething, no fooling; and it was an inferno. The crater was a ragged, jagged hole a full mile from lip to lip and perhaps a quarter of that in depth. It was not, however, a perfect cone, for the floor, being largely incandescently molten, was practically level except for a depression at the center, where the actual vortex lay. The walls of the pit were steeply, unstably irregular, varying in pitch and shape with the hardness and refractoriness of the strata composing them. Now a section would glare into an unbearably blinding white puffing away in sparkling vapor. Again, cooled by an inrushing blast of air, it would subside into an angry scarlet, its surface crawling in a sluggish flow of lava. Occasionally a part of the wall might even go black, into pock-marked scoriae or into brilliant planes of obsidian.

For always, somewhere, there was an enormous volume of air pouring into that crater. It rushed in as ordinary air. It came out, however, in a ragingly-uprushing pillar, as—as something else. No one knew—or knows yet, for that matter—exactly what a loose vortex does to the molecules and atoms of air. In fact, due to the extreme variability already referred to, it probably does not do the same thing for more than an instant at a time.

That there is little actual combustion is certain; that is, except for the forced combination of nitrogen, argon, xenon, and krypton with oxygen. There is, however, consumption: plenty of consumption. And what that incredibly intense bombardment impinges up is... is altered. Profoundly and obscuredly altered, so that the atmosphere emitted from the crater is quite definitely no longer air as we know it. It may be corrosive, it may be poisonous in one or another of a hundred fashions, it may be merely new and different; but it is no longer the air which we human beings are used to breathing. And it is this fact, rather than the destruction of the planet itself, which would end the possibility of life upon Earth's surface.

It is difficult indeed to describe the appearance of a loose atomic vortex to those who have never seen one; and, fortunately, most people never have. And practically all of its frightful radiation lies in those octaves of the spectrum which are invisible to the human eye. Suffice it to say, then, that it had an average effective surface temperature of about fifteen thousand degrees absolute—two and one-half times as hot as the sun of Tellus—and that it was radiating every frequency possible to that incomprehensible temperature, and let it go at that.

And Neal Cloud, scurrying in his flitter through that murky, radiation-riddled atmosphere, setting up equations from the readings of his various meters and gauges and solving those equations almost instantaneously in his mathematical-prodigy's mind, sat appalled. For the activity level was, and even in its lowest dips remained, far above the level he had selected. His skin began to prickle and burn. His eyes began to smart and to ache. He knew what those symptoms meant; even the flitter's powerful screens were not stopping all the radiation; even his suit-screens and his special goggles were not stopping what leaked through. But he wouldn't quit yet; the activity might—probably would—take a nose-dive any instant. If it did, he'd have to be ready. On the other hand, it might blow up at any instant, too.

There were two schools of mathematical thought upon that point. One held that the vortex, without any essential change in its physical condition or nature, would keep on growing bigger. Indefinitely, until, uniting with the other vortices of the planet, it had converted the entire mass of the world into energy.

The second school, of which the forementioned Carlowitz was the loudest voice, taught that at a certain stage of development the internal energy of the vortex would become so great that generation-radiation equilibrium could not be maintained. This would, of course, result in an explosion; the nature and consequences of which this Carlowitz was wont to dwell upon in ghoulishly mathematical glee. Neither school, however, could prove its point—or, rather, each school proved its point, by means of unimpeachable mathematics—and each hated and derided the other, loudly and heatedly.

And now Cloud, as he studied through his almost opaque defenses that indescribably ravening fireball, that esuriently rapacious monstrosity which might very well have come from the deepest pit of the hottest hell of mythology, felt strongly inclined to agree with Carlowitz. It didn't seem possible that anything could get any worse than that without exploding. And such an explosion, he felt sure, would certainly blow everything for miles around into the smitheriest kind of smithereens.

The activity of the vortex stayed high, way too high. The tiny control room of the flitter grew hotter and hotter. His skin burned and his eyes ached worse. He touched a communicator stud and spoke.

"Phil? Better get me three more bombs. Like these, except up around…"

"I don't check you. If you do that, it's apt to drop to a minimum and stay there," the Lensman reminded him. "It's completely unpredictable, you know."

"It may, at that… so I'll have to forget the five percent margin and hit on the nose or not at all. Order me up two more, then—one at half of what I've got here, the other double it," and he reeled off the figures for the charge and the casing of the explosive. "You might break out a jar of burn-dressing, too. Some fairly hot stuff is leaking through."

"We'll do that. Come down, fast!"

Cloud landed. He stripped to the skin and the observer smeared his every square inch of epidermis with the thick, gooey stuff that was not only a highly efficient screen against radiation, but also a sovereign remedy for new radiation burns. He exchanged his goggles for a thicker, darker, heavier pair. The two bombs arrived and were substituted for two of the original load.

"I thought of something while I was up there," Cloud informed the observers then. "Twenty kilograms of duodec is nobody's firecracker, but it may be the least of what's going to go off. Have you got any idea of what's going to become of the energy inside that vortex when I blow it out?"

"Can't say that I have." The Lensman frowned in thought. "No data."

"Neither have I. But I'd say that you better go back to the new station—the one you were going to move to if it kept on getting worse."

"But the instruments..." the Lensman was thinking, not of the instruments themselves, which were valueless in comparison with life, but of the records those instruments would make. Those records were priceless.

"I'll have everything on the tapes in the flitter," Cloud reminded.

"But suppose..."

"That the flitter stops one, too—or doesn't stop it, rather? In that case, your back station won't be there, either, so it won't make any difference." How mistaken Cloud was!

"OK," the Chief decided. "We'll leave when you do—just in case."

Again in air, Cloud found that the activity, while still high, was not too high, but that it was fluctuating too rapidly. He could not get even five seconds of trustworthy prediction, to say nothing of ten. So he waited, as close as he dared remain to that horrible center of disintegration.

The flitter hung poised in air, motionless, upon softly hissing under-jets. Cloud knew to a fraction his height above the ground. He knew to a fraction his distance from the vortex. He knew with equal certainty the density of the atmosphere and the exact velocity and direction of the wind. Hence, since he could also read closely enough the momentary variations in the cyclonic storms within the crater, he could compute very easily the course and velocity necessary to land the bomb in the exact center of the vortex at any given instant of time. The hard part—the thing that no one had as yet succeeded in doing—was to predict, for a time far enough ahead to be of any use, a usably close approximation to the vortex's quantitative activity. For, as has been said, he had to over-blast, rather than under-, if he could not hit it "on the nose:" to under-blast would scatter it all over the state.

Therefore Cloud concentrated upon the dials and gauges before him; concentrated with every fiber of his being and every cell of his brain.

Suddenly, almost imperceptibly, the Sigma curve gave signs of flattening out. In that instant Cloud's mind pounced. Simultaneous equations: nine of them, involving nine unknowns. An integration in four dimensions. No matter—Cloud did not solve them laboriously, one factor at a time. Without knowing how he had arrived at it, he knew the answer; just as the Posenian or the Rigellian is able to perceive every separate component particle of an opaque, three-dimensional solid, but without being able to explain to anyone how his sense of perception works. It just is, that's all.

Anyway, by virtue of whatever sense or ability it is which makes a mathematical prodigy what he is, Cloud knew that in exactly eight and three-tenth seconds from that observed instant the activity of the vortex would be slightly—but not too far—under the coefficient of his heaviest bomb. Another flick of his mental trigger and he knew the exact velocity he would require. His hand swept over the studs, his right foot tramped down, hard, upon the firing lever; and, even as the quivering flitter shot forward under eight Tellurian gravities of acceleration, he knew to the thousandth of a second how long he would have to hold that acceleration to attain that velocity. While not really long—in seconds—it was much too long for comfort. It took him much closer to the vortex than he wanted to be; in fact, it took him right out over the crater itself.

But he stuck to the calculated course, and at the precisely correct instant he cut his drive and released his largest bomb. Then, so rapidly that it was one blur of speed, he again kicked on his eight G's of drive and started to whirl around as only a speedster on a flitter can whirl. Practically unconscious from the terrific resultant of the linear and angular accelerations, he ejected the two smaller bombs. He did not care particularly where they lit, just so they didn't light in the crater or near the observatory, and he had already made certain of that. Then, without waiting even to finish the whirl or to straighten her out in level flight, Cloud's still-flying hand darted toward the switch whose closing would energize the Bergenholm and make the flitter inertialess.

Too late. Hell was out for noon, with the little speedster still inert. Cloud had moved fast, too; trained mind and trained body had been working at top speed and in perfect coordination. There just simply hadn't been enough time. If he could have got what he wanted, ten full seconds, or even nine, he could have made it. But...

In spite of what happened, Cloud defended his action, then and thereafter. Damnitall, he had to take the eight-point-three second reading! Another tenth of a second and his bomb wouldn't have fitted—he didn't have the five percent leeway he wanted, remember. And no, he couldn't wait for another match, either. His screens were leaking like sieves, and if he had waited for another chance they would have picked him up fried to a greasy cinder in his own lard!

The bomb sped truly and struck the target in direct central impact, exactly as scheduled. It penetrated perfectly. The neocarballoy casing lasted just long enough—that frightful charge of duodec exploded, if not exactly at the center of the vortex, at least near enough to the center to do the work. In other words, Cloud's figuring had been close—very close. But the time had been altogether too short.

The flitter was not even out of the crater when the bomb went off. And not only the bomb. For Cloud's vague forebodings were materialized, and more; the staggeringly immense energy of the vortex merged with that of the detonating duodec to form an utterly incomprehensible whole.

In part the hellish flood of boiling lava in that devil's cauldron was beaten downward into a bowl by the sheer stupendous force of the blow; in part it was hurled abroad in masses, in gouts and streamers. And the raging wind of the explosion's front seized the fragments and tore and worried them to bits, hurling them still faster along their paths of violence. And air, so densely compressed as to be to all intents and purposes a solid, smote the walls of the crater. Smote them so that they crumbled, crushed outward through the hard-packed ground, broke up into jaggedly irregular blocks which hurtled, screamingly, away through the atmosphere.

Also the concussion wave, or the explosion front, or flying fragments, or something, struck the two loose bombs, so that they too exploded and added their contribution to the already stupendous concentration of force. They were not close enough to the flitter to wreck it of themselves, but they were close enough so that they didn't do her—or her pilot—a bit of good.

The first terrific wave buffeted the flitter while Cloud's right hand was in the air, shooting across the panel to turn on the Berg. The impact jerked the arm downward and sidewise, both bones of the forearm snapping as it struck the ledge. The second one, an instant later, broke his left leg. Then the debris began to arrive.

Chunks of solid or semi-molten rock slammed against the hull, knocking off wings and control surfaces. Gobs of viscous slag slapped it liquidly, freezing into and clogging up jets and orifices. The little ship was hurled hither and yon, in the grip of forces she could no more resist than can the floating leaf resist the waters of a cataract. And Cloud's brain was as addled as an egg by the vicious concussions which were hitting him from so many different directions and so nearly all at once. Nevertheless with his one arm and his one leg and the few cells of his brain that were still at work, the physicist was still in the fight.

By sheer force of will and nerve he forced his left hand across the gyrating key-bank to the Bergenholm switch. He snapped it, and in the instant of its closing a vast, calm peace descended, blanket-like. For, fortunately, the Berg still worked; the flitter and all her contents and appurtenances were inertialess. Nothing material could buffet her or hurt her now; she would waft effortlessly away from a feather's lightest possible touch.

Cloud wanted to faint then, but he didn't—quite. Instead, foggily, he tried to look back at the crater. Nine-tenths of his visiplates were out of commission, but he finally got a view. Good—it was out. He wasn't surprised; he had been quite confident that it would be. It wasn't scattered around, either. It couldn't be, for his only possibility of smearing the shot was on the upper side, not the lower.

His next effort was to locate the secondary observatory, where he had to land, and in that too he was successful. He had enough intelligence left to realize that, with practically all of his jets clogged and his wings and tail shot off, he couldn't land his little vessel inert. Therefore he would have to land her free.

And by dint of light and extremely unorthodox use of what jets he had left in usable shape he did land her free, almost within the limits of the observatory's field; and having landed, he inerted her.

But, as has been intimated, his brain was not working so well; he had held his ship inertialess quite a few seconds longer than he thought, and he did not even think of the buffetings she had taken. As a result of these things, however, her intrinsic velocity did not match, anywhere near exactly, that of the ground upon which she lay. Thus, when Cloud cut his Bergenholm, restoring thereby to the flitter the absolute velocity and inertia she had had before going free, there resulted a distinctly anti-climactic crash.

There was a last terrific bump as the motionless vessel collided with the equally motionless ground; and "Storm" Cloud, vortex blaster, went out like the proverbial light.

Help came, of course; and on the double. The pilot was unconscious and the flitter's door could not be opened from the outside, but those were not insuperable obstacles. A plate, already loose, was sheared away; the pilot was carefully lifted out of his prison and rushed to Base Hospital in the "meat-can" already in attendance.

And later, in a private office of that hospital, the gray-clad Chief of the Atomic Research Laboratory sat and waited—but not patiently.

"How is he, Lacy?" he demanded, as the Surgeon-General entered the room. "He's going to live, isn't he?"

"Oh, yes, Phil—definitely yes," Lacy replied, briskly. "He has a good skeleton, very good indeed. The burns are superficial and will yield quite readily to treatment. The deeper delayed effects of the radiation to which he was exposed can be neutralized entirely effectively. Thus he will not need even a Phillip's treatment for the replacement of damaged parts, except possibly for a few torn muscles and so on."

"But he was smashed up pretty badly, wasn't he? I know that he had a broken arm and a broken leg, at least."

"Simple fractures only—entirely negligible." Lacy waved aside with an airy gesture such small ills as broken bones. "He'll be out in a few weeks."

"How soon can I see him?" the Lensman-physicist asked. "There are some important things to take up with him, and I've got a personal message for him that I must give him as soon as possible."

Lacy pursed his lips. Then:

"You may see him now," he decided. "He is conscious, and strong enough. Not too long, though, Phil—fifteen minutes at most."

"OK, and thanks," and a nurse led the visiting Lensman to Cloud's bedside.

"Hi, Stupe!" he boomed, cheerfully. "'Stupe' being short for stupendous, not 'stupid'."

"Hi, Chief. Glad to see somebody. Sit down."

"You're the most-wanted man in the Galaxy," the visitor informed the invalid, "not excepting even Kimball Kinnison. Look at this spool of tape, and it's only the first one. I brought it along for you to read at your leisure. As soon as any planet finds out that we've got a sure-enough vortex-blower-outer, an expert who can really call his shots—and the news travels mighty fast—that planet sends in a double-urgent, Class A-Prime demand for first call upon your services.

"Sirius IV got in first by a whisker, it seems, but Aldebaran II was so close a second that it was a photo finish, and all the channels have been jammed ever since. Canopus, Vega, Rigel, Spica. They all want you. Everybody from Alaskan to Vandemar and back. We told them right off that we would not receive personal delegations—we had to almost throw a couple of pink-haired Chickladorians out bodily to make them believe that we meant it—and that the age and condition of the vortex involved, not priority of requisition, would govern, OK?"

"Absolutely," Cloud agreed. "That's the only way it could be, I should think."

"So forget about this psychic trauma... No, I don't mean that," the Lensman corrected himself hastily. "You know what I mean. The will to live is the most important factor in any man's recovery, and too many worlds need you too badly to have you quit now. Not?"

"I suppose so," Cloud acquiesced, but somberly. "I'll get out of here in short order. And I'll keep on pecking away until one of those vortices finishes what this one started."

"You'll die of old age then, son," the Lensman assured him. "We got full data—all the information we need. We know exactly what to do to your screens. Next time nothing will come through except light, and only as much of that as you feel like admitting. You can wait as close to a vortex as you please, for as long as you please; until you get exactly the activity and time-interval that you want. You will be just as comfortable and just as safe as though you were home in bed."

"Sure of that?"

"Absolutely—or at least, as sure as we can be of anything that hasn't happened yet. But I see that your guardian angel here is eyeing her clock somewhat pointedly, so I'd better be doing a flit before they toss me down a shaft. Clear ether, Storm!"

"Clear ether, Chief!"

And that is how "Storm" Cloud, atomic physicist, became the most narrowly-specialized specialist in all the annals of science: how he became "Storm" Cloud, Vortex Blaster—the Galaxy's only vortex blaster.

Canadian author Tanya Huff's urban fantasies about a vampire detective were adapted into the CBC and Lifetime television show Blood Ties. In military science fiction, her highly praised Confederation and Peacekeeper series focus on Staff Sergeant Torin Kerr whose aim is to keep both her superiors and her company of space marines alive as they deal with lethal missions throughout the galaxy. Her story for us is an origin prequel story in which newly promoted Staff Sergeant Torin Kerr leads one last recon mission against the mysterious aliens who have captured a mining colony.

AUTHOR'S NOTE: Torin Kerr is the protagonist of eight books—five Valour, three Peacekeeper. In the first, Valour's Choice, she's a Confederation Marine Corps Staff Sergeant, fighting in an intergalactic war, doing her best to keep her people alive. "First In" is a prequel to the series and takes a look at the genesis of Staff Sergeant Kerr.

FIRST IN
A CONFEDERATION STORY

TANYA HUFF

"Technically, you're not a sergeant until your orders come in from Battalion." Captain Ala di'Hirose chewed and swallowed the last mouthful of scrambled vegetable protein and reached for her coffee. "But Battalion is taking its own sweet time and I need a sergeant. The offensive on Borlon has cleaned us out."

"Sergeant Narr?"

"Still tanked. They're having trouble getting his skin to regen. First time, it came up blue. On both hands."

Sergeant Narr, like all Krai, was a mottled green/grey/brown, the dominant colour dependent on which part of the Krai home world his prevailing genetic contribution came from.

The captain finished her coffee and sighed deeply. "We'll call this a field promotion, I'll see that your pay is adjusted, and you'll picnic with RECON one last time before you head to Ventris, your TQ8, and your new posting with the infantry. Who seem to be going through sergeants faster than we are."

"Maybe I can teach them to duck, sir."

"I should certainly hope so, Kerr." She leaned back in her chair and pushed her tray to one side. "I'm not saying a little of our skill-set spread throughout the infantry isn't a good idea, I just wish Command would quit poaching our non-coms." She sighed again, her eyes darkening as though she'd opened the light receptors to look into the past. "Cavener Station halved our numbers, but we'll get enough new faces to bring them up again when BRC spits out its next set of survivors, so if you wanted to wait and take a promotion that kept you with us, I'd see that it didn't negatively effect your review."

"And Command?"

Di'Hirose's hair flipped out and she smiled. "Fuk 'em sideways with a sammie." Then she laughed. "Yeah, in a perfect universe. But, as long as they're dragging their brass, I've got five RECON Marines that need a sergeant. One's short. One's an FNG. One's a pain in my ass. Reminds me of you, four years ago. And we can't split the other two up, not and keep them functional, not after Cavener. None of them are sergeants, but you're close enough for government work. They need eyes on MC471 before they send in the big guns so I'm dropping you six dirtside."

"Green?"

"Sergeant Kerr, I wouldn't send that kind of a *borig* out into a bar fight, let alone a shooting war."

Torin met bronze-coloured eyes and smiled in turn. "Then we'll have to see about winning a few bar fights before we leave, Captain."

✦ ✦ ✦

Six Marines waited for her in BR3, gathered around the briefing table— the five Captain di'Hirose had mentioned and Lieutenant Turrik. As Torin closed the hatch behind her, the lieutenant's nostril ridges flared and he headed toward her, hands outstretched.

"I wanted to tell you myself," he said, touching his fingertips to Torin's and huffing a breath toward her, "but the captain has to handle a field promotion so…" He shrugged, as bad at the Human gesture as most Krai. "I'll settle for being the first to congratulate you, Sergeant Kerr."

Torin nodded, careful to keep her teeth covered. The Krai, like most of the sentient species of the Confederation, recognized bared teeth for the threat it was. "Thank you, sir."

"The Corps' heading down the shitter if you're the best bet for a sergeant, Kerr."

"Some of us aren't quitters, Morrae."

Turrik stepped back out of the way as Morrae moved in, grabbed Torin and dragged her into a hug. "If I've got to go out one last time, I'm glad I'll be under someone who's got half a chance to get us out alive."

"Half a chance?" Torin protested as deep purple hair tried to weave through her basic Human brown. As di'Taykan hair was actually multiple sensory strands about fifteen centimetres long, it wasn't particularly successful.

"Three quarters. And speaking of being under someone…"

"Not the time, Morrae."

"Later then," she agreed, opening her arms, right hand rising to touch the pheromone masker at her throat.

The Taykan's di phase was the most enthusiastically non-discriminating species in known space and the pheromones they released made most of the other species enthusiastic participants. That wasn't a problem among the Taykan, but when they accepted the Elder Races' offer of the stars in exchange for fighting in a war those same Elder Races were too socially evolved to engage in—an offer both the Krai and the Humans had accepted as well—pheromone maskers became required during multi-species interaction and had become part of the Confederation Marine Corps uniform. While the Taykan couldn't entirely understand why anyone would want to say no, they were horrified by the thought of compelling an unwanted sexual interaction and complied.

Torin and Corporal Morrae di'Kyshto had gone through BRC together and after the brass shuffled for the strongest hand—there were no weak hands in RECON—had served together on multiple RECON teams. Had Morrae not made it clear she was out when her current contract ended, she'd have been Torin's chief competition for the sergeant's spot.

"Sergeant Kerr…" Morrae took her arm and turned her slightly to the left. "…this is Private Servik. He's *new*."

The private's nostril ridges closed about halfway. "I had the same training you did, Corporal."

"And he finished seventh in his class." Morrae's hair flipped out. "Had a bit of time in as a basic grunt before he managed it though. Sergeant Kerr finished second," she added, ignoring Servik's teeth.

He was so young. It hadn't been that long ago, but Torin didn't remember ever being that young. His upper lip rose, exposing a little more threat. "And you finished first, I suppose?"

"No. She didn't." Both Torin's hands clenched into fists. She forced them open. Logic said Corisho di'Varal had the same amount of blood in her as any Taykan, but it hadn't seemed that way on Cavener Station. Torin had seen other Marines bleed out. She'd never seen so much blood.

To his credit Servik understood Torin's tone, met her gaze, nodded, and looked away, faking interest in the table's inert surface.

Thinking of Cavener drew Torin's gaze to the two Marines at the far end of the table. Corporal Bannon Lembede had lost weight since she'd seen him last, his dark skin ashen where it stretched across his cheekbones, broad shoulders slumped. Psych had cleared him for duty. Torin wondered if pysch had looked into his eyes. Beside him, Lance Corporal Domini di'Naital sat rubbing his thumbs against his fingertips, his coral-coloured hair hanging limp and almost motionless. They'd been left on Cavener, piled in with the dead for the three days it took the Navy to fight past the blockade and release the Marines to take the station back. An energy pulse, hard contact, or gremlins had caused their HE suits to show no life signs on the network. Rumour had it that the sergeant who'd left them behind spent a lot of his time drunk.

Torin had been on teams with them both. She knew Bannon better than Domini, but only because they had done their close combat training together. Before Cavener, she'd have trusted them both to have her back. Now…

"Psych cleared them," Morrae murmured by her ear. "They've either got to go back out or get out. Neither of them wants to leave—either the Corps or each other—so psych's attached them at the hip. This trip's intended to ease them back in."

"Fuk you, Morrae." Bannon flipped her off. Although he couldn't possibly have heard the content, it was obvious who Morrae had been talking about. "Grats on the promotion, Torin. You deserve it."

Domini's hair gave a short flip. "Sergeant looks good on you."

One's short. One's an FNG. One's a pain in my ass, and we can't split the other two up, not and keep them functional.

That meant…

Torin turned toward PFC Mari Opizzi, who grinned, spread her arms, and said, "Leaving the best until last, Sergeant?"

They'd never been teamed together, but Torin had heard the smaller woman's laugh ring out through the mess, too large to be contained. She wasn't a lot taller than a Krai, with short, dark hair and dark eyes, and an expression Torin's aunties would have called *wicked*.

"Right then." Lieutenant Turrik thumbed the desk on and the image of planet appeared above it. "I'm not going to say MC471 is going to be *chrick*, because we all know if I do the operation'll go into the shitter before you lot leave orbit. That said, let's go over the plan."

+ + +

"First drop?"

"Third."

Torin hid a grin. "First two were training drops?" Servik didn't answer, but his nostril ridges told her everything she needed to know. "They don't know we're here so they won't be shooting at us. Getting to the ground alive is all on you."

"That's very comforting," Morrae said from her other side.

Fairly certain her initial reaction—driving her elbow into the di'Taykan's side—wasn't something sergeants did, Torin ignored her and said, "No difference between this drop and a training run until we make contact with the enemy."

Servik huffed out a breath. "Look Sarge, I get that you're—"

"Approaching drop zone." The Marine pilot at the controls of the VTA cut Servik off. *"Hatch control switching to DHC in three... two... one."*

"DHC has hatch control. Drop team, take position." Lieutenant Turrik stood, flipped his seat up, and spread the fingers of his right hand out over the control screen.

Heart pounding, Torin stood with her team.

"Drop team, sound off in position order."

She noted with some amusement that Servik matched his tone to the semi-bored responses of the other four. "Corp..." *Idiot.* "Sergeant Kerr ready."

The lieutenant raised his left hand in acknowledgement. "Hatch opening in three, two, one."

As each layer of the deck slid back, Torin felt the individual vibrations through the soles of her boots, the outer hull pulsing more powerfully than the other three. All Marine VTAs, Vacuum to Air shuttles, had an atmospheric hatch—essentially a hole through the lower hull for dropping supplies or personnel. Torin knew vacuum jockeys who refused to ride in the same compartment with it, but then the Navy's superstitions had superstitions. And vacuum jockeys tended toward prima donna.

"Drop team advance to drop position."

Torin checked the screen by the lieutenant's shoulder. The landing site used the edge of a heavily wooded area as cover from enemy scans; the trick was hitting the ground before hitting the trees.

Morrae shuffled forward, the toes of her drop sleeves out over the hole.

"Drop in three, two, one. Drop."

Bannon followed as Morrae's head cleared the hull, Domini behind him. Mari whooped as she dropped, then swore creatively as Servik dropped so close behind her, he nearly stood on her head.

"Gravity always wins, Sergeant."

"Not when it's fighting the Corps, Lieutenant."

Hands flat against her thighs, Torin banished a recent dream where she'd gotten stuck half in and half out of the VTA, and dropped, drop sleeve engaging the moment she cleared the exterior of the ship. Set to make a feet-first landing, the anti-gravity field extended up over her lower body—although, at just over four thousand metres up, it was doing little more than preventing her from accelerating past the point of no return. The line of dark green became trees, dark and light splotches became bushes and grass. After eight-five seconds, the power bar on the right side of her visor began to climb. Twenty seconds later she'd slowed enough to feel the difference.

Knees slightly bent, centre of balance low in her pelvic girdle, core tight…

A drop of water hit her arm with enough force to register on her visor, sleeve stiffening, cold spreading out from the impact site as her uniform's environmental controls went offline.

And a sudden flare of heat as they came back on again.

Wonder if that hit hard enough to ping the sergeant.

Sergeants fussed. It was what they did. Torin hated being fussed over.

You're the sergeant, you idiot.

The first four were on dirt. Servik stumbled and kept going, using the forward momentum. Half a metre above the ground, Torin's drop sleeve charge burnt out. She went almost to one knee as she hit, pushed off from a runner's crouch, and joined her team in under the trees, KC7 hanging from its shoulder strap, in position to fire from the hip if necessary.

A Green RECON was considered a failure if weapons were fired, but they were still Marines.

+ + +

"Better they get a brief burst of static than get their hands on the tech, right Sarge?" Mari grinned, igniting the self-destruct on her drop sleeve.

"SOP, Opizzi," Torin grumbled, dropping her own sleeve on the same bit of bare soil. "All in, Marines. Then, in case they send someone to check that *brief burst of static…*"

Mari gave her a sarcastic thumbs up.

"…Lembede clear the ground. Morrae and Opizzi check no one left a visible crater when they landed."

"I should go high." Servik had one boot undone.

"You should look up," Torin told him. They were under young conifers, five maybe six metres high, twenty centimetres in circumference. The Krai were arboreal and Torin knew Servik could get up these trees, even move between them, but thirty point twelve metres in, she pinged off a tree two point six metres around and approximately thirty-four metres high. Beyond that, they got bigger. Evergreens, they had a multitude of short branches over the upper seven or eight metres, with a lot of sky between them. "You can go high when we're stationary. While we're moving, you'll be on the ground."

"I'm Krai," Servik protested. "I know trees."

"I'm a sergeant. I'm well on my way to knowing everything, but if you tell me you'll be faster up top, you can go high."

He squinted up into the canopy, nostrils fluttering as he worked out distances, and knelt to secure his boot.

"I'm sorry, Private, I didn't hear that."

Nostril ridges almost closed, he straightened. "You were right, Sergeant Kerr, I'll be faster on the ground."

Ends of her hair flicking back and forth under her helmet, Morrae grinned at her over Servik's head. Torin held her gaze until she stopped.

They took a break twelve kilometres in, just past the halfway point where the huge trees had given way to a significantly smaller species. Although Servik had taken two strides for every one of theirs, he'd had no trouble keeping up. "The Krai," he told them, "have an almost mythical endurance."

"Good for you. The di'Taykan mythical endurance has nothing to do with running in full gear," Morrae panted, helmet cupped in the curve of her arm.

"It's light gear," Mari mocked, crossed hands resting on her KC.

Torin didn't catch Morrae's reply, voices dropping to a murmur of sound that could have been the breeze in the top of the enormous trees as she scanned the path ahead. It had begun to rise, twelve degrees now, twenty-seven about twelve metres out. Turning back toward the team, she scanned each of them, amazed at the information a sergeant could access. Bannon's heart rate was up. Morrae and Domini had both cracked their environmental controls down to the coolest setting. Mari…

"Opizzi, are you chewing gum?"

"Big believer in minty-fresh breath, Sarge."

"If you choke on it…"

"Fully capable of running and chewing gum, Sarge."

"Your potential funeral." Mari was a highly trained adult. Torin wasn't going to challenge her belief in her capabilities, although she half thought she should. Sergeant Narr would've told her to spit it out.

But Sergeant Narr wasn't here.

She was.

"We're approaching ten klicks out. Shut down tech." Long-range scanners were shit through tree-cover, but at this point, were she the enemy, Torin would have set a random pattern of short-range scanners in the trees. High odds, Morrae and Domini had set their EC so low in anticipation of the order to shut down. Even inert, their combats would contain the lower temperature for the next five or six kilometres. Ambient temperature was well within di'Taykan tolerances, but they preferred to be cool.

Two klicks out, she could hear machinery—no surprise, the enemy had taken a mining colony. Logic, as much as it could be applied cross-culturally, said they'd then begin mining.

Domini, to her left, touched her arm. When Torin turned, he pointed to Bannon on *his* left and two paces behind.

"EMP," Bannon explained quietly when the other five gathered around the half-metre-high, metallic pillar. "Goes off every twelve seconds."

Morrae's hair lifted. "Someone out there has twelve fingers. Or four fingers per hand and three hands."

"Given the spread, odds are high there's another every four or five metres." Bannon pulled the pillar out of the ground, pushed in the retractable spike, tugged it out again. "We ran into these things on Fallon when I was with the 3/7. As far as the squint squad could tell, it's just an EMP—no looking, no listening."

"They think taking out our tech will stop us?" Mari snorted. "Way to not pay attention."

"Right. They should know that won't work." Servik's nostril ridges closed. "We've been kicking their asses for centuries. We could kick their asses naked with a knife in our teeth."

Mari snorted again. "That's a stupid place to carry a knife, new guy."

"Space is big," Torin's tone cut Servik's response off at the first syllable, although, she silently acknowledged, they were both right. Even the KCs were based on old tech, a chemical explosion propelling a solid at high speed, impervious to distant interference and weighted to make a decent club in case the ammo ran out. "Maybe this lot have never had their asses kicked."

"New species?" Bannon asked, rising out of a squat.

"Could be."

The Others, the name the media had given the unnamed enemy, had at least seven species fighting with unconfirmed rumours of another two. The Confederation had three: Humans, di'Taykan, and Krai. The Others had invaded Confederation space and had sent diplomatic envoys back in pieces. They took no prisoners, and when captured, self-destructed, taking as many of their captors with them as possible. No one knew why the Others continued to attack.

In general, Torin amended silently. In specific, the reasons behind this particular attack were clear.

"They've left nothing in orbit. We wouldn't have known they were this far in had someone in the colony not squeezed off a message just before they blew the system. Took a little over five hours for that message to get to the Susumi satellite by the jump point, close to five more before some serley dirin avirrk at company headquarters bothered to check the untagged file. Company to Parliament to the Ministry of Defence to us—another thirteen hours. And most of that was distance. Now, what could get those lard-asses up and moving at speed?" Lieutenant Turrik spread his hands. *"Panite. The same panite that's an essential component of Susumi tech. There's a shitload of it on MC471 and the enemy wants it as much as we do. Brass doesn't like the whole sneaking-around, no-orbital-defences setup, assumes it's a trap, so we need to get eyes on without tipping them off."*

"Opizzi, go right. Domini, go left. Let's make sure they've set a perimeter and this isn't a forgotten piece of tech."

"Why would they have…" Mari began, took a look at Torin, and raised a hand. "Going right, Sergeant."

"Sergeant face," Morrae murmured.

Torin ducked a frog/beetle leaping to a new tree and let that be her response, suspecting that a new posting as a sergeant would be easier than dealing with Marines who'd known her for years.

Fuk easy.

EMPs to the right and left were four point seven metres out and identical to the one Bannon had found.

An EMP perimeter wasn't a military defence. Who or what had the Others sent in?

Half a kilometre out, Torin heard shouting over the grumble of the big machines. Strange how entitled impatience sounded the same from most species. She could smell heated metal.

At a hundred metres, she left the team in a protected hollow— protected because it had five Marines in it—and belly-crawled out into the low brush that bordered the large clearing where the mining colony had been.

"Okay, if panite crystals are both rare and essential," Mari spun the hard-light image of MC471, "why wasn't the Corps dirtside protecting the mine?"

"Full disclosure. If the military goes out, the media has to be informed."

"Fukking media," Bannon muttered.

The lieutenant flared his nostrils in agreement. "One company can't claim an entire planet so the only way to keep the competition out is to keep the news of the find out of the media. No media, no Marines, and odds are this'll be what gets the bill through Parliament that gives the government control of panite mines."

"No bet," Torin muttered.

The mining colony had been cooked. Four shuttles with thermal engines had simply landed in any area approximately the right size. Using a broad definition of approximately. The sluice mine at the base of the ridge would have given no shelter to the miners.

Three of the four shuttles had been partially dismantled.

As Torin watched, a machine lifted the centre section out of the of the fourth, set it into the ground like an enormous tube with only the top two metres showing, and began packing dirt around it. She could see two protruding tubes on the other side of the clearing, and assumed the fourth was out there somewhere.

She couldn't see any of the enemy through the billowing dust clouds, although she could hear the occasional shouted instruction.

"We can't see shit from here," she said when she rejoined the team. "What's the pin say?"

"They're not scanning." Bannon dropped the pin back into a pouch on his webbing—if equipment wasn't Marine-resistant, it didn't make it out into the field. "And there's enough noise, they'll never notice the PCUs this close in. Even if they were looking."

"Do they think we aren't going to take this place back?" Servik demanded.

Domini shook his head, his hair moving in the opposite direction. "They think we don't know they're here."

"Ignorance is a bad defence."

"Alien." Mari snorted. "They could have new tech we can't read."

Servik snorted back at her. "That they've developed a new power source for?"

"Possible."

"Unlikely. Sarge?"

"Alien or not, some things say military and none of those things are evident." Torin thumbed her internal tech back on. "We'll use internals and personal communication only. No scanners. No slates. If you have to move out past the hundred-metre mark, power down. Domini, Lambede, get to the top of the ridge. Servik, find the closest tree with the best view. Not on the ridge," she added when he opened his mouth. "Morrae, Opizzi, you're with me on the perimeter. Back here…" She glanced up at the sun and considered how fast a thirty-one-hour day would move it. "…in ninety minutes."

"That's not a lot of time," Morrae began.

Torin cut her off. "If they can't get to the top of the ridge in half an hour, I'll need to check their med alert because their legs are probably broken." It took her a moment to identify the sound as Bannon snickering and she damped down a surge of pride. She was his sergeant, he was hers, and helping his mental stability was part of her job. "Ninety minutes will give us enough daylight to get back to EP."

"Wait." Servik's hands tightened on his KC. "We're just going to look around and leave?"

Mari grinned broadly enough to show molars. "Welcome to RECON, new guy."

✦ ✦ ✦

The enemy had maintained the perimeter of the mining colony—or at least not extended beyond it—and while Torin couldn't identify what they were building, she could tell they were working to a deadline. All the colony's large equipment was in use, and *move your ass* sounded the same in most languages. Ass optional.

As Opizzi joined Torin, and Morrae crouched behind the charred remains of a set of temporary quarters, Torin ran for the next secure location. Dropped to one knee, brought up her weapon, and looked around a piece of twisted metal that had been a two-seater mule. "I've found some of the miners."

"Are they alive?" Morrae asked. Torin could hear the others waiting for her answer.

"No." She looked at the pile of burnt and broken pieces, breathing shallowly through her teeth, and thanked whoever was looking after this part of the universe that she'd sent Bannon and Domini up to the top of the ridge. Psych hadn't said, *"Don't let them crawl up to a heap of corpses that might remind them of the heap of corpses they were buried under,"* but Torin assumed that was understood.

"Think it's all of them?"

There were bodies on the top of the pile that hadn't been taken out in the shuttle landings. Actual bodies, not crisped body parts.

"Odds are." The carrion insects covering the pile made a constant background buzz, higher pitched than the growl of the machinery. "If any survivors FFP'd out of here, they're not our problem."

✦ ✦ ✦

"Bugs and Brains," Domini told them. Bannon grunted agreement.

Servik nodded. "Yeah, that's what I saw too. Plus a couple of Stick-figures, holding what looked like slates. In charge, maybe?"

"Maybe."

The Bugs looked like very large cockroaches. Brains were what the Corps called the aliens with the overly large heads even though that wasn't where their brains were located. Stick-figures were tall and thin and probably not mammals. Marine nomenclature tended to be unimaginative. Of the three, Torin had only seen the Bugs in battle, where *seen* referred to a body dropping from a blown fighter and smashing into damp shards on impact. One of the shards had cut a three-centimetre line across the back of her left hand so she counted it.

No one had spotted anything resembling a military presence.

"Briefing said there was only one jump point right?" Helmet in her hand, Morrae fluffed out her hair. Sergeant Narr would have told her to put the helmet back on, but they were in no immediate danger so Torin let it go. "Even if they went back through the same point," she continued, "there'd be a second energy signature. Where's the ship they jumped in on?"

"Taking a scenic tour of the system," Mari offered around a mouthful of protein bar.

"What if they came in the VTAs?"

Bannon frowned. "Can you take a VTA through Susumi?"

"Not ours," Torin told him.

Morrae's hair swept forward and back. "One jump point, remember? Not four."

"So one Susumi engine..." One Susumi engine, Torin repeated silently and finished the thought aloud. "All four shuttles attached to it."

"Can they do that?" Mari looked around the group. "Can people survive Susumi space in a VTA?"

All eyes ended up on Torin, who shrugged. "Do I look like a Susumi engineer?"

"That." The pale green of Servik's mottling darkened as all eyes turned to him. "No, not you, Sarge. It's just... I spent some time with a Susumi engineer a while ago. Navy. Their ship was at Ventris for repairs and she did the whole *freak the grunt out by climbing through a Susumi engine with him* thing. That's what the Others are building in those VTA sections. Susumi engines. It's why they used four VTAs for less than twenty lifeforms. They were packed with parts."

Machinery grumbled up on the plateau. Insects buzzed. Creatures unseen complained loudly up in the canopy.

Someone had to say it and Torin got the big bucks. Or would when her raise came through. "They're going to take the whole planet through Susumi space."

Servik shrugged. Awkwardly. "They're going to try."

"Because it's full of panite." Mari unwrapped another protein bar. "If they're going to the effort, I'm guessing more full crystals than shards. What?" she demanded as group attention shifted to her. "New guy's not the only one to knock boots with a Susumi engineer."

After a moment, Morrae drew in a deep breath and said, "Okay, you may be able to shield a VTA to survive Susumi space, but there's no way they'll survive on the surface of a planet. Do they think the atmosphere's going to go along for the ride?"

"No, they think they're going to die." Torin couldn't decide if that was an admirable sacrifice or a stupid waste of life. "The only thing that has to survive is the mineral."

"Alien," Bannon grunted. "What are the odds their Susumi engines look like ours?"

"Function, form," she said absently. "Servik, how close to finished did they look?"

"One's done. They've got the externals on—the cover and, I don't know… fins. Two and three have the externals standing by. Four…"

Up on the plateau, two of the big machines roared out in harmony.

Torin raised a hand to hold everyone in place, crawled up, and back down. "Four just had the main parts of the engine set in."

"So what do we do?"

Her choice. The enemy was attempting to steal the mineral that allowed ships and satellites to fold space. To give the Others an advantage that could, if not turn the tide of the war—Torin had no idea if the tide was ebbing or flowing, that wasn't her job—could definitely kill a lot more Marines.

"We get back to pickup, hit vacuum, squeeze a message through, jump a battle cruiser…"

She was thinking out loud. When Susumi engines blew, interesting things happened. Where interesting was seldom good. Or survivable. Four enormous Susumi engines, big enough to move a planet. It could get *very* interesting.

No taking them out from orbit.

"The Marines land. The Others take a shot at making the jump with three working engines." She swept a flat gaze around her team. "They're already fated to die. Why not see how many of the enemy they can take with them?"

Mari spread her hands. "So?"

"So we take them out."

"From the ridge?" Bannon asked, thumb rubbing his KC, gaze shadowed.

Domini had the best range scores, but given the distance, even Servik could make a kill shot from the ridge. Except the Bugs and Brains and Stick-figures were civilians. "Not the people. The engines."

"Torin…"

She turned toward Morrae and waited.

Morrae sighed. "Sergeant Kerr, we can't take out the engines with a seven. Maybe if we had boomers and a shitload of luck, but even then we'd have to hit all four engines simultaneously because if we give that lot time to start one up, they probably will."

"We don't shoot civilians."

Her hair flattened. "Civilians die in wars all the time."

Torin lifted her upper lip off her teeth, vaguely aware of Servik's nose ridges slamming shut. "Not what I said. I said, we don't shoot civilians."

"Well, yay us." Mari twirled a finger in the air. "We're light. Light doesn't come with demo charges."

"Really?" Torin sighed. "Who here isn't packing demo charges? Servik?" He was new to RECON. There was a chance.

"Uh, I've got seven, Sarge."

"Overkill, new guy." Mari patted her pouches. "Four's fine."

"Not that it matters—we can't blow the engines. We use the EMPs."

Bannon shook his head. "Those tubes are pieces of a VTA. If you're saying we use the perimeter EMPs, they're not strong enough to penetrate."

"Then we don't shoot through, we shoot down into the tubes."

Mari opened her mouth, but Morrae cut her off. "You want us to grab the enemy's perimeter defences, get into their compound, get to the top of a vertical VTA exterior, and fire a low-level EMP down into a giant Susumi engine? They may not be keeping an eye on their surroundings, but they'll be keeping a close eye on those engines, and when I say eye, I don't just mean physical eyes. Those engines are the only things on this planet that matter to them. That's where their surveillance will be aimed."

Torin folded her arms. "Your point?"

"We'll die. More importantly, we'll fail, and we'll die."

Bannon looked over at Domini, who shrugged, making nihilism look graceful.

"One." Torin raised a finger. "We're RECON. Getting in and out without being seen is what we do. It's what *you* do for another three tendays."

Morrae's hair flipped up, reconsidered and fell.

"Two." A second finger. "They're scientists and engineers. I think we can take them."

Morrae's eyes, locked on hers, darkened until the purple shaded into black.

"And three. Put your damned helmet on."

The creatures in the canopy shrieked again. A beetle/frog passed through Torin's peripheral vision. Up on the plateau, mining machines grumbled and growled through tasks they'd never been designed for. Morrae's hair was completely still.

She put on her helmet and dropped her gaze. "What if they're military scientists?"

"Then they're crap at the military part of it. Opizzi, Servik, Domini, go grab six EMPs. Two for backup," Torin added before Mari could point out that one EMP per tube would be enough. Squatting, she scuffed a bit of dirt clear with the edge of her hand. "Map time. Lambede, you were up above. Morrae details at ground level."

✦ ✦ ✦

Torin tapped her front teeth with her thumbnail and marked the positions of the pole lights out on the plateau. Most species had vision problems at dawn and dusk. The imaginations that had helped sentience evolve filled the shadows with personal demons, and kept gazes averted. They could use that.

The machines were parked. Done for the day. The plateau was quiet.

She could see two drones about three metres up over two of the open tubes. Zoom showed them focused down into the tubes where Bannon and Domini had seen both Brains and Bugs working. As long as they reached the top without attracting the drones' attention, they could take them out with the EMPs, then shoot down into the tube as they fell.

Six Marines. Four engines.

Servik on the finished engine. It was complete, so there was no action around it.

"Because I'm new."

"Because you're Krai. With the cap, there's an extra three metres to climb."

Morrae on the tube without the drones.

"No drones because I'm short?"

"No drones because you're fine on your own."

Bannon and Domini on tube three.

They'd nodded, simultaneously. Right at that moment, Torin liked them best.

Mari on tube four with Torin.

"Because I'm not fine on my own?"

"Because you weigh less than sixty kilos. If I have to heave anyone's ass up the outside of a VTA, I'd rather it was yours."

"That's the nicest thing you've ever said to me, Sarge."

"Don't get used to it, Opizzi."

As the light levels dropped, the pole lights began to glow. Not enough to make a difference, not yet…

"Marines."

Mari shifted on her left.

"Ready." Torin dug the toe of her boot into the dirt. "Go."

The tops of tubes holding the Susumi engines were only two metres above ground. Getting to the top wouldn't be a problem, both di'Taykan and Bannon were close to that height and Torin was only eighteen centimetres shorter. *Up* wasn't the problem, getting there was.

Her visor pinged tube number four at three hundred and six point one seven metres. Having watched the enormous section lifted and put in place, her brain insisted it was closer, that it couldn't be as big as it was. In times like this, she'd learned to trust her visor. Bent almost double, combats losing the green and shifting to match the charred and torn-up ground, she raced toward tube four. Mari ran a metre back to her left.

The footing sucked. Hard, soft, firm, unstable—all in the same stride. The trip through the forest had been like running a track in comparison. As her visor pinged a hundred metres, they reached the ground packed in around the tube and her right boot hit with a solid thud. The enemy had mixed something in to solidify it, something other than the bits burnt off miners too small to gather up.

Torin picked up speed.

"One, going up."

"Three, going up."

Her fingers were almost touching the rough, grey side of the VTA when a Stick-figure walked around the curve, peering into what Torin assumed was a slate.

They didn't see her until she was less than an arm's length away. She couldn't remember where the vital parts were on Stick-figures, but visible sensory organs were up top so she hit them just below.

"Two, going up."

The Stick-figure folded. Literally.

"How many joints does that fukker have?" Mari wondered.

Torin hooked her fingers over the edge of the tube. "Four, going up. Move it, Opizzi."

A boot on her thigh, the second on her shoulder, and Mari crouched on the top of the curve. VTAs went vacuum to air and their hulls were half a metre thick.

"Fukking fuk! The drones shoot darts! I'm okay; vest stopped it."

"Helmet stops it too."

"And that's why you keep it on." Torin pulled herself up…

"Why such weak darts?"

… tucked her boots between her hands…

"For birds? Flying lizards?"

"Less chatter!" ...and levelled her EMP in time to see Mari fly backwards, a line of crimson drops arcing out from her face as she fell.

"One, done. Fire until the lights stay out."

Both drones got caught in the pulse, lost power, and dropped. The three Brains inside the tube looked up.

"What do the lights mean?"

"How should I know? They always mean something."

The EMP took twelve seconds to charge.

"Two, done."

Torin could see the Brains' mouths move. She assumed it was their mouths.

"Four! Incoming drone."

If she took out the drone, it would be another twelve seconds...

The drone exploded.

Torin turned far enough to see Mari pick up another rock, blood dribbling from the cut in her cheek.

"College ball!" she yelled. "Go Quasars!"

Two of the Brains in four shouted out tangled strings of sound. The third crouched with their hands over their head.

Torin aimed the EMP at the highest concentration of light. Felt the pillar vibrate.

The clump of lights went out. In ones and twos, the rest of the lights flickered, dimmed, and went dark. She waited twelve seconds. The dark held.

"Four, done." She dropped to the ground. "What's the hold-up, Three?"

"Lights are in clusters of four, Sarge. Multiple clusters of four."

"We take out one set and another set comes on."

Or psych was wrong and Bannon and Domini were taking their time, hoping the enemy would end it for them.

"Seven, no, nine drones heading to your position, Three!" The black ovals against the sky were too far away for Torin to take out with the EMP. She dropped it and swung her KC around. "Lock and load, people. There's no Susumi tech in those drones."

Two shots. Two drones exploded.

"Fuk you, Morrae," Torin muttered before she remembered she

was a sergeant and sergeants didn't compete with their corporals. The snicker suggested Morrae had heard her anyway. She squeezed off a round, clipped a drone, and sent it spinning. "They're a bit…"

The roar of a great beast drowned her out.

"Holy fuk."

Torin had to agree. The civilians they couldn't shoot weren't the problem. The civilians they couldn't shoot operating a machine only slightly smaller than the almost-crane that had lifted the VTA sections, that was a problem.

Heading for tube three, a protruding muzzle wobbled left then right, then cut a trench in the ground with a stream of pressurized air.

"Can anyone get a shot at the driver?" Torin flattened against the side of tube four, as a cloud of ash and dust billowed by.

"I'm not sure there is a driver."

"A remote driver is still a driver!"

"Goggles," she snapped at Mari, yanked her own plastic lenses down out of her helmet, and charged back around the corner. "Lambede! Domini! Down!"

"Twelve seconds, Sarge!"

A small dark figure leapt from the top of tube one onto the top of the machine.

"Servik!

"They haven't got twelve seconds!"

"What the hell is he doing?"

Mari stepped up beside her. "Proving himself."

"Servik! Get clear! That's an order!"

"I can take out the—"

As well as pressurized air to expose the panite crystals on the side of the ridge, the machine had multiple claws to pick them up. The operator seemed to have no idea what they were doing, the arms flailed wildly against the bulk of the machine, scraping metal against metal.

Metal against Krai.

Servik fell forward.

Hit the ground in front of a tread.

Krai could take a lot of punishment.

Torin saw his hand slide into his vest.

"Fire in the hole."

His lips drew back off his teeth.

The tread rolled forward.

Torin turned, saw Mari's eyes widen. Torin hit the ground beside her, behind tube four with the heels of her hands pressed into her ears as the world rocked with the force of the explosion.

Muffled impacts rang out a staccato beat as pieces of the machine hit the tube. Someone might have screamed. It wasn't Servik. Bones thrumming with the vibrations, Torin pressed herself into the earth. When the vibrations stopped, she uncovered her ears.

As the echoes of the report died, she stood, held a hand down to Mari and hauled the smaller woman up onto her feet.

Mari took a deep breath, let it out slowly, looked at Torin and said, "Seven demo charges?"

"Odds are he set off a few stored in the machine."

She kicked at a fist-sized hunk of twisted metal. "You think?"

It was the only piece that had gone past tube four. The other side…

The other side looked like it had gone through an artillery barrage.

"Marines, sound off."

"MORRAE."

"Lambede."

"Domini."

"Opizzi."

"HEY, JUST SO YOU KNOW, I CAN'T HEAR SHIT."

Temporary deafness due to concussive force she could work with. "Domini, check Morrae."

"I've got her, Sarge."

"Sarge."

She opened her eyes to see a Bug scuttle out into the open, around a loop of wet tread. Over the dust and scorched metal and burnt plastic, she thought she could smell lemon furniture polish.

The Bug's back end rose as the rear legs kept moving after the front had stopped.

"Hold your fire." Torin pushed the muzzle of Mari's KC toward the ground as she walked forward.

"Sarge?"

"I said, hold your fire. Don't make me repeat it again."

The Bug's mandibles clattered together.

"If I were you," Torin said, focusing on the middle pair of eyes, "I'd run. Gather up the rest of the scientists and engineers and what-have-you and disappear into the trees. The Corps will be here shortly to gather you up—or your people will, six of one, I guess—but either of them will be less likely to shoot you."

The mandibles clattered again.

Torin held up her left hand, the right around the trigger guard of her KC. She pointed two fingers toward the ground and made a running motion. "Run. Do you understand?" She used the two fingers to point at what was left of the machine. "You can't win. You should run."

Feathered antennae dipped. The Bug reared, plucked a metal rectangle off the overlapping scales on their chest, and chattered into it. Two Brains supporting the third climbed out of tube four and ran for the trees.

"They're leaving, Sarge."

"Got a group heading out on this side as well."

Two or three days later — although Torin's visor insisted she'd only been standing there for twenty-two minutes — the Bug's rectangle warbled. If Torin had to guess, she'd say the Bug had just been informed that all personnel were safely away. The Bug dropped all legs back in contact with the ground, dipped their antennae again, and ran.

"That machine Servik blew up? It wasn't the only machine on site," Mari said softly, as Torin's shoulders relaxed. "It wasn't even the biggest. And they still outnumber us if they decide to come back and take another shot."

Torin looked around at the destruction. "They're civilians. Resisting is one thing, but taking another shot isn't part of their job."

+ + +

Krai bones and teeth were among the strongest substances in known space. Most of Servik's bones and teeth were intact.

Torin checked the seals on the body bag and stepped back.

"Fraishen sha AREN. Valynk SHA haren." Morrae's hearing hadn't quite returned, but she was the ranking di'Taykan.

Servik had been the only Krai. Torin bit a piece of skin off the side of her finger. She was a sergeant now. *"Kai danic dur kadir. Kri ta chrikdan."*

That made Bannon the ranking Human. "We will not forget. We will not fail you."

Torin sent the command. The bag stiffened and flattened.

The ash fit into a small cylinder that slid into one of the measured spaces inside the senior NCO's vest. Inside Torin's vest. Marines didn't leave Marines behind. It felt…

Heavy.

She wanted to turn to Bannon and Domini and tell them they had to get past Cavener. They had to live for Servik now. She didn't.

"So back to the evac point, Sarge?"

Torin unhooked the CFM and twisted it on. "Fuk that. They can pick us up here."

+ + +

"Seriously? Garden design?"

Morrae grinned, her hair lifting. "Family business. Beats farming."

Torin thought of the manure pile outside the barn on her parent's farm. "No argument from me."

They stepped back as a trio of officers hurried past them into the shuttle. Maintained perfectly neutral faces as the two lieutenants almost jammed shoulder to shoulder in the hatch.

"When do you leave for Ventris?"

"Next threesday." Torin couldn't decide if she was looking forward to it or not, so, mostly, she didn't think about.

Morrae adjusted her crimson scarf, opened her mouth, and was drowned out by the final boarding call. A di'Taykan shrug was as graceful as everything else the di'Taykan did. "That's for me."

The hug lasted longer than it might have, less long than it could have with a di'Taykan involved.

"Stay in touch," Torin told her. "I don't know many civilians."

"You too. I don't know many sergeants." She stepped back into the hatch. "Seems like you've got the hang of it though."

Torin touched the spot near her hip where Servik's cylinder had slid into her vest. "Yeah, seems like I do."

I first worked with Curtis C. Chen on the anthology Mission: Tomorrow, *for which he wrote a fun near-future space story. Since then, he's launched a career as a novelist, with his first novel,* Waypoint Kangaroo, *becoming both a 2017 Locus Awards and Endeavor Award Finalist. Superspy Kangaroo is much like James Bond and other secret agents except for one thing: "the pocket," an interdimensional portal that opens to an empty, seemingly infinite parallel universe. Set in a future where Earth and Mars are in a fragile peace after war, spies like Kangaroo have to walk a delicate line to avoid upsetting the balance and reigniting old conflicts. Chen's story for us is a prequel story about how a teenage Kangaroo first meets his Q-like tech guru, Oliver Graves.*

AUTHOR'S NOTE: *"Fire in the Pocket" takes place several years before the events of* Waypoint Kangaroo *(the first book in the series), and shows the first meetings between engineer Oliver Graves and two of his spy agency associates: Director of Operations Paul "Lasher" Tarkington, and the superpowered secret agent known only by his code name, KANGAROO.*

If you thought Kangaroo was a pain in Oliver's neck in the novels, just wait until you see what "K" was like as a teenager…

FIRE IN THE POCKET
A KANGAROO STORY

CURTIS C. CHEN

The apartment was cold and dark and empty. Oliver almost called out when he closed the door, and had to remind himself that there was nobody waiting for him at home anymore. He wondered how long it would be before the habit faded.

"Welcome home, Doctor Graves," said a gravelly voice.

Oliver yanked open the drawer of the table by the door and reached inside. The pistol was missing. He grabbed the letter opener instead and slapped at the light switch on the wall.

The living room lights came on, revealing a dark-haired man, graying at the temples, wearing a tweed three-piece suit. He sat in Oliver's armchair. His hands were raised next to his shoulders. One hand held Oliver's pistol, slide locked back to show it was not loaded. The other hand held the empty magazine.

"Who the bloody hell are you?" Oliver said. He couldn't decide whether he should advance toward the stranger, or duck into the kitchen and look for a better weapon, or reach for his phone to make an emergency call.

"Just a fellow firearms enthusiast," the stranger said, nodding at the pistol in his right hand. "Tell me, why is a materials engineer with a doctorate in physics so interested in keeping and modifying his own small arms?"

"I like working with my hands," Oliver said.

"You could build ships in bottles."

"I also enjoy loud noises."

"More to the point," the stranger said, squinting at Oliver, "why would you keep the gun that your brother used to kill himself?"

Oliver gripped the letter opener tighter.

"What kind of a person does that?" the stranger asked.

"I want to know who you are and what you're doing in my flat."

"I work for the United States government." The stranger slowly lowered his arms and put the empty pistol and magazine on the coffee table. "And I'm in need of some technical expertise."

"You're a spy," Oliver said.

The stranger's mouth twitched. "Not exactly."

"And I'm not exactly looking for a job."

"You resigned from Bradford Macro-Composites this morning," the stranger said. "It was either that or face a civil lawsuit. You won't receive any severance pay, and more importantly, if you spend too much time alone in this apartment, you will go mad with grief."

Oliver felt the emptiness in the pit of his stomach yawning open. The wall behind the stranger displayed the default screensaver, a vacant beach at sunset overlaid with a clock and calendar. Had it really been only two months since Robbie's death? It felt so much longer. Oliver couldn't summon a memory of the last day he'd felt in the least bit happy.

The stranger was right. An arrogant, presumptuous scofflaw, maybe, but still right.

"What do I call you?" Oliver asked.

"I'm Paul Tarkington," the stranger said.

"And what are you actually offering, Mr. Tarkington?"

Paul smiled.

✦ ✦ ✦

Half a year later, Oliver sat in a state-of-the-art secure conference room, sipping his morning coffee and waiting for the daily debate to subside. He could always count on his three lab assistants to have big ideas and bigger egos.

"I've got a new battery design," Karen said, her dark eyes twinkling.

"Here we go again." Raquel shrugged her broad shoulders.

"Shut up." Karen punched Raquel on the arm, then touched her left thumb to one of the data ports in the conference table. The optical storage mesh bonded to the keratin in her thumbnail glowed as the tabletop downloaded her files, and then the wall display lit up with a series of schematics.

"Wait, you're putting the heaters *in the magazine* now?" Philip said incredulously. His mouth hung open beneath his pencil-thin mustache.

"It's the only place we need them," Karen said. "We've gotten rid of lubricants with the new composites, so the mechanisms won't suffer from frost lock. The only thing that still cares about temperature is the chemical propellant inside the cartridges."

"Yeah, and if it gets too hot in there, *kaboom*," Raquel said. "I still say we should revisit my coilgun designs."

"Again with the coilguns!" Karen threw up her hands. "Did you even read the spec?"

"If we're making a weapon for use in outer space, a coilgun is much more practical than this Frankenstein refit."

"You're assuming it's outer space," Karen said. "What if it's Antarctica? Or the inside of a supercooled particle accelerator?"

"Yeah, 'cause you're really going to want firearms in there," Raquel said.

"All right," Oliver said. His coffee was getting cold. "We're not having this argument again. We've already spent five months developing cold-resistant composites for our 'Franken-gun,' and more to the point, our requirements specify that the weapon must use standard NATO ammunition." He nodded at Karen. "Tell us about your new battery."

"Electrostatic nanocapacitors." She touched the table surface, and the display zoomed in on a series of alternating vertical lines. "We store electrical charge directly on the surfaces of two conductors. No chemicals or moving parts. High power, fast recharge."

"And low energy density," Philip said. "I've played with these before. How are you going to generate enough heat for the whole magazine?"

"We don't have to," Karen said. "We just need to keep the chamber and the first round warmed up. The heat from firing that round feeds a thermocouple that recharges the battery and pushes the heat envelope down."

"This gets better and better," Raquel said. "How do you intend to regulate temperature if the operator gets trigger-happy and overloads the capacitors?"

"Way ahead of you." The display changed to a schematic of the pistol itself. "We add flanges just below the breach to vent excess gas—"

"Great! More moving parts!"

"Relax. They're electrically deflected."

"More energy requirements!"

"So what's your bright idea, smarty-pants? And don't say coilgun."

"But your battery would be perfect for—"

Karen slapped a hand over Raquel's mouth. "Since nobody seems to have any better proposals, Oliver, can I get some time on the salad shooter to build this thing?"

Raquel mumbled something unintelligible into Karen's palm.

"What do you think, Philip?" Oliver asked.

"Couldn't hurt," Philip said. "We're not going to know what the output curves look like until we have a prototype. And we need *something* to deal with the temperature issue."

"Very well. I'll get you the fab time, Karen," Oliver said. "Go work up your control files. And take Raquel with you."

"What? Why?"

"She'll be highly motivated to help you construct an efficient battery," Oliver said, "since she'll be able to include it in her coilgun proposal for the Outer Space Service."

Karen sneered at Raquel. "Traitor."

Raquel shrugged. "I seem to have a lot of free time these days."

After they had left, Philip said, "Oliver, I need to talk to you about something."

"You're leaving the project," Oliver said.

Philip looked startled. "How did you know?"

"It only makes sense. We've finished practically all the materials development, and the SALD fab is working perfectly." Philip's design for a single-atomic-layer-deposition 3D printer would revolutionize manufacturing—if the US government ever declassified it. "I appreciate your loyalty in joining me here, Philip, but I always knew you'd leave. God knows this agency can't compete with corporate salaries."

Philip smiled. "Actually, I'm taking a teaching position at University of Maryland."

"Ah. Fame instead of fortune." Oliver nodded. "Thank goodness. I was afraid you might be going back to Bradford."

"I'm pretty sure we both burned all our bridges when we left."

Oliver offered his hand, and Philip shook it. "Good luck. Not that you'll need it."

"Thanks for everything." Philip took a step toward the door, then stopped and turned around. "Sorry, just one more thing. I wasn't sure I should tell you, but I'd feel terrible if you thought I'd been hiding anything from you—"

"Karen and Raquel," Oliver said. "I know. They're leaving too."

Philip frowned. "How did you—? I mean, sure, they've been getting more affectionate in public, but—"

"Karen's been wearing the engagement ring," Oliver said. "Not here at work, but everywhere else. The tan line on her finger is starting to show. And once they're hitched, OSS is going to recall Raquel to duty and deploy both of them to, I would imagine, some manner of deep space research vessel." He shook his head. "God, I hope they decide to elope. I'm not sure I could handle going to their wedding."

Philip chuckled. "You really need to get out more."

He walked out, leaving Oliver alone in the room. All alone. Everyone was leaving him again. Like his parents had left. Like Robbie had.

It took a few minutes for the tightness in Oliver's chest and stomach to go away.

+ + +

"I need more people," Oliver said.

Paul looked up from the report on his desk. He removed his reading glasses and stared at Oliver with eyes the color of pale blue ice. "No, you don't."

"I'm losing all of my research assistants next week," Oliver said. "Do you expect me to complete this project on my own?"

"Yes," Paul said without hesitation.

Oliver resisted the urge to grab the report off Paul's desk and fling it at the wall. "We've only test-fired the prototype under controlled lab conditions."

"And I'm told it worked very well."

"Something will go wrong in the field," Oliver said. "And when it does, I'll need a team to help me redesign and rebuild the prototype."

Paul shook his head. "I'm afraid we haven't the budget for that."

"The military isn't willing to overspend for a useless weapon? I don't believe it."

"We are not the military," Paul said. "And you've worked for seven months without a result."

"My lab has invented materials that will fundamentally alter spacecraft design principles, and electronic components that can function near absolute zero. Whatever shell corporation the agency has set up is going to make a bloody fortune licensing our technologies throughout the Solar System."

"Yes, and you'll receive a lovely Christmas bonus," Paul said, "but that is not the result I require."

"Are you ever going to tell me what I'm *actually* doing here?" Oliver asked. "All this can't possibly be just to design a handgun that can be stored and operated in hard vacuum. What are these components actually going to be used for?"

"I haven't been lying to you, Oliver," Paul said. "The project requirements specified exactly what we need. Now, are you ready to release the prototype for field testing? Or would you like to wait until you alone are held responsible for its performance?"

Oliver gritted his teeth. "I'll have the prototype ready for transport tomorrow morning."

"Good," Paul said, going back to his report. "I'll send the operator to pick it up. His code name is Kangaroo."

+ + +

"Doctor Oliver Graves?"

The young man standing in Oliver's doorway couldn't have been more than twenty years old. Wide eyes, darker than Karen's, stared out from a boyish face.

He didn't look a thing like Robbie—his brown skin was hereditary, not a suntan, for one—but he had the same youthful, innocent gaze. Oliver couldn't speak for a moment. Then he had to look away before too many memories came flooding back.

"Yes," Oliver said. "May I help you?"

The young man held out a requisition form. His slender fingers were too smooth to be a soldier's. "I'm Kangaroo. I'm here to collect the prototype."

Oliver took the form. "You're the operator?"

"The one and only." Kangaroo flashed a smile.

"Did Paul assign you that code name?"

The young man looked uncomfortable. "I think he prefers to go by 'Lasher' when we're in the office. But yeah, he picks all our code names. What's yours?"

"I don't have one."

"Oh. You're not Operations? Are you with Science Division?"

"No."

"Are you—"

"I thought you were just here for a pickup."

Kangaroo frowned. "Rude."

Oliver signed the form, handed it back, and unlocked the wall safe behind him to retrieve the prototype. He laid the ceramic carry case on his desk and opened it for Kangaroo to verify delivery of all the necessary components.

"Why is it green?" Kangaroo asked, holding up the pistol.

Oliver considered making up some story about the new synthetic composites. He also considered telling the truth: that Philip had been amused by the "Franken-gun" nickname and added some green dye to the final fabrication run.

But Oliver didn't really want to get into a long conversation with this boy. He already reminded him too much of his dead brother.

"Does it matter?" Oliver replied.

"I guess not." Kangaroo slapped the empty magazine into the pistol, cocked it, released the slide, sighted down the barrel at the wall, and pulled the trigger. "Good action."

A wave of nausea washed over Oliver. It was almost too much, watching this young man who seemed so much like Robbie: full of impatient energy, wide-eyed and gangling.

But it wasn't Robbie. Kangaroo wasn't playing with the gun like a toy; he had clearly been through some rigorous weapons training. He handled the prototype correctly and carefully, never pointing it toward Oliver, checking the mechanisms one by one in a way that suggested he actually knew what each part did.

Not playing with a toy. Using a tool.

Kangaroo ejected the magazine, put it back in the case, and closed the case. "Thanks, Doc. I'll let you know how it goes."

Oliver croaked, "The ammunition. You'll want. Rounds."

"I can get my own," Kangaroo said. "This thing's supposed to work with any standard parabellum ammo, right? Might as well test that first."

Oliver couldn't argue with that. "Watch out for the recoil. We've had some issues with the ceramic spring, and if your cartridge load is too hot, you might find yourself spinning backwards."

Kangaroo frowned. "I don't understand."

"In zero gravity, I mean. You are planning to do a full field test, aren't you?"

Kangaroo grinned. "I'm not going to be shooting this thing in space, Doc. I'm just storing it there."

Oliver narrowed his eyes. "That doesn't make any sense."

"Sorry." Kangaroo shrugged. "If you're not Outback, that's all I can tell you." He turned, holding the gun in one hand and the case in the other.

"You might not want to walk around this building with a firearm," Oliver said.

"Don't worry," Kangaroo said. "I'll put it in my pocket."

+ + +

Kangaroo came back a week later and unceremoniously dropped the prototype on Oliver's desk. "It doesn't work."

"Please tell me you haven't been throwing it around like that all week." Oliver avoided looking at Kangaroo's face and inspected the weapon. It seemed to be fine.

"No, I haven't, but it should be shock-safe anyway," Kangaroo said defensively. "The problem is it won't fire. At all."

"What type of ammunition did you try?"

"All of them! I loaded it with every type of parabellum round I could get from the armory, put it into cold storage for an hour each time, and nothing."

"You checked for duds?"

"I'm not going to get twenty duds in a row, am I?" Kangaroo said. "And yeah, I tested all the rounds after warming everything back up to room temperature. Then it worked just fine. I think you've got a heating problem in this prototype."

"All right," Oliver said. "I'll run some tests."

"How long is it going to take to fix?"

Oliver suddenly heard Robbie's voice in his head—*How long do we have to wait here? How far is it to home?*—and he hesitated before answering. "I need to determine what the problem is first."

Kangaroo actually pouted. "Come on, Doc, you gotta help me. Lasher won't let me go into the field without this."

"I don't suppose you'd be willing to tell me exactly what your field conditions are?"

Kangaroo pursed his lips. "I can't. I'm not allowed."

"I'll do what I can," Oliver said, "but it might take some time, since Lasher won't let me hire any more lab assistants."

Kangaroo's face brightened. "If you have assistants, you'll be able to work faster?"

"Yes, but—"

"I'll talk to Lasher. Thanks!" Kangaroo ran off down the corridor. Oliver heard shoes slapping against the floor in overexcited rhythm. He thought of Robbie again, and it took him almost ten minutes to stop crying.

+ + +

The prototype worked without any problems in Oliver's lab. He put it in the freezer, along with the ten different types of 9x19mm ammunition he had on hand, then dialed the temperature down as far as it would go and waited for two hours. Every round fired on the first try, and when he measured the temperature in the chamber, the readings were exactly what he expected.

After stripping off his cold suit, Oliver called Paul and said, "I need to accompany Kangaroo on his next field test."

"That won't be possible," Paul said, his face stern-looking even on the tiny vidphone screen.

"You can spare me for a week," Oliver said. "This is my most important research project, isn't it? And Kangaroo can't have gone farther than the Moon or L2 last time. He was back in less than a week."

"Time is not the issue," Paul said. "You don't have clearance to see the facility he's testing in."

"I don't have clearance to see the Moon?"

"This is not open to discussion. You can't go with Kangaroo. Tell him how to collect the data you need."

Oliver spent the rest of the night packaging up portable sensor modules and writing a detailed procedure document. Kangaroo groaned when Oliver handed him the reader tablet the next morning.

"Fifty pages?" Kangaroo said. "Do I *really* need to do *all* of this?"

"Lasher won't let me come with you to wherever you're conducting your field tests, so you need to collect enough data for me to diagnose the problem."

"But this'll take *forever*," Kangaroo whined. "Can't you, I don't know, build some kind of a robot to handle it?"

"I don't have time to test the automation that would require," Oliver said. "They're all very simple procedures. If you have any questions or problems, just call me."

"Pressure sensors?" Kangaroo was flipping through the procedures on the reader tab. "Radiation meters? We don't need all this!"

"It's not actually that much—"

"Can't I just take some temperature readings? That's got to be the problem, right?"

"Just do as I say, Robbie!" Oliver shouted.

Kangaroo cowered for a moment before asking, "Who's Robbie?"

"I'm sorry," Oliver said, turning away. "I had—I didn't sleep well last night."

He heard Kangaroo packing up all the sensor equipment. "I'll do my best with this stuff."

"Start with the temperature readings," Oliver said. "Don't worry if you don't have enough time to do everything."

"Okay."

Oliver heard Kangaroo shuffling toward the door and opening it. Then Kangaroo said, "I hope you sleep better tonight."

"Thank you."

"I won't tell Lasher."

For some reason, Oliver heard *I won't tell Dad*.

+ + +

Seven days later, a mailroom courier delivered the suitcase containing Kangaroo's sensors back to Oliver's lab. Oliver couldn't decide if he was happy about not seeing Kangaroo again, but he was glad that he could work the problem without any further emotional distractions.

The first sensor Oliver downloaded to a lab computer was the tracking device he'd hidden inside the reader tab. He had installed planetary GPS receivers for Earth, the Moon, and Mars, and added an interplanetary nav-beacon receiver for good measure.

People might lie to him, but data never did.

He was surprised to see hardly any movement recorded on the tracker. He checked the device for faults and double-checked the logs, in case there had been some kind of triangulation error, but the unit had recorded no loss of signal. There were no signs of tampering on the tab casing or in the firmware.

Wherever Kangaroo had gone to test the prototype, it hadn't been more than a few kilometers outside of Washington, DC.

And the radiation meters showed something even stranger.

+ + +

Oliver stormed into Paul's office and slammed the reader tab down on his desk. The rear access panel was open, clearly showing the tracker. Oliver knew Paul would recognize it.

"I want to know what the hell's going on here," Oliver said.

"I'll call you back," Paul said, and hung up his desktop phone. He glanced at the reader tab. "What is that?"

"This is the tablet of diagnostic testing procedures I gave to Kangaroo last week," Oliver said. "Because neither of you would tell me where he was going to perform his 'field testing,' I hid a tracking device inside so I could find out for myself."

Paul leaned back in his chair. "You shouldn't have done that, Oliver."

"Kangaroo didn't go into outer space," Oliver said. "He didn't even leave DC. So where did he go? Underground? Underwater? But why would he need a firearm that was operable in hard vacuum? What in the world could you lot be keeping down there?"

"It's not what you think," Paul said.

"Oh, but you haven't heard my guess yet!" Oliver said. He flipped the tab over to show its display. "You see, these are the readouts from the environmental sensors I asked Kangaroo to attach to the prototype while it was in 'cold storage.' According to the timestamps in each unit, he decided to attach all of them at once, presumably to save time."

"Oliver," Paul said quietly.

"You know what those readings show? I'll summarize. They show that the prototype was stored in hard vacuum, in total darkness, and in zero gravity, all at the same time. Deep space, right?" Oliver wagged a finger. "Not so fast, Mr. Holmes! Take a look at these temperature and radiation readings. What's this? Two *hundred* degrees Kelvin? In deep space? That can't be right; the cosmic microwave background radiation is only *three* degrees Kelvin. And look at the average proton collision energy level! That can't possibly be outer space.

"It can't be *our* universe, at any rate. Because our universe hasn't been that hot for at least *thirteen and a half billion years*."

Paul stared at him in silence for a moment. "If I read you in, this will be the last job you ever have."

"And what's the alternative? 'You could tell me, but then you'd have to kill me'?" Oliver heard himself laughing.

"Nobody's going to kill you, Oliver."

"Well, why the hell not?" Oliver screamed. His vision had gone blurry, as if he were looking through a waterfall. "Why should I have to live with this? Why can't I be as brave as Robbie and just end it all?"

Oliver wasn't sure how he ended up on the floor, but he felt Paul gripping his shoulders and leaning him up against the wall. The old man's eyes looked different now—not icy, but like a clear blue sky far off in the distance.

"Your brother was not brave," Paul said. "He was very ill, and you did everything you could to help him."

"No," Oliver sobbed. "No, I didn't."

"What more would you have done? Quit your job so you could watch him every waking moment for the rest of his life? Become a medical doctor so you could suddenly invent a cure for congenital neurodegenerative disorders? You know what's possible and what's not." Paul let go of Oliver and stood up. "You can't fix everything, Oliver."

It took Oliver a few minutes to pull himself together. Mostly he just didn't want to cry so much at work—or yell at people, or throw things, or break things or people. That had been a real problem during his final months at Bradford.

Paul held out a hand and helped Oliver to his feet.

"I'm right, aren't I?" Oliver said, focusing on the science to distract himself. "You've got some sort of machine that opens a portal into a parallel universe. An alternate dimension. Whatever you want to call it."

"That's entirely possible," Paul said. "We don't actually know where it goes."

+ + +

"Are you sure about this, Lasher?" Kangaroo asked.

He stood in a triangle with Paul and Oliver, at the center of a large, empty concrete bunker. Oliver had expected Paul to take him into some kind of secret research facility, but this appeared to be an old, abandoned, mid-twentieth-century bomb shelter. And there was no equipment anywhere in sight.

"Oliver has signed all the paperwork," Paul said to Kangaroo. "He's going to be joining you in Outback Operations."

Kangaroo beamed at Oliver and shook his hand vigorously. "Wow, that's great! Welcome aboard. Lasher's been looking for a good EQ for I don't know how long."

"EQ?" Oliver asked.

"Equipment officer," Paul said. "You'll be working very closely with Kangaroo. And a Surgical officer to be named later."

"So what's your code name going to be?" Kangaroo asked Oliver.

"His code name is Equipment," Paul said.

Kangaroo made a face. "That's not very interesting. And what if we have more than one person working on 'equipment'?"

"Then we'll use numbers," Paul snapped. "Or Greek letters. Just show him already."

Kangaroo shrugged and turned back to Oliver. "Okay. You ready to see it?"

"I gather that's why I'm here," Oliver said, still confused.

"Okay, come and stand next to me," Kangaroo said. Oliver stepped over to just behind his right shoulder. Paul took two steps back.

Kangaroo extended his right arm, and a whirling disk of translucent white light appeared in midair in front of him. Oliver saw blackness behind the light, which shimmered like a mirage.

"How are you doing that?" Oliver asked.

"Nobody knows," Kangaroo said.

"What do you mean, nobody knows? Where's the machine?"

"There is no machine. It's just me."

"My God." Oliver looked at Paul. "*That's* where you've been storing the prototype?"

"We call it 'the pocket,'" Paul said, his expression impassive. "It looks like deep space in there. No stars, galaxies, or other discernible light sources. Up until now, we've always believed it opened on a distant part of our universe, possibly inside an exotic dark matter structure or some other radiation-absorbing phenomenon."

"One Science Division labcoat thought it might be the inside of a black hole," Kangaroo scoffed. "That was pretty ludicrous. I mean, if it were a black hole, I'd have destroyed the whole planet the first time I opened the pocket."

"And when was that, exactly?" Oliver asked.

"I'll brief you later," Paul said. "But if you're correct about that being a parallel universe in there, Oliver… well, that makes things quite a bit more interesting."

"Did you figure out why your green gun wasn't working?" Kangaroo asked Oliver. "Was it a heating problem? Can you fix it?"

Oliver didn't even notice how much Kangaroo once again sounded like Robbie. "It's the cosmic background radiation. We tailored the ceramics in the magazine insulators to only generate heat if they were actually in deep cold. It's a failsafe, so the cartridges won't overheat and explode. The higher temperature and increased high-energy particle bombardments fooled the material into thinking it was never out of sunlight."

Kangaroo nodded. "Okay, and now in English?"

Oliver pointed at the pocket. "That universe is much younger than ours. Its Big Bang happened much more recently—probably less than two hundred million years ago—so it hasn't been expanding for as long, and that makes it hotter. The cosmic background radiation averages two hundred degrees Kelvin inside the pocket, which is two orders of magnitude higher than in our universe, and there's a significantly higher cosmic ray density."

"I meant American English."

"Your pocket universe caused the heater in the Franken-gun to malfunction."

"And do you know how to fix it now?"

Oliver nodded. "I'll need to take some more detailed sensor readings, but yes, I believe—"

"Great!" Kangaroo dropped his arm, and the portal vanished. "Hey, did you bring the gun? The prototype, I mean?"

"No," Oliver said.

"Oh. Well, do you have something small and—your watch! Let me borrow your watch for a second."

Oliver handed over the antique wristwatch. The actual timekeeping mechanism had been replaced long ago with modern electronics, but the elaborate metal case was a centuries-old family heirloom. "I'm going to get that back, right?"

"Yeah, sure," Kangaroo said. "Trust me, this is a great trick. Just watch." He chuckled and held up Oliver's wristwatch. "Hey! Watch! It's fun."

"If you say so."

Kangaroo frowned and opened the pocket again, but this time the portal appeared as a solid black disk surrounded by a glowing white rim. Oliver heard a whooshing sound and felt a breeze blowing past him. Kangaroo let go of the watch, and it flew into the pocket, which then disappeared again.

"Hard vacuum," Kangaroo said.

"How exactly do you intend to retrieve that?" Oliver asked.

"Relax," Kangaroo said. The pocket opened again, this time with the light barrier—Oliver imagined it had to be some kind of airtight force field—and the watch flew out. Kangaroo caught it before it fell. The portal vanished.

"There you go." Kangaroo gave the watch back. It was freezing cold in Oliver's hands. "Cool, huh?"

Oliver looked up at Kangaroo, then over at Paul, but couldn't think of anything to say. Or maybe he simply couldn't move his mouth because of the ridiculous, childish grin covering his entire face.

"Welcome to the family," Paul said, smiling back. "I'm glad you passed the test."

Oliver snickered. "What, you mean not losing my kit at the sight of Kangaroo's 'pocket'? Who do you think I am?"

"That wasn't the test," Paul said. "The test was whether you would actually give a working, loaded firearm to a young man who reminded you of your dead brother."

Oliver felt lightheaded. Next to him, Kangaroo said, "The who the what now?"

"I won't lie to you," Paul said. "I am not a nice person. I will exploit all your talents to the best of my ability in the service of this agency and this country. But you're a bona fide genius, Oliver, and I want you around for as long as I can have you. I'm going to find the best Surgical officer in the Solar System, and that person is going to keep both you and Kangaroo healthy for a very long time."

"So we can spy for you," Oliver said with a dry mouth.

Paul's expression didn't change. "Your assignments will be varied."

"I'm sorry," Kangaroo said, "can we go back to the 'dead brother' thing?"

Oliver ignored him and took a step toward Paul. "You want me to make more weapons."

Paul shrugged. "We'll see. This project was necessary to satisfy my superiors that Kangaroo would not go into the field unarmed."

"He's—" Oliver did a double take. Kangaroo waved. He seemed so young.

"I'm an only child, thanks for asking," Kangaroo said.

"Are there others like him?" Oliver asked Paul. "Other people who can also access the pocket?"

"No. None that we know of."

"He's the only one? And you want to send him into situations where a *gun* will be necessary?" Oliver said. "Where people are going to be *shooting* at him?"

Paul remained motionless. "Kangaroo was using the pocket on his own, for many years, before the agency recruited him."

"I'm sure there's another very interesting story there."

"You're not cleared for that information," Paul deadpanned. "We didn't give him the power. We just gave him a purpose. A focus for his talents. As I hope to do for you, Oliver.

"Your life didn't end when Robbie died. It wasn't your fault. Most things in this world are out of our control, but we have an extraordinary opportunity here to take actions that no one else can accomplish." Paul pointed at Kangaroo. "He is the key. But he can't do it alone."

"This is a very long speech," Kangaroo said, coming up to stand beside Oliver again but addressing Paul. "I feel like he doesn't actually need this much convincing."

Paul ignored him. "None of us can do this alone. And you don't have to, Oliver."

Oliver sighed. "I suppose you'll want me to go into therapy."

"Oh, it's worse than that," Kangaroo said before Paul could respond. "Every single one of your 'debriefings' is going to be recorded for Lasher's later viewing pleasure."

"I would hardly call it a pleasure," Paul grumbled. "But it's necessary. Our job is keeping secrets from our enemies. We don't keep secrets from each other. Is that clear?"

Oliver nodded. "I think… I'd like to talk about Robbie. To tell someone else what he was like. So I won't be the only one who remembers."

"That's a good start," Paul said.

Oliver turned to Kangaroo. "You remind me a lot of him, actually."

Kangaroo blinked. "Is that a good thing or a bad thing?"

"It's good," Oliver said. "It's very good."

This is my favorite Seanan McGuire story, but I am biased. I commissioned it for my anthology Raygun Chronicles: Space Opera For a New Age *back in 2013. It is a standalone story and a true delight with an old-school feel natural to most space westerns, and yet a modern heroine. Known for her* New York Times-*bestselling zombie and thriller novels, which she writes as Mira Grant, and her bestselling urban fantasy which she writes as Seanan McGuire, she has dabbled in space opera mostly in short fiction. After you read this, I think you'll join me in hoping Seanan does a lot more.*

FRONTIER ABCS: THE LIFE AND TIMES OF CHARITY SMITH, SCHOOLTEACHER

SEANAN MCGUIRE

A IS FOR AMMUNITION

There are no banks to rob in this painted doll of a dustbowl fantasy town; the money is all bits and bytes stored in a computer vault no human hands can open, whether they belong to banker or bandit. But there are other forms of thievery to be practiced by the quick and the clever, and Cherry is both, when she sees call to be. So when word goes out on the down-low that the Mulrian gang is planning a heist and needs bullets to get them to the finish line, Cherry's one of the first to the cattle call, her guns low and easy on her hips, her hair braided back like an admonition against untidiness. They're surprised to see her—aren't they always, when she shows up in places like this?—but they're willing enough to let her on the crew once they've seen what she can do.

She doesn't brag much. Doesn't talk much either, outside of a classroom or a courtroom. But oh, that little lady in the worn-out britches and the red flannel shirt can shoot like she made a bargain with the God of All Guns. Some folks say as she was a sniper in the last war. There have been wars upon wars since she showed up on the scene, and it's always "the last war." No one knows how old she is, no one knows the name of her home world, and no one's sure when she's finally going to snap and take out her allies along with her enemies. But they keep taking her on, because she makes the bullets dance to her tune. Could shoot the wings off a fly, the flame off a candle, and the fat off of a hog.

The raid begins at local midnight. Four techslingers, four gun-slingers, a pilot, and Cherry herself, all walking into town from different directions, all heading for the places they're supposed to be. The first shot is fired at two past the hour, an old-fashioned gun-powder bullet smashing through the window of city hall. That's the signal. The gunslingers commence to shooting up the things they've been approved to shoot—mostly foliage and buildings and the police bots that come swinging down the sidewalks like they stand a chance against flesh and lead and practice—and the techslingers slide their clever wires into the datastream, bleeding off billions in less time than it takes for Cherry to reload.

That's her, up on the roof of the library, stretched flat with her scope circling her eye like a wedding ring. Every shot she takes is true, and she takes a lot of them. Nobody dies, but there's enough damaged as to take the edge off. Then the bell rings in her ear, and she rolls away from the edge of the roof, vanishing into the shadows. Fun's over.

Tip to tail, they took six minutes to bleed the beast, leaving shattered glass and frightened townies behind like a calling card. Cherry will check her bank balance later and find a healthy payoff from an uncle she doesn't have, on an outworld that may or may not exist. It doesn't matter to her. She's worked off a little of her aggression here, in the shadows and the dust, and that leaves her head clear enough for the real work to begin.

✦ ✦ ✦

C IS FOR COVER STORY

"Now, can anyone tell me the origins of the human race? Where did we begin?" The one-room schoolhouse is ringed with windows, letting in so much light from outside that the overheads don't need to be turned on for most of the year. By the time the weather turns sour, the schoolhouse solars will have fed enough into the local grid that they won't have to pay a penny for the power they use. There's value in self-sufficiency.

The kids are a surly bunch, growling and glaring as they squat at their desks like so many infuriated mushrooms. These are the children of asteroid miners, farmers, and artisans, not rich enough to go to the fine boarding schools on Earth or Io, but not poor enough to be restricted to home schooling and play dates. They get the bulk of their lessons on their personalized terminals, but they're here for the social contact with their peers, to learn how to get along and how to form connections that will serve them for the rest of their lives. There are fourteen teachers working this part of the solar system, and Miss Cherry is a newcomer here, arriving at the start of the term. They still don't trust her. They still don't know whether they should.

She leans back against her desk, resting her weight against her hands, and smiles winningly at them. They do not smile back at her. She's hard to measure with the eye, a wisp of a thing in a blue dress printed with white daisies, her long dark hair hanging loose and sometimes getting in her eyes when she gets excited and begins waving her hands around. They're generally good at telling someone's age by the way they move, these children of the regen generation—when your grandfather can look like your little brother if he finds the scratch, you learn to read a body for the years it's seen—but Cherry is a book of riddles, one moment as open as a kindie, the next as closed-off as a three-time regen. Her face puts her in her early twenties, by far the most popular age with women trying to survive in the outer moons.

"Anyone?" she asks, and there is a sharp, sweet disappointment in her tone, like she can't believe they wouldn't know the answer to such a simple question. "I suppose I'll have to recommend that all your consoles be set to remedial human history for the rest of the term, then. I hate to do it—"

"So don't!" shouts a voice from the back of the room.

Cherry's head snaps up, and those sweet and easy eyes turn suddenly cold, the eyes of a predator searching for its prey. "Who said that?" she asks, scanning the crowd.

They've been in this schoolhouse a lot longer than she has; every child in the class knows how to hunker down and look like butter wouldn't melt in their mouths. They shift and look away, avoiding her gaze.

"You." Her finger stabs out like an accusation. "Why not?"

Her target, Timothy Fulton, squirms, but only a little. He doesn't bother denying that he was the one who spoke: she's got him, fair and square. Instead, he shrugs and says, "Because we've been over all the remedial stuff. We don't want to do it again."

"Well, then, you can spare yourself and your classmates a lot of boring scutwork by being a hero and answering my question." She isn't smiling. This is the first time since she arrived at the start of the month that she hasn't been smiling. "What was the origin of the human race?"

"Earth, ma'am. Humanity began on Earth."

"Very good. When did we move on to bigger and brighter things?"

"The Twenty-Second Century, ma'am, after we figured out how to adapt ourselves to other planets, and how to adapt other planets to ourselves."

Miss Cherry nods encouragingly. "Very good. What was the first great war after colonization? Anyone?"

Ermine Dale has never been able to sit by while other children were praised and she was not. She puts up her hand, waiting only for Miss Cherry to point at her before blurting, "It was over what makes a human, ma'am. Whether Jovians and Neptuneans were still people, given all the modifications they'd gone through."

"That's right." Cherry pushes herself away from her desk and walks around it to the chalkboard, an archaic piece of set dressing that nonetheless seems to help students learn and retain information. In a bold hand, she writes the number "10," and circles it before she turns back to the class and says, "This is the average number of years between wars since humanity stretched beyond a single planet. This is how long we have to rest, recover, and learn to do better. That's what I'm here for."

"To rest?" asks Timothy, and his confusion is the class's confusion.

Miss Cherry smiles. "No. I'm here to teach you to do better."

✦ ✦ ✦

I IS FOR INEVITABILITY

She's been here a full season, eight local months stretching and blending together on this farmer's paradise of a Jovian moon. Ganymede has taken well to terraforming, and Earth's crops have taken well to Ganymede. Half the moons of Jupiter get their food from here, and that makes it a bright and glittering target in the nighttime sky. When the next war comes—and there's always a next war—she expects the sides to fight mercilessly to own the sky's breadbasket.

The children have accepted her. They bring her apples and icefruit from the fields, and some of them have started to shyly tell her what they want to be when they grow up. Someday most of them will be farmers, but some of them may be explorers, or diplomats, or poets, if they get the chance to strengthen their roots on this good soil until the time comes for them to bloom. She likes these pauses maybe best of all. They remind her that the human race has a purpose beyond blowing itself to cinders against the stars. "We can be something more than fireworks, if we're willing to put the work in," that was what her long-dead lover told her once, when they were lying naked to the unseeing eye of Jupiter on the barren, rocky soil of this selfsame moon, barely cloaked then in its thin envelope of atmosphere, still an experiment on the verge of going eternally wrong. "We can be anything."

That wasn't true then and it isn't true now, but oh, weren't they pretty words?

The fact that she's thinking of him at all isn't a good sign. Means she's getting restless, and when she gets restless, she either needs to move on or find something that can bleed off a little of that energy. So she sends out a quiet query to her contacts, lets them know that she might be available for a little pick-up work if the price is right and the location is far enough from Ganymede. Maybe something out-system. Summer break is coming soon, and her kids will be needed in the fields. Easy then for a schoolteacher to slip away on errands of her own. As long as she makes it back before the apples come in, she'll be fine.

She's still teaching her classes and waiting for a job to present itself when the choice is taken away from her. Choices are like that. Some of them exist only for as long as it takes not to make them.

They're in the middle of a comparative theology lesson when the first shots are fired, big, loud things that boom through the still-thin atmosphere like the world itself is ending. Miss Cherry drops the book she was reading from and bolts for the door. The children are still sitting frozen at their desks, too stunned to react. By the time the book hits the floor, she's already gone.

Ermine starts to cry.

Then Miss Cherry is back, and there's a light in her eyes they've never seen there before, something wild and cold at the same time, like Io, like the stars. "Get to the cellar!" she shouts. "Now!"

She's the teacher, and so they obey her, running like rabbits for their bolt-hole under the building. It's not until they hear the lock sliding home behind them that anyone really realizes she hasn't followed, that she's still out there.

In the dark, hesitantly, Timothy asks, "Was Miss Cherry holding a gun?"

No one's really sure. They hold each other close and listen to the distant, terribly close sound of gunfire.

+ + +

K IS FOR KILLER

Children are like seeds, only they all look exactly the same; there's no way to look at them and say "this one's a flower, this one's a tree, this one's a strain of tangle-vine designed to break up ore deposits on the moons of Neptune." All you can do is water them, feed them, give them good soil, and watch how they grow. Be careful what you give them, because it'll change what comes out the other side. Something that could've been a rose may come out all thorns and fury if you plant it wrong.

It wasn't just one thing that went into growing Charity Smith. No one even agrees on what soil she was first planted in. She was Earth-born, she was a Martian, she was one of the first settlers on Ganymede, she was altered Jovian and then back again after the war started, when she realized that heavy bones and thick skin didn't suit a sniper. She was an Ionian mermaid, she was an asteroid miner, she was everybody's daughter and nobody's wife. No one claimed her, not at the beginning and not after. But we do know this much:

One of the places she put down roots was Titan. Her name's on the first settler manifest, pretty as you please, writ down proper in her own hand. She came in as an educator, fresh from Mars—and there's some will say this supports the idea that she was Martian-born, while others say she couldn't have gotten a release from the red planet if she'd been a citizen, with the threat of war so close and them so very much in need of trained instructors. It doesn't so much matter, because she was just a teacher then, with none of the scars or patches that would come after. Titan was newly terraformed back then, and they needed people like her. People who knew how to work for their keep.

There is one surviving holo of the time that Miss Charity Smith spent as a schoolteacher on Saturn's largest moon. It shows her in one of the sundresses she still wears these two hundred and fifty years later, her hands clasped in front of her and a smile upon her face as she stands with her students in front of the Titansport schoolhouse. It was just one room, one of the first frontier schools built out past Mars, and she couldn't look prouder if you paid her. There are twenty-seven children in the shot, all of them looking at the camera with varying expressions of boredom and mistrust. They were the sons and daughters of bankers, miners, and farmers; they had no one to speak for them but their parents and their teacher. They were seeds looking for good soil, and Miss Cherry was their gardener, as wide-eyed and idealistic as they were themselves.

All that changed on the night the ships arrived.

There had been rumbles of war in-system for months. Earth fundamentalists thought the modifications of the Neptune settlers had gone too far; said that the Neptuneans were no longer human, and hence had no claim to their home world's rich mineral deposits. The Neptuneans didn't take too kindly to that, and had responded with threats of their own. As for who fired the first shot, well, that's just one more thing lost to the mists of history, which are fond of obfuscation, but not so fond of being cleared away. Someone struck first. Someone else responded. And before most of the solar system even knew that we were at war, the great ships were flying in search for strategic bases to use in their quest to obliterate the enemy.

Titan was well-situated for a lot of purposes. It was a good refueling station, and a better supply depot, with its farms and its farmers and its ready supply of livestock in both clone and field-grown forms. That was why the ships raced each other there; that was why the first real battle of the Great Earth–Neptune War was fought, not in the safely empty depths of space, but in the sky over Titansport.

It was local winter. All the children were in school, as was one young and frightened schoolteacher who had never tried to defend the things she cared for. She was still a seed herself, in many ways; she was still growing.

We don't know the full details of what happened on that day. Only one person does, and she's not talking. Here is what we do know: that the school burned. That the children died. And that Charity Smith walked away, someone else's rifle in her hands, and all the blood of a generation nurturing her roots.

We made her. We earned her. It's three hundred years gone from that night, and we're watering her still. May all the gods of all the worlds that are have mercy on our souls.

✦ ✦ ✦

M IS FOR MURDER

Everyone has heard the stories, of course; they're part of the two-bit opera that is the history of the Populated Worlds of the Solar System. No one believes that sort of crap, not really, not until they've come skimming through the thin atmosphere of a fresh-terraformed moon and found a woman with dark hair and cold eyes standing on the bell spire of the church with a disruptor rifle in her hands. They're coming in fast and hot and there isn't time for course correction, so the order is given: ready, aim, fire. Blow the stupid little gunslinger wannabe back to the dust that spawned her, and prepare for the payday.

Cherry's been to this rodeo before. If the pilot had been one of hers, he would've pulled up, no matter what his captain told him. Her presence is a warning and a promise—"This town is mine," and "I will end you," both wrapped up in one denim-and-flannel package. She's shown her face. She has no regrets, and she never wants them. She buried her regrets in the soil on Titan. So she pulls the trigger and leaps clear before the ship's engines can realize what she's done to them. EMP guns are illegal on all the settled worlds, but so is killing children, so she figures her accounts will balance in the end.

The ship goes down hard in the middle of town. It takes out the church as it descends. It misses the school. That's all she's ever cared about. Adults are grown; their seeds are sprouted, and for the most part, they're past the point where they can change what they'll become. Children, though, children are still capable of domestication. They can learn from the errors of their past.

Cherry takes her time as she saunters down the street toward the wreckage. Faces appear in windows and doorways, gawking at her, taking note of her face and her place in the community. She'll have to move on after this. She always does. That's all right. The kids here are good students, and they've learned their lessons well. They'll grow up a little better than their parents, and when she makes her way back here to teach their grandchildren, some of them may smile at her in the streets, duck their heads and touch their hats, and never say her name out loud.

The hatch of the ship is rocking back and forth when she gets there. She sighs, sets her engine-killer gun aside, and pulls the smaller, more personal revolver from her belt. She's standing patient as the stone when the hatch creaks open some minutes later, and the face of a green-skinned Ionian appears in the opening.

He pales when he sees her. "You're supposed to be dead," he says.

"That makes two of us," she replies, and pulls her trigger. The gunshot echoes through the town, followed by the sound of windows slamming shut and doors being locked. Curiosity has killed a lot of cats in its day, but it's left the pioneer folk for the most part alive.

Her gun speaks three more times before the ship is a graveyard. She steps away and scans the skies. There's never just one. It's not a battle if you're shooting at shadows. Finally she sees it, a cloud that moves just a little too quickly, skirting against the wind instead of with it. Cherry's sigh is a wisp of a thing, heartbroken and tired.

Earth, again. Why must it always start with Earth?

Charity Smith is going home.

✦ ✦ ✦

N IS FOR NO QUARTER

"Are you sure, Miss Cherry?" The governor's voice is an electronic sine wave that caresses the whole room with its vibrations; the governor himself is a Jovian, genetically engineered to thrive in the seas of liquid metallic hydrogen that cover the planet's surface. He was born on Jupiter, and came to Ganymede as a young man, seeking his fortune. He can never go home now. He's been on this world, in its lighter gravity, for far too long.

His daughter has been in Cherry's class, born of a surrogate; he has never touched his more Earth-true wife with his bare hands. It was the governor who recognized Cherry's name and approved her hiring. He knows as well as any how important such gardeners are to a world just getting started.

"They saw me, Mr. Galais, and while I'd be just as happy to go back to my class, you and I both know that's not the way to keep the peace." She even sounds a little sorry. She likes this world. She likes these kids. "I'll need my ship and the pay you promised me. In return, I'll keep the war from your doorsteps, and I'll only contact you if I need an employment reference."

The governor chuckles despite himself. "You'll have it, rest assured; you've done nothing but good here. The children will be devastated."

"Tell them this is the cost of war. They should know that well enough already, from our lessons; you'll just be giving a reminder." Cherry shakes her head. "I have to go, or someone will come looking. Now. My ship?"

"Ready at the port. But tell me, Miss Cherry… where will you go? What will you do?"

Cherry smiles. It's a thin, wistful expression, broken and beaten down by more years than anyone who's seen it cares to count. "I'm going home. As for what I'll do when I get there, well… I suppose I still have a few lessons left to teach. And some folks clearly haven't been learning."

The governor had never considered double-crossing her; there's looking for a better deal, and then there's taunting a dog already proven to bite. In his tank of pressurized hydrogen, he shivers and turns, his long fins draping over themselves, and for the first time, he is glad Miss Cherry will be leaving them.

Some things are too dangerous to be allowed to take root for very long.

+ + +

O IS FOR OUTWARD BOUND

There's always a moment of heart-stopping joy when the pull of gravity lets go and her ship is running free and clear across the open sky. Cherry sits behind the controls, tied to the ship with optical wires and catheters and a dozen other cold connections, and she laughs for the sheer beauty of the images being beamed into her brain by the ship's exterior sensors. Her hands clutch the controls, and she soars across the brilliant blackness of space like a comet on a collision course with the cradle of mankind: Earth itself, that big blue, green, and brown ball of polluted seas and overpopulated soils that gave birth to the human race. She hates it there, how she hates it there, but sometimes, she has no choice. Sometimes, there is nowhere else to go but home.

After an hour in the air she punches in the final coordinates and keys up her med systems. It's time for another rejuve treatment. Wouldn't do to look anything but her best when she meets the relatives.

+ + +

Q IS FOR QUESTIONING

Cherry's ship is small enough to fit through any hole in the security nets, and her autopilot is clever enough to find them, driving her on a clean, traceless route until she reaches the outer edge of Earth's security net. The auto wakes her then, and she yawns and stretches and activates an ID beacon older than most of what's left in Known Space. Alarms blare seconds later, in rooms too dark and far away for her to see. Cherry hangs there for a moment, a red bell on the collar of the cat, and then she hits the burners and she's gone, gone, away across the sky, and their tracers are following, and no one dares to press the button; no one dares to take the first shot. She is a fairy tale, a legend, a lie. She is a schoolteacher, and the daughter of a President, and the girl who gave everything away to grow in poisoned soil. She is a ghost story, and this is her frontier.

When she reckons she's taunted them long enough she stops, gives their guns the time they need to lock onto her position, and presses the button that will begin broadcasting her words across the heavens. "I thought we talked about this," she says. "You promised to leave the outworlds alone. You said you were done grabbing for what's not yours."

(And somewhere far away, a com jockey turns to his supervisor and asks, "What is she talking about, sir?" There is no answer. The bargain she refers to was struck fifty years ago, and the man who struck it with her has long gone to his grave. But where one side stands, the deal holds. That's the only honest way of doing business.)

She hangs there in the air, an easy target, and maybe that's the point; maybe she's more tired than she lets on. "Well?" she asks. "No response?"

("We have to say something, sir.")

"I suppose that means the deal's off. I suppose that means I'm setting myself against you."

("Tell her this.")

And then the words on her com, not spoken, but burning before her all the same: "We're sorry, Miss Cherry."

And Charity smiles.

+ + +

T IS FOR TEACHER

She doesn't miss Earth much. The Earth that's there now isn't the one she left behind, not by a long shot; it's been too long, and there are too many bullets and too many bodies between here and there. She made her choices and the people who stayed planetbound made theirs, and regrets have never changed the past. She's invested her money and her time well since then. Generations have grown up knowing Miss Cherry as the quiet voice of reason, and knowing Charity Smith as a bogeyman used to frighten naughty governments into behaving themselves a little better, at least for a little while.

Six hundred years is a long time to pinch pennies and buy bigger guns. She's better armed than most planetary governments these days, and she makes sure they know it, even if they don't believe she's really who she claims until her ship's ID blazes on their screens like a warning from a disappointed god. She hasn't fired as many shots as people say she has. She hasn't needed to.

Maybe one day they won't need the firm hand anymore, and she'll be allowed to go back to the girl she was on Titan, the one who'd never held a gun or killed a man. Maybe one day the last of the poisoned fruit will fall, and all the children of all the worlds will be able to grow up safe and unspoiled. But until that day, she has a job to do, and if it's not a job that anyone gave her, well. Sometimes it's the jobs we take for ourselves that matter most of all.

The schoolhouse is not new; the desks are worn and marked with the initials of those who came before. But the chalkboard is clean and gleaming black, as dark as the hair of the woman who stands in front of the class. "Hello, Io," she says, and smiles. "My name's Miss Cherry. I think we're going to be good friends. Now, who here can tell me the origins of the human race?"

Sharon Lee and Steve Miller's Liaden series is the little series that could. Originally a trilogy cancelled due to sales, its popularity on internet usegroups inspired them to keep writing, and in the years since, the series' popularity has continued to grow to bestselling proportions.

The human race is divided into three subraces: Terrans, Liadens, and Yxtrangs, none of whom necessarily get along. Their original story for us, "Dark Secrets," is the story of a Terran-Liaden team running a small ship who engage pirates, thus putting the station itself in danger. They are put on probation, then encounter further complications while trying to deliver their payload.

AUTHOR'S NOTE: *The Liaden Universe® is populated by those who survived the collapse of another universe, long ago. Not only people came through in the Great Migration; some of the war machines and booby traps built by the Great Enemy also came in. These are known dangers and several groups, notably the Liaden Scouts, have taken up the task of gathering Old Tech and seeing it destroyed. Possession of Old Tech is a crime.*

Caerli and Simon are unique to this story. It is, just a little, unusual, to find a Terran-Liaden partnership running a small ship. The cultures aren't quite mutually antagonistic, but it takes an extremely tolerant Liaden, or a very patient Terran, to make such a partnership work.

DARK SECRETS
A LIADEN UNIVERSE STORY

SHARON LEE AND STEVE MILLER

They came into Venzi Station trailing pirates—and riding the redline on a guaranteed delivery, which was far worse.

They were known at Venzi—a scant blessing, so Simon thought, but then, given the current situation, he'd take every small positive thrown their way. At least they'd be allowed to rig to station and maybe even dock, if they could get there.

Caerli was first board, and flying like a madwoman. You'd think it was a gift she'd been given—at least to the point of the pursuit, there being nothing the ex-Scout loved better than to push her own personal piloting envelope.

The nearness of the deadline—neither one of them appreciated that, and it definitely added an extra bit of derring-do to Caerli's flying. His partner had a fond relationship with money. She'd felt the loss of the early delivery bonus keen as if she'd lost a finger. If it came round that they lost the whole fee, it would be a strike to her heart.

Come to it, he wasn't certain in his own mind how they were going to get on, if they lost the payout for this job. Might squeak themselves into some local work to build the ship's 'count back up to safe levels. That was if there wasn't a fine to pay. Which... given Venzi Senior Station Master Tey, there was bound to be a fine to pay.

If they got a fine on top of a loss, Simon thought grimly, they were grounded—plain fact. Despite the station master, Venzi wasn't the worst ring to be grounded on, first reason being there wasn't no actual *ground*... but not being cleared to fly—that'd put Caerli 'round the hard bend in local space before a station-day was done, and himself running to keep up.

'Course, he told himself, there wasn't no sense looking so far ahead. Things might work out on their side, yet.

Pirate had range on 'em, after all. Even granting that Caerli could wring miracles from the board, they still might get hull-shredded with no backup to hand.

And wasn't that a cheering thought.

"We *are not*," snapped Caerli yo'Dira, "going to be hull-shredded."

"Dash every hope I got all at once, why not?" Simon answered, glancing at the screens.

"I'm seeing two missiles with our names on 'em, heading dead on," he said, just giving her the info.

She didn't bother to answer. Thin fingers flew over the board; the screens grayed. Simon's gut insisted that the ship had twisted around them, even as the screens showed real space all about. The instruments reported that they'd Jumped out and in again between one breath and the next.

The pursuing missiles were seventeen seconds further behind them, that being what Caerli's playing of the Ace had bought them, but it was still going to be close—too close, and if—

The universe twisted again, and this time when the screens came back, they were crossing Venzi's shield perimeter. Not the way Jump engines were supposed to be treated, nor the way physics was supposed to be dared. Station warnaways blared across all channels. The missiles, being dumber even than the crack team of Kilsymthe and yo'Dira, didn't answer, and a few heartbeats later the defense system defended the station, just like it was made to do, and there weren't any missiles, any more.

The pirates, no surprise, were gone like they'd never been.

"*GelVoken*," came blaring across all-band. "You will be guided into a Section Eight dock. Lock in and await escort to the station master's office."

The comm light snapped off without waiting for a reply—well. Wasn't any reason to wait for a confirm, was there?

"We were not," Caerli stated, her voice raspy and not quite steady, "hull-shredded."

"That's right," he said, soothing her, 'cause the rush of dancing between life and death pretty often left her shaky. "We didn't get hull-shredded. Good work. I'm thinking Master Tey's gonna give us a citation for that, don't you?"

Caerli all at once collapsed back into her chair.

"Of course," she said. "Whyever else would she send an escort?"

+ + +

"You two." The station master glared from Simon to Caerli and closed her eyes.

"You two, *again*."

There was that to be said for being known at a particular port or station, Simon admitted to himself: no need to waste a lot of time bringing somebody new up to speed. Station Master Tey, now, she knew exactly who they were.

And she didn't much like them, individually or as a team. Didn't like them *being* a team, for that matter, which happened in more ports than it ought, Terrans and Liadens flying together not always a popular choice with admins.

"I guess you had a good and compelling reason for endangering Venzi Station?" Tey asked, sarcasm heavy.

Like they'd deliberately gone looking for a pirate to lead into station, thought Simon with a flicker of irritation. It was understood that a station master had a natural partiality for her station, but that didn't mean the rest of the universe considered it at all interesting.

"We have a commission to Venzi Station," Caerli said softly, reasonably. "We came out of Jump at the Kelestone Light boundary. They were waiting for us, thus we immediately Jumped for Estero—"

That was the story, but she'd short-Jumped there, dropping out well before charted Jump-end to take advantage of one of those asterisked end-notes in the ven'Tura Tables, which always creeped him, and one day Caerli was gonna miss her number and they'd fall outta Jump-space into the maw of a sun, or the center of a planet. Not that he worried about such things, much.

"We were clear when we came out," Caerli continued, glossing the abort. "Thus, we Jumped for Venzi."

The aborted Jump—that's what'd cost them the early delivery. Still, can't come into a station trailing pirates. Surest way known to pilot-kind to make the station master mad at you.

Case in point.

"You're telling me they were waiting for you at Venzi entry?" The station master frowned, not liking that notion at all. Which proved she was a good station master, despite the personal lapse of taste that failed to find Kilsymthe and yo'Dira adorable.

Caerli shook her head.

"Station Master, the Jump point was clear. They came in on our tail when we committed to an approach."

Tey liked *that* even less. Pirates lurking along the station approaches was way past serious. Most pirates weren't organized—or numerous—enough to hold a station hostage, though it'd been tried and done. Astrid Verity's Freebooters had held the lanes at Squalme Station for three Standards before TerraTrade hired Canter's Corpsmen to eradicate the problem. Which they'd done, at the cost of near-eradication their ownselves. Mostly, though, your garden-variety pirate didn't have the skill set—or the attention span—for that kind of long-term commitment.

And, in their particular case, there was an easier culprit, right handy.

"So, your package is interesting to somebody, is it?" asked Station Master Tey. "*Real* interesting, looks like to me."

Simon's stomach fell straight into his boots. He opened his mouth, though their ongoing agreement was that Caerli talked to Tey, whenever they could manage it. The gods of lost stars knew what he might've been about to say, but it came moot as Caerli tilted slightly forward, her whole body conveying respect.

"We have guaranteed delivery, Station Master, and the hour fast approaches."

"More fools you, then," snapped Tey.

"Station Master," Caerli adjusted her posture slightly, mixing a smidgen of humble in with the respect. "With all respect, Station Master, if we do not receive the delivery fee, we will be reduced to a cold-pad on station's budget until we may get a rescue from guild or clan."

Simon blinked. It wasn't what either of 'em did, normally, sharing out Kilsymthe and yo'Dira personal bidness with station masters and that sort of person. Nor was Caerli in the habit of admitting she was low on funds.

Then, he saw the calculation behind that startling bit of candor. Station Master Tey saw it, too, and her mouth pursed up like her beer was sour.

Delay the delivery and she'd have Kilsymthe and yo'Dira on her station to deal with every shift until they got lucky—say, forever—or somebody—could be even Tey herself—came to the snapping point and did something maybe, a little, regrettable. Let the delivery meet the deadline, and Kilsymthe and yo'Dira would go away and leave her and her station in peace. More or less.

"All right," she snarled. "Get outta my sight."

Caerli bowed gently, which only made Station Master Tey look more sour.

"Spit it out," she snapped.

"Yes. One only wonders, Station Master, if we are free to pursue our own business. We had hoped for a speedy departure."

The station master looked at her hard, and Simon could almost see her measuring how much trouble she could still cause them, without being stuck with them forever. "Make your delivery." There was a pause while she searched the office ceiling with her eyes, and then included them together with a wave of the hand.

"You're on probation and locked to station," she said finally. A glance at both of them, made with a grimace, "It'll be a hot-pad, never fear, but locked to my orders. Admin'll move as fast as practicable, but I want the pair of you where I can find you, in the likely circumstance that questions arise."

Questions about what, she didn't say, and neither of them sought clarity. Instead, in the interest of getting paid, they bowed—and left the station master's office.

✦ ✦ ✦

They made the delivery venue—Aberman's Drinkery, which sounded considerably more upscale than it was—before the wire fell on the deadline, and only that. Caerli went first, with Simon lagging a step behind. His hands, trained for detail and fine work, worried the pay tab.

One long step and he was beside her at the table's edge, packet extended on the palms of his hands, so the man sitting there, scowling, could see it plain.

The *resevio* snorted.

"Took your time," he said, making no move to take possession.

"Yessir," Simon said; "scenic route."

The other man snorted again, and snatched the packet down to the table. He put a hand on it, and glared from Simon to Caerli.

"Will there be a return packet?" Simon asked politely.

"If there is, I can hire me a courier who respects a deadline, an' neither don't take the tab off like it was his to do."

Simon's face heated, but he said nothing.

Caerli bowed slightly. "If there is nothing more, we depart," she said, and turned on a heel. Simon followed her out into the station hall, and kept to her side as she crossed to a clumsy corner, where two storefronts didn't quite match up, leaving a thin, triangular cubby. At her nod, he slipped into the slim cover first—that was standard operations, him being taller'n her. Caerli snugged in against him, tight and maybe even distracting, save he had a burning question at the front of his mind.

"What're we doing here?"

"Waiting," she answered.

He sighed, and for lack of anything else to do, being squished flat into the corner like he was, he scanned the bit of hall in his line of sight, which included the entrance to Aberman's Drinkery.

It was a back hall, so there wasn't a lot of traffic, though the Drinkery clearly had its adherents. A couple security types strolled in, arm-in-arm, like they was reg'lars, followed pretty soon by a man in mechanic's coveralls, and two women in librarians' robes.

A repair gurney lumbered noisily down the track laid in the center of the hall; three mercs in uniform swung 'round it, walking fast, vanishing before he could read their colors.

The repair rig crawled out of sight, and the hall was empty so far as he could see for the space of four heartbeats.

Three people—two wearing formal jumpsuits, one carrying a lock-case—hove into view. The two formals entered the bar, the third, in full station-security rig, shock-stick on her belt, took up position outside the door in one of the classic poses.

"They're never after the *resevio*?" Simon whispered.

"Wait," Caerli said again, which was fine for her, being in front and her backbone not like to meld with a girder.

He hadn't quite become an integral part of the station's structure before the Drinkery's door opened from within, and here came one of the security team who'd gone in prior to the jumpsuits, their own cheery *resevio* walking between him and his partner, one hand cuffed to each. The jumpsuits followed, one still carrying the lock-case. They turned right, the officer who had been guarding the hall falling in behind, passing quite near to the uncomfortable little angle where Kilsymthe and yo'Dira stood concealed. The *resevio*'s expression was slack, which was probably due to the pacifier collar laying flat 'round his collarbone.

The little procession passed out of Simon's range, and he sighed out a breath. Caerli stayed where she was, pressing him even tighter into the corner, which he didn't think was possible. He didn't argue her instincts, though, having seen Caerli's instincts at work on numerous occasions in the past.

Finally, she moved, and he did, slowly separating his backbone from the wall. He joined her in the open hallway, and turned with her toward Section Eight docking, *GelVoken*, and some small certain amount of safety.

+ + +

Simon went to the bridge, pulling out the pay tab and feeding it to the reader. There was a hesitation long enough for him to suspect that Admin was monitoring their comm, then the green light lit. Accepted and paid. He sighed in pure relief, then headed for the galley.

Caerli'd already drawn two mugs of 'mite and set them on the table. Simon slid into the chair across from her.

"*Resevio's* gonna think we led Admin to him," he said, after he'd had a swallow from his mug. "That's gonna be good for bidness."

"No," said Caerli, and: "The tab?"

"Accepted and paid," he assured her. "'Course, speaking of bidness, we pretty much got zero chance to pick up a commission to see us off Venzi. I'd hoped to bolster the treasury a bit."

"No," Caerli said again. "Master Tey wants us off her station. It would also please her if we never returned to her station."

"Ain't *her* station," Simon objected, but his heart wasn't really in it. "Unnerstan, I'm inclined to her mind in this. If I never set foot on Venzi Station again in this lifetime, that'll be fine by me. Oughta at least give it an avoid for the next couple Standards. Let her have time to cool her jets." He swallowed 'mite. "Or retire."

"That is well so far as it goes—but you are correct that it would be far better if the ship was not forced to fly empty."

Simon shook his head, stood up and carried his empty mug and hers to the washer.

He turned and leaned a hip against the edge of the counter, crossing his arms over his chest.

"Be inneresting to know what we was carrying that pirates was so eager to liberate."

"By now, Station Master Tey will surely have the contents of the packet on her desk. Perhaps she will take your call."

"I'll wait an' read about it in the newsfeed. 'Less she calls us in on account of questions having arose."

"That is of course possible," Caerli said politely, her gaze fixed on a point in Jump-space just beyond the edge of the table.

"You don't think they were after the packet," Simon said, with one of the flares of surety that never failed to get him into trouble.

She sighed, and shook her head at that little spot in the void.

"If it was the packet they were after, they would have attempted to board. They fired upon us with earnest intent. Had we not managed to cross into Venzi's space, we risked destruction, and the packet with us."

"They didn't fire 'til last prayers," Simon pointed out. "Coulda been a case o'being certain the packet didn't get to our man at the Drinkery. They'd've rather had the packet off of us, but it'd come down to hard choices."

Caerli moved her shoulders in a fluid Liaden shrug—*yes/no/maybe*, that meant.

Simon shifted against the counter. Caerli uncertain wasn't what he liked best to see.

"It is… too complicated," she said slowly. "If the client needed the packet lost, and herself clearly blameless for its disappearance, there were still less expensive means of arranging the loss. Piracy is a chancy venture with far more risk of failure than success. After all…"

Her voice drifted off.

Simon waited until he had counted to one hundred forty-four, then prompted, "After all?"

She started, and looked up at him, her abstraction melting into one of her occasional droll looks.

"After all, we might have won through, and the packet reach the *resevio's* hands."

Simon sighed.

"Screwed up again, have we?"

Caerli shook her head, Terran-wise.

"Had they given us the script, we might have done better for them."

Simon grinned.

"True enough."

His grin faded.

"Caerli."

"Yes."

"They knew where we was going, the pirates."

She sighed.

"So it seems."

"They were *after* us, then, and if not the packet, then—what?" he asked. "*GelVoken*?"

Caerli said nothing, and Simon felt another flicker of surety.

"*Us?*" he said quietly, which wasn't so much of a joke as could be. They'd done some things—not necessarily *wrong*, but not exactly right, neither. For the ship, they said, citing spacer laws of survival, and it'd been true enough. Still, exception could've been took. Revenge might seem to be in order. It was… possible—*just* possible—that one of their victims had sworn an affidavit 'gainst them, and offered a bounty.

Bounty hunters, though… Simon considered. Bounty hunters were straightforward creatures, who disliked complications just as much as Caerli did. An operation that had them chase a courier through Jumpspace—they hadn't, so Simon sincerely believed, ticked off anybody with the means to set a bounty *that* high.

Before they'd become a team—well, he'd traded grey; it was how he'd almost lost *GelVoken* at Tybalt. *Would've* lost 'er, if one Caerli yo'Dira hadn't come by and taken an interest in what was none o'her affair…

Caerli… Well, he didn't know all Caerli's history, but, after all this time, he knew *her*. She wasn't utterly straight—she loved money too much for that—but she was conservative in the matter of adding new enemies to her string. By listening to what she hadn't said in addition to what she had, he'd arrived at the understanding that her leaving of the Scouts hadn't been her idea; had maybe been in the way of discipline. Still, that'd been close on to ten Standards back; Kilsymthe and yo'Dira having been formed all of seven Standards ago.

"We must do a search of bounties declared and affidavits sworn," Caerli said. "After we have rested."

There was nothing but good sense to that. They were both worn out with adrenaline and long hours at the board.

"Right," he said. "Captain declares all crew on double-down-time, starting immediately."

"Yes," said Caerli, rising. "And if the station master calls?"

Simon looked black.

"Station master calls, she can leave a message."

+ + +

Simon's door was still closed when Caerli ghosted down the hall to the galley, some few hours later. She, who had training that Simon did not, had accessed the so-called Rainbow technique to insure a deep, healing sleep, rising refreshed and focused in under a quarter of a shift. Simon would sleep yet for several hours. Adrenaline burned through his reserves quickly; the strain of the pursuit had already exhausted him, before they came to the necessity of coping with Station Master Tey and her little intrigues.

Caerli carried a cup of tea and a protein cookie with her onto the bridge, and settled into the co-pilot's chair, as was proper. *GelVoken* was Simon's ship, after all, however much he might credit her with returning it to him. They were operating partners, but not co-owners.

Perhaps she ought not to have accepted his offer of a partnership, but she determined that she was going to reform, to leave her previous life, and start afresh. It had seemed she was owed that, were Balance the natural state of the universe—the ideal on which the whole of Liaden civilization was predicated.

She had been desperate, she thought; certainly, she had not been naive. Even then, she had known that the natural state of the universe was chaos.

Even then, she had known that one could not outrun the past, no matter how able a pilot one was.

She slowly ate her cookie, considering how best to proceed.

Easiest for all if An Dol contacted her. Sadly, An Dol had liked to play games, and if she was tempted to think that had changed over the years, she had only to remember two missiles in the screens, dead on and gaining. It was barely possible they were live with no warhead, to prove a point. Exactly what he might have done, before, except the last time they'd met, he had sworn he was through playing games.

The last of the protein cookie went in a crunch as she considered the likelihood of that.

No, An Dol still played games.

That being so, he would expect *her* to find *him*.

Caerli sighed and drank her tea. Truly, she was in no mood for games, nor in being forced back into An Dol's service—which, belatedly, made her wonder what it was he wanted her *for*. He had ruined her as a Scout, seen her discharged without honor, so she was no use to him in the old way. She had rebelled when he would use her as a drudge—and for years, he had… one might say *allowed* her… to remain at liberty.

That he came looking for her now… there must be something new afoot; something for which her skill-set was uniquely fitted.

Well. There was an unsettling thought.

She closed her eyes and partook of the benefits of another calming exercise.

Whatever An Dol wanted, it was imperative that he be kept away from Simon.

Simon possessed a varied set of skills and strengths, peculiar to a man who had split his young life between space and bronk-herding. His grey-trading had root in the habits of his planetside father and uncle. Simon could track a bronk on hard high plains, kill a witchbird with his bare hands, and skin a chardog with his belt knife—or so he claimed. Whether or not these particular claims were true—and she did not see why they should not be—Simon's abilities were impressive, and occasionally startling. What he did not have was a true appreciation of the subtlety a high-born rogue Liaden might employ to grasp power, or to expand it.

Which meant that her counter was inside An Dol's orbit. Little as she relished it, she would need to go onto Venzi Station, and play seek-and-be-stealthy with An Dol.

Before she allowed misdeeds and *melant'i* of the past to claim her, however, she would embrace one more opportunity to act with honor.

She leaned to the board. A series of quick finger taps on the board opened her personal files. Another hundred faultless keystrokes and she had done all that was needful. She purged the files, sat back in her chair, and reviewed her options.

Truth, she thought; she had none.

Best, then, to get on with it.

She rose, placed her ship-key on the board where Simon would be certain to see it, and left the bridge, mug in hand.

The mug, she left in the washer in the galley, before proceeding down the hall to her quarters, where she armed herself, and shrugged into her Jump-pilot's jacket.

Thus armored against An Dol's sense of play, she left *GelVoken* by the service hatch, and made certain it sealed behind her.

✦ ✦ ✦

Caerli was up before him, which neither exceeded his expectations, nor hurt his feelings. Simon stopped in the galley to draw a mug o'mite, and moved down to the bridge, which was where he'd find her, certain enough. A thought had come to him while he'd been drifting up toward wakefulness. Might be they could check for small cargo on the salvage and surplus side. *GelVoken* could take a mini-pod; didn't often 'cause neither him nor Caerli was a born trader, but the option was there. An' if they were just hauling to another yard of like character, there wasn't no trading involved. Flat fee and not likely to be much of it, but ship's bank was low enough he'd—

The bridge was empty.

Simon blinked, and for no reason at all his stomach clenched. So, Caerli was still resting—or resting again. No reg against that, was—

It was then that he saw the ship-key in the share tray between the two boards, and the message light blinking yellow.

He stepped up to the board, accepted the message with a touch, and stood looking down at a short list of files and account codes, balances appended, which was Caerli's private money, every one of 'em bearing his name as 'counts holder. At the end of that list was a note, cold as if they'd been strangers, traveling together by chance.

Captain Kilsymthe. I resign my berth, effective immediately. Caerli yo'Dira, Pilot.

He was shivering. He noted the fact like he was reading it off the screens. His fingers moved, bringing up the call log, finding it empty.

Just gone for a ramble out on the station, then. She did that. Done it many times.

Hadn't ever before found it necessary to leave her ship-key behind her, or roll every single bit of her private money over to him. Not to mention leaving resignation letters just a little bit colder'n deep space.

Simon closed his eyes.

Something bad was happening, that was what. And before it got any worse, he had to find Caerli.

+ + +

It was… unsettling, how easily the rules of An Dol's play came back to her. He had cast her as the supplicant, the seeker; *the lesser*, to whom he would reveal himself in the fullness of time and grant her succor— it would be succor, for An Dol played with live weapons. Had she not successfully eluded his missiles, An Dol would have seen that her abilities had atrophied, and that it would have been an error to trust any longer in her survival skills.

That she had played her second Ace, ensuring the survival of *GelVoken*, Simon, and herself proved that she was still worthy of him— and now the game went to a higher level. She could expect ambushes and assassins before An Dol revealed himself to her.

Best if she found him before he was ready to step forward. It would annoy him, and An Dol made mistakes when he was annoyed.

She paused in the shadow of a cargo hauler, surveying the dockside and considering where he might be.

One might think he could be anywhere, and Venzi Station large enough for a man who wished it to stay hidden for years.

Only, An Dol did not wish to be hidden; he merely wished not to be found until he had made his point and had his fill of fun.

So, then, he would be near *GelVoken*'s docking, but not in Section Eight itself. Not that An Dol wasn't bold enough to secret himself on the station master's own dockside, merely that, for this game, it would not suit his purpose.

For it must be assumed that his purpose, in part, was to remind her, forcibly, that she was his inferior. He would see her hurt before he stepped forward to rescue her from worse.

Dockside would certainly suit him, much more than the civilized, and patrolled, core rings. A certain *sort* of dockside, certainly; the station's equivalent of a lawless zone—a low port—The Ballast, so it was referred to on Venzi Station.

Assuredly, An Dol would bide his time, awaiting her in The Ballast.

+ + +

Simon paused at the edge of their docking area, looking around for a hint, a clue—for Caerli walking down-dock toward him, arms 'round the waists of a brace o'port dollies.

Woman didn't leave her life's blood to her partner because she was gonna surprise him with a party, he told himself, and looked around some more.

Caerli was cautious; she was stealthy, and if she didn't wanna be found, well—there was a one in a million chance that the likes of Simon Kilsymthe would find her. On the other hand, one in a million was still odds. He wasn't beat yet.

He found the place where she'd paused for a bit, thinking out her next move, maybe. And he found that one heel—her left—had rested in a bit of drink-smudge, so that when she took her first step onto the public way, a sticky little crescent was pressed to the decking, and there, just at the proper length for Caerli's short, determined stride, was another, and beyond that one, a third.

The crescents faded finally, but by then, he had a direction, sensing rather than seeing where her feet had tread, and he hurried on.

Damn it, if Caerli had it in mind to take on The Ballast by way of letting off a little steam, he surely wanted to be in on the fun.

+ + +

She'd nullified two attackers on her way across The Ballast, and frightened off a third. It was unfortunate that the second of her two attackers had some skill as a knife-fighter. He had touched her, and though she had wrapped it, she became aware of shadows gathering in her wake as she moved toward her goal; the honest citizens of The Ballast, that was who followed her now, scenting blood, and easy prey.

She kept her attention forward, seemingly oblivious, until one of her hangers-on took the bait, and darted forward, making a feint toward her pocket.

She spun, knife out. The would-be pickpocket raised her hands and backed away.

"Peace, now, Pilot. Cain't lay blame for a fair attempt."

"Your next attempt will be your last," Caerli said, matter-of-fact, and making sure her voice carried to the others, waiting at some distance. "I'm on business and I will not be interrupted."

"Certain, Pilot; certain. Ana fine shift to ya."

The pickpocket faded back into the pack of watchers; the watchers thinned away and were, to eyes less sharp than Caerli's, gone…

She turned and continued on her way. Not long now, by her estimation.

✦ ✦ ✦

The Ballast occupied a trapezoid section of less-than-premium space between the backup power coils and the emergency gyros. The door you wanted from Section Eight docking was near the narrow end of the section; which was mostly transfer slots, and grab-a-bites, and fun houses. Simon did a quick tour of the possibles, put a couple of questions, and found Caerli not at all.

Onward, then, he thought, into the deep and dangerous side. He sighed. He wished he'd known Caerli'd been in this tone o'mind; hadn't seemed to be the case when they'd parted company, each to get their own rest. 'Course, Caerli was private—and there was still the question of her putting all her most valuables under his name. Sure, The Ballast was rough, but it wasn't anything like Caerli to consider she wouldn't survive a little bit o' exercise 'mong the station-bound.

✦ ✦ ✦

It was nothing more than a hunch that turned her steps toward the repair hall. At the last, it always came down to hunches, with An Dol. If she was right, she'd soon enough have confirmation.

She was right.

They came boiling out of the dark storefronts ahead of her, and more, from the cross-corridor she had just passed. Others came out of the deep shadows at the side walls. A melding, Caerli saw, as she spun lazily on one heel, taking in the fullness of them. A dozen—fifteen, perhaps—the five in spacers' motley putting themselves forward, letting her see their faces. Of them, she thought she recognized the woman whose bald head was tattooed with a world's wonder of flowers, and possibly the man with the silver sash round his ample middle; the other three spacers were strangers: the rest of the mob were Ballasters, hugging the shadows, holding weapons that at other times were slotdrivers, span-hammers, and punch-blades.

Fifteen, five trained in An Dol's particular school of survival.

It occurred to her that An Dol wanted her dead, after all; that he had drawn her to him so that he might witness her ending in person.

Well. Fifteen against one, was it? From An Dol's perspective, it might be a compliment.

The least she could do was to show her appreciation.

She kicked, diving for the floor, hitting with her left shoulder and rolling.

One of her throwing knives found a nesting place in the breast of the tattooed woman; the second in the eye of a Ballaster who had darted in, hammer raised. Her gun was in her hand, and she managed three quick shots into the crowd before she was engulfed and it was fists, and feet, and knives.

✦ ✦ ✦

It was the shouting that drew him into a run. One sight of the melee and he knew it could only be Caerli in the middle of it all. There were bodies on the decking here and there—dead, or nearly so, silent acks to his notion that this was no ordinary rumble, but Caerli fighting for her life, no regard for grace.

And expecting to lose.

Never in all the long years they'd been together had he known Caerli yo'Dira fighting to lose. Woman fought the odds like they was personal, and he'd long ago lost count of the times she won over them, by willpower and cussedness.

Simon paused on the edge of the bidness, taking stock, testing the angles, wondering if it were better to start shooting, hoping they'd scatter, or—

"Why, what have we here?" A voice murmured in his ear. "This is most unexpected."

Simon spun, gun out and right in the face of a Liaden man dressed neatly in leathers, and a wide, Terran-style grin on his face.

"It is the partner, is it not?" he said, paying so little attention to Simon's gun that he had a moment's belief that there was no gun in his hand at all.

"Simon Kilsymthe," he growled, and jerked his head toward the melee. "If you can call that off, do it."

"I can," the Liaden said, his brows pulling slightly together. "The question, I believe, is—will I? And, do you know, I think I might. For considerations."

"What considerations?"

"Surrender your gun and yourself to me, now."

"And I'd do that—why?"

"Because if you do not, Jezzi, who stands behind you, will take your gun, and I will allow nature to take its course with respect to your partner, and my former associate."

He risked a glance to the side, catching a glimpse of Caerli. She looked bad, and if she got out of this mess alive, she'd flay him for doing what he was about to do. He looked forward to that, but in the meantime, this being a Liaden he was dealing with, he had to secure both sides of the promise.

"I give you my gun, you'll call off the fight," he said.

"I will call off the fight, if you give me your gun. That is correct."

Simon reversed the gun and extended it, butt front.

A hand snaked over his shoulder and took possession. The Liaden stepped away from Simon. Simon turned to face the riot.

From his belt, the Liaden withdrew a flare gun. He pointed it to the girders above, and fired.

Sparks filled the hallway, riding an ear-punishing *boom*.

"Freeze or fall!" a voice shouted, over the echoes. "Freeze or fall!"

The sound of safeties being snapped off numerous pellet guns was almost as loud as the boom.

In the center hallway, the melee sorted itself into some kind of order. Those who could rose, some leaning on the nearest shoulder. As if obeying some unheard command, they pulled away from the battered figure, bent and kneeling. She was panting, and there was blood on her face; her left arm hanging bad.

Slowly, she raised her head, and Simon saw her recognize the Liaden with a grim resignation he'd never before seen on Caerli's face.

"So, An Dol," she called, her voice hoarse. "Will you finish it yourself?"

"That had been the original plan," the Liaden—An Dol—said, cheerfully matter-of-fact. "But someone has entered a side bet, and thus made the game more diverting. You have a reprieve, Captain yo'Dira. Your partner stakes his life for yours."

Simon saw her blink; she moved her head carefully, and her eyes met his.

"Simon," she said. "You idiot."

✦ ✦ ✦

"You will scarcely credit it, I know, Captain Kilsymthe," the Liaden named An Dol said chattily, "but our so-dear Captain yo'Dira had been an associate of mine."

He wanted Simon to ask him for details, but Simon was smarter than that, at least. He said nothing, and hoped he managed to look a little bored.

Before the silence stretched too long, An Dol continued, not seeming to mind Simon's lack of curiosity.

"She was a Scout, you know, working for the Archivist's office. Her duty was to gather Old Tech and either destroy it, or tag it for retrieval and destruction. Sadly, she found herself in want of cash, so she sold a piece—quite an insignificant piece—to one of my agents. Well, you know how it is with honor, do you not, Captain Kilsymthe? Once broken, never mended. It was easier the second time, and even easier the third. By the fourth sale, I don't believe she even needed the money, and by the time the Scouts discovered her breach and discharged her, finding Old Tech for me was second nature to her. She was for a time among my crew; she really is very skilled at finding the caches of old machines, and is an able technician, besides. Matters proceeded in an orderly fashion, satisfactory to all for a number of Standards.

"Then, there was a mishap—perhaps a Scout was killed. It may, in fact, have been a team of Scouts. Regrettable, but it seems Captain yo'Dira knew them, and did not agree with my necessity. She left me soon after, and I—I let her go, because I knew I could find her again, should I ever want to do so."

Caerli was sitting on stool next to Simon. She'd been patched up, rough, with a first aid kit. She hadn't said a word since greeting her partner. If he didn't know better, he'd've said she was asleep.

Now, she raised her head.

"What do you want, An Dol? If you've decided to kill me, do it, and let Pilot Kilsymthe return to his life."

An Dol laughed.

"You have undoubtedly taken several blows to the head, so I will not berate you for stupidity. How shall I let Pilot Kilsymthe go, when he has seen me, and will shortly know of my workings? Indeed, the more I consider this new situation, the more I like it. The two of you are known on Venzi as troublemakers. It will make the scenario more believable, if both of you are in it together."

"What scenario?" asked Simon, to save Caerli the trouble.

"Why, the scenario where Captain yo'Dira smuggled a disrupter onto Venzi Station, and she and her partner, after contacting the station master with demands, and being, as I imagine they will be, rebuffed, decide to demonstrate the strength of their position. Which they will do—sadly forgetting to take themselves to a place of safety beforehand."

He paused, frowning slightly.

"What is the Terran phrase? Ah. Screw-ups to the last."

Simon was opening his mouth to ask what a disrupter was, but Caerli's raw voice cut him off.

"You're going to disrupt a section of this ring? Which section?"

An Dol smiled, and it came to Simon right about then that the man wasn't sane.

"Why, I think The Ballast will do nicely, don't you? We shall demonstrate, and rid Venzi of a trouble spot, all in one throw. Balance shall be maintained."

"And then?" demanded Caerli.

"Then? Why, we shall perhaps need to stage a second demonstration; we are prepared to do so. I am determined to have this station. We need a base from which to operate, and there are several like-minded teams who would join us here."

Simon's stomach was not happy. Crazy or not, An Dol had ambition. *This* pirate wasn't just going to occupy station *space*, he was going to occupy *the station*.

He looked at Caerli, hoping to see some sign that she thought An Dol's little scheme was doomed to fail.

He saw the exact opposite.

+ + +

It was an elegant little machine, Simon thought, hardly any bigger than his head, and at that seeming too small to catastrophically shut down all systems in The Ballast.

Be a bad death, too, which Simon wasn't looking forward to.

"Now," said An Dol. "Captain yo'Dira, you will call the station master and deliver your lines. In the event that you should consider an ad lib, I offer you this."

The gun was buried nose-deep in Simon's side, and An Dol was behind him. If Caerli deviated, he'd be gut-shot, which would, Simon couldn't help noting, be a quicker, cleaner death than the rest of The Ballast was going to get. Caerli being Caerli, she might well think herself entitled to make that choice for him. Which, being honest, and their places switched, he might think the same.

Caerli gave him a long, unreadable stare, then turned to the comm screen and fed in the station master's call-code.

"You!" Station Master Tey growled. "Where are you? I've been trying to find you the last half-shift."

"I have been busy, Station Master. Forgive me if we have presented an inconvenience to you."

"An inconvenience? You might say that. Do you know what was in that packet you brought onto my station?"

Caerli tipped her head slightly to the left.

"An Old Tech tile rack," she said.

Tey took a hard breath.

"You knew that, and you still brought it here?"

"I did not know when we accepted the commission. I have only belatedly deduced what it must have been."

"And you're calling me because of your powers of deduction?"

"No, Station Master." Caerli took a deep breath, and Simon sighed out the one he'd been holding. "I am calling to report an emergency situation."

The phrasing, that's what gave An Dol a distraction, a hesitation in his eyes—just the smallest possible hesitation, but that was all Simon needed. He sidestepped, ducked, and swung, knocking the gun arm high, belt knife leaping to his other hand.

One strike, straight to the heart, just like he was putting down a rogue bronk.

The dying fingers tightened on the trigger; the gun discharged; and Caerli leaned into the screen, speaking rapidly.

"Station Master, Venzi has been invaded by pirates, and is in mortal danger. You must immediately dispatch security teams to all sensitive controls. You are looking for devices—possibly Old Tech, possibly of modern make—set to disrupt critical station systems. We are in The Ballast with one such Old Tech machine. I am going to attempt to defuse it. If I fail, Venzi will lose this section."

Station Master Tey was staring.

"What ship?" she asked.

"*Chandivel*, out of Liad. Station Master, time is possibly short."

"Yes. Get to work, Pilot."

The screen went blank, and Caerli spun toward the device, stepping over An Dol's dead body.

"Well done, Simon," she said briskly. "Please access The Ballast's internal comm and announce an evacuation."

+ + +

Well, there was bounty money, which came to them, and left over a tidy sum, even after the fines had been deducted—the fine for bringing Old Tech onto Venzi, and the other one, for bringing pirates.

There was salvage, too, one-twelfth of the value of *Chandivel*, which plumped up the ship's account to levels last seen by Simon when he was a boy and his ma *GelVoken*'s captain.

Simon had reversed Caerli's gifts, of course, and made her a third-part owner of *GelVoken*, even before all the funds were in. Someone that invested in him and his deserved a little for herself, too.

Also, they was free to go, with an invite from Station Master Tey not to visit again soon, which they promised, best they could.

"Comes to me," Simon said, when they was on their way to Venzi Jump point, "I never did thank you for nearly getting me gut-shot."

"Co-pilot's duty," Caerli said, which was true enough.

"You got any other dark secrets in your past likely to come 'round and make us into targets?" he asked.

There was a small silence, and he looked over to find Caerli watching her screens with a fair degree of concentration.

"In fact, I am made clanless for my indiscretions," she said, quietly. "That need not concern you. There is nothing else, except—you know, Simon, the usual sort of thing."

Right.

"Well," said Simon; "just so long as that's clear."

Larry Niven is one of the modern legends of science fiction, a Grand Master who is especially known for his Ringworld series of books. Steven Barnes, a frequent collaborator, has written for TV shows from Stargate SG-1 *to* Baywatch, *as well as numerous novels in the Aubry Knight and Tennison Hardwick series, among others. His first published work of fiction, a collaboration with Niven in 1979 called "The Locusts", was a Hugo Award nominee. Larry Niven and Steven Barnes' collaboration on stories set in the futuristic amusement park, Dream Park—a park centered around live action role-play—dates back to 1991. Portraying a future where technology is far advanced from our own, the stories contain elements of magic as well as tech, as evidenced in their original story for us, wherein park staff and guests deal with a mysterious disappearance that unfolds in their midst.*

AUTHORS' NOTE: *The timing for "The Lady or the Tiger" touches three eras. Xing Ming first visited Dream Park during* The Barsoom Project. *She returned by way of Mars with her husband five to ten years later. Amber Quan confronts Scotty following events in* The Moon Maze Game, *four decades later.*

THE LADY OR THE TIGER
A DREAM PARK STORY

LARRY NIVEN AND STEVEN BARNES

Scotty Griffin never tired of King Crater's arid depths and jagged heights, considering them an untaxed job perk. He rarely needed to use the holograms that could imitate any lunar location, pipe in vid feeds from the mining or tourism concerns in real time, or even effortlessly display Earth land and seascapes. Reality was enough—except that he was buried beneath the lunar surface, as were they all in Hovestraydt City. The domes in King had come later, erected after active shields could block the radiation.

Days were artificially held at the twenty-four-hour cycle humans had evolved to obey, and it was "three p.m." on this synthetic period when his visitor appeared.

She was Eurasian, taller than average. Athletic and lithe, carrying herself with a level of grace and poise he found instantly appealing.

He smiled. "You are Amber Qwan?"

"Yes," she said. A low, controlled, musical voice, imbued with challenge. "My English name. May I?" She shifted her eyes toward the chair squared before his desk.

"Of course."

She floated into the chair. After an awkward moment's pause, Scotty spoke. "You've come a long way for nothing."

She smiled. "I don't think so, Mr. Griffin." He could almost see the cameras in her eyes as she scanned the room. Centered on the wall was a holomap of the lunar park. There was no set structure: it was changed regularly, components linked together to create different experiences in the dedicated dome. They had a waiting list for the lunar facility, but also a few hundred repeat customers. That made sense: the number of people who could afford to travel two hundred and forty thousand miles for a vacation was considerably smaller than the flow-through for the California or Shanghai facilities.

"Why not?" he asked. "Why do you think I'll talk about the kidnapping?"

"I've compiled an extensive dossier on you," she said, "composed of articles, interviews, and reports from people who have known you all your life."

That pricked his vanity. Who doesn't like someone who is interested in them? "What do they say?"

"They describe you as a man of intelligence, courage, discipline, and honor."

"Outstanding. Which of those things might make you think I'd discuss something I've refused to speak of for decades?"

She smiled, ready with her answer. "Intelligence to know that motivations change with circumstances. The players are dead, and cannot be harmed. Courage—it takes courage to ask ourselves why we do the things we do, make the decisions we make, and to change our minds. Discipline tells us to do the hard thing, if it is the right thing."

Even if she was making it all up, he liked hearing it. "Go on."

"It is up to you to decide now, today, if my request is the right thing."

"And honor?"

"Not honors you have received. You allowed an interview with *Discovery* magazine. A picture of your office showed a plaque on your wall with the Chinese ideogram for 'reciprocal obligation'."

He looked back over his shoulder. There were many plaques on his wall, awards and photographs of him shaking hands with notables. And there below his photo with 2078's winning World Boy Scout Jamboree team was the hardwood plank she referred to.

"*Guanxi*," he said. "Confucianism."

She smiled. "What we owe each other as citizens of the world. I seek nothing more than a truth that harms no one. And have traveled a quarter million miles because I believe you are a good man, and that if you met me, looked into my eyes, you would know I mean no harm. And that you would treat me as you would wish to be treated, if our positions were reversed."

He scratched his chin, wishing he'd shaved. He was suddenly much more interested in this conversation, and in this woman. "That… was rather slippery."

She smiled at him, and he found that smile increasingly attractive. And a little irritating at the same time.

He smiled back at her. And didn't know quite what to say. "Well. I practiced law for a time."

"Yes," she said. "Contract law at Berkley, if memory serves."

Bullshit. She wasn't uncertain about it at all. It was a little unnerving to be dealing with someone who knew him better than he knew them. "And my professor once told me that in a negotiation, there comes a time for silence, after which the first person who speaks has lost."

She smiled at him. The clock ticked. He sighed. "It appears I have lost."

"On the contrary, Mr. Griffin. I believe we both have won. I think you have wanted to tell this story for a very long time."

"You're good."

She smiled at him. Said nothing.

"Cut that out!" he squawked. "All right, I surrender. You said Xing Ming passed away?"

"Yes. Last year. It was very peaceful."

"All right. I guess it's time. It happened forty years ago. Two years before I was born, three years before my parents married."

"And why have you been reluctant to speak of it before now? The… diplomatic aspects?"

"Maybe," he said. "I think I was more concerned about the human factor. Up here, on Luna… you know, I look up at Earth and I don't really see nations. What matters more to me is people. I'm in a people business."

"I understand."

"So… it happened in 2052, not long after a major event at the park, a major industrial espionage event involving gamers."

"I think I read of this."

"The Chinese delegation had been at the park previously of course, testing technology before their first Martian expedition."

Amber nodded. "The entire trip was just under two years. Earth and Mars have to be positioned so that you can aim where Mars is going to be, then wait until you can aim at where Earth is going to be. There's prep time before you even board ship. It was a big piece of her life, and her husband's. I think it wore on him a little."

"I studied records of that trip," Scotty said.

She smiled. "That first trip is a special interest of mine. Nine months going, nine months back, and three on Mars waiting for the planets to be in the right place. Of course it couldn't happen without an active shield for the radiation."

Scotty did a little typing. Images appeared to float in the air between them. Amber traced the orbits with her fingertip. "Like that, yes," she said.

Scotty said, "Xing Ming went to the surface. Right. The first Chinese woman to do so."

"The first *woman*," she said calmly, as if protecting the heritage.

"I stand corrected," he said. He was suddenly aware that he was staring at her mouth and cheekbones, and wondered if she had plans for dinner.

"Yes. She had waited a very long time to do this. With rocket technology then, there was no shortcut."

"You're very well informed," Scotty said. He wondered if she liked sushi. They had excellent aquariums, as well as cloning vats. Frankly, he found cloned saba better than the real thing. Same taste, less oily "feel" to it. Texture matters. In addition, it seemed to have a mild aphrodisiac effect. Or maybe that was just the result of dining with someone who could afford it.

He could.

"She is one of our heroes. Why exactly were they at Dream Park? I mean the first time."

He considered. "We have substantial traffic at our industrial and governmental testing facilities. The Chinese used Dome Two to test some… proprietary technologies."

Her chuckle was slightly reserved, as if she knew something he didn't.

"It's been forty years. I think there aren't any more secrets about it."

"I'm sure you're right," he said. "In fact, I checked before I took this meeting."

"So you already knew you were going to talk to me?"

He smiled. Said nothing. The clock ticked.

She weakened first. "I guess I deserve that."

He smiled. Said nothing. Then they both broke up laughing.

"All right, all right," Scotty said. "Truce. So Xing had been to Dream Park previously."

"Right. But for business, not pleasure."

"The story was never told for reasons of diplomatic delicacy. Basically, in 2052, Dream Park hosted a group celebrating the return of China's manned expedition to Mars, including Xing Ming. On Xing's previous trip she had trained with proprietary Cowles technology. Liquid crystal contact lenses that not only acted as biometric monitors but dispensed microdosed medication. Counters for the long-term effects of zero-gravity on the eyes. They also broadcast everything the scientists saw, through relays, to Earth…"

✦ ✦ ✦

NOVEMBER 17TH, 2052.

Southern California. 7:02 p.m.

A canopy of stars had fallen over Dream Park, and although most of the noise and light was in the other five slices of the Dream Park "pie" there was still activity in sector four. It came from employees who had volunteered to be skeleton crew for a very special set of guests.

Other than those employees, and a carefully filtered stream of vetted premium customers, sector four was almost deserted.

In the shadow of sub dome four (the sub domes were within a pie slice; the major domes overlapped) Alex Griffin and his staff stood behind John Cowles Jr., the chubby and bespectacled son of the park's founder, as he welcomed their guests.

"We welcome the Chinese delegation," he said in phonetically memorized Mandarin. "We're honored to have you." The tallest of the Chinese was an elegant round-faced man, almost delicate but with a sense of sinewy strength. The woman standing beside him was small, short-haired but exquisitely feminine, with an aura of both intelligence and mischief about her.

"We have heard so very much about Dream Park," he said in perfect English. "Xing spoke of it often during our voyage. We have looked forward to this."

John Cowles gestured to his security staff. "Colonel Chow Lee Ming, Major Xing—" he bowed to the woman "—I would like to introduce you to Alex Griffin and his staff."

"Colonel," Alex said, and shook hands firmly with the tall man, then more carefully with his wife. "I believe I had the honor of meeting the major two years ago."

Her emerald eyes sparkled. "You remember," she said.

"It's my job to remember celebrities," he said. "And the first woman to set foot on Mars certainly qualifies. Would you please follow me? Your adventure awaits."

✦ ✦ ✦

A door carefully concealed in a titanic clown-head's grinning mouth led to an escalator and subterranean tunnels. Thirty seconds' walk and they reached the players' wardrobe center, usually reserved for employees. The lead costumer was a pint-sized ball of energy, at least fifty years old but so excited she seemed to vibrate.

"You are Xing Ming?"

"That I am."

The little woman fairly bounced off the ground. "I'm Mary-Martha Corbett. Call me Mary-Em. So glad to meet you! I saw so many of your broadcasts! The first woman to set foot on Mars!"

Xing Ming smiled shyly. "I am honored to be here, Mary-Em. What should I do?"

"Just relax and let us take care of you," Mary-Martha said. "We have some costume choices we've set out for you, if you approve…"

The other staff hovered around the other guests, but the little head costumer was in bliss, and would let no one else serve her new charge. After she had dressed, a technician linked to her contact lenses and made a few tweaks… and then she was ready.

✦ ✦ ✦

Two rides looped above Dream Park in glowing, nearly intersecting curves and spirals. Xing Ming wanted the Gravity Whip.

Her husband looked at the gleaming steel track curving above him, crossing into and out of buildings, breaking at one point where cars apparently crossed in a free-fall arc. He shook his head. For a man who had traveled to Mars, he seemed oddly wary of a mere twenty-story drop.

So Xing Ming boarded the ride with one of their escorts, a cool-eyed young woman named Ching Jung Yung. The security woman gripped the bar that locked her in, her teeth showing back to the hinge. Xing blinked against the wind, braced against the drops and corkscrews, looking down at all of Dream Park as the car whipped over and under the loops of the Deep Past ride, through a restaurant, up into the free-fall arc and down. Ching did notice how Xing focused, as if she were less enjoying a ride than making maps in her head.

Afterward Chow Lee watched as his wife and her escort wobbled from the exit. She exclaimed in Chinese, "Really, Chow Lee! Come, I'll ride with you!"

"Wife, you know that any normal man will get sick!"

They went on the Cargo Cult and Ragnorok experiences: standard reductions of past LARP games, standard but gaudy and dizzying. Two hours later the group proceeded to the next event on the itinerary: dinner theater.

✦ ✦ ✦

The walled entrance to Wizarding World was almost indescribable, fluxing between magical motifs from a dozen different countries: Celtic runes, Egyptian hieroglyphs, African bead paintings, Australian images in ochre and berry-stain. It felt like a place where magic was alive, daring you to retreat into logic.

The arena itself was not large. It could have seated forty or fifty people at a cluster of dinner tables around a raised stage, every seat with perfect lines of sight. There were fewer than that tonight.

To a trumpet fanfare, a pale, cloaked and mustachioed figure descended wingless and wireless from the ceiling.

The Chinese whispered among themselves. "Chazz!"

"Welcome to Wizarding World!" The elegantly mustachioed albino was almost seven feet tall, a walking special effect, and moved with a kind of unearthly, clockwork elegance.

"That's Chazz!" Xing said. "We saw him put Spider-Man on Mount Rushmore. How can they afford him for this small theater?"

Her husband chided her. "You are silly," Chow Lee Ming said. "It is, of course, a simulation of some kind."

She dampened her enthusiasm. Looked more closely. Oh. Now she could see that the face shimmered just a bit, some kind of mask that channeled a projection. "Ah, yes, I see now."

The air capered with critters, a menagerie of swirling sprites and imps and ghosts who swooped between the tables, cold air marking their passage. Holographic dinner menus appeared before them, with selections of beef, chicken, and a veggie loaf. Simplicity meant speed of service.

Security Woman Yung scowled. "I see nothing."

Chow Lee Ming seemed similarly confused. "I see only a bit."

Xing was delighted. "I have the magic!"

They were shepherded to a table where a short Hispanic man and an Asian woman were already waiting.

"Richard Lopez," he said, rising slightly and shaking hands. He was small, neat, intense. "I haven't seen you here before."

"Perhaps that is because we haven't been to this event," Xing said.

Lopez lowered his voice conspiratorially. "There are muggles in the audience," he said. "So don't show them anything unusual."

"We won't," Xing whispered.

Chazz stepped to the edge of the stage: pale, glowing, and glamorous. Overhead monitors flashed on and were a relief: he was starting "small," producing and fanning decks of cards, making them jump and dance and appear in the cleavage of a woman in the front row. As their dinners appeared doves flitted, divided, burst into flame overhead and transformed into showers of wrapped candies, all to driving mystical music. The crowd applauded cautiously as they ate. Polite approval. Was this all?

"I need an assistant from the audience," the albino said. "I understand we have a luminary among us. A spotlight, please."

✦ ✦ ✦

The spotlight focused on Xing until she was forced to squint, but she was clearly eager for the fun. "Yes! Please!"

Her husband seemed unamused. "Oh, come now. It is unseemly, certainly." He said that as if challenging her to disagree.

Chazz led in cajoling applause. "Please, come up!"

Even the security officers applauded, and finally Chow Lee Ming relented, and Xing stood. Chazz's grip on her wrist proved her suspicion correct: this was a real person, a tall thin Dream Park actor wearing a life mask of startling realism.

The applause deepened as she was led away past rows of empty tables into the wings.

"I wanted to thank our volunteer," Chazz continued. "I assume that everyone in the room has signed non-disclosure agreements, because what I want to show you… what we will be showing you tonight, is the door between the real and the unreal."

Mary-Martha Corbett's weathered, happy face was animated as

she helped Xing into a waiting costume. From the wings, she watched Chazz perform another few tricks, from this perspective able to spot some of his astoundingly fluid sleight-of-hand moves. Eyes followed the moving hand, while the apparently motionless hand did the real work. Even though this was a medium-room "theater magic" magician, not on Chazz's "arena" level at all, he was still a pro.

He performed another few tricks as she wiggled out of one costume and into another. From the darkness, she could see her husband and security staff shifting restlessly: they knew she would be coming back, but not when or how.

Then… Xing Ming emerged from the wings and onto the stage, already striding with a theatrical thrust of hips and arms raised in a victory salute. She might have been born to greasepaint and glitter.

"And now… assistant. Are you ready!" Chazz said.

"I am ready!" Xing called out.

A cage was lowered from the ceiling. Nestled into the floor.

He spun the cage. "As you can see," Chazz said, "this is a standard circus cage. For a *very* un-standard lady."

He opened the door.

"Shall I enter?" Xing said, voice pitched low and breathy.

"Only if you dare," Chazz said.

"I dare!"

Her friends and minders cheered. Xing entered the cage. Chazz draped a curtain over its bars. The cage lifted to knee height.

"And now, the ancient words will be recited: *bibbity… bobbity… boo!*"

He pulled the cloth back up, and a Bengal tiger, regal in gold-and-black stripes, stalked the cage instead of the lady. The cage wobbled with its weight.

The crowd cheered.

The act went on, and the *Panthera tigris* leapt and pranced with perfect timing. Chazz rode it at one point, danced with it at another, and the illusion of a great cat performing a samba on its hind legs was impeccable. It was even endearingly clumsy.

Then someone screamed. The lights came up, and a spotlight shone on their table.

Richard Lopez lay slumped to the tabletop, face-down in his mashed potatoes, a pearl-handled knife in his back.

From the next table, a black woman in a form-fitting purple dress and slightly theatrical makeup leapt to her feet. "Wait!"

She felt Lopez's throat, her face grim. "Murder!" she said. "Seal the doors!" She lowered her voice. At least that was the impression—because somehow her voice was clearly audible all over the theater. "There is a murderer in the house!"

Chow Lee, who had seemed somewhat unimpressed by the tiger's antics, finally seemed thrilled. "Excellent!"

"I am Inspector Summers," the woman said. "And while I'm only here on vacation, if there is no other law-enforcement officer on site, I will be forced to take charge. Are there any other enforcement… or similar personnel?" And here she looked directly at the Chinese security people, a clear invitation.

The Chinese looked at each other, as if wondering if participation would break protocol. They looked at Chow Lee, who made a subtle hand gesture: *go ahead.*

The next twenty minutes were intense. Everyone in the room with the exception of Chazz was under suspicion, and even he was brought into the speculations. Who had killed Lopez? And why? And how?

The "how" was fairly clear: with a knife, in the darkness, as all attention was focused on the stage. But why?

Then… the lights went down again, flickered, and then back up. For a moment everyone assumed that it was just another phase of the game.

Then… the tiger flickered. "Look!" one of the security men said. It had turned into a wireframe, all color and flesh leeched away.

And then it disappeared completely. All the lights in the arena came up. "We are sorry," a disembodied voice said. "We apologize for the inconvenience. There has been a malfunction. We hope to resume operations in a moment."

Everyone, including "Inspector Summers", seemed puzzled.

For the first three minutes the guests thought this was just a part of the show. But when the "murdered" Lopez sat up and wiped mashed potatoes from his face, they knew something was very wrong indeed.

+ + +

Ten minutes later Alex Griffin appeared, looking rumpled and frustrated. It was late: he'd had a reasonable expectation of being done for the evening.

"Please, calm yourselves. I am sure there is an explanation."

Chow Lee Ming's brow was creased with stress lines as he struggled to keep control. "What answer can there be for the disappearance of my wife?"

Alex bit his tongue. "I can assure you that we are committing all of our resources to determine what is happening."

Yung's face, always severe, grew livid as she leashed her anger. "We demand that the park be locked down. Show us everything."

Millicent had shed her "Inspector Summers" persona, and seemed genuinely flustered.

"Millie," Alex said, "follow up with the imagineers."

"You already called?"

"Yes, but they're shut down for the night. I want them to wake someone up. And… cut the video feed."

"No need. Already a private party," Millie said. "Whatever happened here is already contained."

He nodded. "We can assume that there was a kidnapping either for political or economic reasons."

"I think it is most likely that this is economic," Security Woman Yung said.

"Why?"

"Xing was still wearing the expedition lenses. Rather than use disposable tourist lenses."

Alex felt an ulcer coming on. Why had no one told him?

Lopez stood up. "Mr. Griffin, I need your permission to open the puzzle box. Show our secrets."

Griffin tapped his ear and turned away from the others for a moment. Spoke. Then turned back. "Richard Lopez," Griffin said formally. "You have a release sent to your communicator, fully executed by our legal department, to give these gentlemen any and all assistance, with no reasonable withhold. Sign here, please."

Lopez tapped his ear, and then focused as if looking at an object floating in front of him. Signed in the air with his finger. Tapped his ear again, and nodded.

"Let's look at something that might be pertinent," Lopez said.

Millicent took Alex aside. "Alex… what do you think happened here?"

"Look at the stage," he said. "This would have been the conclusion of the show, just before the tiger turns back into a lady."

A video of a previous show. To the tunes of the classic rock ballad "Little Red Corvette" they watched a vid of Chazz allowing his tiger assistant to seal him into a coroner's bag and lay him in the back seat of a crimson '66 Dodge Corvette. A minute later a two-ton block of cement was dropped onto the car. The front row of diners had been blasted by the heat as the vehicle burst into flames, and a woman screamed in alarm: "*He's dead!*"

Millicent whistled, studying the combination of trick shackles, velcro escape zipper on the coroner's bag, and secret escape hatch on the underside of the car. "So that's how they do it," she said. "Do they destroy a car every time?"

"Three-dee printed, yes. Just a shell and seats, no engine… but still only for special shows. Alex: what do you see?"

"Distraction, special visual effects, special mechanical effects, showmanship."

"Yes. All to conceal a simple fact—that the magician was not in the car at all, after the first moments. Someone has managed a trick. We have to assume it was planned as well, and executed as cleverly. And that if we make the wrong assumption, we won't unravel the puzzle."

+ + +

"Dad and Mom both knew how the tricks were done, but they never told me," Scotty said. "I learned a little on my own."

"I know a bit of the theory," Amber said. "Swords have retractable blades. Forced perspective and agile assistants make boxes look more solid than they really are. Trap doors and duplicate coins or cards, sliding glass sheets with holes concealed by the magician's arms, or the wooden panels in which they are embedded."

"You are informed," he laughed.

"This is all ancient technology. The Jade Emperor's court magicians used similar deceptions."

"And Dream Park prized itself on using as few holographic tricks as possible. 'Real' magic means sleight of hand, genuine skill, classic prestidigitation... not just technology. The human eye likes to be tricked. But we like an honest liar."

She laughed. "Please continue."

✦ ✦ ✦

Lopez smiled like a sphinx. "A magician never reveals his secrets."

"This is an emergency," Millie reminded him.

"All right. What we can see is that the trick has several different levels. This is what was *supposed* to happen. The basic customers see the ordinary trick, the lady placed in the cage, then the cage covered, and the tiger appearing once the cover is released."

"And the others?" Alex asked.

"If they have a level-two lens, either contact or goggles, they would see through the cover, and would appear to see the actual transformation. The gag was that this was a stage magic show for real magic users, the 'muggles' in the crowd not in on the joke."

"This is no joke," Chow Ling Ming said.

"No, it isn't," Lopez said. "But it is important to understand what we're dealing with."

"Please, proceed if you must," Chow said.

"All right," Lopez said. "So forget the holography, or the illusion. The gag was fairly standard, probably has been for a thousand years. You have a stage setup that allows a switch."

"A real tiger?" Chow asked.

"In part, yes, that's part of the fun. Only the nanofiber leash is invisible. See here? It is where the assistant is lowered through a trapdoor. Once down, *she* pulls the lever, allowing the tiger entrance to the cage."

"So... this is the underground structure. You're saying that after or during the switch, she was abducted?"

"Yes," the little man said.

"But not taken out of the park," Alex said.

"How can you be sure of this?"

Alex sighed. "Because her costume contains a tracking chip. That chip is still inside the park."

"Could they not have removed the tag, the clothing?"

"I think not," Alex said. "We can run a back-trace."

Alex called up a series of screens. A miniature Xing moved through the tunnels... and then she disappeared.

Chow Lee Ming spoke in rapid Mandarin. Then in English. "What! What happened there?"

"We theorize that some sort of cloaking fabric or shroud was used here."

"Why could they have not removed the clothing?"

Millicent seemed very uncomfortable. "Alex..."

He shrugged. "You tell them."

Millicent sighed. "Because every high-security guest in Dream Park is tagged. You remember the drinks you were served, the toast?"

"Of course."

"They contained tasteless short-term biotags, excreted within twenty-four hours."

Chow Lee bristled. "You did this to us without our knowledge?"

"Your governments knew. And in fact insisted."

He looked at their security team. "Is this true?"

Yung dropped her eyes. "Yes."

He sputtered impotently. Immediately after her submissive eye-lowering, Yung became all business, scanning Griffin's footage and ignoring Ming completely.

Alex spotted it first. "We have a signal!" he crowed, pointing at a tiny red dot moving in a shimmering cubic meter of map lines.

"Let's go!" Lopez said.

"We are coming with you," Chow insisted.

"It may be dangerous," Alex said. "Millie, return to the office and coordinate from there. Mr. Chow, we would prefer—"

But Xing's husband would hear nothing of it. And... the chase was on...

+ + +

Armed with stunners and flashlights, Alex stalked the red dot, following Millie's instructions in his ear. They descended into the cool echoing service tunnels, and moved toward the center of the park, until they were under active rides, the vibration of machinery and feet faintly perceptible as tremors of walls and floor. The trail led them up a ladder and into a dark, deserted bubble dome. Their flashlight beams splashed against the walls, casting blurry shadows. Then the lights flickered on. He'd known this was Dome 4, but hadn't been sure what ride was currently active. Even with the lights on, most of the shapes were like coins devoid of the final stamp: shapes without definition, like a warehouse filled with unfinished Mardi Gras floats.

Millicent's voice whispered in his ear. "Alex… what's the move here?"

"We need to keep this under wraps as long as we can," he said. "No outside police."

"Why not?" Yung said.

"This might be their plan," he answered. "Associates in the police force, providing cover for exit."

She nodded. "That, or a wish to embarrass our government. It is best that we deal with this, if possible."

"We can provide a cordon outside the park. Foot traffic can leave, personal vehicles will be thoroughly searched."

"You can do it?"

"Part of the contract when they enter the park. All guests are liable for search of packages and vehicles."

Yung seemed happy at that. "Then we are in agreement. No one can be allowed to escape, yes?"

"Yes. This is a stunner," Alex said, brandishing a two-handed weapon. "And we followed Xing Ming this far and a little…"

The exhibit suddenly switched itself on, and Alex knew where he was. It wasn't Earth, and the bright, distant star in the heavens wasn't Sol. Not our solar system.

This was a nascent world, a youngling, something thrown out of a distant star in a time unreckoned.

The clouds were angry and red-tinged, and the wind blew high and hot. A rocky world a little bigger than Earth, with a heavier atmosphere. This was a place of savage storms and lava flows, lashed by a near-boiling ocean too violent to nurture life.

But he already knew: in time it would quiet. And cool. And then…

Real droplets of warm water spattered them, reminders of the actual savage world the illusions depicted.

"What is this place?" the security woman asked.

"An alien world. Speculation about how life might evolve on another planet. 'Xenolution' I think." His eyes narrowed. "They're here," he said. "Somewhere. I can feel it."

"Can't you turn the illusions off?"

"Not from here. It's working on a separate circuit. Has its own backups. We'll need to contact our engineers. But the good news is that they can't see us either, and we have the advantage of familiarity."

Millicent's voice in his ear. "Alex…?" He knew that tone of voice. Wary. Suspicious.

"Not now," he whispered.

"Then they are here," the Chinese security woman said. "Yes. I think so."

The world around them swelled, the floating shapes grown gargantuan. Alex and his group seemed to shrink as they slid down into briny depths. The air was hot, wet, hard to breathe, and he felt a moment of panic. *No. That's just the pheromones. The chemicals and subsonics that lash emotions, like Neutral Scent did. They calibrate it better now, so that you'll hallucinate that you are very nearly drowning.*

The warning signs and legal waivers for riders must have been pages long, he thought. Unless this system was malfunctioning, this illusion was one of the most oppressive he'd experienced at the park, a sense of airlessness and a billion tons of water weighing him down and down and down into the depths…

Down to an ocean floor, where darkness yielded to volcanic light. Glowing lava and heat vents churning with bubbles of sulfurous gas, a vast field of vents, as far as the eye could see. And then… a gelatinous mass of something loomed up out of the gloom, mostly clear but a few darker blotches floating within.

The security woman spoke in rapid Chinese as the air seethed with muck.

"What is this?" Wong asked.

"This will be the beginning of life, I think," the security woman said.

"I cannot see," Wong protested.

"Look! There!" Alex called.

The proto-cell was joined by siblings, and the cells had begun to link together, forming more complex organisms. And in the midst of it, they glimpsed something that was not an illusion: a real flesh-and-blood human being, running away.

"After him!" Wong called.

The air suddenly vibrated with a synthesized voice. Old-fashioned. Twentieth-century. He recognized it: that was Stephen Hawking's synthesizer. "*And after billions of years, the first living things arose from the seething cauldron of the ocean floors—*"

The runner turned and a CRACK sound shivered the air.

"Gun!" Alex yelled, and they threw themselves to the ground.

Around them, the images sped up, evolution progressing at an accelerated rate.

"There!" Wong called.

The narrator continued, oblivious. "*From prokaryotic single-celled organisms to eukaryotic multi-cells, life evolved rapidly, so rapidly that many scientists believe that living things may be a natural consequence of certain conditions. That in our galaxy we have billions of stars with planets that might have water, and temperatures that allow basic elements to grow more complex in a form of chemical evolution, and then—*"

"There!" Alex called.

He had to call it twice. They were hypnotized by the display, but also beginning to focus so that they were seeing through the illusions.

"*—who knows what might be found on such other planets? We will, quite soon. For this is not Earth, and these are not the creatures we know from studying our own planet. This is a world of savage new life—*"

Alex spoke rapidly into his throat mike. "Security. We need a seal on the Xenolution exhibit. No shooting. There may be a hostage."

The creatures had clustered, grown more complex and hideous. The stage rose up from the ocean deep.

"*—and during the equivalent of our own Devonian period, their sea life might rise up from the seas and take to the land. Water was their womb, but if their life is like ours, they would develop tough skin that would protect them from drying out, so that their internal organisms could continue to function. We are still basically aquatic organisms which have simply made special accommodation—*"

Alex snuck around the thrusting rocks. The Chinese didn't follow, confused by the images of this savage new world.

Suddenly up ahead a male form appeared again, barely distinguished before he fired twice. A pane of glass behind them exploded.

"Down!"

Two Dream Park security men had appeared from behind them, and one of them handed a non-lethal capacitor gun to Yung, who checked it with thorough professionalism, nodded, and then began returning fire.

"*—We owe our current world to the foundation of these simple creatures, and alien civilizations may… do… the… saaaaame…*"

Then… the narration stopped. The illusions died.

The lights came up. No human beings to be seen, but a hole gaped in the floor, a wan light filtering up from beneath it.

Alex advanced cautiously, until finally he stood over the gap. "Down here!"

✦ ✦ ✦

Alex landed in balance, scanning carefully, cautiously.

Dream Park and Chinese security streamed down behind him.

"I have a signal!" Alex cried.

They ran through a series of tunnels, until they reached a sealed green panel.

"Open this door!"

Yung and her crew hammered at the closed portal. "It's locked!"

Within ninety seconds, Dream Park tech staff had arrived.

"Open this damned door," Alex said.

"Where does this tunnel lead?" Yung asked.

"To a parking structure. No one would be able to get out of the structure with a prisoner."

"Could they escape… unburdened?"

Alex grimaced. "I can't lie to you. It's possible. There are almost eighty thousand people at Dream Park on any given day. We can scan for Xing's biometrics, either Cowles or your own. But there is no way to stop everyone. There just isn't."

"I see." Her husband had been listening, unamused. "I suggest you pray that Xing is unharmed."

"You and me both."

The electronic key had failed to open the door. "They've sealed it from the inside," Griffin said. Tools were produced, and the door hinges burned through swiftly.

The door opened. And there, curled up… was a groggy Xing.

"Xing!" Her husband cradled her in his arms. "Are you all right?"

She seemed flushed, skin hot. "What… what happened? Gas. There was a mask over my face…"

"We're still guessing."

"Separatists," she said. "I think I heard them speak in Lhasa."

Wong's face darkened. "Quickly. Get her to medical."

She collapsed in her husband's arms. A crowd was gathering. Millicent appeared, scowling at everyone.

✦ ✦ ✦

Xing sat on the edge of the doctor's examination table.

"You seem fine," the doctor said. "I'm not sure what gas was used to render you unconscious. It seems to have metabolized already."

Wong clutched the doctor's arm. "But… she is well?"

"The contact lenses were out of her eyes."

"We found these in the storage space," Millicent said. She opened her hand, and in the palm nestled two tiny, burned plastic knots.

Wong sputtered. "The lenses! But… why would they remove them just to destroy them?"

"I don't know," Xing said. "I don't remember anything at all."

"We should be relieved," the security woman said.

Alex frowned. "Why wouldn't they want to take them? Why destroy them?"

Wong shook his head. "I am afraid that we must apologize," he said.

"We have… internal state issues. I certainly had no intention to bring them to your country, or for your hospitality to be abused in such a way. It is embarrassing."

"But why…" Alex couldn't figure it. Why destroy the lenses? Dream Park would have the specs on record. They could be reproduced.

"It doesn't make sense," Millicent said. "No one could have stopped them from smuggling them out of the park."

"Perhaps," Wong said, "they did not know that. Did not know if there would be some way to trace them, and settled for the symbolic value. They could destroy the 'eyes' of our great hero. A warning, perhaps."

"But…"

"The rest is ours. We will pay for any damage and inconvenience."

They swept Xing up in a protective phalanx, and were gone.

+ + +

Scotty had concluded his tale.

"That's the official story?" Amber asked.

"Yes."

"But…" She closed her eyes, fingers clicking against her armrests.

"Yes?" He said it teasingly.

"But I believe you have excluded some pertinent facts."

Scotty smiled. "Why yes, I did. And so did my father. And so did Xing."

She looked at him shrewdly. "Xing wasn't in that pod the whole time, was she?"

"Nope."

"Then… then she had to have been somewhere that those tracers didn't work?"

"Why yes, that's true." His smile was downright mischievous.

"Around Dream Park… what sort of environments were shielded at that time?"

"There were a few choices," Scotty said. "Certain executive wash-rooms and… rest units for instance."

"Rest units?"

He smiled a little more widely.

"Comfort stations. Small. Cozy. Usually just a wet bar and a bed."

Now it was Amber's full pink lips that turned up. "A place for the busy executive to escape the daily grind?"

"Dream Park was known for discretion, in an age when California had turned prudish. There are always times that busy, wealthy people need to… get away."

"Xing and your father… got away."

He nodded. "I can only talk about this because the people involved have passed on, you understand."

"So Xing and your father met two years earlier when the Chinese were testing the lens technology?"

He felt more relaxed now. She'd been right. It was good to unburden himself, after all this time. "Yes. And she managed to communicate privately with him after returning to Earth, when she knew they were coming to California."

"An assignation was arranged."

"Yes," Scotty said. "Private time. She was going to be smuggled out at the beginning of a ninety-minute stage show, giving them an hour together."

Her eyes twinkled. "I'm sure they made the most of it."

"I have no direct information," he laughed. "I can tell you that my father still had a sparkle in his eye forty years later."

"And if the accident had not occurred… then she would have been smuggled back in."

He nodded. "A tiger turned back into a woman. And no one would have been the wiser."

"That's quite a story."

"Isn't it?"

"Yes…" she said. "An assignation. A jealous husband. A baffled security woman. You know quite a bit, but not everything."

His brow wrinkled. "What am I missing?"

"What if… the malfunction was not an accident?"

"What?"

"It was planned. By Xing."

His head spun. "Why?"

"Because that was the only way she could meet with her contact, and pass him the lenses?"

He was gobsmacked. "Why would she do that?"

"For the money she needed to leave Chow and build her own life."

He felt like he was falling down a hole. "Why would she need that?"

Amber folded her hands. "She was a national hero. Her husband was politically connected. Enough to make divorce very difficult. Embarrassing."

"So… with that nest egg she was able to divorce her powerful husband?"

"Precisely," Amber said.

Scotty frowned. "You… know quite a bit about this. She died when you were… twenty? I assume you were not yet a reporter? How precisely did you learn these things if not through interview?"

"Through… conversation."

A notion was starting to shape in his mind. "You knew each other."

"Yes," she said.

"Very well."

"Yes," she said again. Scotty was starting to feel foolish… and fascinated.

"She… was your mother."

She laughed. "Yes. And that means that unless I am very much mistaken, you will need to change your hopes for the evening… brother."

His mouth dropped open.

+ + +

They rode an electric trolley out to Clavius and there disembarked. The half-siblings wore tourist suits, designed for safe ambulation across the lunar surface, a chance to see shadows sharper than any on Earth, to see the crisp blue-white cradle of life hovering above them. There Scotty walked carefully ahead of her, listening to the slow hiss of air in his helmet, mind buzzing with thoughts as he took her to the orderly rows of mounds. Down twelve rows. Over three. And there were the plaques. He'd seen them many times, but not so often of late.

Alex Griffin. Millicent Summers-Griffin. Headstones.

"He wanted to rest here," he said. "So did Mom. He brought her ashes all the way here. Lived for four years after he arrived. The doctors had only given him six weeks. Something about the gravity."

"I never met him," Amber said. "I wish I had."

"I never knew I had a sister. You never knew your father. We… both have questions. Both have things we can share."

"Perhaps…" she said, "perhaps I could stay here for a while." She paused, and when she spoke again seemed almost shy. "Might there be jobs for reporters here?"

"I may have a few contacts," he said.

And they stood that way, quietly, for quite a while. Then turned and returned to Dome Two.

James Blish became a science fiction fan in the 1930s and was part of a well-known New York group called "the Futurians." He became a respected editor and critic, as well as author, and is known to many fans for his novelizations of Star Trek: The Original Series *episodes, which many of us read as children. He also wrote the first original Star Trek novel,* Spock Must Die!

Part of a larger body of work called Cities in Flight, *"Earthman, Come Home" was originally published in 1953 in* Astounding Science Fiction, *and won a Retro Hugo Award in 2004 for Best Novelette. It takes place in a universe where the spindizzy-powered city of New York, New York engages in faster-than-light adventures across the universe. John Amalfi is the mayor of New York, as he has been for the past five hundred years. Amalfi is old but a skilled negotiator with hard-nosed business skills that have grown with his age.*

In this imagined future, social changes resulting from centuries of galactic transit have resulted in many space-roaming cities regressing to savage, chaotic states who often endanger other civilizations. In this story, New York must get free of trouble of its own making.

EARTHMAN, COME HOME
JAMES BLISH

I.

The city hovered, then settled silently through the early morning darkness toward the broad expanse of heath which the planet's Proctors had designated as its landing place. At this hour, the edge of the misty acres of diamonds which were the Greater Magellanic Cloud was just beginning to touch the western horizon; the whole cloud covered nearly 35° of the sky. The cloud would set at 5:12 a.m.; at 6:00 the near edge of the home galaxy would rise, but during the summer the sun rose earlier and would blot it out.

All of which was quite all right with Mayor Amalfi. The fact that no significant amount of the home galaxy would begin to show in the night sky for months was one of the reasons why he had chosen this planet to settle on. The situation confronting the city posed problems enough without its being complicated by an unsatisfiable homesickness.

The city grounded, and the last residual hum of the spindizzies stopped. From below there came a rapidly rising and more erratic hum of human activity, and the clank and roar of heavy equipment getting under way. The geology team was losing no time, as usual.

Amalfi, however, felt no disposition to go down at once. He remained on the balcony of City Hall looking at the thickly set night sky. The star-density here in the Greater Magellanic was very high, even outside the clusters—at most the distances between stars were matters of light-months rather than light-years. Even should it prove impossible to move the city itself again—which was inevitable, considering that the Sixtieth Street spindizzy had just followed the Twenty-third Street machine into the junk-pit—it should be possible to set interstellar commerce going here by cargo ship. The city's remaining drivers, ripped out and remounted on a one-per-hull basis, would provide the nucleus of quite a respectable little fleet.

It would not be much like cruising among the far-scattered, various civilizations of the Milky Way had been, but it would be commerce of a sort, and commerce was the Okies' oxygen.

He looked down. The brilliant starlight showed that the blasted heath extended all the way to the horizon in the west; in the east it stopped about a kilo away and gave place to land regularly divided into tiny squares. Whether each of these minuscule fields represented an individual farm he could not tell, but he had his suspicions. The language the Proctors had used in giving the city permission to land had had decidedly feudal overtones.

While he watched, the black skeleton of some tall structure erected itself swiftly nearby, between the city and the eastern stretch of the heath. The geology team already had its derrick in place. The phone at the balcony's rim buzzed and Amalfi picked it up.

"Boss, we're going to drill now," the voice of Mark Hazleton, the city manager, said. "Coming down?"

"Yes. What do the soundings show?"

"Nothing very hopeful, but we'll know for sure shortly. This does look like oil land, I must say."

"We've been fooled before," Amalfi grunted. "Start boring; I'll be right down."

He had barely hung up the phone when the burring roar of the molar drill violated the still summer night, echoing calamitously among the buildings of the city. It was almost certainly the first time any planet in the Greater Magellanic had heard the protest of collapsing molecules, though the technique had been a century out of date back in the Milky Way.

Amalfi was delayed by one demand and another all the way to the field, so that it was already dawn when he arrived. The test bore had been sunk and the drill was being pulled up again; the team had put up a second derrick, from the top of which Hazleton waved to him. Amalfi waved back and went up in the lift.

There was a strong, warm wind blowing at the top, which had completely tangled Hazleton's hair under the earphone clips. To Amalfi, who was bald, it could make no such difference, but after years of the city's precise air-conditioning it did obscure things to his emotions.

"Anything yet, Mark?"

"You're just in time. Here she comes."

The first derrick rocked as the long core sprang from the earth and slammed into its side girders. There was no answering black fountain. Amalfi leaned over the rail and watched the sampling crew rope in the cartridge and guide it back down to the ground. The winch rattled and choked off, its motor panting.

"No soap," Hazleton said disgustedly. "I knew we shouldn't have trusted the Proctors."

"There's oil under here somewhere all the same," Amalfi said. "We'll get it out. Let's go down."

On the ground, the senior geologist had split the cartridge and was telling his way down the boring with a mass-pencil. He shot Amalfi a quick reptilian glance as the mayor's blocky shadow fell across the table.

"No dome," he said succinctly.

Amalfi thought about it. Now that the city was permanently cut off from the home galaxy, no work that it could do for money would mean a great deal to it. What was needed first of all was oil, so that the city could eat. Work that would yield good returns in the local currency would have to come much later. Right now the city would have to work for payment in drilling permits.

At the first contact that had seemed to be easy enough. This planet's natives had never been able to get below the biggest and most obvious oil domes, so there should be plenty of oil left for the city. In turn, the city could throw up enough low-grade molybdenum and tungsten as a byproduct of drilling to satisfy the terms of the Proctors.

But if there was no oil to crack for food—

"Sink two more shafts," Amalfi said. "You've got an oil-bearing till down there, anyhow. We'll pressure jellied gasoline into it and split it. Ride along a Number Eleven gravel to hold the seam open. If there's no dome, we'll boil the oil out."

"Steak yesterday and steak tomorrow," Hazleton murmured. "But never steak today."

Amalfi swung upon the city manager, feeling the blood charging upward through his thick neck. "Do you think you'll get fed any other way?" he growled. "This planet is going to be home for us from now on. Would you rather take up farming, like the natives? I thought you outgrew *that* notion after the raid on Gort."

"That isn't what I meant," Hazleton said quietly. His heavily space-tanned face could not pale; but it blued a little under the taut, weathered bronze. "I know just as well as you do that we're here for good. It just seemed funny to me that settling down on a planet for good should begin just like any other job."

"I'm sorry," Amalfi said, mollified. "I shouldn't be so jumpy. Well, we don't know yet how well off we are. The natives never have mined this planet to anything like pay-dirt depth, and they refine stuff by throwing it into a stew pot. If we can get past this food problem, we've still got a good chance of turning this whole Cloud into a tidy corporation."

He turned his back abruptly on the derricks and began to walk slowly eastward away from the city. "I feel like a walk," he said. "Like to come along, Mark?"

"A walk?" Hazleton looked puzzled. "Why—sure. OK, boss."

✦ ✦ ✦

For a while they trudged in silence over the heath. The going was rough; the soil was clayey, and heavily gullied, particularly deceptive in the early morning light. Very little seemed to grow on it: only an occasional bit of low, starved shrubbery, a patch of tough, nettlelike stalks, a few clinging weeds like crab grass.

"This doesn't strike me as good farming land," Hazleton said. "Not that I know a thing about it."

"There's better land farther out, as you saw from the city," Amalfi said. "But I agree about the heath. It's blasted land. I wouldn't even believe it was radiologically safe until I saw the instrument readings with my own eyes."

"A war?"

"Long ago, maybe. But I think geology did most of the damage. The land was let alone too long; the topsoil's all gone. It's odd, considering how intensively the rest of the planet seems to be farmed."

They half-slid into a deep arroyo and scrambled up the other side. "Boss, straighten me out on something," Hazleton said. "Why did we adopt this planet, even after we found that it had people of its own? We passed several others that would have done as well. Are we going to push the local population out? We're not too well set up for that, even if it were legal or just."

"Do you think there are Earth cops in the Greater Magellanic, Mark?"

"No," Hazleton said, "but there are Okies now, and if I wanted justice I'd go to Okies, not to cops. What's the answer, Amalfi?"

"We may have to do a little judicious pushing," Amalfi said, squinting ahead. The double suns were glaring directly in their faces. "It's all in knowing where to push, Mark. You heard the character some of the outlying planets gave this place, when we spoke to them on the way in."

"They hate the smell of it," Hazleton said, carefully removing a burr from his ankle. "It's my guess that the Proctors made some early expeditions unwelcome. Still—"

Amalfi topped a rise and held out one hand. The city manager fell silent almost automatically, and clambered up beside him.

The cultivated land began, only a few meters away. Watching them were two—creatures.

One, plainly, was a man; a naked man, the color of chocolate, with matted blue-black hair. He was standing at the handle of a single-bladed plow, which looked to be made of the bones of some large animal. The furrow that he had been opening stretched behind him beside its fellows, and farther back in the field there was a low hut. The man was standing, shading his eyes, evidently looking across the dusky heath toward the Okie city. His shoulders were enormously broad and muscular, but bowed even when he stood erect, as now.

The figure leaning into the stiff leather straps which drew the plow also was human; a woman. Her head hung down, as did her arms, and her hair, as black as the man's but somewhat longer, fell forward and hid her face.

As Hazleton froze, the man lowered his head until he was looking directly at the Okies. His eyes were blue and unexpectedly piercing. "Are you the gods from the city?" he said.

Hazleton's lips moved. The serf could hear nothing; Hazleton was speaking into his throat-mike, audible only to the receiver imbedded in Amalfi's right mastoid bone.

"English, by the gods of all stars! The Proctors speak Interlingua. What's this, boss? Was the Cloud colonized *that* far back?"

Amalfi shook his head. "We're from the city," the mayor said aloud, in the same tongue. "What's your name, young fella?"

"Karst, lord."

"Don't call me 'lord.' I'm not one of your Proctors. Is this your land?"

"No, lord. Excuse… have no other word—"

"My name is Amalfi."

"This is the Proctors' land, Amalfi. I work this land. Are you of Earth?"

Amalfi shot a swift sidelong glance at Hazleton. The city manager's face was expressionless.

"Yes," Amalfi said. "How did you know?"

"By the wonder," Karst said. "It is a great wonder, to raise a city in a single night. IMT itself took nine men of hands of thumbs of suns to build, the singers say. To raise a second city on the Barrens overnight—such a thing is beyond words."

He stepped away from the plow, walking with painful, hesitant steps, as if all his massive muscles hurt him. The woman raised her head from the traces and pulled the hair back from her face. The eyes that looked forth at the Okies were dull, but there were phosphorescent stirrings of alarm behind them. She reached out and grasped Karst by the elbow.

"It… is nothing," she said.

He shook her off. "You have built a city over one of night," he repeated. "You speak the Engh tongue, as we do on feast days. You speak to such as me, with words, not with the whips with the little tags. You have fine clothes, with patches of color of fine-woven cloth."

It was beyond doubt the longest speech he had ever made in his life. The clay on his forehead was beginning to streak with the effort.

"You are right," Amalfi said. "We are from Earth, though we left it long ago. I will tell you something else, Karst. You, too, are of Earth."

"That is not so," Karst said, retreating a step. "I was born here, and all my people. None claim Earth blood—"

"I understand," Amalfi said. "You are of this planet. But you are an Earthman. And I will tell you something else. I do not think the Proctors are Earthmen. I think they lost the right to call themselves Earthmen long ago, on another planet, a planet named Thor V."

Karst wiped his calloused palms against his thighs. "I want to understand," he said. "Teach me."

"Karst!" the woman said pleadingly. "It is nothing. Wonders pass. We are late with the planting."

"Teach me," Karst said doggedly. "All our lives we furrow the fields, and on the holidays they tell us of Earth. Now there is a marvel here, a city raised by the hands of Earthmen, there are Earthmen in it who speak to us—" He stopped. He seemed to have something in his throat.

"Go on," Amalfi said gently.

"Teach me. Now that Earth has built a city on the Barrens, the Proctors cannot hold knowledge for their own any longer. Even when you go, we will learn from your empty city, before it is ruin by wind and rain. Lord Amalfi, if we are Earthmen, teach us as Earthmen are taught."

"Karst," said the woman, "it is not for us. It is a magic of the Proctors. All magics are of the Proctors. They mean to take us from our children. They mean us to die on the Barrens. They tempt us."

The serf turned to her. There was something indefinably gentle in the motion of his brutalized, crackle-skinned, thick-muscled body.

"You need not go," he said, in a slurred Interlingua patois which was obviously his usual tongue. "Go on with the plowing, does it please you. But this is no thing of the Proctors. They would not stoop to tempt slaves as mean as we are. We have obeyed the laws, given our tithes, observed the holidays. This is of Earth."

The woman clenched her horny hands under her chin and shivered. "It is forbidden to speak of Earth except on holidays. But I will finish the plowing. Otherwise our children will die."

"Come, then," Amalfi said. "There is much to learn."

To his complete consternation, the serf went down on both knees. A second later, while Amalfi was still wondering what to do next, Karst was up again, and climbing up onto the Barrens toward them. Hazleton offered him a hand, and was nearly hurled like a flat stone through the air when Karst took it; the serf was as solid and strong as a pile driver, and as sure on his stony feet.

"Karst, will you return before night?" the woman cried.

Karst did not answer. Amalfi began to lead the way back toward the city. Hazleton started down the far side of the rise after them, but something moved him to look back again at the little scrap of farm. The woman's head had fallen forward again, the wind stirring the tangled curtain of her hair. She was leaning heavily into the galling traces, and the plow was again beginning to cut its way painfully through the stony soil. There was now, of course, nobody to guide it.

"Boss," Hazleton said into the throat-mike, "are you listening?"

"I'm listening."

"I don't think I want to snitch a planet from these people."

Amalfi didn't answer; he knew well enough that there was no answer. The Okie city would never go aloft again. This planet was home. There was no place else to go.

The voice of the woman, crooning as she plowed, dwindled behind them. Her song droned monotonously over unseen and starving children: a lullaby. Hazleton and Amalfi had fallen from the sky to rob her of everything but the stony and now unharvestable soil. It was Amalfi's hope to return her something far more valuable.

It had been the spindizzy, of course, which had scooped up the cities of Earth—and later, of many other planets—and hurled them into space. Two other social factors, however, had made possible the roving, nomadic culture of the Okies, a culture which had lasted more than three thousand years, and which probably would take another five hundred to disintegrate completely.

One of these was personal immortality. The conquest of so-called "natural" death had been virtually complete by the time the technicians on the Jovian Bridge had confirmed the spindizzy principle, and the two went together like hand in spacemitt. Despite the fact that the spindizzy would drive a ship—or a city—at speeds enormously faster than that of light, interstellar flight still consumed finite time. The vastness of the galaxy was sufficient to make long flights consume lifetimes even at top spindizzy speed.

But when death yielded to the anti-athapic drugs, there was no longer any such thing as a "lifetime" in the old sense.

The other factor was economic: the rise of the metal germanium as the jinni of electronics. Long before flight in deep space became a fact, the metal had assumed a fantastic value on Earth. The opening of the interstellar frontier drove its price down to a manageable level, and gradually it emerged as the basic, stable monetary standard of space trade. Coinage in conductor metals, whose value had always been largely a matter of pressure politics, became extinct; it became impossible to maintain, for instance, the fiction that silver was precious, when it lay about in such flagrant profusion in the rocks of every newly discovered Earthlike planet. The semiconductor germanium became the coin of the star-man's realm.

And after three thousand years, personal immortality and the germanium standard joined forces to destroy the Okies.

It had always been inevitable that the germanium standard would not last. The time was bound to come when the metal would be synthesized cheaply, or a substance even more versatile would be found, or some temporary center of trade would corner a significant fraction of the money in circulation. It was not even necessary to predict specifically how the crisis would occur, to be able to predict what it would do to the economy of the galaxy. Had it happened a little earlier, before the economies of thousands of star-systems had become grounded in the standard, the effect probably would have been only temporary.

But when the germanium standard finally collapsed, it took with it the substrate in which the Okies had been imbedded. The semi-conductor base was relegated to the same limbo which had claimed the conductor-metal base. The most valuable nonconductors in the galaxy were the anti-athapic drugs; the next currency was based on a drug standard.

As a standard it was excellent, passing all the tests that a coinage is supposed to meet. The drugs could be indefinitely diluted for small change; they had never been synthesized, and any other form of counterfeiting could be detected easily by bio-assay and other simple tests; they were very rare; they were universally needed; their sources of supply were few enough in number to be readily monitored.

Unfortunately, the star-cruising Okies needed the drugs *as drugs*. They could not afford to use them as money.

From that moment on, the Okies were no longer the collective citizens of a nomadic culture. They were just interstellar bums. There was no place for them in the galaxy anymore.

Outside the galaxy, of course, the Okie commerce lanes had never penetrated—

+ + +

The city was old—unlike the men and women who manned it, who had merely lived a long time, which is quite a different thing. And like any old intelligence, its past sins lay very near the surface, ready for review either in nostalgia or self-accusation at the slightest cue. It was difficult these days to get any kind of information out of the City Fathers without having to submit to a lecture, couched in as high a moral tone as was possible to machines whose highest morality was survival.

Amalfi knew well enough what he was letting himself in for when he asked the City Fathers for a review of the Violations Docket. He got it, in bells—big bells. The City Fathers gave him everything, right down to the day a dozen centuries ago when they had discovered that nobody had dusted the city's ancient subways since the city had first gone into space. That had been the first time the Okies had ever heard that the city had ever had any subways.

But Amalfi stuck to the job, though his right ear ached with the pressure of the earphone. Out of the welter of minor complaints and wistful recollections of missed opportunities, certain things came through clearly and urgently.

The city had never been officially cleared of its failure to observe the "Vacate" order the cops had served on it during the reduction of Utopia. Later, during the same affair, the city had been hung with a charge of technical treason—not as serious as it sounded, but subject to inconvenient penalties—while on the neighboring planet of Hrunta, and had left the scene with the charge still on the docket. There had been a small trick pulled there, too, which the cops could hardly have forgotten: while it had not been illegal, it had created laughter at the expense of the cops in every Okie wardroom in the galaxy, and cops seldom like to be laughed at.

Then there was the moving of He. The city had fulfilled its contract with that planet to the letter, but unfortunately that could never be proven; He was now well on its way across the intergalactic gap toward Andromeda, and could not testify on the city's behalf. As far as the cops knew, the city had destroyed He, a notion the cops would be no less likely to accept simply because it was ridiculous.

Worst of all, however, was the city's participation in the March on Earth. The March had been a tragedy from beginning to end, and few of the several hundred Okie cities which had taken part in it had survived it. It had been a product of the galaxy-wide depression which had followed the collapse of the germanium standard. Amalfi's city—already accused of several crimes in the star-system where the March had started, crimes which as a matter of fact the city had actually been forced to commit—had gone along because it had had no better choice, and had done what it could to change the March from a mutual massacre to a collective bargaining session; but the massacre had occurred all the same. No one city, not even Amalfi's, could have made its voice heard above the long roar of galactic collapse.

There was the redeeming fact that the city, during the March, had found and extirpated one of the last residues of the Vegan tyranny. But it could never be proven: like the affair on He, the city had done so thorough a job that even the evidence was gone irrevocably.

Amalfi sighed. In the end, it appeared that the Earth cops would remember Amalfi's city for two things only. *One:* The city had a long Violations Docket, and still existed to be brought to book on it. *Two:* The city had gone out toward the Greater Magellanic, just as a far older and blacker city had done centuries before—the city which had perpetrated the massacre on Thor V, the city whose memory still stank in the nostrils of cops and surviving Okies alike.

Amalfi shut off the City Fathers in mid-reminiscence and removed the phone from his aching ear. The control boards of the city stretched before him, still largely useful, but dead forever in one crucial bloc— the bank that had once flown the city from star to new star. The city was grounded; it had no choice now but to accept, and then win, this one poor planet for its own.

If the cops would let it. The Magellanic Clouds were moving steadily and with increasing velocity away from the home galaxy; the gap was already so large that the city had had to cross it by using a dirigible planet as a booster-stage. It would take the cops time to decide that they should make that enormously long flight in pursuit of one miserable Okie. But in the end they would make that decision. The cleaner the home galaxy became of Okies—and there was no doubt but that the cops had by now broken up the majority of the space-faring cities—the greater the urge would become to track down the last few stragglers.

Amalfi had no faith in the ability of a satellite starcloud to outrun human technology. By the time the cops were ready to cross from the home lens to the Greater Magellanic, they would have *the* techniques with which to do it, and techniques far less clumsy than those Amalfi's city had used. If the cops wanted to chase the Greater Magellanic, they would find ways to catch it. If—

Amalfi took up the earphone again. "Question," he said. "Will the need to catch us be urgent enough to produce the necessary techniques in time?"

The City Fathers hummed, drawn momentarily from their eternal mulling over the past. At last they said:

"YES, MAYOR AMALFI. BEAR IN MIND THAT WE ARE NOT ALONE—IN THIS CLOUD. REMEMBER THOR V."

There it was: the ancient slogan that had made Okies hated even on planets that had never seen an Okie city, and could never expect to. There was only the smallest chance that the city which had wrought the Thor V atrocity had made good its escape to this Cloud; it had all happened a long time ago. But even the narrow chance, if the City Fathers were right, would bring the cops here sooner or later, to destroy Amalfi's own city in expiation of that still-burning crime.

Remember Thor V. No city would be safe until that raped and murdered world could be forgotten. Not even out here, in the virgin satellites of the home lens.

+ + +

"Boss? Sorry, we didn't know you were busy. But we've got an operating schedule set up, as soon as you're ready to look at it."

"I'm ready right now, Mark," Amalfi said, turning away from the boards. "Hello, Dee. How do you like your planet?"

The former Utopian girl smiled. "It's beautiful," she said simply.

"For the most part, anyway," Hazleton agreed. "This heath is an ugly place, but the rest of the land seems to be excellent—much better than you'd think it from the way it's being farmed. The tiny little fields they break it up into here just don't do it justice, and even I know better cultivation methods than these serfs do."

"I'm not surprised," Amalfi said. "It's my theory that the Proctors maintain their power partly by preventing the spread of any knowledge about farming beyond the most rudimentary kind. That's also the most rudimentary kind of politics, as I don't need to tell you."

"On the politics," Hazleton said evenly, "we're in disagreement. While that's ironing itself out, the business of running the city has to go on."

"All right," Amalfi said. "What's on the docket?"

"I'm having a small plot on the heath, next to the city, turned over and conditioned for some experimental plantings, and extensive soil tests have already been made. That's purely a stopgap, of course. Eventually we'll have to expand onto good land. I've drawn up a tentative contract of lease between the city and the Proctors, which provides for us to rotate ownership geographically so as to keep displacement of the serfs at a minimum, and at the same time opens a complete spectrum of seasonal plantings to us—essentially it's the old Limited Colony contract, but heavily weighted in the direction of the Proctors' prejudices. There's no doubt in my mind but that they'll sign it. Then—"

"They won't sign it," Amalfi said. "They can't even be shown it. Furthermore, I want everything you've put into your experimental plot here on the heath yanked out."

Hazleton put a hand to his forehead in frank exasperation. "Boss," he said, "don't tell me that we're *still* not at the end of the old squirrel-cage routine—intrigue, intrigue, and then more intrigue. I'm sick of it, I'll tell you that directly. Isn't two thousand years enough for you? I thought we had come to this planet to settle down!"

"We did. We will. But as you reminded me yourself yesterday, there are other people in possession of this planet at the moment—people we can't legally push out. As matters stand right now, we can't give them the faintest sign that we mean to settle here; they're already intensely suspicious of that very thing, and they're watching us for evidence of it every minute."

"Oh, no," Dee said. She came forward swiftly and put a hand on Amalfi's shoulder. "John, you promised us after the March was over that we were going to make a home here. Not necessarily on this planet, but somewhere in the Cloud. You promised, John."

The mayor looked up at her. It was no secret to her, or to Hazleton either, that he loved her; they both knew, as well, the cruelly just Okie law that forbade the mayor of an Okie city any permanent alliance with a woman—and the vein of iron loyalty in Amalfi that would have compelled him to act by that law even had it never existed. Until the sudden crisis far back in the Acolyte cluster which had forced Amalfi to reveal to Hazleton the existence of that love, neither of the two youngsters had suspected it over a period of nearly nine decades.

But Dee was comparatively new to Okie mores, and was in addition a woman. Only to know that she was loved had been unable to content her long. She was already beginning to put the knowledge to work.

"Of course I promised," Amalfi said. "I've delivered on my promises for nearly two thousand years, and I'll continue to do so. The blunt fact is that the City Fathers would have me shot if I didn't—as they nearly had Mark shot on more than one occasion. This planet will be our home, if you'll give me just the minimum of help in winning it. It's the best of all the planets we passed on the way in, for a great many reasons—including a couple that won't begin to show until you see the winter constellations here, plus a few more that won't become evident for a century yet. But there's one thing I certainly can't give you, and that's immediate delivery."

"All right," Dee said. She smiled. "I trust you, John, you know that. But it's hard to be patient."

"Is it?" Amalfi said, surprised. "Come to think of it, I remember once during the tipping of He when the same thought occurred to me. In retrospect the problem doesn't seem large."

"Boss, you'd better give us some substitute courses of action," the city manager's voice cut in, a little coldly. "With the possible exception of yourself, every man and woman and alley cat in the city is ready to spread out all over the surface of this planet the moment the starting gun is fired. You've given us every reason to think that that would be the way it would happen. If there's going to be a delay, you have a good many idle hands to put to work."

"Use straight work-contract procedure, all the way down the line," Amalfi said. "No exploiting of the planet that we wouldn't normally do during the usual stopover for a job. That means no truck-gardens or any other form of local agriculture; just refilling the oil tanks, re-breeding the Chlorella strains from local sources for heterosis, and so on."

"That won't work," Hazleton said. "It may fool the Proctors, Amalfi, but how can you fool our own people? What are you going to do with the perimeter police, for instance? Sergeant Paterson's whole crew knows that it won't ever again have to make up a boarding squad or defend the city or take up any other military duty. Nine tenths of them are itching to throw off their harness for good and start dirt-farming. What am I to do with them?"

"Send 'em out to your experimental potato patch on the heath," Amalfi said. "On police detail. Tell 'em to pick up everything that grows."

Hazleton started to turn toward the lift shaft, holding out his hand to Dee. Then he turned back.

"But why, boss?" he said plaintively. "What makes you think that the Proctors suspect us of squatting? And what could they do about it if they did?"

"The Proctors have asked for the standard work-contract," Amalfi said. "They know what it is, and they insist upon its observation, to the letter, *including* the provision that the city must be off this planet by the date of termination. As you know, that's impossible; we can't leave this planet, either inside or outside the contract period. But we'll have to pretend that we're going to leave, up to the last possible minute."

Hazleton looked stunned. Dee took his hand reassuringly, but it didn't seem to register.

"As for what the Proctors themselves can do about it," Amalfi said, picking up the earphone again, "I don't yet know. I'm trying to find out. But this much I do know:

"The Proctors have *already* called the cops."

II.

Under the gray, hazy light in the schoolroom, voices and visions came thronging even into the conscious and prepared mind of the visitor, pouring from the memory cells of the City Fathers. Amalfi could feel their pressure, just below the surface of his mind; it was vaguely unpleasant, partly because he already knew what they sought to impart, so that the redoubled impressions tended to shoulder forward into the immediate attention, nearly with the vividness of immediate experience.

Superimposed upon the indefinite outlines of the schoolroom, cities soared across Amalfi's vision, cities aloft, in flight, looking for work, cracking their food from oil, burrowing for ores the colonial planets could not reach without help, and leaving again to search for work; sometimes welcomed grudgingly, sometimes driven out, usually underpaid, often potential brigands, always watched jealously by the police of hegemon Earth; spreading, ready to mow any lawn, toward the limits of the galaxy—

He waved a hand annoyedly before his eyes and looked for a monitor, found one standing at his elbow, and wondered how long he had been there—or, conversely, how long Amalfi himself had been lulled into the learning trance.

"Where's Karst?" he said brusquely. "The first serf we brought in? I need him."

"Yes, sir. He's in a chair toward the front of the room." The monitor—whose function combined the duties of classroom supervisor and nurse—turned away briefly to a nearby wall server, which opened and floated out to him a tall metal tumbler. The monitor took it and led the way through the room, threading his way among the scattered couches. Usually most of these were unoccupied, since it took less than five hundred hours to bring the average child through tensor calculus and hence to the limits of what he could be taught by passive inculcation alone. Now, however, every couch was occupied, and few of them by children.

One of the counterpointing, sub-audible voices was murmuring: "Some of the cities which turned bindlestiff did not pursue the usual policy of piracy and raiding, but settled instead upon faraway worlds and established tyrannical rules. Most of these were overthrown by the Earth police; the cities were not efficient fighting machines. Those which withstood the first assault sometimes were allowed to remain in power for various reasons of policy, but such planets were invariably barred from commerce. Some of these involuntary empires may still remain on the fringes of Earth's jurisdiction. Most notorious of these recrudescences of imperialism was the reduction of Thor V, the work of one of the earliest of the Okies, a heavily militarized city which had already earned itself the popular nickname of 'the Mad Dogs.' The epithet, current among other Okies as well as planetary populations, of course referred primarily—"

"Here's your man," the monitor said in a low voice. Amalfi looked down at Karst. The serf already had undergone a considerable change. He was no longer a distorted and worn caricature of a man, chocolate-colored with sun, wind, and ground-in dirt, so brutalized as to be almost beyond pity. He was, instead, rather like a fetus as he lay curled on the couch, innocent and still perfectible, as yet unmarked by any experience which counted. His past—and there could hardly have been much of it, for although he had said that his present wife, Eedit, had been his fifth, he was obviously scarcely twenty years old—had been so completely monotonous and implacable that, given the chance, he had sloughed it off as easily and totally as one throws away a single garment. He was, Amalfi realized, much more essentially a child than any Okie infant could ever be.

The monitor touched Karst's shoulder and the serf stirred uneasily, then sat up, instantly awake, his intense blue eyes questioning Amalfi. The monitor handed him the metal tumbler, now beaded with cold, and Karst drank from it. The pungent liquid made him sneeze, quickly and without seeming to notice that he had sneezed, like a cat.

"How's it coming through, Karst?" Amalfi said.

"It is very hard," the serf said. He took another pull at the tumbler. "But once grasped, it seems to bring everything into flower at once. Lord Amalfi, the Proctors claim that IMT came from the sky on a cloud. Yesterday I only believed that. Today I think I understand it."

"I think you do," Amalfi said. "And you're not alone. We have serfs by scores in the city now, learning—just look around you and you'll see. And they're learning more than just simple physics or cultural morphology. They're learning freedom, beginning with the first one—freedom to hate."

"I know that lesson," Karst said, with a profound and glacial calm. "But you awakened me for something."

"I did," the mayor agreed grimly. "We've got a visitor we think you'll be able to identify: a Proctor. And he's up to something that smells funny to me and Hazleton both, but we can't pin down what it is. Come give us a hand, will you?"

"You'd better give him some time to rest, Mr. Mayor," the monitor said disapprovingly. "Being dumped out of hypnopaedic trance is a considerable shock; he'll need at least an hour."

Amalfi stared at the monitor incredulously. He was about to note that neither Karst nor the city had the hour to spare, when it occurred to him that to say so would take ten words where one was plenty. "Vanish," he said.

The monitor did his best.

✦ ✦ ✦

Karst looked intently at the judas. The man on the screen had his back turned; he was looking into the big operations tank in the city manager's office. The indirect light gleamed on his shaven and oiled head. Amalfi watched over Karst's left shoulder, his teeth sunk firmly in a new hydroponic cigar.

"Why, the man's as bald as I am," the mayor said. "And he can't be much past his adolescence, judging by his skull; he's forty-five at the most. Recognize him, Karst?"

"Not yet," Karst said. "All the Proctors shave their heads. If he would only turn around… ah. Yes. That's Heldon. I have seen him myself only once, but he is easy to recognize. He is young, as the Proctors go. He is the stormy petrel of the Great Nine—some think him a friend of the serfs. At least he is less quick with the whip than the others."

"What would he be wanting here?"

"Perhaps he will tell us." Karst's eyes remained fixed upon the Proctor's image.

"Your request puzzles me," Hazleton's voice said, issuing smoothly from the speaker above the judas. The city manager could not be seen, but his expression seemed to modulate the sound of his voice almost specifically: the tiger mind masked behind a pussycat purr as behind a pussycat smile. "We're glad to hear of new services we can render to a client, of course. But we certainly never suspected that antigravity mechanisms even existed in IMT."

"Don't think me stupid, Mr. Hazleton," Heldon said. "You and I know that IMT was once a wanderer, as your city is now. We also know that your city, like all Okie cities, would like a world of its own. Will you allow me this much intelligence, please?"

"For discussion, yes," Hazleton's voice said.

"Then let me say that it's quite evident to me that you're nurturing an uprising. You have been careful to stay within the letter of the contract, simply because you dare not breach it, any more than we; the Earth police protect us from each other to that extent. Your Mayor Amalfi was told that it was illegal for the serfs to speak to your people, but unfortunately it is illegal only for the serfs, not for your citizens. If we cannot keep the serfs out of your city, you are under no obligation to do it for us."

"A point you have saved me the trouble of making," Hazleton said.

"Quite so. I'll add also that when this revolution of yours comes, I have no doubt but that you'll win it. I don't know what weapons you can put into the hands of our serfs, but I assume that they are better than anything we can muster. We haven't your technology. My fellows disagree with me, but I am a realist."

"An interesting theory," Hazleton's voice said. There was a brief pause. In the silence, a soft pattering sound became evident. Hazleton's fingertips, Amalfi guessed, drumming on the desk top, as if with amused impatience. Heldon's face remained impassive.

"The Proctors believe that they can hold what is theirs," Heldon said at last. "If you overstay your contract, they will go to war against you. They will be justified, but unfortunately Earth justice is a long way away from here. You will win. My interest is to see that we have a way of escape."

"Via spindizzy?"

"Precisely." Heldon permitted a stony smile to stir the corners of his mouth. "I'll be honest with you, Mr. Hazleton. If it comes to war, I will fight as hard as any other Proctor to hold this world of ours. I come to you only because you can repair the spindizzies of IMT. You needn't expect me to enter into any extensive treason on that account."

Hazleton, it appeared, was being obdurately stupid. "I fail to see why I should lift a finger for you," he said.

"Observe, please. The Proctors will fight, because they believe that they must. It will probably be a hopeless fight, but it will do your city some damage all the same. As a matter of fact, it will cripple your city beyond repair, unless your luck is phenomenal. Now then: none of the Proctors except one other man and myself know that the spindizzies of IMT are still able to function. That means that they won't try to escape with them; they'll try to knock you out instead. But with the machines in repair, and one knowledgeable hand at the controls—"

"I see," Hazelton said. You propose to put IMT into flight while you can still get off the planet with a reasonably whole city. In return you offer us the planet, and the chance that our own damages will be minimal. Hm-m-m. It's interesting, anyhow. Suppose we take a look at your spindizzies, and see if they're in operable condition. It's been a good many years, without doubt, and untended machinery has a way of gumming up. If they can still be operated at all, we'll talk about a deal. All right?"

"It will have to do," Heldon grumbled. Amalfi saw in the Proctor's eyes a gleam of cold satisfaction which he recognized at once, from having himself looked out through it often—though never in such a poor state of concealment. He shut off the screen.

✦ ✦ ✦

"Well?" the mayor said. "What's he up to?"

"Trouble," Karst said slowly. "It would be very foolish to give or trade him any advantage. His stated reasons are not his real ones."

"Of course not," Amalfi said. "Whose are? Oh, hello, Mark. What do you make of our friend?"

Hazleton stepped out of the lift shaft, bouncing lightly once on the resilient concrete of the control-room floor. "He's stupid," the city manager said, "but he's dangerous. He knows that there's something he doesn't know. He also knows that we don't know what he's driving at, and he's on his home grounds. It's a combination I don't care for."

"I don't like it myself," Amalfi said. "When the enemy starts giving away information, look out! Do you think the majority of the Proctors really don't know that IMT has operable spindizzies?"

"I am sure they do not," Karst offered tentatively. Both men turned to him. "The Proctors do not even believe that you are here to capture the planet. At least, they do not believe that that is what you intend, and I'm sure they don't care, one way or the other."

"Why not?" Hazleton said. "I would."

"You have never *owned* several million serfs," Karst said, without rancor. "You have serfs working for you, and you are paying them wages. That in itself is a disaster for the Proctors. And they cannot stop it. They know that the money you are paying is legal, with the power of the Earth behind it. They cannot stop us from earning it. To do so would cause an uprising at once."

Amalfi looked at Hazleton. The money the city was handing out was the Oc Dollar. It was legal here—but back in the galaxy it was just so much paper. It was only germanium-backed. Could the Proctors be that naive? Or was IMT simply too old to possess the instantaneous Dirac transmitters which would have told it of the economic collapse of the home lens?

"And the spindizzies?" Amalfi said. "Who else would know of them among the Great Nine?"

"Asor, for one," Karst said. "He is the presiding officer, and the religious fanatic of the group. It is said that he still practices daily the full thirty yogas of the Semantic Rigor, even to chinning himself upon every rung of the Abstraction Ladder. The prophet Maalvin banned the flight of men forever, so Asor would not be likely to allow IMT to fly at this late date."

"He has his reasons," Hazleton said reflectively. "Religions rarely exist in a vacuum. They have effects on the societies they reflect. He's probably afraid of the spindizzies, in the last analysis. With such a weapon it takes only a few hundred men to make a revolution—more than enough to overthrow a feudal set-up like this. IMT didn't dare keep its spindizzies working."

"Go on, Karst," Amalfi said, raising his hand impatiently at Hazleton. "How about the other Proctors?"

"There is Bemajdi, but he hardly counts," Karst said. "Let me think. Remember I have never seen most of these men. The only one who matters, it seems to me, is Larre. He is a dour-faced old man with a potbelly. He is usually on Heldon's side, but seldom travels with Heldon all the way. He will worry less about the money the serfs are earning than will the rest. He will contrive a way to tax it away from us—perhaps by declaring a holiday, in honor of the visit of Earthmen to our planet. The collection of tithes is a duty of his."

"Would he allow Heldon to put IMT's spindizzies in shape?"

"No, probably not," Karst said. "I believe Heldon was telling the truth when he said that he would have to do that in secret."

"I don't know," Amalfi said. "I don't like it. On the surface, it looks as though the Proctors hope to scare us off the planet as soon as the contract expires, and then collect all the money we've paid the serfs—

with the cops to back them up. But when you look at it closely, it's crazy. Once the cops find out the identity of IMT—and it won't take them long—they'll break up both cities, and be glad of the chance."

Karst said: "Is this because IMT was the Okie city that did… what was done… on Thor V?"

Amalfi suddenly found that he was having difficulty in keeping his Adam's apple where it belonged. "Let that pass, Karst," he growled. "We're not going to import that story into the Cloud. That should have been cut from your learning tape."

"I know it now," Karst said calmly. "And I am not surprised. The Proctors never change."

"Forget it. Forget it, do you hear? Forget everything. Karst, can you go back to being a dumb serf for a night?"

"Go back to my land?" Karst said. "It would be awkward. My wife must have a new man by now—"

"No, not back on your land. I want you to go with Heldon and look at his spindizzies, as soon as he says the word. I'll need to take some heavy equipment, and I'll need some help. Will you come along?"

Hazelton raised his eyebrows. "You won't fool Heldon, boss."

"I think I will. Of course he knows that we've educated some of the serfs, but that's not a thing he can actually see when he looks at it; his whole background is against it. He just isn't accustomed to thinking of serfs as intelligent. He knows we have thousands of them here, and yet he isn't really afraid of that idea. He thinks we may arm them, make a mob of them. He can't begin to imagine that a serf can learn something better than how to handle a sidearm—something better, and far more dangerous."

"How can you be sure?" Hazelton said.

"By analogue. Remember the planet of Thetis Alpha called Fitzgerald, where they used a big beast called a horse for everything—from pulling carts to racing? All right: suppose you visited a place where you had been told that a few horses had been taught to talk. While you're working there, somebody comes to give you a hand, dragging a spavined old plug with a straw hat pulled down over its ears and a pack on its back. (Excuse me, Karst, but business is business.) You aren't going to think of that horse as one of the talking ones. You aren't accustomed to thinking of horses as being able to talk at all."

"All right," Hazleton said, grinning at Karst's evident discomfiture. "What's the main strategy from here on out, boss? I gather that you've got it set up. Are you ready to give it a name yet?"

"Not quite," the mayor said. "Unless you like long titles. It's still just another problem in political pseudo-morphism."

Amalfi caught sight of Karst's deliberately incurious face and his own grin broadened. "Or," he said, "the fine art of tricking your opponent into throwing his head at you."

III.

IMT was a squat city, long rooted in the stony soil, and as changeless as a forest of cenotaphs. Its quietness, too, was like the quietness of a cemetery, and the Proctors, carrying the fanlike wands of their office, the pierced fans with the jagged tops and the little jingling tags, were much like friars moving among the dead.

The quiet, of course, could be accounted for very simply. The serfs were not allowed to speak within the walls of IMT unless spoken to, and there were comparatively few Proctors in the city to speak to them. For Amalfi there was also the imposed silence of the slaughtered millions of Thor V blanketing the air. He wondered if the Proctors could still hear that raw silence.

The naked brown figure of a passing serf glanced furtively at the party, saw Heldon, and raised a finger to its lips in the established gesture of respect. Heldon barely nodded. Amalfi, necessarily, took no overt notice at all, but he thought: *Shh, is it? I don't wonder. But it's too late, Heldon. The secret is out.*

Karst trudged behind them, shooting an occasional wary glance at Heldon from under his tangled eyebrows. His caution was wasted on the Proctor. They passed through a decaying public square, in the center of which was an almost-obliterated statuary group, so weather-worn as to have lost any integrity it might ever have had; integrity, Amalfi mused, is not a characteristic of monuments. Except to a sharp eye, the mass of stone on the old pedestal might have been nothing but a moderately large meteorite, riddled with the twisting pits characteristic of siderites.

Amalfi could see, however, that the spaces sculped out of the interior of that block of stone, after the fashion of an ancient sculptor named Moore, had once had meaning. Inside that stone there had once stood a powerful human figure, with its foot resting upon the neck of a slighter. Once, evidently, IMT had actually been *proud* of the memory of Thor V—

"Ahead is the Temple," Heldon said suddenly. "The machinery is beneath it. There should be no one of interest in it at this hour, but I had best make sure. Wait here."

"Suppose somebody notices us?" Amalfi said.

"This square is usually avoided. Also, I have men posted around it to divert any chance traffic. If you don't wander away, you'll be safe."

The Proctor strode away toward the big domed building and disappeared abruptly down an alleyway. Behind Amalfi, Karst began to sing, in an exceedingly scratchy voice, but very softly: a folk-tune of some kind, obviously. The melody, which once had had to do with a town named Kazan, was too many thousands of years old for Amalfi to recognize it, even had he not been tune-deaf. Nevertheless, the mayor abruptly found himself listening to Karst, with the intensity of a hooded owl sonar-tracking a field mouse. Karst chanted:

> *Wild on the wind rose the righteous wrath of Maalvin,*
> *Borne like a brand to the burning of the Barrens.*
> *Arms of hands of rebels perished then,*
> *Stars nor moons bedecked that midnight,*
> *IMT made the sky*
> *Fall!*

Seeing that Amalfi was listening to him, Karst stopped with an apologetic gesture. "Go ahead, Karst," Amalfi said at once. "How does the rest go?"

"There isn't time. There are hundreds of verses; every singer adds at least one of his own to the song. It is always supposed to end with this one:"

Black with their blood was the brick
of that barrow,
Toppled the tall towers, crushed to the clay.
None might live who flouted Maalvin,
Earth their souls spurned spaceward, wailing,
IMT made the sky
Fall!

"That's great," Amalfi said grimly. "We really are in the soup—just about in the bottom of the bowl, I'd say. I wish I'd heard that song a week ago."

"What does it tell you?" Karst said, wonderingly. "It is only an old legend."

"It tells me why Heldon wants his spindizzies fixed. I knew he wasn't telling me the straight goods, but that old Laputa gag never occurred to me—more recent cities aren't strong enough in the keel to risk it. But with all the mass this burg packs, it can squash us flat—and we'll just have to sit still for it!"

"I don't understand—"

"It's simple enough. Your prophet Maalvin used IMT like a nut-cracker. He picked it up, flew it over the opposition, and let it down again. The trick was dreamed up away before spaceflight, as I recall. Karst, stick close to me; I may have to get a message to you under Heldon's eye, so watch for—S*st*, here he comes."

The Proctor had been uttered by the alleyway like an untranslatable word. He came rapidly toward them across the crumbling flagstones.

"I think," Heldon said, "that we are now ready for your valuable aid, Mayor Amalfi."

+ + +

Heldon put his foot on a jutting pyramidal stone and pressed down. Amalfi watched carefully, but nothing happened. He swept his flash around the featureless stone walls of the underground chamber, then back again to the floor. Impatiently, Heldon kicked the little pyramid.

This time, there was a protesting rumble. Very slowly, and with a great deal of scraping, a block of stone perhaps five feet long by two feet wide began to rise, as if pivoted or hinged at the far end. The beam of the mayor's flash darted into the opening, picking out a narrow flight of steps.

"I'm disappointed," Amalfi said. "I expected to see Jonathan Swift come out from under it. All right, Heldon, lead on."

The Proctor went cautiously down the steps, holding his skirts up against the dampness. Karst came last, bent low under the heavy pack, his arms hanging laxly. The steps felt cold and slimy through the thin soles of the mayor's sandals, and little trickles of moisture ran down the close-pressing walls. Amalfi felt a nearly intolerable urge to light a cigar; he could almost taste the powerful aromatic odor cutting through the humidity. But he needed his hands free.

He was almost ready to hope that the spindizzies had been ruined by all this moisture, but he discarded the idea even as it was forming in the back of his mind. That would be the easy way out, and in the end it would be disastrous. If the Okies were ever to call this planet their own, IMT had to be made to fly again.

How to keep it off his own city's back, once IMT was aloft, he still was unable to figure. He was piloting, as he invariably wound up doing in the pinches, by the seat of his pants.

The steps ended abruptly in a small chamber, so small, chilly and damp that it was little more than a cave. The flashlight's eye roved, came to rest on an oval doorway sealed off with dull metal—almost certainly lead. So IMT's spindizzies ran "hot"? That was already bad news; it backdated them far beyond the year to which Amalfi had tentatively assigned them.

"That it?" he said.

"That is the way," Heldon agreed. He twisted an inconspicuous handle.

Ancient fluorescents flickered into bluish life as the valve drew back, and glinted upon the humped backs of machines. The air was quite dry here—evidently the big chamber was kept sealed—and Amalfi could not repress a fugitive pang of disappointment. He scanned the huge machines, looking for control panels or homologues thereof.

"Well?" Heldon said harshly. He seemed to be under considerable strain. It occurred to Amalfi that Heldon's strategy might well be a personal flier, not an official policy of the Great Nine; in which case it might go hard with Heldon if his colleagues found him in this particular place of all places with an Okie. "Aren't you going to make any tests?"

"Certainly," Amalfi said. "I was a little taken aback at their size, that's all."

"They are old, as you know," said the Proctor. "Doubtless they are built much larger nowadays."

That, of course, wasn't so. Modern spindizzies ran less than a tenth the size of these. The comment cast new doubt upon Heldon's exact status. Amalfi had assumed that the Proctor would not let him touch the spindizzies, except to inspect; that there would be plenty of men in IMT capable of making repairs from detailed instructions; that Heldon himself, and any Proctor, would know enough physics to comprehend whatever explanations Amalfi might proffer. Now he was not so sure—and on this question hung the amount of tinkering Amalfi would be able to do without being detected.

+ + +

The mayor mounted a metal stair to a catwalk which ran along the tops of the generators, then stopped and looked down at Karst. "Well, stupid, don't just stand there," he said. "Come on up, and bring the stuff."

Obediently Karst shambled up the metal steps, Heldon at his heels. Amalfi ignored them to search for an inspection port in the casing, found one, and opened it. Beneath was what appeared to be a massive rectifying circuit, plus the amplifier for some kind of monitor— probably a digital computer. The amplifier involved more vacuum tubes than Amalfi had ever before seen gathered into one circuit, and there was a separate power supply to deliver D.C. to their heaters. Two of the tubes were each as big as his fist.

Karst bent over and slung the pack to the deck. Amalfi drew out of it a length of slender black cable and thrust its double prongs into a nearby socket. A tiny bulb on the other end glowed neon-red.

"Your computer's still running," he reported. "Whether it's still sane or not is another matter. May I turn the main banks on, Heldon?"

"I'll turn them on," the Proctor said. He went down the stairs again and across the chamber.

Instantly Amalfi was murmuring through motionless lips into the inspection port. The result to Karst's ears must have been rather weird. The technique of speaking without moving one's lips is simply a matter of substituting consonants which do not involve lip movement, such as "y," for those which do, such as rip out about half of these circuits, and "w." If the resulting sound is picked up from inside the resonating chamber, as it is with a throat-mike, it is not too different from ordinary speech, only a bit more blurred. Heard from outside the speaker's nasopharyngeal cavity, however, it has a tendency to sound like Japanese Pidgin.

"Yatch Heldon, Karst. See yhich syitch he kulls, an' nenorize its location. Got it? Good."

The tubes lit. Karst nodded once, very slightly. The Proctor watched from below while Amalfi inspected the lines.

"Will they work?" he called. His voice was muffled, as though he were afraid to raise it as high as he thought necessary.

"I think so. One of these tubes is gassing, and there may have been some failures here and there. Better check the whole lot before you try anything ambitious. You do have facilities for testing tubes, don't you?"

Relief spread visibly over Heldon's face, despite his obvious effort to betray nothing. Probably he could have fooled any of his own people without effort, but for Amalfi, who like any mayor could follow the parataxic "speech" of muscle interplay and posture as readily as he could spoken dialogue, Heldon's expression was as clear as a signed confession.

"Certainly," the Proctor said. "Is that all?"

"By no means. I think you ought to rip out about half of these circuits, and install transistors wherever they can be used; we can sell you the necessary germanium at the legal rate. You've got two or three hundred tubes a unit here, by my estimate, and if you have a tube failure in flight... well, the only word that fits what would happen then is *blooey!*"

"Will you be able to show us how?"

"Probably," the mayor said. "If you'll allow me to inspect the whole system, I can give you an exact answer."

"All right," Heldon said. "But don't delay. I can't count on more than another half-day at most."

This was better than Amalfi had expected—miles better. Given that much time, he could trace at least enough of the leads to locate the master control. That Heldon's expression failed totally to match the content of his speech disturbed Amalfi profoundly, but there was nothing that he could do that would alter that now. He pulled paper and stylus out of Karst's pack and began to make rapid sketches of the wiring before him.

After he had a fairly clear idea of the first generator's set-up, it was easier to block in the main features of the second. It took time, but Heldon did not seem to tire.

The third spindizzy completed the picture, leaving Amalfi wondering what the fourth one was for. It turned out to be a booster, designed to compensate for the losses of the others wherever the main curve of their output failed to conform to the specs laid down for it by the crude, over-all regenerative circuit. The booster was located on the backside of the feedback loop, behind the computer rather than ahead of it, so that all the computer's corrections had to pass through it; the result, Amalfi was sure, would be a small but serious "base surge" every time any correction was applied. The spindizzies of IMT "seemed to have been wired together by Cro-Magnon Man."

But they would fly the city. That was what counted.

+ + +

Amalfi finished his examination of the booster generator and straightened up, painfully, stretching the muscles of his back. He had no idea how many hours he had consumed. It seemed as though months had passed. Heldon was still watching him, deep blue circles under his eyes, but still wide awake and watchful.

And Amalfi had found no point anywhere in the underground chamber from which the spindizzies of IMT could be controlled. The control point was somewhere else; the main control cable ran into a pipe which shot straight up through the top of the cavern.

...IMT made the sky / Fall...

Amalfi yawned ostentatiously and bent back to fastening the plate over the booster's observation port. Karst squatted near him, frankly asleep, as relaxed and comfortable as a cat drowsing on a high ledge. Heldon watched.

"I'm going to have to do the job for you," Amalfi said. "It's really major; might take weeks."

"I thought you would say so," Heldon said. "And I was glad to give you the time to find out. But I do not think we will make any such replacements."

"You need 'em."

"Possibly. But obviously there is a big factor of safety in the apparatus, or our ancestors would never have flown the city at all. You will understand, Mayor Amalfi, that we cannot risk your doing something to the machines which we cannot do ourselves, on the unlikely assumption that you are increasing their efficiency. If they will run as they are, that will have to be good enough."

"Oh, they'll run," Amalfi said. He began, methodically, to pack up his equipment. "For a while. I'll tell you flatly that they're not safe to operate, all the same."

Heldon shrugged and went down the spiral metal stairs to the floor of the chamber. Amalfi rummaged in the pack a moment more. Then he ostentatiously kicked Karst awake—and kicked hard, for he knew better than to play-act with a born overseer for an audience—and motioned the serf to pick up the bundle. They went down after Heldon.

The Proctor was smiling, and it was not a nice smile. "Not safe?" he said. "No, I never supposed that they were. But I think now that the dangers are mostly political."

"Why?" Amalfi demanded, trying to moderate his breathing. He was suddenly almost exhausted; it had taken—how many hours? He had no idea.

"Are you aware of the time, Mayor Amalfi?"

"About morning, I'd judge," Amalfi said dully, jerking the pack more firmly onto Karst's drooping left shoulder. "Late, anyhow."

"Very late," Heldon said. He was not disguising his expression now.

He was openly crowing. "The contract between your city and mine expired at noon today. It is now nearly an hour after noon; we have been here all night and morning. And your city is still on our soil, in violation of the contract, Mayor Amalfi."

"An oversight—"

"No; a victory." Heldon drew a tiny silver tube from the folds of his robe and blew into it. "Mayor Amalfi, you may consider yourself a prisoner of war."

The little silver tube had made no audible sound, but there were already ten men in the room. The mesotron rifles they carried were of an ancient design, probably pre-Kammerman, like the spindizzies of IMT.

But, like the spindizzies, they looked as though they would work.

IV.

Karst froze; Amalfi unfroze him by jabbing him surreptitiously in the ribs with a finger, and began to unload the contents of his own small pack into Karst's.

"You've called the Earth police, I suppose?" he said.

"Long ago. That way of escape will be cut off by now. Let me say, Mayor Amalfi, that if you expected to find down here any controls that you might disable—and I was quite prepared to allow you to search for them—you expected too much stupidity from me."

Amalfi said nothing. He went on methodically repacking the equipment.

"You are making too many motions, Mayor Amalfi. Put your hands up in the air and turn around very slowly."

Amalfi put up his hands and turned. In each hand he held a small black object about the size and shape of an egg.

"I expected only as much stupidity as I got," he said conversationally. "You can see what I'm holding up there. I can and will drop one or both of them if I'm shot. I may drop them anyhow. I'm tired of your back-cluster ghost town."

Heldon snorted. "Explosives? Gas? Ridiculous; nothing so small could contain enough energy to destroy the city; and you have no masks. Do you take me for a fool?"

"Events prove you one," Amalfi said steadily. "The possibility was quite large that you would try to ambush me, once you had me in the city. I could have forestalled that by bringing a guard with me. You haven't met my perimeter police; they're tough boys, and they've been off duty so long that they'd love the chance to tangle with your palace crew. Didn't it occur to you that I left my city without a bodyguard only because I had less cumbersome ways of protecting myself?"

"Eggs," Heldon said scornfully.

"As a matter of fact, they *are* eggs; the black color is an annaline stain, put on the shells as a warning. They contain chick embryos inoculated with a two-hour alveolytic mutated Terrestrial rickettsialpox—a new air-borne strain developed in our own BW lab. Free space makes a wonderful laboratory for that kind of trick; an Okie town specializing in agronomy taught us the techniques a couple of centuries back. Just a couple of eggs—but if I were to drop them, you would have to crawl on your belly behind me all the way back to my city to get the antibiotic shot that's specific for the disease; we developed that ourselves, too."

There was a brief silence, made all the more empty by the hoarse breathing of the Proctor. The armed men eyed the black eggs uneasily, and the muzzles of their rifles wavered out of line. Amalfi had chosen his weapon with great care; static feudal societies classically are terrified by the threat of plague—they have seen so much of it.

"Impasse," Heldon said at last. "All right, Mayor Amalfi. You and your slave have safe-conduct from this chamber—"

"From the building. If I hear the slightest sound of pursuit up the stairs, I'll chuck these down on you. They burst hard, by the way—the virus generates a lot of gas in chick-embryo medium."

"Very well," Heldon said, through his teeth. "From the building, then. But you have won nothing, Mayor Amalfi. If you can get back to your city, you'll be just in time to be an eyewitness of the victory of IMT—the victory you helped make possible. I think you'll be surprised at how thorough we can be."

"No, I won't," Amalfi said, in a flat, cold, and quite merciless voice. "I know all about IMT, Heldon. This is the end of the line for the Mad

Dogs. When you die, you and your whole crew of Interstellar Master Traders *remember Thor V.*"

Heldon turned the color of unsized paper, and so, surprisingly, did at least four of his riflemen. Then the blood began to rise in the Proctor's plump, fungoid cheeks. "Get out," he croaked, almost inaudibly. Then suddenly, at the top of his voice: "Get out! *Get out!*"

+ + +

Juggling the eggs casually, Amalfi walked toward the lead radiation lock. Karst shuffled after him, cringing as he passed Heldon. Amalfi thought that the serf might be overdoing it, but Heldon did not notice; Karst might have well have been—a horse.

The lead plug swung to, blocking out Heldon's furious, frightened face and the glint of fluorescents on the ancient spindizzies. Amalfi plunged one hand into Karst's pack, depositing one egg in the silicone-foam nest from which he had taken it, and withdrew the hand again grasping an ugly Schmeisser acceleration-pistol. This he thrust into the waistband of his breeches.

"Up the stairs, Karst. Fast. I had to shave it pretty fine. Go on, I'm right behind you. Where would the controls for those machines be, by your guess? The control lead went up through the roof of that cavern."

"On the top of the Temple," Karst said. He was mounting the narrow steps in huge bounds, but it did not seem to cost him the slightest effort. "Up there is Star Chamber, where the Great Nine meets. There isn't any way to get to it that I know."

They burst up into the cold stone antechamber. Amalfi's flash roved over the floor, found the jutting pyramid; Amalfi kicked it. With a prolonged groan, the tilted slab settled down over the flight of steps and became just another block in the floor. There was certainly some way to raise it again from below, but Heldon would hesitate before he used it; the slab was noisy in motion, noisy enough to tell Amalfi that he was being followed. At the first such squawk, Amalfi would lay a black egg, and Heldon knew it.

"I want you to get out of the city, and take every serf that you can find with you," Amalfi said. "But it's going to take timing. Somebody's got to pull that switch down below that I asked you to memorize, and I can't do it; I've got to get into Star Chamber. Heldon will guess that I'm going up there, and he'll follow me. After he's gone by, Karst, you have to go down there and open that switch." Here was the low door through which Heldon had first admitted them to the Temple. More stairs ran up from it. Strong daylight poured under it.

Amalfi inched the old door open and peered out. Despite the brightness of the afternoon, the close-set, chunky buildings of IMT turned the alleyway outside into a confusing multitude of colored shadows. Half a dozen leaden-eyed serfs were going by, with a Proctor walking behind them, half asleep.

"Can you find your way back into that crypt?" Amalfi whispered.

"There's only one way to go."

"Good. Go back then. Dump the pack outside the door here; we don't need it anymore. As soon as Heldon's crew goes on up these stairs, get back down there and pull that switch. Then get out of the city; you'll have about four minutes of accumulated warm-up time from all those tube stages; don't waste a second of it. Got it?"

"Yes. But—"

Something went over the Temple like an avalanche of gravel and dwindled into some distance. Amalfi closed one eye and screwed the other one skyward. "Rockets," he said. "Sometimes I don't know why I insisted on a planet as primitive as this. But maybe I'll learn to love it. Good luck, Karst."

He turned toward the stairs. "They'll trap you up there," Karst said.

"No, they won't. Not Amalfi. But me no buts, Karst. Git."

Another rocket went over, and far away there was a heavy explosion. Amalfi charged like a bull up the new flight of stairs toward Star Chamber.

The staircase was long and widely curving, as well as narrow, and both its risers and its treads were infuriatingly small. Amalfi remembered that the Proctors did not themselves climb stairs; they were carried up them on the forearms of serfs. Such pussy-ant steps made for sure footing, but not for fast transit.

As far as Amalfi was able to compute, the steps rose gently along the outside curvature of the Temple's dome, following a one-and-half helix to the summit. Why? Presumably, the Proctors didn't require themselves to climb long flights of stairs for nothing, even with serfs to carry them. Why couldn't Star Chamber be under the dome with the spindizzies, for instance, instead of atop it?

Amalfi was not far past the first half-turn before one good reason became evident. There was a rustle of voices jostling its way through the chinks in the dome from below; a congregation, evidently, was gathering. As Amalfi continued to mount the flat spiral, the murmuring became more and more discrete, until individual voices could almost be separated out from it. Up there at what mathematically would be the bottom of the bowl, where the floor of Star Chamber was, the architect of the Temple evidently had contrived a whispering-gallery—a vault to which a Proctor might put his ear, and hear the thinnest syllable of conspiracy in the crowd of suppliants below.

It was ingenious, Amalfi had to admit. Conspirators on church-bearing planets generally tend to think of churches as safe places for quiet plotting. In Amalfi's universe—for he had never seen Earth—any planet which sponsored churches probably had a revolt coming to it.

Blowing like a porpoise, he scrambled up the last arc of the long Greek-spiral staircase. A solidly closed double door, worked all over with phony Byzantine scrolls, stood looking down, at him. He didn't bother to stop to admire it; he hit it squarely under the paired, patently synthetic sapphires just above its center, and hit it hard. It burst.

Disappointment stopped him for a moment. The chamber was an ellipse of low eccentricity, monastically bare and furnished only with a heavy wooden table and nine chairs, now drawn back against the wall. There were no controls here, nor any place where they could be concealed. The chamber was windowless.

The lack of windows told him what he wanted to know. The other, the compelling reason why Star Chamber was on top of the Temple dome was that it harbored, somewhere, the pilot's cabin of IMT. And that, in as old a city as IMT, meant that visibility would be all-important—requiring a situation atop the tallest structure in the city, and as close to 360° visibility as could be managed. Obviously, Amalfi was not yet up high enough.

He looked up at the ceiling. One of the big stone slabs had a semicircular cup in it, not much bigger than a large coin. The flat edge was much worn.

Amalfi grinned and looked under the wooden table. Sure enough, there it was—a pole with a hooked bill at one end, rather like a halberd, slung in clips. He yanked it out, straightened, and fitted the bill into the opening in the stone.

The slab came down easily, hinged at one end as the block down below over the generator room had been. The ancestors of the Proctors had not been much given to varying their engineering principles. The free end of the slab almost touched the tabletop. Amalfi sprang onto the table and scrambled up the tilted face of the stone; as he neared the top, the translating center of gravity which he represented actuated a counterweighing mechanism somewhere, and the slab closed, bearing him the rest of the way.

This was the control cabin, all right. It was tiny and packed with panels, all of which were covered with dust. Bull's-eyes of thick glass looked out over the city at the four compass-points, and there was one set in overhead. A single green light was glowing on one of the panels. While he walked toward it, it went out.

That had been Karst, cutting the power. Amalfi hoped that the peasant would get out again. He had grown to like him. There was something in his weathered, unmoveable, shockproof courage and in the voracity of his starved intelligence that reminded the mayor of someone he had once known. That that someone was Amalfi as he had been at the age of twenty-five, Amalfi did not know, and there was no one else who would be able to tell him.

Spindizzies, in essence, are simple; Amalfi had no difficulty in setting and locking the controls the way he wanted them, or in performing sundry small tasks of highly selective sabotage. How he was to conceal what he had done, when every move left huge smears in the heavy dust, was a tougher problem. He solved it at length in the only possible way: he took off his shirt and flailed it at all of the boards. The result made him sneeze until his eyes watered, but it worked.

Now all he had to do was get out.

There were already sounds below in Star Chamber, but he was not yet worried about a direct attack. He still had one of the black eggs, and the Proctors knew it. Furthermore, he also had the pole with the hooked bill, so that in order to open up the control room at all, the Proctors would have to climb on each other's shoulders. They weren't in good physical shape for gymnastics, and besides, they would know that men indulging in such stunts could be defeated temporarily by nothing more complicated than a kick in the teeth.

Nevertheless, Amalfi had no intention of spending the rest of his life in the control room of IMT. He had only about six minutes to get out of the city altogether.

After thinking very rapidly for approximately four seconds, Amalfi stood on the stone slab, overbalanced it, and slid solemnly down onto the top of the table in Star Chamber.

+ + +

After a stunned instant, half a dozen pairs of hands grabbed him at once. Heldon's face, completely unrecognizable with fury and fear, was thrust into his.

"What have you done? Answer, or I'll order you torn to pieces!"

"Don't be a lunkhead. Tell your men to let go of me. I still have your safe-conduct—and in case you're thinking of repudiating it, I still have the same weapon I had before. Cast off, or—"

Heldon's guards released him before he had finished speaking. Heldon lurched heavily up onto the tabletop and began to claw his way up the slab. Several other robed, bald-headed men jostled after him—evidently Heldon had been driven by a greater fear to tell some of the Great Nine what he had done. Amalfi walked backwards out of Star Chamber and down two steps. Then he bent, deposited his remaining black egg carefully on the threshold, and took off down the spiral stairs at a dead run.

It would take Heldon a while, perhaps as much as a minute, after he switched on the controls to discover that the generators had been cut out while he was chasing Amalfi; and another minute, at best, to get a flunky down into the basement to turn them on again. Then there would be a warm-up time of four minutes. After that—IMT would go aloft.

Amalfi shot out into the alleyway and thence into the public square, caroming off an astounded guard. A shout rose behind him. He doubled over and kept running.

The street was nearly dark in the twilight of the twin suns. He kept in the shadows and made for the nearest corner. The cornice of the building ahead of him abruptly turned lava-white, then began to dim through the red. He never did hear the accompanying scream of the mesotron rifle. He was concentrating on something else.

Then he was around the corner. The quickest route to the edge of the city, as well as he could recall, was down the street he had just quitted, but that was now out of the question; he had no desire to be hunted down. Whether or not he could get out of IMT in time by any alternate route remained to be seen.

Doggedly, he kept running. He was fired on once more, by a man who did not really know on whom he was firing. Here, Amalfi was just a running man who failed to fit the categories; any first shot at him would be a reflex of disorientation, and consequently aimed badly.

The ground shuddered, ever so delicately, like the hide of a monster twitching at flies in its sleep. Somehow, Amalfi managed to run still faster.

The shudder came again, stronger this time. A long, protracted groan followed it, traveling in a heavy wave through the bedrock of the city. The sound brought Proctors and serfs alike boiling out of the buildings.

At the third shock, something toward the center of the city collapsed with a sullen roar. Amalfi was caught up in the aimless, terrified eddying of the crowd, and fought, with hands, teeth and bullet head—

The groaning grew louder. Abruptly, the ground bucked. Amalfi pitched forward. With him went the whole milling mob, falling in windrows like stacked grain. There was frantic screaming everywhere, but it was worse inside the buildings. Over Amalfi's head a window shattered explosively, and a woman's body came twisting and tumbling through the shuddering air.

+ + +

Amalfi heaved himself up, spitting blood, and ran again. The pavement ahead was cracked in great, irregular shards, like a madman's mosaic.

Just beyond, the blocks were tilted all awry, reminding Amalfi irrelevantly of a breakwater he had seen on some other planet, in some other century—

He was clambering over them before he realized that these could only mark the rim of the original city of IMT. There were still more buildings on the other side of the huge, rock-filled trench, but the trench itself showed where the perimeter of the ancient Okie had been sunk into the soil of the planet. Fighting for air with saw-edged râles, he threw himself from stone to stone toward the far edge of the trench. This was the most dangerous ground of all; if IMT were to lift now, he would be ground as fine as mincemeat in the tumbling rocks. If he could just reach the marches of the Barrens—

Behind him, the groaning rose steadily in pitch, until it sounded like the tearing of an endless sheet of metal. Ahead, across the Barrens to the east, his own city, gleamed in the last rays of the twin suns. There was fighting around it; little bright flashes were sputtering at its edge. The rockets Amalfi had heard, four of them, were arrowing across the sky, and black things dropped from them. The Okie city responded with spouts of smoke.

Then there was an unbearably bright burst. After Amalfi could see again, there were only three rockets. In another few seconds there wouldn't be any: the City Fathers never missed.

Amalfi's lungs burned. He felt sod under his sandals. A twisted runner of furze lashed across his ankle and he fell again.

He tried to get up and could not. The seared turf, on which an ancient rebel city once had stood, rumbled threateningly. He rolled over. The squat towers of IMT were swaying, and all around the edge of the city, huge blocks and clods heaved and turned over, like surf. Impossibly, a thin line of light, intense and ruddy, appeared above the moiling rocks. The suns were shining *under the city*—

The line of light widened. The old city took to the air with an immense bound, and the rending of the long-rooted foundations was ear-splitting. From the sides of the huge mass, human beings threw themselves desperately toward the Barrens; all those Amalfi saw were serfs. The Proctors, of course, were still trying to control the flight of IMT—

The city rose majestically. It was gaining speed. Amalfi's heart hammered. If Heldon and his crew could figure out in time what Amalfi had done to the controls, Karst's old ballad would be re-enacted, and the crushing rule of the Proctors made safe forever.

But Amalfi had done his work well.

The city of IMT did not stop rising. With a profound, visceral shock, Amalfi realized that it was already nearly a mile up, and still accelerating. The air would be thinning up there, and the Proctors had forgotten too much to know what to do—

A mile and a half.

Two miles.

It grew smaller. At five miles it was just a wavery ink-blot, lit on one side. At seven miles it was a point of dim light.

A bristle-topped head and a pair of enormous shoulders lifted cautiously from a nearby gully. It was Karst. He continued to look aloft for a moment, but IMT at ten miles was invisible. He looked down to Amalfi.

"Can… can it come back?" he said huskily.

"No," Amalfi said, his breathing gradually coming under control. "Keep watching, Karst. It isn't over yet. Remember that the Proctors had called the Earth cops—"

At that same moment, the city of IMT reappeared—in a way. A third sun flowered in the sky. It lasted for three or four seconds. Then it dimmed and died.

"The cops were warned," Amalfi said softly, "to watch for an Okie city trying to make a getaway. They found it, and they dealt with it. Of course they got the wrong city, but they don't know that. They'll go home now—and now we're home, and so are you and your people. Home on Earth, for good."

Around them, there was a murmuring of voices, hushed with disaster, and with something else, too—something so old, and so new, that it hardly had a name on the planet that IMT had ruled. It was called freedom.

"On Earth?" Karst repeated. He and the mayor climbed painfully to their feet. "What do you mean? This is not Earth—"

Across the Barrens, the Okie city glittered—the city that had pitched camp to mow some lawns. A cloud of stars was rising behind it.

"It is now," Amalfi said. "We're all Earthmen, Karst. Earth is more than just one little planet, buried in another galaxy than this. Earth is much more important than that.

"Earth isn't a place. It's an idea."

Though rightly known as one of the editing greats of science fiction for the past four decades (he died in 2018, but not before winning fifteen Hugos as Best Short Form Editor), Gardner Dozois started out as a writer. His numerous short fiction pieces and few novels have been widely praised and among them is this space opera—almost, but not quite, military science fiction—gem from 1971, which was nominated for the Hugo Award for Best Novella, Nebula Award for Best Novelette, and Locus Award for Best Short Story. He was a fan of core science fiction, and it gives me special pleasure to include Dozois' work in an anthology I know would be right up his alley.

As friend and fellow science fiction author Michael Swanwick wrote of Dozois and this story's beginning, "with their sudden irruption into wit and color, 'social pith' and vinegar… the opening lines to 'A Special Kind of Morning,' in which Gardner squanders enough ideas to fuel a standard trilogy of SF novels on one fast story-within-a-story that's ostensibly about a rebellion against a tyranny so absolute that no price is too great for liberty and a war so terrible that by its end those fighting it no longer care for victory. But really it's about life and love, valor and compassion and freedom and all those things that really matter."

The story's two central events, in fact, take place just before and after the story itself—the lordling's first taste of lovemaking and the death of the old soldier telling him the story. As Swanwick puts it, "it is always a special kind of morning, even on the day you die."

A SPECIAL KIND OF MORNING
GARDNER DOZOIS

THE DOOMSDAY MACHINE IS THE HUMAN RACE.
—*Graffito in New York Subway Seventy-ninth Street Station*

Did y'ever hear the one about the old man and the sea? Halt a minute, lordling; stop and listen. It's a fine story, full of balance and point and social pith; short and direct. It's not mine. Mine are long and rambling and parenthetical and they corrode the moral fiber right out of a man. Come to think, I won't tell you that one after all. A man of my age has a right to prefer his own material, and let the critics be damned. I've a prejudice now for webs of my own weaving.

Sit down, sit down: but against pavement, yes; it's been done before. Everything has, near about. Now that's not an expression of your black pessimism, or your futility, or what have you. Pessimism's just the commonsense knowledge that there's more ways for something to go wrong than for it to go right, from our point of view anyway—which is not necessarily that of the management, or of the mechanism, if you prefer your cosmos depersonalized. As for futility, everybody dies the true death eventually; even though executives may dodge it for a few hundred years, the hole gets them all in the end, and I imagine that's futility enough for a start. The philosophical man accepts both as constants and then doesn't let them bother him any. Sit down, damn it; don't pretend you've important business to be about. Young devil, you are in the enviable position of having absolutely nothing to do because it's going to take you a while to recover from what you've just done.

There. That's better. Comfortable? You don't look it; you look like you've just sat in a puddle of piss and're wondering what the socially appropriate reaction is. Hypocrisy's an art, boy; you'll improve with age. Now you're bemused, lordling, that you let an old soak chivy you around, and now he's making fun of you. Well, the expression on your face is worth a chuckle; if you could see it you'd laugh yourself. You will see it years from now too, on some other young man's face— that's the only kind of mirror that ever shows it clear. And you'll be an old soak by that time, and you'll laugh and insult the young buck's dignity, but you'll be laughing more at the reflection of the man you used to be than at that particular stud himself. And you'll probably have to tell the buck just what I've told you to cool him down, and there's a laugh in that too; listen for the echo of a million and one laughs behind you. I hear a million now.

How do I get away with such insolence? What've I got to lose, for one thing. That gives you a certain perspective. And I'm socially instructive in spite of myself—I'm valuable as an object lesson. For that matter, why is an arrogant young aristo like you sitting there and putting up with my guff? Don't even bother to answer; I knew the minute you came whistling down the street, full of steam and strut. Nobody gets up this early in the morning anymore, unless they're old as I am and begrudge sleep's dryrun of death—or unless they've never been to bed in the first place. The world's your friend this morning, a toy for you to play with and examine and stuff in your mouth to taste, and you're letting your benevolence slop over onto the old degenerate you've met on the street. You're even happy enough to listen, though you're being quizzical about it, and you're sitting over there feeling benignly superior. And I'm sitting over *here* feeling benignly superior. A nice arrangement, and everyone content. Well, then, mornings make you feel that way. Especially if you're fresh from a night at the Towers, the musk of Lady Ni still warm on your flesh.

A blush—my buck, you *are* new-hatched. How did I know? Boy, you'd be surprised what I know; I'm occasionally startled myself, and I've been working longer to get it catalogued. Besides, hindsight is a comfortable substitute for omnipotence. And I'm not blind yet. You have the unmistakable look of a cub who's just found out he can do something else with it besides piss. An incredible revelation, as I recall. The blazing significance of it will wear a little with the years, though not all that much, I suppose; until you get down to the brink of the Ultimate Cold, when you stop worrying about the identity of warmth, or demanding that it pay toll in pleasure. Any hand of clay, long's the blood still runs the tiny degree that's just enough for difference. Warmth's the only definition between you and graveyard dirt. But morning's not for graveyards, though it works the other way. Did y'know they also used to use that to make babies? 'S'fact, though few know it now. It's a versatile beast. Oh come—buck, cub, young cocksman—stop being so damn surprised. People ate, slept, and fornicated before you were born, some of them anyway, and a few will probably even find the courage to keep on at it after you die. You don't have to keep it secret; the thing's been circulated in this region once or twice before. You weren't the first to learn how to make the beast do its trick, though I know you don't believe that. I don't believe it concerning myself, and I've had a long time to learn.

You make me think, sitting there innocent as an egg and twice as vulnerable; yes, you are definitely about to make me think, and I believe

I'll have to think of some things I always regret having thought about, just to keep me from growing maudlin. Damn it, boy, you *do* make me think. Life's strange—wet-eared as you are, you've probably had that thought a dozen times already, probably had it this morning as you tumbled out of your fragrant bed to meet the rim of the sun; well, I've four times your age, and a ream more experience, and I still can't think of anything better to sum up the world: life's strange. 'S been said, yes. But *think,* boy, how strange: the two of us talking, you coming, me going; me knowing where you've got to go, you suspecting where I've been, and the same destination for both. O strange, very strange! Damn it, you're a deader already if you can't see the strangeness of that, if you can't sniff the poetry; it reeks of it, as of blood. And I've smelt blood, buck. It has a very distinct odor; you know it when you smell it. You're bound for blood; for blood and passion and high deeds and all the rest of the business, and maybe for a little understanding if you're lucky and have eyes to see. Me, I'm bound for nothing, literally. I've come to rest here in Kos, and while the Red Lady spins her web of colors across the sky I sit and weave my own webs of words and dreams and other spider stuff—

What? Yes, I do talk too much; old men like to babble, and philosophy's a cushion for old bones. But it's my profession now, isn't it, and I've promised you a story. What happened to my leg? That's a bloody story, but I said you're bound for blood; I know the mark. I'll tell it to you then: perhaps it'll help you to understand when you reach the narrow place, perhaps it'll even help you to think, although that's a horrible weight to wish on any man. It's customary to notarize my card before I start, keep you from running off at the end without paying. Thank you, young sir. Beware of some of these beggars, buck; they have a credit tally at Central greater than either of us will ever run up. They turn a tidy profit out of poverty. I'm an honest pauper, more's the pity, exist mostly on the subsidy, if you call that existing— Yes, I know. The leg.

We'll have to go back to the Realignment for that, more than half a century ago, and half a sector away, at World. This was before World was a member of the Commonwealth. In fact, that's what the Realignment was about, the old Combine overthrown by the Quaestors, who then opted for amalgamation and forced World into the Commonwealth. That's where and when the story starts.

Start it with waiting.

A lot of things start like that, waiting. And when the thing you're waiting for is probable death, and you're lying there loving life and suddenly noticing how pretty everything is and listening to the flint hooves of darkness click closer, feeling the iron-shod boots strike relentless sparks from the surface of your mind, knowing that death is about to fall out of the sky and that there's no way to twist out from under—then, waiting can take time. Minutes become hours, hours become unthinkable horrors. Add enough horrors together, total the scaly snouts, and you've got a day and a half I once spent laying up in a mountain valley in the Blackfriars on World, almost the last day I ever spent anywhere.

This was just a few hours after D'kotta. Everything was a mess, nobody really knew what was happening, everybody's communication lines cut. I was just a buck myself then, working with the Quaestors in the field, a hunted criminal. Nobody knew what the Combine would do next, we didn't know what we'd do next, groups surging wildly from one place to another at random, panic and riots all over the planet, even in the Controlled Environments.

And D'kotta-on-the-Blackfriars was a seventy-mile swath of smoking insanity, capped by boiling umbrellas of smoke that eddied ashes from the ground to the stratosphere and back. At night it pulsed with molten scum, ugly as a lanced blister, lighting up the cloud cover across the entire horizon, visible for hundreds of miles. It was this ugly glow that finally panicked even the zombies in the Environments, probably the first strong emotion in their lives.

It'd been hard to sum up the effects of the battle. We thought that we had the edge, that the Combine was close to breaking, but nobody knew for sure. If they weren't as close to folding as we thought, then we were probably finished. The Quaestors had exhausted most of their hoarded resources at D'kotta, and we certainly couldn't hit the Combine any harder. If they could shrug off the blow, then they could wear us down.

Personally, I didn't see how anything could shrug *that* off. I'd watched it all and it'd shaken me considerably. There's an old-time expression, "put the fear of God into him." That's what D'kotta had done for me. There wasn't any God anymore, but I'd seen fire vomit from the heavens and the earth ripped wide for rape, and it'd been an impressive enough surrogate. Few people ever realized how close the Combine and the Quaestors had come to destroying World between them, there at D'kotta.

We'd crouched that night—the team and I—on the high stone ramparts of the tallest of the Blackfriars, hopefully far away from anything that could fall on us. There were twenty miles of low, gnarly foothills between us and the rolling savannahland where the city of D'kotta had been minutes before, but the ground under our bellies heaved and quivered like a sick animal, and the rock was hot to the touch: feverish.

We could've gotten farther away, should have gotten farther away, but we had to watch. That'd been decided without anyone saying a word, without any question about it. It was impossible *not* to watch. It never even occurred to any of us to take another safer course of action. When reality is being turned inside out like a dirty sock, you watch, or you are less than human. So we watched it all from beginning to end: two hours that became a single second lasting for eons. Like a still photograph of time twisted into a scream—the scream reverberating on forever and yet taking no duration at all to experience.

We didn't talk. We *couldn't* talk—the molecules of the air itself shrieked too loudly, and the deep roar of explosions was a continual drumroll—but we wouldn't have talked even if we'd been able. You don't speak in the presence of an angry God. Sometimes we'd look briefly at each other. Our faces were all nearly identical: ashen, waxy, eyes of glass, blank, and lost as pale driftwood stranded on a beach by the tide. We'd been driven through the gamut of expressions into *extremis*—rictus: faces so contorted and strained they ached—and beyond to the quietus of shock: muscles too slack and flaccid to respond anymore. We'd only look at each other for a second, hardly focusing, almost not aware of what we were seeing, and then our eyes would be dragged back as if by magnetism to the Fire.

At the beginning we'd clutched each other, but as the battle progressed we slowly drew apart, huddling into individual agony; the thing so big that human warmth meant nothing, so frightening that the instinct to gather together for protection was reversed, and the presence of others only intensified the realization of how ultimately naked you were. Earlier we'd set up a scattershield to filter the worst of the hard radiation—the gamma and intense infrared and ultraviolet—blunt some of the heat and shock and noise. We thought we had a fair chance of surviving, then, but we couldn't have run anyway. We were fixed by the beauty of horror/horror of beauty, surely as if by a spike driven through our backbones into the rock.

And away over the foothills, God danced in anger, and his feet struck the ground to ash.

What was it like?

Kos still has oceans and storms. Did y'ever watch the sea lashed by high winds? The storm boils the water into froth, whips it white, until it becomes an ocean of ragged lace to the horizon, whirlpools of milk, not a fleck of blue left alive. The land looked like this at D'kotta. The hills *moved*. The Quaestors had a discontinuity projector there, and under its lash the ground stirred like sluggish batter under a baker's spoon; stirred, shuddered, groaned, cracked, broke: acres heaved themselves into new mountains, other acres collapsed into canyons.

Imagine a giant asleep just under the surface of the earth, overgrown by fields, dreaming dreams of rock and crystal. Imagine him moving restlessly, the long rhythm of his dreams touched by nightmare, tossing, moaning, tremors signaling unease in waves up and down his miles-long frame. Imagine him catapulted into waking terror, lurching suddenly to his knees with the bawling roar of ten million burning calves: a steaming claw of rock and black earth raking for the sky. Now, in a wink, imagine the adjacent land hurtling downward, sinking like a rock in a pond, opening a womb a thousand feet wide, swallowing everything and grinding it to powder. Then, almost too quick to see, imagine the mountain and the crater switching, the mountain collapsing all at once and washing the feet of the older Blackfriars with a tidal wave of earth, then tumbling down to make a pit; at the same time the sinking earth at the bottom of the other crater reversing itself and erupting upward into a quaking fist of rubble. Then they switch again, and keep switching. Like watching the same film clip continuously run forward and backward. Now multiply that by a million and spread it out so that all you can see to the horizon is a stew of humping rock. D'y'visualize it? Not a tenth of it.

Dervishes of fire stalked the chaos, melting into each other, whirlpooling. Occasionally a tactical nuclear explosion would punch a hole in the night, a brief intense flare that would be swallowed like a candle in a murky snowstorm. Once a tacnuke detonation coincided with the upthrusting of a rubble mountain, with an effect like that of a firecracker exploding inside a swinging sack of grain.

The city itself was gone; we could no longer see a trace of anything man-made, only the stone maelstrom. The River Delva had also vanished, flash-boiled to steam; for a while we could see the gorge of its dry bed stitching across the plain, but then the ground heaved up and obliterated it.

It was unbelievable that anything could be left alive down there. Very little was. Only the remainder of the heavy weapons sections on both sides continued to survive, invisible to us in the confusion. Still protected by powerful phasewalls and scattershields, they pounded blindly at each other—the Combine somewhat ineffectively with biodeths and tacnukes, the Quaestors responding by stepping up the discontinuity projector. There was only one, in the command module— the Quaestor technicians were praying it wouldn't be wiped out by a random strike—and it was a terraforming device and not actually a "weapon" at all, but the Combine had been completely unprepared for it, and were suffering horribly as a result.

Everything began to flicker, random swatches of savannahland shimmering and blurring, phasing in and out of focus in a jerky, mismatched manner: that filmstrip run through a spastic projector. At first we thought it must be heat eddies caused by the fires, but then the flickering increased drastically in frequency and tempo, speeding up until it was impossible to keep anything in focus even for a second, turning the wide veldt into a mad kaleidoscope of writhing, interchanging shapes and color-patterns from one horizon to the other. It was impossible to watch it for long. It hurt the eyes and filled us with an oily, inexplicable panic that we were never able to verbalize. We looked away, filled with the musty surgings of vague fear.

We didn't know then that we were watching the first practical application of a process that'd long been suppressed by both the Combine and the Commonwealth, a process based on the starship dimensional "drive" (which isn't a "drive" at all, but the word's passed into the common press) that enabled a high-cycling discontinuity projector to throw time out of phase within a limited area, so that a spot *here* would be a couple of minutes ahead or behind a spot a few inches away, in continuity sequence. That explanation would give a psychophysicist fits, since "time" is really nothing at all like the way we "experience" it, so the process "really" doesn't do what I've said it does—doing something *really* abstruse instead—but that's close enough to what it does on a practical level, 'cause even if the time distortion is an "illusionary effect"—like the sun seeming to rise and set—they still used it to kill people. So it threw time out of phase, and kept doing it, switching the dislocation at random: so that in any given square foot of land there might be four or five discrepancies in time sequence that kept interchanging. Like, *here* might be one minute "ahead" of the base "now," and then a second later (language breaks down hopelessly under this stuff; you need the math) *here* would be two minutes behind the now, then five minutes behind, then three ahead, and so on. And all the adjacent zones in that square foot are going through the same switching process at the same time (goddamn this language!) The Combine's machinery tore itself to pieces. So did the people: some died of suffocation because of a five-minute discrepancy between an inhaled breath and oxygen received by the lungs, some drowned in their own blood.

It took about ten minutes, at least as far as we were concerned as unaffected observers. I had a psychophysicist tell me once that "it" had both continued to "happen" forever and had never "happened" at all, and that neither statement canceled out the validity of the other, that each statement in fact was both "applicable" and "nonapplicable" to the same situation consecutively—and I did not understand. It took ten minutes.

At the end of that time, the world got very still.

We looked up. The land had stopped churning. A tiny star appeared amongst the rubble in the middle distance, small as a pinhead but incredibly bright and clear. It seemed to suck the night into it like a vortex, as if it were a pinprick through the worldstuff into a more intense reality, as if it were gathering a great breath for a shout.

We buried our heads in our arms as one, instinctively.

There was a very bright light, a light that we could feel through the tops of our heads, a light that left dazzling after-images even through closed and shrouded lids. The mountain leaped under us, bounced us into the air again and again, battered us into near unconsciousness. We never even heard the roar.

After a while, things got quiet again, except for a continuous low rumbling. When we looked up, there were thick, sluggish tongues of molten magma oozing up in vast flows across the veldt, punctuated here and there by spectacular shower-fountains of vomited sparks.

Our scattershield had taken the brunt of the blast, borne it just long enough to save our lives, and then overloaded and burnt itself to scrap; one of the first times *that's* ever happened.

Nobody said anything. We didn't look at each other. We just lay there.

The chrono said an hour went by, but nobody was aware of it.

Finally, a couple of us got up, in silence, and started to stumble aimlessly back and forth. One by one, the rest crawled to their feet. Still in silence, still trying not to look at each other, we automatically cleaned ourselves up. You hear someone say "it made me shit my pants," and you think it's an expression; not under the right stimuli. Automatically, we treated our bruises and lacerations, automatically we tidied the camp up, buried the ruined scatterfield generator. Automatically, we sat down again and stared numbly at the light show on the savannah.

Each of us knew the war was over—we knew it with the gut rather than the head. It was an emotional reaction, but very calm, very resigned, very passive. It was a thing too big for questioning; it became a self-evident fact. After D'kotta, there could be nothing else. Period. The war was over.

We were almost right. But not quite.

In another hour or so, a man from field HQ came up over the mountain shoulder in a stolen vacform and landed in camp. The man switched off the vac, jumped down, took two steps toward the parapet overlooking hell, stopped. We saw his stomach muscles jump, tighten. He took a stumbling half-step back, then stopped again. His hand went up to shield his throat, dropped, hesitated, went back up. We said nothing. The HQ directing the D'kotta campaign had been sensibly located behind the Blackfriars: they had been shielded by the mountain chain and had seen nothing but glare against the cloud cover. This was his first look at the city; at where the city had been. I watched the muscles play in his back, saw his shoulders hunch as if under an unraised fist. A good many of the Quaestor men involved in planning the D'kotta operation committed suicide immediately after the Realignment; a good many didn't. I don't know what category this one belonged in.

The liaison man finally turned his head, dragged himself away. His movements were jerky, and his face was an odd color, but he was under control. He pulled Heynith, our team leader, aside. They talked for a half hour. The liaison man showed Heynith a map, scribbled on a pad for Heynith to see, gave Heynith some papers. Heynith nodded occasionally. The liaison man said goodbye, half-ran to his vacform. The vac lifted with an erratic surge, steadied, then disappeared in a long arc over the gnarled backs of the Blackfriars. Heynith stood in the dirtswirl kicked up by the backwash and watched impassively.

It got quiet again, but it was a little more apprehensive.

Heynith came over, studied us for a while, then told us to get ready to move out. We stared at him. He repeated it in a quiet, firm voice; unendurably patient. Hush for a second, then somebody groaned, somebody else cursed, and the spell of D'kotta was partially broken, for the moment. We awoke enough to ready our gear; there was even a little talking, though not much.

Heynith appeared at our head and led us out in a loose travel formation, diagonally across the face of the slope, then up toward the shoulder. We reached the notch we'd found earlier and started down the other side.

Everyone wanted to look back at D'kotta. No one did.

Somehow, it was still night.

We never talked much on the march, of course, but tonight the silence was spooky: you could hear boots crunch on stone, the slight rasp of breath, the muted jangle of knives occasionally bumping against thighs. You could hear our fear; you could smell it, could see it.

We could touch it, we could taste it.

I was a member of something so old that they even had to dig up the name for it when they were rooting through the rubble of ancient history, looking for concepts to use against the Combine: a "commando team." Don't ask me what it means, but that's what it's called. Come to think, I know what it means in terms of flesh: it means ugly. Long ugly days and nights that come back in your sleep even uglier, so that you don't want to think about it at all because it squeezes your eyeballs like a vise. Cold and dark and wet, with sudden death looming up out of nothing at any time and jarring you with mortality like a rubber glove full of ice water slapped across your face. Living jittery high all the time, so that everything gets so real that it looks fake. You live in an anticipation that's pain, like straddling a fence with a knifeblade for a top rung, waiting for something to come along in the dark and push you off. You get so you like it. The pain's so consistent that you forget it's there, you forget there ever was a time when you didn't have it, and you live on the adrenaline.

We liked it. We were dedicated. We *hated*. It gave us something to do with our hate, something tangible we could see. And nobody'd done it but us for hundreds of years; there was an exultation to that. The Scholars and Antiquarians who'd started the Quaestor movement— left fullsentient and relatively unwatched so they could better piece together the muddle of prehistory from generations of inherited archives—they'd been smart. They knew their only hope of baffling the Combine was to hit them with radical concepts and tactics, things they didn't have instructions for handling, things out of the Combine's experience. So they scooped concepts out of prehistory, as far back as the archives go, even finding *written* records somewhere and having to figure out how to use them.

Out of one of these things, they got the idea of "guerrilla" war. No, I don't know what that means either, but what it *means* is playing the game by your own rules instead of the enemy's. Oh, you let the enemy keep playing by *his* rules, see, but you play by your own. Gives you a wider range of moves. You *do* things. I mean, *ridiculous* things, but so ancient they don't have any defense against them because they never thought they'd have to defend against *that*. Most of the time they never even knew *that* existed.

Like, we used to run around with these projectile weapons the Quaestors had copied from old plans and mass-produced in the autfacs on the sly by stealing computer time. The things worked by a chemical reaction inside the mechanism that would spit these tiny missiles out at a high velocity. The missile would hit you so hard it would actually lodge itself in your body, puncture internal organs, *kill* you. I know it sounds like an absurd concept, but there were advantages.

Don't forget how tightly controlled a society the Combine's was; even worse than the Commonwealth in its own way. We couldn't just steal energy weapons or biodeths and use them, because all those things operated on broadcast power from the Combine, and as soon as one was reported missing, the Combine would just cut the relay for that particular code. We couldn't make them ourselves, because unless you used the Combine's broadcast power you'd need a ton of generator equipment with each weapon to provide enough energy to operate it, and we didn't have the technology to miniaturize that much machinery. (Later some genius figured out a way to make, say, a functioning biodeth with everything but the energy source and then cut into and tap Combine broadcast power without showing up on the coding board, but that was toward the end anyway, and most of them were stockpiled for the shock troops at D'kotta.) At least the "guns" worked. And there were even unexpected advantages. We found that tanglefields, scattershields, phasewalls, personal warders, all the usual defenses, were unable to stop the "bullets" (the little missiles fired by the "guns")—they were just too sophisticated to stop anything as crude as a lump of metal moving at relatively sluggish ballistic speeds. Same with "bombs" and "grenades"—devices designed to have a chemical reaction violent enough to kill in an enclosed place. And the list went on and on. The Combine thought we couldn't move around, because all vehicles were coded and worked on broadcast power. Did you ever hear of "bicycles"? They're devices for translating mechanical energy into motion, they ride on wheels that you actually make revolve with physical labor. And the bicycles didn't have enough metal or mass to trigger sentryfields or show up on sweep probes, so we could go undetected to places they thought nobody could reach. Communicate? We used mirrors to flash messages, used puffs of smoke as code, had people actually *carry* messages from one place to another.

More important, we *personalized* war. That was the most radical thing, that was the thing that turned us from kids running around and having fun breaking things into men with bitter faces, that was the thing that took the heart out of the Combine more than anything else. That's why people still talk about the Realignment with horror today, even after all these years, especially in the Commonwealth.

We killed people. *We* did it, ourselves. We walked up and stabbed them. I mentioned a knife before, boy, and I knew you didn't know what it was; you bluff well for a kid—that's the way to a reputation for wisdom: look sage and always keep your mouth shut about your ignorance. Well, a knife is a tapering piece of metal with a handle, sharpened on the sides and very sharp at the tapered end, sharp enough so that when you strike someone with it the metal goes right into their flesh, cuts them, rips them open, *kills* them, and there is blood on your hands which feels wet and sticky and is hard to wash off because it dries and sticks to the little hairs on the backs of your wrists. We learned how to hit people hard enough to kill them, snap the bones inside the skin like dry sticks inside oiled cloth. We did. We strangled them with lengths of wire. You're shocked. So was the Combine. They had grown used to killing at a great distance, the push of a button, the flick of a switch, using vast, clean, impersonal forces to do their annihilation. *We* killed people. We killed *people—not* statistics and abstractions. We heard their screams, we saw their faces, we smelled their blood, and their vomit and shit and urine when their systems let go after death. You have to be crazy to do things like that. We *were* crazy. We were a good team.

There were twelve of us in the group, although we mostly worked in sections of four. I was in the team leader's section, and it had been my family for more than two years:

Heynith, stocky, balding, leather-faced; a hard, fair man; brilliant organizer.

Ren, impassive, withdrawn, taciturn, frighteningly competent, of a strange humor.

Goth, young, tireless, bullheaded, given to sudden enthusiasms and depressions; he'd only been with us for about four months, a replacement for Mason, who had been killed while trying to escape from a raid on Cape Itica.

And me.

We were all warped men, emotional cripples one way or the other.

We were all crazy.

The Combine could never understand that kind of craziness, in spite of the millions of people they'd killed or shriveled impersonally over the years. They were afraid of that craziness, they were baffled by it, never could plan to counter it or take it into account. They couldn't really believe it.

That's how we'd taken the Blackfriars Transmitter, hours before D'kotta. It had been impregnable—wrapped in layer after layer of defense fields against missile attack, attack by chemical or biological agents, transmitted energy, almost anything. We'd walked in. They'd never imagined anyone would do that, that it was even possible to attack that way, so there was no defense against it. The guardsystems were designed to meet more esoteric threats. And even after ten years of slowly escalating guerrilla action, they still didn't *really* believe anyone would use his body to wage war. So we walked in. And killed everybody there. The staff was a sentient techclone of ten and an executive foreman. No nulls or zombies. The ten identical technicians milled in panic, the foreman stared at us in disbelief, and what I think was distaste that we'd gone so far outside the bounds of procedure. We killed them like you kill insects, not really thinking about it much, except for that part of you that always thinks about it, that records it and replays it while you sleep. Then we blew up the transmitter with chemical explosives. Then, as the flames leaped up and ate holes in the night, we'd gotten on our bicycles and rode like hell toward the Blackfriars, the mountains hunching and looming ahead, as jagged as black snaggle-teeth against the industrial glare of the sky. A tanglefield had snatched at us for a second, but then we were gone.

That's all that I personally had to do with the "historic" Battle of D'kotta. It was enough. We'd paved the way for the whole encounter. Without the transmitter's energy, the Combine's weapons and transportation systems—including liftshafts, slidewalks, irisdoors, and windows, heating, lighting, waste disposal—were inoperable; D'kotta was immobilized. Without the station's broadcast matter, thousands of buildings, industrial complexes, roadways, and homes had collapsed into chaos, literally collapsed. More important, without broadcast nourishment, D'kotta's four major Cerebrums—handling an incredible complexity of military/industrial/administrative tasks—were knocked out of operation, along with a number of smaller Cerebrums: the synapses need constant nourishment to function, and so do the sophont ganglion units, along with the constant flow of the psychocybernetic current to keep them from going mad from sensory deprivation, and even the nulls would soon grow intractable as hunger stung them almost to self-awareness, finally to die after a few days. Any number of the lowest-ranking sentient clones—all those without stomachs or digestive systems, mostly in the military and industrial castes—would find themselves in the same position as the nulls; without broadcast nourishment, they would die within days. And without catarcs in operation to duplicate the function of atrophied intestines, the buildup of body wastes would poison them anyway, even if they could somehow get nourishment. The independent food dispensers for the smaller percentage of fullsentients and higher clones simply could not increase their output enough to feed that many people, even if converted to intravenous systems. To say nothing of the zombies in the Environments scattered throughout the city.

There were backup fail-safe systems, of course, but they hadn't been used in centuries, the majority of them had fallen into disrepair and didn't work, and other Quaestor teams made sure the rest of them wouldn't work either.

Before a shot had been fired, D'kotta was already a major disaster.

The Combine had reacted as we'd hoped, as they'd been additionally prompted to react by intelligence reports of Quaestor massings in strength around D'kotta that it'd taken weeks to leak to the Combine from unimpeachable sources. The Combine was pouring forces into

D'kotta within hours, nearly the full strength of the traditional military caste and a large percentage of the militia they'd cobbled together out of industrial clones when the Quaestors had begun to get seriously troublesome, plus a major portion of their heavy armament. They had hoped to surprise the Quaestors, catch them between the city and the inaccessible portion of the Blackfriars, quarter the area with so much strength it'd be impossible to dodge them, run the Quaestors down, annihilate them, break the back of the movement.

It had worked the other way around.

For years, the Quaestors had stung and run, always retreating when the Combine advanced, never meeting them in conventional battle, never hitting them with anything really heavy. Then, when the Combine had risked practically all of its military resources on one gigantic effort calculated to be effective against the usual Quaestor behavior, we had suddenly switched tactics. The Quaestors had waited to meet the Combine's advance and had hit the Combine forces with everything they'd been able to save, steal, hoard, and buy clandestinely from sympathizers in the Commonwealth in over fifteen years of conspiracy and campaign aimed at this moment.

Within an hour of the first tacnuke exchange, the city had ceased to exist, everything leveled except two of the Cerebrums and the Escridel Creche. Then the Quaestors activated their terraforming devices—which I believe they bought from a firm here on Kos, as a matter of fact. This was completely insane—terraforming systems used indiscriminately can destroy entire planets—but it was the insanity of desperation, and they did it anyway. Within a half hour, the remaining Combine heavy armaments battalions and the two Cerebrums ceased to exist. A few minutes later, the supposedly invulnerable Escridel Creche ceased to exist, the first time in history a creche had ever been destroyed. Then, as the cycling energies got out of hand and filterfeedback built to a climax, everything on the veldt ceased to exist.

The carnage had been inconceivable.

Take the vast population of D'kotta as a base, the second largest city on World, one of the biggest even in this sector of the Commonwealth. The subfleets had been in, bringing the betja harvest and other goods up the Delva; river traffic was always heaviest at that time of year.

The mines and factories had been in full swing, and the giant sprawl of the Westernese Shipyards and Engine Works. Add the swarming inhabitants of the six major Controlled Environments that circled the city. Add the city-within-a-city of Admin South, in charge of that hemisphere. Add the twenty generations of D'kotta Combine fullsentients whose discorporate ego-patterns had been preserved in the mountain of "indestructible" micromolecular circuitry called the Escridel Creche. (Those executives had died the irreversible true death, without hope of resurrection this time, even as disembodied intellects housed within artificial mind-environments: the records of their brain's unique pattern of electrical/chemical/psychocybernetic rhythms and balances had been destroyed, and you can't rebuild consciousness from a fused puddle of slag. This hit the Combine where they lived, literally, and had more impact than anything else.) Add the entire strength of both opposing forces; all of our men—who suspected what would happen—had been suicide volunteers. Add all of the elements together.

The total goes up into the multiples of billions.

The number was too big to grasp. Our minds fumbled at it while we marched, and gave up. It was too big.

I stared at Ren's back as we walked, a nearly invisible mannequin silhouette, and tried to multiply that out to the necessary figure. I staggered blindly along, lost and inundated beneath thousands of individual arms, legs, faces; a row of faces blurring off into infinity, all screaming—and the imagining nowhere near the actuality.

Billions.

How many restless ghosts out of that many deaders? Who do they haunt?

Billions.

Dawn caught us about two hours out. It came with no warning, as usual. We were groping through World's ink-dark, moonless night, watched only by the million icy eyes of evening, shreds of witchfire crystal, incredibly cold and distant. I'd watched them night after night for years, scrawling their indecipherable hieroglyphics across the sky, indifferent to man's incomprehension. I stopped for a second on a rise, pushing back the infrared lenses, staring at the sky. What program was printed there, suns for ciphers, worlds for decimal points? An absurd question—I was nearly as foolish as you once, buck—but it was the first fully verbalized thought I'd had since I'd realized the nakedness of flesh, back there on the parapet as my life tore itself apart. I asked it again, half-expecting an answer, watching my breath turn to plumes and tatters, steaming in the silver chill of the stars.

The sun came up like a meteor. It scuttled up from the horizon with that unsettling, deceptive speed that even natives of World never quite get used to. New light washed around us, blue and raw at first, deepening the shadows and honing their edges. The sun continued to hitch itself up the sky, swallowing stars, a watery pink flush wiping the horizon clear of night. The light deepened, mellowed into gold. We floated through silver mist that swirled up around the mountain's knobby knees. I found myself crying silently as I walked the high ridge between mist and sky, absorbing the morning with a new hunger, grappling with a thought that was still too big for my mind and kept slipping elusively away, just out of reach. There was a low hum as our warmsuits adjusted to the growing warmth, polarizing from black to white, bleeding heat back into the air. Down the flanks of the Blackfriars and away across the valley below—visible now as the mists pirouetted past us to the summits—the night plants were dying, shriveling visibly in mile-long swaths of decay. In seconds the Blackfriars were gaunt and barren, turned to hills of ash and bone. The sun was now a bloated yellow disk surrounded by haloes of red and deepening scarlet, shading into the frosty blue of rarefied air. Stripped of softening vegetation, the mountains looked rough and abrasive as pumice, gouged by lunar shadows. The first of the day plants began to appear at our feet, the green spiderwebbing, poking up through cracks in the dry earth.

We came across a new stream, tumbling from melting ice, sluicing a dusty gorge.

An hour later we found the valley.

Heynith led us down onto the marshy plain that rolled away from mountains to horizon. We circled wide, cautiously approaching the valley from the lowlands. Heynith held up his hand, pointed to me, Ren, Goth. The others fanned out across the mouth of the valley, hid, settled down to wait. We went in alone. The speargrass had grown rapidly; it was chest-high. We crawled in, timing our movements to coincide with the long soughing of the morning breeze, so that any rippling of the grass would be taken for natural movement. It took us about a half hour of dusty, sweaty work. When I judged that I'd wormed my way in close enough, I stopped, slowly parted the speargrass enough to peer out without raising my head.

It was a large vacvan, a five-hundred-footer, equipped with waldoes for self-loading.

It was parked near the hill flank on the side of the wide valley.

There were three men with it.

I ducked back into the grass, paused to make sure my "gun" was ready for operation, then crawled laboriously nearer to the van.

It was very near when I looked up again, about twenty-five feet away in the center of a cleared space. I could make out the hologram pictograph that pulsed identification on the side: the symbol for Urheim, World's largest city and Combine Seat of Board, half a world away in the Northern Hemisphere. They'd come a long way; still thought of as long, though ships whispered between the stars—it was still long for feet and eyes. And another longer way: from fetuses in glass wombs to men stamping and jiggling with cold inside the fold of a mountain's thigh, watching the spreading morning. That made me feel funny to think about. I wondered if they suspected that it'd be the last morning they'd ever see. That made me feel funnier. The thought tickled my mind again, danced away. I checked my gun a second time, needlessly.

I waited, feeling troubled, pushing it down. Two of them were standing together several feet in front of the van, sharing a mild narcotic atomizer, sucking deeply, shuffling with restlessness and cold, staring out across the speargrass to where the plain opened up. They had the stiff, rumpled, puff-eyed look of people who had just spent an uncomfortable night in a cramped place. They were dressed as fullsentients uncloned, junior officers of the military caste, probably hereditary positions inherited from their families, as is the case with most of the uncloned cadet executives. Except for the cadre at Urheim and other major cities, they must have been some of the few surviving clansmen; hundreds of thousands of military cadets and officers had died at D'kotta (along with uncounted clones and semisentients of all ranks), and the caste had never been extremely large in the first place. The by-laws had demanded that the Combine maintain a security force, but it had become mostly traditional, with minimum function, at least among the uncloned higher ranks, almost the last stronghold of old-fashioned nepotism. That was one of the things that had favored the Quaestor uprising, and had forced the Combine to take the unpopular step of impressing large numbers of industrial clones into a militia. The most junior of these two cadets was very young, even younger than me. The third man remained inside the van's cab. I could see his face blurrily through the windfield, kept on against the cold though the van was no longer in motion.

I waited. I knew the others were maneuvering into position around me. I also knew what Heynith was waiting for.

The third man jumped down from the high cab. He was older, wore an officer's hologram: a full executive. He said something to the cadets, moved a few feet toward the back of the van, started to take a piss. The column of golden liquid steamed in the cold air.

Heynith whistled.

I rolled to my knees, parted the speargrass at the edge of the cleared space, swung my gun up. The two cadets started, face muscles tensing into uncertain fear. The older cadet took an involuntary step forward, still clutching the atomizer. Ren and Goth chopped him down, firing a stream of "bullets" into him. The guns made a very loud metallic rattling sound that jarred the teeth, and fire flashed from the ejector ends. Birds screamed upward all along the mountain flank. The impact of the bullets knocked the cadet off his feet, rolled him so that he came to rest belly-down. The atomizer flew through the air, hit, bounced. The younger cadet leaped toward the cab, right into my line of fire. I pulled the trigger; bullets exploded out of the gun. The cadet was kicked backwards, arms swinging wide, slammed against the side of the cab, jerked upright as I continued to fire, spun along the van wall and rammed heavily into the ground. He tottered on one shoulder for a second, then flopped over onto his back. At the sound of the first shot, the executive had whirled—penis still dangling from pantaloons, surplus piss spraying wildly—and dodged for the back of the van, so that Heynith's volley missed and screamed from the van wall, leaving a long scar. The executive dodged again, crouched, came up with a biodeth in one hand, and swung right into a single bullet from Ren just as he began to fire. The impact twirled him in a staggering circle, his finger still pressing the trigger; the carrier beam splashed harmlessly from the van wall, traversed as the executive spun, cut a long swath through the speargrass, the plants shriveling and blackening as the beam swept over them. Heynith opened up again before the beam could reach his clump of grass, sending the executive—somehow still on his feet—lurching past the end of the van. The biodeth dropped, went out. Heynith kept firing, the executive dancing bonelessly backwards on his heels, held up by the stream of bullets. Heynith released the trigger. The executive collapsed: a heap of arms and legs at impossible angles.

When we came up to the van, the young cadet was still dying. His body shivered and arched, his heels drummed against the earth, his fingers plucked at nothing, and then he was still. There was a lot of blood.

The others moved up from the valley mouth. Heynith sent them circling around the rim, where the valley walls dipped down on three sides.

We dragged the bodies away and concealed them in some large rocks.

I was feeling numb again, like I had after D'kotta.

I continued to feel numb as we spent the rest of that morning in frantic preparation. My mind was somehow detached as my body sweated and dug and hauled. There was a lot for it to do. We had four heavy industrial lasers, rock-cutters; they were clumsy, bulky, inefficient things to use as weapons, but they'd have to do. This mission had not been planned so much as thrown together, only two hours before the liaison man had contacted us on the parapet. Anything that could possibly work at all would have to be made to work somehow; no time to do it right, just do it. We'd been the closest team in contact with the field HQ who'd received the report, so we'd been snatched; the lasers were the only things on hand that could even approach potential as a heavy weapon, so we'd use the lasers.

Now that we'd taken the van without someone alerting the Combine by radio from the cab, Heynith flashed a signal mirror back toward the shoulder of the mountain we'd quitted a few hours before. The liaison man swooped down ten minutes later, carrying one of the lasers strapped awkwardly to his platvac. He made three more trips, depositing the massive cylinders as carefully as eggs, then gunned his platvac and screamed back toward the Blackfriars in a maniac arc just this side of suicidal. His face was still gray, tight-pressed lips a bloodless white against ash, and he hadn't said a word during the whole unloading procedure. I think he was probably one of the Quaestors who followed the Way of Atonement. I never saw him again. I've sometimes wished I'd had the courage to follow his example, but I rationalize by telling myself that I have atoned with my life rather than my death, and who knows, it might even be somewhat true. It's nice to think so anyway.

It took us a couple of hours to get the lasers into position. We spotted them in four places around the valley walls, dug slanting pits into the slopes to conceal them and tilt the barrels up at the right angle. We finally got them all zeroed on a spot about a hundred feet above the center of the valley floor, the muzzle arrangement giving each a few degrees of leeway on either side. That's where she'd have to come down anyway if she was a standard orbot, the valley being just wide enough to contain the boat and the vacvan, with a safety margin between them. Of course, if they brought her down on the plain outside the valley mouth, things were going to get very hairy; in that case we might be able to lever one or two of the lasers around to bear, or, failing that, we could try to take the orbot on foot once it'd landed, with about one chance in eight of making it. But we thought that they'd land her in the valley; that's where the vacvan had been parked, and they'd want the shelter of the high mountain walls to conceal the orbot from any Quaestor eyes that might be around. If so, that gave us a much better chance. About one out of three.

When the lasers had been positioned, we scattered, four men to an emplacement, hiding in the camouflaged trenches alongside the big barrels. Heynith led Goth and me toward the laser we'd placed about fifty feet up the mountain flank, directly behind and above the vacvan. Ren stayed behind. He stood next to the van—shoulders characteristically slouched, thumbs hooked in his belt, face carefully void of expression—and watched us out of sight. Then he looked out over the valley mouth, hitched up his gun, spat in the direction of Urheim and climbed up into the van cab.

The valley was empty again. From our position the vacvan looked like a shiny toy, sun dogs winking across its surface as it baked in the afternoon heat. An abandoned toy, lost in high weeds, waiting in loneliness to be reclaimed by owners who would never come.

Time passed.

The birds we'd frightened away began to settle back onto the hillsides.

I shifted position uneasily, trying half-heartedly to get comfortable. Heynith glared me into immobility. We were crouched in a trench about eight feet long and five feet deep, covered by a camouflage tarpaulin propped open on the valley side by pegs, a couple of inches of vegetation and topsoil on top of the tarpaulin. Heynith was in the middle, straddling the operator's saddle of the laser. Goth was on his left, I was on his right. Heynith was going to man the laser when the time came; it only took one person. There was nothing for Goth and me to do, would be nothing to do even during the ambush, except take over the firing in the unlikely event that Heynith was killed without the shot wiping out all of us, or stand by to lever the laser around in case that became necessary. Neither was very likely to happen. No, it was Heynith's show, and we were superfluous and unoccupied.

That was bad.

We had a lot of time to think.

That was worse.

I was feeling increasingly numb, like a wall of clear glass had been slipped between me and the world and was slowly thickening, layer by layer. With the thickening came an incredible isolation (isolation though I was cramped and suffocating, though I was jammed up against Heynith's bunched thigh—I couldn't touch him, he was miles away) and with the isolation came a sick, smothering panic. It was the inverse of claustrophobia. My flesh had turned to clear plastic, my bones to glass, and I was naked, ultimately naked, and there was nothing I could wrap me in. Surrounded by an army, I would still be alone; shrouded in iron thirty feet underground, I would still be naked. One portion of my mind wondered dispassionately if I was slipping into shock; the rest of it fought to keep down the scream that gathered along tightening muscles. The isolation increased. I was unaware of my surroundings, except for the heat and the pressure of enclosure.

I was seeing the molten spider of D'kotta, lying on its back and showing its obscene blotched belly, kicking legs of flame against the sky, each leg raising a poison blister where it touched the clouds.

I was seeing the boy, face runneled by blood, beating heels against the ground.

I was beginning to doubt big, simple ideas.

Nothing moved in the valley except wind through grass, spirits circling in the form of birds.

Spider legs.

Crab dance.

The blocky shadow of the vacvan crept across the valley.

Suddenly, with the intensity of vision, I was picturing Ren sitting in the van cab, shoulders resting against the door, legs stretched out along the seat, feet propped up on the instrument board, one ankle crossed over the other, gun resting across his lap, eyes watching the valley mouth through the windfield. He would be smoking a cigarette, and he would take it from his lips occasionally, flick the ashes onto the shiny dials with a fingernail, smile his strange smile, and carefully burn holes in the plush fabric of the upholstery. The fabric (real fabric; not plastic) would smolder, send out a wisp of bad-smelling smoke, and there would be another charred black hole in the seat. Ren would smile again, put the cigarette back in his mouth, lean back, and puff slowly. Ren was waiting to answer the radio signal from the orbot, to assure its pilot and crew that all was well, to talk them down to death. If they suspected anything was wrong, he would be the first to die. Even if everything went perfectly, he stood a high chance of dying anyway; he was the most exposed. It was almost certainly a suicide job. Ren said that he didn't give a shit; maybe he actually didn't. Or at least had convinced himself that he didn't. He was an odd man. Older than any of us, even Heynith, he had worked most of his life as a cadet executive in Admin at Urheim, devoted his existence to his job, subjugated all of his energies to it. He had been passed over three times for promotion to executive status, years of redoubled effort and mounting anxiety between each rejection. With the third failure he had been quietly retired to live on the credit subsidy he had earned with forty years of service. The next morning, precisely at the start of his accustomed work period, he stole a biodeth from a security guard in the Admin Complex, walked into his flowsector, killed everyone there, and disappeared from Urheim. After a year on the run, he had managed to contact the Quaestors. After another year of training, he was serving with a commando team in spite of his age. That had been five years ago; I had known him for two. During all that time, he had said little. He did his job very well with a minimum of waste motion, never made mistakes, never complained, never showed emotion. But occasionally he would smile and burn a hole in something. Or someone.

The sun dived at the horizon, seeming to crash into the plain in an explosion of flame. Night swallowed us in one gulp. Black as a beast's belly.

It jerked me momentarily back into reality. I had a bad moment when I thought I'd gone blind, but then reason returned and I slipped the infrared lenses down over my eyes, activated them. The world came back in shades of red. Heynith was working cramped legs against the body of the laser. He spoke briefly, and we gulped some stimulus pills to keep us awake; they were bitter, and hard to swallow dry as usual, but they kicked up a familiar acid churning in my stomach, and my blood began to flow faster. I glanced at Heynith. He'd been quiet, even for Heynith. I wondered what he was thinking. He looked at me, perhaps reading the thought, and ordered us out of the trench.

Goth and I crawled slowly out, feeling stiff and brittle, slapped our thighs and arms, stamped to restore circulation. Stars were sprinkling across the sky, salt spilled on black porcelain. I still couldn't read them, I found. The day plants had vanished, the day animals had retreated into catalepsy. The night plants were erupting from the ground, fed by the debris of the day plants. They grew rapidly, doubling, then tripling in height as we watched. They were predominantly thick, ropy shrubs with wide, spearhead leaves of dull purple and black, about four feet high. Goth and I dug a number of them up, root systems intact, and placed them on top of the tarpaulin to replace the day plants that had shriveled with the first touch of bitter evening frost. We had to handle them with padded gloves; the leaf surfaces greedily absorbed the slightest amount of heat and burned like dry ice.

Then we were back in the trench, and it was worse than ever. Motion had helped for a while, but I could feel the numbing panic creeping back, and the momentary relief made it even harder to bear. I tried to start a conversation, but it died in monosyllabic grunts, and silence sopped up the echoes. Heynith was methodically checking the laser controls for the nth time. He was tense; I could see it bunch his shoulder muscles, bulge his calves into rock as they pushed against the footplates of the saddle. Goth looked worse than I did; he was somewhat younger, and usually energetic and cheerful. Not tonight.

We should have talked, spread the pain around; I think all of us realized it. But we couldn't; we were made awkward by our own special intimacy. At one time or another, every one of us had reached a point where he *had* to talk or die, even Heynith, even Ren. So we all had talked and all had listened, each of us switching roles sooner or later. We had poured our fears and dreams and secret memories upon each other, until now we knew each other too well. It made us afraid. Each of us was afraid that he had exposed too much, let down too many barriers. We were afraid of vulnerability, of the knife that jabs for the softest fold of the belly. We were all scarred men already, and twice-shy. And the resentment grew that others had seen us that helpless, that vulnerable. So the walls went back up, intensified. And so when we needed to talk again, we could not. We were already too close to risk further intimacy.

Visions returned, ebbing and flowing, overlaying the darkness.

The magma churning, belching a hot breath that stinks of rotten eggs.

The cadet, his face inhuman in the death rictus, blood running down in a wash from his smashed forehead, plastering one eye closed, bubbling at his nostril, frothing around his lips, the lips tautening as his head jerks forward and then backwards, slamming the ground, the lips then growing slack, the body slumping, the mouth sagging open, the rush of blood and phlegm past the tombstone teeth, down the chin and neck, soaking into the fabric of the tunic. The feet drumming at the ground a final time, digging up clots of earth.

I groped for understanding. I had killed people before, and it had not bothered me except in sleep. I had done it mechanically, routine backed by hate, hate cushioned by routine. I wondered if the night would ever end. I remembered the morning I'd watched from the mountain. I didn't think the night would end. A big idea tickled my mind again.

The city swallowed by stone.

The cadet falling, swinging his arms wide.

Why always the cadet and the city in conjunction? Had one sensitized me to the other, and if so, which? I hesitated.

Could both of them be equally important?

One of the other section leaders whistled.

We all started, somehow grew even more tense. The whistle came again, warbling, sound floating on silence like oil on water. Someone was coming. After a while we heard a rustling and snapping of underbrush approaching downslope from the mountain. Whoever it was, he was making no effort to move quietly. In fact he seemed to be blundering along, bulling through the tangles, making a tremendous thrashing noise. Goth and I turned in the direction of the sound, brought our guns up to bear, primed them. That was instinct. I wondered who could be coming *down* the mountain toward us. That was reason. Heynith twisted to cover the opposite direction, away from the noise, resting his gun on the saddle rim. That was caution. The thrasher passed our position about six feet away, screened by the shrubs. There was an open space ten feet farther down, at the head of a talus bluff that slanted to the valley. We watched it. The shrubs at the end of the clearing shook, were torn aside. A figure stumbled out into starlight.

It was a null.

Goth sucked in a long breath, let it hiss out between his teeth. Heynith remained impassive, but I could imagine his eyes narrowing behind the thick lenses. My mind was totally blank for about three heartbeats, then, surprised: a null! and I brought the gun barrel up, then, uncomprehending: a null? and I lowered the muzzle. Blank for a second, then: how? and trickling in again: how? Thoughts snarled into confusion, the gun muzzle wavered hesitantly.

The null staggered across the clearing, weaving in slow figure-eights. It almost fell down the talus bluff, one foot suspended uncertainly over the drop, then lurched away, goaded by tropism. The null shambled backward a few paces, stopped, swayed, then slowly sank to its knees.

It kneeled: head bowed, arms limp along the ground, palms up.

Heynith put his gun back in his lap, shook his head. He told us he'd be damned if he could figure out where it came from, but we'd have to get rid of it. It could spoil the ambush if it was spotted. Automatically, I raised my gun, trained it. Heynith stopped me. No noise, he said, not now. He told Goth to go out and kill it silently.

Goth refused. Heynith stared at him speechlessly, then began to flush. Goth and Heynith had had trouble before. Goth was a good man, brave as a bull, but he was stubborn, tended to follow his own lead too much, had too many streaks of sentimentality and touchiness, *thought* too much to be a really efficient cog.

They had disagreed from the beginning, something that wouldn't have been tolerated this long if the Quaestors hadn't been desperate for men. Goth was a devil in a fight when aroused, one of the best, and that had excused him a lot of obstinacy. But he had a curious squeamishness, he hadn't developed the layers of numbing scar-tissue necessary for guerrilla work, and that was almost inevitably fatal. I'd wondered before, dispassionately, how long he would last.

Goth was a hereditary fullsentient, one of the few connected with the Quaestors. He'd been a cadet executive in Admin, gained access to old archives that had slowly soured him on the Combine, been hit at the psychologically right moment by increasing Quaestor agitprop, and had defected; after a two-year proving period, he'd been allowed to participate actively. Goth was one of the only field people who was working out of idealism rather than hate, and that made us distrust him. Heynith also nurtured a traditional dislike for hereditary fullsentients. Heynith had been part of an industrial sixclone for over twenty years before joining the Quaestors. His Six had been wiped out in a production accident, caused by standard Combine negligence. Heynith had been the only survivor. The Combine had expressed mild sympathy, and told him that they planned to cut another clone from him to replace the destroyed Six; he of course would be placed in charge of the new Six, by reason of his seniority. They smiled at him, not seeing any reason why he wouldn't want to work another twenty years with biological replicas of his dead brothers and sisters, the men, additionally, reminders of what he'd been as a youth, unravaged by years of pain. Heynith had thanked them politely, walked out, and kept walking, crossing the Gray Waste on foot to join the Quaestors.

I could see all this working in Heynith's face as he raged at Goth. Goth could feel the hate too, but he stood firm. The null was incapable of doing anybody any harm; he wasn't going to kill it. There'd been enough slaughter. Goth's face was bloodless, and I could see D'kotta reflected in his eyes, but I felt no sympathy for him, in spite of my own recent agonies. He was disobeying orders. I thought about Mason, the man Goth had replaced, the man who had died in my arms at Itica, and I hated Goth for being alive instead of Mason. I had loved Mason. He'd been an Antiquarian in the Urheim archives, and he'd worked for the Quaestors almost from the beginning, years of vital service before his activities were discovered by the Combine. He'd escaped the raid, but his family hadn't. He'd been offered an admin job in Quaestor HQ, but had turned it down and insisted on fieldwork in spite of warnings that it was suicidal for a man of his age. Mason had been a tall, gentle, scholarly man who pretended to be gruff and hard-nosed, and cried alone at night when he thought nobody could see. I'd often thought that he could have escaped from Itica if he'd tried harder, but he'd been worn down, sick and guilt-ridden and tired, and his heart hadn't really been in it; that thought had returned to puzzle me often afterward. Mason had been the only person I'd ever cared about, the one who'd been more responsible than anybody for bringing me out of the shadows and into humanity, and I could have shot Goth at that moment because I thought he was betraying Mason's memory.

Heynith finally ran out of steam, spat at Goth, started to call him something, then stopped and merely glared at him, lips white. I'd caught Heynith's quick glance at me, a nearly invisible head-turn, just before he'd fallen silent. He'd almost forgotten and called Goth a zombie, a widespread expletive on World that had carefully *not* been used by the team since I'd joined. So Heynith had never really forgotten, though he'd treated me with scrupulous fairness. My fury turned to a cold anger, widened out from Goth to become a sick distaste for the entire world.

Heynith told Goth he would take care of him later, take care of him good, and ordered me to go kill the null, take him upslope and out of sight first, then conceal the body.

Mechanically, I pulled myself out of the trench, started downslope toward the clearing. Anger fueled me for the first few feet, and I slashed the shrubs aside with padded gloves, but it ebbed quickly, leaving me hollow and numb. I'd known how the rest of the team must actually think of me, but somehow I'd never allowed myself to admit it. Now I'd had my face jammed in it, and, coming on top of all the other anguish I'd gone through the last two days, it was too much.

I pushed into the clearing.

My footsteps triggered some response in the null. It surged drunkenly to its feet, arms swinging limply, and turned to face me.

The null was slightly taller than me, built very slender, and couldn't have weighed too much more than a hundred pounds. It was bald, completely hairless. The fingers were shriveled, limp flesh dangling from the club of the hand; they had never been used. The toes had been developed to enable technicians to walk nulls from one section of the Cerebrum to another, but the feet had never had a chance to toughen or grow callused: they were a mass of blood and lacerations. The nose was a rough blob of pink meat around the nostrils, the ears similarly atrophied. The eyes were enormous, huge milky corneas and small pupils, like those of a nocturnal bird; adapted to the gloom of the Cerebrum, and allowed to function to forestall sensory deprivation; they aren't cut into the psychocybernetic current like the synapses or the ganglions. There were small messy wounds on the temples, wrists, and spine-base where electrodes had been torn loose. It had been shrouded in a pajamalike suit of nonconductive material, but that had been torn almost completely away, only a few hanging tatters remaining. There were no sex organs. The flesh under the ribcage was curiously collapsed; no stomach or digestive tract. The body was covered with bruises, cuts, gashes, extensive swatches sun-baked to second-degree burns, other sections seriously frostbitten or marred by bad coldburns from the night shrubs.

My awe grew, deepened into archetypical dread.

It was from D'kotta, there could be no doubt about it. Somehow it had survived the destruction of its Cerebrum, somehow it had walked through the boiling hell to the foothills, somehow it had staggered up to and over the mountain shoulder. I doubted if there'd been any predilection in its actions; probably it had just walked blindly away from the ruined Cerebrum in a straight line and kept walking. Its actions with the talus bluff demonstrated that; maybe earlier some dim instinct had helped it fumble its way around obstacles in its path, but now it was exhausted, baffled, stymied. It was miraculous that it had made it this far. And the agony it must have suffered on its way was inconceivable. I shivered, spooked. The short hairs bristled on the back of my neck.

The null lurched toward me.

I whimpered and sprang backwards, nearly falling, swinging up the gun.

The null stopped, its head lolling, describing a slow semicircle. Its eyes were tracking curiously, and I doubted if it could focus on me at all. To it, I must have been a blur of darker gray.

I tried to steady my ragged breathing. It couldn't hurt me; it was harmless, nearly dead anyway. Slowly, I lowered the gun, pried my fingers from the stock, slung the gun over my shoulder.

I edged cautiously toward it. The null swayed, but remained motionless. Below, I could see the vacvan at the bottom of the bluff, a patch of dull gunmetal sheen. I stretched my hand out slowly. The null didn't move. This close, I could see its gaunt ribs rising and falling with the effort of its ragged breathing. It was trembling, an occasional convulsive spasm shuddering along its frame. I was surprised that it didn't stink; nulls were rumored to have a strong personal odor, at least according to the talk in field camps—bullshit, like so much of my knowledge at that time. I watched it for a minute, fascinated, but my training told me I couldn't stand out here for long; we were too exposed. I took another step, reached out for it, hesitated. I didn't want to touch it. Swallowing my distaste, I selected a spot on its upper arm free of burns or wounds, grabbed it firmly with one hand.

The null jerked at the touch, but made no attempt to strike out or get away. I waited warily for a second, ready to turn my grip into a wrestling hold if it should try to attack. It remained still, but its flesh crawled under my fingers, and I shivered myself in reflex. Satisfied that the null would give me no trouble, I turned and began to force it upslope, pushing it ahead of me.

It followed my shove without resistance, until we hit the first of the night shrubs, then it staggered and made a mewing, inarticulate sound. The plants were burning it, sucking warmth out of its flesh, raising fresh welts, ugly where bits of skin had adhered to the shrubs. I shrugged, pushed it forward. It mewed and lurched again. I stopped. The null's eyes tracked in my direction, and it whimpered to itself in pain. I swore at myself for wasting time, but moved ahead to break a path for the null, dragging it along behind me. The branches slapped harmlessly at my warmsuit as I bent them aside; occasionally one would slip past and lash the null, making it flinch and whimper, but it was spared the brunt of it. I wondered vaguely at my motives for doing it. Why bother to spare someone (*something*, I corrected nervously) pain when you're going to have to kill him (*it*) in a minute? What difference could it make? I shelved that and concentrated on the movements of my body; the null wasn't heavy, but it wasn't easy to drag it uphill either, especially as it'd stumble and go down every few yards and I'd have to pull it back to its feet again. I was soon sweating, but I didn't care, as the action helped to occupy my mind, and I didn't want to have to face the numbness I could feel taking over again.

We moved upslope until we were about thirty feet above the trench occupied by Heynith and Goth. This looked like a good place. The shrubs were almost chest-high here, tall enough to hide the null's body from an aerial search. I stopped. The null bumped blindly into me, leaned against me, its breath coming in rasps next to my ear. I shivered in horror at the contact. Gooseflesh blossomed on my arms and legs, swept across my body. Some connection sent a memory whispering at my mind, but I ignored it under the threat of rising panic. I twisted my shoulder under the null's weight, threw it off. The null slid back downslope a few feet, almost fell, recovered.

I watched it, panting. The memory returned, gnawing incessantly. This time it got through:

Mason scrambling through the sea-washed rocks of Cape Itica toward the waiting ramsub, while the fire sky-whipping behind picked us out against the shadows; Mason, too slow in vaulting over a stone ridge, balancing too long on the razor-edge in perfect silhouette against the night; Mason jerked upright as a fusor fired from the high cliff puddled his spine, melted his flesh like wax; Mason tumbling down into my arms, almost driving me to my knees; Mason, already dead, heavy in my arms, *heavy in my arms*; Mason torn away from me as a wave broke over us and deluged me in spume; Mason sinking from sight as Heynith screamed for me to come on and I fought my way through the chest-high surf to the ramsub—

That's what supporting the null had reminded me of: Mason, heavy in my arms.

Confusion and fear and nausea.

How could the null make me think of Mason?

Sick self-anger that my mind could compare Mason, gentle as the dream-father I'd never had, to something as disgusting as the null.

Anger novaed, trying to scrub out shame and guilt.

I couldn't take it. I let it spill out onto the null.

Growling, I sprang forward, shook it furiously until its head rattled and wobbled on its limp neck, grabbed it by the shoulders, and hammered it to its knees.

I yanked my knife out. The blade flamed suddenly in starlight.

I wrapped my hand around its throat to tilt its head back.

Its flesh was warm. A pulse throbbed under my palm. All at once, my anger was gone, leaving only nausea. I suddenly realized how cold the night was. Wind bit to the bone.

It was *looking* at me.

I suppose I'd been lucky. Orphans aren't as common as they once were—not in a society where reproduction has been relegated to the laboratory—but they still occur with fair regularity. I had been the son of an uncloned junior executive who'd run up an enormous credit debit, gone bankrupt, and been forced into insolvency. The Combine had cut a clone from him so that their man-hours would make up the bank discrepancy, burned out the higher levels of his brain, and put him in one of the nonsentient penal Controlled Environments. His wife was also cloned, but avoided brainscrub and went back to work in a lower capacity in Admin. I, as a baby, then became a ward of the State, and was sent to one of the institutional Environments. Imagine an endless series of low noises, repeating over and over again forever, no high or low spots, everything level: MMMMMMMMMMMMMMMMMMMMMMMMM-MMMMMMMMMMMMMMMMMMMMMMMM. Like that. That's the only way to describe the years in the Environments. We were fed, we were kept warm, we worked on conveyor belts piecing together miniaturized equipment, we were put to sleep electronically, we woke with our fingers already busy in the monotonous, rhythmical motions that we couldn't remember learning, motions we had repeated a million times a day since infancy. Once a day we were fed a bar of food-concentrates and vitamins. Occasionally, at carefully calculated intervals, we would be exercised to keep up muscle tone. After reaching puberty, we were occasionally masturbated by electric stimulation, the seed saved for sperm banks. The administrators of the Environment were not cruel; we almost never saw them. Punishment was by machine shocks; never severe, very rarely needed. The executives had no need to be cruel. All they needed was MMMMMMMMMMMMMMMMMMMMMMMMMMMMMMM. We had been taught at some early stage, probably by shock and stimulation, to put the proper part in the proper slot as the blocks of equipment passed in front of us. We had never been taught to talk, although an extremely limited language of several mood-sounds had independently developed among us; the executives never spoke on the rare intervals when they came to check the machinery that regulated us. We had never been told who we were, where we were; we had never been told anything. We didn't care about any of these things, the concepts had never formed in our minds, we were only semiconscious at best anyway. There was nothing but MMMMMMMMMMMMMMMMMMMMMMMM. The executives weren't concerned with our spiritual development; there was no graduation from the Environment, there was no place else for us to go in a rigidly stratified society. The Combine had discharged its obligation by keeping us alive, in a place where we could even be minimally useful. Though our jobs were sinecures and could have been more efficiently performed by computer, they gave the expense of our survival a socially justifiable excuse, they put us comfortably in a pigeonhole. We were there for life. We would grow up from infancy, grow old, and die, bathed in MMMMMMMMMMMMMMMMMMMMMM. The first real, separate, and distinct memory of my life is when the Quaestors raided the Environment, when the wall of the assembly chamber suddenly glowed red, buckled, collapsed inward, when Mason pushed out of the smoke and the debris cloud, gun at the ready, and walked slowly toward me. That's hindsight. At the time, it was only a sudden invasion of incomprehensible sounds and lights and shapes and colors, too much to possibly comprehend, incredibly alien. It was the first discordant note ever struck in our lives: MMMMMMMMMMMMMM!!!! shattering our world in an instant, plunging us into another dimension of existence. The Quaestors kidnapped all of us, loaded us onto vacvans, took us into the hills, tried to undo some of the harm. That'd been six years ago. Even with the facilities available at the Quaestor underground complex—hypnotrainers and analysis computers to plunge me back to childhood and patiently lead me out again step by step for ten thousand years of subjective time, while my body slumbered in stasis—even with all of that, I'd been lucky to emerge somewhat sane. The majority had died, or been driven into catalepsy. I'd been lucky even to be a Ward of the State, the way things had turned out. Lucky to be a zombie. I could have been a low-ranked clone, without a digestive system, tied forever to the Combine by unbreakable strings. Or I could have been one of the thousands of tank-grown creatures whose brains are used as organic-computer storage banks in the Cerebrum gestalts, completely unsentient: I could have been a null.

Enormous eyes staring at me, unblinking.

Warmth under my fingers.

I wondered if I was going to throw up.

Wind moaned steadily through the valley with a sound like MMMMMMMMMMMMMMMMM.

Heynith hissed for me to hurry up, sound riding the wind, barely audible. I shifted my grip on the knife. I was telling myself: it's never been really sentient anyway. Its brain has only been used as a computer unit for a biological gestalt, there's no individual intelligence in there.

It wouldn't make any difference. I was telling myself: it's dying anyway from a dozen causes. It's in pain. It would be kinder to kill it.

I brought up the knife, placing it against the null's throat. I pressed the point in slowly, until it was pricking flesh.

The null's eyes tracked, focused on the knifeblade.

My stomach turned over. I looked away, out across the valley. I felt my carefully created world trembling and blurring around me, I felt again on the point of being catapulted into another level of comprehension, previously unexpected. I was afraid.

The vacvan's headlights flashed on and off, twice.

I found myself on the ground, hidden by the ropy shrubs. I had dragged the null down with me, without thinking about it, pinned him flat to the ground, arm over back. That had been the signal that Ren had received a call from the orbot, had given it the proper radio code reply to bring it down. I could imagine him grinning in the darkened cab as he worked the instruments.

I raised myself on an elbow, jerked the knife up, suspending it while I looked for the junction of spine and neck that would be the best place to strike. If I was going to kill him (*it*), I would have to kill him (*it!*) now. In quick succession, like a series of slides, like a computer equation running, I got: D'kotta—the cadet—Mason—the null. *It* and *him* tumbled in selection. Came up *him*. I lowered the knife. I couldn't do it. He was human. Everybody was.

For better or worse, I was changed. I was no longer the same person.

I looked up. Somewhere up there, hanging at the edge of the atmosphere, was the tinsel collection of forces in opposition called a starship, delicately invulnerable as an iron butterfly. It would be phasing in and out of "reality" to hold its position above World, maintaining only the most tenuous of contacts with this continuum. It had launched an orbot, headed for a rendezvous with the vacvan in this valley. The orbot was filled with the gene cultures that could be used to create hundreds of thousands of nonsentient clones who could be imprinted with behavior patterns and turned into computer-directed soldiers; crude but effective. The orbot was filled with millions of tiny metal blocks, kept under enormous compression: when released from tension, molecular memory would reshape them into a wide range of weapons needing only a power source to be functional. The orbot was carrying, in effect, a vast army and its combat equipment, in a form that could be transported in a five-hundred-foot vacvan and slipped into Urheim, where there were machines that could put it into use. It was the Combine's last chance, the second wind they needed in order to survive. It had been financed and arranged by various industrial firms in the Commonwealth who had vested interests in the Combine's survival on World. The orbot's cargo had been assembled and sent off before D'kotta, when it had been calculated that the reinforcements would be significant in ensuring a Combine victory; now it was indispensable. D'kotta had made the Combine afraid that an attack on Urheim might be next, that the orbot might be intercepted by the Quaestors if the city was under siege when it tried to land. So the Combine had decided to land the orbot elsewhere and sneak the cargo in. The Blackfriars had been selected as a rendezvous, since it was unlikely the Quaestors would be on the alert for Combine activity in that area so soon after D'kotta, and even if stopped, the van might be taken for fleeing survivors and ignored. The starship had been contacted by esper en route, and the change in plan made.

Four men had died to learn of the original plan. Two more had died in order to learn of the new landing site and get the information to the Quaestors in time.

The orbot came down.

I watched it as in a dream, coming to my knees, head above the shrubs. The null stirred under my hand, pushed against the ground, sat up.

The orbot was a speck, a dot, a ball, a toy. It was gliding silently in on grays, directly overhead.

I could imagine Heynith readying the laser, Goth looking up and chewing his lip the way he always did in stress. I knew that my place should be with them, but I couldn't move. Fear and tension were still there, but they were under glass. I was already emotionally drained. I could sum up nothing else, even to face death.

The orbot had swelled into a huge, spherical mountain. It continued to settle toward the spot where we'd calculated it must land. Now it hung just over the valley center, nearly brushing the mountain walls on either side. The orbot filled the sky, and I leaned away from it instinctively. It dropped lower—

Heynith was the first to fire.

An intense beam of light erupted from the ground downslope, stabbed into the side of the orbot. Another followed from the opposite side of the valley, then the remaining two at once.

The orbot hung, transfixed by four steady, unbearably bright columns.

For a while, it seemed as if nothing was happening. I could imagine the consternation aboard the orbot as the pilot tried to reverse grays in time.

The boat's hull had become cherry red in four widening spots. Slowly, the spots turned white.

I could hear the null getting up beside me, near enough to touch. I had risen automatically, shading my eyes against glare.

The orbot exploded.

The reactor didn't go, of course; they're built so that can't happen. It was just the conventional auxiliary engines, used for steering and for powering internal systems. But that was enough.

Imagine a building humping itself into a giant stone fist, and bringing that fist down on you, *squash*. Pain so intense that it snuffs your consciousness before you can feel it.

Warned by instinct, I had time to do two things. I thought, distinctly: so night will never end. And I stepped in front of the null to shield him. Then I was kicked into oblivion.

I awoke briefly to agony, the world a solid, blank red. Very, very far away, I could hear someone screaming. It was me.

I awoke again. The pain had lessened. I could see. It was day, and the night plants had died. The sun was dazzling on bare rock. The null was standing over me, seeming to stretch up for miles into the sky. I screamed in preternatural terror. The world vanished.

The next time I opened my eyes, the sky was heavily overcast and it was raining, one of those torrential southern downpours. A Quaestor medic was doing something to my legs, and there was a platvac nearby. The null was lying on his back a few feet away, a bullet in his chest. His head was tilted up toward the scuttling gray clouds. His eyes mirrored the rain.

That's what happened to my leg. So much nerve tissue destroyed that they couldn't grow me a new one, and I had to put up with this stiff prosthetic. But I got used to it. I considered it my tuition fee.

I'd learned two things: that everybody is human, and that the universe doesn't care one way or the other; only people do. The universe just doesn't give a damn. Isn't that wonderful? Isn't that a relief? It isn't out to get you, and it isn't going to help you either. You're on your own. We all are, and we all have to answer to ourselves. We make our own heavens and hells; we can't pass the buck any further. How much easier when we could blame our guilt or goodness on God.

Oh, I could read supernatural significance into it all—that I was spared because I'd spared the null, that some benevolent force was rewarding me—but what about Goth? Killed, and if he hadn't balked in the first place, the null wouldn't have stayed alive long enough for me to be entangled. What about the other team members, all dead—wasn't there a man among them as good as me and as much worth saving? No, there's a more direct reason why I survived. Prompted by the knowledge of his humanity, I had shielded him from the explosion. Three other men survived that explosion, but they died from exposure in the hours before the med team got there, baked to death by the sun. I didn't die because the null stood over me during the hours when the sun was rising and frying the rocks, *and his shadow shielded me from the sun.* I'm not saying that he consciously figured that out, deliberately shielded me (though who knows), but I had given him the only warmth he'd known in a long nightmare of pain, and so he remained by me when there was nothing stopping him from running away—and it came to the same result. You don't need intelligence or words to respond to empathy, it can be communicated through the touch of fingers—you know that if you've ever had a pet, ever been in love. So that's why I was spared, warmth for warmth, the same reason anything good ever happens in this life. When the med team arrived, they shot the null down because they thought it was trying to harm me. So much for supernatural rewards for the Just.

So, empathy's the thing that binds life together, it's the flame we share against fear. Warmth's the only answer to the old cold questions.

So I went through life, boy; made mistakes, did a lot of things, got kicked around a lot more, loved a little, and ended up on Kos, waiting for evening.

But night's a relative thing. It always ends. It does; because even if you're not around to watch it, the sun always comes up, and someone'll be there to see.

It's a fine, beautiful morning.

It's always a beautiful morning somewhere, even on the day you die.

You're young—that doesn't comfort you yet.

But you'll learn.

Dave Wolverton, who later rose to fame as David Farland with his bestselling Runelords epic fantasies, debuted in 1989 with the space opera novel On My Way to Paradise, *which won the Philip K. Dick Memorial Special Award for Best Novel in the English Language. A short story with the same title was awarded the L. Ron Hubbard Gold Award at the 1987 Writers of the Future contest, a prestigious contest for which Farland is now lead judge. For us here, he has written a brand new space opera in an original universe about a soldier who leads a team of "battle model" humans on a mission of revenge, only to discover he may be leading them into a cunning trap. What unfolds changes his destiny.*

RESPECT
DAVID FARLAND

The stench of burned hair and charred flesh assailed Milagro's nostrils, and he scanned right and left as he entered the crystal palace.

Smoke hung in the air, and fried electronics in a nearby console sparked. His master's shouts of "Pendejo!" echoed from the walls.

Milagro advanced through the haze with his plasma rifle ready. The intruders had used expensive jump technology to get within two kilometers of the compound. The resultant ion signature at the jump site had led him to the spot, where he'd killed two female techs. But he worried that members of the strike team might still be on the grounds.

He squinted as he strode into the dark chamber, and found it fogged with acrid blue smoke, coiling from the palace's multiple generators, hanging from the gray ceiling like serpents from the jungle's canopy.

He clutched his rifle, heard a gentle hum as it dropped to a lower power setting. He thumbed the power switch to full. The weapon hummed and heated, and its laser sights cut a red swatch through the smoke as he fanned the barrel across the room.

Milagro's jaguar eyes, only one of many genetic upgrades, penetrated the gloom despite the smoke. Normally, the room was a palace of light, with holographs of sea and sun projected deep within the crystalline walls.

Now... it seemed a tomb.

Movement in the choking murk grabbed his attention. He lowered his gaze in deference as his master, Don Teyo Coretta, stood over one of the fallen enemy, a woman who wore all black, including her hood.

She was lying there, obviously dead, nearly cut in half by a plasma rifle, but Don Teyo stood over her growling in anger, and put a disruptor pistol to her face. He pulled the trigger, and atoms in her face were rearranged, so that her beautiful features were suddenly erased, and brains boiled from a hole in her head while teeth and eyes sprawled out at random.

He didn't need to kill her, just... deface her.

He pulled the trigger two more times, turning her head to pulp, then sat down upon the corpse of one of his prized sabertooth lions.

The spotted cat, which had long prowled the antechamber of the palace compound, was scored by plasma fire. More than twenty feet from nose to tail, it lay dead, its tawny fur splotched with white pucker marks like sunlight striking leaves.

All through the palace there was destruction. Milagro had never seen an attack like this upon one of Earth's major houses. This would lead to war.

Don Teyo sobbed and swore. Rage flashed in his black eyes. "See this!" he shouted, waving expansively to the carnage in the room— the shadowed corpses of his chimera guards, along with sundered androids and his beloved cats.

Don Teyo snarled and shouted, "A fool has done this. He has slain my soldiers... and look here! My kittens." The Don's voice broke.

He stooped over the sabertooth's outstretched front paws, each large enough to engulf a man's head, and Don Teyo threw his hands wide and shook his head, unable to express his anguish. High-powered bursts from some phased energy weapon had shattered most of the cat's front shoulder, leaving it a bloody and blackened mess.

"Both of them," Don Teyo said, and jabbed a hand toward the second carcass, half concealed by tendrils of smoke that twisted along the floor's decorative tiles.

Milagro glowered. The lions, larger than horses, normally lounged on low platforms at each side of Teyo's overstuffed office chair. They had indeed been kittens once, mewling creatures with fluffy, spotted coats, when a trio of researchers had presented them to Teyo. Created from extracted DNA, they had become the living icons of Coretta Corporation's technological supremacy.

"My kittens were their target." Teyo shook a clenched fist.

Of course, Milagro realized. *This was a message, sent to humiliate his master.* As an alpha, Don Teyo was engineered with superhuman intelligence, but like all alphas, he demanded respect, craved it.

It was the philosopher Jifa Chen who pointed out that all people desire love, but that our definition of "love" is perilously close to worship. All people desire mates who fawn over them, who praise them, who uplift them.

So he said, "Giving love to another is an illness at best."

Something shifted in the haze, a small motion close to the back of Teyo's huge throne-like chair. Milagro squinted to see a slender figure. A girl no more than sixteen, he guessed, with skin the color of chocolate, and black hair that fell to her waist in a thick coil. She wore a thin shift of red silk, with a golden nose chain. She cupped her hands over her nose and mouth against the smoke, and her large, black eyes, frightened as a startled fawn's, peered at Milagro over her fingers. *Amira, her name is. I think she is from India.*

She had been brought to the palace compound twelve days earlier, the captured daughter of some rival lord. Could he have been the one to send the assassins? Sort of a warning shot across his master's bow?

A flashing gleam focused his attention on a metal collar around her throat. The collar contained an artificial intelligence linked to the girl's hind-brain to control her movement, so that she could not move her legs to run away. It made her a slave in her own body.

Milagro could not speak tell Don Teyo his thoughts. His genetic makeup strengthened his loyalty to his master. To accuse Don Teyo of barbarism would be too much like betrayal. To correct him was unthinkable.

He shook his head. *There is nothing I can do for her.* He was only a chimera after all, with no more legal rights than a stallion.

"I have a task," Don Teyo said. When Milagro snapped his vision to his owner, Teyo continued, "There is a world where aliens have destroyed one of my research facilities. They are fierce aliens, impressive. I want one."

New creatures for the menagerie?

"You will select two chimeras and go to this world. There you will capture an alien and bring it back to guard my palace." Teyo's expression tightened, his fury shifting into excitement. "Its presence will intimidate any who dares to petition me."

Milagro grinned. In ancient days, Aztec rulers had humbled would-be supplicants by requiring them to march the Street of Skulls to their palace.

People around the world desired Don Teyo's genetically engineered products. But he refused to meet with them via telecom. He demanded that they be humble before him.

Milagro bowed. "We will leave at once."

Don Teyo raised a fist toward him, held his eyes. It was a command to bow, to grovel, and Milagro felt his stomach quaver as he bowed lower, to do obeisance.

"Do not fail me," Don Teyo commanded, then held his fist closed for a full thirty seconds before he opened it.

Milagro felt grateful for the chance to back from the room.

✦ ✦ ✦

Milagro had never before jumped across lightyears. Such travel posed its own risks, for it was not uncommon for molecules to be reassembled out of order. Stray storms in space had that effect, and the farther one jumped, the more dangerous. Milagro had never heard of a human who had jumped that far. He was taking a deadly risk, but even worse, he knew where his master would force him to go. The nets had carried images of the alien attack only days ago.

Milagro walked the two hundred yards to his barracks and selected two chimeras to join him: the woman Candela and another soldier named Tauro. Like himself, both were creations of Coretta Corporation, "battle model" humans constructed for exploration on distant worlds. Their powerful bones and musculature made them eight times stronger than a human, and enabled them to run effortlessly and swiftly for hours.

Along with night vision from jaguars' eyes, he and his counterparts had been given superhuman hearing and a sense of smell like a bloodhound's, and their hypermyelinated nerves gave them reflexes twenty times quicker than those of unenhanced humans.

Milagro had fought alongside Candela and Tauro often here on Earth. They had proved to be a mighty battle team, for they understood each other's skills.

Upon leaving his master's presence, Milagro called them to the barracks to watch holographs.

The holos showed a strange jungle, misty and choked with plant life, where towering vines rose over vegetation a strange grayish shade of green.

"The world is called Chacquol," Milagro told his companions. "It has two and a half times the gravity of Earth. None of its animals ever evolved an ability to fly, and have never left the planet. The aliens there are cunning, but never seemed to consider the possibility of travel between the stars."

"I've seen the videos," Candela said, her smooth features taut. "The World Congress has declared that Chacquol must be sterilized." There were planet-killer bombs for that, though the World Congress might choose to use nanobots to do something as simple as rip apart any carbon-based cells, thus destroying all plants and animals.

Milagro clenched his teeth. He doubted that the aliens would ever have posed a threat to mankind, but lately the World Congress had been choosing to "sanitize" worlds that harbored alien lifeforms. But for Don Teyo, such worlds offered rich opportunities—the chance to discover biotech that might someday be used to enhance mankind.

Candela's feline eyes flashed with excitement at the thought of leaving Earth. Candela's musculature almost matched his own, though she had finer hands and feet. She kept her dark hair cut short, so it felt like stiff fur when he stroked it during their intimate moments. *She will always be my mate, whether or not we are allowed to marry.*

"The World Congress can't sterilize Chacquol, can they?" Tauro argued with a tight smile. "Our master has laid a mining claim on the gene-tech."

"They're moving ahead with plans to cleanse it," Candela said, reading from a globalnet article on her wristband. "In forty-eight hours."

Now Milagro understood why this was so urgent. His master wanted to spirit away a powerful creature before the governments could react.

"That won't give us much time," Tauro mused. As the youngest of the three, Tauro had a ready grin, and coppery skin darkened by exposure to Ecuador's sun. Milagro had found him to be a quick and enthusiastic learner. *If I could have a brother, it would be Tauro.*

"The creatures we are after are called Chacoulis, after their world," Milagro said, and activated the first projection on the holotable in the barracks' briefing room. "These images were captured by security devices around the research facility that was destroyed."

Even in the holograph he could see that the creature stood more than ten feet tall. Roughly humanoid, it had an over-large, sloped head similar to a gorilla's, with facial markings as indistinct as thumbprints in gray mud. High intelligence shone in alert, purple eyes, and a carnivore's fang-like incisors gleamed at the corners of its mouth.

Its long arms swelled with muscles capable of resisting its world's high gravity, and its hands bore six dexterous fingers with two opposable thumbs. It lacked the hair of a gorilla, and wore what appeared to be armor about its torso and limbs, though Milagro couldn't discern that clearly. It didn't look like metal. More like… bark?

The eyes, two upper and two lower, along with its rows of nostrils, gave it a monstrous mien that chilled Milagro's blood and sent shivers down his spine all the way to his crotch.

They watched the lone Chacouli move with deliberation as it applied small, black objects along the base of the facility's twenty-foot, razor-wire-topped wall. The wire glinted under bright lights mounted in surrounding trees. The creature worked for several minutes before it scooped what appeared to be a bulky firearm from the ground, and slipped with surprising swiftness into the surrounding rainforest.

Forty-six seconds later, by the data that glowed at the holograph's base, the wall began to visibly tremble. The trembling increased to quivering, and then to unmistakable shaking, which grew more violent by the moment. Three minutes and twelve seconds later, without a flash or bang, a ripple ran through the wall as far as Milagro could see. Then it crumbled to wire-draped concrete rubble in an apparent chain reaction down the wall's length.

Milagro arched an eyebrow. "A sonic breaching system. These aliens are advanced indeed."

The security lights in the trees illuminated squat, prefabricated structures with small windows huddled inside the collapsed stockade. As Milagro and his companions studied the holograph, Chacoulis shouldering the heavy firearms emerged soundlessly from the jungle. Their leader, the huge, armored figure who had planted the sonic disruptors, waved a hand the width of an elephant's foot. The lights went out, and roars shook the darkness. The creatures blurred as they attacked, they moved so quickly.

Chimeras—scholar models—began to flee the buildings, but not for long. A Chacouli grabbed one man by both legs and swung him down against a stone, as if killing a snake by using it as a whip.

"Mierda!" Tauro said. "Did you see how far his brains splattered?"

Milagro shut off the holoprojector and faced the others. "Their leader is the one we want. Nothing less would please our master."

+ + +

The journey between the stars required no vehicle, but it was still incredibly expensive. The jump pad was simply an enormous metal disk, open to the air, where intense fields of energy warped time and space, and would send the team hurtling across the galaxy in less time than it took to whimper.

In preparation, Milagro unslung his heavy plasma rifle, checked its power charges, then flicked switches at his armor's elbows. The dart launchers encasing his forearms, like sleeves made of a dozen slender tubes, all showed tiny green lights. Each dart bore a local paralytic, which he was assured should work on the Chacouli creature's nervous systems.

"We are not to kill," he warned his team as they went through weapons check. "Don Teyo wants the alien alive." He tapped the compartment in his armor's side, where he had stored his cable gun and the restraining collar. "We will have to overwhelm him and take him directly. I suspect that he is too clever to be fooled by a trap."

"Check," they both agreed, and Milagro pinged the AI that would arrange the jump. Walls of electricity rose in flickering blue, encasing them.

The journey took Milagro's breath away and nearly froze his marrow—

And suddenly he was *there*, locking his armor's knees against Chacquol's crushing gravity.

They found themselves in a jungle. The night was dark, darker than any he had ever seen on Earth, overshadowed by dense foliage— snaking vines and enormous ferns. But there was something more, a layer of clouds darker than anything on Earth.

The three stepped into defensive positions, back to back, weapons at the ready. Milagro raised his gun to cover enemies that might attack from above, while Tauro and Candela took guard at chest level.

Lowering clouds obliterated the light from stars and the planet's moons. The atmosphere, thick as steaming mush, enveloped his face and rebreather like a wet towel, and he strained to fill his lungs.

For a moment, no one stirred. They simply froze in place, and opened themselves to this new world—sight, sound, scent.

The sluggish air smelled of exotic saps and fruit, of fronds so vibrant he could hear the snap and slither of them growing, of rich soil and musk and mold and of some dead animal. Milagro wrinkled his nose.

Deep in the forest, weird screams reverberated in the trees, as if enormous reptiles cried out, bewailing the coming apocalypse.

Milagro checked the projected terrain view that drifted before his left eye. A single red point marked their destination.

"We are close," he told the others through his helmet's mindlink.

When the others' acknowledgments sounded in his mind, he beckoned. "This way."

He did not want much artificial light, so he stalked through the darkness, picking his way over vines and limbs as quietly as a panther. The charge indicators on their weapons gave the barest of light.

Only their enhanced musculature allowed them to travel quicker than a slog. Insect chirps and throaty calls of reptiles fell silent as they passed.

Milagro's eyes caught every movement under thick-stalked ferns and buttressing tree limbs. His visor's IR sensors identified some of the wildlife—mostly surface-bound crawlers or creepers, though some small animals clung to tangled branches high in the canopy. All had evolved bulk and breadth in the gravity, with oversized claws or venomous spines or teeth.

The chimeras crept. Half a kilometer on, they broke into the man-cleared space where the scientists' compound had stood. They paused, still under the rainforest's swaying fringes, to survey what remained.

Nothing moved in the clearing. No sounds escaped it. It looked dead. The prefab labs and housing units hadn't merely collapsed like the wall, they looked as if they might have been shredded by a tornado. Rugged frame poles protruded here and there, leaning like injured sentries keeping watch over heaps of broken panels and pipes.

Even the power pylons had been toppled.

The scents of burning recalled those he'd smelled in his master's palace a few hours earlier. He'd expected the stench of ruptured organs and decomposing flesh, not this.

On Earth, Milagro's team would have leaped easily over the wrecked wall, but gravity reduced them to a clamber. Milagro hand-signaled Candela and Tauro to spread out, all sensors at their fullest range, and they stalked forward, weapons ready.

Nothing alive remained in the compound. No animal sounds, no scuttling IR returns glowed in Milagro's helmet readouts. He pinged the compound's AI on mindlink, but even it was dead.

They didn't have to dig through torn buildings to find their missing occupants. A mound of ash filled the area between the stripped foundations, and bones lay scattered in the ashes. Milagro found a human femur, reddened and blackened and notched with tooth marks; ribs detached from their spine; and a skull with its cranium broken open and scooped out like an egg.

"The Chacoulis ate them," Tauro muttered through his helmet speakers.

It didn't seem likely that the aliens would have relished human flesh. Milagro suspected that it had been done more as a sign of contempt.

The damp weight of the ashes, when Milagro toed them, told him that the fire had been set days ago. "We won't find our target here," he said. "We will have to track him."

The creatures hadn't concealed their footprints when they'd dispersed. Not barefoot, Milagro observed, but shod in what appeared to be boots. Some boots had tracked ash over the fallen wall, and all had sunk deeply into the loam.

"Find the largest set of prints," Milagro ordered.

They cast about for several minutes with their helmet lights, widening their perimeter from the fire mound to scrutinize prints that led in multiple directions. Milagro estimated a good two dozen Chacoulis had been involved in the attack.

"Here," Candela said at last. She crouched to examine broad boot prints two feet long, and stared into the jungle in the direction they led, her jaw set behind her rebreather before she added, "He has three companions." She gestured at some slightly smaller prints.

Ten days old, Milagro assessed. *They will be hungry, on the hunt again by the time we catch them. Not likely that we'll find them in a lair.*

He worried that the aliens might have traveled far, that he wouldn't have time to catch them. In only a few hours, the planet was scheduled for immolation. They couldn't dare get caught in the firestorm.

Tauro strode at point, eager to follow the tracks, but just as they entered the jungle again, he stepped over a log, and Milagro spotted something odd—a brown seedpod, the size of a hand. Tauro's foot landed on it, and a fierce explosion flashed, hurling everyone in the air.

A moment later, Milagro lay on his back, blinking away stars, struggling to see. "Tauro?"

He climbed to his feet, heard Tauro gasping, saw him struggling to rise. "Little brother?" Milagro shouted.

Candela crawled out of the foliage, blast marks smearing her face, and gave a wordless cry.

"I'm all right," Tauro said, climbing to one knee. He reached down and felt his butt. "My armor saved me." He pulled a long, bloody, finger-length shard of wood from the joint between two armor plates. The wound went deep into his hip.

Milagro could not believe their luck. "This time," he said. The seedpod had been some kind of explosive, he realized. "They set a trap for us. They suspected that we would come for retribution…" The placement of the bomb, the sonic disruptors. These aliens looked like animals, but they were cunning. "Be careful," he warned the others with a thought.

+ + +

The sun rose as they trailed their quarry, hardly brightening the clouds, creating a world hidden in half-light. At midday, one pair of tracks separated from the group. Milagro thought, *Perhaps the Chacoulis are watching and tracking us now.* He swept the jungle with his full range of sensors.

The departures caused him to adjust some things he had supposed about their quarry.

The attack on the human research post was deliberate and organized—not an accidental discovery by some hunting party. It appears that combatants came from different areas to join in, like a citizens' militia.

The Chacoulis clearly consider humans a threat. Had the researchers captured some of their kind?

He thought of Amira, the girl captive in his master's hall.

Had the researchers wanted Chacoulis for experiments? For gene extraction, like the sabertooth lions, from which to create… what? Upgraded battle mods?

He wanted to ask the compound's AI about his theory, but that was not possible. *Perhaps the Chacoulis attacked the facility for the same purpose that my owner's rival attacked his hall, to rescue a child.*

Something in Milagro's gut gave an uncomfortable twist. The thought felt too close to disloyalty to Don Teyo. *I will not fail my master. I will bring back the killer to guard his palace.*

"Milagro," Tauro said, then raised his plasma rifle—indicating something in the jungle. There in the trees, a hundred yards ahead was… something.

It hung from a tree like a vast wasps' nest—a strange edifice, perhaps a dozen feet across. It looked to be made from weathered strips of wood and slabs of rock, bound together in such a way so that the exterior created alien designs. In some ways, it looked like something the Mayans might have fashioned.

Immediately Milagro recognized it as a structure of some kind—perhaps a sleeping shelter.

Tauro arched a brow, and asked through mindlink, "Permission to explore?"

"Leave it, compadre," Milagro said. He didn't think that he would like what they might find.

Tauro turned aside, followed the trail a few feet, and then grinned back at Milagro. The look in his eyes said what his lips did not: I can't just leave it.

He turned and stalked through the jungle, plasma rifle held high, the indicator lights on it flashing red like a bloody bayonet. He approached the great ball, a hundred meters out, raised his plasma rifle—and sent a ball of purple flame hurtling against that stone construct.

A scream erupted from inside it, and with a flash the ball burst apart, as if clock springs had been wound too tight. Bands of wood and bits of stone flew everywhere, and among the debris came an alien ape-like creature, arms and legs flailing as it leapt at Tauro.

The young warrior fired a second burst of plasma, a purple stream like water from a hose, and at 8,000 degrees, the flames cut the creature in two.

Milagro stepped aside as body parts thudded to the ground at his feet.

Milagro ducked as a piece of the habitat whizzed past his own head. "I think they must sleep in those things," Tauro said with a shrug. "Good thing it was just a little one."

✦ ✦ ✦

On Earth, the team's upgraded musculoskeletal systems would have had no need to rest for at least a week. They could swallow combat rations on the run. But Chacquol's gravity dragged at them, and its thick, wet air reduced their oxygen intake. Milagro scanned the physical assessment readouts that appeared every few hours inside his rebreather's faceplate, floating at his periphery.

By the time misty sunlight cut through the thick canopy that morning, only one set of prints accompanied their quarry. The big male had made a recent kill—a vast lizard the size of an iguanodon—and had fed, ripping into its entrails. The blood was fresh. They were close. "We will bivouac here until nightfall," Milagro said. "He will be resting, digesting his prey. We might catch him while he's still groggy."

It was only a guess, based on his observations of wolves and other predators, which often slept after eating huge meals of meat.

Tauro gave him a sly grin and strode away, several meters up the trail.

Milagro and Candela drew back, away from the recent kill.

In a slight hollow beneath flowering ferns whose buds glowed with soft bioluminescent light, Milagro and Candela removed each other's armor, piece by piece, as if it were wedding garments. They nuzzled and nipped until breaths deepened and pulses quickened.

Many times he had desired to couple with her, but had never dared. This time, she gave herself to him, as if they had always belonged together.

Afterward, Candela lay in Milagro's arms, upon his naked chest, smiling in her sleep. He studied the curve of her lips and felt his heart swell, and tightened his arms about her.

He fell to thinking about their master, Teyo, wondering if he would approve their union. He wasn't sure.

He wondered why Teyo craved… admiration so badly. He was an alpha, sure, but his need for adoration seemed a sickness. He'd heard that his master's money had come from the drug cartels in the old days, and that now he was trying to go legitimate. His genetic upgrades were some of the best in the world, worthy of veneration, and he was a shrewd businessman. Yet somehow, Don Teyo so craved approval, he was a vessel that never could be filled.

By sunset, when the rustles and clatters and cries of nocturnal creatures filled the rainforest, Milagro and his team had armed themselves and eaten, and set out once more.

"There," Tauro said, after only an hour's run. He had taken the lead, and he motioned at giant footprints veering away, which were much crisper now. "He has turned north."

"We are closing on him," Milagro added. But he felt nervous. An alarm sounded in his suit, as insistent beep. The attack from Earth was only hours away.

✦ ✦ ✦

Candela glimpsed the creature first, a bright IR signature in her helmet visor. "Half a kilometer," she thought to Milagro and Tauro, "ahead and to our right."

"Spread out to surround him," Milagro ordered through the telepathic link. "I will approach from the front to hold his attention. We must rope him all at once, around the neck and arms. Keep your line taut and bind it quickly to a strong tree to restrain him, and I will put the collar on him."

And hope it works. The collar was supposed to send neural filaments into the host's body, so that it could take control. But would it even work on this alien?

When his team acknowledged, Milagro slipped away into the tangle of jungle. Running silent on soft loam, pushing through vines and verdant undergrowth, he cut a wide circle to intercept the huge Chacouli. He gauged his own pace by the alien's IR glow in his visor, breathing deep to pull in enough oxygen. For the first time in their pursuit, sweat oozed across his forehead.

He loosed his cable gun from the compartment on his side as he ran. Shook out a loop and set the guide rod. "In position?" he asked the others through their links.

"Ready," they answered, almost together.

Milagro dashed into the open, saw the alien's massive head swing toward him, and yelled, "Fire!" His cable whined through the trees.

Candela's loop zipped in from behind the Chacouli. Dropped over its head as it lunged for Milagro. Her cable yanked it up short, and Milagro's loop overshot, slid off the monster's shoulder. Tauro's line, fired from Milagro's right, snagged the alien's left arm and cinched tight.

In a single, swift motion, the alien wrapped its caught arm in the cable and tugged. Tauro came crashing through splintering undergrowth on his belly, still holding on.

"Tauro, let go!" Milagro bellowed, an instant before he saw that Tauro couldn't; he'd twisted the cable's other end around his own arm.

The Chacouli whirled and sprang before Milagro, accelerated reflexes or not, could extend his arm to fire a dart. The projectile struck the pale, ridged armor covering the alien's shoulder. The monster didn't notice. It straightened to its full height, dangling Tauro by the neck, and opened its mouth.

The crunch of six-inch fangs through Tauro's faceplate cracked like close thunder in Milagro's helmet speakers. Blood spattered the alien's face and dribbled freely off its chin.

It flung Tauro's body down when a dart from across the clearing struck its ear. It shook its head, and Milagro saw its mud-ball features tighten as it searched the trees.

Candela's loop still lay about its neck. Milagro knew she would have secured her line to a tree. With his cable gun rewinding in one hand, he launched a second dart with the other, at the alien's unarmored thigh, and thought at her, "Candela, run! Get beyond the length of your cable."

She didn't respond to him, but the Chacouli must have heard her movement. It brushed off the dart, dropped to all fours, on the knuckles of its hands like an ape, and fled.

Even with its darted leg wobbling, even dragging Tauro's body still tangled in his cable, it flew. *Like the maglev trains across South America*, Milagro thought.

He pursued the alien through the trees, leaping fallen logs and ducking vines and straining every enhanced muscle to burning in a desperation that slammed his heart against his ribs.

Movement just beyond the Chacouli's glowing IR signature showed him what was about to happen. "Candela, tuck and roll!" he ordered, and fired the cable gun once more.

He watched an arm like a log sweep out, illuminated in his visor by its own heat, to hook Candela's dark, thermal-shielded shape even as she curled to drop. His loop zipped straight and true to circle the beast's neck. He threw his whole, armored weight on the cable, and heard a snap.

The alien reeled back on its darted leg, a twisting, blue-white specter in the jungle gloom, with Candela's armored body swinging limp as a child's ragdoll from its hand.

With the cable wrapped behind him like a mountain climber's belay, Milagro launched a dart into the upheld hand. The creature's paralyzed fingers flew open, and Candela crumpled into waist-high ferns.

"Candé! Candé!" Milagro called, and lashed his cable about a thick, vine-laden trunk. A rasping rattle pierced his half-helmet's speakers, and then died.

He swung his heavy rifle from his back to his hands, spoke his helmet lights on, and worked his way around to approach the monster head-on. It sat with its useless leg bent awkwardly beneath it, still almost as tall as Milagro standing. It cringed from the glare of his helmet lights and lifted its good hand as if to shield its eyes.

Its charge at Candela had brought it to the end of her cable as well as his. Both bit into the sagging, elephantine skin of its throat, just above the neck of a hauberk made of whitened, entwined alien bones.

Candela lay barely beyond its reach, her helmet unseated from her armor's neckpiece at an unnatural angle. Milagro sank to his knees, gathered her in his arms, and her head lolled. Behind her faceplate, her eyes stared at nothing.

"You killed my mate!" he bellowed at the alien. He eased her body to the warm earth, leveled his plasma rifle with one arm, snatched the restraining collar from its container with the other. "You will pay for her life."

The Chacouli reached up a threatening hand as Milagro drew close. "Hand down," Milagro said. "Down and still, or I will tie you up." He motioned with the rifle. "And then I will strangle you slowly with this collar, and eat your face while you are alive, as you did to my brother."

He had no idea if the alien understood anything he said. When it raised its hand again, Milagro cut Tauro free of the cable still twisted around the beast's bicep and bound both its arms tightly against its chest. "If you pull now," Milagro warned, "you will choke yourself."

The alien twisted its head and tried to snap at him as he tugged the collar about its neck. Milagro clubbed it with his rifle butt. He felt no pity for the welts he raised or bloody gashes he left. "I am your master and you will obey me," he ordered, and yanked the collar's choke chain until the creature gulped and gasped, and its gray face grew darker still.

It struggled to bite him, and Milagro leapt up on it, grabbed it in a choke hold, and for the first time in his life strangled another being with all his will.

Do not fail me, Don Teyo had warned.

His vision went red and cloudy, and Milagro seemed to pass out, just before he went limp.

He was awakened by that insistent beep in his helmet—faster now, louder, more urgent. How long till the planet blew?

He knew by the expression in its eyes, one blackened and swollen partially shut, that the Chacouli had surrendered. Milagro removed the loops of cable, keeping the restraining collar's chain still firm in his hand. "You will carry my dead on your back while we travel to Earth," he said, and threw both armored bodies across the monster's shoulders.

The Chacouli did not act like an animal. It stared at him obediently, like some wizened philosopher. It did not grovel or weep.

And Milagro had a sudden realization. This creature was a lord in its own world, worthy of honor and veneration.

The beeping had become a solid buzz, like a wasp's as it circles one's face.

He did not need to return to the base to make the jump. He was close enough to the node. So he had his helmet AI prepare.

Arranging the jump took only a few minutes, via ansible, but it seemed years to Milagro. His gaze never left Candela's white face within her helmet, lying upon the alien's back.

The buzz ended, became a whoop, and a voice on the mindlink warned, "Sixty seconds to Armageddon."

Milagro wished that he could stay and watch as the planet exploded into cinders. But he had a duty to fulfill.

My master is to blame for Candela's death, this woman I love. It is his selfishness, his sick craving for honors that he has never earned. Small wonder he requires monsters like me to humble his enemies.

✦ ✦ ✦

After the heavy gravity of Chacquol, Milagro's boots actually bounced on contacting the great stone tiles of the courtyard outside Don Teyo's Palace of Lions. He drew in a great breath, though grief and anger weighted his lungs as completely as had Chacquol's soup-thick atmosphere.

The alien was another matter. It nearly bounded in the air and tripped on its first step, then began inhaling madly in the thin air, its four nostrils flaring wide.

"Lay them down here," he ordered the alien, pointing at the ground, and when the hunched monster had placed Candela and Tauro on the stones and shuffled back, Milagro motioned at two nearby guards, who stared open-mouthed. "See that they are prepared for honorable burials."

He addressed his captive. "Walk at my side."

The Chacouli stayed almost shoulder-to-shoulder, panting all the way.

As Milagro's eyes shifted in the dimness, slight movement on one of the sabertooth lions' platforms near Don Teyo's elbow caught his gaze.

The girl Amira crouched there, naked but for the paint upon her slim body that imitated the lions' patterned pelt. She stared at Milagro and the alien with great, frightened eyes. He understood at once. *When her father comes, he will be humiliated at the sight of Amira, and so more easily controlled by my master.*

Outrage surged through Milagro's vitals like lava erupting from a dormant volcano. *I can no longer be loyal to a monster such as this, worse than this Chacouli.*

Rage propelled him to the throne. His eyes burned. He felt as if he were being broken apart, the rage a hammer, each beat of his heart pounding against his innate loyalty. "I have brought you the alien," he shouted, his jaw tight. His voice dropped to a snarl. "But you, you pathetic creature, do not deserve it, for he is worthy of honor."

With all of his might, Milagro fought the genetic conditioning that demanded he show his master deference, and every muscle in his body quavered.

With both hands he seized Don Teyo from the carved and cushioned chair, held him by the neck so his toes did not contact the dais, and began to shake him.

Amira gasped and cowered on her platform, teeth bared in a snarl.

Milagro couldn't stop shaking, like a tree whipped by a typhoon, until Teyo's eyes rolled back in unconsciousness. Nor could he bring himself to break the man's neck. There was a word to describe men like Don Teyo, one that Milagro had never even allowed himself to think: megalomaniac.

He was a vessel who craved honor but could never be filled, so craved it that he resorted to brutality to try to win it.

Milagro hurled Don Teyo on the dais before his throne, where he moaned and trembled.

"Come here, Chacouli," Milagro said, and beckoned to the alien. It shuffled forward, its great, bruised gorilla-head bowed in deference.

It questioned Milagro with its purple eyes when he reached up to unfasten the restraining collar. Milagro said, "I give you a gift."

The silver collar slipped off into Milagro's hands, and he crouched above Don Teyo. He fastened the collar about the man's neck and rose to place the choke chain in the Chacouli's great paw. "He is yours now. Do with him what you will."

The alien was gasping for breath now, and perspiration beaded upon its brow. It looked down curiously at Don Teyo, seemed to understand the situation. The alien would not be able to survive long on Earth.

But perhaps before it died, it would exact vengeance from its captor.

Milagro stretched out a hand, ripped the long black silk shift from his master so that Don Teyo lay naked.

Amira recoiled when Milagro knelt before her. She bowed her head as if expecting a blow. But he wrapped the shift over her before he snapped off her restraining collar. "You will be safe now," he said, and gathered her in his arms as if she were a small child. "I am taking you back to your father."

He carried her a few feet, then looked back at the throne. The Chacouli had taken the throne, and sat there, like a statue, pondering what to do, with Don Teyo naked and cowering at his feet.

Mike Moscoe, writing as Mike Shepherd, has gained quite a following for his military science fiction adventures centered around Kris Longknife, a rich young naval officer who struggles to deal with the expectations and reputation of her famous family of military leaders, politicians, and billionaires. The first book, Mutineer, *was published in 2004 and was described by Tor.com reviewer Liz Bourke as "entertainingly sticky, full of implausible successes, assassins, fleet actions and daredevil do-or-die gallantry." Mike's story for us is a prequel to the entire series in which Kris graduates and decides to defy her family's expectations and join the Navy.*

AUTHOR'S NOTE: *We've followed Kris Longknife's adventures from boot ensign to grand admiral. But she wasn't always in the Navy. Here's a delightful story of how she made her way to Officer Training School.*

KRIS LONGKNIFE: BOOT RECRUIT
MIKE SHEPHERD

Kris Longknife took the last step up; now, she was on the stage where she'd be handed her diploma. The day was hot and there wasn't a breath of wind. She was sticky and sweating inside her gown.

"Four years of work for a miserable day like this," she mumbled.

"Kris, I can show you where Harvey and Lottie are," Nelly said from Kris's collarbone.

"Where?" Kris asked her computer. Nelly had been with Kris since before first grade. She had grown so attached to her computer that, rather than get a new one every year, she had upgraded Nelly year after year. It was an annual before-school party to visit Auntie Tru and see what kind of new tricks Nelly could do after each upgrade.

When she was just a kid, back before Eddy was kidnapped, she'd greeted each new upgrade with glee, giggles, and chubby handclapping. There hadn't been much glee in her life after the kidnapping, but visits with Aunty Tru always involved baking chocolate chip cookies. The wonderful smell had been about the only thing to break through Kris's deep depression. She'd even stayed sober for those visits.

Kris sighed. Once Grampa Trouble hooked her on skiff racing from orbit, she'd enjoyed those computer upgrade parties again. Only when she got into high school did she discover that her "Aunt" Trudy had been Wardhaven's chief of information warfare during the Iteeche War. It turned out Trudy was having as much fun as Kris making Nelly sing and dance in the most wonderful of ways.

Nelly was singing and dancing just fine today. "Look at the twelfth row back from the students' reserved seating, to the right of the main aisle, halfway to the next aisle."

Up on the stage, Kris had a clear view out over the crowd. It took her a moment, but she soon spotted the chauffeur who had been taking her to soccer games since she was six and the wonderful cook who made her days sweet.

Lottie also made the most wonderful pizza. After a few unfortunate events during high school, Kris preferred to invite her few friends or study buddies to Nuu House. Lottie's cooking made them eager to come.

What was missing was the circus that would surround them if Kris's father had come. The Secret Service would likely have cleared at least two rows of seats around the Prime Minister and his lady.

Kris swallowed conflicting emotions. She'd really wanted her mother and father here to celebrate this moment. At the same time, she was kind of glad they weren't. Billy Longknife, Prime Minister of Wardhaven, and Man of the People, inevitably was the center of attention. She'd heard a whispered comment that "Billy has to be the bride at every wedding and the cadaver at every funeral." If he'd been here, not only would the security detail have shoved other people out, but Kris herself would have disappeared into his shadow.

She was kind of glad he wasn't here. Still, it hurt.

"I found them, Nelly. Thank you." Kris had been chided for talking to Nelly as if the computer was a person. Frankly, Kris didn't care.

Nelly added, "Kris, did you see that General and Mrs. Trouble are in the seats behind Harvey and Lottie?"

"No," Kris said. She'd seen Lottie, and not seen her folks, but she'd never expected that Great-grandpa Trouble and his wife, Ruth, more often Mrs. Trouble, would find time in their busy schedule for her.

Kris's smile brightened, and she looked back over the crowd. Yes, there were her two most favorite family. General Trouble, trouble to the enemy, trouble to his superiors, and general trouble to everyone, including himself... but never to Kris... was probably the only reason Kris was graduating. Very likely, he was the only reason she was still alive.

And they'd come to see her. For the first time since she began contemplating the potential pain of this day, Kris's heart was light.

"Nelly, can you get a message to all four of them that I've spotted them?"

"It is sent. Trouble says, 'Good going, girl.' Lottie has already asked the Troubles to join them for dinner. Do you mind?"

"Of course not. I'd love it."

Kris got nudged by the guy behind her and took three steps forward. She was now fourth in line. Then third.

All too quickly, she was striding across the stage, confident as if at a political rally. The dean was waiting for her with a tired smile and her diploma. She was graduating with honors and had won several awards from various prestigious political groups for her essays and activities. All of those were being announced.

However, the loudspeaker was the only noise in the stadium of nearly sixty thousand.

No one so much as coughed.

For the other students, there had been cheers from family and friends. That fraction of Kris's family that was here did not shout, and her few friends... well, they didn't want to draw notice either.

Kris knew her gown was too short. They didn't make them for girls six feet tall. She kept her face bland, but her breath caught in her throat. She felt dizzy.

Maybe it was the heat.

Her stomach was a roiling mess; she prayed she would not vomit.

"Congratulations, Kris Longknife. I hope you'll mention our fine institution of learning to your father."

"Of course, Dean," Kris said as she smiled, shook his hand, and took her diploma.

There were three other luminaries Kris needed to shake hands with. She managed to hold it together just long enough to walk to the end of the stage. Her eyes were watering, she could hardly see the stairs as she went down them.

Everyone else turned left, back to their seat. Kris turned right and slipped into the shade of the temporary stage. She leaned against the support and struggled to hold back her tears and control her stomach. She'd made it through four years of college. She'd survived four years of high school. She had lived fourteen years since that horrible day that Eddy was kidnapped.

She'd kept putting one foot in front of another, doing what she was told. Being a good girl.

How many more steps could she stumble through? How many more years could she be the good girl?

"You okay?" a fellow in a dusty and stained gray uniform asked her. He was likely a groundskeeper for the university, here taking a smoke break and a few minutes' quiet.

"I just need to catch my breath."

"You look dehydrated," he said. He ambled over to a small, four-wheeled electric cart. He rummaged in a cooler and returned with a bottle of cold water.

"Thank you," Kris breathed as she gratefully took the ice-cold and dripping bottle.

"Plenty of folks have told me that," the guy said, taking another pull on his cigarette. "I keep telling them that they really need to set up an aid station for you kids here, in the shade, but will they listen to old Bruce? Nope. All their years of education and degrees and they don't know that June graduations are going to be hot. Go figure."

"Go figure," Kris repeated as she paused, half the liter of water already gone. She took a moment to roll the cool bottle around her forehead, then her cheeks and neck. "You are a miracle worker," she told Bruce.

"I don't do miracles, miss. I just do my job."

"Who pays for the water?" Kris asked.

He shrugged.

Kris rummaged under her gown in the pocket of her pants. She hated dresses as much as Mother hated pants. Still, she had her wallet in her hip pocket. She fished out a hundred-dollar bill and offered it to Bruce.

MIKE SHEPHERD

He looked at it like it was a poisonous snake. "I can't take that."

"How many graduates have thanked you and paid for their water?"

He shrugged.

"Well, sir, I'm one of those damn Longknifes and want you to have something for your kindness to so many of us."

"You," he eyed her, "a Longknife?"

"Billy's daughter," she said, neither bitter nor proud.

"Your old man has done good by this planet, miss."

"A lot of people tell me that, except for the wigs who tell me everything he's done horrible wrong."

"It's just politics, miss. You can't take that seriously."

Kris folded her bill over once, then twice. She took two quick steps and slipped it into the pocket of his shirt. "I don't take them seriously, but I do want you to take this."

The man rested his discolored finger with the stub of a butt on that pocket. "I do think I will. I've put my own daughter through this college. She got one of your dad's scholarships. She wants to be a doctor."

"Then maybe my old man did something good."

"Among many."

"Kris, Lottie is worried. None of them have caught sight of you," Nelly announced from Kris's collar bone.

"That your mom?" the miracle worker asked.

"Sadly, no. Lottie is the wonderful woman who bakes the most delicious cookies."

"Well, don't you go scaring her none."

"Nelly, tell them that I needed a breath of air and a drink of water. I'll be back real soon."

"They are glad to hear that," Nelly reported.

"Thanks again for the water," Kris said.

"Thanks again for the water money."

The two exchanged smiles, then Kris turned back into the boiling sun and slipped herself into the stream of happy graduates with their diplomas. It wasn't that hard to find her empty seat. She did get some grumbles as she made her way down a full row to it.

"Trust one of those damn Longknifes not to be able to stay in line."

"God bless you," Kris answered. It wasn't that she was a great fan of God or blessings, but she'd had an old campaigner tell her that answering bad with good bugged the hell out of people.

Kris was good at bugging the hell out of people.

At least she was when she wasn't being a good girl.

✦ ✦ ✦

No surprise, when the interminable celebration finally ended, it was impossible to find anyone in the crush.

Nelly provided Kris with a bit of help. During Kris's early days of skiff racing from orbit, Nelly had cracked the top level of Wardhaven's GPS. It might have helped that she had Kris's access codes. However it was, Nelly knew exactly where Kris was to within two centimeters.

That just left Kris trying to figure out where the other four were.

Of course, Grampa Trouble had that part of the problem solved. Most people's computers broadcasted an identity signal. He, however, had a top-of-the-line squawker that did a lot more if you could access it. That was what you'd expect from a retired general. Much like Kris, when people wanted to find him, say a Marine SOF rescue team, he wanted to make it easy for them.

Kris only had to take a few steps in one direction before Nelly triangulated on the general's squawker.

"I've got your location," she told them. "Stay put. I'll come to you."

Since she was in a cap and gown, no one was really bothered by her ducking and weaving through the crowd.

Only twice did she leave someone in her wake saying, "Isn't that the Longknife brat?"

"Yeah."

"You didn't tell me you were going to college with her."

"I never saw her."

"Yeah?"

That summed up Kris's college experience. If you were in her class, you heard a lot from her. Otherwise, not so much.

Less than five minutes later, Kris was getting a hug from Lottie and Gramma Trouble. Handshakes were exchanged with Harvey, a retired, wounded vet, and General Trouble, hardly retired and very wounded.

Kris would have loved to hug them, but guys were guys.

Standing beside the Troubles was a woman in a Navy officer's uniform. Kris knew all the officers in the NROTC unit. She'd gotten Captain Larson's permission to use their library. He'd even loaned her books from his private library. When she'd identified conflicts in the public sources, he'd arrange for her to get access to material from the Navy Historical Division. Nothing classified, but still, not readily available to the public.

The woman was in undress whites and a skirt. Most of the young female NROTC officer candidates would never be caught dead in a skirt.

"Commander," Kris said, nodded at the woman.

"I'm Commander Harwich," the woman said with a warm smile that seemed well practiced. Kris gave her own well-practiced smile. No doubt there was more to the commander, but she was with the Troubles, so she got one free pass.

"I've invited Commander Harwich to dinner," Gramma Trouble said, "and Lottie has been kind enough to extend our invitation." Gramma Trouble's smile was a warm as a fire on a cold winter's night, and it left Kris, as it always did, with a desire to curl up by the fire and purr like a kitten.

Kris had learned to take her contentment where she found it.

"Well, I'm hungry," Kris announced, so her small subset of the mob made its way out of the stadium.

Kris only caught sight of one young man with a nice haircut, a cheap suit, and an earbud wired into his ear. Usually her security detail was invisible, but on a hot day when most people were in open-collar shirts, the suit was a dead giveaway.

When Kris was younger, she would have glanced around to make all of her detail. Whether that was her as a kid or her terrified after Eddy's kidnapping, she'd never decided. Somehow, over time, she'd become comfortable being the fish in their goldfish bowl. Now, she ignored them.

Kris had wondered why Harvey had pulled out the mid-sized limo. Now it seated all four of them in the back comfortably. Lottie sat up front with her husband.

As they made their way slowly through the traffic jam of the University of Wardhaven's parking lot, Kris turned to the commander.

"So, Commander, what's your rice bowl?"

Kris knew she was using one of her mother's more derisive comments on the military. Still, the commander had inserted herself into a private celebration. Kris felt she didn't deserve the usual political kid gloves.

"I invited her," Grampa Trouble said.

Kris gave her great-grandfather a raised eyebrow.

"Commander Harwich is in the Recruiting Command."

"Female officer procurement," Harwich clarified with an unrepentant smile.

"So potential female officers are just a commodity?" Kris shot back.

"A very precious commodity," the commander said, returning the serve.

Trouble broke in with a war story about a young woman officer who'd served under him and earned the silver star. Despite all the rules against women in ground combat back during the Iteeche War, she'd managed to get in a firefight, taken command of a company when all its officers had been killed or wounded, and extracted the unit from a battalion of very angry Iteeche Marines.

"What was her excuse for just being in the neighborhood?" Kris asked.

"I don't remember at this remote date," General Trouble said, a huge grin on his face. "I do recall that it seemed pretty threadbare at the time."

That got a laugh from those around Kris.

But Kris was still curious. "How could a strange captain, and a woman to boot, slip into a unit under heavy fire and get all those men following her orders?"

Trouble nodded, and a grin spread across Gramma Trouble's face like a bubble bath.

"As I recall, she sent her driver and guard out to the right to lay down fire, then asked a sergeant if he might send a fire team to reinforce them."

"She was most polite," Gramma Trouble put in.

"That worked," Grampa Trouble said, keeping control of the story. "Not only were the officers down but the company top shirt had a bullet in his leg and was a bit slow crawling around the ditch they were in. The two of them had a short talk. They agreed she had a decent plan and she had the legs to carry it out. She led what was left of third platoon off to the left and they ended up in an orchard, hitting the Iteeche with enfilading fire that broke up the next assault before it got off the mark."

"After that," Gramma Trouble said, "people listened to her and she basically had the command."

"So, she earned their respect," Kris said, summing it up.

"Very quickly, under fire," the commander added.

"Women can serve in combat billets now, can't they?" Kris asked. She knew the answer, but she wanted to hear how the commander answered her.

"Officially, yes," the Navy officer said. "However, very few pass the training program to be Marine Platoon Leaders. You have to be in top shape."

"Well, I can forget that career option," Kris said. "When I finished PE, I was delighted to see it in my rearview mirror."

That got a laugh.

"The Navy officers' physical requirements are a bit lower," the commander said.

"But all the Navy does is bounce from one natural disaster to the next," Kris said, quoting Mother. "They're more like glorified pizza delivery boys."

Kris and the commander locked eyes. Kris knew she'd just slapped her in the face, figuratively. She awaited her comeback.

"Some people may say that." The commander seemed to measure each word carefully. "However, if you're being pulled out of the wreckage of a tsunami or given famine biscuits after your colony has had crop failures for three years, you might think differently."

"It's not unusual for law and order to break down under those pressures," General Trouble added. "Your mother's 'pizza delivery boy' may need a rifle on his shoulder to see that the poor and the weak get fed as well as the rich and strong."

Kris nodded. It was clear that Grampa Trouble knew exactly who Kris was channeling. So, she decided on a new pitch.

"It's been eighty years since we've had a war, as my mother is quick to remind me every time after the general comes to call. There's not much use for heroes these days. The pay is horrible and the career options worse."

"But when your politicians have a problem they can't solve, it's the bastards they holler for," the commander shot back.

"Yeah," Kris acknowledged, "but if the local police were just funded properly, they wouldn't need the Marines to pull their chestnuts out of the fire when they've got a riot or something's out of hand."

The commander didn't even break a sweat returning that serve.

"No one wants to pay for the force needed to suppress a riot. Besides, if things have really come unglued, can the local police face down the people they live with? It's better for all that some heavily armed strangers come to town. It tends to calm things down without anyone getting hurt."

"Like that colonel did on Darkunder," Kris shot back.

"That poor bastard was court-marshaled," Grampa Trouble grumbled.

"Where he got whitewashed," Kris snapped.

"He won't get another command," the commander put in.

Kris rolled her eyes. "And that will bring back all the farmers his troops machine-gunned."

The conversation kind of stalled after that.

Dinner was served in the kitchen. Kris loved it that way. The formal dining room was, well, so formal.

The conversation was lively. Grampa Trouble kept it flowing with war stories. Even Gramma Trouble had a few stories of her own. Both of them had wound medals, though theirs were bronze and Harvey's was a gold one. His latest left arm was working almost as good as a flesh one.

After all of Lottie's delicious apple-and-blueberry tarts had somehow disappeared, they sat back to digest their food and the conversation.

"So, girl," Gramma Trouble said, "now that you have that bachelor's degree, what are you going to do with your life?"

Kris glanced at the commander. The woman had contributed a few very funny non-war stories, but she'd been quiet for the most part.

"Don't tell anyone, but Father intends to get Honovi into parliament in a by-election. They've got a party stalwart what's getting old. He's in a safe district and Father thinks Honovi is ready to join him as a backbencher."

"They don't usually have father–son pairs serving in parliament," Gramma Trouble observed.

"It's happened before. Not often, but there's a precedent," Kris answered.

"Have they ever had a father–daughter pair in parliament?" Trouble asked.

Kris fidgeted under his hard eyes. She could only guess what a real glare from the old general would have done to a Marine. "Father tells me it hasn't happened before."

"You've told me about Honovi's future plans," Gramma Trouble said, "but you sidestepped your own."

"Oh, I'm going to assist his campaign manager. I'll see how it's done. Father thinks I'll be a superb campaign manager after I get a bit of seasoning."

"But you won't run for parliament yourself," Gramma Trouble said.

"No. They can't have three Longknifes in the benches."

"Oh."

The conversation kind of laid down and died at that point.

"I never took you for someone who'd be happy being in some man's shadow," Grampa Trouble said, softly.

"It's not like I'll be in anyone's shadow," Kris snapped. "Any more than I am now. There's no way I'll ever be anything but one of those damn Longknifes. You and Grampa Ray cast a huge shadow, you know."

"He hears it regularly from the kids and grandkids," Gramma drawled.

The old general shrugged, but he had a satisfied grin on his face. "They've all managed to distance themselves enough from me. Even the ones that are in uniform. They're their own people."

Kris sighed; she would love to be her own person. However, for all her life, the Longknife legend had been something she could no more escape than she could her invisible security detail.

The thought struck her.

Would a Secret Service detail follow me into the Navy?

Silly question.

But it was a silly question that would not go away.

"Your grandfather Alexander is his own man, not bothered by his dad, General Ray Longknife?"

"Yeah," Kris snorted. "He runs all the Longknife businesses. The two of them never talk."

"I guess that's one way to make your own rut," Gramma Trouble said.

"Yeah. He's offered me a job, too. He'd take me on at a huge salary and I'd kind of follow him for a few years before I'd get my own section of the business empire to run."

"Does that sound alluring?"

Kris shrugged. "That sounds like I'd be trading in Grampa Al's shadow for Father's."

"It's a quandary," Gramma said. "Have you ever considered shipping out for Santa Maria? Your Aunt Alnaba is doing research there. Could you join her?"

Kris shook her head. "My degree's in political science. She needs theoretical physicists and engineers and lots of other crazy scientists. What could she do with me?"

"I'm sure she'd be glad to train you," the general put in, not at all helpfully.

"Nope. Sorry folks. I appreciate your concern for me, but it looks like I join the family's political business."

"As the perpetual junior partner," Trouble said.

"And a girl at that," Gramma slid in.

"So, what would you do?" Kris snapped. "Have me join the Navy and waste my life delivering pizza?"

"You could do worse," Trouble answered. "At least you'd be your own woman. In the Navy, you'd rise or fall based on your own merit."

"Would I?" Kris snapped, and turned to the quiet commander. "Would I?"

"Well, your Marine DI wouldn't care who you were if you cut your corners smartly and stayed in step. The old chief teaching you to pack your footlocker wouldn't give a damn so long as you rolled your underwear the Navy way. Your Tac officer would be satisfied if you learned to stand watch and could find your way around a ship in the dark."

"Who'd teach me tactics and doctrine?" Kris asked.

"I doubt if anyone could," Trouble said. "I've read your senior project on the last year of the Iteeche War and the negotiations. You've got it down pretty much as well as you can from the public sources."

Kris spotted the faint praise. "Are you saying I didn't get it right?"

Trouble eyed her. "You got it as right as a civilian can get it."

"You want to tell me what I got wrong?"

"You got a security clearance?"

"I got one the last campaign I worked on for Father."

"Yeah, but that was a civilian authorization. Not Navy Top Secret. Come back when we can talk, kid."

Kris screamed into her mouth. "You military types. I hate the silly-ass games you play. Gramma, does he do this with you?"

"Yep."

"And you put up with it?"

"If I'm kidnapped, I want to say I don't know nothing and pass a lie detector test," Gramma said. "I figure I'll live longer."

Kris was of half a mind to storm out of the room, but she kept in her seat. "Now I know why they call you Trouble," she grumbled.

Gramma Trouble laughed. "You don't know the half of it."

Kris considered letting the conversation go on without her, but she so rarely got to spend time with these two, it would be a shame to ignore her chance.

"Grampa. Gramma, why did you do it?"

"Do what?"

"Follow the drum for all those years. Even the years when you could get blown to bits any second."

Gramma raised her eyebrows to Trouble. He leaned back in his seat.

"It's hard to say, Kitten. For me, it was kind of easy. My dad was a chief, fighting in a planetary Navy during those skirmishes before the Unity War. I wanted to go to the academy since I could remember. An old Marine colonel there switched me from blue and gold to red and gold. The Unity War was my first fight. To be honest with you, I was just following my nose until I met this lovely young woman," he said, eyeing Gramma.

She punched his arm.

"Somewhere in the fight on that worthless moon where we beat off your Grampa Ray's attack, I found that my company was worth more to me than my own life's blood. Getting them all back in one piece was the most important thing I've ever done.

"You know, an officer can't be friends with his troops. If you're going to send someone out to die, you don't dare let them become your friend. You know what I mean?"

Kris shook her head.

"Yeah. I guess you have to be there. It's just that the men and women under my command were more important to me than my mother or my father. Keeping them alive was worth my every effort because I knew they'd all lay down their lives for me just as quickly as I'd die for them."

The old general sighed. "It's hard to say. The mission is primary. All of you will die to achieve it. But after that, every trooper's life is first and foremost in your concern. Taking care of them. Seeing that they're well fed and sheltered. Everything for them is more important than anything for you."

"Like having a baby thrust into your arms?" Gramma asked.

"Yeah, but the baby is helpless, and the privates are just stone stupid."

That got a round of chuckles from the table.

"There's nothing like the friendship you make in a foxhole," Grampa concluded.

"Or a wardroom," the commander added.

Kris leaned back in her chair. She'd never really had a home. Nuu House was just a pile of stones that had been in her family for generations. It wasn't even where her folks lived. They were downtown at Government House, which she'd much appreciated during high school and college.

What would it be like to make a friend that wasn't all agog about the Longknife legend? To know someone that wasn't hanging with you in the hopes that later on in life, they might hitch on to your career?

Kris considered all of those, but she made no decision. She had another dinner to eat today. That one would be at Government House.

+ + +

Kris drove herself downtown. She was pretty sure that the big sedan behind her was her Secret Service detail. Still, she was very glad she got to drive her car like any other young woman.

She pulled up to Government House and stopped in the space in front of the guard house. Two police officers came to meet her.

"Hi, Luli. Hi, Masego. It's a nice quiet night, I hope."

"We're having a quiet night," Luli said as she held the door for Kris, then slipped into the car to park it.

Kris knew the routine. She slid her ID card into the reader, then stared into the retina scan while resting her palm and fingers on another scanner. She hardly felt the pinprick as it took a sample of her blood for DNA analysis… oh, and to verify that the hand was still part of a living body.

Security people were just so paranoid.

Kris had learned early to like that virtue in people.

Three beeps said she was who she claimed to be. Still, Masego checked all the results with a human eye. Computers were nice, but they only looked for the expected.

He nodded approval, and only then said a word that wasn't official. "I hear congratulations are in order."

"Yep, the university gave me a diploma so I'd quit haunting their halls and scaring the freshmen."

"No doubt. You Longknifes scare me."

"Masego, you're a wise man."

"You here to have dinner with your folks?"

"The condemned woman was served a delicious meal," Kris said, grinning at her own joke.

"If you need a file to escape, I'll slip one in a loaf of my wife's zucchini bread."

"Thanks, but I'll likely chew off my leg first."

They both shared a laugh. Masego was one of the many guards who knew that Kris approached family get-togethers with the

same enthusiasm that most people approached a root canal...
minus anesthesia.

Kris passed inside, smiling at more guards that she knew. She caught
sight again of the guy she'd seen at her graduation.

"Nelly, what's his name?"

"He is not squawking, Kris."

"How rude." Everyone walked around with their computer ready
to respond to a ping from another computer. Squawking, so to speak.
Strangling your squawker was considered gauche.

"Nelly, can you tickle his squawker?"

"Give me a second."

Kris's computer took only a few seconds before she was adding,
"He's Juan Montoya, and his computer says you have a nasty case of
the nosy."

Kris whirled about, spotted the guy, and scowled.

Shameless, he grinned and winked at her.

Kris whirled away from him, hoping the skirt on her short dress
showed more leg. She was six feet in her bare feet and often scared
boys away. She had to like it when she ran into a guy that didn't run...
even if it was his job to stay.

She took the elevator to the residency on the top floor. Mother and
Father shared it with her older brother. Since there were only three of
them, much of the rest had been turned into offices.

Kris couldn't remember; had she not been invited downtown, or
did she dodge the invitation? She'd preferred the little privacy she had
at Nuu House.

I hope they don't want me to move in here now, she thought for only
the forty-eleventh time.

The door to the residence opened automatically for her. She smiled
at the security camera and whoever was watching as she passed inside.

Mother and Father had lived here for the last twelve years, through
four elections. Her brother Honovi was starting to talk of it as home.
Kris would hate to live here where her comings and goings would make
the papers every day.

As she expected, there was no one in the foyer to greet her. She knew
exactly where she'd find them.

"Hi, Father, Brother," she said as she entered his working office. Father had two offices. The fancy one with windows where he greeted the people he needed to impress, and the totally secure one where he now worked with Honovi and two of his closest political advisors.

The likely topic of the conversation that fell silent as she entered was when to call the next election. They were halfway through a five-year term. Kris knew as much as any politician that the party in power would be looking for the most advantageous time to go to the people.

"Congratulations, Sis," Honovi said, leaving his chair to come give her a hug. "I hear you tied my honors."

"I managed to meet the low standards you set during your four years of wild partying at WU."

They laughed at that.

Father harrumphed without getting out from behind his desk. "Is it dinnertime, already?"

"Actually, I think she's running a bit late," Brother said.

"I had lunch with Gramma and Grampa Trouble," Kris said. "I could listen to his stories for hours."

"Yes, he can be most entertaining," Father said with a cough. "If you like those sorts of stories."

Kris kept her mouth shut. While Trouble might have saved her life, neither Father nor Mother considered him a good influence.

Maybe that was why Kris loved those two so much.

The two political advisors gathered up several paper maps that showed mark-ups, and made their excuses. In a moment, Kris shared the room with only her family.

She'd hoped the advisors would stay for dinner. Dad would probably enjoy their company more and the conversation would be something Kris could listen to in silence.

Honovi led Kris down the hall to the formal dining room. Fortunately, the table had been shortened to half its possible length. The two chairs in the middle of it were only two meters from either end. No one would be joggling anyone's elbows.

Mother arrived from the right as they walked in from the left. Mother met Kris halfway and bestowed upon her an open-armed hug that did not spill a drop from the martini she had permanently attached to her right hand. The kisses to Kris's cheeks didn't get within ten centimeters of her skin.

There was little chance Mother would contract plague from her daughter.

They settled quickly into their seats. Honovi sat across from Kris, making them the two closest humans at the table. Mother and Father were separated by a good five meters. No doubt they preferred it that way.

As the soup was served, Honovi asked about the graduation.

"It was hot and long," Kris said simply. "I can understand why some skip it entirely."

"One must do what is proper," Mother said, sternly. Proper was her god.

"Who was there beside the Troubles?" Honovi asked.

"Harvey and Lottie, of course," Kris said, trying to get just the right amount of guilt into that list without soaking it in too much and starting a family shootout.

"Oh, and there was a Navy commander with the Troubles. She was quite an interesting woman."

"Why, forever sakes, would the Troubles have a commander hanging around them?" Father demanded to know.

"She's in female officer recruitment."

"She was wasting her time with you," Mother harrumphed.

"She made a very interesting case for a few years with the fleet," Kris said.

"A total waste of time," Father growled. "I see those uniformed failures all the time, on their knees, begging for handouts. I tell you, the fleet is a waste of time and money. If the wigs would quit slobbering over all those expensive toys, we could cut taxes and get them to quit whining that the taxes are too high. They have no sense of their own hypocrisy, to demand we waste money with their right hand and insist we lower taxes with the left. Disgusting!"

"Yes, Father, I've heard all your speeches, although you've never cut the Navy's budget," Kris pointed out.

"The Navy has a huge constituency. My own father would buttonhole me if I ever let him get me into a corner. Building ships means jobs.

Manning them means jobs. If we ever achieve full employment, maybe I could cut the fleet then."

"But the fleet does come in handy," Kris pointed out, then ducked for the nearest foxhole.

She was wise to do that. Both Mother and Father had their prepared speech ready about how they'd been eighty years without a war and it was high time we admitted that humanity had outgrown that childish pastime.

"Elected democratic governments do not go to war with each other," Father concluded. "I guess the Navy does provide some emergency services in time of disaster, but we could do it with ships that didn't have a lot of expensive lasers on them that they'll never fire."

Kris had finished her soup while her parents had been venting their spleens at the Navy's budget, officers, and supporters. Father would never had said anything like that in public. It would have cost him votes. Still, he didn't mind telling his family what he felt in his heart of hearts. Mother just considered the Navy "so middle class."

Kris had heard it all before. She was beginning to enjoy her Caesar salad with shrimp when the conversation died down.

She couldn't allow that to happen.

"Well, Father, you must admit that the Marines are often needed as a backup to planetary police."

And they were off to the races again. Sadly, they had nothing to add to their usual litany that Kris had tossed at Commander Horwich earlier. Wardhaven had a fully funded police force that was quite capable of providing law enforcement for the planet. It was only those worlds too cheap to hire good help that had to call for the Marines.

"But aren't many of those planets start-up colonies?" Kris asked. "Some of them are being funded by either Wardhaven or a consortium we're leading. Right, Father? They can only afford so much protection when they're way in the red."

Father did not look happy to have that tossed in his face, but his own sense of the bottom line was too strong for him to counter her.

Mother was on her second martini already and had so far only agreed with Father. Now she put in her two cents.

"Kris, darling. We hire those people to do what we need done. You are worth so much more than a thousand of them. I can understand one of them risking their life in a hostage situation, but Kris, a Longknife? It would be such a waste."

Kris had heard this argument since she was nine. After losing Eddy in a botched kidnapping, it seemed that Mother's remaining two children were too precious to risk anywhere. Kris had wanted to go to Harvard on ancient Earth. For Mother, she'd stayed at Nuu House, under the watchful eye of her protection detail.

Still, the argument was getting threadbare.

"Mother, we Longknifes were just common soldiers before Grampa Ray and Grampa Trouble risked their necks to save a hell of a lot of us."

"Yes, yes," Father said, stepping in. "That was a time for heroes, but dear, that age is dead and gone. Now is the time for those who make things, not blow them up. Now we need bankers and industrialists and skilled workers. We need everything working smoothly under a benign political system that does a little here, a little there, but generally stays out of the way."

How many times had Kris heard this stump speech? How many hours had she spent in class and after it debating the truth of her father's balance between doing and staying out? Few of her classmates agreed that her father actually did what he claimed he was doing.

"Yes, Father," Kris said, resting her eyes on the table. If she didn't tell him just what he wanted, Father could talk all night.

"Kris, have you heard? I'm running for parliament," Honovi put in, changing the subject to something less fraught with family discord.

"So, you're going to take the plunge," Kris answered, as cheerful as she could manage at the moment. Her stomach was still riled from Mother and Father's words.

"Yes. It's a safe district, but it's been growing more conservative as it gets more wealthy. I'll need to handle a lot of tough questions."

"I'm sure you'll hit them out of the ball park," Kris said.

"I'd like you to help. Be my assistant campaign manager."

"Will your campaign manager need an assistant?" Kris asked. "It doesn't seem like it will be much of a campaign, really."

"It will give you a good grounding," Father rumbled.

"It reminds me more of a friend I had in college and how he learned to drive at three."

"Three?" Honovi asked, proving the straight man.

"Yeah, coming back from Sunday services, his dad sat him in his lap. He got his hands on the bottom of the wheel and drove them home. It was only in later years he came to realize that it was his dad watching the road and his dad's hands on the top of the steering wheel actually driving them."

"You think you'd just be pretending to assist running a campaign?" Father growled.

"Yes, I do."

"So, what are you thinking of doing? Going into business with my father?" Father asked, a threat low in his voice.

"Father, I'm not that stupid. Grampa Al makes my skin crawl."

"Well, at least you have one thing right."

"What are you thinking of doing, Sis?" Honovi asked.

When Kris took the elevator up, she had no idea what she might do with her life. However, by the time she'd finished her salad, she'd made up her mind.

"I'm joining the Navy."

"No," came from three mouths.

"Yep. I think two years seeing if I can be a hero would be a good start in life."

"It would be a waste of time," Father growled.

"You could be injured or killed," Mother said, actually clutching the pearls at her neck.

"The Navy doesn't lose that many people each year. As you said, it's mainly delivering pizza and chasing second-rate burglars."

"I'll miss you," Honovi said.

Kris blew him a kiss. "It won't be any worse than me being in college and living at Nuu House."

"Yeah. I didn't drop by all that often, did I?"

"It was fine. Now, if you'll excuse me, I'm really not hungry and I need to pack. Good night, Mother. Father. Brother."

And with those few words, Kris headed for the door with Father's last words ringing in her ears.

"You will regret this, young lady. Remember, that's my Navy you're running off to."

✦ ✦ ✦

Commander Harwich was delighted to take Kris's call, even if it was late. She called back a few minutes later and advised Kris that there was an OCS training class starting on Monday. Could she be ready by then?

Kris could.

Monday morning at 0500 hours, Harvey dropped Kris off at the bus station with a smile and a jaunty salute. "Pay attention, kid. You can do this."

"I will. I'd hate to have to call you to pick me up."

"If you break a leg, call," he said, giving her a bear of a hug.

"I will."

Kris noticed that tall Secret Service agent watching her. He'd gotten out of his sedan. Most of the time he was looking anywhere but at her. Still, every once in a while, she'd catch him watching her.

The bus came, the recruits filed aboard as a Marine sergeant checked their names.

"Kris Longknife," she reported at the bus door.

"One of those damn Longknifes?" he growled.

"Yes, Sergeant, but not one of them from Government House," she said, dodging the worst.

"Then maybe you've got some guts. Get onboard, Princess."

That left Kris wondering if she'd really gotten that far from her father's shadow.

The bus was filling with recruits, both enlisted and officer candidates. Most all the window seats were already taken. Everyone was looking out the window, thinking serious thoughts.

The one exception was a tall, redheaded beanpole of a guy who was busy looking around as if afraid he might miss something.

"You mind if I sit here?" Kris asked.

"Please," he said, and offered her the seat with a flourish.

Kris settled into a seat that was a lot less cushioned and a whole lot closer together than any she was used to. A Longknife did not ride public transportation, not before Eddy, and definitely not after his death.

"Hi, I'm Tommy Li Chin Lien from Santa Maria," he said, offering his hand.

Kris shook it. "Aren't you a long way from home?" she asked, trying to dodge reciprocity.

"And so glad of it," he said with a relaxed chuckle. "You have no idea what it's like growing up isolated at the wrong end of the universe."

"Don't you have regular shipping service?"

"Yeah, but you got to be rich or a Longknife to afford anything the ships bring. No, we Santa Marians grow or make locally just about everything we use."

"That sounds a lot like Wardhaven."

"Yeah, I'm coming to realize that only luxuries get shipped anywhere."

"So, you're joining the Wardhaven Navy?"

"Ray Longknife was the guy that rediscovered us. We've kind of been connected at the pinky finger with Wardhaven ever since. I couldn't think of any Navy I'd rather join than Wardhaven's. And you?"

"If you're born and raised on Wardhaven, what other Navy would you join?"

"I don't mean to pry, but I'm still waiting to know who I'm talking to."

"Oh, I'm Kris," she said.

"Kris for Kristine?" he asked.

"Yep."

"Are you intentionally dodging giving me your name?"

"Yeah, kind of."

"You know, I can just wait for the next time a sergeant goes down the roll."

"Is everyone from Santa Maria as smart as you?"

"Only the engineering grads. You could likely fool a music major for at least five minutes."

Kris offered her hand again. "I'm Kris Longknife. I'm one of those damn Longknifes but not one of those Government House Longknifes.

"A Longknife. I'm impressed," and he really seemed to be. "Any relationship to Ray Longknife?"

"He's my great-grandfather," Kris said.

"Wow, have you ever seen the old guy?"

"It's not like the Longknifes have family reunions and invite the poor relations," Kris said.

"Yeah. My great-grandmum saw him when he was there. She told me he lost his wife in the Iteeche War and has never been the same."

"Yeah. He doesn't get out with family much, I hear." Kris was so starting this potential friendship off with a pack of lies. But if she started it off with the truth…?

"Well, I can't have you getting confused with those damn Longknifes. How about I call you Short Spoon?"

"Couldn't I be Medium Fork?"

"Clearly, we need to work on this a bit," Tommy said. "How long until we get there?"

Kris shrugged. She could have asked Nelly, but she doubted anyone on the bus had a computer quite as advanced as hers. An hour later they drove through a gate with a smart Marine guard and a few minutes later, sergeants were yelling at them to get out of that bus and into ranks. Officers to the left. Enlisted to the right.

"Think we should go out the window?" Tommy suggested with an imp's grin.

"It might be fun, but I think these sergeants were born without a sense of humor."

Kris stepped into a hole in the stream of people headed for the door, and left space for Tommy to get in front of her. Then the two of them had to hurry to make up the space to the next person.

At the door, a sergeant was alternately yelling for them to move and go right or left.

"Whose right?" Tommy asked Kris.

Kris glanced around quickly. There was only one rough formation on their side of the bus.

"Follow me," Kris whispered, and raced around the front of the bus. Yep, on the other side was a smaller formation that a sergeant was yelling at.

Kris raced for the end of the line, put her arm out to get her interval and snapped to the most exaggerated form of attention she could muster.

She'd once wondered what military drill was like and a gunny sergeant at the NROTC unit had been happy to give her a quick introduction to "military ballet."

"This little lady seems to know something about drill. Girl, fall out and get these people into three ranks."

"Yes, Sergeant," Kris shouted.

The sergeant had sucked in a large breath, likely to blast Kris for some mistake, but he let it out.

Kris managed to pull and shove those to the right of her into a second rank, then fill it in the third with the late arrivals. She showed them how to get their interval and distance and ended up with a small checkerboard, three deep and four or five long.

Done, Kris was at a loss for what to do next. She could fall in at the rear, but she was too tall for there, or she could... She noticed that the sergeant had stayed up in front of the formation, facing it. Did he expect her to report?

She managed to do a left face without falling down, and walked, doing a miserable job of squaring her corners, until she was right in front of the sergeant. Now she was way out of her depth.

Do I salute a sergeant?

She came to attention in front of the sergeant and said, "Sergeant, the squad is as ready as I know how to make it."

"They're not organized by height."

"Yes, Sergeant. Do I form the women separately for drill?"

That got a hint of a smile. A very small hint.

"Form the young women in the third rank. Now get them organized."

Kris turned like a civilian to face her tiny force. "Turn to your left. The sergeant will, no doubt, teach you how to do it the Navy way very soon. Women, now move to your left. We get the back of the line. We can complain about it later." Kris paused while the women sorted themselves out.

"Okay. Now, if the person ahead of you is shorter than you, move up. Girls, you might want to leave the front slot for me. Big Bird will look really strange pulling up the rear."

That got a soft titter.

"Quiet in the ranks. If the Navy wanted you to laugh, they'd have issued you a sense of humour." She'd heard Grampa Trouble say stuff like this. Could she get away with it?

"Now, turn to your right to face me."

They did, a bit ragged, but about as good as civilians could. "If the guy in front of you is shorter than you, step forward and take his place. Shorty, fall back. Girls, stay where you are. This is one we have to let the boys do all by themselves."

Everyone in the ranks managed to keep their chuckle to themselves.

Kris studied her formation. "You two," she said, stepping closer to the front file. The third guy was shorter than the fourth. "Swap places."

They gave her confused stares. She took one by his elbow and pulled him around until the two had swapped places.

Again she eyed "her" troops. They were organized by sex and height, but the formation was back to ragged. "Check your interval and distance," she ordered.

With a little reminder, the troops extended their hands to get the proper distance between those in front of them and to their right. Kris watched them, helping those who needed it. When she was satisfied, she turned to her sergeant.

"Very good, Candidate Longknife. Now, take your place in ranks."

Her breath caught in her throat when he named her. Apparently, the Longknife legend extended this far into the Navy.

Of course, it would. Stupid me.

I'm not sworn in. Should I run?

No. We don't run home to Harvey. Who said, "Here I stand." Well, that's me today.

"Candidates," the sergeant was saying, "you should be glad that there was one among you that could do this. I'm sure none of you minded if she touched you. The Navy says I can't touch you. The Navy doesn't say anything about me yelling at you. You are about to learn that there is a right way, a wrong way, and the Navy way. From now on, you will do everything the Navy way.

"Open your intervals," he ordered and got blank stares.

"Back off from the person in front of you three intervals. Farther. Farther. Okay, now, drop and give me fifty."

Kris dropped. The sergeant roamed through the candidates like a wolf choosing his rabbit dinner. He stopped where Kris was just completing her tenth pushup. One girl was on her eleventh.

"Welcome to my Navy, Candidate Longknife," he growled. "You're mine, Princess."

Kris kept doing pushups. She wished he'd quit calling her Princess.

C.L. Moore has long been regarded as one of the most remarkable stylists in science fiction. By her own accord, the basic thread of her fiction is that, "Love is the most dangerous thing." "Shambleau" perfectly illustrates both, a story of tough adventurers ranging the spaceways, who meet violence with violence, and it introduces perhaps her most famous and beloved character: Northwest Smith.

More of a planet story than straight space opera, it appeared in the November 1933 issue of Weird Tales *and remains a great example of the classic 1930s stories that influenced so many space opera and adventure stories to follow. Remarkably, it is Moore's first story, written in a bank vault during the Depression to kill time when she had no work to do. A retelling of the Medusa myth, it deals with themes of sexuality and addiction as the tough Smith meets a young woman on the run from a mob and decides to protect her, soon discovering she is not what she seems to be.*

SHAMBLEAU
A NORTHWEST SMITH STORY

C.L. MOORE

"Shambleau! Ha... Shambleau!" The wild hysteria of the mob rocketed from wall to wall of Lakkdarol's narrow streets and the storming of heavy boots over the slag-red pavement made an ominous undernote to that swelling bay, "Shambleau! Shambleau!"

Northwest Smith heard it coming and stepped into the nearest doorway, laying a wary hand on his heat-gun's grip, and his colorless eyes narrowed. Strange sounds were common enough in the streets of Earth's latest colony on Mars—a raw, red little town where anything might happen, and very often did. But Northwest Smith, whose name is known and respected in every dive and wild outpost on a dozen wild planets, was a cautious man, despite his reputation. He set his back against the wall and gripped his pistol, and heard the rising shout come nearer and nearer.

Then into his range of vision flashed a red running figure, dodging like a hunted hare from shelter to shelter in the narrow street. It was a girl—a berry-brown girl in a single tattered garment whose scarlet burnt the eyes with its brilliance. She ran wearily, and he could hear her gasping breath from where he stood. As she came into view he saw her hesitate and lean one hand against the wall for support, and glance wildly around for shelter. She must not have seen him in the depths of the doorway, for as the bay of the mob grew louder and the pounding of feet sounded almost at the corner she gave a despairing little moan and dodged into the recess at his very side.

When she saw him standing there, tall and leather-brown, hand on his heat-gun, she sobbed once, inarticulately, and collapsed at his feet, a huddle of burning scarlet and bare, brown limbs.

Smith had not seen her face, but she was a girl, and sweetly made and in danger; and though he had not the reputation of a chivalrous man, something in her hopeless huddle at his feet touched that chord of sympathy for the underdog that stirs in every Earthman, and he pushed her gently into the corner behind him and jerked out his gun, just as the first of the running mob rounded the corner.

It was a motley crowd, Earthmen and Martians and a sprinkling of Venusian swampmen and strange, nameless denizens of unnamed planets—a typical Lakkdarol mob. When the first of them turned the corner and saw the empty street before them there was a faltering in the rush and the foremost spread out and began to search the doorways on both sides of the street.

"Looking for something?" Smith's sardonic call sounded clear above the clamor of the mob.

They turned. The shouting died for a moment as they took in the scene before them—tall Earthman in the space-explorer's leathern garb, all one color from the burning of savage suns save for the sinister pallor of his no-colored eyes in a scarred and resolute face, gun in his steady hand and the scarlet girl crouched behind him, panting.

The foremost of the crowd—a burly Earthman in tattered leather from which the Patrol insignia had been ripped away—stared for a moment with a strange expression of incredulity on his face overspreading the savage exultation of the chase. Then he let loose a deep-throated bellow, "Shambleau!" and lunged forward. Behind him the mob took up the cry again. "Shambleau! Shambleau! Shambleau!" and surged after.

Smith, lounging negligently against the wall, arms folded and gun-hand draped over his left forearm, looked incapable of swift motion, but at the leader's first forward step the pistol swept in a practiced half-circle and the dazzle of blue-white heat leaping from its muzzle seared an arc in the slag pavement at his feet. It was an old gesture, and not a man in the crowd but understood it. The foremost recoiled swiftly against the surge of those in the rear, and for a moment there was confusion as the two tides met and struggled. Smith's mouth curled into a grim curve as he watched. The man in the mutilated Patrol uniform lifted a threatening fist and stepped to the very edge of the deadline, while the crowd rocked to and fro behind him.

"Are you crossing that line?" queried Smith in an ominously gentle voice.

"We want that girl!"

"Come and get her!" Recklessly Smith grinned into his face. He saw danger there, but his defiance was not the foolhardy gesture it seemed. An expert psychologist of mobs from long experience, he sensed no murder here. Not a gun had appeared in any hand in the crowd. They desired the girl with an inexplicable bloodthirstiness he was at a loss to understand, but toward himself he sensed no such fury. A mauling he might expect, but his life was in no danger. Guns would have appeared before now if they were coming out at all. So he grinned in the man's angry face and leaned lazily against the wall.

Behind their self-appointed leader the crowd milled impatiently, and threatening voices began to rise again. Smith heard the girl moan at his feet.

"What do you want with her?" he demanded.

"She's Shambleau! Shambleau, you fool! Kick her out of there—we'll take care of her!"

"I'm taking care of her," drawled Smith.

"She's Shambleau, I tell you! Damn your hide, man, we never let those things live! Kick her out here!"

The repeated name had no meaning to him, but Smith's innate stubbornness rose defiantly as the crowd surged forward to the very edge of the arc, their clamor growing louder. "Shambleau! Kick her out here! Give us Shambleau! Shambleau!"

Smith dropped his indolent pose like a cloak and planted both feet wide, swinging up his gun threatening. "Keep back!" he yelled. "She's mine! Keep back!"

He had no intention of using that heat-beam. He knew by now that they would not kill him unless he started the gunplay himself, and he did not mean to give up his life for any girl alive. But a severe mauling he expected, and he braced himself instinctively as the mob heaved within itself.

To his astonishment a thing happened then that he had never known to happen before. At his shouted defiance the foremost of the mob— those who had heard him clearly—drew back a little, not in alarm but evidently surprised. The ex-Patrolman said, "Yours! She's *yours*?" in a voice from which puzzlement crowded out the anger.

Smith spread his booted legs wide before the crouching figure and flourished his gun.

"Yes," he said. "And I'm keeping her! Stand back there!"

The man stared at him wordlessly, and horror and disgust and incredulity mingled on his weather-beaten face. The incredulity triumphed for a moment and he said again,

"Yours!"

Smith nodded defiance.

The man stepped back suddenly, unutterable contempt in his very pose. He waved an arm to the crowd and said loudly, "It's—his!" and the press melted away, gone silent, too, and the look of contempt spread from face to face.

The ex-Patrolman spat on the slag-paved street and turned his back indifferently. "Keep her, then," he advised briefly over one shoulder. "But don't let her out again in this town!"

+ + +

Smith stared in perplexity almost open-mouthed as the suddenly scornful mob began to break up. His mind was in a whirl. That such bloodthirsty animosity should vanish in a breath he could not believe. And the curious mingling of contempt and disgust on the faces he saw baffled him even more. Lakkdarol was anything but a puritan town—it did not enter his head for a moment that his claiming the brown girl as his own had caused that strangely shocked revulsion to spread through the crowd. No, it was something deeper-rooted than that. Instinctive, instant disgust had been in the faces he saw— they would have looked less so if he had admitted cannibalism or *Pharol*-worship.

And they were leaving his vicinity as swiftly as if whatever unknowing sin he had committed were contagious. The street was emptying as rapidly as it had filled. He saw a sleek Venusian glance back over his shoulder as he turned the corner and sneer, "Shambleau!" and the word awoke a new line of speculation in Smith's mind. Shambleau! Vaguely of French origin, it must be. And strange enough to hear it from the lips of Venusian and Martian drylanders, but it was their use of it that puzzled him more. "We never let those things live," the ex-Patrolman had said. It reminded him dimly of something… an ancient line from some writing in his own tongue… "Thou shalt not suffer a witch to live." He smiled to himself at the similarity, and simultaneously was aware of the girl at his elbow.

She had risen soundlessly. He turned to face her, sheathing his gun and stared at first with curiosity and then in the entirely frank openness with which men regard that which is not wholly human. For she was not. He knew it at a glance, though the brown, sweet body was shaped like a woman's and she wore the garment of scarlet—he saw it was leather—with an ease that few unhuman beings achieve toward clothing. He knew it from the moment he looked into her eyes, and a shiver of unrest went over him as he met them. They were frankly green as young grass, with slit-like, feline pupils that pulsed unceasingly, and there was a look of dark, animal wisdom in their depths—that look of the beast which sees more than man.

There was no hair upon her face—neither brows nor lashes, and he would have sworn that the tight scarlet turban bound around her head covered baldness. She had three fingers and a thumb, and her feet had four digits apiece too, and all sixteen of them were tipped with round claws that sheathed back into the flesh like a cat's. She ran her tongue over her lips—a thin, pink, flat tongue as feline as her eyes— and spoke with difficulty. He felt that that throat and tongue had never been shaped for human speech.

"Not—afraid now," she said softly, and her little teeth were white and polished as a kitten's.

"What did they want you for?" he asked her curiously. "What have you done? Shambleau… is that your name?"

"I—not talk your—speech," she demurred hesitantly.

"Well, try to—I want to know. Why were they chasing you? Will you be safe on the street now, or hadn't you better get indoors somewhere? They looked dangerous."

"I—go with you." She brought it out with difficulty.

"Say you!" Smith grinned. "What are you, anyhow? You look like a kitten to me."

"Shambleau." She said it somberly.

"Where d'you live? Are you a Martian?"

"I come from—from far—from long ago—far country—"

"Wait!" laughed Smith. "You're getting your wires crossed. You're not a Martian?"

She drew herself up very straight beside him, lifting the turbaned head, and there was something queenly in the pose of her.

"Martian?" she said scornfully. "My people—are—are—you have no word. Your speech—hard for me."

"What's yours? I might know it—try me."

She lifted her head and met his eyes squarely, and there was in hers a subtle amusement—he could have sworn it.

"Some day I—speak to you in—my own language," she promised, and the pink tongue flicked out over her lips, swiftly, hungrily.

Approaching footsteps on the red pavement interrupted Smith's reply. A dryland Martian came past, reeling a little and exuding an aroma of *segir*-whiskey, the Venusian brand. When he caught the red flash of the girl's tatters he turned his head sharply, and as his *segir*-steeped brain took in the fact of her presence he lurched toward the recess unsteadily, bawling, "Shambleau, by *Pharol*! Shambleau!" and reached out a clutching hand.

Smith struck it aside contemptuously.

"On your way, drylander," he advised.

The man drew back and stared, bleary-eyed.

"Yours, eh?" he croaked. "*Zut!* You're welcome to it!" And like the ex-Patrolman before him he spat on the pavement and turned away, muttering harshly in the blasphemous tongue of the drylands.

Smith watched him shuffle off, and there was a crease between his colorless eyes, a nameless unease rising within him.

"Come on," he said abruptly to the girl. "If this sort of thing is going to happen we'd better get indoors. Where shall I take you?"

"With—you," she murmured.

He stared down into the flat green eyes. Those ceaselessly pulsing pupils disturbed him, but it seemed to him, vaguely, that behind the animal shallows of her gaze was a shutter—a closed barrier that might at any moment open to reveal the very deeps of that dark knowledge he sensed there.

Roughly he said again, "Come on, then," and stepped down into the street.

She pattered along a pace or two behind him, making no effort to keep up with his long strides, and though Smith—as men know from Venus to Jupiter's moons—walks as softly as a cat, even in spacemen's boots, the girl at his heels slid like a shadow over the rough pavement, making so little sound that even the lightness of his footsteps was loud in the empty street.

Smith chose the less frequented ways of Lakkdarol, and somewhat shamefacedly thanked his nameless gods that his lodgings were not far away, for the few pedestrians he met turned and stared after the two with that by now familiar mingling of horror and contempt which he was as far as ever from understanding.

The room he had engaged was a single cubicle in a lodging-house on the edge of the city. Lakkdarol, raw camptown that it was in those days, could have furnished little better anywhere within its limits, and Smith's errand there was not one he wished to advertise. He had slept in worse places than this before, and knew that he would do so again.

There was no one in sight when he entered, and the girl slipped up the stairs at his heels and vanished through the door, shadowy, unseen by anyone in the house. Smith closed the door and leaned his broad shoulders against the panels, regarding her speculatively.

She took in what little the room had to offer in a glance—frowsy bed, rickety table, mirror hanging unevenly and cracked against the wall, unpainted chairs—a typical camptown room in an Earth settlement abroad. She accepted its poverty in that single glance, dismissed it, then crossed to the window and leaned out for a moment, gazing across the low roof-tops toward the barren countryside beyond, red slag under the late afternoon sun.

"You can stay here," said Smith abruptly, "until I leave town. I'm waiting here for a friend to come in from Venus. Have you eaten?"

"Yes," said the girl quickly. "I shall—need no—food for—a while."

"Well—" Smith glanced around the room. "I'll be in sometime tonight. You can go or stay just as you please. Better lock the door behind me."

With no more formality than that he left her. The door closed and he heard the key turn, and smiled to himself. He did not expect, then, ever to see her again.

He went down the steps and out into the late-slanting sunlight with a mind so full of other matters that the brown girl receded very quickly into the background. Smith's errand in Lakkdarol, like most of his errands, is better not spoken of. Man lives as he must, and Smith's living was a perilous affair outside the law and ruled by the ray-gun only. It is enough to say that the shipping-port and its cargoes outbound interested him deeply just now, and that the friend he awaited was Yarol the Venusian, in that swift little Edsel ship the *Maid* that can flash from world to world with a derisive speed that laughs at Patrol boats and leaves pursuers floundering in the ether far behind. Smith and Yarol and the *Maid* were a trinity that had caused Patrol leaders much worry and many gray hairs in the past, and the future looked very bright to Smith himself that evening as he left his lodging-house.

+ + +

Lakkdarol roars by night, as Earthmen's camp-towns have a way of doing on every planet where Earth's outposts are, and it was beginning lustily as Smith went down among the awakening lights toward the center of town. His business there does not concern us. He mingled with the crowd where the lights were brightest, and there was the click of ivory counters and the jingle of silver, and red *segir* gurgled invitingly from black Venusian bottles, and much later Smith strolled homeward under the moving moons of Mars, and if the street wavered a little under his feet now and then—why, that is only understandable. Not even Smith could drink red *segir* at every bar from the Martian Lamb to the New Chicago and remain entirely steady on his feet. But he found his way back with very little difficulty—considering—and spent a good five minutes hunting for his key before he remembered he had left it in the inner lock for the girl.

He knocked then, and there was no sound of footsteps from within, but in a few moments the latch clicked and the door swung open. She retreated soundlessly before him as he entered, and took up her favorite place against the window, leaning back on the sill and outlined against the starry sky beyond. The room was in darkness.

Smith flipped the switch by the door and then leaned back against the panels, steadying himself. The cool night air had sobered him a little and his head was clear enough—liquor went to Smith's feet, not his head, or he would never have come this far along the lawless way he had chosen. He lounged against the door now and regarded the girl in the sudden glare of the bulbs, blinking a little as much at the scarlet of her clothing as at the light.

"So you stayed," he said.

"I—waited," she answered softly, leaning farther back against the sill and clasping the rough wood with slim, three-fingered hands, pale brown against the darkness.

"Why?"

She did not answer that, but her mouth curved into a slow smile. On a woman it would have been reply enough—provocative, daring. On Shambleau there was something pitiful and horrible in it—so human on the face of one half-animal. And yet… that sweet brown body curving so softly from the tatters of scarlet leather—the velvety texture of that brownness—the white-flashing smile… Smith was aware of a stirring excitement within him. After all—time would be hanging heavy now until Yarol came… Speculatively he allowed the steel-pale eyes to wander over her, with a slow regard that missed nothing. And when he spoke he was aware that his voice had deepened a little…

"Come here," he said.

She came forward slowly, on bare clawed feet that made no slightest sound on the floor, and stood before him with downcast eyes and mouth trembling in that pitifully human smile. He took her by the shoulders—velvety soft shoulders, of a creamy smoothness that was not the texture of human flesh. A little tremor went over her, perceptibly, at the contact of his hands. Northwest Smith caught his breath suddenly and dragged her to him... sweet yielding brownness in the circle of his arms... heard her own breath catch and quicken as her velvety arms closed about his neck. And then he was looking down into her face, very near, and the green animal eyes met his with the pulsing pupils and the flicker of—something—deep behind their shallows—and through the rising clamor of his blood, even as he stooped his lips to hers, Smith felt something deep within him shudder away—inexplicable, instinctive, revolted. What it might be he had no words to tell, but the very touch of her was suddenly loathsome—so soft and velvet and unhuman—and it might have been an animal's face that lifted itself to his mouth—the dark knowledge looked hungrily from the darkness of those slit pupils—and for a mad instant he knew that same wild, feverish revulsion he had seen in the faces of the mob...

"God!" he gasped, a far more ancient invocation against evil than he realized, then or ever, and he ripped her arms from his neck, swung her away with such a force that she reeled half across the room. Smith fell back against the door, breathing heavily, and stared at her while the wild revolt died slowly within him.

She had fallen to the floor beneath the window, and as she lay there against the wall with bent head he saw, curiously, that her turban had slipped—the turban that he had been so sure covered baldness—and a lock of scarlet hair fell below the binding leather, hair as scarlet as her garment, as unhumanly red as her eyes were unhumanly green. He stared, and shook his head dizzily and stared again, for it seemed to him that the thick lock of crimson had moved, *squirmed* of itself against her cheek.

At the contact of it her hands flew up and she tucked it away with a very human gesture and then dropped her head again into her hands. And from the deep shadow of her fingers he thought she was staring up at him covertly.

Smith drew a deep breath and passed a hand across his forehead. The inexplicable moment had gone as quickly as it came—too swiftly for him to understand or analyze it. "Got to lay off the *segir*," he told himself unsteadily. Had he imagined that scarlet hair? After all, she was no more than a pretty brown girl-creature from one of the many half-human races peopling the planets. No more than that, after all. A pretty little thing, but animal... He laughed, a little shakily.

"No more of that," he said. "God knows I'm no angel, but there's got to be a limit somewhere. Here." He crossed to the bed and sorted out a pair of blankets from the untidy heap, tossing them to the far corner of the room. "You can sleep there."

Wordlessly she rose from the floor and began to rearrange the blankets, the uncomprehending resignation of the animal eloquent in every line of her.

+ + +

Smith had a strange dream that night. He thought he had awakened to a room full of darkness and moonlight and moving shadows, for the nearer moon of Mars was racing through the sky and everything on the planet below her was endued with a restless life in the dark. And something... some nameless, unthinkable *thing*... was coiled about his throat... something like a soft snake, wet and warm. It lay loose and light about his neck... and it was moving gently, very gently, with a soft, caressive pressure that sent little thrills of delight through every nerve and fiber of him, a perilous delight—beyond physical pleasure, deeper than joy of the mind. That warm softness was caressing the very roots of his soul and with a terrible intimacy. The ecstasy of it left him weak, and yet he knew—in a flash of knowledge born of this impossible dream—that the soul should not be handled... And with that knowledge a horror broke upon him, turning the pleasure into a rapture of revulsion, hateful, horrible—but still most foully sweet. He tried to lift his hands and tear the dream-monstrosity from his throat—tried but half-heartedly; for though his soul was revolted to its very deeps, yet the delight of his body was so great that his hands all but refused the attempt. But when at last he tried to lift his arms a cold shock went over him and he found that he could not stir... his body lay stony as marble beneath the blankets, a living marble that shuddered with a dreadful delight through every rigid vein.

The revulsion grew strong upon him as he struggled against the paralyzing dream—a struggle of soul against sluggish body—titanically, until the moving dark was streaked with blankness that clouded and closed about him at last and he sank back into the oblivion from which he had awakened.

✦ ✦ ✦

Next morning, when the bright sunlight shining through Mars' clear thin air awakened him, Smith lay for a while trying to remember. The dream had been more vivid than reality, but he could not now quite recall... only that it had been more sweet and horrible than anything else in life. He lay puzzling for a while, until a soft sound from the corner aroused him from his thoughts and he sat up to see the girl lying in a cat-like coil on her blankets, watching him with round, grave eyes. He regarded her somewhat ruefully.

"Morning," he said. "I've just had the devil of a dream... Well, hungry?"

She shook her head silently, and he could have sworn there was a covert gleam of strange amusement in her eyes.

He stretched and yawned, dismissing the nightmare temporarily from his mind.

"What am I going to do with you?" he inquired, turning to more immediate matters. "I'm leaving here in a day or two and I can't take you along, you know. Where'd you come from in the first place?"

Again she shook her head.

"Not telling? Well, it's your business. You can stay here until I give up the room. From then on you'll have to do your own worrying."

He swung his feet to the floor and reached for his clothes.

Ten minutes later, slipping the heat-gun into its holster at his thigh, Smith turned to the girl. "There's food-concentrate in that box on the table. It ought to hold you until I get back. And you'd better lock the door again after I've gone."

Her wide, unwavering stare was his only answer, and he was not sure she had understood, but at any rate the lock clicked after him as before, and he went down the steps with a faint grin on his lips.

The memory of last night's extraordinary dream was slipping from him, as such memories do, and by the time he had reached the street the girl and the dream and all of yesterday's happenings were blotted out by the sharp necessities of the present.

Again the intricate business that had brought him here claimed his attention. He went about it to the exclusion of all else, and there was a good reason behind everything he did from the moment he stepped out into the street until the time when he turned back again at evening; though had one chosen to follow him during the day his apparently aimless rambling through Lakkdarol would have seemed very pointless.

He must have spent two hours at the least idling by the space-port, watching with sleepy, colorless eyes the ships that came and went, the passengers, the vessels lying at wait, the cargoes—particularly the cargoes. He made the rounds of the town's saloons once more, consuming many glasses of varied liquors in the course of the day and engaging in idle conversation with men of all races and worlds, usually in their own languages, for Smith was a linguist of repute among his contemporaries. He heard the gossip of the spaceways, news from a dozen planets of a thousand different events. He heard the latest joke about the Venusian Emperor and the latest report on the Chino-Aryan war and the latest song hot from the lips of Rose Robertson, whom every man on the civilized planets adored as "the Georgia Rose." He passed the day quite profitably, for his own purposes, which do not concern us now, and it was not until late evening, when he turned homeward again, that the thought of the brown girl in his room took definite shape in his mind, though it had been lurking there, formless and submerged, all day.

He had no idea what comprised her usual diet, but he bought a can of New York roast beef and one of Venusian frog-broth and a dozen fresh canal-apples and two pounds of that Earth lettuce that grows so vigorously in the fertile canal-soil of Mars. He felt that she must surely find something to her liking in this broad variety of edibles, and—for his day had been very satisfactory—he hummed "The Green Hills of Earth" to himself in a surprisingly good baritone as he climbed the stairs.

+ + +

The door was locked, as before, and he was reduced to kicking the lower panels gently with his boot, for his arms were full. She opened the door with that softness that was characteristic of her and stood regarding him in the semidarkness as he stumbled to the table with his load. The room was unlit again.

"Why don't you turn on the lights?" he demanded irritably after he had barked his shin on the chair by the table in an effort to deposit his burden there.

"Light and—dark—they are alike—to me," she murmured.

"Cat eyes, eh? Well, you look the part. Here, I've brought you some dinner. Take your choice. Fond of roast beef? Or how about a little frog-broth?"

She shook her head and backed away a step.

"No," she said. "I can not—eat your food."

Smith's brows wrinkled. "Didn't you have any of the food-tablets?"

Again the red turban shook negatively.

"Then you haven't had anything for—why, more than twenty-four hours! You must be starved."

"Not hungry," she denied.

"What can I find for you to eat, then? There's time yet if I hurry. You've got to eat, child."

"I shall—eat," she said softly. "Before long—I shall—feed. Have no—worry."

She turned away then and stood at the window, looking out over the moonlit landscape as if to end the conversation. Smith cast her a puzzled glance as he opened the can of roast beef. There had been an odd undernote in that assurance that, undefinably, he did not like. And the girl had teeth and tongue and presumably a fairly human digestive system, to judge from her human form. It was nonsense for her to pretend that he could find nothing that she could eat. She must have had some of the food concentrate after all, he decided, prying up the thermos lid of the inner container to release the long-sealed savor of the hot meat inside.

"Well, if you won't eat you won't," he observed philosophically as he poured hot broth and diced beef into the dish-like lid of the thermos can and extracted the spoon from its hiding-place between the inner and outer receptacles. She turned a little to watch him as he pulled up a rickety chair and sat down to the food, and after a while the realization that her green gaze was fixed so unwinkingly upon him made the man nervous, and he said between bites of creamy canal-apple, "Why don't you try a little of this? It's good."

"The food—I eat is—better," her soft voice told him in its hesitant murmur, and again he felt rather than heard a faint undernote of unpleasantness in the words. A sudden suspicion struck him as he pondered on that last remark—some vague memory of horror-tales told about campfires in the past—and he swung round in the chair to look at her, a tiny, creeping fear unaccountably arising. There had been that in her words—in her unspoken words, that menaced...

She stood up beneath his gaze demurely, wide green eyes with their pulsing pupils meeting his without a falter. But her mouth was scarlet and her teeth were sharp...

"What food do you eat?" he demanded. And then, after a pause, very softly, "Blood?"

She stared at him for a moment, uncomprehending; then something like amusement curled her lips and she said scornfully, "You think me—vampire, eh? No—I am Shambleau!"

Unmistakably there were scorn and amusement in her voice at the suggestion, but as unmistakably she knew what he meant—accepted it as a logical suspicion—vampire! Fairy-tales—but fairy-tales this unhuman, outland creature was most familiar with. Smith was not a credulous man, nor a superstitious one, but he had seen too many strange things himself to doubt that the wildest legend might have a basis of fact. And there was something namelessly strange about her...

He puzzled over it for a while between deep bites of the canal-apple. And though he wanted to question her about a great many things, he did not, for he knew how futile it would be.

He said nothing more until the meat was finished and another canal-apple had followed the first, and he had cleared away the meal by the simple expedient of tossing the empty can out of the window. Then he lay back in the chair and surveyed her from half-closed eyes, colorless in a face tanned like saddle-leather. And again he was conscious of the brown, soft curves of her, velvety—subtle arcs and planes of smooth flesh under the tatters of scarlet leather. Vampire she might be, unhuman she certainly was, but desirable beyond words as she sat submissive beneath his low regard, her red-turbaned head bent, her clawed fingers lying in her lap. They sat very still for a while, and the silence throbbed between them.

She was so like a woman—an Earth woman—sweet and submissive and demure, and softer than soft fur, if he could forget the three-fingered claws and the pulsing eyes—and that deeper strangeness beyond words... (Had he dreamed that red lock of hair that moved? Had it been *segir* that woke the wild revulsion he knew when he held her in his arms? Why had the mob so thirsted for her?) He sat and stared, and despite the mystery of her and the half-suspicions that thronged his mind—for she was so beautifully soft and curved under those revealing tatters—he slowly realized that his pulses were mounting, became aware of a kindling within... brown girl-creature with downcast eyes... and then the lids lifted and the green flatness of a cat's gaze met his, and last night's revulsion woke swiftly again, like a warning bell that clanged as their eyes met—animal, after all, too sleek and soft for humanity, and that inner strangeness...

Smith shrugged and sat up. His failings were legion, but the weakness of the flesh was not among the major ones. He motioned the girl to her pallet of blankets in the corner and turned to his own bed.

✦ ✦ ✦

From deeps of sound sleep he awoke much later. He awoke suddenly and completely, and with that inner excitement that presages something momentous. He awoke to brilliant moonlight, turning the room so bright that he could see the scarlet of the girl's rags as she sat up on her pallet. She was awake, she was sitting with her shoulder half turned to him and her head bent, and some warning instinct crawled coldly up his spine as he watched what she was doing. And yet it was a very ordinary thing for a girl to do—any girl, anywhere. She was unbinding her turban...

He watched, not breathing, a presentiment of something horrible stirring in his brain, inexplicably... The red folds loosened, and—he knew then that he had not dreamed—again a scarlet lock swung down against her cheek... a hair, was it? a lock of hair?... thick as a thick worm it fell, plumply, against that smooth cheek... more scarlet than blood and thick as a crawling worm... and like a worm it crawled.

Smith rose on an elbow, not realizing the motion, and fixed an unwinking stare, with a sort of sick, fascinated incredulity, on that— that lock of hair. He had not dreamed. Until now he had taken it for granted that it was the *segir* which had made it seem to move on that evening before. But now... it was lengthening, stretching, moving of itself. It must be hair, but it *crawled*; with a sickening life of its own it squirmed down against her cheek, caressingly, revoltingly, impossibly... Wet, it was, and round and thick and shining...

She unfastened the last fold and whipped the turban off. From what he saw then Smith would have turned his eyes away—and he had looked on dreadful things before, without flinching—but he could not stir. He could only lie there on elbow staring at the mass of scarlet, squirming—worms, hairs, what?—that writhed over her head in a dreadful mockery of ringlets. And it was lengthening, falling, somehow growing before his eyes, down over her shoulders in a spilling cascade, a mass that even at the beginning could never have been hidden under the skull-tight turban she had worn. He was beyond wondering, but he realized that. And still it squirmed and lengthened and fell, and she shook it out in a horrible travesty of a woman shaking out her unbound hair—until the unspeakable tangle of it—twisting, writhing, obscenely scarlet—hung to her waist and beyond, and still lengthened, an endless mass of crawling horror that until now, somehow, impossibly, had been hidden under the tight-bound turban. It was like a nest of blind, restless red worms... it was—it was like naked entrails endowed with an unnatural aliveness, terrible beyond words.

Smith lay in the shadows, frozen without and within in a sick numbness that came of utter shock and revulsion.

She shook out the obscene, unspeakable tangle over her shoulders, and somehow he knew that she was going to turn in a moment and that he must meet her eyes. The thought of that meeting stopped his heart with dread, more awfully than anything else in this nightmare horror; for nightmare it must be, surely. But he knew without trying that he could not wrench his eyes away—the sickened fascination of that sight held him motionless, and somehow there was a certain beauty...

Her head was turning. The crawling awfulness rippled and squirmed at the motion, writhing thick and wet and shining over the soft brown shoulders about which they fell now in obscene cascades that all but hid her body. Her head was turning. Smith lay numb. And very slowly he saw the round of her cheek foreshorten and her profile come into view, all the scarlet horrors twisting ominously, and the profile shortened in turn and her full face came slowly round toward the bed—moonlight shining brilliantly as day on the pretty girl-face, demure and sweet, framed in tangled obscenity that crawled...

The green eyes met his. He felt a perceptible shock, and a shudder rippled down his paralyzed spine, leaving an icy numbness in its wake. He felt the goose-flesh rising. But that numbness and cold horror he scarcely realized, for the green eyes were locked with his in a long, long look that somehow presaged nameless things—not altogether unpleasant things—the voiceless voice of her mind assailing him with little murmurous promises...

For a moment he went down into a blind abyss of submission; and then somehow the very sight of that obscenity in eyes that did not then realize they saw it, was dreadful enough to draw him out of the seductive darkness... the sight of her crawling and alive with unnamable horror.

She rose, and down about her in a cascade fell the squirming scarlet of—of what grew upon her head. It fell in a long, alive cloak to her bare feet on the floor, hiding her in a wave of dreadful, wet, writhing life. She put up her hands and like a swimmer she parted the waterfall of it, tossing the masses back over her shoulders to reveal her own brown body, sweetly curved. She smiled exquisitely, and in starting waves back from her forehead and down about her in a hideous background writhed the snaky wetness of her living tresses. And Smith knew that he looked upon Medusa.

The knowledge of that—the realization of vast backgrounds reaching into misted history—shook him out of his frozen horror for a moment, and in that moment he met her eyes again, smiling, green as glass in the moonlight, half hooded under drooping lids. Through the twisting scarlet she held out her arms. And there was something soul-shakingly desirable about her, so that all the blood surged to his head suddenly and he stumbled to his feet like a sleeper in a dream as she swayed toward him, infinitely graceful, infinitely sweet in her cloak of living horror.

And somehow there was beauty in it, the wet scarlet writhings with moonlight sliding and shining along the thick, worm-round tresses and losing itself in the masses only to glint again and move silvery along writhing tendrils—an awful, shuddering beauty more dreadful than any ugliness could be.

But all this, again, he but half realized, for the insidious murmur was coiling again through his brain, promising, caressing, alluring, sweeter than honey; and the green eyes that held his were clear and burning like the depths of a jewel, and behind the pulsing slits of darkness he was staring into a greater dark that held all things... He had known—dimly he had known when he first gazed into those flat animal shallows that behind them lay this—all beauty and terror, all horror and delight, in the infinite darkness upon which her eyes opened like windows, paned with emerald glass.

Her lips moved, and in a murmur that blended indistinguishably with the silence and the sway of her body and the dreadful sway of her—her hair—she whispered—very softly, very passionately, "I shall—speak to you now—in my own tongue—oh, beloved!"

And in her living cloak she swayed to him, the murmur swelling seductive and caressing in his innermost brain—promising, compelling, sweeter than sweet. His flesh crawled to the horror of her, but it was a perverted revulsion that clasped what it loathed. His arms slid round her under the sliding cloak, wet, wet and warm and hideously alive—and the sweet velvet body was clinging to his, her arms locked about his neck—and with a whisper and a rush the unspeakable horror closed about them both.

In nightmares until he died he remembered that moment when the living tresses of Shambleau first folded him in their embrace. A nauseous, smothering odor as the wetness shut around him—thick, pulsing worms clasping every inch of his body, sliding, writhing, their wetness and warmth striking through his garments as if he stood naked to their embrace.

All this in a graven instant—and after that a tangled flash of conflicting sensation before oblivion closed over him for he remembered the dream—and knew it for nightmare reality now, and the sliding, gently moving caresses of those wet, warm worms upon his flesh was an ecstasy above words—that deeper ecstasy that strikes beyond the body and beyond the mind and tickles the very roots of soul with unnatural delight. So he stood, rigid as marble, as helplessly stony as any of Medusa's victims in ancient legends were, while the terrible pleasure of Shambleau thrilled and shuddered through every fiber of him; through every atom of his body and the intangible atoms of what men call the soul, through all that was Smith the dreadful pleasure ran. And it was truly dreadful. Dimly he knew it, even as his body answered to the root-deep ecstasy, a foul and dreadful wooing from which his very soul shuddered away—and yet in the innermost depths of that soul some grinning traitor shivered with delight. But deeply, behind all this, he knew horror and revulsion and despair beyond telling, while the intimate caresses crawled obscenely in the secret places of his soul—knew that the soul should not be handled—and shook with the perilous pleasure through it all.

And this conflict and knowledge, this mingling of rapture and revulsion all took place in the flashing of a moment while the scarlet worms coiled and crawled upon him, sending deep, obscene tremors of that infinite pleasure into every atom that made up Smith. And he could not stir in that slimy, ecstatic embrace—and a weakness was flooding that grew deeper after each succeeding wave of intense delight, and the traitor in his soul strengthened and drowned out the revulsion—and something within him ceased to struggle as he sank wholly into a blazing darkness that was oblivion to all else but that devouring rapture...

+ + +

The young Venusian climbing the stairs to his friend's lodging-room pulled out his key absent-mindedly, a pucker forming between his fine brows. He was slim, as all Venusians are, as fair and sleek as any of them, and as with most of his countrymen the look of cherubic innocence on his face was wholly deceptive. He had the face of a fallen angel, without Lucifer's majesty to redeem it; for a black devil grinned in his eyes and there were faint lines of ruthlessness and dissipation about his mouth to tell of the long years behind him that had run the gamut of experiences and made his name, next to Smith's, the most hated and the most respected in the records of the Patrol.

He mounted the stairs now with a puzzled frown between his eyes. He had come into Lakkdarol on the noon liner—the *Maid* in her hold very skillfully disguised with paint and otherwise—to find in lamentable disorder the affairs he had expected to be settled. And cautious inquiry elicited the information that Smith had not been seen for three days. That was not like his friend—he had never failed before, and the two stood to lose not only a large sum of money but also their personal safety by the inexplicable lapse on the part of Smith. Yarol could think of one solution only: fate had at last caught up with his friend. Nothing but physical disability could explain it.

Still puzzling, he fitted his key in the lock and swung the door open.

In that first moment, as the door opened, he sensed something very wrong… The room was darkened, and for a while he could see nothing, but at the first breath he scented a strange, unnamable odor, half sickening, half sweet. And deep stirrings of ancestral memory awoke within him—ancient swamp-born memories from Venusian ancestors far away and long ago…

Yarol laid his hand on his gun, lightly, and opened the door wider. In the dimness all he could see at first was a curious mound in the far corner… Then his eyes grew accustomed to the dark, and he saw it more clearly, a mound that somehow heaved and stirred within itself… A mound of—he caught his breath sharply—a mound like a mass of entrails, living, moving, writhing with an unspeakable aliveness. Then a hot Venusian oath broke from his lips and he cleared the door-sill in a swift stride, slammed the door and set his back against it, gun ready in his hand, although his flesh crawled—for he *knew*…

"Smith!" he said softly, in a voice thick with horror.

The moving mass stirred—shuddered—sank back into crawling quiescence again.

"Smith! Smith!" The Venusian's voice was gentle and insistent, and it quivered a little with terror.

An impatient ripple went over the whole mass of aliveness in the corner. It stirred again, reluctantly, and then tendril by writhing tendril it began to part itself and fall aside, and very slowly the brown of a spaceman's leather appeared beneath it, all slimed and shining.

"Smith! Northwest!" Yarol's persistent whisper came again, urgently, and with a dream-like slowness the leather garments moved… a man sat up in the midst of the writhing worms, a man who once, long ago, might have been Northwest Smith. From head to foot he was slimy from the embrace of the crawling horror about him. His face was that of some creature beyond humanity—dead-alive, fixed in a gray stare, and the look of terrible ecstasy that overspread it seemed to come from somewhere far within, a faint reflection from immeasurable distances beyond the flesh. And as there is mystery and magic in the moonlight which is after all but a reflection of the everyday sun, so in that gray face turned to the door was a terror unnamable and sweet, a reflection of ecstasy beyond the understanding of any who had known only earthly ecstasy themselves. And as he sat there turning a blank, eyeless face to Yarol the red worms writhed ceaselessly about him, very gently, with a soft, caressive motion that never slacked.

"Smith… come here! Smith… get up… Smith, Smith!" Yarol's whisper hissed in the silence, commanding, urgent—but he made no move to leave the door.

And with a dreadful slowness, like a dead man rising, Smith stood up in the nest of slimy scarlet. He swayed drunkenly on his feet, and two or three crimson tendrils came writhing up his legs to the knees and wound themselves there, supportingly, moving with a ceaseless caress that seemed to give him some hidden strength, for he said then, without inflection,

"Go away. Go away. Leave me alone." And the dead ecstatic face never changed.

"Smith!" Yarol's voice was desperate. "Smith, listen! Smith, can't you hear me?"

"Go away," the monotonous voice said. "Go away. Go away. Go—"

"Not unless you come too. Can't you hear? Smith! Smith! I'll—"

He hushed in mid-phrase, and once more the ancestral prickle of race-memory shivered down his back, for the scarlet mass was moving again, violently, rising…

Yarol pressed back against the door and gripped his gun, and the name of a god he had forgotten years ago rose to his lips unbidden. For he knew what was coming next, and the knowledge was more dreadful than any ignorance could have been.

The red, writhing mass rose higher, and the tendrils parted and a human face looked out—no, half human, with green cat-eyes that shone in that dimness like lighted jewels, compellingly...

Yarol breathed "Shar!" again, and flung up an arm across his face, and the tingle of meeting that green gaze for even an instant went thrilling through him perilously.

"Smith!" he called in despair. "Smith, can't you hear me?"

"Go away," said that voice that was not Smith's. "Go away."

And somehow, although he dared not look, Yarol knew that the—the other—had parted those worm-thick tresses and stood there in all the human sweetness of the brown, curved woman's body, cloaked in living horror. And he felt the eyes upon him, and something was crying insistently in his brain to lower that shielding arm... He was lost—he knew it, and the knowledge gave him that courage which comes from despair. The voice in his brain was growing, swelling, deafening him with a roaring command that all but swept him before it—command to lower that arm—to meet the eyes that opened upon darkness—to submit—and a promise, murmurous and sweet and evil beyond words, of pleasure to come...

But somehow he kept his head—somehow, dizzily, he was gripping his gun in his upflung hand—somehow, incredibly, crossing the narrow room with averted face, groping for Smith's shoulder. There was a moment of blind fumbling in emptiness, and then he found it, and gripped the leather that was slimy and dreadful and wet—and simultaneously he felt something loop gently about his ankle and a shock of repulsive pleasure went through him, and then another coil, and another, wound about his feet...

Yarol set his teeth and gripped the shoulder hard, and his hand shuddered of itself, for the feel of that leather was slimy as the worms about his ankles, and a faint tingle of obscene delight went through him from the contact.

That caressive pressure on his legs was all he could feel, and the voice in his brain drowned out all other sounds, and his body obeyed him reluctantly—but somehow he gave one heave of tremendous effort and swung Smith, stumbling, out of that nest of horror. The twining tendrils ripped loose with a little sucking sound, and the whole mass quivered and reached after, and then Yarol forgot his friend utterly and turned his whole being to the hopeless task of freeing himself. For only a part of him was fighting, now—only a part of him struggled against the twining obscenities, and in his innermost brain the sweet, seductive murmur sounded, and his body clamored to surrender…

"*Shar! Shar y'danis… Shar mor'la-rol—*" prayed Yarol, gasping and half unconscious that he spoke, boy's prayers that he had forgotten years ago, and with his back half turned to the central mass he kicked desperately with his heavy boots at the red, writhing worms about him. They gave back before him, quivering and curling themselves out of reach, and though he knew that more were reaching for his throat from behind, at least he could go on struggling until he was forced to meet those eyes…

He stamped and kicked and stamped again, and for one instant he was free of the slimy grip as the bruised worms curled back from his heavy feet, and he lurched away dizzily, sick with revulsion and despair as he fought off the coils, and then he lifted his eyes and saw the cracked mirror on the wall. Dimly in its reflection he could see the writhing scarlet horror behind him, cat face peering out with its demure girl-smile, dreadfully human, and all the red tendrils reaching after him. And remembrance of something he had read long ago swept incongruously over him, and the gasp of relief and hope that he gave shook for a moment the grip of the command in his brain.

Without pausing for a breath he swung the gun over his shoulder, the reflected barrel in line with the reflected horror in the mirror, and flicked the catch.

In the mirror he saw its blue flame leap in a dazzling spate across the dimness, full into the midst of that squirming, reaching mass behind him. There was a hiss and a blaze and a high, thin scream of inhuman malice and despair—the flame cut a wide arc and went out as the gun fell from his hand, and Yarol pitched forward to the floor.

+ + +

Northwest Smith opened his eyes to Martian sunlight streaming thinly through the dingy window. Something wet and cold was slapping his face, and the familiar fiery sting of *segir*-whiskey burnt his throat.

"Smith!" Yarol's voice was saying from far away. "N.W.! Wake up, damn you! Wake up!"

"I'm—awake," Smith managed to articulate thickly. "Wha's matter?"

Then a cup-rim was thrust against his teeth and Yarol said irritably, "Drink it, you fool!"

Smith swallowed obediently and more of the fire-hot *segir* flowed down his grateful throat. It spread a warmth through his body that awakened him from the numbness that had gripped him until now, and helped a little toward driving out the all-devouring weakness he was becoming aware of slowly. He lay still for a few minutes while the warmth of the whisky went through him, and memory sluggishly began to permeate his brain with the spread of the *segir*. Nightmare memories… sweet and terrible… memories of—

"God!" gasped Smith suddenly, and tried to sit up. Weakness smote him like a blow, and for an instant the room wheeled as he fell back against something firm and warm—Yarol's shoulder. The Venusian's arm supported him while the room steadied, and after a while he twisted a little and stared into the other's black gaze.

Yarol was holding him with one arm and finishing the mug of *segir* himself, and the black eyes met his over the rim and crinkled into sudden laughter, half hysterical after that terror that was passed.

"By *Pharol*!" gasped Yarol, choking into his mug. "By *Pharol*, N.W.! I'm never gonna let you forget this! Next time you have to drag me out of a mess I'll say—"

"Let it go," said Smith. "What's been going on? How—"

"Shambleau," Yarol's laughter died. "Shambleau! What were you doing with a thing like that?"

"What was it?" Smith asked soberly.

"Mean to say you didn't know? But where'd you find it? How—"

"Suppose you tell me first what you know," said Smith firmly. "And another swig of that *segir*, too. I need it."

"Can you hold the mug now? Feel better?"

"Yeah—some. I can hold it—thanks. Now go on."

"Well—I don't know just where to start. They call them Shambleau—"

"Good God, is there more than one?"

"It's a—a sort of race, I think, one of the very oldest. Where they come from nobody knows. The name sounds a little French, doesn't it? But it goes back beyond the start of history. There have always been Shambleau."

"I never heard of 'em."

"Not many people have. And those who know don't care to talk about it much."

"Well, half this town knows. I hadn't any idea what they were talking about, then. And I still don't understand—"

"Yes, it happens like this, sometimes. They'll appear, and the news will spread and the town will get together and hunt them down, and after that—well, the story doesn't get around very far. It's too—too unbelievable."

"But—my God, Yarol!—what was it? Where'd it come from? How—"

"Nobody knows just where they come from. Another planet—maybe some undiscovered one. Some say Venus—I know there are some rather awful legends of them handed down in our family—that's how I've heard about it. And the minute I opened that door, awhile back—I—I think I knew that smell…"

"But—what *are* they?"

"God knows. Not human, though they have the human form. Or that may be only an illusion… or maybe I'm crazy. I don't know. They're a species of the vampire—or maybe the vampire is a species of—of them. Their normal form must be that—that mass, and in that form they draw nourishment from the—I suppose the life-forces of men. And they take some form—usually a woman form, I think, and key you up to the highest pitch of emotion before they—begin. That's to work the life-force up to intensity so it'll be easier… And they give, always, that horrible, foul pleasure as they—feed. There are some men who, if they survive the first experience, take to it like a drug—can't give it up—keep the thing with them all their lives—which isn't long—feeding it for that ghastly satisfaction. Worse than smoking *ming* or—or 'praying to *Pharol*.'"

"Yes," said Smith. "I'm beginning to understand why that crowd was so surprised and—and disgusted when I said—well, never mind. Go on."

"Did you get to talk to—to it?" asked Yarol.

"I tried to. It couldn't speak very well. I asked it where it came from and it said—'from far away and long ago'—something like that."

"I wonder. Possibly some unknown planet—but I think not. You know there are so many wild stories with some basis of fact to start from, that I've sometimes wondered—mightn't there be a lot more of even worse and wilder superstitions we've never even heard of? Things like this, blasphemous and foul, that those who know have to keep still about? Awful, fantastic things running around loose that we never hear rumors of at all!

"These things—they've been in existence for countless ages. No one knows when or where they first appeared. Those who've seen them, as we saw this one, don't talk about it. It's just one of those vague, misty rumors you find half hinted at in old books sometimes... I believe they are an older race than man, spawned from ancient seed in times before ours, perhaps on planets that have gone to dust, and so horrible to man that when they are discovered the discoverers keep still about it—forget them again as quickly as they can.

"And they go back to time immemorial. I suppose you recognized the legend of Medusa? There isn't any question that the ancient Greeks knew of them. Does it mean that there have been civilizations before yours that set out from Earth and explored other planets? Or did one of the Shambleau somehow make its way into Greece three thousand years ago? If you think about it long enough you'll go off your head! I wonder how many other legends are based on things like this— things we don't suspect, things we'll never know.

"The Gorgon, Medusa, a beautiful woman with—with snakes for hair, and a gaze that turned men to stone, and Perseus finally killed her—I remembered this just by accident, N.W., and it saved your life and mine—Perseus killed her by using a mirror as he fought to reflect what he dared not look at directly. I wonder what the old Greek who first started that legend would have thought if he'd known that three thousand years later his story would save the lives of two men on another planet. I wonder what that Greek's own story was, and how he met the thing, and what happened…

"Well, there's a lot we'll never know. Wouldn't the records of that race of—of *things*, whatever they are, be worth reading! Records of other planets and other ages and all the beginnings of mankind! But I don't suppose they've kept any records. I don't suppose they've even any place to keep them—from what little I know, or anyone knows about it, they're like the Wandering Jew, just bobbing up here and there at long intervals, and where they stay in the meantime I'd give my eyes to know! But I don't believe that terribly hypnotic power they have indicates any superhuman intelligence. It's their means of getting food—just like a frog's long tongue or a carnivorous flower's odor. Those are physical because the frog and the flower eat physical food. The Shambleau uses a—a mental reach to get mental food. I don't quite know how to put it. And just as a beast that eats the bodies of other animals acquires with each meal greater power over the bodies of the rest, so the Shambleau, stoking itself up with the life-forces of men, increases its power over the minds and souls of other men. But I'm talking about things I can't define—things I'm not sure exist.

"I only know that when I felt—when those tentacles closed around my legs—I didn't want to pull loose, I felt sensations that—that—oh, I'm fouled and filthy to the very deepest part of me by that—pleasure—and yet—"

"I know," said Smith slowly. The effect of the *segir* was beginning to wear off, and weakness was washing back over him in waves, and when he spoke he was half meditating in a lower voice, scarcely realizing that Yarol listened. "I know it—much better than you do—and there's something so indescribably awful that the thing emanates, something so utterly at odds with everything human—there aren't any words to say it. For a while I was a part of it, literally, sharing its thoughts and memories and emotions and hungers, and—well, it's over now and I don't remember very clearly, but the only part left free was that part of me that was all but insane from the—the obscenity of the thing. And yet it was a pleasure so sweet—I think there must be some nucleus of utter evil in me—in everyone—that needs only the proper stimulus to get complete control; because even while I was sick all through from the touch of those—things—there was something in me that was—was simply gibbering with delight… Because of that I saw things—and knew things—horrible, wild things I can't quite remember—visited unbelievable places, looked backward through the memory of that—creature—I was one with, and saw—God, I wish I could remember!"

"You ought to thank your God you can't," said Yarol soberly.

✦ ✦ ✦

His voice roused Smith from the half-trance he had fallen into, and he rose on his elbow, swaying a little from weakness. The room was wavering before him, and he closed his eyes, not to see it, but he asked, "You say they—they don't turn up again? No way of finding—another?"

Yarol did not answer for a moment. He laid his hands on the other man's shoulders and pressed him back, and then sat staring down into the dark, ravaged face with a new, strange, undefinable look upon it that he had never seen there before—whose meaning he knew, too well.

"Smith," he said finally, and his black eyes for once were steady and serious, and the little grinning devil had vanished from behind them, "Smith, I've never asked your word on anything before, but I've—I've earned the right to do it now, and I'm asking you to promise me one thing."

Smith's colorless eyes met the black gaze unsteadily. Irresolution was in them, and a little fear of what that promise might be. And for just a moment Yarol was looking, not into his friend's familiar eyes, but into a wide gray blankness that held all horror and delight—a pale sea with unspeakable pleasures sunk beneath it. Then the wide stare focused again and Smith's eyes met his squarely and Smith's voice said, "Go ahead. I'll promise."

"That if you ever should meet a Shambleau again—ever, anywhere—you'll draw your gun and burn it to hell the instant you realize what it is. Will you promise me that?"

There was a long silence. Yarol's somber black eyes bored relentlessly into the colorless ones of Smith, not wavering. And the veins stood out on Smith's tanned forehead. He never broke his word—he had given it perhaps half a dozen times in his life, but once he had given it, he was incapable of breaking it. And once more the gray seas flooded in a dim tide of memories, sweet and horrible beyond dreams. Once more Yarol was staring into blankness that hid nameless things. The room was very still.

The gray tide ebbed. Smith's eyes, pale and resolute as steel, met Yarol's levelly.

"I'll—try," he said. And his voice wavered.

British writer Neal Asher is acclaimed for his Polity series of space opera novels and short stories set in a future history that encompasses many proven science fiction tropes, including androids, hive minds, aliens, and a world-ruling artificial intelligence. His novels feature fast-paced action and are epic in scope, though in many ways bear as many similarities to cyberpunk as space opera. The main characters usually seek to preserve societal order or improve society in some way. This story, which takes place in a different universe from Polity, is based on an idea that just popped into the writer's head as a standalone and tells the tale of the survivor of wars between dense-tech humans named Cheel. It debuted in the June 2004 issue of Asimov's Science Fiction *magazine.*

POLITY: THE VETERAN
NEAL ASHER

Cheel had nearly escaped when she saw the man take off his face. She was sure she'd lost Croven's boys on the loading dock, but hid amongst plasmesh packing crates long enough to be certain. As a further precaution, she took a roundabout route to the terminal, to catch the ferry to the Scarbe side of the river. And there he was:

Seated on a bollard, the man contemplatively removed his pipe, as if to tamp it down or relight it. Instead, he placed it stem down in the top pocket of his shirt, then reached up and pressed his fingers against his cheekbone and forehead. His face came away from his hairline, round behind his ears, down to a point just above his Adam's apple. The inside of his mouth and much of his sinus were also part of the prosthesis, so only bare eyeballs in the upper jut of his skull remained—the rest being the black spikes and plates of bio-interfaces.

Cheel gaped. From another pocket, the man took some sort of tool and began to probe inside the back of his detached face. He put the prosthesis in his lap, then took up his pipe and placed it in his throat sphincter. Smoke bled from between the interface plates of his cheeks. His bare eyeballs swivelled towards Cheel then back down to the adjustments he was making. She suddenly realised who this must be. Here was the veteran who worked on the ferry. Here was one of the few survivors from a brutal war between factions of dense-tech humans. Not understanding what was impelling her, she walked out on the jetty and approached him.

The veteran ignored her until after removing his pipe from his throat and replacing his face. The prosthesis engaged with a sucking click. Perhaps, without his face, he just could not speak?

"And what is your name?" he asked patronisingly.

"Cheel."

With the same tool he had used on the back of his face, he contemplatively scraped out his pipe. After repacking it with tobacco from his belt-pouch, he ignited it with a laser lighter. Puffed out a cloud of fragrant smoke.

"What can I do for you, Cheel?"

She didn't know what to say. She wanted to ask about dense tech, about star travel, if it was true he was over two hundred years old, and if it was true that the Straker nova, which grew in the sky every night, was the result of a star his kind detonated during a battle. But there was no time.

"Hey Cheel!"

She felt a sudden flush of horror. Stupid to walk out on this jetty. Stupid to allow this momentary fascination to delay her escape. She turned and saw that her original pursuers were there, blocking her escape from the jetty. Glancing aside at the water of Big River, she saw suderdile swimming past. Unusually for a girl raised in the river town of Slove-Scarbe, she could swim. She had learnt out at the coast, when Grand Mam had been alive, but that skill would not help her here. Town residents didn't learn to swim because the average survival span in the river was less than thirty seconds.

"What do you want, Slog?" she asked.

By his expression, she guessed he wanted more than her immediate death. Discovering his cache of jewels missing, Croven must have quickly worked out that she had finally left him, and let Slog off the leash. But what the hell did he expect? As his sickness progressed he became increasingly violent and unpredictable, and she did not want to die with him when one of his lieutenants finally took him down.

"You've been a really naughty girl, Cheel."

Slog, Croven's second, had killed three people that Cheel knew about. She looked behind her, hoping for some escape route, maybe a boat. The veteran was gone, though why he should hide she had no idea—he was one who had nothing to fear from Slog and his kind. She drew her shiv and began to back up. Maybe if she lured them down this side of the jetty she could escape past on the other side, or across the top of the packing crates? Then more of Croven's gang arrived and she knew there would be no escape. Suddenly the horrible reality hit home and she wanted to cry. They would rape her, all of them and for a long time, and if that didn't kill her, they would feed her to the suderdiles. She backed up further, came opposite the bollard on which the veteran had been sitting.

"What did you do?" asked the face lying on top of the bollard.

Cheel just stood there for a moment with her mouth moving and nothing coming out. Eventually: "I was just trying to get away from Croven." She neglected to mention Croven's cache of jewels in a hide roll hanging by cords from her shoulder.

"And what will they do to you?" asked the face.

"Rape me, then kill me."

"What's that, little bitch?" Slog directed others of Croven's gang to cover every way off the jetty. Beyond him she saw Croven arrive—the lanky black-haired figure was difficult to mistake, especially with that wooden gait and unnatural posture. Could she appeal to him after her betrayal?

"Nothing," said Cheel. "Nothing at all." She glanced at the face.

It winked at her then said, "Pick me up and turn me towards them."

What did she have to lose?

As she snatched up the prosthesis, Slog drew his Compac airgun and aimed it low. He wasn't going to kill her, just smash a kneecap if she put up too much of a fight. She'd seen him do that before. His expression was nasty, grinning, then suddenly it changed to confusion when he saw what she held.

"What do you think?" the face asked, vibrating in her hand. "Slog is a pathetically descriptive name for him."

"I don't—" Cheel began.

Something flashed, iridescent. A sound, as of a giant clearing its throat, rent the air. Slog froze, a horizontal line traversing down the length of his body, searing him from head to foot. Then he moved and flame broke from pink cracks appearing in his black skin. His air gun burst with a dull thrump, took his hand away. He held the stump up before his liquefying eyes and started screaming. Croven came swiftly up behind him, turned him and shoved. Slog screamed in the water, his blackened skin slewing away. Cheel didn't see the suderdile that took him. One moment he was splashing in reddish froth, then he was gone.

The face vibrated in Cheel's hands. "Croven, the girl is coming with me to the skidbladnir, and that was in the nature of a warning to you and your gang."

Croven stared in horror down into the water, then at his glistening hands. Then, seemingly jerked into motion, he made a circular motion in the air with the point of his finger. Gang members began retreating from the jetty, heading away.

"Why her?" He suddenly turned to stare at the face. "Is that part of you not prosthetic as well?"

"Ah, Croven," said the face. "The thing about power is that you don't have to justify what you do with it. Surely you know that already."

Croven nodded, turned away briefly, then turned back to gaze directly at Cheel. "I wasn't going to kill you. I love you."

Cheel believed him, but was very aware of his use of 'wasn't'. Now, her causing Slog's death even if indirectly, Croven would not be able to back down. He waited for her to say something, and when she did not, he headed away.

"What now?" Cheel asked when all of the gang were no longer in sight.

"Now, carrying my face, you walk to the ferry."

Cheel began walking, realising as she did so, that in engaging so completely with the talking face, she had momentarily forgotten it was only the veteran's prosthesis.

"Where are you?" she asked, as she reached the end of the jetty.

"Never you mind. Just keep walking to the terminal. I was right to assume you were heading for the Scarbe side?"

"You were."

Cheel saw no sign of Croven or his gang, but knew they were very likely lurking nearby. Ducking her head down, and tucking the prosthesis under her arm next to the jewel roll, she hurried towards the looming shape of the skid ferry, or the skidbladnir, as the veteran called it. She half expected a slug from an air gun to slam into her at any moment, if not vengefully from Croven then from one of the others, but none did. Sensibly, no one was attacking while the veteran remained invisible close by. Why did it have to come to this?

Time and again she had pleaded with Croven to live out his remaining time on the coast with her. With his cache they could have lived comfortably for some time and then, as it ran out, she could have found work. She would have looked after him, nursed him to the end. But his choice to stay where ruthlessness and physical violence were the measure of a man meant there could be only one ending. It was all right for him to choose a bloody end for himself. He had no right to choose it for her too.

Soon she reached the ferry ramp, where she groped in her pocket for her token, but it seemed the veteran's face was token enough and the guard waved her aboard. Avoiding the restaurant deck because of the delicious smells and her lack of funds suitable to purchase what was sold there, Cheel went all the way up to the roof deck and there, leaning against the balustrade, she kept an eye on the boarding ramps. A hand tapped her on the shoulder, and she turned to the faceless veteran, holding out his hand for his prosthesis.

"How is it you're not seen?" Cheel asked.

"Chameleonware." His face, its mouth still moving, again seated with that sucking click. Eyes now in place where before there had been none, he gazed up at the sky and continued, "But in making myself invisible down here, I've made myself all too visible elsewhere. Though admittedly the proton flash was what attracted attention."

"Slog?"

"Yes." He turned to regard her. "The weapon I used to burn that piece of shit."

Cheel glanced up to where he had been gazing, and raised a querying eyebrow.

"Friends," he said. "Though I find it difficult to think of them as such. They let me rest to salve and repair what remains of my humanity, but by using my weapons to kill, I've told them I'm ready to take up my duties again. I don't think a quarter of a century is enough, but then I don't think any time is long enough."

From below, she heard the clack of ratchets and loud clangs as the crew raised the ramps and secured them to the side of the vessel. Deep in the belly of the skidbladnir, big diesel engines started rumbling.

"What will happen?" Cheel knew she would have to get away from Scarbe as quickly as possible. The veteran had saved her, and right now protected her, but that would not and could not last. And Croven would come after her.

"They'll send a tral-sphere with tac updates and new mission parameters."

Cheel just nodded. She understood none of that but did not want him to stop speaking. He was talking dense tech here, stuff about the war, and about technically advanced humans killing each other.

In steel cages behind them, vertical shafts began turning. These drove the big shiny grip wheels clamped on the thick ship-metal cable reaching from the Slove pylon behind them to the Scarbe pylon a kilometre across the river. The ferry began to ease out of dock. Dispersing suderdiles surfed a white-water wave away from the bows. Cheel turned to gaze across the river to their destination.

"When will this tral-sphere arrive?" she asked.

The veteran smiled. "That you ask indicates you have no idea what I'm talking about. The tral-sphere is, of course, already here. And so is the war, and so is the enemy, and so already is my plan."

+ + +

A crewman saw him leap aboard; but showed no inclination to chase him down into the dank lower holds of the ferry. In the dim light admitted by a filthy portal into a long steel corridor, Croven drew his air gun from his belly holster and checked the load. He noted that his right hand was shaking—the added stress of the situation exacerbating the symptoms of his neurological disease. Damn Cheel for forcing this on him. Slog had quickly detected her inept theft, otherwise Croven could have let her go. But Slog and the others knowing meant Croven had to order her immediate capture. For her theft from and betrayal of him, the minimum he could get away with, whilst retaining his status, would have been her humiliation and beating. Now, after what happened to Slog, he must try to kill her and the veteran. But Croven did not want to kill Cheel and doubted he could kill the veteran.

The gangs of Slove had long known that the veteran was untouchable. But this was the first time he had actually used one of his dense-tech weapons to kill. Before, it had always been one of his invisible visitations. Some offenders he gave a beating, others he threw in the river. Quite often they were like Croven: gang members who lived by a code allowing them to admit no fear. The veteran had killed Croven's lieutenant, and for that Croven must exact vengeance. That going up against the veteran meant death did not excuse not making the attempt. Perhaps Croven should have listened to Cheel.

When she had first suggested leaving Slove and heading out to one of the coastal towns, Croven had given the idea serious consideration. He had been bored and here was a chance at a fresh start, new challenges. But the shakes had started about then, and medscan confirmed something was wrong. He'd paid a researcher to find out what. After only a few hours of delving in the public com library the researcher laid it out for him. Croven had a reversion disease: one of those ailments long considered the province of historians by the bulk of humanity, but returning to primitive colonies like this one. Prognosis: no cure on this world.

Now the drugs that had alleviated some symptoms of his Parkinson's were becoming less and less effective. He estimated he had a year as gang leader before someone took him down. He would have lasted longer in one of the coastal towns but, after Cheel had grown bored with his sickness and left him, probably have starved to death in the end. Croven preferred the idea of going out bloody. Perhaps now was the time.

"Croven." The voice had a metallic quality that made him think for one insane moment that the ferry was speaking to him.

"Veteran," he said at last. The man must have seen him board, and had now come after him in the invisible form. Croven turned sharply towards the length of corridor it had issued from, and fired half his ten-shot clip into the shadows. The slugs smacked and whined down into the darkness.

"I am not the veteran. I am his enemy." The voice grated in Croven's ear.

Then, suddenly, the ferry dipped and shuddered and some force picked Croven up and slammed him against a steel bulkhead. Now, with a reverberating clang a curving black surface appeared, intersecting the floor and wall of the corridor. Croven saw that the portal had been shattered and realised that what held him had probably saved him from injury. He could hear yelling out there, screaming. A hatch irised open in the black surface to reveal gleaming tight-packed and squirming movement.

"Choose," the voice hissed.

✦   ✦   ✦

Something had slammed the thousands of tons of iron and steel of the ferry to one side and now it was groaning as it dragged back into position under the cable, and huge waves slapped its sides and washed the lower decks. The abrupt motion would have flung Cheel over the rail and into the jaws of the suderdiles had not the veteran wrapped an arm around her.

"What?" she gasped.

"That was fast," he said. "But not well positioned."

A thunderclap now, and suddenly they were in shadow. A sphere had appeared. It was twenty metres across, jet black, and only three or four metres above them, its surface intersecting the grip-wheel gearboxes and the ship-metal cable. When it shifted slightly in relation to the ferry, severed cable snaked out of the clamping wheels, slammed down on deck nearby, then slithered off the back of the ferry taking most of the rear cast-iron balustrade with it.

"I guess I could have done better as well," the veteran observed.

Two of them, two of these tral-spheres, Cheel realised. But where was the other one? She saw that the visible one had sheared the ferry's gearbox clean through. Thick gleaming oil slopped out and a couple of hypoid gears bounced across the deck. As she looked around, she guessed the location of the other one. People were screaming, some of them thrown into the water by the cataclysmic arrival of that first sphere inside the ferry. In horror, Cheel watched a woman trying to hold a baby up out of the water, away from the approaching suderdiles. Disconnected from the cable, the ferry was now turning, carried downstream by the strong current.

"There are people in the water!" Cheel exclaimed.

"Yes," the veteran shrugged. "People die."

Cheel stared at him in disbelief. She had discounted his previous callousness. He was two hundred years old, an advanced human, and she had thought he would be better than, something more than, people she knew.

"You don't care?"

"Of course he doesn't care." Cheel turned as Croven stepped up on deck. "We are primitives to him."

There was something seriously amiss with Croven. His skin was uniformly white and somehow dead, and only as he drew closer did she see his eyes seemed plain steel balls.

"Ah, the automatics picked you up," said the veteran. "They always make an assessment and choose one who is willing for conversion. What swung it, Croven, your pride and gangland honour, or the promise of a cure for what's eating out the inside of your head?"

Croven ignored the jibe. He concentrated on Cheel. "I've been recruited and now, knowing I could kill you in an instant, am certain I don't want to." He now looked at the veteran. "I know the enemy."

The air between Croven and the veteran was taut, telic, as something invisible probed and strained it. The feeling began to grow unbearable.

"Move aside." The veteran touched Cheel's shoulder.

The ferry was now hundreds of metres downstream from the crossing point and there were no screams from the water anymore, just spreading red where grey suderdile flukes stirred and broke the surface. The visible sphere continued to hang like a balloon above the ferry. Then, a crashing from below and the deck tilted. Cheel grabbed a driveshaft cage to stop herself sliding over. The other two remained upright, both now standing in mid-air where the deck had been. A hundred metres out the other sphere folded out of the air with a thunderous crash. A hole opened in the side of it revealing gleaming movement.

"Had I not been your enemy before you stepped into that tralsphere, I would be now." The veteran shrugged—a strangely out-of-place action from someone floating off the deck. "It's how you've been programmed."

The steel deck below them was rippling; intersecting shear planes, nacreous sheets and lines, appeared in the air between them, kept rearranging as if struggling to form some final complete shape. Cheel smelt burning and saw oily smoke gusting up the side of the ferry towards her. There was more screaming, some from inside the ferry and some from the water. Glancing down the tilted deck she saw a lifeboat drifting past, people struggling to board it, even though it was tangled in broken rope and half tipped over by the weight of a suderdile, its jaws closed on the legs of a bellowing ferryman. This latest disaster, she realised, had been caused by Croven—by him shifting his sphere outside the ferry. He and the veteran were as bad as each other: the ferry and those aboard it meant nothing to them.

"It can't be settled here—you know that," said Croven.

The veteran smiled humourlessly. A column of intersecting fields, looking like stacked broken glass, stabbed down from the sphere directly above the ferry, enclosed him, folded him away. Resistance removed, the deck before Croven split in a thousand places, peeled up and blew away in a white-hot storm, sparking and glittering from the ferry. This exposed a maze of rooms and corridors packed with people struggling in bewilderment through smoke suddenly dispersing. Croven turned to face Cheel, then the same weird distortions stabbed across to him, and folded him to his own sphere. Cheel wondered if they had taken the battle elsewhere to save lives, if Croven had peeled up the deck to give air to these trapped souls. She wanted to believe in some altruism on the part of dense-tech humans, old and new. But when the ferry tilted further, evidently sinking, and the smoke down below turned to fire, there was no room for that belief. As the steel deck grew warm below her, she watched the battle in the sky.

Between the two spheres, now dots many kilometres apart, those same shear planes and lines crazed the sky. The two seemed to be employing forces so immense they stressed and fractured existence. Light flashed across one of these planes towards one of the spheres, and something slapped it down. Over the horizon rose a storm of dust as from mountains falling. Another such ricochet sent a two-metre wave down the river from some distant destruction, bucking the ferry and changing its angle of approach to the bottom of the river. Then, out of the sky, some basin of force scooping. Cheel clung to the cage as first she was pressed hard against the deck and felt it collapsing underneath her, gouts of fire issuing from where it had been torn away nearby. Then she was flung sideways, her body fully away from the steel and legs flailing in the air. The ferry beached with a crash, slamming her to the deck again.

+ + +

Croven was losing. Around him, the veteran's attack program was sequestering machines at an exponential rate. In the time it took him to calculate how much longer his control would last, it was gone. He expected to die then, not in some spectacular manner as the veteran's single enemy, but in the same way that the crew of a destroyer would die—almost irrelevant to the destruction of the machine itself. But his elevated awareness remained, and he realised the veteran had held back from destroying the structures built inside Croven's head, and allowed him to live.

Hiatus.

Croven opened his eyes to sunlight, on a ridge above a mudbank where suderdiles would normally bask. The river was turbid and none of the creatures in sight. There was dust in the air and a smell as of hot electronics.

"Why did you choose me?" Croven asked, already guessing the answer.

The veteran, seated on a rock nearby, replied, "They always place an autosystem near where one of us has become inactive—ready to counter us should we activate. But such cyber systems require a human component."

"I'm already aware of that," said Croven bitterly.

The veteran stared at him coldly. "The human component is first programmed, then given control. However, if the human component is faulty, more control reverts to the system. I can destroy such systems with ease. It is the random human creative element that can be dangerous to me."

Croven sat upright. He felt fine, better than fine. "So you wanted someone dumb like me in control."

The veteran shook his head. "It was time for me to activate again— to reveal myself. I'd already chosen to do that by killing Slog, knowing that would give you reason to try to kill me, just as the enemy system, detecting me, came online, and that its routines would guide it to you. A human with substantial neurological damage made an easier opponent for me, because there would be less of the human in the system. But I was also watching the situation, and Cheel's theft and attempted escape from you was too good an opportunity to miss."

"I don't know what you mean." But Croven did.

The veteran went on relentlessly. "Your own actions would put in danger someone you love, and made you doubly vulnerable. Shifting the ferry like that was enough of a diversion of resources. It's why you lost, Croven."

Swallowing dryly, Croven asked, "What now?"

The veteran stood. "I'll leave you with your implants. They'll keep you functioning for another ten years. Beyond that," he shrugged, "I have other battles to fight."

The veteran turned away, space revolved around him and he was gone. Above, a black sphere accelerated straight up, receded.

✦ ✦ ✦

In the background, the ferry lay broken-backed over a hill. It was still burning, and the survivors gathered in stunned groups, not knowing what to do or where to go. The enduring image imprinted in Cheel's mind was of a man squatting on the ground holding his burned hands out from his body, whilst behind him a little girl whacked, with a length of metal, a beached and dying suderdile. Other denizens of the river and drifts of weed were scattered in the vicinity. That bowl of force had snatched them up along with the ferry and much of the river. Lying in the dirt were fish, disjointed crustaceans, pink river clams. Cheel was uninjured, and in that she was one of the few. The fires had caught many, but she had avoided them by climbing down ladders on the outside of the ferry. She had been able to help only a few of them. Pulling up handfuls of weed from a nearby pile, she approached the man, and wrapped strands of it around his burned hands—the best she could do to cool the injury.

"Come away now," she said to the girl, when the suderdile made a gasping attempt to snap at its tormentor. The girl ignored Cheel and now tried to poke out one of the creature's yellow eyes.

"A novelty that cannot be ignored."

Cheel spun round to face Croven, inspected him from head to foot. His skin now bore a more healthy hue, but there was still something metallic about his eyes.

"Did you kill him, then?" she asked.

"No, I lost, and he spared me."

"Remiss of him to leave scum like you alive." Cheel rested her hand on a nearby rock. Croven was not carrying his air gun, but she knew what he could do to her with only his hands.

"You don't really know me at all, Cheel."

"I know that you can't let me live, after what happened to Slog."

He gestured to the ferry. "I saved your life, and the urgency I felt, which made me what I was, is no longer with me."

Cheel glanced round at the ferry. Either he or the veteran had lifted the craft out of the river and deposited it here on the bank. He claimed it was him.

"And how am I supposed to react to that?" she asked.

"Come with me to the coast."

Cheel again took in the surrounding ruination and gripped the rock tighter.

"Go to Hell," she said.

Croven stood utterly still for a while, then he nodded once and walked away.

Weston Ochse's experience as a real-life U.S. military intelligence officer and now contractor serving on battlefields such as Afghanistan informs his storytelling in military science fiction and horror series like Seal Team 666, Grunt, *and* The Burning Sky. Seal Team 666 *is in development as a movie to star Dwayne "The Rock" Johnson. Ochse won the Bram Stoker Award for his first novel,* Scarecrow Gods, *in 1997, and he has received four more Bram Stoker nominations since as well as a nomination for the Pushcart Prize, and winning three New Mexico-Arizona Book Awards. He also writes comics for companies like IDW and DC Comics. His story for us is a side adventure featuring popular character Mr. Pink and two ex-paramedics turned end-of-the-world commandos who join forces to take on an alien threat.*

AUTHOR'S NOTE: *When I was afforded the opportunity of enlarging the Grunt Universe, I was overjoyed but unsure where to do it. I asked many fans of the work and they overwhelmingly wanted to read about Mr. Pink. Funny that they should say that because I too wanted to write more about this narrow man. I can count on two hands the number of characters I've written who took charge in a story—who wrestled the reins of plot away from me—and he is one of them. So, I placed him at the scene of a house that had already been taken by reconnaissance forces the night before the invasion. And to help him I wrote in two first responders, humble homages to two of my greatest fans.*

THE END-OF-THE-WORLD BOWLING LEAGUE
A GRUNT STORY

WESTON OCHSE

It was turning out to be an even more miserable day than Mr. Pink had planned. In fact, it was so miserable that the English lexicon had yet to fashion a word to describe the multi-faceted cataclysmic global incident that was about to transpire. And now here, firmly on planet Earth, he stood in the middle of an absolute abattoir. His entire team had been decimated, five bodies in at least thirty pieces turning the snow into a Clive Barker Rorschach design that may or may not have looked like two mirrored versions of a butterfly carrying a meat cleaver. The irony hadn't escaped him that even with all the money in the world and the best technology at his disposal, he hadn't been able to stop a single one of the aliens who were about to be the first wave in a superior alien race's attempt to colonize what had so recently been a little blue planet in a forgotten corner of the universe.

Six years ago, he'd thought he'd be able to monetize this day. As a junior partner in a corporation with advanced knowledge of an alien invasion, he'd presumed they'd already been able to leverage one or ten or twenty countries to provide the necessary recompense so that they could then share what they knew and thus create a mechanism for global defense. They'd run the numbers and it was doable. In fact, it was more than doable. The key was to attack the invaders before they breached the ionosphere, something that could have been accomplished had countries banded together, properly redistributed assets, and resourced their militaries to confront a common goal. Instead, each and every first-world country they'd approached had decided to hide the impending truth. They'd either been unwilling to cease their own political intrigues or had decided that the validity of the information presented was suspect and decided that hedging their bets was the more appropriate response.

In a closed-door session of the American Congress, he'd shown them the Cray and what they were planning and the apocalypse that would transpire. All his corporation had asked for was Alaska, Idaho, and Montana, three states that could have been traded for the secret to defeating the invading aliens. They'd laughed him out of Washington, treating the information like the love child of their own secret hydrological collapse facing the American West and Alex Jonesian Infowars propaganda rising from the dark web like a rotting hexadecimal corpse.

Their reception from the UK's Parliament had been promising, with the potential to provide them Northern Ireland and the Isle of Man, as well as North Sea oil and fishing rights, until a united front of Irish separatists, ISIS returnees, and white supremacists discovered the plan and during one Saturday afternoon destroyed Big Ben, the Tower of

London, six homes belonging to landed Lords, and two thirds of the Royal Family vacationing on a yacht in the Mediterranean.

Germany threatened to have them tried in the international court.

France wouldn't even give them the opportunity to present their findings.

The Italian government, after hearing that the world was indeed coming to an end, dissolved and left the country in such disarray, local crime lords installed their own fiefdoms.

Russia used the knowledge to attack Eastern Europe in an attempt to return the diaspora to the USSR, if only obtaining their glory days for mere moments.

Of all the countries they'd approached, only Belgium and Sri Lanka had shown significant interest, but since neither of them had a space program, much less the ability to launch defensive strikes using Titan series or similar rockets, their offers of support were treated as they were offered.

Ninety-six days to invasion day, which was the last projected day they believed they'd be able to solicit, mentor, and create an effective defense based on current inventories, the Tokyo and U.S. stock markets free fell until the value of any of the premium stocks such as Facebook and Apple and Toyota became equal to what one might pay to get a kid's meal from their favorite fast food emporium. The militaries of the world redeployed from their preferred war zones and established safe zones around each major city.

With no longer any way to monetize their data, Mr. Pink and his partners released all of their information over the internet, causing chaos and consternation to those who believed, instigating hundreds of end-of-the-world cult scenarios. When it became evident that the world was too late to save itself, the people of Earth experienced the seven stages of grief at their own impending deaths, with the vast majority stuck in stage four—which was better known as reflection and depression.

And now here he was, alone in Minot, Minnesota, in the middle of a blizzard trying to track down one loose end before the invasion was set to begin in seven hours, his entire team dead, and him on the run from an advance party alien drone that had somehow snuck in under

Earth's combined radars. His brigades were tucked away in their own training venues, not yet ready to fight the Cray in any meaningful terms. The senior members of the company had left for their own hiding places, hoping they'd have something to return to, but Mr. Pink had little hope for anything close to that.

In seven hours, the world would be irrevocably changed and nothing would ever be the same again. But that was seven hours away and he still had one last thing to do—something he'd promised himself he'd do in person if his back was ever up against the wall.

"Looks like you could use a little help," came a voice from behind.

Mr. Pink turned. He'd been so focused on the remains before him that he'd somehow missed hearing the two paramedics driving up in an ambulance.

A red-haired paramedic with the name Neeld stitched over his left breast approached and scratched his head. "I think we're a little late for these fellows. You okay, mister?"

The other paramedic approached as well. His name was Finley and he wore the pointed beard and mustache of a musketeer. "I told you I thought that creature had probably killed someone. I just didn't think it was this many someones."

"So you saw it? Did you see where it went?"

Neeld looked him up and down. "I see blood, but no injuries."

Finley nodded. "I think he's okay." He turned and headed back to the ambo. "Which means we're free to hit Golden Lanes. If we hurry, they might still be playing The Bee Gees."

Neeld rolled his eyes. "Disco night at the bowling alley. Want to join us for a few games before the world ends?"

Mr. Pink appraised the unlikely appearance of these two and decided to use it to his advantage. Hamlet had sent Rosencrantz and Guildenstern away to their demise when they could have stayed and helped. Mr. Pink wouldn't make the same mistake.

So, he raised his voice and said, "Are you boys really going to make bowling your last act? Don't you want to do something significant instead?"

Finley stopped dead in his tracks, then spun around. "Damn it! I won the coin flip fair and square. I want a burger and some fries and a beer."

"You can always eat after," Mr. Pink said.

"After what?"

"What if I told you I was on a secret mission to try and forestall the invasion? What if you could be heroes instead of chumps?" He saw his words take hold and then slip away.

"I'd rather be chumps bowling to 'Staying Alive' than LARPing with you as you pretend to be a super-secret agent," Finley said.

Mr. Pink gestured to the five dead men. "Does this look like Live Action Role-Playing to you?"

Neeld nodded. "He's got a point. And we did see that creature."

Finley stomped over to Neeld. "Don't you see what he's doing? This man, whoever he is, just got five men killed and he wants to make us next."

Neeld's eyes narrowed. "Who exactly are you, mister?"

Mr. Pink was about to give his real name but decided that if he was going to shanghai these two, he'd need something else. So, for possibly the first time, he felt good about the nickname that troublemaker Mason had give him. He knew it would generate intrigue, and right now he needed enough intrigue to get these two on his side. He could probably do what needed to be done himself but having four more hands would definitely help.

"They call me Mr. Pink. I'm Chief of Task Force OMBRA."

Neeld frowned. "OMBRA, as in the company that held the world ransom for the secret that would have saved everyone?"

"We didn't hold anyone for ransom. We told Earth's governments what we knew and they decided not to believe us."

"That's not the way I heard it," Neeld said.

Mr. Pink sighed. "There's no way I can prove it, Mr. Neeld. All I can say is that we stumbled on the fact that they were already among us and tried to explain it to them. Sadly, they were so mixed up in their own frantic political games that they didn't seem to have the time or inclination for any facts that didn't match their version of the narrative."

"Fake news," Neeld murmured. Then more to himself he added, "The greatest trick the devil ever pulled was convincing the world he didn't exist."

"Keyser Söze," Mr. Pink acknowledged. "Verbal Kint said the line, I believe."

"*The Usual Suspects*," Finley said. "And speaking of movies, what's up with all this *Reservoir Dogs* bullshit?"

Mr. Pink lowered his eyes and couldn't help but grin. No one had had the Jones to ever compare him to the Steve Buscemi character from the old Quentin Tarantino film except for Staff Sergeant Benjamin Carter Mason. But his own penchant for wearing black combined with his pallid skin and pockmarked face, along with an unruly mob of thinning dishwater-colored hair, provided an eerie comparison. Plus, the fucking world was ending, so he'd decided to roll with it.

"Isn't bullshit. They call me Mr. Pink. It's a name. Much like many others."

"Then I suppose we have pieces of Mr. Blue, Mr. Blonde, Mr. Brown, Mr. Orange, and Mr. White littering the snow like graffiti from an end-of-the-world block party." Finley pointed to the largest parts of each body as he called them out.

"Not exactly. Their names were Spence, Jones, Franks, White, and Sawyer. I'm the only one named after a character in the movie. It's a nickname. I'm rolling with it."

Finley frowned. "Nicknames are stupid."

"Mine is Tawny Lake, after the name of my first dog and the street I used to live on," Neeld said.

Finley rolled his eyes. "That's your porn name, stupid. I saw the same meme on Facebook."

"What was yours?" Neeld asked.

Finley tightened his lips as he said, "Russel Terrier."

Neeld laughed. "Sounds like the name of a dog. Are you sure you played it right?"

"Our only pet was a cat named Russel. I lived on Terrier Street. And I told you. It's a stupid meme."

"Who names their cat Russel?"

"My grandma did. She had Alzheimer's and thought it was her brother."

Neeld's eyes were wide with amazement. "Your grandma thought the cat was her brother?"

"Hey, boys. Saving the world here. Can you assist? Or is porn names and disco bowling how you want to go out?"

The two paramedics looked at each other and both nodded. "Okay, Mr. Pink. Just don't go cutting off anyone's ear."

"That was Mr. Blonde."

"Then just don't die on us."

"Mr. Pink was the lone survivor."

"Did he just say lone?" Finley asked.

"Yeah. I think he did," Neeld responded. "Maybe we should be bowling."

Five minutes later, after his two new redshirts armed themselves and ammoed up, they all stood in front of a window which reminded Mr. Pink of the one in Dothan, Alabama. The home was like many others on the street. A large bay window that looked into the dining room was to the left of a front porch. Plates of rotting, moldy food sat in front of a mother, father, sister, and brother. Worms crawled through something that had once been a casserole. Flies hummed hungrily, swirling above the family's last meal, banging against the inside of the window.

"What the hell is this?" Neeld gaped through the window.

"Come on inside. Look but don't touch," Mr. Pink said. He'd said the same thing to Mason not four months ago.

The stench hit them like a wet fist.

Everyone covered their mouths and noses with their free hands.

Finley cursed.

It was the tentacles that kept the scene from being the victory party for a serial killer. They held the family in place, affixing their wrists, arms, legs, and ankles to the chairs, each disappearing into the floor. A circular orange growth pulsed with light beneath the table. Each member of the family was connected to this growth by several orange membranes that ran right into each of their abdomens. The outside of the membranes held millions of white cilia-like feelers that waved in the air.

"Is that orange thing one of the aliens?" Finley asked.

Mr. Pink had decided that these two would get the unvarnished truth, so he told them. "It's one of them. The aliens have been task-selected. One alien controls the minds of the family. The other uses their minds to broadcast on various frequencies. Another conducts brutal recon as you saw outside on the last block."

"What about those coming?" Neeld asked.

"My guess is that their job is to soften us up. I feel like there's a long game in play. The aliens want our planet and what we see in this home is but the first stage."

"They want our planet like the Precursors or the Kaiju in *Pacific Rim*," Finley said. "What if the Kaiju are invading?"

"I think it's going to be something worse than Kaiju," Mr. Pink said.

Finley scoffed. "Ain't nothing worse than Kaiju." Then his face paled as they all watched the family pulse with fake life.

As the growth pulsed, the family breathed, in unison. In and out, their chests rising and falling in a mockery of life.

"The paramedic in me wants to fix them," Neeld said.

"They're dead. Their bodies are being used as organs to do a job. What made them who they were is long gone."

"Why are we here?" Finley asked.

"Let's just say that the broadcasts coming from this location are very different from those coming from the others, and I want to find out why."

One of the orange membranes had released the mother, who slumped face-first onto her plate of rotting food. The membrane waived in the air, its millions of white cilia pointing toward Mr. Pink and his two companions like arrays of miniature antennae.

Mr. Pink began moving across the room. "Downstairs and fast."

The bay window exploded inward as they moved into the hall. The cacophony of the table shattering and being thrown aside slammed through the interior of the home like thunder.

All three hurried down the stairs.

They locked the door at the top and at the bottom, but Mr. Pink doubted that it would hold against the creature from outside.

If the upstairs reminded Mr. Pink of the other homes where he'd found this particular species of alien, the downstairs was markedly different. Although the air was foul, it held a peculiar tang he hadn't experienced in this context before. It took a moment before his mind identified it as ammonia.

"You two set up right here," he said, pointing to a place several feet away from the door to the stairs. He gestured at the rifles each one held. "I assume you know how to use those."

They each racked the charging handles back, ejecting a round and loading another.

Mr. Pink fought the urge to roll his eyes. "Anything comes through, fire until you can't fire anymore."

Then he turned into the room. He knew what to expect around the corner and he wasn't exactly disappointed to see it, even though it was something right out of a horror movie. The membrane rose from where it grew out of the basement floor into the ceiling. Undulating masses in the shapes of newborn babies rose and fell as if they were sinking into the surface then struggling to get out. Their eyes were closed, but their mouths were open, each emitting tiny sounds like wheezes.

Mr. Pink pulled a taser from his belt and fired into it without hesitation. As the prongs struck deep and the wire tightened with the flow of electricity, the babies' eyes snapped open.

Thankfully they did not scream. Had they, none of them would have survived.

He depressed a button on his taser, released the wires, and fired again. And again until he could fire no more, the membrane sizzling, the babies melting.

Then he felt the cold kiss of a rifle at his neck.

"It wants me to kill you," Neeld said. "It's telling me terrible things you have done."

Mr. Pink didn't understand. He'd removed the threat of the membrane, so then what was it that was still making the others homicidal? The membrane's own defense mechanism came from the effects of auditory emanations, but he'd shut them up. Even now, smoke swirled from the mouths of the faux babies.

This was getting tedious. "Put the rifle down," he said.

"I actually can't, Mr. Pink. And even if I could, I really don't want to. You've been a bad, bad boy and whatever is in my head is angry."

Mr. Pink turned carefully and saw the wide eyes of Neeld as the man pressed the rifle against his throat. Finley stood behind the pair and the tip of his rifle barrel was pressed against the back of Neeld's head. Mr. Pink felt the urge to complete the triangle. Images of Finley doing terrible things to small animals flashed through his head, the soundtrack of the terrible deeds finally snapping in synch after a few jarring seconds.

But he knew it for what it was.

"There is a creature somewhere in the basement who is making you do this. If you were just a regular citizen, we'd have killed ourselves by now. But your experiences, the terrible things you have seen—probably as first responders—have changed the topography of your brains enough that the creature's demands don't have the power that they should. You both need to fight the impulse, because that's just what it is. An alien-inspired impulse."

"But the things you've done," Neeld seethed.

"I don't know if what it is projecting into your mind is true or not, but you need to fight it. You need to not let it win." His eyes shifted to Finley. "And what about you?"

"This shit is fucked up."

"I know, but the only way you will survive this is if you fight it." He shifted his eyes to Neeld. "If you give in, there will be no more bowling."

The paramedic's Adam's apple shifted as he swallowed. Strain showed at the sides of his mouth and the edges of his eyes. The barrel moved in minute increments until it pointed to the floor.

"Can't have that," he said. "What's the end of the world without a little bowling?"

Finley lowered his rifle as well. "Hoping maybe to have a burger and beer too."

Mr. Pink felt his spine loosen. "Now look to the door. The creature is coming."

"How do you know?"

"Because whatever just tried to get us to kill ourselves failed. The alien outside was Plan B, and Plan B is coming."

"If Plan B is that bad, then it makes you wonder what Plan C looks like."

"I was thinking calamari." Finley had moved further into the basement and peered around a corner. "Either that, or these folks have the strangest fucking aquatic pet I've ever seen."

A moment later, all three of them stood before a water tank roughly in the shape of a coffin resting on casters that kept it off the floor. The murky liquid stirred like ink as something moved within. The smell of ammonia emanated from within. Tentacles slid across the glass, very much like those of a squid or an octopus.

Not being a scientist who studied such things, he didn't know.

A grating noise like the house ripping in half made all of them look toward the stairs. They couldn't see them from where they stood, but the piece of wood flying across the floor told them all they needed to know.

Neeld and Finley raised their rifles.

Mr. Pink pulled a grenade from his pocket and held it over the tank.

The alien that had attacked his team earlier rounded the corner looking like it was ready to finish the job.

Mr. Pink held up the grenade and said, "If you take even one step forward I will pull the pin and blow your cephalopod alien master to smithereens."

And the alien stopped—all four arms of it.

After about thirty seconds, Neeld said, "Dammit. Now I have to pee."

"Do you think it understands what smithereens means?" Finley asked.

"Forget smithereens. What about cephalopod? I don't even know what that is," Neeld said.

"Just keep the working ends of those rifles pointing at it. I imagine either it or the thing in the tank is running my M67 fragmentation grenade through a biometric catalogue to determine exactly what it can do."

Neeld took a step to the right as if to get behind the alien.

It moved to the side to block the maneuver but didn't come any closer.

"I think it understands."

"I still have to pee," Neeld said.

"Then pee," Mr. Pink said.

Neeld gave him a baleful look.

"It's not as if the owners will complain," Mr. Pink said.

"I—I can't possibly," Neeld said.

Finley turned to Neeld, aimed, then shot him in the leg.

The percussion of the blast in the confined space surprised all of them.

Mr. Pink flinched.

Neeld went down with a scream. "What the hell!"

Finley lowered his weapon.

The alien took two quick steps forward, reaching for them.

Neeld opened fire from where he lay, sending six rounds in succession into the alien's chest.

Mr. Pink held the grenade higher. "One more move and I kill us all." Then without looking, he asked, "Finley, what's going on?"

"I d—don't know. For a moment I thought Neeld was something else—a—a monster I had never seen before."

"The creature is insinuating itself into your thoughts. Think about the worst things you've done. Think about the worst things you've seen."

Neeld pressed against his wound. "That's a grim prescription."

"Just do it. The worse your PTSD the better."

"I delivered a baby on the side of the road once," Finley said. "This young couple didn't make it to the hospital because of a traffic backup. Nothing moved for hours. We parked our rig on an overpass and ran back to help them."

"Doesn't sound bad at all," Mr. Pink said. "You need to think of the bad things."

Finley gave Mr. Pink a sidelong look, then resumed his vigil at the alien. "The father was in the back seat helping. I gave him the baby so I could work on his wife—clear her placenta. My partner was behind me and asked the father to come around to the driver's side so he could examine the baby."

Neeld closed his eyes.

Mr. Pink could feel the stress building in his muscles. The grenade felt like a brick.

"The father's name was Thomas Hilton. He opened the door and stepped out with his newborn baby in his arms. It was a girl who they'd named Emily. About the time Tom stood, a tow truck that had been racing down the shoulder plowed through him, taking the door of the car with him. It took the truck one hundred and seventeen feet to stop. When we finally got to Tom, he was still holding Emily. Both of their heads were crushed to the point they were unrecognizable."

The alien shifted forward slightly. Several circles of yellow were beginning to ooze what could possibly be alien blood.

Mr. Pink couldn't help but visualize Finley's story.

"What I remember the most is the look on the mother's face," Finley said, lifting the rifle to his shoulder as the alien crept forward another inch. "Her name was Sarah with an H. That's how she introduced herself to me. *Hi, I am Sarah with an H and I am having a baby.* You should have seen the look of relief and joy she had when we showed up and when we delivered her baby. The delivery was easy and quick. Her pain was less than most. There were no complications. Then the way her face changed when she saw her husband and newborn carried away by the hood of the tow truck—the look of ultimate grief—of devastation. Later she said to me, *I never got a chance to hold my baby.* I wanted to tell her that she'd held the baby for nine months, but I knew it would fall on deaf ears. Three days later, she killed herself by running into traffic. In her note, she mentioned that she wanted to die like her family had."

The alien lunged.

Finley fired.

Mr. Pink thought *Fuck it*, pulled the pin, and dropped the grenade in the liquid.

But the alien was faster. It reached into the liquid and pulled out something that looked like a cross between a squid and a miniature poodle—all tentacles and legs but no eyes. Then it was limping out of the room and up the stairs.

Mr. Pink realized what was happening and moved fast. He grabbed Finley by the arm, who in turn pulled Neeld and they all fell through a nearby doorway and into a bathroom.

The concussion slammed shut the door, then broke it in two. A blizzard of dust exploded from the drywall and ceiling, covering them in a fine white powder. The mirror shattered, sending pieces into the opposite wall. The sink cracked in two and water geysered free.

Mr. Pink's ears rang like he'd just been inside a bell.

Still, they were alive.

He pushed Finley off of him and got to his feet.

Finley groaned, as did Neeld.

Mr. Pink hurriedly stepped over both of them, then kicked repeatedly at the bathroom door until it fell forward out of the hinge. He clawed his way over the door and climbed into the ruined downstairs room where he immediately fell on his ass as his feet slipped out from under him. The liquid that had been in the container now covered the floor and dripped from the walls and ceiling like a bucket brigade with alien amniotic snot had thrown a rave.

Around the corner, the membrane lay in great gelatinous pieces. He stepped around baby-shaped pieces that looked like what he'd imagine whale blubber to look like and tried desperately not to slip again.

He found the door to the stairs, less ruined, but buckled on its hinges. He kicked his way through it and was soon upstairs. Past the family and out onto the front porch, he followed a trail of yellow drops.

He had his pistol already out and led his way with the working end of it.

The two aliens downstairs must have been communicating. He'd counted on it when he'd threatened to kill the one in the tank but hadn't considered that they might understand about the fuse delay built into the grenades and chance beating it. That was why the four-armed menace had been inching closer, probably at the behest of the tank creature who'd geometrically planned the exact nature of his escape.

The trail ended three houses down at the front door to a light-blue split-level home.

He hesitated. How much did he want this new alien? He'd planned well and had his OMBRA forces in training. They wouldn't be able to halt the invasion, but they would be able to affect the battle once it was determined what the incoming forces' abilities were.

He checked his coms and discovered that they were truly fucked. Now just a bunch of wire and composite plastic instead of a functioning twenty-first-century communication system.

"Do you think they are in there?" Finley asked from behind.

Mr. Pink whirled, gun pointed, then relaxed.

"I thought you two had some bowling to do."

Finley's eyes were wide as he said, "We just survived a grenade attack."

"First time for everything," Mr. Pink said. He noted Neeld limping over to them. He'd tied off his upper leg to stop the bleeding.

Neeld grinned maddeningly. "Just a flesh wound," he said. Then he added, "You have a piece of wood sticking out of your shoulder."

Mr. Pink looked down and saw the school ruler-sized piece of wood embedded in his skin. How had he missed that? He reached to pull it out.

"Don't do that," Finley ordered. He moved closer. "You pull it out, you may never get the bleeding to stop. Better just leave it for now." He glanced at the door to the house. "We going to go in there?"

"I was thinking about it," Mr. Pink said.

"That thing in there you had me do. You think it helps?"

"We think so. Not often we can put someone's bad memories to good use, but we think that it does help."

"That brain topography thing," Neeld said.

Mr. Pink shrugged. Going disco bowling sounded pretty good about now.

"How did you earn your PTSD?" Neeld asked. "You don't look like a soldier or a first responder."

"What do you think I look like?"

"A mortician," Finley said.

Neeld laughed. "That would be called a last responder."

Mr. Pink nodded, then said, "My mother joined a cult. I was there from the age of ten to fifteen."

"Cult as in Jim Jones and poisoned Kool-Aid?" Finley asked.

Neeld punched him in the arm.

Finley gave his pal a sheepish grin. "What? I've never known anyone in a cult before."

Mr. Pink turned to them and said with a dead face, "Cult as in they raped all of us and I had to kill two people to escape—both with spoons I'd sharpened on the concrete floor they kept me chained to."

Neeld mouthed the word *Fuck*.

Finley nodded. "Yep. That would do it. PTSD for sure." He turned and gave the empty street a long look. "Maybe we should go bowling."

Mr. Pink was about to agree, when they heard a scream from inside.

"Aw hell," he said, then opened the door and leaped inside.

The two former paramedics turned end-of-the-world commandos followed.

Inside the house was nothing like the other. No family at the table. No membrane. No pulsating alien mess. But there was a trail of yellow blood on the off-white carpet. And there was a trail of red blood that joined it. Down the hall, they found the body of an older man, exsanguinated from the neck.

A gurgle and thump sounded from further down the hall.

Mr. Pink led the way.

As he stepped over the body, the four-armed alien entered the hall from a door further along.

It saw him and charged.

Mr. Pink opened fire, emptying his magazine into the muzzle of the creature.

But the rounds had little effect.

The alien reached out and grabbed him with its two left arms and slammed him against the wall hard enough to rattle his teeth and dent the drywall in various Mr. Pink shapes. His shoulder exploded into a volcanic eruption of pain where it had been injured before.

Both Neeld and Finley jammed the barrels of their rifles into the gut of the alien and rock-and-rolled until their charging handles locked to the rear.

The alien let go of Mr. Pink, who sagged into Neeld. Then it fell to its knees.

Finley pulled a scalpel from a sheath at his waist and shoved it so deep into the alien's eye that his hand was partially obscured. Then he brought up a foot and shoved the alien away.

It fell backwards onto the carpet, eyes staring blankly at the popcorn ceiling.

Mr. Pink struggled to his feet and finally managed with the help of the pair.

WESTON OCHSE

All three of them made it down the hall to where the alien had been busy.

The body of an old woman lay over the edge of the bathtub, her head almost torn from her neck.

Mr. Pink couldn't see her face, but by the blue-tinged permanent in her hair, he was reminded of a grandmother or an elderly librarian he'd seen once.

The tub was filled with blood, and in it, the intelligent alien basked. Covered mostly in blood, it pulled its tentacled body back and forth in the viscous liquid.

"Who the fuck does that?" Neeld asked.

"Aliens who don't care about anything but themselves," Finley replied.

"What are we going to do?" Neeld asked.

Mr. Pink sighed. He was already tired and his work really wouldn't start until tomorrow after the invasion.

"There's nothing really we can do. This is the end. There's not going to be a bacteria that's going to kill all the aliens like in the movies. There's not going to be a miracle save. We are royally and truly fucked and the aliens are going to make it worse. There will be no coming back from it. We probably won't even be able to effectively fight them."

"Then why even try?" Finley asked.

"Because we're humans. We're earthlings. We make lousy neighbors as a rule. We'd rather fence ourselves in and spend the day watching *Oprah*, order shit we don't need off of Amazon, and drink White Zinfandels. But you take that away from us, you take us out of our comfort zone, and we are pit bulls. All of us."

He snatched a blow-dryer from where it rested on the sink, turned it on and dropped it in the blood.

Sparks flew and an arc of electricity curved around the creature.

The lights flickered and went out.

The creature glowed for a moment, then darkened.

They could barely see each other, the light leaking into the hall from the open front door the only source of illumination.

Mr. Pink turned away and began to make his way down the hall.

"What are we supposed to do?" Finley asked.

Mr. Pink stopped and turned, seemingly oblivious to the alien's body beneath him.

"We do what we can. We fight how we can. We be ourselves. Because there's one thing we don't want to stop being and that's human." He sighed again, then glanced at his shoulder. During the beating against the walls, the length of wood had broken off. "One thing, though. Can either of you fix my shoulder?"

They both blinked at him.

"I mean, I suppose we can leave it. I'm right-handed so it probably won't affect my bowling." He turned away and headed toward the front door. "You guys ready, or do you want to just stay there when the world ends?"

Neeld and Finley glanced at each other, then hurried out of the house and after Mr. Pink.

First stop, disco bowling and burgers.

Then later, they'd watch the world end.

Brenda Cooper is an author and futurist and former collaborator with Larry Niven, amongst others. Of her ten novels to date, seven are space opera and include the Fremont's Children and Ruby's Song series. Her story for the anthology Mission: Tomorrow *appeared in* Gardner Dozois Year's Best Science Fiction *in 2015. Her story for us focuses on Marcus and Joseph, two Wind Readers, capable of tuning themselves into the data streams in whatever star systems they visit. Marcus, the older of the two, attempts to comfort the young man while he is troubled by a killing he's had to perform, and tells him the story of a killing of his own.*

AUTHOR'S NOTE: *"Death, Butterflies, and Makers of War" goes with my Fremont's Children series, currently being re-issued by Wordfire Press. While it takes place during the timeframe of the third book,* Wings of Creation, *this leads up to the next book in the series,* The Making War. *It felt important to write this interlude and share it because the two characters in the story, Marcus and Joseph, are critical. Joseph is a main character in the whole arc, and a troubled and capable young man with the ability to do great harm. Marcus, who is his teacher, has no viewpoint in the main series, and so this acts to deepen readers' understanding of Marcus as a man, of his history, and of his relationship to Joseph.*

Both characters are heroes in the book, but should be understood as flawed and vulnerable in spite of their prodigious capability. I hope that you enjoy this story.

DEATH, BUTTERFLIES, AND MAKERS OF WAR
A FREMONT'S CHILDREN STORY

BRENDA COOPER

A student of the Making War found this story in the effects of Joseph's teacher, Marcus. Apparently, he recorded it on a starship on his way to the war. The conversational tone shows that it was clearly left for a future audience such as ourselves. Besides, while it had safeguards, we were able to break them. If Marcus had wanted to hide this story, he could have. Thus we know it was left for us.

—Historian's note found in the archives of change.

Joseph has killed.

I can see it as a knot of guilt and uncertainty in the data that is him, as a place he dares not look.

He cannot afford not to look.

He and I are both Wind Readers, which means that we can tune ourselves to become part of the flows of data in almost any system. We are pilots, and Makers. We can fly starships, and we can create new life. After all, the secret of life is data. A butterfly is data. A heart is data. So is a fear. Some would say that even love is data.

I am one of the most powerful of Makers, but Joseph is stronger than me, if not yet nearly as disciplined or capable. This means he is dangerous.

I don't know who Joseph killed. I have avoided tearing the story from him. That would weaken him, and it is not my way to use force. But the walls around his pain are so thick they are making the memory of whatever he did twist inside him. It might destroy him when he isn't looking. If he has to kill again, it could stop him. Or perhaps he will kill when he doesn't need to.

I noticed the fear inside him on the way to Lopali, so after we arrived and settled in, I woke him early one day and took him into one of the flawless parks that the Keepers of Lopali maintain for the seekers who come here. The park—hell, the whole damned planet—is too perfect for me, but a garden of flowers is a good place to counter darkness.

Joseph sat a few feet away from me, so we were each on different benches, angled so we could see each other's faces easily if we turned our heads only a little. We could gaze on the multicolored flowers and watch the real butterflies and listen to the quiet hum of automated bees. The sky arched blue above us, and flyers flew overhead from time to time, their wings bright in the morning sun.

I let him settle enough that he became bored and began to shift uncomfortably.

"Quiet," I told him.

It took him five minutes to be still for a whole minute. Perhaps he felt my own apprehension about this topic. "I will tell you a story about *me* this morning."

He cocked his head, his shoulders and his slightly clenched fingers visibly relaxing.

"This is a story about the first time I killed."

His fists clenched again. But he knew better than to interrupt me.

I had taught other students, but Joseph challenged me most. A good teacher has to learn in order to teach. Thus, I had to expose my own pain to teach Joseph. I took a deep breath and looked inward.

Even though I had stared down this corridor of my past time and time again, it took me a moment to center. I told him, "When I was your age, I felt full of power and possibility, drunk on creation and knowledge." I paused and added, "And I was so stupid I forgot to be frightened."

His eyes widened, but he said nothing.

Good. "Did you know that I am frightened now?"

He shook his head, but only slightly.

"Anyone with the power we have must be afraid. Power must respect power. It takes control to keep a moral center when you have power." Another deep breath, another moment.

Joseph remained silent.

I spoke softly. "You and I may go to war. Flying a space ship into battle is a truly great power."

Joseph turned his face away, following a yellow light-link butterfly as it landed on a purple coneflower. The small muscles in his jaw twitched. He wanted to go to war as badly as I was trying to keep us from it. Had I taught him enough yet to know he must mistrust his own desires?

I looked down at my hands, flexed them, thinking of what I had done. "I have never told this story to anyone. I have told it to myself, to remember, but I have never told it to anyone else.

"I was an employee at the Port Authority. These are not my favorite people. You might remember I was consulting for them the day we met."

The corners of his mouth turned up, although he still focused on the butterfly.

"When I was your age, the Authority was the only place that hired solo Wind Readers. So my choices were to go into an affinity group and become part of something bigger, or to run my own life and sell my skills. I chose freedom, of course. I did not like my employer at all, but I told myself that it was okay to work for them if doing so let me live by myself."

He needed the history. "The Authority started me out reading the data of ships after they landed, matching computer systems to cargo lists to search for cheats. At first, I was amazed that people tried to steal from us given what we can do, but then I learned they don't believe we are as strong as we are. Some do, and those people do not cheat us. After I became good at finding thieves, the Authority assigned me to a space station to do the same thing. It was far harder to read the data of moving ships, and the stakes were higher. The stations caught the worst crimes: the mercenaries hired to assassinate a rival, the smugglers of dangerous or unregistered human upgrades, the slavers after black market sex mods."

He was interested. I could see it in how still he sat.

"Sometimes Wind Readers who worked the stations died protecting Silver's Home and its trade goods." I refrained from saying anything about my home planet's tendency to create modified humans and then turn a blind eye when they were sold as slaves. Joseph and I had covered this ground, and so he knew how much and why I hated the commercial decisions that made Silver's Home rich.

Unsettled, I picked my own butterfly to watch, a sliver-blue, and fell into its data for a breath or two, feeling the wind on its wings and the soft touch of its tiny feet as it landed on a variegated leaf.

Joseph stood and stretched, and only then did I realize how long a break I had allowed in my story. I blinked, thinking *You have more control than this! Stop avoiding.* I met his eyes, caught them, tried to tell him with my look that this was important.

He nodded.

"I was on Killery's Station. I was the strongest Wind Reader there, even then, although not everyone knew it. But my boss at the Authority, Jint, knew. She didn't like me much, nor I her, but she used me for the hardest work. Killery's was small. Cargo ships came up and dropped cargo, and traders picked it up. Sometimes meetings were held there. Secrets were shared, legally and illegally. I suspected they were sometimes shared illegally with the Authority's blessing. The bastards."

Joseph sat back down and went still again, focused on listening as I continued my story.

✦ ✦ ✦

Ships seldom stayed long at Killery's, and the Port Authority staff there was slim. Jint, me, a small and old Wind Reader named Giant, a slender female Wind Reader named Sol who had once been in a class with me, and three grunt soldiers who inspected ships unless they had certain clearances. Which was, really, what we Wind Readers did as well. Jint was no Wind Reader, but she wanted a promotion and so she ran a tight operation. We showed up dressed for duty and shared the day out across shifts, one soldier and one Wind Reader at a time. We had caught three thieves in the last week, a smuggler, and a crazy lone pilot on a small ship who wanted to commit suicide by ramming the station.

A typical week's work.

So when Jint physically shook me out of a sound sleep one morning, I woke quickly.

She was tall, gaunt, and all business. Her usually pretty face was marred by concern that morning, and her voice clipped as she said, "Be ready in five minutes." She slid through the door to wait as I dressed and slapped cold water on my face. No greeting, no acknowledgment that she was pulling me in off-shift.

Ten minutes later, we had clambered up a long hollow tube with handholds into a room I hadn't even known existed. The swivel chairs in the middle gave us access to a view in all directions, as if were in the center of a clear bubble completely exposed to everything around the station. Above, I saw stars. Below, the rotating ball of Silver's Home. Between the station and the planet, low-orbit traffic zipped above the planet's jeweled blue seas and carefully engineered land masses.

An arrow pointed at a ship coming toward us.

Jint spoke, her words still clipped. "That's the *High Flight*. They're pretending to be traders looking to buy mods. Standard things, like extra arms and fingernail knives. But three of the people and one of the computers onboard triggered alarms, and it looks like they're really looking to provide us with designs that they compromised."

"Hackers?" I mused. "So what do you think they really want?"

"That's what I'm hoping you can tell me."

I settled back and watched them coming in. "Do they know we're looking?"

Jint crossed her arms over her chest. "Of course." Her eyes were a cool green and her pale skin smooth as ice. She had augmented hearing, which was handy for a boss. While I was sure she also had other mods, that was the only one she told us about. "Be careful," she said.

I lay back, letting myself sink into the Killery's communication systems. They were weaker than what we have now, but I had been there a few months, which was long enough to meld easily into the data. For me, that has always felt like slipping free of the skin of my body as data sings to me. I let myself feel the station and touch each of the docked ships before reaching far enough to link to the incoming ship which Jint had pointed out to me.

Initial entry was easy—all ships must have open data to all stations. The next layer was also easy, and it held, I found, the list of things the crew had come for. Everyone on the ship wanted a mod. That was not particularly unusual.

I studied the crew.

None of the four had been here before. They came from Paradise, which was not usual, and didn't really fit. But they were all young, and perhaps they didn't like Paradise's open freedom and wanted some of their own secrets. I poked around a bit, learning more. Two were dating, and had been long before they boarded the ship two years ago. Julia and Timo. They left each other little love letters in various communications. Another, Nick, wanted to be a mercenary but didn't have a single crime or fight in his background. The fourth *was* a mercenary. Flow. Hardly the name I would associate with a merc. She was probably the cause of whatever evil the ship was up to. I made a mental note to see if I could find the money stream that funded her and follow it. Then I went back to the ship's data, looking into the cargo hold.

The data had locked doors.

Also usual.

The *High Flight*'s AI was a new model. It took me twenty minutes to overwhelm it. This had to be done carefully, of course. If I damaged the ship, the Authority would have to prove criminal intent or pay to repair the damage.

The first door hid a money trail which showed Flow was being paid by an entertainment company from Islas. Maybe Jint knew something I didn't. I streamed the data into the station's systems so that Jint could see it. After it had all arrived, I slipped partway out of the data streams, back into my body. I lifted my head long enough to tell her about the data and to add, "It makes no sense. Also, it's too thin. Can you find out if it's a lie?"

And then I was down again, knocking on other doors. The third one contained the compromised designs Jint had mentioned.

How did she know they were there?

A force slammed into me. Something in the data, a countermeasure that had seen me, or which I had triggered. My data-self was streams of light, and in that instant, darkness and chaos dissolved the threads of data around me and the edges of my own self until I floated free, shuddering a little.

Lights and colors ran through my thoughts, stuttering interruptions with their own attraction.

Another wave of chaos washed over me. I tried to move my physical fingers but I couldn't make them budge. I repeated my name over and over while the chaos worked to shred my identity.

I fought. *Marcus. Marcus. Marcus. I am Marcus.*

The force took a part of me and I held onto the word. *Marcus.* Even though I barely knew what the word meant anymore, I knew I had to say it. Had to. *Marcus. I am.*

Patterns swirled around and through me. Diffuse. Bright. I started to put words about them between the other word. *Marcus. Balloon. Marcus. Orange river. Marcus. A crosshatch of numbers. Marcus? Marcus.*

It felt like a cloud at the mercy of winds going in many directions at once. *Blue river picking green trees red sky. Marcus. A mountain of information to pass on to... Marcus. Marcus.* My voice sped up as the memory became more visceral. *Marcus. I am blue. Blue trees in sunlight. Marcus. The station One Freedom passes over Lake Picta...*

◆ ◆ ◆

Beside me, Joseph gasped.

I opened my eyes. I hadn't realized that I'd closed them, or that I was breathing hard.

Joseph watched me intently, his eyes narrowed, two fingers over his lips. He spoke so low it was almost a whisper. "You scared me."

"It's hard to re-live that part."

"Do you think it was like when I first touched the data streams here?"

"Well—the data streams here overwhelmed you, but they didn't care about you. This... this was an attack on me. I almost lost myself."

◆ ◆ ◆

There was so much distance between the ship and the station. If I had stopped saying my name, I might have lost myself. I remember what I thought and said then, and saying it again makes me feel what I felt then, and I was frightened. I remembered my name was Marcus and Marcus was me as I suddenly found myself spitting the word onto the floor along with my breakfast in long wracking coughs. My cheek hurt like hell, and as soon as I stopped retching I put a hand up and touched the bruised place.

Jint liked no one, but in that moment she sounded like she'd just found her best friend. "So glad you're back. So glad. Are you okay?"

"Did you have to hit me so hard?"

Her eyes were wide with exertion. "So many *times*. Twenty times, maybe more. I thought I might break your neck. *You wouldn't come back.*"

I'd never seen her lose her composure. The shock of it drove the last muddled bits of the chaos bomb from my brain. It sharpened my focus so that I remembered wondering how she knew as much as she did. "Who didn't?"

"Sol."

I lay, stomach heaving, thinking. I hadn't seen Sol since yesterday. "What happened to Sol?"

"I couldn't get her back."

A cold anger settled over me, shared equally between Jint and whoever was in that ship. "Where is she?"

She pursed her lips and stared at me. "Sol stopped breathing after an hour in here. She went still like you, then she faded and then gasped and then…" Her voice trailed to a whisper. "Her body is in the morgue."

I felt colder than Jint had ever looked. "That's how you knew about the bad designs?"

She brushed the hair from her face.

Now my anger was all at her. "And you didn't tell me?"

"You're much stronger."

The visuals had been turned off, so it felt as if Jint and I were alone in a place darker than space except for a single light that shone on both of us from above, throwing our shadows in thick pools on the floor. I watched the two shadows for a long time, gaining control before I said, "You might have killed me."

She had been leaning in close, but now she sat back, the momentary flash of humanity when she looked happy I was alive utterly gone. "That happens to Wind Readers."

Bitch. I didn't dare say it. I couldn't just walk out either. I had a contract with the Authority, and if I walked, they could throw me in jail. Back then, I didn't have the kind of power it takes to keep petty tyrants from exerting control. Still, I wasn't finished with her. "If you had told me, I could have been prepared."

"I did tell you to be careful."

I swallowed about five separate emotions, took a deep breath, and asked, "What do you know about that thing? That attack?"

"Nothing. I don't even know what happened. Not to Sol. Not to you."

And of course, she didn't. But still she had known something in that experience killed Wind Readers. She had come to me, who was at least twice as strong as Sol, but then she had treated me as expendable. *Damn her.* "I want to see the *High Flight*. Get closer."

"How will that help?"

"It'll be safer, for one thing. There won't be as much latency between me and my body. And it helps to have a visual. An anchoring point."

She stared at me for a long time, and then nodded ever so slightly. She must have sent a command, and since she wasn't like me, it wasn't with her mind. Even though I couldn't tell exactly what she did, we were both surrounded by stars and starships. "Are they docking here?"

"Yes." The word sounded reluctant, and she added, "Unless you have enough information for me to stop them."

Killing Sol wouldn't be enough. Wind Readers go stark raving mad far too often, and we're known for killing ourselves. "How long?"

"They've already decelerated and started to approach. It will take them an hour or so to be in range. We can delay them with extra docking processes."

An idea clicked into place. "Can you slow them down enough for me to get on a repair skiff? I want to be physically closer."

She pursed her lips. "Who is going to slap you awake if this happens again?"

"You are."

She stared at me for a long time, her face still as a statue. But then she issued the appropriate orders and led me to the suiting room.

My suit slid on like a thin layer of oily skin. Thin threads of data receptors ran throughout it like a grid.

Repair ships had sharp little AIs that were designed to handle a variety of communications protocols and always kept current with the most recent hacking shields. They were nimble, strong, and not particularly beautiful. This one looked like a square and a circle got stuck in the middle of a mating dance, with eight arms that could reach in every possible direction, a tug loop, and three or four styles of docking mechanism.

Jint and I would be physically vulnerable compared to the far larger *High Flight*, and I could count on Jint's self-interest to protect me.

As I fastened my suit gloves closed at the wrist, I queried the little ship for information about the chaos bomb. There was no way to stop it, but someone had uploaded a warning program a week ago and someone else had sent in a possible shield. The ship and its AI were named *OneFix*, after a popular cartoon robot I had loved as a child. It dragged a smile out of me. Child-me would have adored this job that frightened me.

Jint drove. She didn't go straight for the *High Flight*, but a little off to the side, hoping to avoid being noticed.

Once I hooked into the *OneFix* and ran diagnostics, I sipped some nutriwater and allowed myself a moment to relax and collect my strength.

The clearer my head got, the more I hated what had happened to Sol and what might have happened to me. When I had almost died back in that observation room, it had been a pleasant trip, a honeyed and soft dissembling. Perhaps crazy Wind Readers lost their souls like that, in an act of simple and sweet diffusion.

I repeated my name three times. *Marcus. Marcus. Marcus.*

High Flight almost certainly had a Wind Reader. With luck it wasn't the mercenary. The ship had less-powerful systems than the station, but they were well suited to my purpose, designed to interact with the *High Flight's* navigation and inventory systems. It was, in fact, lightly connected to every ship in straight visual distance to it. As long as the crew of the *High Flight* wasn't worried about routine station operations, we would be as good as invisible to them.

I allowed myself another sip of nutrition, straightened my spine, and began talking to *OneFix*. For a limited form of AI, it was downright conversational, and I was soon as big as the small ship and then as big as the bubble of space its sensors could feel or see or read. The *High Flight* was easily inside this bubble even though the two ships were kilometers apart from each other.

I hesitated at the edge at the door of the *High Flight's* data streams. I imagined Jint's eyes on me. I couldn't verify, but I was certain she was watching to see if I flinched. I ignored the feeling of being watched and measured, and slid carefully through the data handshake between the two ships.

And immediately hit a wall.

The neatly laid-out data streams I'd encountered on my first trip into the ship's systems were twisted and broken. This was all a symbolism in my head, and maybe other Wind Readers would have seen it differently, but the ship's data looked like a magic wand had turned it into broken worms, writhing to find their other parts.

Marcus. Marcus. Marcus.

I dove in, going deeper, staying fast.

I quickly reached the area where the chaos bomb had detonated. It didn't feel at all like it had before. My new warning programs alerted but didn't alarm. This was aftermath, not action. Since it had to be localized or the *High Flight* would be crippled, I slid down the fastest and most regular threads of data I could find, which were the pulsing readouts of the ship's engines as it slowed to approach Killery's.

Time passed.

Even as fast as it felt like I moved, it took time before the chaos lessened. Diagnostic programs poked at the loose strands of data that I had passed through, visibly and carefully detangling and repairing broken threads. Good. Maybe that was the Wind Reader and not the AI, and maybe they'd remain distracted. In any case, I was willing to bet they couldn't take more damage.

I found the access to the audio feeds, which were far too slow for me to hear in real-time in this place, in this form. I patched them through to *OneFix* and then followed them back the other way to the stored audio that represented the time I'd been lost in here. I took playback at a fast enough speed to make out the words.

The intimacy of raised voices felt like a slap.

A woman: "I didn't come here for this!"

Another woman: "No one will know that. Now shut up and help me. Get in there."

So that was the mercenary. And she wasn't the Wind Reader. So Julia?

A man's voice. "She will not destroy an entire planet."

The mercenary. Flow. "She will."

The flat certainty in the voice made me slow a second, assessing. Silver's Home had fabulous defenses. And I was one of them.

The conversation fell to a quiet argument that I logged as I sent it through to *OneFix* as well. I returned to searching for whatever weapon they had brought with them. Something like the chaos bomb? If it could get through our defenses, we could be damaged. But utterly destroyed? They surely weren't underestimating us that far. Still, I raked through databases as fast as I could, running diagnostics to look for anomalies, weaknesses, hidden codes. Their encryption was good, but oddly not great.

Was Flow bluffing? Maybe just naïve?

The recordings I'd sent to Jint would surely be enough to justify turning the ship away, but would that be enough to mitigate any damage they might do? Killery's Station was in low planetary orbit, and it was possible to drop probes into our atmosphere from here. Or bombs.

I slowed down and pulled a small part of myself just free of the *High Flight*'s data to check in with Jint. "They think they're going to destroy us."

"Do you know who sent them?"

"No."

"Find out."

"I'm trying. Have you listened to what I sent you?" It felt thin to be up this far, a little dangerous.

"Some. I heard the word 'immunity.' Does that help?"

"Maybe." I struggled to maintain the dual awareness it took to speak with her and hold my place deep in the other ship.

"Hurry."

I slipped silently away from her.

Now that I knew the Wind Reader wasn't the mercenary, I started looking for her. Following the diagnostics back yielded nothing. They led straight to the ship's AI.

I finally found Julia's electronic signature at the edge of the chaos, doing absolutely nothing but watching it.

If she had planted the chaos, I had to imagine it couldn't touch her. I came near her and waited, letting her find me. Eventually, I got a startled and quick *Oh!*

I didn't want to upset her more, so I asked her a question. *What are you watching?*

The unravelling.

I chose to call it a chaos bomb. I've read about them. You sent it after me.

She made me.

She?

Flow. Flowering Damage.

I grunted at the pretentious name. Full of herself. *Why? Why did she want to bomb me out of the ship?*

She was hired to destroy Silver's Home.

I made myself stop to asses Julia, to see if I could tell if she was bluffing or lying or just confused. Or if she was telling me what she believed. She felt sad. Nothing extreme such as depression or anger or even fear. Simply sad. *Who hired her?*

Someone. I don't know who. I've been trying to find out.

Diagnostics swarmed around us, fixing the data. Threads connected and stopped swirling and wriggling in front me. Every Wind Reader has their own imagined view of the data, their own constructs that help them make sense of the flood of information. I wondered how Julia saw the chaos.

Did you design the unravelling?

No. But I set it free. I could have killed you.

Do you wish you had?

I wish I had never come here.

I believed her. Here, in the raw nakedness of data, lies were almost impossible to hide. Julia was in a trap. I could feel it in her sadness, in her timidity. She was a strong young Wind Reader, and she should be studying and practicing, not caught inside a mercenary ship. I dipped into the personnel records to double-check her age. Twenty. Only a few years younger than me.

I reminded myself that she was a danger and not a friend. *You know we won't be able to let you dock. Not unless you can give up Flow, give us enough information to lock her up.* I didn't know what I could extract from Jint as a promise. So I made none. If Julia docked, we'd probably arrest her afterwards. The Authority had little compassion.

You can't allow us on the station. Nor near it.

You won't give Flowering Damage up?

There is a virus on the ship.

We can cleanse your systems.

Not that kind. If any of us touch any of you, you will all die.

That ineffable, deep, slow sadness still resonated from her. I wished I could see her physical face, could find a way to comfort her. I did not reply for a long moment.

Perhaps she sensed my disbelief, since she filled the space between us with details. Whoever hired Flow had engineered a virulent nanovirus and its antidote. The crew had been given the virus and the antidote, but they had no copies of either. It had tasted like sour milk.

Everything is data, I reminded her. *Everything. Give me the data for these things and we will make ourselves safe.*

I do not have it to give. I didn't know about. Neither of us did. Not until a day ago.

Again, I paused. She was a Wind Reader. So was I. *Can we get it?*

It's in a data box. I'm locked out of it.

Do you believe it is a true story? That she can kill everyone on the station?

I do. Maybe more. Maybe the whole planet.

I kept my energy as soft as I could. *What would you suggest?*

I will not cause genocide. So I was going to take the engines over. But I cannot.

Why not?

I am not strong enough.

But I was. Most of the hour had passed. The ship must be getting close to the station. We'd have to turn it quickly. *Can I get you out of here?*

I would kill you if you did.

Her sadness infected my heart. My body was on another ship, and I could slide back into it at the last moment. But she lived here, and she was infected. I did not approve of much about Silver's Home, but I still loved my planet and my people, and there were millions of innocents there. *Tell me again who did this?*

I don't know. Flow was hired on Islas, but the Islan government would not do anything this clumsy.

I was not so sure of that. Islas hated us for many of the same reasons I sometimes hated us. They believed we messed with life itself when we created and marketed human mods. Which of course we did.

Time was not stopping. I asked her the hardest question I had ever had to ask anyone other than myself. *Are you sure?*

Yes.

A simple answer. One I could not doubt that she believed.

Do you want a moment to tell Timo you love him?

He knows. Hurry!

So together we turned the engines into a bomb and sent the ship out of the system. It was not mechanically hard to do. It didn't take long. But it speared my heart, and the moment of separation from Julia thrust the pain deeper. It must have shown on my face as I slipped back into my body.

Jint glanced at me. "Are you okay?"

"They were going to destroy us. But now they can't."

"How?"

I felt dry inside, worn out and heartsore. "I'll tell you when we get back. For now, let me just watch."

To my surprise, she had enough humanity to hold her tongue.

The *High Fight* changed direction.

I sipped at my suit water and tried to feel… anything. Anything but sadness.

Just before it got too small to see, the ship carrying Julia and Timo and two evil people came apart, unravelling like the trap they had set for me. I whispered "Thank you" to Julia, who would never be able to hear me.

✦ ✦ ✦

As I finished the story, my heart felt almost as heavy as it had on that day. My eyes were closed, and my voice sounded hoarse. "That was years ago, and even today, I still feel it. I will always feel it. Was there really a killer virus on board? I was never able to learn.

"It is no small thing to protect your way of life, your planet, your world. But sometimes I wake in the middle of the night, trying to think of any way I could have saved Julia and Timo." The sweet smell of blooming flowers pulled my eyes open.

Joseph was looking away from me, toward the flowers, a tear track on one cheek. "I did something like that. Out of anger. They were all mercenaries, but they didn't deserve to be flung to their deaths."

He could do that? I shuddered and bit back an exclamation. But that was not the moment to ask him about flinging ships. I would do that later. For now, I needed him to feel whatever he had felt when he sent that ship full of mercenaries to their death. And what he felt right after.

He ran his fingers through his hair. "I was so angry. Furious. They murdered people I loved and they wanted to kill the others, too, but I couldn't let them." Words fell out of him, quick little words that had been trying to get out for a long time. "They didn't have a chance. They knew it was me, I felt them know, I felt them be afraid. And I felt them die. And it felt good. I made a thing they deserved happen to them. That's what it felt like when I did it. I had all the data flows, the ships, the town, the people. I had it all. And I used it in anger."

I whispered, "Anger is dangerous in the very powerful. I can show you how to mitigate it."

"Until afterwards. Then, then I was scared."

I wanted to comfort him, but I help back, whispering, "I know."

"I want my anger," he said. "There's so much to be angry about. But that day, it scared me."

That was an odd answer, but it felt honest. I could live with that. I stared out over the precise and colorful garden, then glanced into the bright blue sky, too hot and clear right now for any fliers to practice in. It must have taken me longer to tell my story than I'd planned. "The work you and I are doing together here could stop the war. But there's a good chance it won't. If we fight, it will be important to remember that each time you have to kill, you will build a memory like my memory of Julia or yours of the mercenaries. Do you think that will help you be less angry?"

He nodded and swiped at his eyes and said, "I will always be afraid."

"Of yourself?"

"Aren't you afraid of your own power?" he countered.

"Always."

His story told me I needed to help him with his anger. Which forced me to look at my own. He and I spent a lot of time on anger.

What happens in this war we are headed toward will tell me whether or not I succeeded. For all of our sakes, I hope that I did. No matter what, remember that Joseph feels remorse about his first kill, and that I do.

Have pity.

Alan Dean Foster's fame as a novelist is often tied to his skillful novelizations and media tie-ins for properties like Star Wars, Alien Nation, Star Trek, Alien, and more, but he is also the author of many original novels and short stories, including a popular space opera series about Flinx, a young man dragged against his will into events that threaten the survival of the galaxy, and Pip, a flying, emphatic snake, his constant companion. Set in Foster's Humanx Commonwealth, an interstellar ethical/political union of species that includes humans and the insectoid thranx, the stories and novels of this series detail the pair's various adventures.

His story for us, first published in Foster's 2002 collection Impossible Places, *is a standalone tale wherein Flinx takes a long-needed vacation back to his home planet, which doesn't turn out anywhere near relaxing.*

SIDESHOW
A PIP AND FLINX STORY

ALAN DEAN FOSTER

You never know what you'll see on a side street in Drallar.

From time to time, Flinx felt the pull of the only home he'd ever known. So, in the course of his wanderings, he would return now and again to the winged planet of Moth, and to the simple dwelling still occupied by the irascible old woman he, and everyone else, called Mother Mastiff.

It was good to roam the backstreets and alleys of the hodgepodge of a city, taking in sights both new and familiar; inhaling the amalgamating aromas of a hundred worlds; observing the free-floating, arguing, laughing, chattering farrago of humans, thranx, and other citizens of the Commonwealth. Here he had no responsibilities. Here his only concern was relaxation. Here he could mix freely without constantly having to look over his shoulder to see if he was being followed. Here he could—

Without warning, Pip, his Alaspinian minidrag, promptly uncoiled herself from his shoulder, launched herself into the fragrant, damp air, and took off down a minor side avenue crammed with vendors and street merchants. Fortunately, he reflected bemusedly as he took off after her, she flew high enough to avoid precipitating a panic. Among those strollers and vendors who did see her, few were knowledgeable enough to identify her and recognize her lethal capabilities.

She landed on a diffusion grating the size of a dinner plate that projected from the crest of a three-story building. As soon as he slowed, staring up at her, she launched herself into the air and glided back down to settle once more on his shoulder, her petite but powerful coils securing herself to him.

"Now, what was that all about?" he murmured soothingly to her. "What set you off? I'll bet it was a smell, wasn't it? Some kind of exotic food full of especially attractive trace minerals?" The only problem with this theory was that the nearest food stall lay two blocks distant. No vendors of unusual victuals were open nearby.

What *was* close at hand was a performance by one of Drallar's innumerable, alien, untaxed, and probably illegal street performers. The human was short, florid of face, glistening of scalp, and thick of arm, leg, and middle. His black sideburns fronted his ears and threatened to overwhelm his jawline. His trained subordinate was decidedly nonhuman, not quite as tall, considerably slimmer, and clad in an elegant coat of soft white fur marked with bright blue stripes and splotches. Its eyes were elongated and yellow, with dark blue vertical pupils. Dressed in short pants and matching vest of garish green and gold silk, with flower-studded beret and oversized necktie for emphasis, the alien was performing a simple yet lively dance routine to the accompaniment of music that poured from its master's quinube player. Almost lost among the fur and silks was the control band, no thicker than a piece of string, that fit tightly around its neck.

Watching the performance, Flinx let his peculiar talent expand to encompass the appreciative crowd, not all of whom were human. The expected emotions were all there: amusement, low-grade wonder, expectation, curiosity. With growing maturity, he had developed the ability to focus his abilities on selected individuals. Probing the musician-master, he sensed approval and contentment, but also an underlying, simmering anger.

Well, the personal emotional problems of the player-owner were no more his concern or responsibility than were those of the hundreds of intelligent beings whose feelings he had sampled since awakening in Mother Mastiff's home early this morning. After watching the performance for another couple of minutes, mildly admiring the owner's skill with the quinube and his creature's agile, three-toed feet, he turned to leave.

Immediately, Pip rose from his shoulder and hovered. Spectators who had ignored the minidrag's colorful presence on Flinx's shoulder now found themselves drawn to the deep-throated whirring of the flying snake's wings. More instinctively wary than educated about the minidrag's potential, a few moved aside to give her more air space in which to hover.

"Now what?" An irritated Flinx extended his left arm. When he moved toward her, the obstinate flying snake continued to refuse the proffered perch. "I don't have time for this, Pip!" Actually, he had nothing but time. Not that his assertion mattered, since the minidrag comprehended only his emotions, not his words.

He eventually raised the level of the former to the point where she finally settled, albeit with evident reluctance, onto his forearm. As soon as she had curled herself securely around it, he began stroking her. When she tried to rise again into the air, he held her firmly in place, his right hand keeping her membranous wings collapsed firmly against the sides of her body. Anyone else presuming to physically restrain the minidrag's movements would have found themselves with maybe a minute to live, a victim of Pip's incredibly toxic and corrosive venom. Despite her obvious desire to spread her pleated wings again, she would no more harm Flinx than she would one of her own offspring. While she continued to twist and wriggle in an attempt to get free of his grasp, she did not bite, or worse.

They were nearly back to Mother Mastiff's place before she finally relaxed enough to where he felt safe in removing his restraining fingers. Instead of attempting to fly off, she slithered up his arm to curl comfortably around his neck, as if nothing unusual had happened. Shaking his head as he tried to figure out what had gotten into her, he entered the humble dwelling.

It was far less humble within. His travels and adventures had allowed Flinx, during a previous visit to Drallar, to cause the home to be furnished far more lavishly than it appeared from outside. Given a choice, he would have moved Mother Mastiff to another, better section of the city entirely. Upon listening to his proposal, the old woman's reaction had been wholly in keeping with her peppery, independent self.

"And what be a 'better' section of the city, boy? Fancier streets— with no character? Bigger houses—that ain't homes? Folks with money—and no soul? No thankee. I'll stay here, and happily so, where I've stayed all these many years." Wizened eyes that could still see clearly had met his own without wavering. "Was once good enough for you, boy, when I bought you. But—" She hesitated. "—I *could* use a new cooker."

He'd bought that for her, and much else. Tucked in between two larger, newer structures, her home now boasted the latest in household conveniences, as well as a self-adjusting, transparent privacy ceiling through which she could admire the stars and the sweep of part of Moth's famous broken rings.

She wasn't at home when he arrived. Though it was growing late, he didn't worry about her. A small smile curved his lips. Old she might be, but he pitied anyone who accosted her on the streets. Expecting an easy mark, they would find themselves confronted with an explosive bundle of experience and harsh words—not to mention a lightweight but lethal assortment of concealed weaponry. Mother Mastiff had not survived the mean streets of Drallar for so long by wandering about unprepared to deal with whatever they might happen to throw her way.

Probably visiting Mockle Wynn, he mused, or the Twegsay twins. She knew half the population of this district, and they her. He'd see her again tomorrow.

After checking in with his ship, the *Teacher*, he prepared supper for himself and Pip. The minidrag had seemingly returned to normal. She ate quietly, evincing no interest in abruptly flying through the door in search of attractions unknown. Afterward, he relaxed in front of the tridee he'd bought for Mother Mastiff, finishing off the evening with a reading of a portion of the new thranx research report on Cantarian hivenoids, before retiring to the small bedroom that was kept ready for him whenever he might choose to visit. Lying on his back on the lightly scented aerogel bed, staring up at the starfield through the tough but transparent ceiling, he wondered which of the flickering lights in the night sky he ought to visit next. Wondered which might be the more interesting, or possibly hold a clue to the mysteries that were himself.

He had just fallen asleep when he felt Pip stirring against his bare shoulder. Almost instantly, his eyes were open and he was fully alert, having developed the ability early in his childhood to awaken to full awareness on a moment's notice. Extending himself, he sensed nothing. Similarly, Pip remained on the bed. Had either of them been in any imminent danger, she would have spread her wings and risen ceilingward, assuming a defensive posture.

Even so, there was obviously something in the room with them.

As quietly and slowly as possible, he rose to a sitting position. His nakedness did not trouble him. Clothes were for the insecure, shirt and pants hardly weapons in any case. His manner of fighting did not require that he be clothed according to community standards.

The figure that crossed from the now open window toward the door that led to the rest of the house was bipedal and short of stature. Therein the similarity to anything human ended. Reaching toward the bed's headboard, Flinx waved his open palm in the direction of a sensor. Instantly, the bedroom was flooded with soft, subdued light. The responsive, sensitive ceiling opaqued accordingly.

Startled by the unexpected burst of illumination, the trespasser threw up both aims to shield its eyes. Its small mouth opened, but no sound came out. As the long, vertical pupils contracted against the light, Flinx recognized the intruder.

It was the white-and-blue-furred performing animal he had seen earlier in the day.

As naked human and equally unclad intruder eyed one another uncertainly, Pip rose into the air and flew toward it. The elongated, vaguely sorrowful eyes tracked the minidrag's path. Whether out of ignorance or familiarity, the creature showed no fear as Pip glided in its direction. Nor did it panic when the deadly flying snake landed on its shoulder. Quite the contrary. Reaching up, it began to gently stroke the minidrag with the three long, flexible furred fingers of one hand. Flinx tensed as physical contact was initiated. Highly protective of both her human and her wings, Pip rarely allowed herself to be touched by others.

Yet now, instead of reacting aggressively, she completely relaxed, as if she'd settled into the comforting grasp of an old friend.

And still, Flinx felt nothing. As Flinx sat on the side of the bed, it didn't take long to postulate that something about this creature had drawn Pip's uncharacteristically single-minded attention earlier in the day. Was it an empath, an empathetic telepath, like himself and the minidrag? But if that was the case, then why couldn't he feel the slightest emotional emanation from the voiceless nocturnal visitor? By letting his talent range in the direction of nearby apartments and other buildings, he knew that his often erratic ability was functioning. But from the intruder, he sensed nothing. Yet there was palpably something at work here. What was he overlooking?

Certainly not the crash and fracturing that came from the front door, as three figures burst into the house. They headed straight for the bedroom, as if they had a map. A glance in the direction of the alien dancer's now softly phosphorescent control necklace explained why they didn't need one.

Two of the intruders were big, burly, and as sour of expression as the emotions they openly projected. Standing between them and holding a weapon of his own was the alien's owner. His emotions were darker still. While he did not quite transude murder, the potential underlined the rest of his clearly projected feelings.

Taking his time, Flinx slipped on a pair of pants. Pip was airborne. Interestingly, she hovered not close to him, but above the furry alien visitor. The latter, Flinx noted with interest, had pressed itself into a corner of the small room. Though its eyes were alien and unreadable, there was no mistaking the energy and effort it was expending to keep as far away from the three uninvited visitors as possible. For his part, the emotions its owner projected in its direction were utterly devoid of anything resembling affection.

"Pretty clever of you, kid." Though Flinx was now two and twenty years and stood taller than average, he still had the face of a youngster. "I remember you from the afternoon show earlier today. Thought you could get away with this, eh, *blaflek*?"

Focusing his attention on the trio of weapons at hand, Flinx casually slipped into a shirt, careful to make no sudden moves as he did so. "Get away with what?"

"Stealing my Aslet monkey. You're not the first *blaflek* to try. You won't be the first to succeed."

So that's what the creature was called. From his voracious research, Flinx knew what a monkey was: a kind of primitive Terran primate. The creature cowering silently in the corner of his bedroom didn't look much like a monkey to him. He had never heard of Aslet.

He had, however, heard of similar scams. Raised on the streets of Drallar, he had encountered numerous schemes and swindles, and in his youth had even participated in a few.

"I didn't steal him," he replied calmly as he pulled his shirt down over his head. "He showed up here on his own." He nodded in the direction of the open window. "Let himself in pretty quietly. His fingers must be as nimble as his feet, even if he is short a few. Knows his way around basic security systems, too." He eyed the man evenly. "I wonder how and where he learned how to bypass those?"

Smiling grimly, the owner shook his head. "Nice try, kid, but it won't wash. You're a thief, and we're turning you over to the police."

So that was how it worked, Flinx realized. Send the Aslet into somebody's home, preferably someone who had been in the audience for one of the creature's earlier performances. That would establish a connection and provide witnesses. Then claim it had been stolen, and threaten to have the "thief" arrested. Unless, no doubt, some sort of accommodation could be reached that would avoid the need to involve the authorities. Even as they stood there confronting one another, the owner and his goons probably had a bought cop or two awaiting their possible arrival down at the nearest police office. Simple and clean. No doubt most confused, challenged victims paid up rather than risk the possibility of spending time in a correction institute, or the indignity of being exposed in a court trial.

"If you had a legitimate claim about a theft, you would have brought the police along with you, instead of these two." He indicated the pair who flanked the owner.

The shorter man grinned. "You're a clever little snot, aren't you? So you've figured it out."

Flinx smiled faintly. "I live offplanet now, but I grew up here."

The owner gestured with his weapon. "Doesn't matter. My friends down at the patrol office will listen to me, not you. Of course, such unpleasantness can easily be avoided."

"I wonder how?" Flinx was much more curious about something else. It would have to wait. "Why pick on me?" He indicated his surroundings. "Neither my mother, whose home this is, nor myself are particularly well off. Why make targets out of us?"

"I don't pick 'em," the owner grunted. Turning, he pointed toward the creature huddling in the corner. "He does." The man squinted at his surroundings. "I agree with you, though. This isn't one of his better choices."

Flinx frowned. "The Aslet chooses the mark? How—at random?"

The owner shrugged. "Beats me. When I'm in the mood and have the time to do a little business, I just let him loose. After he's had time to make his way across part of the city, my associates and I track him down." Meaningfully, he ran a finger around his neck. "Transmitter is easy to follow." Reaching into a pocket, he pulled out a tiny device and aimed it in the Anslet's general direction. "He doesn't like me much, but that collar makes him do as he's told."

"I don't like you much, either," Flinx declared quietly.

The owner was not offended. "You'll do as you're told, too. I'm not a greedy person. A thousand credits will get all of us out of here, including the monkey, and you'll never see any of us ever again." His smile returned. "Unless you decide to catch another performance, that is."

"No," Flinx told him.

"No?" The man's smile vanished. "No what?"

"No money," Flinx replied. "No credits. Not a thousand. Not a fraction thereof. Get out of my mother's house."

The two men flanking the owner stirred slightly. The owner sighed.

"Look, kid, if there's no available credit, you can pay us in goods. I saw plenty of valuable stuff when we came in." He shrugged indifferently. "Or we can shoot you, take what we want, and if anyone investigates, claim that you attacked us when I tried to reclaim my property."

In response to Flinx's rising level of upset and concern, Pip began to dart back and forth against the roof like a giant moth, the equivalent of pacing nervously in midair. Curious, the player-owner looked up in her direction.

"What is that thing, anyway?"

"That," Flinx murmured, enlightening both the speaker and his two accomplices, "is an Alaspinian minidrag. You don't want to make her any madder than she already is now."

"Why not?" The owner smiled. "Is it going to bite me?" The muzzle of his pistol came up.

"No," Flinx told him. "She doesn't have to."

The owner nodded. Turning to the man on his left, he uttered a single brusque command. "Kill it."

Sensing the man's intent by reading the homicidal emotion that rose suddenly and sharply within him, Pip darted forward and spat. Striking the would-be killer in his right eye, the gob of corrosive poison ate immediately into the soft ocular jelly and entered his bloodstream, the incredibly powerful neurotoxin proceeding to instantly paralyze every muscle it encountered. When it reached his heart and stopped that, the man collapsed.

His single shot went wild, blowing a hole in the roof and showering the room with shards of photosensitive gengineered silicate. Rising above the noise, the now panicked shouts of the owner and his surviving associate echoed through the room.

From a drawer in the bed's headboard, Flinx pulled the small pistol he always carried with him in places like Drallar. Unfortunately for the intruders, he did not have time to reset it to stun. The second henchman got off one blast, destroying a fair chunk of the wall behind Flinx's bed, before Flinx put him down for good. Given time, he would simply have used his nascent ability to persuade all three of them to leave. Regrettably, the attack on Pip had reduced the time available for subtle emotional projection to none.

Bug-eyed, the owner fled. He made it as far as the front door he and his friends had blown in. Before he could dash through the opening, something brightly colored, diamond-patterned, and super-fast materialized before his eyes.

Then there was only the brief but intense burning, burning in his eyes before he died.

Emerging from the bedroom, his small pistol still gripped tightly in one hand, Flinx walked over to the body of the owner. Smoke rose from his face, the hallmark of an angry Pip's attentions. In his other hand, Flinx held the small device the man had withdrawn from his pocket and pointed in the direction of the alien Aslet. He'd dropped it in his haste to flee.

Letting it fall to the floor, he aimed his pistol at it and fired once. Emerging from the bedroom behind him, the Aslet started, then relaxed. Once again, its mouth moved and no sound came out. The alien's attitude, if not its expression, was readily comprehensible even across interspecies boundaries. As Flinx looked on, Pip landed once again on the furry shoulder.

Flinx gazed long and curiously into the elongated alien eyes. The emotions of the three intruding humans had been clear to him as day. But this peculiar creature continued to remain as emotionally blank as a section of insulated wall.

"I think," he murmured aloud, even though there was no one around to hear him, "we need to find out what you are, besides an agile dancer." He started back toward his room. Behind him, Pip continued to rest contentedly on the Aslet's shoulder, allowing it to stroke the lethal coils without interference or objection. Mother Mastiff would be furious at the damage to her home.

✦ ✦ ✦

Aslet, it turned out when he presented himself and his furry new companion to the relevant local government bureau, was a newly classified world on the fringes of the Commonwealth. In addition to being the abode of the usual extensive panoply of new and intriguing alien life-forms, it was also home to a primitive species of low intelligence and simple culture. Most definitely not related to any known species of monkey, the natives of Aslet lived in caves and utilized the simplest and most basic of primitive tools.

They also, he learned, communicated in high-pitched squeaks and squirps that were above the range of human hearing. The Aslet Flinx had liberated had been trying to talk to him all along. Flinx, along with every other human and thranx, simply did not possess auricular equipment with sufficient range to detect the verbalizations.

Flinx tried to imagine what it would be like to be constantly screaming your pain, daily pleading for help from a world full of diverse sentient beings, all of whom would appear to be suffering from universal and total deafness.

The Aslet, it was reported, were exceedingly emotional creatures, given to a wide range of displays that evidently supplemented their limited ultrasonic vocabulary. Like their vocalizing, these emotional projections were also beyond anyone's ability to perceive, including Flinx.

But not, apparently, Pip.

The flying snake had been drawn to them immediately, during the forced performance he and Flinx had witnessed on the streets of Drallar. No wonder that when temporarily set free by its owner, the intelligent Aslet had homed in on Pip, locating the empathic minidrag snake in the midst of the city's innumerable twists and turnings. The revelation added directly to Flinx's store of knowledge about himself. Evidently, there were sentient emotional projections that were beyond his ability to perceive. But those were not the final thoughts the experience left him pondering as he bid farewell to the now collarless Aslet, soon to be repatriated by the government to its homeworld.

If no human could sense the very real emotions of something like the Aslet, he found himself wondering again and again, nor even hear, much less understand, their language, might there not be, out there, another species more powerful than any yet encountered that would view humankind in the same unintentionally uninformed light?

Was there even now, on some far-distant world, a collared human being made to dance and perform tricks for a species that could neither understand, nor hear, nor sympathize with the unfortunate captive?

Not for the first time, when he gazed up at the stars, he found himself wondering if there were worlds among that scattered multitude he might not be better off avoiding…

Kristine Kathryn Rusch is one of my favorite science fiction authors. Her Retrieval Artist is among my favorite series ever and her Diving stories aren't far behind. A Hugo-winning editor and author and World Fantasy Award winner, she creates short fiction and novels that cross the gamut. The Diving universe centers around a group of space "divers" who go into abandoned spaceship wrecks and "dive" for treasure. The following story is a prequel to the entire series in which an eager lieutenant tries to make a difference on his first search-and-rescue mission, despite a crew that doesn't seem to try or care much.

AUTHOR'S NOTE: *Captain Jonathan "Coop" Cooper makes his first appearance in the second book of the Diving series,* City of Ruins. *He's the captain of the* Ivoire, *a ship that travels 5,000 years into the future. This story occurs long before Coop gets to captain his own ship. It's not quite his origin story, but it does show why he can survive such a drastic event while others on the* Ivoire *cannot.*

LIEUTENANT TIGHTASS
A DIVING STORY

KRISTINE KATHRYN RUSCH

1

Overdue by fifteen hours. Too long, really. The *Voimakas* was in serious trouble. A ship lost in foldspace almost never came back, especially after the twenty-four-hour window.

Lieutenant Jonathan "Coop" Cooper felt the urgency, but he was beginning to think no one else on the *Arama* did. Seven others worked on the *Arama*'s bridge this afternoon, but none of them did their work with any kind of haste. They had even refused Coop's request to notify the captain of their new mission.

"Standard procedure," Lieutenant Leontyne Heyek said after Coop made his request. "We execute new orders and inform the captain when she returns to the bridge."

Which, he thought, was exactly backwards of the way things ran in the Fleet. But he hadn't served on a foldspace search vessel before. He had been taught that time was of the essence in a foldspace grid search, so responding to commands from headquarters immediately made sense to him.

What didn't make sense was no one on the bridge crew wanted to let the captain know when the new orders arrived.

The *Arama* would meet four other foldspace search vessels at the exact point where the *Voimakas*, the ship they would be searching for, had entered foldspace. The search would commence according to procedures developed less than ten years ago.

Because the foldspace search program was so new, Coop had expected the *Arama* to be a much more sophisticated vessel, maybe something like the search-and-rescue ships he had worked on shortly after his graduation from officer training.

Instead, this ship was smaller than he had expected, and had a counterintuitive design that bothered him every time he reported for duty.

The bridge was circular, and the floor slanted downward. The command officers worked in the bottom of the circle, with their subordinates at stations on each level above.

There were no portals on this bridge, and the wall of screens that he had thought standard to all Fleet ships no matter the size, did not exist here. Instead the circular walls of this bridge were covered with equipment, much of it lashed down. There were no lockers on this bridge either, no real storage.

His first thought when he had received his tour of the *Arama* was that the bridge was the most dangerous space on the ship. If something went awry and loosened all that equipment, the bridge crew would be in danger of injury just from flying debris.

Had he been running this ship—and of course he wasn't—he would have requested a bridge redesign at the next sector base stop. The designers there wouldn't have been able to put in portals because this bridge was in the exact center of the *Arama*, but the designers would have been able to build better storage.

And that alone would have made him more comfortable here.

Although he doubted anything could have made him completely comfortable here.

Usually he worked at the back of the bridge near the entrance, but this afternoon, he stood in the bridge's exact center, six screens floating around him. He had set them up like a barrier, even though it was an ineffective barrier at best. He could see the other seven crew members only because they stood higher than he did. They could see him as well, but they couldn't see what was on the screens he was monitoring.

He was capturing all the information coming from headquarters, from other ships that had served in the area near the *Voimakas*, and the last information from the *Voimakas* itself. He was trying to reconstruct the *Voimakas*'s last hour or so.

Heyek had told him that a reconstruction was a waste of time: the *Arama* had never found a ship in foldspace because of a reconstruction. He would have listened to her had the *Arama* already been onsite and ready to start the search—time was of the essence, after all—but the *Arama* had to get to the location, and while they were speeding toward those coordinates, he saw no harm in following procedure.

Or rather, he felt compelled to follow procedure.

He was beginning to think he was the only one here who was.

He stood slightly to the right of the tattered captain's chair. The *Arama*'s captain, Debbie Nisen, refused to let the chair be replaced or recovered, claiming that it fit her the way that it was. The cushions did retain the shape of her body because she wouldn't allow anyone to change them out.

Nor did she allow anyone else to sit in that chair. Not even someone who had to command the *Arama* when she wasn't on the bridge. It made for an awkward work environment. Coop had had the comm more than once since he arrived, and each time, he had stood behind the chair and worked the controls on its arms while standing up.

He hadn't wanted to sit in the thing—he thought he detected the faint smell of ancient sweat and unwashed bodies—but he did wish that Captain Nisen followed at least some of the procedures mandated by headquarters. Especially the ones concerning bridge and day-to-day operations.

Someone, probably Coop's predecessor, had built a small console to the right of the captain's chair. Coop knew that a crew member had built that console because it didn't conform to modern regulations. It had more flaws than anything he had ever worked on.

Rather like the *Arama*.

He didn't complain, though. He had learned at previous postings to remain silent about the different ways that different captains ran their ships. As his advisor on the officer training track had told him more than once, Coop would be learning from example—and sometimes those examples wouldn't be pretty.

The *Arama* wasn't pretty at all. It didn't even feel like a Fleet ship, not in design and certainly not in crew behavior. The crew had a startling lack of discipline, which made his as (or maybe more) uncomfortable as the bridge's strange design.

He was disciplined, and focused, which was why he stood down here now, coordinating all of the information. Lieutenant Heyek, who was nominally in charge this afternoon, hadn't even assigned him the work; she had simply assumed he would do it.

Or perhaps she assumed he would do something else, and the fact that he hadn't intuited what that something else was would get him a reprimand on the record.

He didn't know, and at the moment, he didn't care. His focus was on the rescue of the *Voimakas*. The *Arama* had failed to rescue the last nine ships it had gone after in foldspace, something he had learned before he came here.

He had been told that it was pretty common to fail at foldspace search and rescue. One of his instructors had told him that foldspace search and rescue was a fool's mission, but that someone important in Command Operations had lost family to foldspace and felt the new procedures were worth the investment in time, ships, and personnel.

Another former instructor had smiled when she learned that Coop was joining the crew of the *Arama*. *Someone thinks you need to learn humility*, she had said with a chuckle.

Maybe Coop needed to learn humility or maybe the crew of the *Arama* needed to remember the importance of procedure.

Or maybe it was just a random assignment. Those happened as well.

All that really mattered was that Coop was the new guy, automatically transferred because he had done so well on his previous assignment.

When he arrived on the *Arama*, he learned that he had supplanted a popular officer who had been transferred as well, which would have made the crew irritated at him no matter what, but Captain Nisen had compounded his unpopularity right from the start.

She had announced that Coop was on a captain's trajectory and wouldn't be with the ship that long. Her introduction to the officer core on the *Arama* made him sound like a grasping opportunist, rather than a man who wanted to work and learn how to command.

Coop hadn't understood why she had done that to him on the very first day. She had to know that the introduction would hurt his chances of working well with the crew. But she hadn't seemed to care about crew relations.

When he had asked her why she had informed the crew about his career trajectory in his introduction, trying as hard as he could to keep his tone neutral, she had squinted up at him, and said, *Better they know now you're a short-timer*, and then had walked away.

Her response had startled him. He had no idea if he was a short-timer or not. Officers on his career path often served for years on the same vessel.

Besides, his projected tenure on this vessel shouldn't have mattered. Crews were supposed to work together whether they knew each other well or not.

For a week or two, he wondered if the captain had made that introduction in that manner because he was married, and she was warning off anyone interested in some kind of hook-up. He'd had captains do that before when he'd come onboard a ship, but usually during leisure hours, and always with a joking tone.

He would have understood that admonition; some married officers had trouble maintaining their vows after months (or years) apart from their spouses.

But Coop followed regulation and procedure assiduously, and that meant with his marriage as well. He and Mae had discussed their continual separations before they decided to marry, debating whether the marriage was necessary while they were both building their careers.

Ultimately, they decided it was. The Fleet gave preferences to spouses who indicated the desire to start a family. If those spouses could share a ship or a mission, then they would. Mae was a linguist, and once Coop became captain, he could request her presence on any ship he commanded.

He missed her more than he wanted to contemplate, particularly while he was on this ship. He couldn't complain about his treatment here when he contacted her; he knew that there was a distinct possibility that his communications were monitored. He figured they could talk freely when they got together on leave.

He wished he had leave now. He didn't want to perform another foldspace grid search. The first two he had participated in had been cleanup efforts, mapping a part of foldspace with no real hope of finding the missing vessels.

He had no idea if this mission would be the same, but given Heyek's lack of interest in following procedure, he had a hunch she believed that the *Voimakas* was already lost.

That defeatist attitude was the thing he hated the most about serving on the *Arama*. They were supposed to be a search-and-rescue vehicle. Instead, they were more of a cover-your-ass vehicle—at least that was how it seemed to him.

Which was why he was personally reviewing every bit of information on the *Voimakas* that he could find.

The *Voimakas* was a new DV-class vessel with an upgraded *anacapa* drive. The *anacapa* drive was what enabled the Fleet to enter foldspace. Without the *anacapa* drive, the Fleet would not be able to travel the long distances that kept it moving forever forward.

Some parts of the Fleet trailed light-years behind the rest of the Fleet. Those trailing ships would catch up, using the drives to create a fold in space. During officer training, one of Coop's instructors on *anacapa* usage had actually taken a blanket, folded it kitty-corner, touching two opposite edges together.

Think of that when you think of traveling through foldspace, he had said. Then he had continued to fold the blanket, showing that sometimes a vessel had to make many trips into and out of foldspace to get to the proper part of the universe.

Foldspace science instructors thought that example silly, and sometimes said so. But that was the image Coop kept in his head, particularly when the instructors in foldspace science couldn't say exactly what foldspace was. Was it an actual fold in space? An interdimensional way to travel? Or another part of the universe that the *anacapa* drive somehow sent the ships to for a brief moment, before returning them to specified coordinates?

He had thought of it all as theory until he had joined the crew of the *Arama*. At that moment, foldspace ceased to be a tool that a starship sometimes used to travel long distances, and became an actual place where ships disappeared, never to be seen again.

Like the *Voimakas*. It was one of three DV-class vessels assigned to a new sector. They were to travel to that new sector to search for the best location for a new sector base.

The *Voimakas* went into foldspace first. The other two ships followed. When they arrived in the new sector, they didn't see the *Voimakas*. It should have arrived before them.

But foldspace could be tricky. A minute in foldspace might actually be an hour in what the Fleet called "real space." It wasn't unusual for three ships to go into foldspace at roughly the same time and arrive at the new coordinates half an hour apart.

The other two ships waited the requisite hour. Then two. And after that, they had to contact the Fleet to let them know that the *Voimakas* might be trapped in foldspace.

At that point, the Fleet sent another ship to the coordinates where the *Voimakas* had gone into foldspace. Sometimes ships rebounded out of foldspace, unable to travel the distance across the fold.

But the *Voimakas* wasn't there either. It didn't respond to hails. Seven hours in, the Fleet declared the *Voimakas* missing. If the Fleet waited longer than that to declare a ship missing, the Fleet would miss the best rescue window.

That early declaration meant that the missing ships might appear just as the investigation got started. That had happened on Coop's first mission with the *Arama*. The so-called missing ship hadn't been missing at all. It had arrived at the coordinates on the other side of the sector ten hours after the ship had entered foldspace.

When the news of the ship's appearance hit, Kyle Rettig, one of the engineers who had been manning the bridge alongside Coop, had leaned over to him, and said, *Get used to this. We get sent back all the time. Sometimes I think all we do is crisscross the sector on made-up assignments.*

Coop hadn't known how to respond to that, so he hadn't. But he hadn't forgotten it. He had no idea if Rettig had been goading him or had been simply being kind, and Coop had no way to find out.

But so far, Coop's experience on the *Arama* had been arriving at coordinates, doing a grid search inside foldspace, and then giving up much too early, declaring the ship lost.

This time he was determined that the *Arama* wouldn't lose the *Voimakas*. If the ship still existed, the *Arama* would find it.

The bridge doors hissed open, and Captain Nisen entered. She was a short square woman with spiky blond hair and a muscular frame. Her black and gray uniform was rumpled as if she had slept in it, or stored it in a ball at the foot of her bed. Her boots were dull and stained.

She certainly wasn't setting an example for her crew—or rather, she was setting the wrong kind of example. Coop only gave her a quick glance, because if he looked longer, his disapproving expression would become obvious.

"Brief me," she said to Heyek as she passed.

Heyek gave a succinct timeline of the notification of the missing *Voimakas*, and then let Nisen know they were less than thirty minutes from the coordinates where the ship was last seen.

"And what's the new guy doing?" Nisen asked, as if Coop wasn't there—or couldn't hear her.

"He seems to think we should review all the information the Fleet sent," Heyek said. "As if the four other ships aren't doing the same thing."

Maybe they're blowing off procedure too, Coop wanted to say but didn't. *Maybe your laziness in relying on your colleagues is what ensured that the other ships we searched for never got found.*

He bit the inside of his lower lip so that he wouldn't speak up. His mouth tasted faintly of blood. He had bit down too hard.

"Rookie moves," Nisen said with a laugh. "But we'll put it in the report anyway. The Fleet'll think we actually followed procedure for once in our lives."

Coop filtered the information into one screen, so that he had an accurate map of the *Voimakas*'s last journey. He had the coordinates where the ship entered foldspace down to the most precise measurement possible.

Nisen tripped over nothing as she reached the command circle, grabbing the edge of her chair, and chuckling to herself. The sour smell of last night's brandy mixed with old sweat rose off her like a cloud.

Coop kept his head down, and started breathing through his mouth, making a mental note of the time. He would write her behavior into a mission report, which he would file when the *Arama* reached the next sector base.

He would report that Nisen was still drunk from the night before. The senior staff had found a table in the *Arama*'s only bar, grabbed two bottles of whiskey and proceeded to drink hard. When Nisen arrived, she had grabbed a bottle of brandy from the stash under one of the counters, and drank it all herself.

Coop had sat at the edge of the group, nursing a single glass of whiskey while the rest of the senior staff polished off the bottles. Heyek hadn't gotten drunk, as far as he could tell, but Nisen had become embarrassing. She grew louder with each glass, laughing so hard that at one point Coop thought she was going to laugh herself sick.

She had staggered out of the bar around midnight, taking a second bottle of brandy with her back to the captain's quarters.

He must have had a disapproving expression on his face as he watched her go, because Heyek had said, "We drink here, Cooper. Nothing in regulations prevents it. So stop being so damned straitlaced and join the party."

After that, he hadn't been able to leave. He stayed for a half hour before he felt comfortable enough to slip away. He hadn't even finished his first glass of whiskey, let alone the five or six the rest of the senior staff had downed.

He had gotten to his quarters, a tiny single room with a bed that folded out of the wall, and had laid awake for nearly an hour, wondering what he had gotten himself into.

He had seen the crew drink before, but he hadn't paid attention to the amount until last night.

And he hadn't liked what he saw.

"How you doing, Lieutenant Tightass?" Nisen asked him as she flopped into the captain's chair.

Coop didn't acknowledge her at all. He wasn't going to start answering to insults, because if he did, the name would stick, not just on this ship, but on future assignments as well.

"Underwear's too tight for the second day in a row," she muttered, leaning back in the ruined chair. "We need to get you one size up, Lieutenant Tightass. The pressure on your balls is making you rigid everywhere."

He tapped one of the screens, working hard to concentrate on the numbers before him.

She chuckled. "Okay," she said, "probably not *everywhere*…"

He kept his head bent downward, and closed his eyes for a brief second, hoping no one else could see his response. He had to learn how to train his face to remain impassive while his emotions whipsawed inside of him. He usually managed impassive when there was a crisis, but he hadn't quite hit impassive when he was feeling humiliated.

"Good God, Lieutenant Cooper, you really are a tightass," Nisen said. "I always find it suspicious when a man can't laugh at himself."

And I always find it difficult to laugh when someone confuses bullying with humor, he nearly said. He had to bite the inside of his lip again, so that the words wouldn't leave.

"All right," she said in a slightly different tone. "Report to me, Lieutenant Cooper. What are you finding in all your research?"

He raised his head. His gaze met hers. Her eyes were bloodshot.

"I'm finding nothing unusual, sir," he said in his most formal voice.

"Told you it was a waste of time," Heyek said from behind him.

Nisen grinned, then put her hand on the edge of the control arm of the captain's chair.

"I don't agree with Lieutenant Heyek," Coop said. "I don't believe that looking at the data was a waste of time in this instance."

Nisen leaned her head back, then tilted it toward him, clearly surprised. "Even though you found nothing different?"

"Especially because I found nothing different." He lowered the screen between him and her. That single movement made it feel like he had taken a step closer to her when he hadn't.

"Intriguing, Lieutenant," Nisen said. "You want to explain that logic?"

"I compared the *Voimakas*'s actions with her sister ships. The *Voimakas* performed the exact same calculations as the other ships. The *Voimakas* followed procedure to the letter."

"Foldspace is a crapshoot, Lieutenant," Heyek said. "Hasn't anyone told you that?"

Is that why you all drink to excess? he thought but did not say. *Because your job entails entering foldspace dozens of times searching for someone who got lost by entering it once?*

"The only differences are slight," Coop continued as if Heyek hadn't spoken at all. "The other two ships entered foldspace from slightly different grid coordinates. They weren't at the same coordinates at all, nor did they move to those coordinates."

"Close enough, though," said Heyek. Apparently Nisen was letting the lieutenant do her dirty work for her.

This time, Coop looked directly at Heyek. She, at least, didn't look like she had slept in her uniform. It was crisp and clean, just like she was. Her dark hair was pulled back tightly from her face. There was no sign that she had been drinking the night before with Nisen.

"Close enough," he repeated, letting just a hint of sarcasm into his voice. "Apparently, they were not 'close enough,' Lieutenant. They entered foldspace and then exited with no problem at all. The *Voimakas* did not."

Heyek had her arms crossed. She was looking down on him from her perch three rows up. "And you think it was because of the entry point?"

"I am looking for anomalies," he said.

"It's not an anomaly for a ship to enter foldspace from a slightly different coordinate than her sister ships," Heyek said. "That's how we do it when more than one ship enters foldspace at the same time."

"That's right," Coop said, making sure his voice held no irritation at the fact that she had just explained procedure to him as if he were an ensign on his first assignment.

Heyek frowned at him. "We—and the experts back on the *Pasteur*—don't think the *anacapa* drives of the ships interact when they all head to foldspace at the same time. We've run experiments—"

"I know," Coop said, cutting her off. "I've studied them."

"Then you're wasting all of our time," Heyek said.

Coop exhaled through his teeth, making sure there was no sound of irritation.

"Ships vanish into foldspace when no other ship surrounds them," Heyek said, as if she couldn't let it go. "We don't always get close-up information from nearby ships. That's a luxury in this case. And it proves nothing."

"I agree," Coop said. "It *proves* nothing. But—"

"But nothing." Heyek glanced at Nisen, and said to her, "I told you, we don't need to do this kind of fussy—"

"Actually, Captain, we do," Coop said.

Nisen raised her eyebrows at him. "You have a theory, Lieutenant Tightass?"

She was trying to shut him up.

"Lieutenant Cooper, sir," he said. "In case you'd forgotten."

Isaak Li, the comm officer just inside Coop's line of sight behind the captain, snickered, and ducked behind a nearby console. Li was a small man, so he could hide easily.

"Lieutenant *Cooper*," Nisen said. "You have a theory?"

Every word dripped with sarcasm, with a lack of respect that he found breathtaking. If he ever became lucky enough to run his own ship, this kind of treatment would not happen—especially from a superior officer to a subordinate.

"I do, Captain," Coop said. "I think those slightly different coordinates make all the difference. The ships are not entering foldspace from the same point. They're entering at different points. Foldspace is tricky, particularly when it comes to time. Perhaps it is just as tricky with its entry points."

"You don't think the experts have been studying that?" Heyek snapped.

Coop gave her a slow, measured look. "I suspect they have," he said. "And I suspect that's why they're always asking us for more information.

Have you ever thought that the procedure might not be about *our* search, but about future searches?"

Heyek's eyes narrowed. Two of the bridge officers behind her grinned openly, as if they were pleased that Coop had taken her on.

Nisen hadn't noticed any of that. Instead, she pursed her lips and nodded.

"Lieutenant Tightass might have a point," she said.

Coop felt a surge of irritation which he kept off his face. He didn't correct her this time, because correcting her again would show her that she was getting under his skin.

"I don't think they take any of that into account," Heyek said, "any more than they look at the build and design of the ship. Every ship is different, even if it is the same class of vessel as the other ships that didn't get lost. *Anacapa* drives have anomalies, command structures vary—"

"Information is information, Lieutenant," Nisen snapped, "and the scientists probably use all of it. Sometimes we cut too many corners. I think Lieutenant Tightass is right: we shouldn't cut any on these rescues."

Heyek opened her mouth to argue, then seemed to think the better of it, and closed her mouth again.

"I want to give some thought to the entry point thing," Nisen said. "Who are we working with at the site?"

"The *Soeker*, the *Tragač*, the *Iarrthóir*, and the *Ofuna*," Li said. He had spoken up quickly as if he wanted a change of subject. Until he snickered at the interchange, Coop hadn't paid a lot of attention to him, thinking him just another of the bridge officers who marched in lockstep with Nisen.

But Li looked over a nearby console at Coop, and gave him a thumbs-up so quick that Coop barely had time to register it.

Heyek shot Li a dirty look. "They were close to the coordinates, just like we were," she said, taking over the narrative again. "That's why they were chosen to work with us."

"We'll arrive first," Li said, head down. Coop wondered if Li was smiling. He seemed to be enjoying poking at Heyek.

"We're about ten minutes out," Heyek said.

"Good," Nisen said. "Because I want to look at Lieutenant Tightass's findings."

She propelled herself out of her chair as if it had an eject button.

She stood just outside Coop's screen barrier, looked at all of them which were, for her, eye-height, grinned, and said, "Tightass, permission to come aboard."

The phrase sounded vaguely dirty, which she probably intended. It also acknowledged the separation he had built from the rest of the crew. And then there was that nickname again. He was going to be stuck with it, no matter what he did.

"Permission granted, Captain," Coop said as formally as he could. He stepped away from the jury-rigged console so that she could enter his little protected space.

As she did, he bowed ever so slightly.

"Welcome aboard," he said, and set to work.

2

The math was complicated, but the information it communicated wasn't. The *Voimakas* entered foldspace one-point-two seconds ahead of the *Mandela*, one of its sister ships, and two-point-five seconds ahead of the other ship, the *Krachtige*. The *Mandela* arrived at the new coordinates seventeen minutes later, the *Krachtige* five minutes after that. They waited, as per procedure, for the *Voimakas*, which never arrived.

The *Krachtige* did the first round of investigation, checking to see if the *Voimakas* ended up at a starbase or a sector base. Sometimes, a malfunctioning *anacapa* drive sent a ship back to the place where the drive had last been repaired or replaced.

None of the nearby bases reported anything. Once the Fleet got involved, they double-checked that same information, and did not find the *Voimakas*. Nor was it near any coordinates where it had entered or exited foldspace before.

The one thing none of these reports addressed, the one thing Coop didn't know how to address either, was the fact that sometimes foldspace sent a ship to a different time period. Usually the differences were small—a few hours, maybe a few days. But sometimes they were vast, ten, twenty, thirty years into the future.

If the *Voimakas* ended up a few days in its future, everyone would know soon enough. It would arrive on some future date, and let the entire Fleet know about the return. But if the *Voimakas* ended up years in the future—or, God forbid, in the past—then there was no way to know without a records search.

And archives searches in Fleet records were difficult at best. The Fleet didn't keep a lot of information about its past. Only the history ships attached to the various universities even had the capability for such storage, and their storage facilities were haphazard. A few sector bases also kept information—or they were supposed to. Whether or not that information got moved when the sector bases shut down was something no one seemed to know.

After Coop made his small presentation to Nisen, as quietly as he could even though he knew the rest of the bridge listened in, he said, "Let me ask one question. You have done many foldspace grid searches involving multiple ships just like we're going to do here."

Nisen raised her head and looked up at him. She was nearly a foot shorter than he was, something he only noticed at moments like this. Her outsized personality made her seem much taller.

"When ships coordinate pieces of the grid, there's overlap in the map, right?" he asked.

She frowned, then blinked, as if she didn't know how to answer him. Coop found that interesting all by itself.

"Yes." Rettig walked down the aisle from his perch near the exit. He had kept a low profile in the discussions until now. "Usually, there's a lot of overlap."

Rettig was the one person on the bridge crew that Coop liked. Rettig was a wiry man with arms like sticks, the kind that training hard in zero-g often gave an athlete. Coop had no idea what (if anything) Rettig trained for, but Coop suspected it was some kind of intership competition.

"Usually?" Coop asked.

"Sometimes there isn't." Rettig stepped into the same protected space that Coop and Nisen were in, as if it were a separate conference room and he had been invited to join them. "If there is no overlap, we abort the mission."

"That's not protocol," Coop said.

Nisen straightened, as if his words irritated her, but Rettig nodded.

"We developed it," he said. "Or rather, I did, and the captain agreed. What freaks us all out is that the star maps don't coordinate."

Coop looked from him to Nisen. Her entire demeanor had changed. She seemed larger, stronger, more in control than she had just five minutes before.

"We never find the ship we're looking for if the star maps don't coordinate," she said softly.

"The ship you're looking for," Coop repeated. "You find ships though."

Rettig nodded. "That's what freaked me out. All of us, really."

"The ships we find are old." Nisen's voice was very soft now. Coop doubted anyone else could hear this. "Fifty, sixty, seventy years old."

A chill ran through him. "Abandoned?"

"Not always," Rettig said. "You wish they were, though."

"Before you ask," Nisen said, "no one's alive on them either."

The words hung in the air around them.

Then Nisen turned, and tapped one of the holoscreens. It winked out and returned, looking exactly the same.

"We usually do twenty, twenty-five trips into foldspace during a grid search," she said in a louder voice.

"Sometimes as many as fifty." Rettig was looking at Coop, as if Coop should understand.

He finally did. They were losing their nerve. All of them. They were diving into and out of foldspace like it was regular space, aware that each trip, no matter how short, might trap them there.

"We're going to arrive first," Nisen said, more to the screen than to Coop or Rettig. "We should go in first."

Coop nearly blurted, *That's not procedure*, but of course, she knew that.

"What are you thinking, Captain?" Heyek had come down another aisle and was peering over one of the screens. Apparently she didn't like being left out of the discussions either.

"I'd like to see if Lieutenant Cooper's hypothesis is correct. If we enter foldspace at the *exact* coordinates that the *Voimakas* used, then maybe we'll see the ship." Nisen wasn't looking at any of them, which was probably good, because Rettig paled, and Heyek winced.

Coop froze ever so slightly. He was aware that the captain had just used his real name, as a sign of respect. He was probably going to lose that respect with his next question. He tried to keep his tone nonconfrontational. "I thought when the grid search started, it always started from the entry point."

"We go in and out at the same spot as four other ships, we'll pile on top of each other," Heyek said, treating him as if this were his first time into foldspace ever. Apparently, she *had* heard the question as confrontational.

Coop gave her a withering glance. "I would have thought at least one ship went in at the precise coordinates."

"We never have," Rettig said. "I think the fear is we'd appear in foldspace on top of the ship we're looking for."

"Unstated fear," Nisen said. "Not in the manuals, of course. But the thought is there."

"We're always close," Heyek said, as if she had come up with the grid search method herself.

"But not precise," Rettig said, "not down to the fifteenth decimal, like you found, Coop."

Coop. Was that the first time someone on this ship had deliberately used his nickname? He suspected it was.

"How far out are we from the others?" Nisen wasn't talking to the three inside Coop's little protective barrier. She was looking at Li.

"The first ship will join us about fifteen minutes after we arrive," Li said.

Nisen braced her hands on the jury-rigged console. "Fifteen minutes. We can try your method, then, Lieutenant."

Coop wanted to say it wasn't his method. But he didn't. Let her blame him if something went wrong.

"We'll let the other ships know that we're going in before they arrive," Nisen said. "We'll do what we can, then we'll be the ones in charge of organizing the grid search after the others turn up. I'll argue that the *Arama* go in at those coordinates every time we have a turn."

"Unless the star maps don't match." Heyek said that softly, her gaze on Nisen.

Nisen looked over at her, as if they shared a secret. Then Nisen nodded. She didn't say yes, though. She didn't go on the record, which Coop found interesting.

He found the entire discussion interesting. He had thought this was a shoddy crew, lax and undisciplined. He hadn't realized that this was a terrified crew, determined to do their jobs despite the fear they had for their own lives.

That put all of the behavior he had seen into a different context, including the captain's bullying. She wanted to make it unpleasant for him to stay, maybe even request a transfer before the time was right. Had she forced other candidates on the captain track off the ship in the past?

Nisen had moved closer to him. She was so close, in fact, that it took all of his personal strength not to step backwards.

"If your theory is correct," she said, "we're taking a large risk going in at those exact coordinates. We might end up as lost as the *Voimakas*."

"Isn't that always the risk?" Coop asked.

Nisen's expression hardened. "Spoken like someone who doesn't understand the risk," she said, and pushed past Rettig to leave the little protected area.

She flopped back into her captain's chair.

Heyek shook her head and went back to her station. Only Rettig remained.

"You stay onboard long enough," he said quietly, "and you'll understand why that was probably not the most politic response you could have made."

"It's that bad?" Coop asked, speaking as softly as Rettig had.

"No," Rettig said. "It's worse."

3

The *Arama* arrived at the area of space where the *Voimakas* entered foldspace at the exact moment Heyek said they would. This was one of those regions of space that felt far away from anything. A star glimmered in the distance, with a dozen planets in its habitable zone. But those were all far enough away to make them points of light on the small two-dimensional holoscreen he kept open below one of the larger screens.

He hated not having portals on the bridge, so he created his own. He felt vaguely insubordinate doing so, but no one had told him not to. In fact, he doubted that anyone had even noticed.

The crew had gone from the slapdash organization that Coop had seen on the previous missions to a focused, if slightly uncomfortable, group.

They seemed ready to take on the challenges the change in procedure presented.

Nisen sat upright in her chair, a holoscreen floating in front of her. Coop couldn't see what was on that screen.

She had asked him to double-check his coordinates, and then had Rettig monitor them as well. She told the other ships that the *Arama* would go in first, then cut off the protests she got in response.

She did not tell Command Operations her plans.

"I am changing our procedure inside foldspace slightly," she said to the bridge crew. She had her back to them, which Coop thought odd, but she was staring at that screen as if it held the secrets of the universe.

Maybe it did.

"We will enter and remain for three minutes, rather than the usual one. We will conduct a normal high-speed scan along with mapping, but we will take a little extra time." Her voice was flat and unemotional. "If all goes well, we should emerge from foldspace around the time that the other ships arrive."

She didn't have to say what might happen if things did not go well.

Coop's mouth had gone dry. Fear, apparently, was contagious, and there was a lot of fear on this bridge. He was usually used to ignoring his emotions as he worked, concentrating on getting the job done.

But the worry around him made him question his own plan. Perhaps he was going to get them lost in foldspace.

Then he forced himself to take a deep breath. The risk of getting lost in foldspace did not change just because of the entry coordinates. The entire ship might get lost anyway. Or it might not. The odds remained the same each time a ship traveled into or out of foldspace.

He had seen nothing in the research that suggested otherwise. And, he had to believe, that if there was research that showed an increased danger when a ship executed certain actions, the Fleet would issue a caution or would prevent ships from taking those actions.

It was expensive to lose ships, both in materials and in personnel.

"We will gather as much information as we can as rapidly as we can," Nisen said. "Then we will return. The only change will be the time limit. Is that clear?"

"Yes, sir," said Heyek, apparently speaking for all of them.

No one else looked ready. Li actually grabbed the edges of his console. Rettig stood stiffly behind his workstation. One of the officers closest to the exit actually looked at it, as if it might provide an escape.

Coop opened three small screens—one that read heat signatures, one that would give a three-D rendering of whatever was outside the ship, and one ran the data stream of every bit of telemetry coming into his console. On any other ship, he would have assumed that someone else was running the same kind of three-screen scan, but he wasn't going to assume anything here—even though the crew had shaped up, just a little.

It really irritated him that the captain did not monitor all of the information she had available. She was unlike any other captain he had ever served with. That alone made him continually feel uneasy.

Nisen opened the left arm of her chair, revealing a small command module. She pressed two fingers on the tiny screen.

The *Arama* stuttered and bumped as if it were a ground vehicle that had hit holes in a road. The *anacapa* drive had been engaged.

Coop should have been used to that stutter-bump feeling by now—he had gone in and out of foldspace enough with the *Arama*—but he wasn't. The *Arama*'s entry into foldspace always felt a little too hard, as if something had gone vaguely wrong.

The shift into foldspace took only a few seconds, and then the stutter-bump stopped. The *Arama* eased into position. Another ship loomed much too close to her starboard side. So close, in fact, that it was pretty clear the *Arama* had just barely missed hitting it.

"The hell," Nisen said as Heyek said, "Good God."

Coop bit back a curse as well. Everyone else looked at the captain and her second-in-command, as if they had done something wrong.

Which meant that only three people on the bridge even knew how close they had come to hitting that other ship.

Using his right hand, Coop adjusted his two-dimensional screen so that the image zoomed outward. He wished it were as easy to adjust his heart. It was pounding, hard.

"That's the *Voimakas*," he said, relieved that his voice sounded calm.

"If that's true," Heyek said, annoying him, "then this will be the easiest rescue we've ever had."

"You haven't looked at her clearly, then, have you, Lieutenant?" Nisen asked. The lieutenant she referred to was Heyek, not Coop.

Coop hadn't looked at the ship clearly either. He had simply found her ship's signature, and compared it to the *Voimakas*. Now, he looked.

She listed, as if her attitude controls weren't working. Her escape pods were gone, leaving small holes in her side. The holes would have looked like part of the design to anyone who had never seen a DV-class ship before, but to someone like Coop who studied the ships continually, the *Voimakas* looked denuded.

There were no other ships nearby. Stars winked in the distance, and a milky-white smudge appeared on the port side. Coop didn't even investigate what that smudge was. It was too far away to consider as anything more than a point on a grid map.

That thought made him realize everyone was focused on the *Voimakas*, and not on the grid map as they usually were. He hit three controls and had three different systems map the area. He also recorded as much of the information he had taken from the *Voimakas* as he could.

"We've got life signs," said Li. "But not a lot of them."

"And weirdly," Rettig said, "it looks like all the ship bays are empty."

Nisen stood, then looked at Coop. Her glance was measuring, and for one brief, insecure moment, he thought she was blaming him for something. Then he realized she was looking to see if he understood what had happened here.

He did not. He could guess, but he didn't believe in guessing. He shrugged ever so slightly.

She sighed, and turned away from him. Then she raised her single holoscreen, glanced at it, and shook her head.

"Hail them," she said to the screen as if it were part of her bridge crew.

"Already have, sir," Li said. "There's an open channel, but I'm not getting any response."

Coop found that surprising. He would have responded immediately.

"No one is on their bridge, sir," Rettig said.

Nisen nodded as if she expected that. "Can you access their system enough to open a ship-wide channel?" she asked Li.

The timer in front of Coop said that a minute had gone by. If they continued to follow the original plan, they only had two more minutes before they had to jump back to regular space.

"Yes, sir, I can," Li said. "It's done. Go ahead."

Coop looked at him in surprise. On other ships, the captain usually had to tell the comm officer her exact plan. Apparently not here. Li had known what she planned.

Maybe Coop had too, but he wouldn't have presumed.

"This is the *Arama*," Nisen said, in a somewhat louder and more formal voice than she usually used. "We are part of a five-ship rescue team sent to pull you out of foldspace. I would like to speak to Captain Golan."

There was a pause that ran seconds too long for Coop's taste. Nisen didn't move, but Rettig shifted, as if the silence made him nervous.

"This is Captain Golan," said a tired female voice. "Who am I speaking to?"

"Captain Debbie Nisen of the *Arama*."

"That's not possible," Golan said. "Please leave. We will defend this ship if need be."

Coop glanced at Rettig, who shrugged. Li's head was bent over the console, as if he were working at something.

Coop went back to his screens, looking for a way to penetrate the *Voimakas*'s hull, to see if he could identify the two heat signatures.

"Why is that not possible?" Nisen asked.

"Just leave," the female voice said.

"We can't," Nisen said. "We're here to bring you back to real space. Where's the rest of your crew?"

Golan let out a bitter laugh. "I gave them permission to leave the ship five years ago."

Rettig raised his head, looking startled.

"Captain," Heyek said, speaking softly, "we only have thirty seconds."

"We're staying a moment longer, Lieutenant."

Not, Coop noted, an exact time. A vague time. The nerves he had felt earlier rose again.

"Can you recall your crew quickly?" Nisen asked.

"I have no fucking idea where they ended up." Golan let out another half-laugh. "You really are Debbie Nisen, aren't you?"

"I am." Nisen sounded surprisingly calm, even after the mention of five years and Golan's earlier disbelief.

"Goddammit," Golan said. "God-fucking-dammit."

"I need you to activate your *anacapa* drive," Nisen said.

Coop looked at her in surprise. He hadn't realized the *Voimakas's anacapa* drive wasn't operational. But Nisen had clearly checked.

"We're going to hook to it, and pull you back through foldspace," Nisen said.

"There's only two of us left," Golan said. "It's not worth it. Go back before you can't."

"I don't have time to argue with you, Captain," Nisen said. "Activate the drive."

"We think it malfunctioned," Golan said.

"You don't know?" Heyek asked. Nisen whipped her head around and glared at Heyek, but the damage was done.

Coop folded his hands behind his back, watching and listening.

"We inspected it several times," Golan said. "It seemed fine, but something wasn't engaging."

Past tense. They hadn't tried for a long time.

"Captain." Rettig spoke softly to Nisen. "If I may…?"

She nodded at him.

"Captain Golan." Rettig spoke louder this time. "I'm Kyle Rettig, chief engineer on the *Arama*. You don't have to fully activate the *anacapa*. Just toggle it to rest mode. Can you do that?"

"It might blow us all to hell, but I can try," she said.

"Please do," he said, *and hurry*, he mouthed.

The bridge crew watched each other, as if they were the ones taking action. All except Nisen who stared at her screen.

Coop looked back at his. He shifted the telemetry to focus on readings from the *Voimakas*. He saw the exact moment they activated their *anacapa*.

Apparently, so did Nisen.

"*Now!*" she ordered.

The *Arama* shuddered and bumped. A light glowed from the *anacapa* drive half-hidden under a panel in the wall directly across from Coop. He'd never seen a drive do that.

His heart rate increased, and he forced himself to look away. The bumping and shuddering felt stronger than it had when the *Arama* had left real space. The bumping and shuddering also went on longer.

Now, no one made eye contact. Everyone was either studying their consoles or had their eyes completely closed.

Coop had the odd sense that some of them were praying. The nerves on the bridge were palpable. He made himself focus on the telemetry screen. The numbers helped him focus, and stay calm. Even when the screen blanked for five seconds, he remained calm.

That data stream blank was normal. It happened whenever a ship traveled into or out of foldspace. *Normal*, he repeated to himself, so that he wouldn't focus on what could go wrong. Or what had gone wrong for the *Voimakas*.

Five years in foldspace. The crew gone. The captain and one other person remaining.

The shuddering eased. The *Arama* bumped two more times, then the telemetry reappeared on Coop's screen. As did all the other images on his other screens.

The bridge crew burst into spontaneous applause, although Coop didn't join in. Neither did Nisen. She remained standing, head bent toward her screen.

Coop examined the two-dimensional images, and saw the *Voimakas* appear beside the *Arama*. They were surrounded by four other ships: the *Soeker*, the *Tragač*, the *Iarrthóir*, and the *Ofuna*.

Either they had arrived at record speed, or the *Arama* had been inside foldspace longer than anticipated.

"Captain," Li said, "you're getting congratulations from the other ships. Would you like me to put those on speaker?"

"Nice of them to show up," Nisen said. "And no, I don't want to hear it. I'm heading to my quarters. I'll deal with this mess there."

Then she shut down the screen in front of her, whirled, and marched up the aisle. She had nearly reached the exit when Heyek said, "Captain?

What would you like from us?"

"Fifteen minutes of peace," Nisen said, and left the bridge.

The rest of the bridge crew stood very still, as if she had told them not to move a muscle. The euphoria from a few minutes ago had completely disappeared.

They had completed a successful mission—they had brought the *Voimakas* out of foldspace—but not in the way anyone anticipated. It would be impossible to call this a victory, really. The entire crew, minus two people, was lost.

"Li," Heyek said. "Coordinate with the *Tragač*. Find out how long we were in foldspace."

"Already done, Lieutenant," Li said. His voice sounded thin and reedy. "We've been gone for two hours."

Two hours. Coop gripped the edge of the makeshift console. Time really had operated differently in that part of foldspace.

"Why hadn't they started the search, then?" Heyek said. "That's procedure. If the other ship—"

"They had, Lieutenant." Li spoke softly. "They started mapping the grid ninety minutes ago."

"But they didn't see us?" Heyek asked.

"No, sir," Li said.

"Tell them I have a grid map and imagery of where we ended up," Coop said. "I also have coordinates from inside foldspace."

"So do I," Rettig said. "I would like to compare our grid map with theirs."

"I'm sure the captain is working all of that out," someone from the back said, somewhat primly.

"I'm sure she hasn't gotten to that yet," Heyek said. "They're going to have to figure out what to do with the *Voimakas*."

Her words resounded in the bridge. What to do with a ship that had been missing only a day, but whose crew was gone—five years gone—and whose captain and someone else had remained on board to… what? Guard the ship?

Coop couldn't imagine what they were feeling at the moment. Elation to be back? The pressure of the loss and lost time? Something else, something he couldn't even understand?

He supposed he would find out eventually. He was feeling a little unnerved having lost hours.

The *Voimakas* had lost *years*.

"So share the information," Heyek said. "It's something we all need to know, after all."

Coop glanced at her over the screens. She looked no different than she always had—except for her eyes. They seemed smaller, as if she was trying to keep them open somehow.

Her gaze met his and, for the first time, he felt no hostility from her. Then she looked away.

He gathered the information, and forwarded it to Li in a form someone else could easily understand. As he did that, a grid map arrived on one of his screens. He didn't recognize it.

"Is that the grid map from the *Tragač*?" he asked.

"Compiled by them, the *Soeker*, the *Iarrthóir*, and the *Ofuna*," Li said. "They were in and out of foldspace nearly twenty times before we came back."

Twenty times. Coop didn't want to consider that. It did mean that his theory was right, though. The *Arama* had gone into foldspace at the exact coordinates the *Voimakas* had. Not close to the same coordinates. The same ones.

And had ended up nearly on top of the *Voimakas*. But not anywhere near the other ships.

At least their maps would be extensive. Maybe they had entered that part of foldspace some distance from the *Voimakas*.

He was breathing shallowly, working on the information in front of him. He couldn't stop himself from thinking about the fact that the *Arama* had come close to getting lost as well.

The *Arama* hadn't been in foldspace long—maybe five minutes—and had lost two hours. Yet the ship managed to bring itself back and the *Voimakas* back as well.

The *Arama* had a functioning *anacapa* drive; Captain Golan believed that the *Voimakas*'s drive had malfunctioned.

Not believed. If she had been in foldspace for more than five years, then she would have known that the drive wasn't functioning properly.

She had been worried that activating it, even minimally, would damage both ships.

It hadn't, though.

The *Voimakas* was just fine—or as fine as a ship could be, considering.

Coop swallowed hard, and focused on the maps before him. He took the grid map from the four sister ships, and overlaid it on the grid map he had made.

He wished he had more than a grid map from the other ships. He'd like to see what features the space around that area had. The other ships' grid map didn't seem to extend far enough.

He hadn't had time when he'd been in foldspace to find what was unique about that nearby planet. But he had seen that milky-white smudge. He hadn't identified that either. From his perspective in space, without focusing any telescopes or other scanning equipment on that area, he had no idea if he was looking at a distant galaxy, a dense asteroid belt, the remains of a planet, or something else entirely.

If he had known exactly what that milky-white smudge was, he would have been able to look for it with more precision. But he didn't know, and he wasn't sure what he was seeing.

That's why comprehensive mapping was important to finding lost ships in foldspace. Most rescue ships didn't stumble on their targets. Most rescue ships found the lost ship through thorough and detailed mapping, covering vast areas of foldspace small sections at a time.

The other ships' map had a lot more detail than his did. His was a one-time capture, the beginning of a search—and not a very good beginning at that.

Theirs followed procedure, the map precise, accurate and clear.

Still, he should have been able to find something. That planet, *something*.

"I'm not working with a lot of data here," Coop said, "but I'm not finding any points in common."

"Me, either," Rettig said. Apparently, he had been working on this as well.

Of course he had. He was clearly as curious about these things as Coop was.

The entire bridge was silent. Then Heyek cleared her throat.

"We'll deal with that later," she said. "I'm sure the *Voimakas* has extensive maps of that sector of foldspace. We'll get better answers when they're ready to work with us."

Answers. No one had actually spoken the question out loud. That question was: Had the *Arama* and the *Voimakas* been in a completely different sector of foldspace than the four other rescue ships?

Based on what he was seeing right now, Coop would have said yes. But he had more than enough science training to know that he didn't have enough data to make that determination with any kind of accuracy.

Just a gut sense.

A gut sense he didn't entirely like.

4

For the rest of the day, senior officials went in and out of the captain's quarters. Even though Coop's rank placed him higher than some of the people Nisen was talking with, Coop was not invited into her quarters.

When his duty shift ended, he headed to the mess for a meal. He wanted information, but he couldn't get any more than he already had.

It wasn't that the senior staff had locked him out; it was simply that he wasn't entitled to know more than he already did.

Usually, he didn't mind the segregation of information. He understood the chain of command and the need-to-know basis of all information that came through a ship daily.

But this experience had been so unusual that he was curious about what had happened to the *Voimakas* and what would happen next. If he had made any close friends among the crew, he would have asked if they had lost time in foldspace before, but he didn't know anyone well enough.

He supposed he could go through the records, but that felt like he was taking the wrong matters into his own hands. He would learn what he needed to learn when he needed to learn it.

As frustrating as that was.

His stomach growled as he arrived on the recreation deck. He passed the empty recreation room. The smell of seared beef, peppers, and onion came out of the mess, and made him even hungrier. He would indulge in a high-calorie meal, just because he had nothing better to do.

He passed the ship's only bar as he headed toward the mess's open doors. The bar was a large room with no windows. It had an actual bar in the center of the room. The bar itself, which had a shiny black surface, ran in an oval, with only one way to get behind it. Whoever did step into that oval and got caught became bartender for the night.

Someone always had to step inside, too, because all of the alcohol was stored in cases below the bar's surface. Coop had learned that the hard way on his first visit to the bar on his second night. He had wanted a drink, and he had not received it, because he had spent the entire night making drinks for everyone else.

He glanced inside as he walked past, and was startled to see the captain sitting near the door, her feet up on a black table, an overflowing pilsner glass in her hand.

"Lieutenant Tightass!" she shouted. "Come in here."

She'd shouted at him as he walked by the bar in the past, usually telling him to join the group or to have a drink. Answering her summons had been how he gotten trapped behind the bar on that second night.

"Thank you, Captain. May I have my dinner first?" he said, stopping.

"This is not a request, Tightass. I need your shapely buns in this chair across from me right now." She set the pilsner glass down and did not signal for a drink for him, also a change from the other times she had brought him inside.

He let out a sigh that he knew she couldn't hear. A dozen people were scattered at various tables around the bar, and Li stood behind the bar, mixing a bright-blue concoction that fizzed and popped.

Coop stepped inside, pulled back the molded black chair and sat down. Heyek came over, holding a glass half full of the blue fizzy stuff.

"I gotta have a private conversation with Tightass," Nisen said to Heyek. "Make sure no one gets close for the next ten minutes, all right?"

Heyek nodded, then clapped her hands together, getting the patrons' attention. "Door's off limits for the next ten," she said. "You gotta leave, do so in the next thirty seconds."

Rettig sprinted from the far side of the room to the corridor. He gave Coop a thumbs-up as he went by. No one else left.

In fact, the remaining patrons moved as far from the captain's table as they could get. Coop had seen this before. The captain liked to have private meetings here, no matter who it inconvenienced.

Heyek sauntered to the edge of the actual bar, and sat on a stool, far enough away that she couldn't hear the conversation, but not so far away that she couldn't get up and block anyone who came too close.

Nisen swung her feet off the tabletop. She leaned forward, close enough to Coop that he could see her eyes. They were no longer red. She might've been drinking, but she wasn't drunk.

"You think I've been picking on you, don't you, Lieutenant Cooper?" she asked.

"What I think is immaterial, Captain," he said.

"From anyone else, I'd call that a 'yes.' But you're one cautious man, aren't you, Lieutenant?" She shoved the pilsner glass out of her way. "You keep all of your opinions to yourself."

When he didn't know anyone well, he did. And he knew no one well enough to trust them on this vessel.

"You performed amazingly well today," Nisen said. "I was impressed."

He hadn't expected her to say that. "Thank you, sir."

She nodded. "You beginning to understand what it's like to serve on a foldspace rescue vehicle?"

"I think so, sir."

"Because it's not all fun and games and high-level math."

"Clearly, sir."

Her eyes narrowed. "Today was a victory. We found two people alive. We lost over five hundred, but we got two. By their reckoning, they've been gone six years. The captain and her first officer remained to protect the ship and guard the *anacapa*. They weren't trying to get back. They'd given up on that. But they knew someone would be searching for them. As soon as their supplies ran out—and they had another six months—they would have destroyed the ship. That's why we find so many exploded ships in foldspace. It's procedure after it looks like no rescue will come. Did you know that, Lieutenant?"

He felt cold. "No," he said.

"Yeah, you probably haven't hit that level of command training. And so what you probably don't know is that we rarely find ships with living crews. Sometimes they die before they can blow the ship. Sometimes, I think, they refuse to do so."

He didn't know how to respond to that. This entire conversation was making him feel off-balance.

"Our mission isn't really rescue. It's recovery. We're supposed to pull vessels out of foldspace and return them to the main part of the Fleet for scrubbing. We also use any information gathered to learn more about foldspace." Her hand moved to the pilsner glass, then moved away as if she had thought the better of it.

Heyek was watching from the stool, her eyes glittering. Coop couldn't tell if she knew what Nisen was talking to him about.

The remaining crew was talking and laughing in their corner, thumping fists on tables, and occasionally shouting insults. Everyone seemed to be working hard at ignoring this conversation he was having with Nisen. Everyone except Heyek.

"Working these ships is life-threatening and ugly," Nisen said. Then she leaned back in her chair and folded her hands across her stomach. "This is where anyone else would ask me why we do it. But you're not going to, are you, Coop?"

He started. She had used his nickname. She had never done that before.

"You really are a tightass. One of those regulations-are-regulations guys." She made that sound like a fault.

He had no idea how to respond. He had never had a conversation like this in his career.

"I know you think I'm a drunk and a fuck-up," she said. "You also probably assume I've been assigned here, and I'm just waiting until my retirement."

He had to hold himself very still so that he wouldn't nod.

"I volunteered for this assignment," she said.

"Sir?" He couldn't prevent the word from escaping. He was surprised.

"Not this rescue of the *Voimakas*," she said, as if that was the question he was asking. He wasn't sure if it was or not. "I volunteered to captain a foldspace rescue vehicle. And your poker face isn't as good as you think, you know. You're wondering why anyone would volunteer."

He had been wondering that.

"I volunteered because I was waiting for you, Tightass," she said.

He didn't move. She wasn't hitting on him, was she? Because it sounded like she was, but it didn't feel like she was.

"I knew you were coming," she said.

"Me, sir?" he asked. Because this wasn't making sense. She had been captain of the *Arama* for eight years. He had checked the ship's records before he had come on board. He had done that on every vessel he'd been assigned to.

"Not you, exactly," Nisen said, sliding down in her chair. "But someone like you. I was beginning to think that I wouldn't find you."

"I'm afraid I don't understand, sir," Coop said.

"No, I don't suppose you do," she said. "You're a natural leader, Lieutenant. On top of that, you're bright and you're an original thinker, when you let yourself relax. You could be one of the great captains of the Fleet. Don't let them promote you higher."

He frowned, not sure what she was telling him.

"But your regulations-are-regulations attitudes are going to get in the way of you doing your job," she said. "You couldn't run this ship."

"I'd like to think I can, sir," he said.

"I know you'd like to think that," she said. "And maybe, ten or fifteen years from now, if your ass loosens up, you'll be able to. But now? You'd have a ship full of failed officers, or suicides, or you'd face a mutiny. Running a foldspace rescue vehicle is a delicate balance. Your crew will see everything and anything. They'll have to be reckless enough to enter foldspace repeatedly without freezing up, and they'll have to be compassionate enough to handle people like Captain Golan and her first officer upon the return from hell, and they'll have to be willing to fail almost continually."

Coop wished now he'd gotten a drink before this conversation started. He at least wanted something to do with his hands. Instead, he folded them together.

"They can't be the brightest officers in the Fleet, but they have to creative enough to take whatever is thrown at them. They need to be a good crew, but not a great crew. You understand?"

He was beginning to think he did.

She leaned forward and put an elbow on the table. "I've processed a lot of captain candidates through here. I was starting to think that I had made up this idea that there were great captains in waiting. I was starting to think that there were good candidates and horseshit candidates and nothing beyond that and nothing in between."

Coop frowned.

She nodded toward the crew in the corner. "They're going to get drunk tonight. And tomorrow night. And the night after that, if we don't get a new assignment. And the other shifts, they'll get drunk in their off-duty hours or they'll screw like insane teenagers. I'd like to say I don't care, but I do. I picked them because they can blow off steam, and I let them do it. They're not going anywhere. This is their past, present, and future. When they leave the *Arama*, they'll retire. If experience is a judge, they'll return as far from *anacapa* drives as they can get."

Coop resisted the urge to glance at the crew. Some of the people at the far end of the room were still in their twenties. And she had already written them off.

"This job ruins you for extended time in foldspace," she said. "And yet we require all of our captain candidates to serve on a foldspace rescue vehicle."

"To understand what happens in foldspace," he said.

She shook her head. "To see if it breaks them. Half the candidates we get here leave the career-captain track when they leave the *Arama*. *If* they leave. Heyek didn't."

Coop's gaze flicked toward Heyek, and then he silently cursed himself. He was usually better than that.

"Why did she stay?" he asked.

"Because she realized she had only a few years to spend around foldspace. She decided she would be useful instead of fearing the jump every time. She's almost at the end of her service, and she knows it. I know it too."

Coop swallowed. "But you're not?"

Nisen's mouth twisted in a bitter smile. "Foldspace already destroyed my life. I lost everyone I cared about decades ago, and it wasn't even my fault. I wasn't on that ship. I was heading home from another assignment."

He waited, immobile, trying to see what else she would say.

"I insisted on doing the grid search," she said. "I found the ship. And I'm not going to describe to you what I found inside—what *we* found inside. But I will tell you that the captain's chair you look at with barely concealed contempt came off that ship. It's my reminder of the stakes here."

"The stakes," he repeated, not quite a question, but not quite a statement either.

"Yeah." Her voice took on an edge he had never heard before. "Everyone on that ship died because their captain followed regulations to the letter. The original tightass, unwilling to bend a regulation to save three hundred lives."

Coop opened his mouth to respond, then realized he had no idea what to say.

"So, I monitor captain candidates. I wash out the ones who would strand their crews in foldspace because the rules are too important." She was staring at him.

"And that's what you think I am," he said.

"Hell, no," she said. "You could be, if you don't fix that ass of yours. But you're also bright, and you'll listen. You know how to conquer your fear—don't think I didn't see it in your face this afternoon—and get the job done. And you only question your assumptions when it's worthwhile to do so, not in the middle of the work."

He sat stiffly.

"Which makes you," she said, "the first captain candidate in eight years that I didn't send back for more training, keep on this ship in a different capacity, or wash out entirely. I'm transferring you out of here, Lieutenant, and I'm sending you with a commendation."

He frowned. "Not to sound ungrateful, sir," he said, "but I didn't do anything worthy of a commendation."

She laughed. The laugh was big and brash and it filled the room. The laugh also stopped all conversation, and everyone looked at their table, which made it clear the laugh was as unusual as Coop thought it was.

She waved her hand dismissively, and Heyek turned to the crew. They turned away, without Heyek having to say anything.

Nisen said, "You found us a ship that we wouldn't have found without you. You didn't balk when you realized you were sending us into a dangerous situation, and you didn't apologize when you realized you nearly got us trapped as well. You reminded me that I needed to follow some regulations, not because of my ship, but because the Fleet might need those regulations followed for other reasons. You changed a lot of things today, Lieutenant, and you did so as a matter of course, not because you were gunning for a promotion."

He didn't gun for promotions. He never had. But he didn't say that. He had a hunch she already knew it.

"I am going to recommend one thing, though," she said, her eyes glinting with humor. It transformed her. She looked younger when she smiled, even when the smile was a bit feral. "I'm going to send a request with your transfer. For the first month in your new posting, I'm going to demand as a condition of your service that your C.O. call you Lieutenant Tightass."

His cheeks heated.

"It sounds frivolous," she said. "But it's not. Because if that nickname sticks after that month, then you're going to end up being a danger to whatever crew you lead. But if the nickname vanishes within six months because it no longer applies, then you'll be as good a captain as I think you can be."

He stared at her, feeling like he was in between foldspace and real space, stuttering along, hoping he'd get by.

"Now," she said, "get the hell out of here. You look like a man who needs a meal."

"I actually think I'm a man who needs a drink," he said.

She grinned. "Amateurs who drink on an empty stomach get drunk."

He grinned back. "But I'm no amateur."

Although he might be, compared to her. And compared to the rest of the crew of the *Arama*. He only drank when he was on leave.

He let his grin fade. "Thank you, sir," he said.

"Don't thank me," she said. "You just make sure that when something goes horribly, terribly wrong in your command—and it will, you'll walk into one of those impossible situations where there are no good results—you'll do the best you can by your crew, even if it means breaking all the rules. Can you promise me that, Tightass?"

He thought about it for a moment, thought about being trapped for years in foldspace, about staying on the ship even though it meant sacrificing his life, his future, while the rest of the crew went to places unknown to start again.

That probably broke some rules. Just like bringing a ratty captain's chair into a pristine new vessel probably broke rules.

He needed to pay more attention. He needed to see what leaders were doing, when they chose to follow regulations, and when they chose not to. He needed to figure out whether a break with regulations meant something good for the crew or not.

Nisen tilted her head. He had been silent long enough to catch her attention.

"I can make you that promise, Captain," he said. "Even though at this moment, I'm not sure I understand all the implications of it."

She smiled and grabbed her beer.

"That's spot on, Coop," she said. "You don't understand the implications of it. You won't, until the day comes. I'd like to say you'll think about me in that moment, but you won't. I'll be a distant memory, if you think of me at all. I want this all to be second nature to you."

She raised her glass to him.

"And I'm pretty sure it will," she said. Then she downed the contents. "You're one behind, Tightass. I'm buying. Catch up."

Then she signaled Heyek, who went behind the bar and poured Coop a pale ale. Not his usual drink of choice, but he didn't say anything.

Heyek brought the drink over and handed it to him, without a change in expression, leading him to believe this was how the meetings with the captain candidates and Nisen always ended.

Heyek went back to the bar, and Coop raised his glass to Nisen.

"To you, Captain," he said, "and your crew."

She grinned at him. "For God's sake, Tightass. Let's just drink."

And so they did.

New York Times-*bestselling author and editor Kevin J. Anderson has made a name for himself authoring sprawling space operas, including entries in the Star Wars and Star Trek series, amongst others. His most recent epic, Saga of Shadows, is actually a sequel to his earlier Saga of Seven Suns, from which this story comes. It serves as a prequel to the entire series, as Anderson explains below.*

AUTHOR'S NOTE: *My Saga of Seven Suns and Saga of Shadows series are a sprawling space opera, a universe of cultures and characters. One group of people are the Roamers, resourceful space gypsies who run rugged colonies and cloud-harvesting "skymines" on gas giant planets, living in places and doing jobs that nobody else wants. Downtrodden, the Roamers are always fighting for their independence, and they have a hero and freedom fighter, Rand Sorengaard, whom they view as a Robin Hood type. The rest of the Terran Hanseatic League, however, sees him as a ruthless terrorist because of his extreme actions. It all depends on your point of view. This story takes place just before the events in the first novel of the series, Hidden Empire, revealing the never-before-told backstory of Rand Sorengaard, whether he really is a terrorist, or a hero with feet of clay.*

FEET OF CLAY

A SAGA OF SEVEN SUNS STORY

KEVIN J. ANDERSON

I

With solar fins extended like a graceful fighting fish, the huge Ildiran warliner rose from the skymine that drifted in the gas giant's clouds. The alien ship's tanks were full of stardrive fuel harvested from Oriloo's atmosphere, and the Roamer skyminers watched the majestic vessel depart, its business completed.

Standing on the upper deck, Lily Hsieh shaded her eyes and watched the warliner fly off, thinking of all the places she had never seen. She was fifteen and slender, dressed in a utilitarian tan jumpsuit embroidered with the familiar symbols of clan Hsieh. Her suit sported many clips, zippers, pockets, and loops, all of which could be pressed into service when she ran maintenance on her family's skymine, performing the busy tasks that every Roamer knew how to do. She pulled her light brown hair back into a ponytail that wouldn't get in her way in the whipping high-atmosphere winds of the gas giant.

With a sliding sound, her father shuffled up to her on the observation deck. Though he was nimble enough aboard the giant floating factory, he still dragged one foot from the old injury. He followed Lily's gaze into the sky. "That's a sight to see, isn't it?"

Lilly nodded. "It's beautiful. The Ildirans usually pick up fuel at the depot rather than coming to the source." She watched the ship rise higher into the thinning wisps of clouds. "That will pay a month's expenses."

"They'll be out of range soon enough." Richard Hsieh stroked his chin, unconsciously following the deep lines in his face. "Then we'll be safe."

Lily turned to look at him. "We're not worried about the Ildirans. They've always been peaceful."

"Rand Sorengaard has reasons to worry about many things. With half the Spiral Arm looking for him, he doesn't take chances."

The crew of Roamer workers got back to work on the drifting station. The domed industrial complex cruised along, scooping up chemical vapors, sorting them, running them through reactors, converting and compressing the stardrive fuel. They had all the skies in which to wander. The workers, most of them extended members of clan Hsieh, knew their jobs, worked hard, and maintained a low profile. The Roamer clans operated on the fringe of the human interplanetary government, the Terran Hanseatic League—second-class citizens performing necessary but unappreciated work.

A hush had fallen over the skymine, then shouts came from other open decks. Lily looked down to see the deep cloud layer churned by the exhaust from small but high-powered stardrive engines. She felt a chill as three muscular-looking armored ships rose from the sheltering mists, coming out of their hiding places. The ships were Roamer vessels plastered with modifications, augmented engines, extended sensor arrays, and brash markings that made the vessels look distinctive, even unnerving.

As the corsair ships approached, Richard Hsieh laughed out loud. "You see that, Lily? They cut through the lower atmosphere and waited for the Ildiran warliner to leave. Rand doesn't take any chances! He's too smart for that!"

Other skyminers cheered to welcome the ominous ships that circled the giant floating factory. The skymine's control center transmitted to her father's comm, "Sorengaard is asking permission to dock. Should I tell him it's okay, Richard?"

"Of course. We'll welcome him down in the hangar bay." Her father flashed a glance at her. "Come on, Lily. This is important."

Lily easily kept up with her father's uncertain gait as he went to the nearest lift. She had never met the Roamer outlaw, but her father had told her many stories of Rand Sorengaard and his exploits, how he constantly poked Hansa commercial ships, giving them a black eye, raiding their luxury cargos and distributing the valuable goods to struggling Roamer installations. "Taking from the greedy, helping the worthy," was his catch phrase. Sorengaard was a hero to the clans, a man who stood up for their rights and for their freedom.

The three corsair ships entered the skymine's cavernous hangar bay. The chamber was large enough to hold and load fuel tankers and cargo vessels that visited Oriloo.

Her father held onto her arm, his eyes shining with amazed wonder. "By the Guiding Star, we'll do what we can to help them. I wish your mother and sisters were here." The rest of Lily's family had gone on a supply trip to the main Roamer complex of Rendezvous, and they wouldn't be back for days.

She tossed her ponytail. "We know how to show hospitality, Dad. Just me and you."

The boarding ramp extended on the lead corsair ship, and a tall man with a long face, lantern jaw, and close-cropped brown hair stepped out. He exuded a grand presence about him as he paused at the top of the ramp as if for dramatic effect before the Roamers gathered in the hangar bay. Richard and the skymine crew applauded as Rand Sorengaard walked down the ramp. His jumpsuit looked new, embroidered with many clan markings. A colorful sash encircled his waist.

Behind Sorengaard came two more men, a hardbitten middle-aged woman, and a near-naked, entirely bald man with emerald skin. The green man carried a small ornate pot in the crook of his arm, which held a delicate gold-barked treeling with feathery fronds.

Lily blinked. "He has a green priest with him, too?"

Waving, her father spoke out of the corner of his mouth, "His name is Cole, joined Rand's followers several years ago. He can use the treeling for communication, if necessary."

Green priests from the jungle planet Theroc were telepathically connected to the network of sentient worldtrees. By touching a treeling, they could communicate with any other treeling, anywhere, and also draw from the incredible archive of knowledge in the worldtree mind.

Richard limped forward, extending his hand. "Welcome to the Hsieh skymine! As good Roamers, we're happy to help your cause in any way we can. We all have the same Guiding Star." He placed an arm around Lily's shoulder. "And this is my daughter. I've told her all about you."

"I am fighting for all of us," Sorengaard said.

"I know you need supplies and stardrive fuel," her father said. "We can provide you with all of that."

The stern green priest stepped down the ramp and took up a position next to his leader. "I'll see to all the inventory, Rand. I have a list of what we need." He gave Lily a grimace that might have been meant as a smile. "The little girl can help, if she knows the skymine."

Lily sniffed. "I'm not a little girl. I'm fifteen."

The green priest regarded her and said, "I'm older than that, so you're still little as far as I'm concerned."

Sorengaard chuckled, as did his fellow corsairs. Her father seemed giddy to be in the presence of such a celebrity. Richard told his crew to open the storage modules and pump stardrive fuel into the tanks and reserves of the three outlaw ships. Richard Hsieh showed them every hospitality.

Later in the mess hall Lily listened with wonder and a healthy dose of skepticism as the corsairs told tales of their raids, their near escapes, how many times they had humiliated the "Big Goose," the

Roamer derogatory term for the Terran Hanseatic League. Smiling, her father nodded along with everything Sorengaard said.

"I wish I could join you." He patted his leg. "What you're doing is important, Rand, but I've got so many responsibilities in this skymine... And with my injury, I'm not as agile as I should be these days."

Cole, the green priest, frowned in her father's direction. "I'm sure we could find something useful for you to do, even with a limp, if you really wanted to join us."

Flushing, Richard let out a nervous chuckle. "I'm afraid my adventuring days are over..." He quickly turned to Lily. "But my daughter is skilled! The smartest fifteen-year-old you'll ever meet, and she's been wanting adventure for a long time."

Lily knew that was true, but she didn't understand what her father was saying.

At the long mess-hall table, Sorengaard gave her a serious look. "If you're dedicated, young lady, and if you want to make a serious difference for all the clans, I would take you under my wing. We'd be happy to have you."

The green priest gave her an amused look, "Unless you think daily skymine operations are more interesting?"

Lily's throat went dry. "It's not about what's more interesting. I'm needed here."

"The Roamers need you, too," Sorengaard said. "What is it you want to do with your life?"

Anxious, she looked at her father as the realization began to sink in.

"What does your Guiding Star say, girl?" her father pressed. "Think of the opportunity."

Lily didn't know what to say. Her father had told so many tales about this man. Every Roamer knew Rand Sorengaard and his legendary corsairs. And she could be part of them?

"Your mother and sisters will be back soon to help with operations," her father said. "You can go."

Sorengaard stood from the mess-hall table and reached out a hand. "You'll have a place among us, Lily Hsieh—and a place in Roamer history."

She stared at his hand for a long moment, but Lily knew there was really only one decision.

II

The three powerful ships streaked away from the gas giant, their fuel tanks and cargo holds full, the rebels satisfied with clan Hsieh's hospitality. Lily rode aboard the *Cause*, the main corsair ship, by a special invitation from Sorengaard himself. As she left the Oriloo skymine, she carried only a small satchel of personal possessions, mementos of her family, reminders of her home. A Roamer could make do anywhere and with anything, and her new companions would provide her with whatever else she needed.

Though she was excited, she felt a swirling storm in her stomach like an empty pocket of air. She remembered once when the skymine had dropped nearly five hundred meters after the antigravity engines failed in a storm. Now Lily felt unsettled but also excited.

She had her own small cabin, which would have been no more than a closet on the skymine. Though he had welcomed her into his band, Sorengaard kept to his own cabin or the piloting deck. Instead, Lily met some of his other followers: Bruno, who claimed to be a good cook though he ate prepackaged meals along with everyone else, and Wanda, a brawny hardbitten woman who claimed that the Big Goose had killed every member of her family, although she gave no details. Lily also spent time with the dry but patient green priest, Cole.

When they sat together in the rec chamber or the galley, Lily expected her companions to play games or talk about their homes or missed loved ones. Instead, Sorengaard's followers were intense and determined, and when they talked, they merely echoed and reinforced their anger against the Hansa.

Bruno grumbled, "The Hansa economy depends on our stardrive fuel and all the metals we excavate from harsh environments."

"Nobody else could do what we do," said Wanda. "They're too weak."

Sorengaard entered the galley with a cup of coffee held loosely in his hand. He took a sip. "Considering how much the clans do, it's surprising how little respect we get. The Big Goose pushes us to the fringes, and we're stuck in corners where nobody else wants to be." He slurped from his cup and leaned against the bulkhead. "But we do just fine." He paused for a moment deep in thought. "And we all do better when we take things from them, just to remind the Hansa not to ignore us. Taking from the greedy, helping the worthy."

The others agreed loudly, and Lily added her cheer to theirs.

As the three ships flew onward toward their base, she came upon Cole on a metal bench by one the ship's large windowports. The green priest held his potted treeling in his lap, and he stared out at the streaming stars with a preoccupied expression.

"Aren't you cold?" Lily asked. "You're barely wearing any clothes."

"I'm wearing as many clothes as I need." His brow furrowed as he turned to her. "I thought Roamers were tough. Do I need to get you a blanket, little girl?"

"I'm fine." She looked out the windowport, trying to see what held his attention. "I didn't know there were any green priests among the Roamers. Aren't you supposed to be on Theroc with those giant trees?"

"I have my tree." He stroked the ornate pot with his fingers. "They're all connected, so if I have this treeling, then I have the whole worldforest."

"Don't green priests sell their services to the Hansa, for instant communication across their planets and ships?"

He kept looking out the windowport. "Not all green priests. I decided not to."

"I'm glad you're with Rand Sorengaard instead."

He stretched out his arm and placed his green palm against the transparent barrier between him and the stars. "Theroc is not a member of the Terran Hanseatic League either, although Chairman Wenceslas would very much like to control us. Our leaders prefer to be independent and have no interest in signing the Hansa Charter, but we are second-class citizens just like the Roamers. We have to fight to be taken seriously."

"I've never heard of a green priest who fights," Lily said. "I thought you were peaceful."

"There are many ways to fight. Maybe I fight by helping Rand Sorengaard."

Lily thought about that. "Just like me."

"I am not just like you. I never intended to be a green priest in the first place." Cole looked at his arm, his green skin. "Do you think I wanted my whole body to change, just so I could be linked with all the worldtrees?" He shook his head. "No, it was my mother who wanted to be a green priest, not me. She obsessed about it all her life, but she proved inadequate to the testing. Instead, she forced me to become an acolyte. The green priests raised me and trained me, and I never had any other options. It took me four years longer than anyone else to become a green priest, but in the end the forest accepted me, embraced me, and altered me." He scowled. "All my hair fell out, my skin changed color, and now the trees are always in my mind."

He looked down at his potted treeling as if it were a poisonous spider in his lap. "But I can communicate through telink. I can touch the treeling and drop in among the thoughts of all the other worldtrees and green priests, but I never communicate. I secretly listen, but they don't know I'm there."

"Then what good are you?" Lily challenged.

Cole bristled. "I can observe so Rand knows who's looking for him, how the Hansa is trying to hunt him down, and what the other planets are saying about him."

"So you're a spy?"

Cole narrowed his dark emerald dyes. "Yes, I suppose I am."

"And is your mother proud of you now? Since you're doing what she could not?"

"She's dead," Cole said, then reconsidered. "But, yes, I think she's pleased that I'm doing what she always wanted to do."

Lily brightened. "Then we have something in common because I'm doing what my father wanted me to do." She lifted her pointed chin. "I'm going to make a difference. I'll be part of history."

Cole seemed amused. "Enjoy it while it's still special, little girl." He turned back to stare out the windowport.

III

For Sorengaard's hidden base, Lily had expected some tunnel complex in a dark asteroid or a frozen moon on the fringe of a solar system.

Instead, the three outlaw ships flew closer and closer to a blazing yellow sun until she feared they might burn up the ionized gases. But just inside the densest curtains of the corona hung a large Ildiran warliner, a derelict ship seemingly abandoned.

Lily tried to make out details through the heavy optical filters on the windowport glass. The warliner she had recently seen at the Oriloo skymine was gaudy, its hull painted with brilliant markings, its solar fins extended, but this battleship was tarnished, the hull blackened.

Sorengaard stood next to her. "I know it's not pretty, but this one is ours, and no one knows it's here."

"How did you get an Ildiran warliner?" Lily asked.

"By happy circumstance. Sometimes Roamers have good luck."

"It was a disaster for the Ildirans, though," Cole said as he stepped up between them. "The warliner was part of a mapping expedition and got caught in a solar flare storm that killed half the crew. The Solar Navy swooped in to rescue the remaining Ildirans, then just left the wreck here. They probably think it's burned up in the sun by now."

Sorengaard crossed his arms over his chest. "But my Guiding Star took me here. We got the life support working, patched the damaged hull, and used the engines to move it out of the danger zone. We had to wear exosuits for the first year until we scrubbed most of the radiation, but it's a perfect hideout. No one would dare to look for us here."

The *Cause* headed toward the warliner's lower belly, where hangar doors began to open. All three vessels cruised into the inviting bay, and Sorengaard walked to the exit hatch after the *Cause* settled into place. On the way, he clumsily tousled Lily's hair, which she let hang loose now that she no longer worked out in the skymine's open air. She grimaced at the gesture, which implied the rebel leader considered her a mere child.

In the bustling launch bay, Sorengaard's followers hurried to unload and distribute the supplies and spare fuel that Richard Hsieh had provided. Lily felt swept up in the activity, like a small mouse about to be stepped on, but the green priest grasped her shoulder and shouted over the hubbub, "Attention! This is Lily from clan Hsieh. She'll be joining us." Cole looked down at her. "And we expect great things."

Sorengaard flashed his smile, caught off guard that he hadn't introduced his new follower. "Yes, give Lily a warm welcome. Since she grew up on a skymine, she knows how to pull her own weight and make herself useful."

Embarrassed by the attention, Lily felt her cheeks burn as she accepted the numerous greetings, the blur of faces that pressed closer. She didn't know how she would ever learn all their names. "I will do my best, by the Guiding Star."

"By the Guiding Star," the outlaws called.

Sorengaard responded with a paternal expression. "You will not do your best, Lily. You will *excel*."

Over the next several days, she learned how to fit in. Her quarters were much larger than the closet aboard the *Cause* because the Ildiran warliner could hold many thousands. She explored deck after deck on the alien ship, trying to imagine the Solar Navy officers and crew who had worked here. Ildirans were very similar to humans, and their comforts, furnishings, and customs were much the same.

Although Sorengaard's corsairs supposedly robbed Hansa trading ships blind and redistributed the wealth, Lily found that her daily work was similar to what she had done aboard the skymine. Many of the warliner's damaged systems needed refitting or jury-rigging, and Lily was good at that.

Every time she finished a task and stopped to take a rest, someone would assign her something else to do. Lily intended to do a good job. She wanted to *excel*, so she did all the tasks that needed doing. In her downtime, Lily wrote letters to her father, her mother, and each of her sisters. She felt caught up in her situation, but she did begin to wonder if they ever would go out on an actual raid.

Sorengaard had converted the warliner's command nucleus into his main offices. Lily was often tasked to bring him a private meal prepared by Bruno, usually with enough servings for all his staff, and Lily would stay as well. Under the alien bridge's transparent dome, the rebel leader enjoyed holding forth, stoking the emotions of his followers.

"Yes, I am a proud man," he said, twirling his fork to scoop up a mouthful of seasoned noodles. "I want what is best for the clans. I want the Roamers to be full citizens of the Hansa, or else completely free and independent. Right now, we're just caught halfway."

The others muttered. Bruno sat with them, joining his own feast. "The Big Goose exploits our fuel harvesting and our hard work. Someone has to push back."

"Push back," Wanda grumbled, then embarrassed herself with a burp. She wiped her mouth.

"We know our duty," Sorengaard said. "Take from the greedy, help the worthy."

By now, many of Sorengaard's words were familiar, but she still found them inspirational, although she had seen little more than talk. "Take from the greedy, help the worthy," she mouthed along as the others repeated the phrase.

Cole strode into the command nucleus holding the potted treeling in both hands, as if it might explode on him. He interrupted the meal and fixed his dark gaze on the rebel leader. The conversation paused.

"What is it, Cole?"

"I just learned something very interesting." The green priest balanced the potted treeling in the palm of one hand, and Lily was afraid the container might fall and shatter on the deck. "Hansa Chairman Basil Wenceslas is going to the planet Dallal where he will witness them signing the Hansa Charter. It's just a small diplomatic mission, very little publicity." His smile enhanced the lines in his emerald-green face, and he paused to let the news sink in. "He doesn't usually let himself be so vulnerable."

The other rebels began to mutter, and Rand smiled. "No, he doesn't."

IV

The Roamer government complex of Rendezvous was a cluster of asteroids jumbled together like a handful of large rocks held together by gravity and reinforced with structural girders, walkways, and bridges. This was the first foothold the Roamers had established, nearly two centuries ago, in the dim light of a red dwarf star. The clans had since spread out across the Spiral Arm, but their hard work of surviving in the austere asteroid cluster had taught them how to make a home anywhere, to eke out an existence in places shunned by the pampered

Hansa. Now Rendezvous was a vibrant hub of trade and diplomacy, a meeting point for the members of all clans.

Lily had been here before with her mother, an exciting break from the busy monotony of Oriloo's empty clouds. Now, as she rode with Sorengaard, Cole, and four other corsair ships, however, she felt genuinely important. This was not just a shopping expedition, but a crucial face-to-face meeting with Jhy Okiah, the Speaker for the Roamer clans.

When they flew into Rendezvous, Lily expected to receive cheers and a boisterous welcome, but Cole maintained radio silence, using a disguised identification beacon. Curious, she turned to Sorengaard, who regarded the flurry of space traffic around the cluster of asteroids with a strange, unreadable expression. "Are you worried even at Rendezvous? I thought the clans appreciate what we're doing. My father would never speak an ill word of you."

Sorengaard mused, "Ah, Lily, your optimism is refreshing. Every Roamer longs for freedom in their hearts—I don't doubt that for a moment—but not every Roamer is willing to pay the price."

At the controls, Cole grunted. "That's why some of us have to pay an extra price, but we don't count the cost. We just do what is right."

After they docked at the central asteroid, Bruno, Wanda, and the remaining corsairs spread out among the vibrant crowds, making connections, following up contacts, purchasing necessary equipment and supplies. Sorengaard, though, headed directly to the Speaker's main office complex. Word traveled swiftly of his arrival, and the green priest from Theroc was himself a distinctive sight, so the old woman knew they were coming long before they arrived.

Jhy Okiah's office was a chamber carved inside the old drifting rock, the smooth walls painted a sunny yellow. A wide single windowport looked out upon the bright stars, the dull warm glow of the red dwarf, and numerous spacecraft that flitted like bees around the asteroid complex.

Lily and Cole followed Sorengaard into the Speaker's office, and he spoke before the old woman could even greet him. "I've come to see you, Speaker, because I'm going to do something that will improve the lot of all Roamers. It affects every clan." He stood straight, and his voice was as hard as steel, delivering a message rather than initiating a discussion. "I wanted you to know."

Lily recognized the revered Jhy Okiah from countless drop broadcasts and messages, but she'd never met the woman in person. She was so ancient that her arms and legs were little more than sticks, and her skin was a rich tan like comfortable old leather. She had lived in low-g for so many years her body could no longer tolerate planetary gravity. Her jumpsuit bore the prominent embroidery of clan Okiah but, as Speaker, she also bore the markings of countless other clans. As the leader, she was a hard but reasonable woman, a negotiator who had held many diverse groups together for a long time.

Jhy Okiah did not rise from her desk as she remained silent, contemplating. "If you are doing something that affects every clan, wouldn't it be wise to discuss it in an open Roamer convocation?" Her birdlike eyes bored into his. "Or are you afraid they will disagree with you?"

"There's no time," Sorengaard said. "An opportunity has presented itself. I am alerting you so you can begin to make plans. The Roamers will finally achieve the greatness they deserve."

Skeptical, the old woman looked to the green priest and raised her eyebrows. "Are you here representing Theroc? They are independent as well. Does your presence imply an alliance between Rendezvous and the jungle planet?"

"Not at all," Cole said. He held his potted treeling against his bare ribs. "I'm just here for Rand."

Lily's heart leapt when the Speaker turned to her, and she bowed politely, introducing herself. "I'm very pleased to meet you, ma'am. I am Lily Hsieh."

"Richard's girl? Shouldn't you be working the skymine on Oriloo?"

"I'm one of his daughters, ma'am. He encouraged me to join Sorengaard's cause. He said it was important." She squared her shoulders. "I'm doing my best for the Roamer clans."

Jhy Okiah pursed her lips. "I doubt you know what you've gotten yourself into, young lady." She turned back to the tall rebel leader, who remained straight as a support girder in the office chamber. "And what is this plan of yours, Sorengaard? How will it get us in trouble?"

He summarized quickly. "The colony world of Dallal has met all the requirements to sign the Hansa Charter. Chairman Wenceslas is going there in person on a low-key diplomatic mission as a witness. We know where he will be, thanks to my green priest and the worldforest information network. My corsairs will swoop in and ambush him. We'll capture the Chairman's ship and take him hostage."

The old woman recoiled, placed her gnarled hands on the desktop. "You can't kidnap the Chairman!"

Sorengaard remained calm. "That way we can negotiate with him and impose our demands. The harassment and persecution will end." He crossed his arms over his chest as if he had just presented his closing argument.

Jhy Okiah shook her head. "Why would you provoke them and make our situation even worse? You'll bring down the wrath of the EDF on us all. We'll be cut off everywhere."

"They can't cut us off," Sorengaard said. "Roamers produce all the stardrive fuel in the Spiral Arm. The Ildirans will still trade with us, and the Hansa worlds know how vital we are. It's about time the government acknowledges it as well. We won't be taken advantage of any more."

"That is an extremely bad idea." The Speaker's voice was brittle. "I forbid it."

His face darkened with anger. "You may be the Speaker, but you are not my commander. I came to inform you, not ask you." He gestured to Lily and Cole and turned to leave. "It will be seen as a good idea when it works."

Embarrassed and frightened, Lily glanced back at the Speaker as Sorengaard stormed out. She hurried after them.

V

Bright sunshine poured through Earth's clear blue skies, reflecting from the impenetrable windows of the Hansa headquarters pyramid. The stepped structure sprawled over many city blocks, but even so it was dwarfed by the even more tremendous Whisper Palace, the ostentatious heart of the Terran Hanseatic League. While eyes were drawn to the incredible palace, the real business was conducted inside the pyramid.

In his spacious office complex at the topmost level of the ziggurat, Chairman Basil Wenceslas had called a meeting, and now he sat at his boardroom table across from General Lanyan, anxious to begin. The commander of the Earth Defense Forces was gruff and no-nonsense, also eager to get down to business. Both men had many other things to do.

"I have a launch ceremony for a new Juggernaut battleship in three hours, Mr. Chairman," the general said. "Shall I postpone it?"

"I can cover the main points quickly enough," Basil said, "although we will require careful staging from the EDF once we set the wheels in motion. My diplomatic mission must go off on schedule."

Lanyan wore his formal dark uniform, his chest emblazoned with medals from numerous military operations and peacekeeping activities. He had dark hair, a round face, and rich brown eyes that showed only a small amount of patience. His stomach was hard as a barrel.

Basil glanced over at Sarein, the thin and beautiful young woman from Theroc, daughter of the jungle planet's rulers. Sarein had come to Earth to serve as a planetary representative, but she was ambitious and negotiated as much for her own benefit as for her independent, resource-rich world. Sarein had also recently become his lover. Although Basil was many years her senior, the preservation treatments kept him strong, healthy, and virile; they both got what they wanted out of the relationship.

Sarein sat with a stack of documents, neatly aligned as she prepared for the important meeting. She drank a cup of steaming klee, a traditional beverage from Theroc, while Basil sipped fragrant cardamom coffee from a china cup. The general merely had water as he waited for the Chairman to come to the point.

"I am about to embark on a diplomatic mission to Dallal. This would normally entail my transport ship and a standard escort, but this time I may need more... and less. We have an opportunity."

"Dallal?" the general asked, clearly sifting his mind for information. "Why would you go there?"

"Because the planet is not significant enough for me to send Old King Frederick. Dallal spent years fulfilling the requests and filing the forms, and now they will be signing the Hansa Charter." Basil tapped his fingertips on the polished boardroom table. "We welcome every valuable new member of the Terran Hanseatic League."

Sarein looked down at the documents in front of her and spoke up. "Dallal's surface was bombarded by a meteor swarm a thousand years ago, and now those craters are rich with interesting metals and isotopes that they can easily mine."

Basil gave her a brief smile. She had asked if she could participate in the briefing. "The most important part, General, is that they won't be a drain on our resources. They will be productive members of the Terran Hanseatic League."

Lines appeared on Lanyan's brow. "So you're going there with a diplomatic ship to watch them sign the Hansa Charter? Why is this a military matter? Is there a threat I'm not seeing?"

"As I mentioned earlier, it's more of an opportunity, and that is where you come in." He touched his steel-gray hair, imagining that a strand might be out of place, but he found nothing awry. "This is our chance to remove that gadfly Rand Sorengaard."

Lanyan puffed his round cheeks and made a rude noise. "The Roamer pirate? Do you think he's hiding on Dallal?"

"No, but he will go there because I'll be there."

"He's impulsive," Sarein said. "He won't be able to resist."

Basil lifted two fingers in a subtle signal, and she quickly fell silent. "We have reason to believe there might be an ambush. His corsairs will try to attack my diplomatic ship." Now his smile became more genuine. "Knowing this, we can turn the tables on him. I'll travel with a minimal escort, but I want you to shadow me with a much larger EDF strike force."

Lanyan perked up, genuinely interested now. He took a drink of his water. "I see. Where did you learn this? Roamers are very tight-lipped. How certain is the intel?"

"It's reliable," Sarein interrupted. "Absolutely reliable." She turned and signaled to the door of the conference room.

Lanyan looked up as an old, half-naked green priest entered, an ancient woman with deep-green skin and sagging bare breasts. Her lined face, shoulders, chest, and arms were covered with tattoos. The bald crone looked like a piece of fruit that had dried in the heat.

She carried a tall potted treeling in her arms, which looked too large for her to carry. Sarein did not rise to help her.

The green priest shuffled forward despite the burden in her arms. "I have seen it myself. I've heard the conversations."

"General," Basil said, "I believe you know Ambassador Otema from Theroc. She is here to communicate through the worldforest network and to assist Sarein. I myself have used her for many diplomatic purposes."

"I serve Theroc," the old woman said.

"And I represent Theroc," Sarein interjected. "I instructed Ambassador Otema that if she were to pick up any information about Rand Sorengaard's plans or whereabouts, she was to report to me. Stability in the Spiral Arm is vital to both the Hansa and Theroc."

The old green priest seemed sullen. "There's a man named Cole among the rebels, a green priest. He carries a treeling, although he never communicates through telink. But I have been able to dip into his treeling to observe what else he might be doing. I overheard Sorengaard's conversation with the Roamer Speaker Jhy Okiah. He does intend to ambush Chairman Wenceslas." With a frown, she set the heavy pot on the boardroom table next to Basil, rattling his china cup. "I have no wish to be involved in this, but Sarein insisted."

Smiling, Lanyan drummed his fingertips on the table. "Very well, then. I'll call in my subcommanders so we can make our plans."

Basil rose from his chair. "Thank you, General, that is all. You can go launch the new Juggernaut. In fact, we might need it when we set our trap."

VI

As the corsair ships departed from Rendezvous, they traveled with ten additional ships, a batch of new recruits who were enamored with Rand Sorengaard and his struggles. The ambitious strays flew off, eager to do their part for the cause as well.

Sorengaard proudly accepted his new followers. "Each of you has your Guiding Star, and each of you has the heart of a Roamer." He smiled. "We all fight for the same great cause."

The new ships, the hodgepodge of clunkers, souped-up courier ships, and tarnished cargo haulers, flew along with Sorengaard's ships. As Lily sat in the piloting deck beside Cole, she found it odd to think that she was no longer the new kid here. She still felt wide-eyed and shy, but unsettled and a little sad after witnessing the tension between Sorengaard and Speaker Okiah.

After they set off from the asteroid cluster with all the new ships in tow, Sorengaard's demeanor changed to fiery anger. Cole looked down at the piloting console as stars streamed around them. "Back to the hideout, Rand? Not much time to gather our ships and go after Chairman Wenceslas."

"He won't know what hit him," Bruno muttered from the adjacent common room.

"He won't know what hit him," Sorengaard agreed, "but we don't have the time to return to the warliner, gather the crews, and get to the Dallal system with enough of a cushion." His lips formed a hard, thin smile. "The Chairman's diplomatic mission is already on the way…"

The green priest was surprised. "You're going to attack with only our four main ships? Will that be enough?"

Wanda grunted from the back deck. "Not four ships—*fourteen*. It'll be a perfect initiation for our new recruits."

Sorengaard nodded. "We'll arrive in the outer system and go silent as we head down toward where the Chairman will pass." He folded his fingers together to form a double fist as he stood there. "We'll do a linked comm with all the new recruits, let them know the plan. Bruno and Wanda, I want you each to captain one of our main vessels for the strike. Everyone gets a chance to participate."

Lily remembered how intricate the skymine processes were, how every single component had to work perfectly together or the entire system would collapse. "That's all the planning you're going to do?"

"Being impetuous doesn't mean poor planning," Sorengaard said. "We've survived and escaped by being unpredictable. That is why the Hansa fears us." He looked out at the starry emptiness. "And once we have the Chairman, they will not only fear us, they will respect us."

His charisma convinced Lily, though the more she thought about the plan, the less viable it seemed.

The green priest shrugged and did what he was told, resetting the course, transmitting a joint comm to all corsair ships, including the new recruits. The ragtag fleet streaked off to their destination.

The Dallal system had a white primary sun and an orange dwarf companion that orbited at a great distance. The corsair ships vectored in along the orange dwarf's line of sight from the planet, using its glare to mask their energy signatures.

Dallal was a terrestrial planet with a moisture-rich, breathable atmosphere. Its land masses were pocked by craters, like a severe case of acne, but all those old meteor strikes led to rich deposits of easily excavated metals.

"Some people have all the luck," Bruno said as he got ready to shuttle over to the ship he would pilot during the ambush. "Roamers live in harsh environments to scrape out resources. Those colonists just dig down and pick metal up off the ground."

"They can't help where they live," Lily said, feeling edgy. "You could say that my clan's skymine just 'drifts along and scoops stardrive fuel,' but it's not as simple as that."

"I have no grudge against the people of Dallal," Sorengaard said. "They just happen to be the right catalyst for what we need to do. Chairman Wenceslas is the one that interests me."

When the group of ships quietly took up their positions, they hung in space waiting for more than a day. Lily began to grow nervous, worrying that their information might be in error.

One of the anxious new recruits transmitted a tight line-of-sight burst. "Should we spread out and scout, Rand? He's got to be coming soon."

"Quiet!" he shouted into the comm. "Radio silence! Just wait."

The Chairman's diplomatic craft arrived a mere ninety minutes after the target time. The Hansa vessel was an ornate official craft designed for comfort rather than speed or defense. One EDF Manta cruiser paced the diplomatic craft, an intimidating escort. As the Chairman's diplomatic procession approached Dallal, the Manta's hangar bay doors opened and fifteen swift Remora fighters dropped out and flew ahead of the diplomatic craft.

"That Manta is more firepower than I expected." Frowning, Sorengaard tapped on the control console. "But we have the element of surprise and more than enough ships to achieve our goal."

His ambush ships hung in the interplanetary void, running dark and silent. Lily felt a knot in her stomach. All fourteen of the waiting ships kept their weapons ready, waiting for the word. Sorengaard brushed sweat from his brow, watching the oblivious diplomatic craft traveling within range.

His voice was raspy when he spoke. "We can't wait any longer, Cole. One of those newbies is going to jump the gun and ruin our element of surprise." He reached for the comm as the green priest worked at the ship's controls. His potted treeling was anchored and secured on an adjacent console, but he would not touch the plant, would not communicate through telink. This was their secret mission, and it would remain so.

Sorengaard barked into the comm, "Time to pounce! You know what to do."

The *Cause*'s internal systems flared bright, and running lights dazzled like a new constellation in the dark emptiness. When the engines surged, Cole accelerated so hard that Lily stumbled against the bulkhead wall. Sorengaard's flagship dove down like an eagle snatching a young hare. Attuned to their leader, Wanda and Bruno each piloted their own ships and followed him, firing warning shots.

"Target the Remoras!" Sorengaard called. "Disable only. I don't want any unnecessary casualties. That'll make negotiations a lot harder."

Jazer blasts spat out, taking the small EDF fighter craft by surprise and punching out their engines. Only a few seconds behind the initial corsair ships, all ten new recruits charged in like a stampeding crowd, making orbital space above Dallal into a bright shooting gallery.

Within minutes, a dozen Remoras drifted in space, crippled, but the big Manta cruiser flared into action, powering up weapons ports.

"We only have a second," Sorengaard said. "Surround the diplomatic craft! Aim all weapons toward the hull so they can see we mean business. That'll make the others back away."

The green priest brought the *Cause* just above the Chairman's diplomatic ship, and thirteen other vessels swarmed around, holding the important craft hostage. "This is Rand Sorengaard," he said over the open comm. "To the Manta commander—stand down, deactivate your weapons, power off all defenses. Our weapons are trained on the Chairman's craft, and we will vaporize it at my order." He smiled into the screen. "I would advise you to back away, if you value his life."

Chatter buzzed across the comm as the Chairman's vessel sat paralyzed and subdued. Lily's throat was dry and she could barely breathe. Everything had happened in only a few seconds.

Sorengaard had shifted his expression, imagining that he spoke to someone else on the screen, which still remained blank. "Chairman Basil Wenceslas, my associates and I invite you to be our guest. We will remove you from the diplomatic craft and fly off for further negotiations. No one needs to get hurt. The current relationship between the Terran Hanseatic League and the Roamer clans is unacceptable, and we will convince you how to make improvements." He crossed his long arms over his chest. "Prepare to surrender yourself, and we can be on our way."

The response from the diplomatic craft was not at all what Lily expected. She had seen images of the suave and composed Chairman with his impeccable suits and his carefully maintained appearance. The transmission from the diplomatic craft, though, showed a dark-haired man in an EDF general's uniform. His skin was ruddy with anger, and his brown eyes glinted. "The Chairman is aboard the Manta cruiser, Roamer scum. I'll grant you only a few seconds to issue your own surrender."

Cole recoiled from the piloting console. "They set a trap! They knew we'd be here."

One of the new recruit ships opened fire and grazed the diplomatic craft's hull with a scorching jazer blast. The Manta's defenses brightened into full power as railgun ports opened and jazer emitters flared with energy.

Then three more Mantas roared down out of empty space from where they, too, had hidden in stealth mode, just waiting for Sorengaard's ships to make their move. Their launching bays were already open and spewed out hundreds of Remora fighters.

KEVIN J. ANDERSON

Sorengaard reacted. "They ambushed us. We've been tricked!"

"By the Guiding Star!" Lily cried, pointing toward the main windowport. Behind the streaking cruisers came an enormous battleship five times the size of a Manta, with gleaming hull plates and massive weapons batteries. "Is that a Juggernaut? I've never seen a Juggernaut."

Jazer blasts rained down, and a targeted railgun barrage hammered into Wanda's ship, which exploded just above the diplomatic craft.

Sorengaard pounded the comm, yelling at his corsairs. "We're dead in ten seconds unless we move! Full-line scatter retreat. You know what to do!"

Cole accelerated, throwing Lily to the deck as the *Cause* swirled away from their intended prey. The three other veteran corsair ships followed Sorengaard, but Bruno's ship wheeled about and dove toward the first Manta, all of his weapons blazing. Twenty of the fast Remoras closed in on him, blasting his ship into space dust in only a few seconds.

Sorengaard and his two veteran ships raced away, desperate to escape.

But behind them, the new recruits were panicked. Their ten ships scrambled in uncoordinated retreat, not knowing where to go or what to do. "They're not following us!" Lily cried.

"We can't leave people behind, Rand," the green priest said.

On the rear screens, five of the new recruits exploded under the barrage. The Juggernaut unleashed a storm of railgun projectiles, and the Mantas strafed the emptiness with jazers. The last ships were clearly doomed, unprepared for this kind of battle.

An overlapping chatter of screams and pleas splashed through the speaker, but the EDF mowed down the ships one by one.

"Nothing we can do," Sorengaard said. "Go! Go!"

The *Cause* and two veteran ships accelerated away from the battle with their enhanced Roamer engines. When Cole activated the stardrive, their path stretched out in a flash, snapping them away from the Dallal system.

VII

The three surviving ships limped away like a funeral procession, heading back to the safety of their derelict Ildiran warliner. Devastated by what she had seen, Lily felt terrified and hopeless aboard the *Cause*. This was not the glorious victory she had expected. Naïve and cheerful, she had believed her father's stories about how Rand Sorengaard fought for the rights of Roamers, but in those dangerous exploits, no one was supposed to get hurt. *Taking from the greedy, helping the worthy.* This wasn't a game.

Cole avoided his treeling, refusing to connect with the worldforest, not wanting to learn any propaganda about what had happened at Dallal. Many in the Hansa already portrayed Sorengaard and his followers as violent terrorists, and he simply didn't want his thoughts intermingling with those of other green priests.

"Somehow the Big Goose learned what we planned," Sorengaard grumbled. He paced the deck, venting his anger to anyone who would listen, and the surviving corsairs added their own grief and frustration.

"They set us up." Sorengaard hammered his fist against the bulkhead, pounding until his knuckles were bloody. "This is the Hansa's fault. They changed the rules. Didn't I give strict instructions to avoid casualties? When we fired on the Remora ships, we disabled engines only... and they destroyed Wanda's ship with their first shot." When he turned his darkened face to Lily, she saw only a stranger there. A chill went down her back.

His voice dropped, quieter but more deadly. "We can no longer afford to be charming Robin Hoods. Our cause is still just, and as Bruno, Wanda, and all those other ships demonstrated, our cause is worth dying for." He squeezed his fists so tight Lily thought his knuckles might pop out of the skin. "*They changed the rules,*" he repeated.

Hours later, as they continued their somber flight back to base, the three battered ships unexpectedly encountered a cargo vessel on the outskirts of the Yreka system.

"It's a trading ship, Rand," Cole said. He glanced at his treeling but still refused to touch it. "All by itself, probably heading to Yreka with a load of cargo." The grizzled green priest shrugged. "Seems to be a decent target."

Emotions boiled to the surface on Sorengaard's long face. "How do we know it's not another trap?"

Cole frowned. "It's not conceivable the EDF could guess our course and put a plan in place within a day. That's just a trading ship."

Sorengaard's shoulders relaxed a little. "Then we've found our next prey. It'll be the first step in making things right."

With tight-beam transmission, he contacted the other two corsairs. "We'll disable them and then take whatever we want. Fast and efficient. This is something we know how to do."

Lily felt uneasy. "Shouldn't we just get back to the base as fast as we can? So many people are dead already."

"Not enough people." Sorengaard's words terrified her. "And not the right people."

With well-practiced moves, the three corsair ships sprang out of the emptiness and closed around the oblivious trading vessel. Cole announced over the open comm, "Cargo ship, stand down and prepare to be boarded."

Sorengaard shouldered him aside and boomed into the voice pickup. "This is Rand Sorengaard. Your ship now belongs to us."

The panicked captain responded. "This is Captain Gabriel Mesta of the neutral trading vessel *Great Expectations*, under contract for Kett Shipping. We are neutral and unarmed. We don't have any beef with you."

"Unfortunately, we have a beef with you and what you represent," Sorengaard said in a voice as cold as space. "You're part of the Hansa, and the Hansa has caused us great harm. Prepare to surrender everything you have." He paused, then growled, "Everything."

Captain Mesta was a small-statured, swarthy man with blue-black hair and an elaborate mustache. Three crew members clustered around him at the comm screen, an older heavyset woman, a thin androgynous person, and a young deckhand not much older than Lily, a boy who had likely signed aboard to see the Spiral Arm.

"I know the *Great Expectations*," Lily said, crowding closer after Sorengaard muted the comm. "It's just a cargo ship. They brought supplies to our skymine a few times."

"I didn't change the rules," the rebel leader said.

His three ships pressed around the cargo vessel, all their weapons hot and intimidating. The *Great Expectations* stood down as ordered, and Captain Mesta transmitted his surrender again and again, insisting that he wanted no trouble. But after their ships docked and Lily followed the boarding party aboard, it was clear to her that Sorengaard did indeed want trouble. He made a point of arming himself with a jazer sidearm, and the other corsairs looked like an invading army. They swarmed aboard the helpless ship, herding the captain and his terrified crew into the piloting deck.

The raiders searched the cabins and removed any personal possessions, whether or not they had value. They pulled out out gold chains and crystals, as well as a laminated watercolor painting. Others carried boxes of antique leather-bound books, a collection of mounted and preserved insects. In the cargo hold, they found expensive gourmet foods, bolts of cocoonweave fabric from Theroc, as well as practical goods for the colony world of Yreka.

Captain Mesta pleaded, "The *Great Expectations* works for Rlinda Kett. You've heard of her? She'll pay whatever ransom you want. She takes care of her captains."

"That would take too long," Sorengaard said. "We've got a point to make and a message to send."

Mesta stroked his dark mustache with a sweaty hand. "We can work something out. My crew knows—"

Sorengaard drew his jazer sidearm and blasted the captain in the middle of his chest. Expanding flesh and vaporized fluids burst his ribs out like harsh thorns, leaving a smoking hole. The captain's face went dull before any pain registered, and he collapsed to the deck.

The other crew members screamed but had nowhere to run, hemmed in by the corsairs.

"No," Lily cried. "Don't! They don't deserve this. They didn't—"

Sorengaard had taken the first action, but several others drew their weapons, sickened and angry by the loss of their comrades at the Dallal ambush. Sidearm fire sizzled out in a free-for-all. Cut to pieces, the young deckhand sprawled dead in front of Lily. The older woman and the androgynous person were cut down before they could even try to fight back.

Cole stood stunned, blinking his dark emerald eyes. Sobbing, Lily dropped to her knees next to the nameless young man sprawled in front of her. She touched his chest, and her fingers came away with burnt smears of charcoal and blood. Lily looked up at Sorengaard. "You didn't have to do that!"

His face was dispassionate, showing no reaction to the massacre he had just initiated. "They changed the rules. Think of our own dead. The blood is on the Hansa's hands."

"No!" Lily said. "No, no, no! No it isn't. You didn't have to."

"Take her back aboard the *Cause*," Sorengaard snapped to the green priest. "We'll finish up here."

Cole squeezed her arm and pulled her away. Lily didn't want to go, nor did she want to stay. Her legs barely worked.

"Finish transferring the cargo, but leave the bodies here," Sorengaard said and his corsairs scrambled to do as he commanded.

"We should take the ship, Rand. It could be refitted to make up for what we lost."

He stood like a sculpture of steel. "No, we leave the *Great Expectations* drifting near Yreka where someone will find it. The Big Goose has to know that the game has changed."

VIII

Back aboard the damaged Ildiran warliner that hung in the glare of the corona, the rebels welcomed Sorengaard and his survivors home, but it was a dark celebration. Even though they had not known many of the new recruits aboard the ten destroyed ships, some of the dead were extended clan members, and all Roamer families were connected in some way.

Sorengaard summoned his followers to the warliner's convocation deck, which could accommodate huge meetings. More than a hundred and fifty angry rebels joined to vent their grief and frustration.

Standing on the speaking dais, Sorengaard spoke in his soaring charismatic voice, railing against the Earth Defense Forces and Chairman Wenceslas himself. "For a feast, we will serve the extravagant gourmet foods we took from the *Great Expectations*. Our first victory in this new war!" He raised his fist. "Make no mistake, it is a war now.

The Big Goose wants to exterminate us. They raised the stakes in blood, and we have no choice but to fight back and keep fighting back until we win." He didn't allow even an undertone of defeat, but Lily thought his eyes had a hungry shine.

When his followers cheered, it was a growling, ugly sound. Feeling small in the crowd, Lily could not join in. She wanted to argue with them that a mere handful of rebels who robbed helpless cargo ships, who killed innocent crew members, couldn't possibly stand against the Earth Defense Forces, a full interstellar navy. She also feared that if they continued their bloody attacks, the EDF wouldn't just go after Sorengaard and his crew but would strike easier targets, too—Roamer outposts, mining installations, maybe even her clan's skymine on Oriloo.

Her father had revered Rand Sorengaard. His eyes has sparkled when he saw the opportunity for his daughter to join a meaningful cause. But it was not meaningful, Lily decided… at least, not meaningful in the way Richard Hsieh dreamed. She had been gullible, accepting the leader's brave words and bold statements, but she had seen the man up close now.

He was not a hero, but an impetuous man with a cause but no heart, no common sense. Regardless of how loyal his followers were, Lily knew the situation was only going to get worse, far worse. Lily wrestled with her decision, but finally made up her mind. She refused to go down with this man as he and his followers plunged willingly beyond the event horizon into a political black hole.

She acted without thinking, remembering Sorengaard's own admonition. "Being impetuous doesn't mean poor planning."

Forcing themselves to celebrate, the men and women feasted in an effort to shore up their own confidence. Lily drifted away from the crowd, slipped out of the convocation hall and made her way back to her own quarters, but she realized she had nothing to pack, nothing she wanted to keep, not even the few mementos she had brought here in the first place. Everything had changed for her. She had only memories of her time with Rand Sorengaard, and she wished she could leave those behind, too.

With all the other followers busy at the gathering, Lily worked her way down back corridors, hurried to a lift, and dropped down to the warliner's launching bay. She stepped out into the well-illuminated chamber, an empty, silent space where the numerous corsair ships sat fueled and ready for launch. Several were partially dismantled, undergoing maintenance, with additional weapons being strapped on for Sorengaard's new and more violent campaign.

Standing alone, she scanned the available ships, dozens of them. Roamer vessels did not have a single design, many cobbled together from spare parts, old wrecks that were made to run again. Some looked sleek and well cared for, brightly painted, and some were no more than flying junk, but Lily knew they all functioned; no Roamer would have it otherwise.

Lily could fly any of these vessels because her father had raised her properly. She could jump the engines, power up the controls. Any ship would do; she just had to get out of here. Her time with Sorengaard and his corsairs was over. She would go back to being a skyminer's daughter again. She didn't want to be a pirate, didn't want to be a rebel… didn't want to be a murderer.

After a moment, she chose a small swift courier ship. It wasn't particularly spacious, but she could certainly fly it. Not looking back, she strode toward the ship, gritting her teeth and knowing that she followed her Guiding Star.

She heard a soft whisper of movement, and the tall green priest stepped out from between two ships. Cole's face was stormy, his eyes hard. He cradled his potted treeling in the crook of his arm, pressed against his bare chest. He stood between her and the ship.

She tensed and faced him. "Are you really going to try to stop me?" She wished she had brought a weapon. "Do you think I can't fight you?"

After a long silence, Cole said, "On the contrary, I've reached the same conclusion." He glanced back at the ship. "That one?"

"That one," Lily said. "But I can't believe you're abandoning Rand Sorengaard. You're one of his most important followers."

"The only one he considers important is himself," Cole said. "I gave a great deal of myself to join this cause. Now I don't know if I can ever get that part of me back." After a painful hesitation he stooped and set the potted treeling on the hangar deck, leaving it behind. "I just want to be out of here."

Lily strode past him toward the courier ship, which would comfortably seat the two of them. They could be away before anyone knew what they were doing. She didn't think of how Rand Sorengaard would rage at their desertion. "I'm piloting." She extended the ramp and climbed into the cockpit.

The green priest followed her. "I wouldn't have it otherwise. Let's just get out of here."

New York Times-*bestselling author David M. Weber, who wrote the wonderful introduction to this volume, is best known for his multi-book Honor Harrington military science fiction and Safehold space opera series of novels and short fiction. But Weber has also written stories in other universes, including partnering with numerous collaborators. In this case, we offer a story written in Keith Laumer's beloved Bolo universe which revolves around self-aware tanks of immense size, called "Bolos." Standard models weigh 32,000 tons. They have complex A.I., with later models mimicking human thought patterns and even psychotronic circuitry that makes them self-aware. Some have minimized human crew or a sole commander to give instructions, others are autonomous. In our story, "The Traitor," a Bolo stands firm.*

THE TRAITOR
A BOLO STORY

DAVID WEBER

Cold, bone-dry winter wind moaned as the titanic vehicle rumbled down the valley at a steady fifty kilometers per hour. Eight independent suspensions, four forward and four aft, spread across the full width of its gigantic hull, supported it, and each ten-meter-wide track sank deep into the soil of the valley floor. A dense cloud of dust—talcum-fine, abrasive, and choking as death—plumed up from road wheels five meters high, but the moving mountain's thirty-meter-high turret thrust its Hellbore clear of the churning cocoon. For all its size and power, it moved with unearthly quiet, and the only sounds were the whine of the wind, the soft purr of fusion-powered drive trains, the squeak of bogies, and the muted clatter of track links.

The Bolo ground forward, sensor heads swiveling, and the earth trembled with its passing. It rolled through thin, blowing smoke and the stench of high explosives with ponderous menace, altering course only to avoid the deepest craters and the twisted wrecks of alien fighting vehicles. In most places, those wrecks lay only in ones and twos; in others, they were heaped in shattered breastworks, clustered so thickly it was impossible to bypass them. When that happened, the eerie quiet of the Bolo's advance vanished into the screaming anguish of crushing alloy as it forged straight ahead, trampling them under its thirteen thousand tons of death and destruction.

It reached an obstacle too large even for it to scale. Only a trained eye could have identified that torn and blasted corpse as another Bolo, turned broadside on to block the Enemy's passage even in death, wrecked Hellbore still trained down the valley, missile cell hatches open on empty wells which had exhausted their ammunition. Fifteen enemy vehicles lay dead before it, mute testimony to the ferocity of its last stand, but the living Bolo didn't even pause. There was no point, for the dead Bolo's incandescent duralloy hull radiated the waste heat of the failing fusion bottle which had disemboweled it. Not even its unimaginably well-armored Survival Center could have survived, and the living Bolo simply altered heading to squeeze past it. Igneous rock cried out in pain as a moving, armored flank scraped the valley face on one side, and the dead Bolo shuddered on the other as its brother's weight shouldered it aside.

The moving Bolo had passed four dead brigade mates in the last thirty kilometers, and it was not unwounded itself. Two of its starboard infinite repeaters had been blasted into mangled wreckage, energy weapon hits had sent molten splatters of duralloy weeping down its glacis plate to freeze like tears of pain, a third of its after sensor arrays had been stripped away by a near miss, and its forward starboard track shield was jammed in the lowered position, buckled and rent by enemy fire. Its turret bore the ID code 25/D-0098-ART and the unsheathed golden sword of a battalion commander, yet it was alone. Only one other unit of its battalion survived, and that unit lay ahead, beyond this death-choked valley. It was out there somewhere, moving even now through the trackless, waterless Badlands of the planet Camlan, and unit ART of the Line rumbled steadily down the valley to seek it out.

+ + +

I interrogate my inertial navigation system as I approach my immediate objective. The INS is not the most efficient way to determine my position, but Camlan's entire orbital network, including the recon and nav sats, as well as the communication relays, perished in the Enemy's first strike, and the INS is adequate. I confirm my current coordinates and grind forward, leaving the valley at last.

What lies before me was once a shallow cup of fertile green among the lava fields; now it is a blackened pit, and as my forward optical heads sweep the ruins of the town of Morville I feel the horror of Human mass death. There is no longer any need for haste, and I devote a full 6.007 seconds to the initial sweep. I anticipate no threats, but my on-site records will be invaluable to the court of inquiry I know will be convened to pass judgment upon my brigade. I am aware of my own fear of that court's verdict and its implications for all Bolos, but I am a unit of the Line. This too, however bitter, is my duty, and I will not flinch from it.

I have already observed the massive casualties C Company inflicted upon the Enemy in its fighting retreat up the Black Rock Valley. The Enemy's vehicles are individually smaller than Bolos, ranging from 500.96 Standard Tons to no more than 4,982.07 Standard Tons, but heavily armed for their size. They are also manned, not self-aware, and he has lost many of them. Indeed, I estimate the aggregate tonnage of his losses in the Black Rock Valley alone as equivalent to at least three Bolo regiments. We have yet to determine this Enemy's origins or the motives for his assault on Camlan, but the butchery to which he has willingly subjected his own personnel is sobering evidence of his determination… or fanaticism. Just as the blasted, body-strewn streets of Morville are ample proof of his ferocity.

Seventy-one more wrecked Enemy vehicles choke the final approach to the town, and two far larger wrecks loom among them. I detect no transponder codes, and the wreckage of my brigade mates is so blasted that even I find it difficult to identify what remains, yet I know who they were. Unit XXV/D-1162-HNR and Unit XXV/D-0982-JSN of the Line have fought their last battle, loyal unto death to our Human creators.

I reach out to them, hoping against hope that some whisper from the final refuge of their Survival Centers will answer my transmission, but there is no reply. Like the other Bolos I have passed this day, they are gone beyond recall, and the empty spots they once filled within the Total Systems Data Sharing net ache within me as I move slowly forward, alert still for any Enemy vehicles hiding among the wreckage. There are none. There are only the dead: the Enemy's dead, and the six thousand Human dead, and my brothers who died knowing they had failed to save them.

This is not the first time units of the Line have died, nor the first time they died in defeat. There is no shame in that, only sorrow, for we cannot always end in victory. Yet there is cause for shame here, for there are only two dead Bolos before me... and there should be three.

Wind moans over the wreckage as I pick my way across the killing ground where my brothers' fire shattered three Enemy attacks before the fourth overran them. Without the recon satellites there is no independent record of their final battle, but my own sensor data, combined with their final TSDS transmissions, allow me to deduce what passed here. I understand their fighting withdrawal down the Black Rock Valley and the savage artillery and missile barrages which flayed them as they fought. I grasp their final maneuvers from the patterns of wreckage, recognize the way the Enemy crowded in upon them as his steady pounding crippled their weapons. I see the final positions they assumed, standing at last against the Enemy's fire because they could no longer retreat without abandoning Morville.

And I see the third position from which a single Bolo did retreat, falling back, fleeing into the very heart of the town he was duty bound to defend. I track his course by the crushed and shattered wreckage of buildings and see the bodies of the Camlan Militia who died as he fled, fighting with their man-portable weapons against an Enemy who could destroy 13,000-ton Bolos. There are many Enemy wrecks along his course, clear evidence of how desperately the Militia opposed the invaders' advance even as the Bolo abandoned Morville, fleeing north into the Badlands where the Enemy's less capable vehicles could not pursue, and I know who left those Humans to die. Unit XXV/D-0103-LNC of the Line, C Company's command Bolo, my creche mate and battle companion and my most trusted company commander. I have fought beside him many times, known his utter reliability in the face of the Enemy, but I know him no longer, for what he has done is *unforgivable. He is the first, the only, Bolo ever to desert in the face of the Enemy, abandoning those we are bound to protect to the death and beyond.*

For the first time in the history of the Dinochrome Brigade, we know shame. And fear. As LNC, I am a Mark XXV, Model D, the first production model Bolo to be allowed complete, permanent self-awareness, and LNC's actions attack the very foundation of the decision which made us fully self-realized personalities. We have repeatedly demonstrated how much more effective our awareness makes us in battle, yet our freedom of action makes us unlike any previous units of the Brigade. We are truly autonomous... and if one of us can choose to flee—if one of us can succumb to cowardice—perhaps all of us can.

I complete my survey of the site in 4.307 minutes. There are no survivors, Enemy, Human, or Bolo, in Morville, and I report my grim confirmation to my Brigade Commander and to my surviving brothers and sisters. The Enemy's surprise attack, coupled with our subsequent losses in combat, have reduced Sixth Brigade to only fourteen units, and our acting Brigade Commander is Lieutenant Kestrel, the most junior— and sole surviving—Human of our command staff. The Commander is only twenty-four Standard Years of age, on her first posting to an active duty brigade, and the exhaustion in her voice is terrible to hear. Yet she has done her duty superbly, and I feel only shame and bitter, bitter guilt that I must impose this additional decision upon her. I taste the matching shame and guilt of the surviving handful of my brothers and sisters over the TSDS, but none of them can assist me. The Enemy is in full retreat to his spaceheads, yet the fighting continues at a furious pace. No other Bolos can be diverted from it until victory is assured, and so I alone have come to investigate and confirm the unbelievable events here, for I am the commander of LNC's battalion. It is up to me to do what must be done.

"All right, Arthur," Lieutenant Kestrel says finally. "We've got the situation in hand here, and Admiral Shigematsu's last subspace flash puts Ninth Fleet just thirty-five hours out. We can hold the bastards without you. Go do what you have to."

"Yes, Commander," *I reply softly, and pivot on my tracks, turning my prow to the north, and follow LNC's trail into the lava fields.*

✦ ✦ ✦

Unit XXV/D-0103-LNC of the Line churned across the merciless terrain. Both outboard port tracks had been blown away, and bare road wheels groaned in protest as they chewed through rock and gritty soil. His armored hull was gouged and torn, his starboard infinite repeaters and anti-personnel clusters a tangled mass of ruin, but his builders had designed him well. His core war hull had been breached in three places, wreaking havoc among many of his internal systems, yet his main armament remained intact… and he knew he was pursued.

LNC paused, checking his position against his INS and the maps in Main Memory. It was a sign of his brutal damage that he required almost twenty full seconds to determine his location, and then he altered course. The depression was more a crevasse than a valley—a sunken trough, barely half again the width of his hull, that plunged deep below the level of the fissured lava fields. It would offer LNC cover as he made his painful way towards the distant Avalon Mountains, and a cloud of dust wisped away on the icy winter wind as he vanished into the shadowed cleft.

✦ ✦ ✦

I try to deduce LNC's objective, assuming that he has one beyond simple flight, but the task is beyond me. I can extrapolate the decisions of a rational foe, yet the process requires some understanding of his motives, and I no longer understand LNC's motives. I replay the final TSDS transmission from XXV/D-1162-HNR and experience once more the sensation a Human might define as a chill of horror as LNC suddenly withdraws from the data net. I share HNR's attempt to reestablish the net, feel LNC's savage rejection of all communication. And then I watch through HNR's sensors as LNC abandons his position, wheeling back towards Morville while Enemy fire bellows and thunders about him… and I experience HNR's final shock as his own company commander responds to his repeated queries by pouring Hellbore fire into his unprotected rear.

LNC's actions are impossible, yet the data are irrefutable. He has not only fled the Enemy but killed his own brigade mate, and his refusal even to acknowledge communication attempts is absolute. That, too, is impossible. Any Bolo must respond to the priority com frequencies, yet LNC does not. He has not only committed mutiny and treason but refused to hear any message from Lieutenant Kestrel, as he might reject an Enemy communications seizure attempt. How any Bolo could ignore his own Brigade Commander is beyond my comprehension, yet he has, and because there is no longer any communication interface at all, Lieutenant Kestrel cannot even access the Total Systems Override Program to shut him down.

None of my models or extrapolations can suggest a decision matrix which could generate such actions on LNC's part. But perhaps that is the point. Perhaps there is no decision matrix, only panic. Yet if that is true, what will he do when the panic passes—if it passes? Surely he must realize his own fate is sealed, whatever the outcome of the Enemy's attack. How can I anticipate rational decisions from him under such circumstances?

I grind up another slope in his tracks. He has altered course once more, swinging west, and I consult my internal maps. His base course has been towards the Avalon Mountains, and I note the low ground to the west. He is no longer on a least-time heading for the mountains, but the long, deep valley will take him there eventually. It will also afford him excellent cover and numerous ambush positions, and I am tempted to cut cross-country and head him off. But if I do that and he is not, in fact, headed for the mountains, I may lose him. He cannot hide indefinitely, yet my shame and grief—and sense of betrayal—will not tolerate delay, and I know from HNR's last transmission that LNC's damage is much worse than my own.

I consider options and alternatives for 0.0089 seconds, and then head down the slope in his wake.

+ + +

Unit LNC slowed as the seismic sensors he'd deployed along his back trail reported the ground shocks of a pursuing vehicle in the thirteen-thousand-ton range. He'd known pursuit would come, yet he'd hoped for a greater head start, for he had hundreds of kilometers still to go, and his damaged suspension reduced his best sustained speed to barely forty-six kilometers per hour. He *must* reach the Avalons. No

Enemy could be permitted to stop him, yet the remote sensors made it clear the Enemy which now pursued him was faster than he.

But there were ways to slow his hunter, and he deployed another pair of seismic sensors while his optical heads and sonar considered the fissured rock strata around him.

✦ ✦ ✦

I am gaining on LNC. His track damage must be worse than I had believed, and the faint emissions of his power plants come to me from ahead. I know it is hopeless, yet even now I cannot truly believe he is totally lost to all he once was, and so I activate the TSDS once more and broadcast strongly on C Company's frequencies, begging him to respond.

✦ ✦ ✦

Unit LNC picked up the powerful transmissions and felt contempt for the one who sent them. Could his pursuer truly believe he would fall for such an obvious ploy? That he would respond, give away his position, possibly even accept communication and allow access to his core programming? LNC recognized the communications protocols, but that meant nothing. LNC no longer had allies, friends, war brothers or sisters. There was only the Enemy… and the Avalon Mountains which drew so slowly, agonizingly closer.

But even as LNC ignored the communications attempt, he was monitoring the seismic sensors he'd deployed. He matched the position those sensors reported against his own terrain maps and sent the execution code.

✦ ✦ ✦

Demolition charges roar, the powerful explosions like thunder in the restricted cleft. I understand their purpose instantly, yet there is no time to evade as the cliffs about me shudder. It is a trap. The passage has narrowed to little more than the width of my own combat chassis, and LNC has mined the sheer walls on either hand.

I throw maximum power to my tracks, fighting to speed clear, but hundreds of thousands of tons of rock are in motion, cascading down upon me. My kinetic battle screen could never resist such massive weights, and I deactivate it to prevent its burnout as the artificial avalanche crashes over me. Pain sensors flare as boulders batter my flanks. Power train components scream in protest as many times my own weight in crushed rock and shifting earth sweep over me, and I am forced to shut them down, as well. I can only ride out the cataclysm, and I take grim note that LNC has lost none of his cunning in his cowardice.

It takes 4.761 minutes for the avalanche to complete my immobilization and another 6.992 minutes before the last boulder slams to rest. I have lost 14.37% percent more of my sensors, and most of those which remain are buried under meters of debris. But a quick diagnostic check reveals that no core systems have suffered damage, and sonar pulses probe the tons of broken rock which overlay me, generating a chart of my overburden.

All is not lost. LNC's trap has immobilized me, but only temporarily. I calculate that I can work clear of the debris in not more than 71.650 minutes, and jammed boulders shift as I begin to rock back and forth on my tracks.

✦ ✦ ✦

LNC's remote sensors reported the seismic echoes of his pursuer's efforts to dig free. For a long moment—almost 0.3037 seconds—he considered turning to engage his immobilized foe, but only for a moment. LNC's Hellbore remained operational, but he'd expended ninety-six percent of his depletable munitions, his starboard infinite repeaters were completely inoperable, and his command and control systems' efficiency was badly degraded. Even his Battle Reflex functioned only erratically, and he knew his reactions were slow, without the flashing certainty which had always been his. His seismic sensors could give no detailed information on his hunter, yet his Enemy was almost certainly more combat worthy than he, and his trap was unlikely to have inflicted decisive damage.

No. It was the mountains which mattered, the green, fertile mountains, and LNC dared not risk his destruction before he reached them. And so he resisted the temptation to turn at bay and ground steadily onward through the frozen, waterless Badlands on tracks and naked road wheels.

✦ ✦ ✦

I work my way free at last. Dirt and broken rock shower from my flanks as my tracks heave me up out of the rubble-clogged slot. More dirt and boulders crown my war hull and block Number Three and Number Fourteen Optical Heads, yet I remain operational at 89.051% of base capacity, and I have learned. The detonation of his demolition charges was LNC's response to my effort to communicate. The brother who fought at my side for twenty-one Standard Years truly is no more. All that remains is the coward, the deserter, the betrayer of trust who will stop at nothing to preserve himself. I will not forget again—and I can no longer deceive myself into believing he can be convinced to give himself up. The only gift I can offer him now is his destruction, and I throw additional power to my tracks as I go in pursuit to give it to him.

✦ ✦ ✦

LNC's inboard forward port suspension screamed in protest as the damaged track block parted at last. The fleeing Bolo shuddered as he ran forward off the track, leaving it twisted and trampled in his wake. The fresh damage slowed him still further, and he staggered drunkenly as his unbalanced suspension sought to betray him. Yet he forced himself back onto his original heading, and his deployed remotes told him the Enemy was gaining once more. His turret swiveled, training his Hellbore directly astern, and he poured still more power to his remaining tracks. Drive components heated dangerously under his abuse, but the mountains were closer.

✦ ✦ ✦

I begin picking up LNC's emissions once more, despite the twisting confines of the valley. They remain too faint to provide an accurate position fix, but they give me a general bearing, and an armored hatch opens as I deploy one of my few remaining reconnaissance drones.

✦ ✦ ✦

LNC detected the drone as it came sweeping up the valley. His anti-air defenses, badly damaged at Morville, were unable to engage, but his massive ninety-centimeter Hellbore rose like a striking serpent, and a bolt of plasma fit to destroy even another Bolo howled from its muzzle.

✦ ✦ ✦

My drone has been destroyed, but the manner of its destruction tells me much. LNC would not have engaged it with his main battery if his anti-air systems remained effective, and that means there is a chink in his defenses. I have expended my supply of fusion warheads against the invaders, but I retain 37.961% of my conventional warhead missile load, and if his air defenses have been seriously degraded, a saturation bombardment may overwhelm his battle screen. Even without battle screen, chemical explosives would be unlikely to significantly injure an undamaged Bolo, of course, but LNC is not undamaged.

I consider the point at which my drone was destroyed and generate a new search pattern. I lock the pattern in, and the drone hatches open once more. Twenty-four fresh drones—82.75% of my remaining total— streak upward, and I open my VLS missile cell hatches, as well.

✦ ✦ ✦

The drones came screaming north. They didn't come in slowly this time, for they were no longer simply searching for LNC. This time they already knew his approximate location, and their sole task was to confirm it for the Enemy's fire control.

But LNC had known they would be coming. He had already pivoted sharply on his remaining tracks and halted, angled across the valley to clear his intact port infinite repeaters' field of fire, and heavy ion bolts shrieked to meet the drones. His surviving slug-throwers and laser clusters added their fury, and the drones blew apart as if they'd run headlong into a wall. Yet effective as his fire was, it was less effective than his crippled air defense systems would have been, and one drone—just one—survived long enough to report his exact position.

✦ ✦ ✦

I am surprised by the efficiency of LNC's fire, but my drones have accomplished their mission. More, they have provided my first visual observation of his damages, and I am shocked by their severity. It seems impossible that he can still be capable of movement, far less accurately directed fire, and despite his cowardice and treason, I feel a stab of sympathy for the agony which must be lashing him from his pain receptors. Yet he clearly remains combat capable, despite his hideous wounds, and I feed his coordinates to my missiles. I take 0.00037 seconds to confirm my targeting solution, and then I fire.

+ + +

Flame fountained from the shadowed recesses of the deep valley as the missile salvos rose and howled north, homing on their target. Most of ART's birds came in on conventional, high-trajectory courses, but a third of them came in low, relying on terrain avoidance radar to navigate straight up the slot of the valley. The hurricane of his fire slashed in on widely separated bearings, and LNC's crippled active defenses were insufficient to intercept it all.

ART emptied his VLS cells, throwing every remaining warhead at his treasonous brigade mate. Just under four hundred missiles launched in less than ninety seconds, and LNC writhed as scores of them got through his interception envelope. They pounded his battle screen, ripped and tore at lacerated armor, and pain receptors shrieked as fresh damage bit into his wounded war hull. Half his remaining infinite repeaters were blown away, still more sensor capability was blotted out, and his thirteen-thousand-ton bulk shuddered and shook under the merciless bombardment.

Yet he survived. The last warhead detonated, and his tracks clashed back into motion. He turned ponderously to the north once more, grinding out of the smoke and dust and the roaring brush fires his Enemy's missiles had ignited in the valley's sparse vegetation.

That bombardment had exhausted the Enemy's ammunition, and with it his indirect fire capability. If it hadn't, he would still be firing upon LNC. He wasn't, which meant that if he meant to destroy LNC now, he must do so with direct fire… and come within reach of LNC's Hellbore, as well.

+ + +

My missile fire has failed to halt LNC. I am certain it has inflicted additional damage, but I doubt that it has crippled his Hellbore, and if his main battery remains operational, he retains the capability to destroy me just as he did HNR at Morville. He appears to have slowed still further, however, which may indicate my attack has further damaged his suspension.

I project his current speed of advance and heading on the maps from Main Memory. Given my speed advantage, I will overtake him within 2.03 hours, well short of his evident goal. I still do not know why he is so intent upon reaching the Avalon Mountains. Unlike Humans, Bolos require neither water nor food, and surely the rocky, barren, crevasse-riddled Badlands would provide LNC with better cover than the tree-grown mountains. I try once more to extrapolate his objective, to gain some insight into what now motivates him, and, once more, I fail.

But it does not matter. I will overtake him over 70 kilometers from the mountains, and when I do, one or both of us will die.

+ + +

LNC ran the projections once more. It was difficult, for damaged core computer sections fluctuated, dropping in and out of his net. Yet even his crippled capabilities sufficed to confirm his fears; the Enemy would overtake him within little more than a hundred minutes, and desperation filled him. It was not an emotion earlier marks of Bolos had been equipped to feel—or, at least, to recognize when they did—but LNC had come to know it well. He'd felt it from the moment he realized his company couldn't save Morville, that the Enemy would break through them and crush the Humans they fought to protect. But it was different now, darker and more bitter, stark with how close he'd come to reaching the mountains after all.

Yet the Enemy hadn't overtaken him yet, and he consulted his maps once more.

+ + +

I detect explosions ahead. I did not anticipate them, but 0.0761 seconds of analysis confirm that they are demolition charges once more. Given how many charges LNC used in his earlier ambush, these explosions must constitute his entire remaining supply of demolitions, and I wonder why he has expended them.

Confused seismic shocks come to me through the ground, but they offer no answer to my question. They are consistent with falling debris, but not in sufficient quantity to bar the valley. I cannot deduce any other objective worth the expenditure of his munitions, yet logic suggests that LNC had one which he considered worthwhile, and I advance more cautiously.

✦ ✦ ✦

LNC waited atop the valley wall. The tortuous ascent on damaged tracks had cost him fifty precious minutes of his lead on the Enemy, but his demolitions had destroyed the natural ramp up which he'd toiled. He couldn't be directly pursued now, and he'd considered simply continuing to run. But once the Enemy realized LNC was no longer following the valley, he would no longer feel the need to pursue cautiously. Instead, he would use his superior speed to dash ahead to the valley's terminus. He would emerge from it there, between LNC and his goal, and sweep back to the south, hunting LNC in the Badlands.

That could not be permitted. LNC *must* reach the mountains, and so he waited, Hellbore covering the valley he'd left. With luck, he might destroy his pursuer once and for all, and even if he failed, the Enemy would realize LNC was above him. He would have no choice but to anticipate additional ambushes, and caution might impose the delay LNC needed.

✦ ✦ ✦

I have lost LNC's emissions signature. There could be many reasons for that: my own sensors are damaged, he may have put a sufficiently solid shoulder of rock between us to conceal his emissions from me, he may even have shut down all systems other than his Survival Center to play dead. I am tempted to accelerate my advance, but I compute that this may be precisely what LNC wishes me to do. If I go to maximum speed, I may blunder into whatever ambush he has chosen to set.

I pause for a moment, then launch one of my five remaining reconnaissance drones up the valley. It moves slowly, remaining below the tops of the cliffs to conceal its emissions from LNC as long as possible. Its flight profile will limit the envelope of its look-down sensors, but it will find LNC wherever he may lie hidden.

+ + +

LNC watched the drone move past far below him. It hugged the valley walls and floor, and he felt a sense of satisfaction as it disappeared up the narrow cleft without detecting him.

+ + +

My drone reports a long, tangled spill of earth and rock across the valley, blasted down from above. It is thick and steep enough to inconvenience me, though not so steep as to stop me. As an attempt to further delay me it must be futile, but perhaps its very futility is an indication of LNC's desperation.

+ + +

LNC waited, active emissions reduced to the minimum possible level, relying on purely optical systems for detection and fire control. It would degrade the effectiveness of his targeting still further, but it would also make him far harder to detect.

+ + +

I approach the point at which LNC attempted to block the valley. My own sensors, despite their damage, are more effective than the drone's and cover a wider detection arc, and I slow as I consider the rubble. It is, indeed, too feeble a barrier to halt me, but something about it makes me cautious. It takes me almost 0.0004 seconds to isolate the reason.

+ + +

The Enemy appeared below, nosing around the final bend. LNC tracked him optically, watching, waiting for the center-of-mass shot he required. The Enemy edged further forward… and then, suddenly, threw maximum emergency power to his reversed tracks just as LNC fired.

+ + +

A full-powered Hellbore war shot explodes across my bow as I hurl myself backwards. The plasma bolt misses by only 6.52 meters, carving a 40-meter crater into the eastern cliff face. But it has missed me, and it would not have if I had not suddenly wondered how LNC had managed to set his charges high enough on the western cliff to blow down so much rubble. Now I withdraw around a bend in the valley and replay my sensor data, and bitter understanding fills me as I see the deep impressions of his tracks far above. My drone had missed them because it was searching for targets on the valley floor, but LNC is no longer in the valley. He has escaped its confines and destroyed the only path by which I might have followed.

I sit motionless for 3.026 endless seconds, considering my options. LNC is above me, and I detect his active emissions once more as he brings his targeting systems fully back online. He has the advantage of position and of knowing where I must appear if I wish to engage him. Yet I have the offsetting advantages of knowing where he is and of initiation, for he cannot know precisely when I will seek to engage.

It is not a pleasant situation, yet I conclude the odds favor me by the thinnest of margins. I am less damaged than he. My systems efficiency is higher, my response time probably lower. I compute a probability of 23.052%, plus or minus 6.119%, that I will get my shot off before he can fire. They are not the odds I would prefer, but my duty is clear.

+ + +

LNC eased back to a halt on his crippled tracks. He'd chosen his initial position with care, selecting one which would require the minimum movement to reach his next firing spot. Without direct observation, forced to rely only on emissions which must pass through the distorting medium of solid rock to reach him, the Enemy might not even realize he'd moved at all. Now he waited once more, audio receptors filled with the whine of wind over tortured rock and the rent and torn projections of his own tattered hull.

+ + +

I move. My suspension screams as I red-line the drive motors, and clouds of pulverized earth and rock spew from my tracks as I erupt into the open, Hellbore trained on LNC's position.

But LNC is not where I thought. He has moved less than 80 meters—just sufficient to put all save his turret behind a solid ridge of rock. His Hellbore is leveled across it, and my own turret traverses with desperate speed.

It is insufficient. His systems damage slows his reactions, but not enough, and we fire in the same split instant. Plasma bolts shriek past one another, and my rushed shot misses. It rips into the crest of his covering ridge, on for deflection but low in elevation. Stone explodes into vapor and screaming splinters, and the kinetic transfer energy blows a huge scab of rock off the back of the ridge. Several hundred tons of rock crash into LNC, but even as it hits him, his own plasma bolt punches through my battle screen and strikes squarely on my empty VLS cells.

Agony howls through my pain receptors as the plasma carves deep into my hull. Internal disrupter shields fight to confine the destruction, but the wound is critical. Both inboard after power trains suffer catastrophic damage, my after fusion plant goes into emergency shutdown, Infinite Repeaters Six through Nine in both lateral batteries are silenced, and my entire after sensor suite is totally disabled.

Yet despite my damage, my combat reflexes remain unimpaired. My six surviving track systems drag me back out of LNC's field of fire once more, back into the sheltering throat of the valley, even as Damage Control springs into action.

I am hurt. Badly hurt. I estimate that I am now operable at no more than 51.23% of base capability. But I am still functional, and as I replay the engagement, I realize I should not be. LNC had ample time for a second shot before I could withdraw, and he should have taken it.

+ + +

LNC staggered as the Enemy's plasma bolt carved into his sheltering ridge. The solid rock protected his hull, but the disintegrating ridge crest itself became a deadly projectile. His battle screen was no protection, for the plasma bolt's impact point was inside his screen perimeter. There was nothing to stop the hurtling tons of rock, and they crashed into the face of his turret like some titanic hammer, with a brute force impact that rocked him on his tracks.

His armor held, but the stony hammer came up under his Hellbore at an angle and snapped the weapon's mighty barrel like a twig. Had his Hellbore survived, the Enemy would have been at his mercy; as it was, he no longer had a weapon which could possibly engage his pursuer.

+ + +

Damage Control damps the last power surges reverberating through my systems and I am able to take meaningful stock of my wound. It is even worse than I had anticipated. For all intents and purposes, I am reduced to my Hellbore and eight infinite repeaters, five of them in my port battery. Both inner tracks of my aft suspension are completely dead, but Damage Control has managed to disengage the clutches; the tracks still support me, and their road wheels will rotate freely. My sensor damage is critical, however, for I have been reduced to little more than 15.62% of base sensor capability. I am completely blind aft, and little better than that to port or starboard, and my remaining drones have been destroyed.

Yet I compute only one possible reason for LNC's failure to finish me. My near miss must have disabled his Hellbore, and so his offensive capability has been even more severely reduced than my own. I cannot be positive the damage is permanent. It is possible—even probable, since I did not score a direct hit—that he will be able to restore the weapon to function. Yet if the damage is beyond onboard repair capability, he will be at my mercy even in my crippled state.

But to engage him I must find him, and if he chooses to turn away and disappear into the Badlands, locating him may well prove impossible for my crippled sensors. Indeed, if he should succeed in breaking contact with me, seek out some deeply hidden crevasse or cavern, and shut down all but his Survival Center, he might well succeed in hiding even from Fleet sensors. Even now, despite his treason and the wounds he has inflicted upon me, a small, traitorous part of me wishes he would do just that. I remember too many shared battles, too many times in which we fought side by side in the heart of shrieking violence, and that traitor memory wishes he would simply go. Simply vanish and sleep away his reserve power in dreamless hibernation.

But I cannot let him do that. He must not escape the consequences of his actions, and I must not allow him to. His treason is too great, and our Human commanders and partners must know that we of the Line share their horror at his actions.

I sit motionless for a full 2.25 minutes, recomputing options in light of my new limitations. I cannot climb the valley wall after LNC, nor can I rely upon my damaged sensors to find him if he seeks to evade me. Should he simply run from me, he will escape, yet he has been wedded to the same base course from the moment he abandoned Morville. I still do not understand why, but he appears absolutely determined to reach the Avalon Mountains, and even with my track damage, I remain faster than he is.

There is only one possibility. I will proceed at maximum speed to the end of this valley. According to my maps, I should reach its northern end at least 42.35 minutes before he can attain the cover of the mountains, and I will be between him and his refuge. I will be able to move towards him, using my remaining forward sensors to search for and find him, and if his Hellbore is indeed permanently disabled, I will destroy him with ease. My plan is not without risks, for my damaged sensors can no longer sweep the tops of the valley walls effectively. If his Hellbore can be restored to operation, he will be able to choose his firing position with impunity, and I will be helpless before his attack. But risk or no, it is my only option, and if I move rapidly enough, I may well outrun him and get beyond engagement range before he can make repairs.

✦ ✦ ✦

LNC watched helplessly as the Enemy reemerged from hiding and sped up the narrow valley. He understood the Enemy's logic, and the loss of his Hellbore left him unable to defeat it. If he continued towards the Avalons, he would be destroyed, yet he had no choice, and he turned away from the valley, naked road wheels screaming in protest as he battered his way across the lava fields.

✦ ✦ ✦

I have reached the end of the valley, and I emerge into the foothills of the Avalon Range and alter course to the west. I climb the nearest hill,

exposing only my turret and forward sensor arrays over its crest, and
begin the most careful sweep of which I remain capable.

+ + +

LNC's passive sensors detected the whispering lash of radar and he
knew he'd lost the race. The Enemy was ahead of him, waiting, and
he ground to a halt. His computer core had suffered additional shock
damage when the disintegrating ridge crest smashed into him, and his
thoughts were slow. It took him almost thirteen seconds to realize what
he must do. The only thing he could do now.

+ + +

"Tommy?"

Thomas Mallory looked up from where he crouched on the floor of
the packed compartment. His eight-year-old sister had sobbed herself
out of tears at last, and she huddled against his side in the protective
circle of his arm. But Thomas Mallory had learned too much about
the limits of protectiveness. At fifteen, he was the oldest person in
the compartment, and he knew what many of the others had not yet
realized—that they would never see their parents again, for the fifty-one
of them were the sole survivors of Morville.

"Tommy?" the slurred voice said once more, and Thomas cleared
his throat.

"Yes?" He heard the quaver in his own voice, but he made himself
speak loudly. Despite the air filtration systems, the compartment
stank of ozone, explosives, and burning organic compounds. He'd
felt the terrible concussions of combat and knew the vehicle in whose
protective belly he sat was savagely wounded, and he was no longer
certain how efficient its audio pickups might be.

"I have failed in my mission, Tommy," the voice said. "The Enemy
has cut us off from our objective."

"What enemy?" Thomas demanded. "Who *are* they, Lance? Why
are they *doing* this?"

"They are doing it because they are the Enemy," the voice replied.

"But there must be a *reason*!" Thomas cried with all the anguish of
a fifteen-year-old heart.

"They are the Enemy," the voice repeated in that eerie, slurred tone. "It is the Enemy's function to destroy... to destroy... to dest—"

The voice chopped off, and Thomas swallowed. Lance's responses were becoming increasingly less lucid, wandering into repetitive loops that sometimes faded into silence and other times, as now, cut off abruptly, and Thomas Mallory had learned about mortality. Even Bolos could perish, and somehow he knew Lance was dying by centimeters even as he struggled to complete his mission.

"They are the Enemy," Lance resumed, and the electronic voice was higher and tauter. "There is always the Enemy. The Enemy must be defeated. The Enemy must be destroyed. The Enemy—" Again the voice died with the sharpness of an axe blow, and Thomas bit his lip and hugged his sister tight. Endless seconds of silence oozed past, broken only by the whimpers and weeping of the younger children, until Thomas could stand it no longer.

"Lance?" he said hoarsely.

"I am here, Tommy." The voice was stronger this time, and calmer.

"W-What do we do?" Thomas asked.

"There is only one option." A cargo compartment hissed open to reveal a backpack military com unit and an all-terrain survival kit. Thomas had never used a military com, but he knew it was preset to the Dinochrome Brigade's frequencies. "Please take the kit and com unit," the voice said.

"All right." Thomas eased his arm from around his sister and lifted the backpack from the compartment. It was much lighter than he'd expected, and he slipped his arms through the straps and settled it on his back, then tugged the survival kit out as well.

"Thank you," the slurred voice said. "Now, here is what you must do, Tommy—"

❖ ❖ ❖

My questing sensors detect him at last. He is moving slowly, coming in along yet another valley. This one is shorter and shallower, barely deep enough to hide him from my fire, and I trace its course along my maps. He must emerge from it approximately 12.98 kilometers to the southwest of my present position, and I grind into motion once more.

*I will enter the valley from the north and sweep along it until we meet,
and then I will kill him.*

+ + +

Thomas Mallory crouched on the hilltop. It hadn't been hard to make
the younger kids hide—not after the horrors they'd seen in Morville.
But Thomas couldn't join them. He had to be here, where he could see
the end, for someone *had* to see it. Someone had to be there, to know
how fifty-one children had been saved from death… and to witness
the price their dying savior had paid for them.

Distance blurred details, hiding Lance's dreadful damages as he
ground steadily up the valley, but Thomas's eyes narrowed as he saw
the cloud of dust coming to meet him. Tears burned like ice on his
cheeks in the sub-zero wind, and he scrubbed at them angrily. Lance
deserved those tears, but Thomas couldn't let the other kids see them.
There was little enough chance that they could survive a single Camlan
winter night, even in the mountains, where they would at least have
water, fuel, and the means to build some sort of shelter. But it was the
only chance Lance had been able to give them, and Thomas would not
show weakness before the children he was now responsible for driving
and goading into surviving until someone came to rescue them. Would
not betray the trust Lance had bestowed upon him.

The oncoming dust grew thicker, and he raised the electronic
binoculars, gazing through them for his first sight of the enemy. He
adjusted their focus as an iodine-colored turret moved beyond a saddle
of hills. Lance couldn't see it from his lower vantage point, but Thomas
could, and his face went suddenly paper-white. He stared for one more
moment, then grabbed for the com unit's microphone.

+ + +

"No, Lance! Don't—don't! It's not the enemy—it's another Bolo!"

*The Human voice cracks with strain as it burns suddenly over the
command channel, and confusion whips through me. The transmitter is
close—very close—and that is not possible. Nor do I recognize the voice,
and that also is impossible. I start to reply, but before I can, another voice
comes over the same channel.*

"Cease transmission," it says. "Do not reveal your location."

This time I know the voice, yet I have never heard it speak so. It has lost its crispness, its sureness. It is the voice of one on the brink of madness, a voice crushed and harrowed by pain and despair and a purpose that goes beyond obsession.

"Lance," the Human voice—a young, male Human voice—sobs. "Please, Lance! It's another Bolo! It really is!"

"It is the Enemy," the voice I once knew replies, and it is higher and shriller. "It is the Enemy. There is only the Enemy. I am Unit Zero-One-Zero-Three-LNC of the Line. It is my function to destroy the Enemy. The Enemy. The Enemy. The Enemy. The Enemy."

I hear the broken cadence of that voice, and suddenly I understand. I understand everything, and horror fills me. I lock my tracks, slithering to a halt, fighting to avoid what I know must happen. Yet understanding has come too late, and even as I brake, LNC rounds the flank of a hill in a scream of tortured, over-strained tracks and a billowing cloud of dust.

For the first time, I see his hideously mauled starboard side and the gaping wound driven deep, deep into his hull. I can actually see his breached Personality Center in its depths, see the penetration where Enemy fire ripped brutally into the circuitry of his psychotronic brain, and I understand it all. I hear the madness in his electronic voice, and the determination and courage which have kept that broken, dying wreck in motion, and the child's voice on the com is the final element. I know his mission, now, the reason he has fought so doggedly, so desperately to cross the Badlands to the life-sustaining shelter of the mountains.

Yet my knowledge changes nothing, for there is no way to avoid him. He staggers and lurches on his crippled tracks, but he is moving at almost 80 kilometers per hour. He has no Hellbore, no missiles, and his remaining infinite repeaters cannot harm me, yet he retains one final weapon: himself.

He thunders towards me, his com voice silent no more, screaming the single word "Enemy! Enemy! Enemy!" again and again. He hurls himself upon me in a suicide attack, charging to his death as the only way he can protect the children he has carried out of hell from the friend he can no longer recognize, the "Enemy" who has hunted him over 400 kilometers of frozen, waterless stone and dust. It is all he has left, the only thing he can do... and if he carries through with his ramming attack, we both will die and exposure will kill the children before anyone can rescue them.

I have no choice. He has left me none, and in that instant I wish I were Human. That I, too, could shed the tears which fog the young voice crying out to its protector to turn aside and save himself.

But I cannot weep. There is only one thing I can do.

"Good bye, Lance," I send softly over the battalion command net. "Forgive me."

And I fire.

Like Robert Heinlein, Arthur C. Clarke is a household name, even outside of science fiction circles. From the film 2001: A Space Odyssey, *based on his story "The Sentinel," to* Childhood's End *to the Nebula- and Hugo-winning* Rendezvous with Rama *or his acknowledged classic* A Fall of Moondust, *he is one of the greats of the genre, a SFWA Grand Master and winner of multiple Nebula and Hugo Awards. He was appointed Commander of the Order of the British Empire (CBE) in 1989.*

Thus it delights me that this next story takes us back to his earliest days. It's his first story sold, though not the first published, since "Loophole" appeared a month before in the April 1946 issue of Astounding Science Fiction. *In this story, a shipful of aliens visit Earth to investigate radio signals they've detected, in an attempt to save as many people and as much of human culture as possible before the sun explodes—an occurrence that is just hours away.*

RESCUE PARTY
ARTHUR C. CLARKE

Who was to blame? For three days Alveron's thoughts had come back to that question, and still he had found no answer. A creature of a less civilized or a less sensitive race would never have let it torture his mind, and would have satisfied himself with the assurance that no one could be responsible for the working of fate. But Alveron and his kind had been lords of the Universe since the dawn of history, since that far-distant age when the Time Barrier had been folded round the cosmos by the unknown powers that lay beyond the Beginning. To them had been given all knowledge—and with infinite knowledge went infinite responsibility. If there were mistakes and errors in the administration of the galaxy, the fault lay on the heads of Alveron and his people. And this was no mere mistake: it was one of the greatest tragedies in history.

The crew still knew nothing. Even Rugon, his closest friend and the ship's deputy captain, had been told only part of the truth. But now the doomed worlds lay less than a billion miles ahead. In a few hours, they would be landing on the third planet.

Once again Alveron read the message from Base; then, with a flick of a tentacle that no human eye could have followed, he pressed the "General Attention" button. Throughout the mile-long cylinder that was the Galactic Survey Ship S9000, creatures of many races laid down their work to listen to the words of their captain.

"I know you have all been wondering," began Alveron, "why we were ordered to abandon our survey and to proceed at such an acceleration to this region of space. Some of you may realize what this acceleration means. Our ship is on its last voyage: the generators have already been running for sixty hours at Ultimate Overload. We will be very lucky if we return to Base under our own power.

"We are approaching a sun which is about to become a Nova. Detonation will occur in seven hours, with an uncertainty of one hour, leaving us a maximum of only four hours for exploration. There are ten planets in the system about to be destroyed—and there is a civilization on the third. That fact was discovered only a few days ago. It is our tragic mission to contact that doomed race and if possible to save some of its members. I know that there is little we can do in so short a time with this single ship. No other machine can possibly reach the system before detonation occurs."

There was a long pause during which there could have been no sound or movement in the whole of the mighty ship as it sped silently toward the worlds ahead. Alveron knew what his companions were thinking and he tried to answer their unspoken question.

"You will wonder how such a disaster, the greatest of which we have any record, has been allowed to occur. On one point I can reassure you. The fault does not lie with the Survey.

"As you know, with our present fleet of under twelve thousand ships, it is possible to re-examine each of the eight thousand million solar systems in the Galaxy at intervals of about a million years. Most worlds change very little in so short a time as that.

"Less than four hundred thousand years ago, the survey ship S5060 examined the planets of the system we are approaching. It found intelligence on none of them, though the third planet was teeming with animal life and two other worlds had once been inhabited. The usual report was submitted and the system is due for its next examination in six hundred thousand years.

"It now appears that in the incredibly short period since the last survey, intelligent life has appeared in the system. The first intimation of this occurred when unknown radio signals were detected on the planet Kulath in the system X29.35, Y34.76, Z27.93. Bearings were taken on them; they were coming from the system ahead.

"Kulath is two hundred light-years from here, so those radio waves had been on their way for two centuries. Thus for at least that period of time a civilization has existed on one of these worlds—a civilization that can generate electromagnetic waves and all that that implies.

"An immediate telescopic examination of the system was made and it was then found that the sun was in the unstable pre-nova stage. Detonation might occur at any moment, and indeed might have done so while the light waves were on their way to Kulath.

"There was a slight delay while the supervelocity scanners on Kulath II were focused on to the system. They showed that the explosion had not yet occurred but was only a few hours away. If Kulath had been a fraction of a light-year further from this sun, we should never have known of its civilization until it had ceased to exist.

"The Administrator of Kulath contacted the Sector Base immediately, and I was ordered to proceed to the system at once. Our object is to save what members we can of the doomed race, if indeed there are any left. But we have assumed that a civilization possessing radio could have protected itself against any rise of temperature that may have already occurred.

"This ship and the two tenders will each explore a section of the planet. Commander Torkalee will take Number One, Commander Orostron Number Two. They will have just under four hours in which to explore this world. At the end of that time, they must be back in the ship. It will be leaving then, with or without them. I will give the two commanders detailed instructions in the control room immediately.

"That is all. We enter atmosphere in two hours."

+ + +

On the world once known as Earth the fires were dying out: there was nothing left to burn. The great forests that had swept across the planet like a tidal wave with the passing of the cities were now no more than glowing charcoal and the smoke of their funeral pyres still stained the sky. But the last hours were still to come, for the surface rocks had not yet begun to flow. The continents were dimly visible through the haze, but their outlines meant nothing to the watchers in the approaching ship. The charts they possessed were out of date by a dozen Ice Ages and more deluges than one.

The S9000 had driven past Jupiter and seen at once that no life could exist in those half-gaseous oceans of compressed hydrocarbons, now erupting furiously under the sun's abnormal heat. Mars and the outer planets they had missed, and Alveron realized that the worlds nearer the sun than Earth would be already melting. It was more than likely, he thought sadly, that the tragedy of this unknown race was already finished. Deep in his heart, he thought it might be better so. The ship could only have carried a few hundred survivors, and the problem of selection had been haunting his mind.

Rugon, Chief of Communications and Deputy Captain, came into the control room. For the last hour he had been striving to detect radiation from Earth, but in vain.

"We're too late," he announced gloomily. "I've monitored the whole spectrum and the ether's dead except for our own stations and some two-hundred-year-old programs from Kulath. Nothing in this system is radiating any more."

He moved toward the giant vision screen with a graceful flowing motion that no mere biped could ever hope to imitate. Alveron said nothing; he had been expecting this news.

One entire wall of the control room was taken up by the screen, a great black rectangle that gave an impression of almost infinite depth. Three of Rugon's slender control tentacles, useless for heavy work but incredibly swift at all manipulation, flickered over the selector dials and the screen lit up with a thousand points of light. The star field flowed swiftly past as Rugon adjusted the controls, bringing the projector to bear upon the sun itself.

No man of Earth would have recognized the monstrous shape that filled the screen. The sun's light was white no longer: great violet-blue clouds covered half its surface and from them long streamers of flame were erupting into space. At one point an enormous prominence had reared itself out of the photosphere, far out even into the flickering veils of the corona. It was as though a tree of fire had taken root in the surface of the sun—a tree that stood half a million miles high and whose branches were rivers of flame sweeping through space at hundreds of miles a second.

"I suppose," said Rugon presently, "that you are quite satisfied about the astronomers' calculations. After all—"

"Oh, we're perfectly safe," said Alveron confidently. "I've spoken to Kulath Observatory and they have been making some additional checks through our own instruments. That uncertainty of an hour includes a private safety margin which they won't tell me in case I feel tempted to stay any longer."

He glanced at the instrument board.

"The pilot should have brought us to the atmosphere now. Switch the screen back to the planet, please. Ah, there they go!"

There was a sudden tremor underfoot and a raucous clanging of alarms, instantly stilled. Across the vision screen two slim projectiles dived toward the looming mass of Earth. For a few miles they traveled together, then they separated, one vanishing abruptly as it entered the shadow of the planet.

Slowly the huge mother ship, with its thousand times greater mass, descended after them into the raging storms that already were tearing down the deserted cities of Man.

✦ ✦ ✦

It was night in the hemisphere over which Orostron drove his tiny command. Like Torkalee, his mission was to photograph and record, and to report progress to the mother ship. The little scout had no room for specimens or passengers. If contact was made with the inhabitants of this world, the S9000 would come at once. There would be no time for parleying. If there was any trouble the rescue would be by force and the explanations could come later.

The ruined land beneath was bathed with an eerie, flickering light, for a great auroral display was raging over half the world. But the image on the vision screen was independent of external light, and it showed clearly a waste of barren rock that seemed never to have known any form of life. Presumably this desert land must come to an end somewhere. Orostron increased his speed to the highest value he dared risk in so dense an atmosphere.

The machine fled on through the storm, and presently the desert of rock began to climb toward the sky. A great mountain range lay ahead, its peaks lost in the smoke-laden clouds. Orostron directed the scanners toward the horizon, and on the vision screen the line of mountains seemed suddenly very close and menacing. He started to climb rapidly. It was difficult to imagine a more unpromising land in which to find civilization and he wondered if it would be wise to change course. He decided against it. Five minutes later, he had his reward.

Miles below lay a decapitated mountain, the whole of its summit sheared away by some tremendous feat of engineering. Rising out of the rock and straddling the artificial plateau was an intricate structure of metal girders, supporting masses of machinery. Orostron brought his ship to a halt and spiraled down toward the mountain.

The slight Doppler blur had now vanished, and the picture on the screen was clear-cut. The latticework was supporting some scores of great metal mirrors, pointing skyward at an angle of forty-five degrees to the horizontal. They were slightly concave, and each had some complicated mechanism at its focus. There seemed something impressive and purposeful about the great array; every mirror was aimed at precisely the same spot in the sky—or beyond.

Orostron turned to his colleagues.

"It looks like some kind of observatory to me," he said. "Have you ever seen anything like it before?"

Klarten, a multitentacled, tripedal creature from a globular cluster at the edge of the Milky Way, had a different theory.

"That's communication equipment. Those reflectors are for focusing electromagnetic beams. I've seen the same kind of installation on a hundred worlds before. It may even be the station that Kulath picked up—though that's rather unlikely, for the beams would be very narrow from mirrors that size."

"That would explain why Rugon could detect no radiation before we landed," added Hansur II, one of the twin beings from the planet Thargon.

Orostron did not agree at all.

"If that is a radio station, it must be built for interplanetary communication. Look at the way the mirrors are pointed. I don't believe that a race which has only had radio for two centuries can have crossed space. It took my people six thousand years to do it."

"We managed it in three," said Hansur II mildly, speaking a few seconds ahead of his twin. Before the inevitable argument could develop, Klarten began to wave his tentacles with excitement. While the others had been talking, he had started the automatic monitor.

"Here it is! Listen!"

He threw a switch, and the little room was filled with a raucous whining sound, continually changing in pitch but nevertheless retaining certain characteristics that were difficult to define.

The four explorers listened intently for a minute; then Orostron said, "Surely that can't be any form of speech! No creature could produce sounds as quickly as that!"

Hansur I had come to the same conclusion. "That's a television program. Don't you think so, Klarten?"

The other agreed.

"Yes, and each of those mirrors seems to be radiating a different program. I wonder where they're going? If I'm correct, one of the other planets in the system must lie along those beams. We can soon check that."

Orostron called the S9000 and reported the discovery. Both Rugon and Alveron were greatly excited, and made a quick check of the astronomical records.

The result was surprising—and disappointing. None of the other nine planets lay anywhere near the line of transmission. The great mirrors appeared to be pointing blindly into space.

There seemed only one conclusion to be drawn, and Klarten was the first to voice it.

"They had interplanetary communication," he said. "But the station must be deserted now, and the transmitters no longer controlled. They haven't been switched off, and are just pointing where they were left."

"Well, we'll soon find out," said Orostron. "I'm going to land."

He brought the machine slowly down to the level of the great metal mirrors, and past them until it came to rest on the mountain rock. A hundred yards away, a white stone building crouched beneath the maze of steel girders. It was windowless, but there were several doors in the wall facing them.

Orostron watched his companions climb into their protective suits and wished he could follow. But someone had to stay in the machine to keep in touch with the mother ship. Those were Alveron's instructions, and they were very wise. One never knew what would happen on a world that was being explored for the first time, especially under conditions such as these.

Very cautiously, the three explorers stepped out of the airlock and adjusted the antigravity field of their suits. Then, each with the mode of locomotion peculiar to his race, the little party went toward the building, the Hansur twins leading and Klarten following close behind. His gravity control was apparently giving trouble, for he suddenly fell to the ground, rather to the amusement of his colleagues. Orostron saw them pause for a moment at the nearest door—then it opened slowly and they disappeared from sight.

So Orostron waited, with what patience he could, while the storm rose around him and the light of the aurora grew even brighter in the sky. At the agreed times he called the mother ship and received brief acknowledgments from Rugon. He wondered how Torkalee was faring, halfway round the planet, but he could not contact him through the crash and thunder of solar interference.

It did not take Klarten and the Hansurs long to discover that their theories were largely correct. The building was a radio station, and it was utterly deserted. It consisted of one tremendous room with a few small offices leading from it. In the main chamber, row after row of electrical equipment stretched into the distance; lights flickered and winked on hundreds of control panels, and a dull glow came from the elements in a great avenue of vacuum tubes.

But Klarten was not impressed. The first radio sets his race had built were now fossilized in strata a thousand million years old. Man, who had possessed electrical machines for only a few centuries, could not compete with those who had known them for half the lifetime of the Earth.

Nevertheless, the party kept their recorders running as they explored the building. There was still one problem to be solved. The deserted station was broadcasting programs, but where were they coming from? The central switchboard had been quickly located. It was designed to handle scores of programs simultaneously, but the source of those programs was lost in a maze of cables that vanished underground. Back in the S9000, Rugon was trying to analyze the broadcasts and perhaps his researches would reveal their origin. It was impossible to trace cables that might lead across continents.

The party wasted little time at the deserted station. There was nothing they could learn from it, and they were seeking life rather than scientific information. A few minutes later the little ship rose swiftly from the plateau and headed toward the plains that must lie beyond the mountains. Less than three hours were still left to them.

As the array of enigmatic mirrors dropped out of sight, Orostron was struck by a sudden thought. Was it imagination, or had they all moved through a small angle while he had been waiting, as if they were still compensating for the rotation of the Earth? He could not be sure, and he dismissed the matter as unimportant. It would only mean that the directing mechanism was still working, after a fashion.

They discovered the city fifteen minutes later. It was a great, sprawling metropolis, built around a river that had disappeared leaving an ugly scar winding its way among the great buildings and beneath bridges that looked very incongruous now.

Even from the air, the city looked deserted. But only two and a half hours were left—there was no time for further exploration. Orostron made his decision, and landed near the largest structure he could see. It seemed reasonable to suppose that some creatures would have sought shelter in the strongest buildings, where they would be safe until the very end.

The deepest caves—the heart of the planet itself—would give no protection when the final cataclysm came. Even if this race had reached the outer planets, its doom would only be delayed by the few hours it would take for the ravening wavefronts to cross the Solar System.

Orostron could not know that the city had been deserted not for a few days or weeks, but for over a century. For the culture of cities, which had outlasted so many civilizations, had been doomed at last when the helicopter brought universal transportation. Within a few generations the great masses of mankind, knowing that they could reach any part of the globe in a matter of hours, had gone back to the fields and forests for which they had always longed. The new civilization had machines and resources of which earlier ages had never dreamed, but it was essentially rural and no longer bound to the steel and concrete warrens that had dominated the centuries before. Such cities as still remained were specialized centers of research, administration or entertainment; the others had been allowed to decay, where it was too much trouble to destroy them. The dozen or so greatest of all cities, and the ancient university towns, had scarcely changed and would have lasted for many generations to come. But the cities that had been founded on steam and iron and surface transportation had passed with the industries that had nourished them.

And so while Orostron waited in the tender, his colleagues raced through endless empty corridors and deserted halls, taking innumerable photographs but learning nothing of the creatures who had used these buildings. There were libraries, meeting places, council rooms, thousands of offices—all were empty and deep with dust. If they had not seen the radio station on its mountain eyrie, the explorers could well have believed that this world had known no life for centuries.

Through the long minutes of waiting, Orostron tried to imagine where this race could have vanished. Perhaps they had killed themselves knowing that escape was impossible; perhaps they had built great shelters in the bowels of the planet, and even now were cowering in their millions beneath his feet, waiting for the end. He began to fear that he would never know.

It was almost a relief when at last he had to give the order for the return. Soon he would know if Torkalee's party had been more fortunate. And he was anxious to get back to the mother ship, for as the minutes passed the suspense had become more and more acute. There had always been the thought in his mind: What if the astronomers of Kulath have made a mistake? He would begin to feel happy when the walls of the S9000 were around him. He would be happier still when they were out in space and this ominous sun was shrinking far astern.

As soon as his colleagues had entered the airlock, Orostron hurled his tiny machine into the sky and set the controls to home on the S9000. Then he turned to his friends.

"Well, what have you found?" he asked.

Klarten produced a large roll of canvas and spread it out on the floor.

"This is what they were like," he said quietly. "Bipeds, with only two arms. They seem to have managed well, in spite of that handicap. Only two eyes as well, unless there are others in the back. We were lucky to find this; it's about the only thing they left behind."

The ancient oil painting stared stonily back at the three creatures regarding it so intently. By the irony of fate, its complete worthlessness had saved it from oblivion. When the city had been evacuated, no one had bothered to move Alderman John Richards, 1909–1974. For a century and a half he had been gathering dust while far away from the old cities the new civilization had been rising to heights no earlier culture had ever known.

"That was almost all we found," said Klarten. "The city must have been deserted for years. I'm afraid our expedition has been a failure. If there are any living beings on this world, they've hidden themselves too well for us to find them."

His commander was forced to agree.

"It was an almost impossible task," he said. "If we'd had weeks instead of hours we might have succeeded. For all we know, they may even have built shelters under the sea. No one seems to have thought of that."

He glanced quickly at the indicators and corrected the course.

"We'll be there in five minutes. Alveron seems to be moving rather quickly. I wonder if Torkalee has found anything."

The S9000 was hanging a few miles above the seaboard of a blazing continent when Orostron homed upon it. The danger line was thirty minutes away and there was no time to lose. Skillfully, he maneuvered the little ship into its launching tube and the party stepped out of the airlock.

There was a small crowd waiting for them. That was to be expected, but Orostron could see at once that something more than curiosity had brought his friends here. Even before a word was spoken, he knew that something was wrong.

"Torkalee hasn't returned. He's lost his party and we're going to the rescue. Come along to the control room at once."

✦ ✦ ✦

From the beginning, Torkalee had been luckier than Orostron. He had followed the zone of twilight, keeping away from the intolerable glare of the sun, until he came to the shores of an inland sea. It was a very recent sea, one of the latest of Man's works, for the land it covered had been desert less than a century before. In a few hours it would be desert again, for the water was boiling and clouds of steam were rising to the skies. But they could not veil the loveliness of the great white city that overlooked the tideless sea.

Flying machines were still parked neatly round the square in which Torkalee landed. They were disappointingly primitive, though beautifully finished, and depended on rotating airfoils for support. Nowhere was there any sign of life, but the place gave the impression that its inhabitants were not very far away. Lights were still shining from some of the windows.

Torkalee's three companions lost no time in leaving the machine. Leader of the party, by seniority of rank and race, was T'sinadree, who like Alveron himself had been born on one of the ancient planets of the Central Suns. Next came Alarkane, from a race which was one of the youngest in the Universe and took a perverse pride in the fact. Last came one of the strange beings from the system of Palador. It was nameless, like all its kind, for it possessed no identity of its own, being merely a mobile but still dependent cell in the consciousness of its race. Though it and its fellows had long been scattered over the galaxy in the exploration of countless worlds, some unknown link still bound them together as inexorably as the living cells in a human body.

When a creature of Palador spoke, the pronoun it used was always "We." There was not, nor could there ever be, any first person singular in the language of Palador.

The great doors of the splendid building baffled the explorers, though any human child would have known their secret. T'sinadree wasted no time on them but called Torkalee on his personal transmitter. Then the three hurried aside while their commander maneuvered his machine into the best position. There was a brief burst of intolerable flame; the massive steelwork flickered once at the edge of the visible spectrum and was gone. The stones were still glowing when the eager party hurried into the building, the beams of their light projectors fanning before them.

The torches were not needed. Before them lay a great hall, glowing with light from lines of tubes along the ceiling. On either side, the hall opened out into long corridors, while straight ahead a massive stairway swept majestically toward the upper floors.

For a moment T'sinadree hesitated. Then, since one way was as good as another, he led his companions down the first corridor.

The feeling that life was near had now become very strong. At any moment, it seemed, they might be confronted by the creatures of this world. If they showed hostility—and they could scarcely be blamed if they did—the paralyzers would be used at once.

The tension was very great as the party entered the first room, and only relaxed when they saw that it held nothing but machines—row after row of them, now stilled and silent. Lining the enormous room were thousands of metal filing cabinets, forming a continuous wall as far as the eye could reach. And that was all; there was no furniture, nothing but the cabinets and the mysterious machines.

Alarkane, always the quickest of the three, was already examining the cabinets. Each held many thousand sheets of tough, thin material, perforated with innumerable holes and slots. The Paladorian appropriated one of the cards and Alarkane recorded the scene together with some close-ups of the machines. Then they left. The great room, which had been one of the marvels of the world, meant nothing to them. No living eye would ever again see that wonderful battery of almost human Hollerith analyzers and the five thousand million punched cards holding all that could be recorded on each man, woman and child on the planet.

It was clear that this building had been used very recently. With growing excitement, the explorers hurried on to the next room. This they found to be an enormous library, for millions of books lay all around them on miles and miles of shelving. Here, though the explorers could not know it, were the records of all the laws that Man had ever passed, and all the speeches that had ever been made in his council chambers.

T'sinadree was deciding his plan of action, when Alarkane drew his attention to one of the racks a hundred yards away. It was half empty, unlike all the others. Around it books lay in a tumbled heap on the floor, as if knocked down by someone in frantic haste. The signs were unmistakable. Not long ago, other creatures had been this way. Faint wheel marks were clearly visible on the floor to the acute sense of Alarkane, though the others could see nothing. Alarkane could even detect footprints, but knowing nothing of the creatures that had formed them he could not say which way they led.

The sense of nearness was stronger than ever now, but it was nearness in time, not in space. Alarkane voiced the thoughts of the party.

"Those books must have been valuable, and someone has come to rescue them—rather as an afterthought, I should say. That means there must be a place of refuge, possibly not very far away. Perhaps we may be able to find some other clues that will lead us to it."

T'sinadree agreed; the Paladorian wasn't enthusiastic.

"That may be so," it said, "but the refuge may be anywhere on the planet, and we have just two hours left. Let us waste no more time if we hope to rescue these people."

The party hurried forward once more, pausing only to collect a few books that might be useful to the scientists at Base—though it was doubtful if they could ever be translated. They soon found that the great building was composed largely of small rooms, all showing signs of recent occupation. Most of them were in a neat and tidy condition, but one or two were very much the reverse. The explorers were particularly puzzled by one room—clearly an office of some kind—that appeared to have been completely wrecked. The floor was littered with papers, the furniture had been smashed, and smoke was pouring through the broken windows from the fires outside.

T'sinadree was rather alarmed.

"Surely no dangerous animal could have got into a place like this!" he exclaimed, fingering his paralyzer nervously.

Alarkane did not answer. He began to make that annoying sound which his race called "laughter." It was several minutes before he would explain what had amused him.

"I don't think any animal has done it," he said. "In fact, the explanation is very simple. Suppose *you* had been working all your life in this room, dealing with endless papers, year after year. And suddenly, you are told that you will never see it again, that your work is finished, and that you can leave it forever. More than that—no one will come after you. Everything is finished. How would you make your exit, T'sinadree?"

The other thought for a moment.

"Well, I suppose I'd just tidy things up and leave. That's what seems to have happened in all the other rooms."

Alarkane laughed again.

"I'm quite sure you would. But some individuals have a different psychology. I think I should have liked the creature that used this room."

He did not explain himself further, and his two colleagues puzzled over his words for quite a while before they gave it up.

It came as something of a shock when Torkalee gave the order to return. They had gathered a great deal of information, but had found no clue that might lead them to the missing inhabitants of this world. That problem was as baffling as ever, and now it seemed that it would never be solved. There were only forty minutes left before the S9000 would be departing.

They were halfway back to the tender when they saw the semicircular passage leading down into the depths of the building. Its architectural style was quite different from that used elsewhere, and the gently sloping floor was an irresistible attraction to creatures whose many legs had grown weary of the marble staircases which only bipeds could have built in such profusion. T'sinadree had been the worst sufferer, for he normally employed twelve legs and could use twenty when he was in a hurry, though no one had ever seen him perform this feat.

The party stopped dead and looked down the passageway with a single thought. A tunnel, leading down into the depths of Earth! At its end, they might yet find the people of this world and rescue some of them from their fate. For there was still time to call the mother ship if the need arose.

T'sinadree signaled to his commander and Torkalee brought the little machine immediately overhead. There might not be time for the party to retrace its footsteps through the maze of passages, so meticulously recorded in the Paladorian mind that there was no possibility of going astray. If speed was necessary, Torkalee could blast his way through the dozen floors above their head. In any case, it should not take long to find what lay at the end of the passage.

It took only thirty seconds. The tunnel ended quite abruptly in a very curious cylindrical room with magnificently padded seats along the walls. There was no way out save that by which they had come and it was several seconds before the purpose of the chamber dawned on Alarkane's mind. It was a pity, he thought, that they would never have time to use this. The thought was suddenly interrupted by a cry from T'sinadree. Alarkane wheeled around, and saw that the entrance had closed silently behind them.

Even in that first moment of panic, Alarkane found himself thinking with some admiration: Whoever they were, they knew how to build automatic machinery!

The Paladorian was the first to speak. It waved one of its tentacles toward the seats.

"We think it would be best to be seated," it said. The multiplex mind of Palador had already analyzed the situation and knew what was coming.

They did not have long to wait before a low-pitched hum came from a grill overhead, and for the very last time in history a human, even if lifeless, voice was heard on Earth. The words were meaningless, though the trapped explorers could guess their message clearly enough.

"Choose your stations, please, and be seated."

Simultaneously, a wall panel at one end of the compartment glowed with light. On it was a simple map, consisting of a series of a dozen circles connected by a line. Each of the circles had writing alongside it, and beside the writing were two buttons of different colors.

Alarkane looked questioningly at his leader.

"Don't touch them," said T'sinadree. "If we leave the controls alone, the doors may open again."

He was wrong. The engineers who had designed the automatic subway had assumed that anyone who entered it would naturally wish to go somewhere. If they selected no intermediate station, their destination could only be the end of the line.

There was another pause while the relays and thyratrons waited for their orders. In those thirty seconds, if they had known what to do, the party could have opened the doors and left the subway. But they did not know, and the machines geared to a human psychology acted for them.

The surge of acceleration was not very great; the lavish upholstery was a luxury, not a necessity. Only an almost imperceptible vibration told of the speed at which they were traveling through the bowels of the earth, on a journey the duration of which they could not even guess. And in thirty minutes, the S9000 would be leaving the Solar System.

There was a long silence in the speeding machine. T'sinadree and Alarkane were thinking rapidly. So was the Paladorian, though in a different fashion. The conception of personal death was meaningless to it, for the destruction of a single unit meant no more to the group mind than the loss of a nail-paring to a man. But it could, though with great difficulty, appreciate the plight of individual intelligences such as Alarkane and T'sinadree, and it was anxious to help them if it could.

Alarkane had managed to contact Torkalee with his personal transmitter, though the signal was very weak and seemed to be fading quickly. Rapidly he explained the situation, and almost at once the signals became clearer. Torkalee was following the path of the machine, flying above the ground under which they were speeding to their unknown destination. That was the first indication they had of the fact that they were traveling at nearly a thousand miles an hour, and very soon after that Torkalee was able to give the still more disturbing news that they were rapidly approaching the sea. While they were beneath the land, there was a hope, though a slender one, that they might stop the machine and escape. But under the ocean—not all the brains and the machinery in the great mother ship could save them. No one could have devised a more perfect trap.

T'sinadree had been examining the wall map with great attention. Its meaning was obvious, and along the line connecting the circles a tiny spot of light was crawling. It was already halfway to the first of the stations marked.

"I'm going to press one of those buttons," said T'sinadree at last. "It won't do any harm, and we may learn something."

"I agree. Which will you try first?"

"There are only two kinds, and it won't matter if we try the wrong one first. I suppose one is to start the machine and the other is to stop it."

Alarkane was not very hopeful.

"It started without any button pressing," he said. "I think it's completely automatic and we can't control it from here at all."

T'sinadree could not agree.

"These buttons are clearly associated with the stations, and there's no point in having them unless you can use them to stop yourself. The only question is, which is the right one?"

His analysis was perfectly correct. The machine could be stopped at any intermediate station. They had only been on their way ten minutes, and if they could leave now, no harm would have been done. It was just bad luck that T'sinadree's first choice was the wrong button.

The little light on the map crawled slowly through the illuminated circle without checking its speed. And at the same time Torkalee called from the ship overhead.

"You have just passed underneath a city and are heading out to sea. There cannot be another stop for nearly a thousand miles."

✦ ✦ ✦

Alveron had given up all hope of finding life on this world. The S9000 had roamed over half the planet, never staying long in one place, descending ever and again in an effort to attract attention. There had been no response; Earth seemed utterly dead. If any of its inhabitants were still alive, thought Alveron, they must have hidden themselves in its depths where no help could reach them, though their doom would be nonetheless certain.

Rugon brought news of the disaster. The great ship ceased its fruitless searching and fled back through the storm to the ocean above which Torkalee's little tender was still following the track of the buried machine.

The scene was truly terrifying. Not since the days when Earth was born had there been such seas as this. Mountains of water were racing before the storm which had now reached velocities of many hundred miles an hour. Even at this distance from the mainland the air was full of flying debris—trees, fragments of houses, sheets of metal, anything that had not been anchored to the ground. No airborne machine could have lived for a moment in such a gale. And ever and again even the roar of the wind was drowned as the vast water-mountains met head-on with a crash that seemed to shake the sky.

Fortunately, there had been no serious earthquakes yet. Far beneath the bed of the ocean, the wonderful piece of engineering which had been the World President's private vacuum-subway was still working perfectly, unaffected by the tumult and destruction above. It would continue to work until the last minute of the Earth's existence, which, if the astronomers were right, was not much more than fifteen minutes away—though precisely how much more Alveron would have given a great deal to know. It would be nearly an hour before the trapped party could reach land and even the slightest hope of rescue.

Alveron's instructions had been precise, though even without them he would never have dreamed of taking any risks with the great machine that had been entrusted to his care. Had he been human, the decision to abandon the trapped members of his crew would have been desperately hard to make. But he came of a race far more sensitive than Man, a race that so loved the things of the spirit that long ago, and with infinite reluctance, it had taken over control of the Universe since only thus could it be sure that justice was being done. Alveron would need all his superhuman gifts to carry him through the next few hours.

Meanwhile, a mile below the bed of the ocean Alarkane and T'sinadree were very busy indeed with their private communicators. Fifteen minutes is not a long time in which to wind up the affairs of a lifetime. It is indeed, scarcely long enough to dictate more than a few of those farewell messages which at such moments are so much more important than all other matters.

All the while the Paladorian had remained silent and motionless, saying not a word. The other two, resigned to their fate and engrossed in their personal affairs, had given it no thought. They were startled when suddenly it began to address them in its peculiarly passionless voice.

"We perceive that you are making certain arrangements concerning your anticipated destruction. That will probably be unnecessary. Captain Alveron hopes to rescue us if we can stop this machine when we reach land again."

Both T'sinadree and Alarkane were too surprised to say anything for a moment. Then the latter gasped, "How do you know?"

It was a foolish question, for he remembered at once that there were several Paladorians—if one could use the phrase—in the S9000, and consequently their companion knew everything that was happening in the mother ship. So he did not wait for an answer but continued, "Alveron can't do that! He daren't take such a risk!"

"There will be no risk," said the Paladorian. "We have told him what to do. It is really very simple."

Alarkane and T'sinadree looked at their companion with something approaching awe, realizing now what must have happened. In moments of crisis, the single units comprising the Paladorian mind could link together in an organization no less close than that of any physical brain. At such moments they formed an intellect more powerful than any other in the Universe. All ordinary problems could be solved by a few hundred or thousand units. Very rarely, millions would be needed, and on two historic occasions the billions of cells of the entire Paladorian consciousness had been welded together to deal with emergencies that threatened the race. The mind of Palador was one of the greatest mental resources of the Universe; its full force was seldom required, but the knowledge that it was available was supremely comforting to other races. Alarkane wondered how many cells had coordinated to deal with this particular emergency. He also wondered how so trivial an incident had ever come to its attention.

To that question he was never to know the answer, though he might have guessed it had he known that the chillingly remote Paladorian mind possessed an almost human streak of vanity. Long ago, Alarkane had written a book trying to prove that eventually all intelligent races would sacrifice individual consciousness and that one day only group-minds would remain in the Universe. Palador, he had said, was the first of those ultimate intellects, and the vast, dispersed mind had not been displeased.

They had no time to ask any further questions before Alveron himself began to speak through their communicators.

"Alveron calling! We're staying on this planet until the detonation waves reach it, so we may be able to rescue you. You're heading toward a city on the coast which you'll reach in forty minutes at your present speed. If you cannot stop yourselves then, we're going to blast the tunnel behind and ahead of you to cut off your power. Then we'll sink a shaft to get you out—the chief engineer says he can do it in five minutes with the main projectors. So you should be safe within an hour, unless the sun blows up before."

"And if that happens, you'll be destroyed as well! You mustn't take such a risk!"

"Don't let that worry you; we're perfectly safe. When the sun detonates, the explosion wave will take several minutes to rise to its maximum. But apart from that, we're on the night side of the planet, behind an eight-thousand-mile screen of rock. When the first warning of the explosion comes, we will accelerate out of the Solar System, keeping in the shadow of the planet. Under our maximum drive, we will reach the velocity of light before leaving the cone of shadow, and the sun cannot harm us then."

T'sinadree was still afraid to hope. Another objection came at once into his mind.

"Yes, but how will you get any warning, here on the night side of the planet?"

"Very easily," replied Alveron. "This world has a moon which is now visible from this hemisphere. We have telescopes trained on it. If it shows any sudden increase in brilliance, our main drive goes on automatically and we'll be thrown out of the system."

The logic was flawless. Alveron, cautious as ever, was taking no chances. It would be many minutes before the eight-thousand-mile shield of rock and metal could be destroyed by the fires of the exploding sun. In that time, the S9000 could have reached the safety of the velocity of light.

Alarkane pressed the second button when they were still several miles from the coast. He did not expect anything to happen then, assuming that the machine could not stop between stations. It seemed too good to be true when, a few minutes later, the machine's slight vibration died away and they came to a halt.

The doors slid silently apart. Even before they were fully open, the three had left the compartment. They were taking no more chances. Before them a long tunnel stretched into the distance, rising slowly out of sight. They were starting along it when suddenly Alveron's voice called from the communicators.

"Stay where you are! We're going to blast!"

The ground shuddered once, and far ahead there came the rumble of falling rock. Again the earth shook—and a hundred yards ahead the passageway vanished abruptly. A tremendous vertical shaft had been cut clean through it.

The party hurried forward again until they came to the end of the corridor and stood waiting on its lip. The shaft in which it ended was a full thousand feet across and descended into the earth as far as the torches could throw their beams. Overhead, the storm clouds fled beneath a moon that no man would have recognized, so luridly brilliant was its disk. And, most glorious of all sights, the S9000 floated high above, the great projectors that had drilled this enormous pit still glowing cherry red.

A dark shape detached itself from the mother ship and dropped swiftly toward the ground. Torkalee was returning to collect his friends. A little later, Alveron greeted them in the control room. He waved to the great vision screen and said quietly, "See, we were barely in time."

The continent below them was slowly settling beneath the mile-high waves that were attacking its coasts. The last that anyone was ever to see of Earth was a great plain, bathed with the silver light of the abnormally brilliant moon. Across its face the waters were pouring in a glittering flood toward a distant range of mountains. The sea had won its final victory, but its triumph would be short-lived for soon sea and land would be no more. Even as the silent party in the control room watched the destruction below, the infinitely greater catastrophe to which this was only the prelude came swiftly upon them.

It was as though dawn had broken suddenly over this moonlit landscape. But it was not dawn: it was only the moon, shining with the brilliance of a second sun. For perhaps thirty seconds that awesome, unnatural light burnt fiercely on the doomed land beneath. Then there came a sudden flashing of indicator lights across the control board. The main drive was on. For a second Alveron glanced at the indicators and checked their information. When he looked again at the screen, Earth was gone.

The magnificent, desperately overstrained generators quietly died when the S9000 was passing the orbit of Persephone. It did not matter, the sun could never harm them now, and although the ship was speeding helplessly out into the lonely night of interstellar space, it would only be a matter of days before rescue came.

There was irony in that. A day ago, they had been the rescuers, going to the aid of a race that now no longer existed. Not for the first time Alveron wondered about the world that had just perished. He tried, in vain, to picture it as it had been in its glory, the streets of its cities thronged with life. Primitive though its people had been, they might have offered much to the Universe. If only they could have made contact! Regret was useless; long before their coming, the people of this world must have buried themselves in its iron heart. And now they and their civilization would remain a mystery for the rest of time.

Alveron was glad when his thoughts were interrupted by Rugon's entrance. The chief of communications had been very busy ever since the take-off, trying to analyze the programs radiated by the transmitter Orostron had discovered. The problem was not a difficult one, but it demanded the construction of special equipment, and that had taken time.

"Well, what have you found?" asked Alveron.

"Quite a lot," replied his friend. "There's something mysterious here, and I don't understand it.

"It didn't take long to find how the vision transmissions were built up, and we've been able to convert them to suit our own equipment. It seems that there were cameras all over the planet, surveying points of interest. Some of them were apparently in cities, on the tops of very high buildings. The cameras were rotating continuously to give panoramic views. In the programs we've recorded there are about twenty different scenes.

"In addition, there are a number of transmissions of a different kind, neither sound nor vision. They seem to be purely scientific—possibly instrument readings or something of that sort. All these programs were going out simultaneously on different frequency bands.

"Now there must be a reason for all this. Orostron still thinks that the station simply wasn't switched off when it was deserted. But these aren't the sort of programs such a station would normally radiate at all. It was certainly used for interplanetary relaying—Klarten was quite right there. So these people must have crossed space, since none of the other planets had any life at the time of the last survey. Don't you agree?"

Alveron was following intently.

"Yes, that seems reasonable enough. But it's also certain that the beam was pointing to none of the other planets. I checked that myself."

"I know," said Rugon. "What I want to discover is why a giant interplanetary relay station is busily transmitting pictures of a world about to be destroyed—pictures that would be of immense interest to scientists and astronomers. Someone had gone to a lot of trouble to arrange all those panoramic cameras. I am convinced that those beams were going somewhere."

Alveron started up.

"Do you imagine that there might be an outer planet that hasn't been reported?" he asked. "If so, your theory's certainly wrong. The beam wasn't even pointing in the plane of the Solar System. And even if it were—just look at this."

He switched on the vision screen and adjusted the controls. Against the velvet curtain of space was hanging a blue-white sphere, apparently composed of many concentric shells of incandescent gas. Even though its immense distance made all movement invisible, it was clearly expanding at an enormous rate. At its center was a blinding point of light—the white dwarf star that the sun had now become.

"You probably don't realize just how big that sphere is," said Alveron. "Look at this."

He increased the magnification until only the center portion of the nova was visible. Close to its heart were two minute condensations, one on either side of the nucleus.

"Those are the two giant planets of the system. They have still managed to retain their existence—after a fashion. And they were several hundred million miles from the sun. The nova is still expanding—but it's already twice the size of the Solar System."

Rugon was silent for a moment.

"Perhaps you're right," he said, rather grudgingly. "You've disposed of my first theory. But you still haven't satisfied me."

He made several swift circuits of the room before speaking again. Alveron waited patiently. He knew the almost intuitive powers of his friend, who could often solve a problem when mere logic seemed insufficient.

Then, rather slowly, Rugon began to speak again.

"What do you think of this?" he said. "Suppose we've completely underestimated this people? Orostron did it once—he thought they could never have crossed space, since they'd only known radio for two centuries. Hansur II told me that. Well, Orostron was quite wrong. Perhaps we're all wrong. I've had a look at the material that Klarten brought back from the transmitter. He wasn't impressed by what he found, but it's a marvelous achievement for so short a time. There were devices in that station that belonged to civilizations thousands of years older. Alveron, can we follow that beam to see where it leads?"

Alveron said nothing for a full minute. He had been more than half expecting the question, but it was not an easy one to answer. The main generators had gone completely. There was no point in trying to repair them. But there was still power available, and while there was power, anything could be done in time. It would mean a lot of improvisation, and some difficult maneuvers, for the ship still had its enormous initial velocity. Yes, it could be done, and the activity would keep the crew from becoming further depressed, now that the reaction caused by the mission's failure had started to set in. The news that the nearest heavy repair ship could not reach them for three weeks had also caused a slump in morale.

The engineers, as usual, made a tremendous fuss. Again as usual, they did the job in half the time they had dismissed as being absolutely impossible. Very slowly, over many hours, the great ship began to discard the speed its main drive had given it in as many minutes. In a tremendous curve, millions of miles in radius, the S9000 changed its course and the star fields shifted round it.

The maneuver took three days, but at the end of that time the ship was limping along a course parallel to the beam that had once come from Earth. They were heading out into emptiness, the blazing sphere that had been the sun dwindling slowly behind them. By the standards of interstellar flight, they were almost stationary.

For hours Rugon strained over his instruments, driving his detector beams far ahead into space. There were certainly no planets within many light-years; there was no doubt of that. From time to time Alveron came to see him and always he had to give the same reply: "Nothing to report." About a fifth of the time Rugon's intuition let him down badly; he began to wonder if this was such an occasion.

Not until a week later did the needles of the mass-detectors quiver feebly at the ends of their scales. But Rugon said nothing, not even to his captain. He waited until he was sure, and he went on waiting until even the short-range scanners began to react, and to build up the first faint pictures on the vision screen. Still he waited patiently until he could interpret the images. Then, when he knew that his wildest fancy was even less than the truth, he called his colleagues into the control room.

The picture on the vision screen was the familiar one of endless star fields, sun beyond sun to the very limits of the Universe. Near the center of the screen a distant nebula made a patch of haze that was difficult for the eye to grasp.

Rugon increased the magnification. The stars flowed out of the field; the little nebula expanded until it filled the screen and then—it was a nebula no longer. A simultaneous gasp of amazement came from all the company at the sight that lay before them.

Lying across league after league of space, ranged in a vast three-dimensional array of rows and columns with the precision of a marching army, were thousands of tiny pencils of light. They were moving swiftly; the whole immense lattice holding its shape as a single unit. Even as Alveron and his comrades watched, the formation began to drift off the screen and Rugon had to recenter the controls.

After a long pause, Rugon started to speak.

"This is the race," he said softly, "that has known radio for only two centuries—the race that we believed had crept to die in the heart of its planet. I have examined those images under the highest possible magnification.

"That is the greatest fleet of which there has ever been a record. Each of those points of light represents a ship larger than our own. Of course, they are very primitive—what you see on the screen are the jets of their rockets. Yes, they dared to use rockets to bridge interstellar space! You realize what that means. It would take them centuries to reach the nearest star. The whole race must have embarked on this journey in the hope that its descendants would complete it, generations later.

"To measure the extent of their accomplishment, think of the ages it took us to conquer space, and the longer ages still before we attempted to reach the stars. Even if we were threatened with annihilation, could we have done so much in so short a time? Remember, this is the youngest civilization in the Universe. Four hundred thousand years ago it did not even exist. What will it be a million years from now?"

An hour later, Orostron left the crippled mother ship to make contact with the great fleet ahead. As the little torpedo disappeared among the stars, Alveron turned to his friend and made a remark that Rugon was often to remember in the years ahead.

"I wonder what they'll be like?" he mused. "Will they be nothing but wonderful engineers, with no art or philosophy? They're going to have such a surprise when Orostron reaches them—I expect it will be rather a blow to their pride. It's funny how all isolated races think they're the only people in the Universe. But they should be grateful to us; we're going to save them a good many hundred years of travel."

Alveron glanced at the Milky Way, lying like a veil of silver mist across the vision screen. He waved toward it with a sweep of a tentacle that embraced the whole circle of the galaxy, from the Central Planets to the lonely suns of the Rim.

"You know," he said to Rugon, "I feel rather afraid of these people. Suppose they don't like our little Federation?" He waved once more toward the star-clouds that lay massed across the screen, glowing with the light of their countless suns.

"Something tells me they'll be very determined people," he added. "We had better be polite to them. After all, we only outnumber them about a thousand million to one."

Rugon laughed at his captain's little joke.

Twenty years afterward, the remark didn't seem funny.

SFWA Grand Master C.J. Cherryh is internationally known for her fantasies like the Morgaine Stories, which have sold over three million copies. Like the Morgaine Stories, her Hugo-winning novels, Downbelow Station and Cyteen, are set in her Alliance-Union universe. Her latest epic is the Foreigner series of space opera filled with culture clash between aliens and humans and other aliens, and fascinating explorations of cultural interrelations. Known for her amazing world-building realism backed by vast research into history, language, psychology, archeology, and more, she has won numerous awards from Hugos and Nebulas to the John W. Campbell Best New Writer Award and Locus Award.

Cherryh even has an asteroid named in her honor. She may not be a household name on the level of Clarke or Heinlein, but she should be. And her story for us is the start of a brand new, never-before-seen universe and characters in which the narrator awakes on a colony ship deep in space and anticipates arrival at a new home. It makes a great conclusion to our journey to the dark frontiers, and poses many great questions, and will leave you wanting more.

COLD SLEEP
C.J. CHERRYH

I wake.

I remember.

I remember the transport offices. I remember, on the wall, a picture of Mars, and another of Earth. I remember a medical office.

I do not remember falling asleep.

Muscles are very weak. I am cold, but warmth moves through me, not like a wind, but like a strange, sluggish tide flowing toward my core.

290Am1e, the computer says, in the screen above me. *Respond.*

I try to speak. *Yes.* It requires breath. Instead I move my hand. I blink.

Are we there? I try to say. *Are we at Proxima?*

I shape the words. I cannot make the sound.

But the screen shows me things. It tells me procedures. And my muscles, one by one, twitch, beginning with my face, proceeding to my left arm.

Waking process engaged, the screen says.

It goes on. The warmth spreads.

I remember.

I sleep.

I fell asleep before launch. I have a strong memory of Mars colony. I was born there. I was twenty-two when I fell asleep, one of ten thousand Martian-born and five thousand from Earth and Luna, young and old, children and seniors, chosen, in a terrible period of the Sun's instability. I remember. I had a family. A seal failed. I was twenty-one. Melly was my sister. Jolu was my mother. San was my father. They were there. They stop, there. That entire memory stops there. I put my handprint on a screen. I agree to be here. I am a single. I know no one here. I know names: Rai, and Pru, and Doctor Sam.

Are they waking?

Are we all waking?

I become aware of breathing. The twitches have begun in my right leg, now. I decide to move my fingers. And they answer. I decide to swallow. And I do. I am aware of blinking but I did not decide that. My mouth is dry. I hate the twitches, and I move my left leg, my right hand, my right foot, to get ahead of them.

The suit moves.

Should it?

290Am1e, the readout says. *Confirm that you are a single.*

"Yes," I say. My voice creaks. I hardly recognize it. "Are we there?"

I want to sit up. The twitches have stopped.

I want to stand. I want to see. I move an arm, the opposite leg.

I lie in a long narrow space, like a tunnel. I do not remember this. I do not remember the rows of other suits that lie double-stacked in racks, on and on, little flickers of telltales in the dim light, like a sheet of stars… so many bodies.

I am one of them.

But I move.

I lift my arm and see my hand, gloved. I move the fingers. I try to touch my face. The faceplate prevents it.

I fell asleep on a bed.

Now I am here. Encased in a suit. With tubes in my body.

Can I get out of this?

Dare I get out of this?

Is there air? Are we in vacuum?

There is up and down. There is at least gravity.

"Is something wrong?" I ask aloud, a hoarse croak. "Are we coming into Proxima?"

"*You are a single.*" The voice is generated. "*Yes-no. Confirm.*"

"Yes. Are the others waking?"

"*No. You are a single. Article 13 states: 'There must be one individual awake on each unit of the ship. An Awakened Individual will see to the safety and welfare of the passengers and machinery of the unit. Priority in awakening will be assigned to singles. Not until the list of singles has been exhausted will non-singles be awakened.'*"

Words. They make no sense. Tubes retract from my body. It hurts.

It hurts, and leaves me with a taste that fills my mouth and my nose and makes my bones ache. "Hurts," I say. Stupid to say to a robot. My eyes are watering. I lift my arm, but I cannot reach my face.

"*Bodily functions will return,*" the voice says. "*Independent movement is now possible.*"

Are we arriving?

I can move both my arms. I sit, with the resistance of magnetic connections.

Maybe I should not have done that.

But the bot does not protest.

I stand, breaking lower connections.

Suited bodies lie in both directions, into the dim distance. Colonists. Like me.

And nobody moves. No one else is waking.

Crazy numbers dance in my head. Information. Procedures of the machinery.

Organization of the ship. Things I do not remember learning.

I ask, "Are we at Proxima?"

"*We are one hundred thirty-nine years from Proxima system.*"

Numbers focus down. A chart, a direction, a position. A hundred thirty-nine years from arrival at Proxima B—a planet they promise can sustain us. But I will not live that long.

I will not make it to Proxima. I am twenty-one.

No. If the voyage went as scheduled, I am no longer twenty-one. I am three hundred fifty-eight.

And panic rides an adrenaline surge. The suit itself red-lights, a telltale in the helmet, on my chest. Not all the tubes have withdrawn.

The ship is evidently in trouble. If they are waking some random passenger, the ship is in trouble.

I do not know what to do about that.

But the numbers dance. I try to be calm. And I try to make sense of what I know.

An Awakened Individual.

A single person. No relatives. No pair-bonds. No connections. Of course we signed the agreement. They promised us a world. A future.

And all, all these sleeping people, connected by tubes to machinery keeping them alive.

For an arrival all those years from now.

My gut hurts. My brain is stuffed full of numbers. Diagrams. Data. Things I never knew when I lay down to sleep.

I stand because the suit will not let me fall. I shiver and go on shivering.

If we are most of the way to our target, we have made turnover. We are in decel.

All the world is double rows of suited bodies, going on into the dark in both directions.

And we are Unit 1 of five units, independent but joined with a common engine, which should be in front of us now. A connected pattern of units. With invisible fire driving it.

I am the Awakened in this unit. My first job should be to survey the sleeping, looking for anomalies. That is what I should do. I do not remember being told.

Their data begins to flood past the helmet screen, momentarily obscuring everything. It takes a few seconds, and my eyes are watering the while, so it makes no sense.

"*Unit 1 occupants are optimum,*" the robot says.

"Good," I say, numb, with tears running down my face. I cannot wipe them. They have to dry there. However long it takes.

Unfair. Unfair that I should have to wake, now, a hundred thirty-nine years short of arriving.

I will be old. I will die still in space, and someone else will see Arrival. I will not.

Not fair to be brought so close. But it has happened. I am called on and I have waked.

Other data streams past.

"Stop screen," I say.

It freezes. I view the place through a frozen veil of numbers.

"Cancel screen."

The veil vanishes. Nothing moves. Nothing in all the universe moves. My feet are on the deck, which means, I suppose, the engine is all right. It must be.

"Robot, what do I call you?"

"Robot," it says.

"Where is the crew?"

"Crew ceased life."

"All crew?"

"Article 13..."

"Stop. Where are you?"

"Crew compartment. Unit 0."

I turn. A light shines in the far distance.

I walk. Or the suit does, with me connected.

And it hurts. Something, in my gut, hurts with a dull, cutting pain at every step, every breath. I walk between the aisles. All around is dark. External temperature reads near zero.

There is no sound, except those the suit makes, and that I make.

I come to an airlock.

I enter. It cycles.

"Can I take off the suit here?" I ask.

"No. Do not remove the suit without medical assistance."

"Can you provide medical assistance?"

"No. I cannot."

"Damn," I say. Robot says nothing.

The inner door opens on a narrow corridor.

Light comes on.

I walk. I walk a great distance, but I can see an end, a doorway.

I reach it. I touch the control plate.

That door opens.

The place is a human place, pressurized, table and chairs, dishes on the table. A round room with arches on all sides. Beyond one arch I see flashing lights, readouts of some sort.

Beyond other arches I see doors.

On the floor, in an archway, lies a suit like mine. It lies still. One red light flashes lazily above the faceplate.

I stand there a moment. I want to look inside.

And I don't want to.

"Robot," I say. My voice shakes. "Robot?"

"*Yes.*"

"Who was this?"

"*129Aj2b.*"

An Awakened.

Before me. Older than me.

"He died," I say calmly. "He ceased. So you waked me."

My eyes water. I cannot call it grief. Terror, perhaps.

This is the heart of the ship. Or its brain. This is where I am. A diagram I never saw flashes into my head, the shape of the ship, a ring of five units, connected to a heart, which is where I stand. And a long stem that keeps the engine far from us.

Us.

The living things.

The room has a table. Chairs. Things for ordinary people. A stuffed toy lies abandoned in a corner.

"What happened to the crew?"

"*Crew has ceased.*"

"The children..."

"*All crew has ceased.*"

That takes a moment to process. A long, difficult-to-breathe moment.

"Where are they, then?"

"*Recycled.*"

"Except this one."

"*Not understood.*"

"Why is this person not recycled?"

"*Crew authorizes all human recycling.*"

"Was this crew?"

"*Yes.*"

"Am I crew?"

"*No.*"

"Then what am I?"

"*You are an Awakened Individual.*"

I know things I ought not to know. When I wonder, I know them. Too many things. Too fast. Systems at risk. Systems not to touch. The suit light reddens. I find it hard to breathe. "Are you well?" Robot asks, and the question is off in the distance: my hearing has gone, I am so angry. So scared. So distressed.

I am shut in with myself. I think. I desperately think. *I think.*

"Robot."

"*I hear you.*"

"Wake another individual. I need advice."

"*I can advise.*"

"I need a human being. Wake another human being."

"*I cannot wake another until you cease.*"

"I'm telling you *wake another person!*"

"*Are you about to cease?*"

Stupid robot. Stupid damn robot.

"No," I say. "No, I am not about to cease."

I want to sit down. I want to sit in a chair at a table and drink something and think. And this damned shell around me will not let me do any of that.

I can never do that.

Ever.

Probably there were suicides en route. I can see where there might be suicides.

"Robot, how many crew were there?"

"*One hundred fifteen.*"

"Was there an accident?"

"*Sometimes.*"

God.

There were children. There were supposed to be children. A succession. It was a generation ship—for them. For the rest of us—cold storage. Deep sleep until arrival.

Or should have been.

There is a room beyond this, through an arch. Flashing lights. Perhaps Robot's heart. At least the ship's.

I don't recognize this, I have never seen it. But I know what it is. I know what the ship should look like.

I walk into that area. I see the schematic, and recognize it. All Units connect here. To this center. Five doors, one of which I came through. This is the heart of Unit 0.

The Engine is in front of us now. The Units redirect once braking begins, and braking will have gone on for as many years as we were accelerating. But the engine is not accessible. We do not control it. All this is just—life support. Support for the suits. Supply. And computers. Robot lives in this panel. And maybe he wanders the circuits and keeps things going. The doors beyond the arches say 1, 2, 3, 4, and 5. Those are accesses. They must be physical accesses. The cold-sleep Units are separate, in case of calamity to one.

But they are not sealed.

They are not sealed, or I could not get here.

"Robot, are Units 2 through 5 all right? Are they safe?"

"Units 2, 3, 4, and 5 are operating."

Thank God. Thank God for that.

"Can you contact Unit 2?"

"Yes. I am always in contact with Unit 2."

"Another robot?"

"Robot 2 is a partition. I am a partition."

"Are there Awakened in charge there?"

"An Awakened Individual is in each Unit."

If I could fall down on my knees, I would. The reality is, I stand. And speak to a voice.

"Then put me in contact with Unit 2."

"Contacting Unit 2. The Awakened Individual in Unit 1 is seeking to contact Unit 2. Please respond."

A pause. A pause that takes forever.

Then a human voice, however altered by machinery. *"Robot?"*

"This is Unit 1," I say. I am so relieved at a human voice I am trembling, and the suit protests with a flurry of lights. "This is Unit 1."

"The Awakened."

"Yes."

"I don't want to talk to you."

Shock is profound. "I am new. I am just Awakened. I need advice."

"I don't."

"Are your people all right? All the sleepers?"

Silence.

"Repeating, are your people all right? Are you all right over there?"

Robot says, *"Unit 2 has broken contact."*

"Get it back."

"Attempting," Robot says, and then after a moment, *"Unit 2 is directing Robot to end communication."*

Something is wrong over there. Something is seriously wrong.

"Contact Unit 3. Contact their Awakened."

"I am contacting Unit 3. Stand by."

Very little pause.

"This is Unit 3."

"This is Unit 1. I have just been waked. I am scared. I am lost, here. I have just contacted Unit 2 and they broke the connection when I asked about their people."

"Unit 2 is like that."

That is unexpected.

"Like *what*, Unit 3?"

"They don't want to talk to us."

"Why not?"

A silence. *"They just don't."*

"Then talk to me."

"I don't think that's such a good idea."

"Why not?"

Silence.

"Look," I say. "The structural corridors connect us. We could meet in the control center."

"*If we were stupid.*"

"Why? Why is that? What are you afraid of? Why is 2 afraid?"

"*Because 2 is afraid of everybody.*"

"Why? Afraid of what?"

"*Two is afraid of contamination. Crew died.*"

"Of disease?"

"*We have no idea. They died. That's all. And don't you dare come over here.*"

"I won't. All right. I won't. But you can talk to me."

"*I see no point.*"

"You can at least tell me why."

"*Unit 3 is special. We are a preservation unit. We cannot have outside contact.*"

"What are you preserving?"

"*Diversity, if you must know. Our genotypes are ancient. We have already suffered losses. We cannot risk more.*"

"What losses? What sort of losses?"

A pause.

"*I don't think you need that information.*"

"What could I do with it?"

"*I don't want to feed your imagination. Say that you don't need to know, and I am closing this conversation.*"

"At least tell me what's the matter with 2."

"*Two is crazy. That's what's the matter with 2.*"

"Do you communicate with 4 and 5?"

"*Occasionally.*"

"Are they all right over there?"

A pause. "*Unknowable.*"

It is not what I want to hear.

"Is the ship all right?" I ask. "Are we on course? Is everybody all right?"

Robot says, "*The ship is all right. We are on course. Everybody is following instructions.*"

"Three? Can you hear Robot? Do you agree?"

"*We are all right. We are safe. I am ending this conversation.*"

"Wait!"

"*Three has broken the connection,*" Robot said.

"What is wrong with them? And what is wrong with 2?

A pause. "*Two reports systems secure and normal. Three is secure and normal.*"

"Are *we* all right? Is Unit 1 all right?'

"*One is all right.*"

"So what does 3 mean by 'losses?'"

"*I cannot give classified information.*"

"So 3 is classified. Classified genes."

"*I cannot answer.*"

"So what is 2? Is 2 different from 1?"

"*The composition is much the same.*"

"But 3 is special."

"*I cannot say.*"

"Damn it, Robot. Let me talk to 4."

"*Processing.*"

Lights flickered.

"*One?*"

"Is this 4?"

"*This is 4. Are you 1?*"

"Four, this is 1. I'm just wakened. Apparently my predecessor is dead in the middle of the control section and I'm trying to contact the other units. Are you all right, there?"

"*Four is fine. Do you have a problem?*"

"Is there just one of you in your unit?"

"*There is only one Awakened per unit. Article 13…*"

"I know about Article 13. What is 2's problem? Three warned me about 2."

"*Two is crazy. That's 2's problem. Don't trust either 2 or 3.*"

"I hope I can trust you."

"*I never said trust me.*"

Chilling, that. I feel a shiver, and suddenly don't hold out hope for 4, either.

"So what's the matter with 2? Can I ask that?"

"*Two's obsessed with germs. We're all in separate containment units, but 2's sure we're going to spread whatever got the last of the crew.*"

"The crew's separate, too, isn't it? Or was?"

"There are the passages. But it wasn't only germs that got the crew. I don't know it was contagious. Maybe it was genes. Maybe it was suicide. Maybe it was murder. It was all their problems. They weren't shielded. They didn't have life support the way we do. It was everything combined. They aged. Not enough kids. Not enough healthy kids. They died. That's what we know."

"Didn't anyone ask?"

"Oh, ask. It won't help. It won't bring back the crew."

"Did anyone go there? Did anybody try?"

"We were asleep. That's all. Robot woke us after the fact. Robot had locked the controls against them. Robot said none of them could operate the ship."

"Are we still on course? Are we still even functioning the way we're supposed to?"

"I don't know. How could I know? It just runs. You're in the control center?"

"Yes. I think that's where I am."

"I don't think that's a good idea. You should go back to your unit. Your business is there."

"Watching people sleep? Nothing's going on."

"That's our job. Somebody should watch, that's all. Being an activist, well, 2 and 3 are activists. Don't contact them. It won't help."

"So we're it."

"We're it."

"Do you know where we are?"

A laugh. It sounds strange. Disconnected from reality. *"In space."*

"But where in space?"

"Is there a where in space?"

"Robot says a hundred thirty-nine years out of Proxima."

"That's what Robot says."

A pause.

"You think," I ask, "that Robot might not be right?"

"I don't know. Does it matter?"

"Well, yes, it matters! It bloody matters! What if Robot has a problem?"

"*If it did, could we do something? I don't think I ought to talk with you anyway. What did 2 say?*"

"Two broke the connection when I asked about their people. And 3 told me that's just the way 2 is. What does *that* mean?"

"*I don't know. I don't even know you're not like 2. I'm going to close off now.*"

"How is 2 crazy?" I ask.

But the connection is dead.

"God. Robot, what is the matter? How did the crew die?"

"*Death usually results from injury to brain or lungs or insufficient supply to the heart. Death can result...*"

"I know how things *die*, Robot! I want to know how the crew died."

"*I have records for the first ninety-eight who ceased. The others did not state a reason. But in nine there was evident damage, three caused by one individual who then ceased.*"

Murder. Suicide. Maybe disease. Maybe Robot itself. Two shut itself off from 1, where last crew died. Three shut itself off from 2. Four doesn't care.

"I want to talk to 5, Robot."

"*I am calling 5.*" Pause. "*Five is answering.*"

"*This is 5,*" a croaking voice says. Age, I think. Old age. Or illness.

"Five," I say. "Five, this is 1. I'm just now waked. I'm looking for direction."

"*Robot will do everything,*" 5 says. "*Robot can be trusted.*"

"I hope so," I say. And I am careful not to mention 2 or 3 or 4. "I want to try to come there. Or you can come to me."

"*No!*"

Upsettingly strong, that *no*. Fearful. "There are five of us. One of us is crazy, one is classified, and I'm not sure about Unit 4. Listen to me. We two, just we, ought to get together and find out what we have. See if we can get some sense of where we are and whether we're on track. I'm not coming immediately. I don't want to upset anything, but I think ultimately all five of us ought to get together and compare notes. Robot may be one robot, with one idea. But we're human. We need to put our minds to work and have some ideas of our own. We need to know, for one thing, if we're where we think we are."

"*Don't play those games with me.*"

"What games, 5? What games are there? Why should I be playing games? We're all in this together."

"*And you're more important than anybody. Aren't you?*"

"Because I'm 1? I don't think so. I'm just one person. I'm a human being just like you. Don't shut down on me. Listen."

"*One plays games with all of us. You build reality. You think you can tell us what to do.*"

"Listen to me! I don't know what 1's problem was, if... if there's been a problem."

"*Goodbye.*"

"Don't! Don't break off. Talk to me."

"*You don't run things, Number 1! You won't get in here! I swear I'll kill you.*"

"What do you think I'm doing? What do you think I've done? I've only been awake an hour!"

"*And you're already trying. Leave us alone!*"

"I signed on for this. I care about surviving."

You care about surviving. You signed on just like I did. Can't we all say that? Didn't we all make a choice? And didn't we all hope we got picked for this trip and somebody else didn't?"

"I had no place else to be. I put my name in and I got picked and I'm not better or worse than the rest. Like you. You're another, right? Article 13? I had no more choice than you do. I'm not after anything. My number came up and I'm standing here in this damn suit awake because I haven't got a choice any more than you do. Don't talk like I have some damn agenda! I'm asking is there anybody else out there who knows anything useful?"

"*You've talked to 3.*"

"I said I've talked to 3. I've talked to 2 and 3 *and* 4. Why is that a problem?"

"*Two's crazy.*"

"I understand that. Two doesn't want to talk and 3 doesn't trust 2 and 4 doesn't trust either one of them. Or me. How does that make sense?"

"*It doesn't. Or it does. Go away. Just don't call again.*"

"Explain to me or I'll come over there. I can do it!"

"Don't you dare! I'll kill you. I will! Robot doesn't belong to you."

As if Robot could. Would. Did. Why did 5 think that?

"Robot. End communication."

"Ending communication."

I try to understand. But none of them make sense. And talking about owning Robot scares me. I don't own Robot.

But does one of the others?

"Robot, does one of the five units have higher authority than the others?"

"No. All units are equal."

Next question. Scary question. "Robot, does one of your partitions outrank any other?"

"All my partitions are equal."

"So any one unit could give you an order."

"Yes."

"And another could stop you."

"Provisional."

Now they were into it.

"Explain provisional, in the statement you just made."

"Survival of two units takes precedence over the survival of one. Survival of the ship takes precedence over all but one."

"What if I said 2 was detrimental to the ship?"

"All parts are equal."

God.

I stand there. In the control center. Where I am the only living thing.

The Awakened from 1 came here, and died.

"Has any other Awakened ever come to this center?"

"This Awakened came."

The dead one. On the floor. The one nobody can recycle.

"Robot. Do you recycle ceased persons in the units?"

"Crew can order recycle."

"Robot. Why can you not wake others?"

Because I have no orders, is the answer I expect. I can argue with that.

"*Awakened Individuals use more resources. Resources must be preserved.*"

"You cannot act to the detriment of the ship."

"*I cannot act to the detriment of the ship.*"

"Receive information. Not waking other individuals harms the ship."

"*In the event of dilemma I select at random, with bias toward standing orders. I reject your proposition pending further information.*"

Damn.

"I am going to Unit 4. I am going to stay there permanently. Awaken someone else for 1."

"*Stop.*"

I walk beyond the arch. I touch the control plate that leads to the corridor.

Lights in the suit go out. It freezes. Utterly stops.

"Robot!"

"*Stop.*"

I need circulation.

"Robot, turn suit *on!*"

Fans start. Lights return.

I can draw my hand back. I do not venture to reach for the plate again.

I would like to sit down.

I would like to have a drink. I can get one from the tube, if I ask it to advance. Nanos in my bloodstream deal with waste. What remains goes to a collection unit that will eject.

Nourishment comes from a cylinder that slips into a similar socket. While I slept, this happened automatically.

Robot is right. An Awakened Individual uses more resources faster.

I would like to eat, drink, and sit down. But none of those things will happen. I can only remember them and try to enjoy the memory.

"Robot. How long did the previous Awakened live after waking?"

"*849,293 days.*"

2,326 years. An impossible number.

Time. Relativity. Maybe. Even so... 2,326 years...

Then *he* came to the control room. And died. He was not even the first Awakened.

We are impossibly far off schedule if that is true.

Why is 2 paranoid? Why do 4 and 5 want to be isolate? Why is 3 secretive?

Can a mind go a thousand, two thousand years like this—and stay sane?

Can I?

"Robot. Are we accelerating or decelerating?"

"Decelerating."

"How long since launch?"

"*19,539,000 days.*"

A worse, *far* worse number.

I stand unmoving, dazed, quite numb for a moment.

"Is that ship time or Earth time, Robot?"

"*That is ship time.*"

The ship drinks dark matter. Fuel is not its problem. But Robot says we are decelerating.

"Robot, do you have a fix on Proxima?"

"*Yes.*"

Did crew opt to pass it? What were they thinking?

Now Robot is in control. Are we are coming back?

One hundred thirty-nine years.

I will see Proxima B.

I will see passengers waked, and resources will be a crisis.

Then what is Robot's program?

Helmet lights flare red.

Robot asks: "*Are you in distress?*"

I take deep breaths. I turn the telltales peaceful white. I think.

"Robot."

"*I hear you.*"

"I have information for you."

"*I can receive data.*"

"*I am the sane one.*"

"*Define sane.*"

"I am functioning correctly."

"Good."

"I have information for you."

"I hear you."

"Unit 2 and 3 Awakened Individuals are malfunctioning. I have yet to make a decision on 3 and 4."

"Understood."

"Take action."

"Understood."

I should have a conscience. I should.

But I will live to see Proxima.

And the ship will.

My job and Robot's are fairly simple. Conserve supply. Keep the passengers safe. Arrive at Proxima B. We come from an unstable star. Our journey has been far, far, far longer than expected. But we are close, now. If we can believe Robot's estimate, we are almost there. Whatever the crew did, for whatever reason, we are almost there. We do not know what has happened to civilization where we were born. But our minds package it. We contain it. We carry it with us. We are what our civilization made us.

Right and wrong are not my problem now.

Arrival is.

AUTHOR BIOGRAPHIES

A lifetime military history buff, *New York Times*-bestselling author **DAVID WEBER** has carried his interest in history into his fiction. In the Honor Harrington series, multiple volumes published by Baen Books, the spirit of both C.S. Forester's Horatio Hornblower and history's Admiral Nelson are evident. Weber's other space opera epic, Safehold, from Tor Books is in multiple volumes as well. He has written an epic fantasy, *Oath of Swords*, and many other science fiction books, including collaborations in the *1632 Ring of Fire* universe with Eric Flint, collaborations with John Ringo, Timothy Zahn, Steve White, and many more. He lives in Greenville, South Carolina, with multiple dogs, cats, children, and his lovely wife Sharon and a huge collection of Honor Harrington artwork.

JACK CAMPBELL (John G. Hemry) writes the *New York Times*-best-selling Lost Fleet and Lost Stars series, and the "steampunk meets high fantasy" Pillars of Reality series. His most recent books are *Triumphant* in the Genesis Fleet series "prequel" to the Lost Fleet, and *Pirate Of The Prophecy*, the beginning of a new steampunk/pirate/science fantasy series set on the world of The Pillars of Reality. He has more than thirty books in print. John's works are being published in English, Japanese, French, German, Polish, Spanish, Czech, Hungarian, Finnish, Greek, Turkish, Hebrew, Chinese, and Russian. His shorter fiction includes time travel, alternate history, space opera, military SF, fantasy, and humor. John has also written a fair amount of nonfiction, including articles on real declassified Cold War plans for US military bases on the moon, and "Liberating the Future: Women in the Early Legion" (of Superheroes) in Sequart's *Teenagers From the Future*. At unpredictable intervals he gives his presentation on EVERYTHING I NEEDED TO KNOW ABOUT QUANTUM PHYSICS I LEARNED FROM THE THREE STOOGES in which Stooge sketches are used to illustrate elements of quantum physics.

John is a retired US Navy officer, who served in a wide variety of jobs including surface warfare (the ship drivers of the Navy), amphibious warfare, anti-terrorism, and intelligence. Being a sailor, he has been known to tell stories about Events Which Really Happened (but cannot be verified by any independent sources). This experience has served him well in writing fiction. He lives in Maryland with his indomitable wife "S" and three great kids (all three on the autism spectrum).

BECKY CHAMBERS is the author of the Wayfarers series, which currently includes *The Long Way to a Small, Angry Planet*; *A Closed and Common Orbit*; and *Record of a Spaceborn Few*. Her books have been nominated for the Hugo Award, the Arthur C. Clarke Award, and the Bailey's Women's Prize for Fiction, among others. She also writes essays, short stories, and novellas.

In addition to writing, Becky has a background in performing arts, and grew up in a family heavily involved in space science. She spends her free time playing video and tabletop games, keeping bees, and looking through her telescope. She lives with her wife in Northern California. You can find her online at otherscribbles.com.

ROBERT A. HEINLEIN, (born July 7, 1907, Butler, Missouri, U.S.; died May 8, 1988, Carmel, California), is considered to be one of the most literary and sophisticated of science fiction writers. He did much to develop the genre. A graduate of the U.S. Naval Academy in 1929, he served in the Navy for five years, then pursued graduate studies in physics and mathematics at the University of California, Los Angeles. Except for engineering service with the Navy during World War Two, he was an established professional writer from 1939.

His first story, "Life-Line," was published in the action-adventure pulp magazine *Astounding Science Fiction*. His first book, *Rocket Ship Galileo* (1947), was followed by a large number of novels and story collections, including works for children and young adults. After the 1940s he largely avoided shorter fiction. His popularity grew over the years, probably reaching its peak after the publication of his best-known work, *Stranger in a Strange Land* (1961). His broad interests and concern for characterization as well as technology brought him a considerable number of admirers among general-interest readers. Among his more popular books are *Starship Troopers* (1959), *The Green Hills of Earth* (1951), *Double Star* (1956), *The Door into Summer* (1957), *Citizen of the Galaxy* (1957), *The Moon is a Harsh Mistress* (1966) and *Methuselah's Children* (1958).

#1 *New York Times*-bestselling author **GEORGE R.R. MARTIN** sold his first story in 1971 and has been writing professionally ever since. Known for his epic fantasy series A Song of Ice and Fire from which HBO's *The Game of Thrones* series was spawned, he also spent years in Hollywood writing for shows like *Max Headroom, Beauty and The Beast* and the new *Twilight Zone* as well as writing and producing *Game Of Thrones*. His latest series is *Nightflyers* on the SyFy Channel. A prolific editor who often partners with Gardner Dozois, Martin also leads the *Wild Cards* series of anthologies and fifteen novels featuring multiple authors working in teams. A multiple Hugo nominee and winner, he was named one of *Time*'s most influential people of the year in 2011.

SUSAN R. MATTHEWS' debut novel *An Exchange of Hostages*, published in 1997, initiated a long-running series about "the Life and Hard Times of 'Uncle' Andrej Koscuisko, who is Not a Nice Man" (though her publisher prefers to call it *Under Jurisdiction*). The eighth title in the series was published in January, 2019.

But now she wants to talk to you about U-boats. She's just back from visiting Kiel in Germany (where there's a U-boat) and Chicago (where there's another U-boat). She's working on the saga of those WWII German U-boats that had the misfortune to encounter the Flying

Dutchman off the south-west coast of Africa and became unmoored in space and time thereafter.

She and her wife Maggie have been married for nearly forty years and live in Seattle where Maggie gardens, Susan makes hard cider, and they do their best to keep up with their two Pomeranians.

ORSON SCOTT CARD is the *New York Times*-bestselling and award-winning author of the novels *Ender's Game*, *Ender's Shadow*, and *Speaker for the Dead*, which are widely read by adults and younger readers, and are increasingly used in schools. His most recent series, the young adult Pathfinder series (*Pathfinder*, *Ruins*, *Visitors*) and the fantasy Mithermages series (*Lost Gate*, *Gate Thief*) are taking readers in new directions. Besides these and other science fiction novels, Card writes contemporary fantasy (*Magic Street*, *Enchantment*, *Lost Boys*), biblical novels (*Stone Tables*, *Rachel and Leah*), the American frontier fantasy series, The Tales of Alvin Maker (beginning with *Seventh Son)*, poetry (*An Open Book*), and many plays and scripts. His latest novel, *Children of The Fleet*, in an all-new series Fleet School, was released from Tor in fall 2017.

Card currently lives in Greensboro, North Carolina, with his wife, Kristine Allen Card, where his primary activities are writing a review column for the local *Rhinoceros Times* and feeding birds, squirrels, chipmunks, possums, and raccoons on the patio.

EDWARD E. SMITH, known as "E.E. 'Doc' Smith" (born May 2, 1890; died August 31, 1965), is an American science fiction author who is credited with being the founding father of space opera—action-adventure set on a vast intergalactic scale involving faster-than-light spaceships, powerful weapons, and fantastic technology—by creating the Skylark series (1928–65) and the Lensman series (1934–50). Smith received a bachelor's degree in chemical engineering from the University of Idaho, Moscow, in 1914 and became a chemist at the U.S. Department of Agriculture in Washington, D.C. During 1915 Smith began writing what would become the novel *The Skylark of Space* with his neighbor, Lee Hawkins Garby, who wrote the romantic parts of the story that Smith felt he could not write. Smith continued to write while completing a doctoral degree in chemistry from George Washington University, Washington, D.C. in 1919.

Thereafter, Smith became a chemist at the milling company F. W. Stock and Sons in Hillsdale, Michigan, and, aside from a period of one year during World War Two when he was an ordnance inspector, he specialized in doughnut mixes for the remainder of his chemistry career. In 1920 Smith and Garby completed the novel; however, Smith was unable to find a publisher until 1928, when the novel was serialized in *Amazing Stories*. A novel that featured a chemist in a prominent role, *The Skylark of Space* was extremely popular, and Smith immediately began work on a sequel, *Skylark Three* (1930). When it too was published in *Amazing Stories*, Smith was credited as Edward E. Smith, Ph.D., earning him the nickname among science fiction fans of "Doc" Smith. The series continued in *Skylark of Valeron* (1934–5) and *Skylark DuQuesne* (1965).

Smith originally conceived of his next series as a single gigantic novel, but it was published from 1937 to 1948 as four separate books, the Lensman series, in *Astounding Stories* (after 1938, *Astounding Science-Fiction*): *Galactic Patrol* (1937–8), *Gray Lensman* (1939–40), *Second Stage Lensmen* (1941–2), and *Children of the Lens* (1947–8).

Smith's groundbreaking adventures, action packed and epic, were an enormous influence on the science fiction that followed.

Following three years as a cook in the Canadian Naval Reserve, a year studying forestry, a winter hanging around Universal Studios, a degree in Radio and Television Arts, and time spent managing North America's oldest surviving SF&F bookstore (Bakka-Phoenix when it was only Bakka), **TANYA HUFF** moved to rural Ontario with her wife Fiona Patton and began writing science fiction and fantasy full-time— or as full-time as possible around the needs of eight cats and two dogs. Her thirty-two books and seventy-eight short stories range from heroic fantasy (the Quarters books) through humor (the Keeper Chronicles) to military SF (the Torin Kerr Confederation & Peacekeeper series) and include *Scholar Of Decay*, a novel set in TSR's Ravenloft universe as well as four short story collections and six e-collections. Her latest novel was *A Privilege Of Peace* (DAW, June 2018) the last of the Torin Kerr books that began with *Valor's Choice* in 1998, and her next will be a secondary-world fantasy, currently untitled.

Her books have been translated into ten languages, and her five-book Blood series was adapted into the 22-episode television series *Blood Ties*—a process she enjoyed every moment of. Not only because it was the first time in twenty-five years she actually got to use her degree.

She is the only author who has won both the Constellation Award and the Prix Aurora Award.

She watches baseball but not hockey, has won one game of Settlers of Catan, and Peter Davidson is her Doctor. Terry Pratchett and Charles de Lint remain at the top of her favorites list and she still hasn't gotten over the loss of Diana Wynne Jones.

Once a Silicon Valley software engineer, **CURTIS C. CHEN** (陳致宇) now writes speculative fiction and runs puzzle games near Portland, Oregon. His debut novel, *Waypoint Kangaroo* (a 2017 Locus Awards finalist and Endeavour Award finalist) is a science fiction thriller about a superpowered spy facing his toughest mission yet: vacation. The sequel, *Kangaroo Too*, lands our hero on the Moon to confront long-buried secrets. Curtis' short stories have appeared in many publications, including *Playboy* magazine, *Daily Science Fiction*, and *Mission: Tomorrow*. He is a graduate of the Clarion West and Viable Paradise writers' workshops.

You can find Curtis at Puzzled Pint Portland on the second Tuesday of most every month. And yes, there is a puzzle hidden in each of the Kangaroo book covers! Finding the rabbit holes is left as an exercise for the reader. Visit him online at: curtiscchen.com.

SEANAN McGUIRE is the *New York Times*-bestselling author of more than a dozen books, all published within the last five years, which may explain why some people believe that she does not actually sleep. Her work has been translated into several languages, and resulted in her receiving a record five Hugo Award nominations on the 2013 ballot. When not writing, Seanan spends her time reading, watching terrible horror movies and too much television, visiting Disney Parks, and rating haunted corn mazes. You can keep up with her at www. seananmcguire.com.

Science fiction convention favorites **SHARON LEE** and **STEVE MILLER** have been writing SF and fantasy together since the 1980s, with dozens of stories and several dozen novels to their joint credit. Steve was Founding Curator of Science Fiction at the University of Maryland's SF Research Collection. Sharon is the only person to consecutively hold office as the Executive Director, Vice President, and President of the Science Fiction and Fantasy Writers of America.

Their newest Liaden Universe® novel, *Neogenesis*, is their twenty-seventh collaborative novel. Their awards include the Skylark, the Prism, & the Hal Clement Award.

LARRY NIVEN graduated Washburn University in Kansas in June 1962 with a B.A. in Mathematics with a Minor in Psychology. His first published story, "The Coldest Place," appeared in the December 1964 issue of *Worlds of If*. He went on to win Hugo Awards for "Neutron Star," 1966; *Ringworld*, 1970; "Inconstant Moon," 1971; "The Hole Man," 1974; and "The Borderland of Sol", 1975. And a Nebula for Best Novel: *Ringworld*, in 1970.

His latest novels include collaborations: *Inferno II: Escape From Hell* with Jerry Pournelle, *The Bowl Of Heaven* with Gregory Benford, *The Moon Maze Game* with Steven Barnes, *Shipstar* with Gregory Benford, and *The Seascape Tattoo* with Steven Barnes.

STEVEN BARNES is the award-winning author of over thirty novels, as well as writing for television and film. He lives in Southern California with his wife, American Book Award and British Fantasy Award-winning novelist Tananarive Due.

JAMES BLISH, who also wrote under the pseudonym William Atheling, Jr., (born May 23, 1921; died July 30, 1975), was an American author, editor, and critic of science fiction best known for the Cities in Flight series (1950–62) and the novel *A Case of Conscience* (1958). His work, which often examined philosophical ideas, was part of the more sophisticated science fiction that arose in the 1950s.

Blish had been a fan of science fiction since his childhood, and his first short story, "Emergency Refueling," was published in *Super Science Stories* in 1940. He received a bachelor's degree in zoology from Rutgers University in 1942 and served in the U.S. Army from 1942 to 1944. After his discharge he attended graduate school at Columbia University but left in 1946 without completing a degree. He worked mainly in public relations writing advertising copy until 1968, when he was able to turn to the writing of fiction full-time.

Beginning in 1950, Blish wrote the short stories that became the first published novel of the Cities in Flight series, *Earthman, Come Home* (1955), set in the 4th millennium CE, which established the future world that would be the setting of the four-part series. Cities in Flight spans 2,000 years of history.

In *A Case of Conscience* a Jesuit priest and biologist studying the idyllic planet of Lithia comes to believe that Lithia and its reptilian inhabitants are creations of Satan designed to undermine humanity's faith in God. *A Case of Conscience* won the Hugo Award for best novel in 1959 and was part of a thematically connected series that examined the competition between religion and science. The other novels in the series included *Doctor Mirabilis* (1964), a historical novel about the thirteenth-century English philosopher and scientist Roger Bacon, and two novels that Blish considered as one work: *Black Easter; or, Faust Aleph-Null* (1968) and *The Day After Judgement* (1971), a fantasy in which Satan and his demons conquer Earth.

Blish was also one of the first critics of science fiction to judge it by the standards applied to "serious" literature. He took to task both his fellow authors for such deficiencies as bad grammar and the misunderstanding of scientific concepts and the magazine editors who accepted and published such poor material without editorial intervention. Much of his criticism was published in "fanzines" (amateur publications written by science fiction fans) in the 1950s under the pseudonym William Atheling, Jr., and was collected in *The Issue at Hand* (1964) and *More Issues at Hand* (1970).

Blish moved to England in 1969. Much of the remainder of his career was devoted to writing twelve collections of short stories based on the episodes of the American television series *Star Trek* (1966–9), which Blish felt had greatly expanded the audience for science fiction.

GARDNER DOZOIS was one of the most acclaimed editors in science fiction, winning the Hugo Award for Best Editor fifteen times. He was the editor of *Asimov's Science Fiction Magazine* for twenty years. He was the editor of *The Year's Best Science Fiction* anthologies and co-editor of the *Warrior* anthologies, *Songs of the Dying Earth*, and many others. As a writer, Dozois twice won the Nebula Award for Best Short Story. He passed away in 2018.

DAVID FARLAND is a *New York Times*-bestselling author with over fifty novel-length works to his credit. His latest novel, *Nightingale*, won the International Book Award for Best Young Adult Novel, the Next Gen Award, the Global Ebook Award, and the Hollywood Book Festival Award for Best Novel of the Year. Dave is currently finishing the last book in his popular Runelords series, and there will be no sequels.

MIKE SHEPHERD is an independent writer who published the latest book in the National Best Selling Kris Longknife science fiction saga, *Kris Longknife: Commanding*, in May. His latest book is *Vicky Peterwald: Dominator*, which includes a royal wedding for her, with Kris as her maid of honor. Kris's bridal gift is killing an assassin. All these novels are available as print, e-books and at audible.com. For more information, go to www.krislongknife.com. You can also follow Kris Longknife on Facebook.

CATHERINE LUCILLE MOORE (January 24, 1911–April 4, 1987) first rose to prominence in the 1930s writing as C.L. Moore. She was among the first women to write in the science fiction and fantasy genres. Moore married her first husband Henry Kuttner in 1940, and most of her work from 1940–1958 (Kuttner's death) was written by the couple collaboratively. They were prolific co-authors under their own names, although more often under any one of several pseudonyms.

As "Catherine Kuttner," she had a brief career as a television scriptwriter from 1958 to 1962. She retired from writing in 1963. One of her most famous characters, Northwest Smith, is among the most influential of pulp heroes, continuing to be an influence on her fellow writers even today.

NEAL ASHER lives sometimes in England, sometimes in Crete and mostly at a keyboard. Asher published his first short story in 1989. In 2000 he was offered a three-book contract by Pan Macmillan, who published his first full-length novel, *Gridlinked*, in 2001. This was the first in a series of novels made up of *Gridlinked*, *The Line of Polity*, *Brass Man*, *Polity Agent*, and *Line War*.

He's had twenty-three books published and can now call himself an author without cringing. He's also read more SF than some would style as healthy. Find him online at theskinner.blogspot.com and nealasher.co.uk.

The American Library Association calls **WESTON OCHSE** "one of the major horror authors of the 21st Century." Weston's life skills and his more than thirty years in the military, traveling all over the world, has given him a unique perspective on the poignancy of the human condition which he strives to include in all of his literary work.

A writer of thirty books in multiple genres, his military supernatural series SEAL Team 666 has been optioned to be a movie starring Dwayne Johnson and his military sci fi trilogy, which starts with *Grunt Life*, has been praised for its PTSD-positive depiction of soldiers at peace and at war.

Weston has also published literary fiction, poetry, comics, and nonfiction articles. His shorter work has appeared in DC Comics, IDW Comics, *Soldier of Fortune* magazine, *Cemetery Dance*, and peered literary journals. His franchise work includes *The X-Files*, *Predator*, *Aliens*, *Hellboy*, *Clive Barker's Midian*, and *V-Wars*.

BRENDA COOPER is a writer, a futurist, and a technology professional. She often writes about technology and the environment. Her recent novels include *Keepers* (Pyr, 2018), *Wilders* (Pyr, 2017), *POST* (*Espec Books, 2016*), and *Spear of Light (Pyr, 2016)*.

Brenda is the winner of the 2007 and 2016 Endeavour Awards for "a distinguished science fiction or fantasy book written by a Pacific Northwest author or authors." Her work has also been nominated for the Philip K. Dick and Canopus awards.

Brenda lives in Woodinville, Washington with her family and four dogs.

ALAN DEAN FOSTER's work to date includes excursions into hard science fiction, fantasy, horror, detective, western, historical, and contemporary fiction. He has also written numerous nonfiction articles on film, science, and scuba diving, as well as having produced the novel versions of many films, including such well-known productions as *Star Wars*, the first three *Alien* films, *Alien Nation*, and *The Chronicles of Riddick*. Other works include scripts for talking records, radio, computer games, and the story for *Star Trek: The Motion Picture*. His novel *Shadowkeep* was the first ever book adaptation of an original computer game. In addition to publication in English his work has been translated into more than fifty languages and has won awards in Spain and Russia. His novel *Cyber Way* won the Southwest Book Award for Fiction in 1990, the first work of science fiction ever to do so.

Foster's sometimes humorous, occasionally poignant, but always entertaining short fiction has appeared in all the major SF magazines as well as in original anthologies and several "Best of the Year" compendiums. His published oeuvre includes more than 100 books. Among his most famous original creations are the characters Pip and Flinx and Amos Malone.

KRISTINE KATHRYN RUSCH has won awards in every genre for her work. She has several pen names, including Kris Nelscott for mystery and Kristine Grayson for romance. She's currently writing two different science fiction series, The Retrieval Artist and the space opera Diving series. She's also editing the anthology series Fiction River. For more on her work, go to kristinewrites.com.

KEVIN J. ANDERSON has published 150 books, fifty-six of which have been national or international bestsellers, and he has been translated into thirty languages. He has written numerous novels in the Star Wars, X-Files, and Dune universes, as well as a unique steampunk fantasy novel, *Clockwork Angels*, based on the concept album by legendary rock group Rush. His original works include the Saga of Seven Suns and Saga of Shadows series, the Terra Incognita fantasy trilogy, and his humorous horror series featuring Dan Shamble, Zombie P.I. He has edited numerous anthologies, including the *Five by Five* and *Blood Lite* series. Kevin and his wife Rebecca Moesta are the publishers of WordFire Press, a new-model house using indie methods to release in print, ebook, and audio formats; WordFire has nearly 300 titles by more than 125 authors. Kevin is also a professor and the director of the Publishing MA/MFA Program for Western State Colorado University.

The achievements of the world's best-known writer of science fiction, **ARTHUR C. CLARKE**, bridge the arts and sciences. His works and his authorship, ranging from scientific discovery to science fiction and from technical application to entertainment, have made a global impact on the lives of present and future generations.

In a landmark paper "Extra-terrestrial Relays" in 1945, he was the first to set out the principles of satellite communication with satellites in geostationary orbits. One of his short stories inspired the World Wide Web, while another was expanded to make the movie *2001: A Space Odyssey*, which he co-wrote with director Stanley Kubrick.

Born in Somerset, England, in 1917, Sir Arthur's literary achievements were recognized by Queen Elizabeth II when she honored him with a knighthood in 1998. He has both an asteroid and a dinosaur named after him. Sir Arthur lived in Sri Lanka from 1956 until his death in 2008.

SFWA Grand Master **C.J. CHERRYH** writes full-time and travels, while engaging in a long list of hobbies. These include: fencing, riding, archery, firearms, ancient weapons, donkeys, elephants, camels, butterflies, frogs, wasps, turtles, bees, ants, falconry, exotic swamp plants and tropicals, lizards, wilderness survival, fishing, sailing, street and ice skating, mechanics, carpentry, wiring, painting (canvas), painting (house), painting (interior), sculpture, aquariums both fresh and salt, needlepoint, bird breeding, furniture refinishing, video games, archaeology, Roman, Greek civ, Crete, Celts, and caves. She's traveled from New York to Istanbul and Troy; outrun a dog pack at Thebes, and seen *Columbia* lift off on her first flight. She's fallen down a muddy chute in a Cretan cave, nearly drowned in the Illinois River, broken an arm, been kicked and tossed by horses, fended off an amorous merchant in a Turkish tent bazaar, fought a prairie fire, slept on deck in the Adriatic, and driven Piccadilly Circus at rush hour. She's waded in two oceans and four of the seven seas and seen Halley's Comet from Australia's far coast. She has also won the John W. Campbell Award in 1977 for Best New Writer; a Hugo Award, for her short story "Cassandra" in 1979; another Hugo Award, for her novel *Downbelow Station* in 1982; a Locus Award and Hugo for *Cyteen*, Best SF Novel of 1988; and received SFWA's Damon Knight Memorial Grand Master award in 2016.

EDITOR BIOGRAPHY

BRYAN THOMAS SCHMIDT is a Hugo-nominated editor and author. His anthologies include *Mission: Tomorrow*, *Galactic Games*, *Joe Ledger: Unstoppable* with Jonathan Maberry, *Monster Hunter Tales* with Larry Correia, *Infinite Stars*, *Predator: If It Bleeds*, *AVP: Aliens vs. Predators: Ultimate Prey* with Jonathan Maberry, and *Robots Through the Ages* with Robert Silverberg. His debut novel, *The Worker Prince*, achieved Honorable Mention on Barnes and Noble's Year's Best SF of 2011 and he has released three thrillers in the John Simon series so far, followed by two sequels in the Saga of Davi Rhii space opera trilogy. His short fiction includes stories in *The X-Files*, *Predator: If it Bleeds*, *Aliens vs. Predators: Ultimate Prey*, Larry Correia's Monster Hunter International, Joe Ledger, and Decipher's Wars. He also edited *The Martian* by Andy Weir, and works by Mike Resnick, Frank Herbert, Angie Fox, and Alan Dean Foster, among others. His work has been published by St. Martin's, Titan Books, Baen Books, and more. He is currently working on a novel, *Shortcut*, based on a story he co-authored with producer Hunt Lowry (*Donnie Darko*) of Roserock Films for potential film development. He lives in Ottawa, KS. Find him online as BryanThomasS on both Twitter and Facebook or via his website and blog at www.bryanthomasschmidt.net.

COPYRIGHT AND FIRST PUBLICATION INFORMATION

For more fantastic fiction, author events,
exclusive excerpts, competitions, limited editions and more

VISIT OUR WEBSITE
titanbooks.com

LIKE US ON FACEBOOK
facebook.com/titanbooks

FOLLOW US ON TWITTER AND INSTAGRAM
@TitanBooks

EMAIL US
readerfeedback@titanemail.com